Blood & Bondage

Published by
Two Realms Publishing LLC
Irmo, SC 29063
https://tworealmspublishingllc.com
Cover Designer: We Got You Covered Book Design

Interior Designer: Two Realms Publishing LLC

Editor: Michelle's Edits

Illustrator: Nicodemus Holroyd

Cartographer: Jog Brogzin

Special Edition

ISBN: 978-1-955106-48-1

Printed in the United States of America

Trigger Warning

This story contains a lot of sex, curse words, dominance, submission, blood, and more. It depicts scenes of mutual fucking and debauchery. As these are fantasy characters and this is a world without humans, human diseases don't exist. And to these creatures, a change from back to front is nothing to fret over. Below is a list of what you can expect.

Continue reading at your own risk.

BDSM	CNC
Non-Con/Child Abuse/PTSD (Memories)	
Dom/Switch	Erotica
Brothel	OCD
Age-gap (she's older)	Abuse of Authority
Off-limits	Blood K!nk
Impact Play	Weapon Play (claws/nails)
Wax Play	An@l
Anti-hero	Morally gray
UnAl!iving/fratricide	

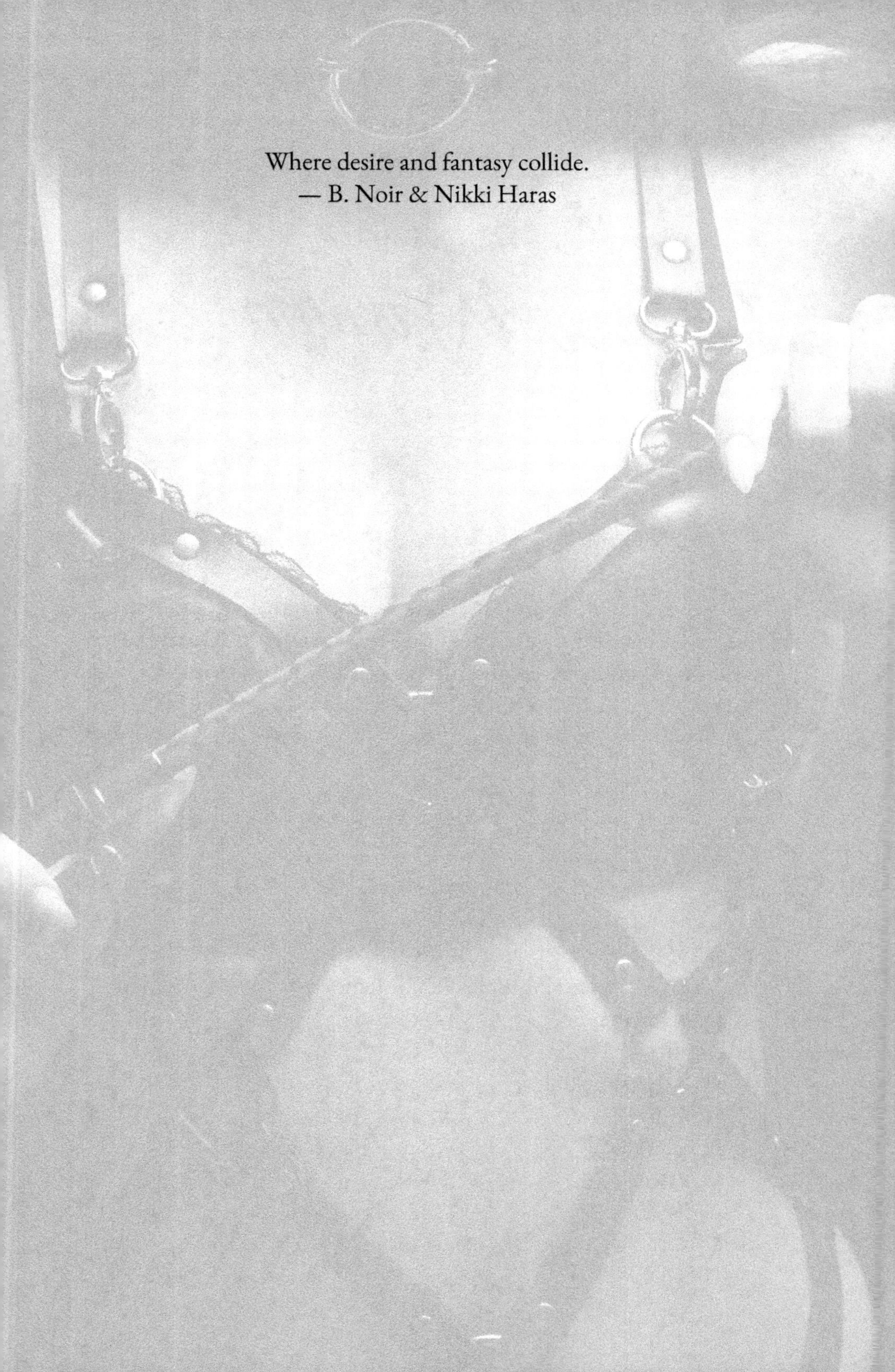
Where desire and fantasy collide.
— B. Noir & Nikki Haras

Trigger Warning

This story contains a lot of sex, curse words, dominance, submission, blood, and more. It depicts scenes of mutual fucking and debauchery. As these are fantasy characters and this is a world without humans, human diseases don't exist. And to these creatures, a change from back to front is nothing to fret over. Below is a list of what you can expect.

Continue reading at your own risk.

BDSM
Non-Con/Child Abuse/PTSD (Memories)
Dom/Switch
Brothel
Age-gap (she's older)
Off-limits
Impact Play
Wax Play
Anti-hero
UnAl!iving/fratricide

CNC

Erotica
OCD
Abuse of Authority
Blood K!nk
Weapon Play (claws/nails)
An@l
Morally gray

Where desire and fantasy collide.
— B. Noir & Nikki Haras

Blood & Bondage

THE EMPYREAL DEN CHRONICLES

A PRISMA ISLE™ SERIES SPIN-OFF

BOOK ONE

B. NOIR & NIKKI HARAS

TWO REALMS PUBLISHING LLC

To the paths not taken.

TERMINOLOGY

Adolescent: term in shape shifter culture for children ten years of age to twenty years of age

Aphros [af-rows]: the second cycle of the Vernal Equinox (the spring)

Cycle: approximately one month or from one full moon to the next

Full-fledged: term in shape shifter culture for adults; those twenty years of age and older

Guiler [guy-lure]: a humanoid species with elemental abilities

Hades: the Greek god of the underworld; sometimes used as a sort-of curse word by the shape shifters

Informant: soldier to the shape shifter king, Markham

Julunna [jew-lew-na]: the first cycle of the Luminos Equinox (the summer)

Lacuna [la-KEW-na]: an hour of time

Luminos Equinox [lum-OH-nose]: summer

Marana: the second cycle (month) of the year

Métamorphe [met-a-mor-fey]: the shape shifter village

Mindlink: a telepathic connection between twins and some mates

Nestling: term in the shape shifter culture for children one year of age to five years of age

Newling: term in the shape shifter culture for newborns to one year of age

Nymph: one of three species of fae that helped build the ecosystem of Prisma Isle, they were created by the goddess Aphrodite; there are three types (Water, Forest, and Celestial) and they are known for their beauty and sexual prowess

Penumbra(s) [pah-num-BRAH]: week(s)

Seelie: one of three species of fae that helped build the ecosystem of Prisma Isle, it is unknown which celestial created them; they have extremely long lives and are highly intelligent; they are among those who keep to themselves, protecting the fae borders for *all* intruders

Solaris: year, which comprises sixteen cycles (months) for the inhabitants of Prisma Isle

Umbra(s) [um-BRAH]: day(s)

Vernal Equinox [ver-NAL]: spring

Youngling: term in shape shifter culture for children five years of age to ten years of age

The Rules

Welcome to the Empyreal Den.

By completing an exchange, you fully acknowledge and agree to follow the rules below.

1. Do not get emotionally invested or attached.
2. Consent is required for all interactions and can be revoked without penalty at any point.
3. Refrain from providing gifts, personal or emotional.
4. Avoid any intentional actions that would permanently cause damage.
5. No weapons, magical artifacts/items are permitted on the premises.

Should you break a rule, you accept any and all consequences, including a complete ban from this establishment.

Welcome

to

The Empyreal Den

One

Hunter arrived at the brothel alone—par for the course. Nine months ago, he'd brought Maddox along, and there was only one other similar instance. That male had needed something he couldn't find anywhere else. But Gregor had found it here, and seemed much happier for it, too.

Opening the door to the second floor with a creak, Hunter headed inside and nodded to the dark-haired and red-headed females leaning against the wall, their figures silhouetted in the dim light. Maddox hadn't ever returned. Not that he knew of, anyway. Just the one time. Hades, how could the male stand it? Hunter couldn't see how once a year worked for anyone. If he had sex so infrequently, he'd go insane. *More* insane than he already was.

Crossing to the receptionist, he dipped his chin at Shalla, the scent of wood polish rising as he leaned a hip against the desk. Ivory was to meet him after preparing the new female, but she hadn't arrived. Which meant she was with a client. Because nothing else but coin in her pocket—so to speak—would keep her from spending even a few seconds with him.

"Evening. I am supposed to be meeting someone new tonight." A small smirk played on his face as he set a bag of coins on the counter with a satisfying thud—enough for two hours. If he didn't enjoy his newest plaything, or the session ended early, he'd get half back. This just ensured the session wouldn't get interrupted for more payment.

"Of course." Shalla collected the pouch and tucked it away inside a drawer, the scent of old wood rising as it opened. "A few things before

Ivory escorts you back. If things go well this session, the cost goes up by a hundred gold coins per hour for those that follow. While we allot some room for unexpected visits and overage, you must adhere to whatever time you've scheduled. Understood?"

"Not a problem." None of that was new to him. He'd been coming here for decades. It wasn't like he ever argued about any of the rules here, major or minor. He needed, as much as wanted, to come here; that was all there was to it.

If this visit went well, he would gladly pay whatever he had to in order to continue returning. From Ivory's veiled hints about the female he was to meet, Hunter gleaned a feeling, a tickle of excitement, that promised he wouldn't be disappointed. Not in the least.

And money was no object, thanks to his side job that had filled his coin storage over the years far better than being an Informant ever had. Plus, the new queen *gifted* them wealth after Markham's demise. Hunter hadn't even finished counting yet, it was so much. Yet still a drop in the bucket compared to what he'd hidden beneath his floorboards for years.

"Good."

Ivory sauntered toward them. She flashed Hunter a sultry smile and winked. "She's ready for you. If you'll follow me."

Hunter smirked down at her as he trailed her down the hall. Gods, this must eat away at her. No matter how much Ivory grinned when telling him about a new female, or taking him to their room for an introduction, he could tell that she hated it. He had gone to her off and on for over twenty-five years. Basically, she was his backup. When things didn't go as planned with a new female, he returned to Ivory. Always. Not that he could even pinpoint *why*. It was just something he'd always done. Returned to the familiar when the new and hopeful turned to dust. Ivory wasn't even *great*, just *good enough*. Barely.

Unlike the times when he was going to have a session with her, Ivory didn't wrap her body around his, and he didn't put his arm around her. They just walked side-by-side. Anything else would have been completely inappropriate considering the circumstances. "And how are you doing today, sweetness?"

"I can't complain." She rounded the corner to the right, then led him down the next hallway on the left. "Her room is toward the back. She's one of our most exclusive workers."

"Good." Not that the thought entered his mind much, or that he ultimately cared, but 'exclusive' meant fewer dicks inside her. Most of the females here were good at acting, but a couple over the years had presented as sloppy seconds. Not on purpose, but that changed nothing. And they hadn't lasted long—with him, or the den.

Ivory stopped in front of a black door. "Here we are." She leaned against the doorframe, stretching her arm above her head, and arched her back. "Though I'm positive you'll be happy with her, I'm always available if you ever change your mind."

With his eyes on hers, Hunter reached forward. Just the tips of the fur on the back of his hand brushed against one of her breasts. The material of the covering she wore was so sheer that there really wasn't a point in wearing anything at all. Even if she had on something else, he still could have seen how easily her nipples hardened. For fuck's sake, all he had to do was look at her and she got wet. Ivory would never truly be happy because she was continually chasing something that just wouldn't happen for her—the perfect male. Or, perfect fuck, rather. Someone who would be exclusive only to her, and would raise her station here far above where she hoped to get. Someone who would make her feel like she was more than a paid whore. No one enjoyed her enough to give her all that, though, or it would have occurred by now.

Hunter placed his hand on the door above hers and ever-so-slowly leaned in. He whispered into her ear, "I know, sweetness. But that day will not be today. So, you should probably open the door." He flicked the tip of his tongue against her earlobe before straightening up.

Smile fixed, she pushed away from the wall. "Suit yourself." With a creak, Ivory opened the door, entered, and stepped aside, revealing his new submissive.

As soon as he entered the room, a visible change came over his body. It was always like this; almost like, in moments of sexuality, he became a completely different person. No more teasing or playing around. No pet names or smiles. He became harder. Harsher. He had to be fully, totally, 100% in control. Fighting back, the word *no*, refusal to comply with a demand pissed him off. Which was never a good thing.

Blood excited him, but he'd treated the females here as *well* as he could. Not that he hadn't drawn it a few times in the throes of ecstasy, but never anywhere near life-threatening. Never anything that wouldn't heal quickly.

Once he drew blood on a female, though, they were done with him. And so he had to move on to someone else. Except for Ivory. He'd drawn blood on her once and she'd ended it for a while, then allowed him to return to her after a few months.

No one could touch him during sex. He just couldn't stand it. It made his skin crawl. The sex he needed, craved, made him feel powerful. Like a god. Gods took what they wanted without remorse. They didn't get punished. They didn't care about the disgusting things they'd done. Had no scars. He was covered head-to-toe in them, and this was the only time he couldn't handle being reminded they existed. Sex—sex like this—was the only time he forgot.

And once they started fucking, they could moan, cry out, and scream as much as they wanted. But no talking. 'Yes, Sir,' 'please' when they begged, their safe word, and those kinds of things were acceptable. Other than that, it killed the mood.

He was fucked up, that was for sure. But at least he was one of the rare few who could admit it.

His gaze fell on the female kneeling on the floor in front of him. Her hands rested on her thighs and her head bowed. All she had on was a pair of sheer underwear, nothing else. Sometimes, he liked them to wear more when he started fucking his females, but it would do for the first time.

Fuck, just staring down at her had his cock thickening and hardening. He resisted the urge to lick his lips as the sweet scent of her perfume tickled his nose. The subtle highlights in the female's hair shimmered beneath the flickering flames of the black candles along the wall. Her skin was utterly flawless. The swells of her breasts were ripe for the bite of his fangs. Her lips were plump and pouty, just slightly wet, and begging to wrap themselves around his cock. He wanted to graze those slender hips with his claws, grip them in his hands, and hold tight while he fucked the shit out of her.

It was exactly what he was going to do over the two hours he'd paid to spend with her. "Does she know my preferences?"

"She's been apprised. The items in her repertoire are hanging on the wall." Ivory gestured to the area to his right. "She will not move until you give her permission."

"Good. Leave us." Hunter remained there until Ivory disappeared, the click of the closing door echoing in the silence. He stared down at the female for another moment, just drinking her in. "Get up."

She stood with great ease, her gaze remaining lowered and her hands at her side.

Hunter strolled around her full circle, taking his time. Once he stopped in front of her, he paused for another beat before speaking. "You will do." Oh, but she would more than do. Hades, she was perfectly exquisite. He lifted her chin so their eyes met, taking a moment to drink in the minuscule nuances of their color—jade-green with tiny flecks of yellow. Bathed in candlelight, they appeared golden. "My name is Hunter. When we are not playing, you may use my name. When we are playing, you will call me 'Sir.' Do you understand?"

"Yes, Sir."

Nothing outwardly showed on his face, or in his demeanor, but internally, he practically drowned in pleasure already. Her voice was positively heavenly. The way 'Sir' just rolled off of her tongue. "I want your name and your safe word before we begin. I do not use gags, so you will always be able to use your safe word if needed." Oh, but he hoped to all the gods she wouldn't. He had a feeling about this one. This one...she would be perfection.

"I am called Nia. My safe word is blue, Sir."

Blue. A color she preferred, for sure.

Nia wasn't her real name. Even if that wasn't a rule, he could just tell. She didn't state the name as if it *belonged* to her. It was just a name to be used. And as she'd stated, it was what she was *called*. Likely, she hadn't even chosen it for herself. Not using their real names kept the intimacy levels nonexistent.

They weren't supposed to learn anything about one another. A rule he'd never broken. Even when he massaged the females afterward, he didn't talk about himself. At all. He would brush their questions off with half-answers, never truly revealing anything about himself. That wasn't for any of them to know.

They were playthings. Not friends. Not lovers.

That wasn't what this was about.

Which was why he came here. Anywhere else, the females expected things from him he couldn't give. They wanted *relationships*. Something that would always be beyond his reach. He wasn't truly good for anyone and never would be. At least he recognized that about himself and spared all the unsuspecting bitches on the isle the heartache.

The draw, the danger of being with a male like him, entranced many. A male who wore the Informant brand, who'd survived Métamorphe under Markham. A savage who thrived on violence. If they knew what they were getting into when they came onto him, they'd tuck tail and run as if their lives depended on it.

Because they did.

Only here—with rules, expectations, limits—this was the only place he could truly let himself go.

How long had he stood here, staring at her? He was wasting coin. They needed to start. "Get on the bed."

"Yes, Sir."

Hunter stayed in place as she climbed onto the bed and lay down. His tail twitched in anticipation as he waited for her to reach the center of the king-sized four-poster bed, the crisp, black sheets rustling as she moved. This bed was special, and only in the rooms that required a dominant male or female. There were bars and shackles on the headboard and footboard, bars on top, and even a top-to-bottom 'X' on one side. A few other details added to it ensured it functioned the way they desired.

Once she was comfortable, Hunter closed the distance between them and strode around to the top of the bed. "Extend your arms."

Nia followed his instructions without pause. This was a new room for him, just as the female was, but the bed was basically the same as those in the other rooms he'd frequented. Pulling up the chains with leather straps on the ends, he laid one on the mattress as he got the first one situated. Her wrists were so damn tiny, but the straps fit her perfectly. He adjusted the buckle tightly, but not enough to cut off her circulation, and then did the same to the other. Hunter tugged on the chains, so they were taut. Her arms pulled straight above her head.

Already, his cock hardened more. Her scent alone had been enough to start that, then the view of her on the floor. Moving around to the foot of the bed, Hunter located the straps for her thighs before climbing on the bed. First her right, and then her left. He buckled the leather straps just above her knees, then drew the chains tight, spreading her thighs wide. Then, kneeling there for a minute, he took her in from head to toe, his eyes lingering. It was a stark contrast to seeing her in that submissive pose, a sight he hadn't anticipated. A whole other experience.

His eyes passed over every dip and curve of her body. Each slight fluctuation in her tan skin tone. The slenderness of her neck. The way her collarbones jutted out just slightly. Not that she was malnourished at all, just small. Her body was completely hairless, just the way he liked. Female shape shifters had never attracted his attention. Not that it was something he'd ever spoken aloud. She had a tiny, almost invisible dot on her left hip bone. A barely discernible scar on her waist. On her right arm, there was a tattoo of three intricately detailed roses. On her left leg was an ornate design of woven vines. Her rounded breasts were magnificent, nice, and perky, the tips a bright pink.

This first session wouldn't get too rough or out of control. The first one with a female never did. She needed to feel him out, to see if she was comfortable with even the lowest levels of what he desired. And he had to feel her out, too. Test her. Push the limits *just* a little before things escalated.

Hunter inched down, so he sat closer between her legs. As he breathed in deeply, her perfume filled his senses, his nostrils flaring at the potent aroma. Her panties were black, the color standing out in stark relief with her skin tone. There were some decorative lace curlicues on the sheer material, too, just above her slit. His tongue darted out, wetting his dry lips. With just one finger, he traced over the top of her panties, from the curlicues all the way down the length of her cleft.

A slight gasp left her mouth.

As her back arched, his eyes shot up to meet hers, capturing the sudden movement. That was new. Not once had a female reacted to him that quickly. Not like this. Like she was on the verge of coming already. And all he'd done was graze a finger over her sex.

Oh, this was going to be fantastic.

His eyes darkened as he stroked her slit again, still just one finger, but with more pressure than before. The flimsy material would be gone soon, once he ripped it off of her, but not just yet.

The sharp sound of her gasp made his cock harden, a pulsating throb up and down his erection. If he had a little less control over himself, he might have growled right then. The noise was there, on the edge, but didn't leave his lips. He didn't make noise during sex. Not much, anyway. The cause eluded him. He'd been around dozens, maybe even hundreds, of males when they'd fucked a female and their noises could split eardrums. He hadn't met a female who could make his carefully constructed composure crumble so completely. To where his growls shook walls and rattled windows. And he'd never moaned. Not once. No matter how much pleasure fucking brought him.

And Nia wasn't faking in the least. Wasn't that just hot as fuck? Those gasps at the gentle touches were 100% natural. He'd dismissed females before and never given them the time of day again for faking even a slight noise when they'd had sex with him. He didn't want fake. If he didn't please them, so be it. But faking it was as good as lying to his face, and he didn't tolerate that. It was insulting.

Time to take things up a notch. True, he had two hours, but he didn't intend to spend the entirety of his time teasing her. Hunter stretched, keeping his knees planted, until he was looming over her, his shadow falling across her face. Replacing his finger with the heel of his palm, he rubbed her clit through her panties, slow and gentle at first. That wouldn't last long at all. He wanted her writhing, panting, begging beneath him. Only then would he taste her pussy. He could just imagine how sweet she would taste. Her scent alone had him practically salivating.

Hunter leaned over and, before she could react, the soft pressure of his mouth was on her right breast. He dug his fangs in slightly, not enough to pierce through her skin, but enough that she would feel a small bite of pain. Sliding his tongue out, he stroked her nipple, twirled and flicked it as he rubbed her nub.

Nia moaned. Gently, she tugged on the leather cuffs as she arched her back, pressing her breast more into his mouth. He bit down harder with his fangs as he sucked, his tongue a rapid flutter against her nipple. As the heat in her pussy intensified, the speed and pressure of his palm increased. She hadn't come yet, nor did he think she would dare until he gave her permission, but she was definitely wet.

As Nia strained against her wrist restraints, her moans grew louder and more frequent, echoing around the room. The throbbing of his cock intensified. A growl rose to the tip of his tongue. Holy fuck. Removing his hand from her pussy, he gave it three quick, hard smacks before moving the heel of his palm back to her clit. He rubbed her nub even harder and faster as he lathered her other breast with attention. He didn't bite gently this time, though still not enough to draw blood. Nearly, but not quite hard enough.

Her back arching, Nia yanked at both ends of the straps. "Please, Sir... please, may I come... please...Sir..." the words came out between whimpers and cries of ecstasy.

His cock pulsated. That noise alone was just about enough to pull the threatening growl out of him. But the way she begged—his mouth watered. Hunter released her breast, slowly sweeping his tongue over her nipple, the sensation causing her to groan as he met her gaze. Gods, the way her body writhed and arched, her arms and legs tugged at her restraints—fucking gorgeous. He continued to rub her nub, his palm moving hard and fast. With his gaze locked on hers, he licked his lips and growled out, "Come for me, Nia. Now."

As if her body was powerless to ignore his demands, her orgasm gushed out of her, soaking her panties and his fingers with it. *Holy fuck.* He couldn't wait any longer. He needed his tongue in her pussy immediately. As he sat up, Hunter brought his hand to his mouth and licked his palm clean. The taste of her cum was an explosion on his taste buds. Hunter scooted down the bed so he could bend over. If he laid down fully, with how stiff his cock was right now, that would be a level of discomfort he could do without.

With his face an inch from her crotch, her scent slammed into him, electrifying his veins. Holy fucking shit, she smelled delicious. He refused to waste a single drop of her sweet juices. Hunter closed his mouth around her pussy, panties and all, and sucked hard. He stroked his tongue along her slit and outer lips, a shudder shooting down his spine. Once he'd gotten out as much as he could, he ripped her panties off. And he wasn't gentle. The remnants went somewhere off the bed. He gripped her thighs and drove his tongue as deep inside her as he could. A low rumble sounded in his chest.

A whimper slipped through as she bit down on her bottom lip and strained against her bindings. "Please, Sir..." Nia pled. "Please, Sir, may I come?"

Hunter snarled against her pussy. He couldn't help it. Fucking mind-boggling. He'd barely driven his tongue into her sex, and another release geared up. He didn't want to punish her on their very first meeting. No, she needed to beg more before he let her come again.

As he withdrew his tongue from her pussy, he gazed up at her while delicately parting her lips and softly blowing on her clit. "No," he said before he bit down on her nub. He flicked his tongue against it, then twirled it around. After one hard suck, he drew back again and blew on her clit.

Nia strained against the straps with a grunt, the leather creaking under the pressure. "Please, Sir, please may I come? Please, Sir... please... please, Sir..." she uttered between whimpered moans.

He tormented her, flicking his tongue lightly while their eyes met, savoring every sound she uttered. It was some of the most beautiful music he'd ever heard. Hunter shoved two fingers into her ass as he bit her clit. "You may come." He closed his mouth over her sex and sucked hard. Driving his tongue deep inside her, he fucked her pussy with it while he simultaneously fucked her ass with his fingers.

Hades. Between her echoing moan, vibrating through the room, and the potent taste of her release, he nearly lost control. He hadn't even gotten his dick inside her yet. What the *fuck* was this female doing to him?

He tightened his grip on her thigh, his claws scraping against her skin with a faint rasping sound. Scratches immediately appeared. The sight of them did something to him. Something more intense than seeing blood on any other female. He intensified his movements, thrusting his fingers deeper and faster into her while delving his tongue further inside her, emitting a continuous low growl. He couldn't get enough of her taste. All he knew was that he needed *more*. And when he'd had his fill—for the moment—he was going to make her forget what it felt like to have any other cock inside of her.

With the straps restricting her movements, Nia tugged at both of them against her wrists and legs. As her nipples pebbled, her back arched, pushing her ass more against his fingers. "More, please, Sir," she moaned.

It was just three words. Words he'd heard dozens of times before. However, what emerged from *her* mouth caught Hunter's attention, causing him to look up at her while he skillfully stimulated her with his fingers and tongue. If she wanted more, he'd give her more.

And he knew exactly where he wanted his cock first.

Removing his fingers and tongue from her simultaneously, Hunter sat up and ensured her restraints were still tight. Yep, just as he'd left them. He moved up on the bed until he sat next to her head. With a firm grip on her hair, he inserted his cock into her mouth, sliding it in until it hit the back of her throat. A deep, guttural groan immediately expelled from his mouth. Holy fuck. Even the noises coming out of him were brand new. No one had ever felt like her before. She was fucking magnificent.

Turning carefully so he didn't dislodge her mouth from his cock, he placed one knee on either side of her head and leaned down. The remnants of her orgasm glistened on her pussy, drawing another growl out of him. Beneath her, he firmly held onto her ass, dug his claws in, and pushed her slit toward his mouth. While sliding two fingers back into her ass, he didn't stop sucking and licking at her sex.

Nia took in the full length of his cock, swirled her tongue around the head, and then sealed her lips around his shaft, moving her mouth back to the base. A soft purr accompanied the graze of her teeth as they moved from base to tip, and then she restarted.

Hunter's eyes rolled back into his head. He almost hissed—something he had absolutely never done before with a female. He groaned as he buried his face deeper in her sex, devouring her vigorously. The pressure of his grip on her ass increased. Blood beaded on his claws. He pounded his fingers into her ass as he fucked her mouth, drilling the head of his cock into the back of her throat. A growl rose in his chest. Holy fucking shit, he was already on the verge of coming.

Extending her tongue, Nia moved it along the length of his shaft until it reached his balls. With a soft hiss, she swirled her tongue around each testicle, then traced it along his shaft as it slid back into her mouth.

His head jerked back and he let out a hiss of his own. "Come. Right now," he snarled before a burst of pleasure exploded out of him. His mouth reclaimed her sex, his tongue exploring her depths with fervor. Once she gave him those sweet pussy juices, it wouldn't be his fingers penetrating her ass.

Hunter skillfully pleasured her, ensuring he didn't miss a single drop of her orgasm, as she returned the favor on his erection. Holy fucking shit. Good gods, she was incredible. His cock hadn't even been inside her pussy or her ass yet, and already he knew—she was his favorite submissive.

It took a great deal of effort to remove his mouth from her pussy. He could stay there for hours, savoring every delicate flavor she offered, never growing tired. Perhaps another day. Right now... *Fuck yes*, right now, he needed to be somewhere else.

Positioning himself between her legs, Hunter wrapped his arms around her thighs, pressed the head of his cock to her asshole, and thrust hard inside of her until she completely sheathed him. Nia cried out in ecstasy. There was no starting out slowly and working up a steady rhythm. He slammed into her ass repeatedly. Holy fuck, she was tight, so fucking tight. Tighter than any female he had ever had before.

Every new moan she made for him, each one louder than the last, intensified the pleasure coursing through his veins. He'd usually enjoyed sex; even if it wasn't the greatest, it all held some level of enjoyment. But this... Nia drove him to new heights. And this session—this first session—this was mild. What would it be like when things escalated further? When he showed her the depths of what he truly desired from a submissive? He'd already drawn blood—not much at all—and she hadn't seemed to care in the least. It had only turned her on more.

Unwrapping one arm from her thigh, Hunter smacked her pussy a few times and slid three fingers inside it. Although he increased the speed of his thrusts, he never fucked the ass too hard. It was all about pleasure. If he wished to draw blood, his gaze raked over Nia's form, missing no curve or vulnerability. "Come for me, Nia," he growled.

Nia's cry of ecstasy almost made him come. Her juices completely coated her pussy, his fingers and hand, as well as her inner thighs. Fuck yes, that was a beautiful sight. Removing his digits, he brought them to his mouth and licked them clean. He withdrew his cock out of her and made quick work of the straps around her ankles, loosened the chains, and then carefully flipped her over onto her stomach, ensuring he didn't dislocate her shoulders. Shoving her knees up underneath her, he spread her legs wider and repositioned his cock at her entrance. With a deep growl, he slammed his cock inside her as her moan echoed off the walls. They were far from finished. Though the warning light was set for sooner than five minutes, he would soak in every second of the paid time until the light blinked off.

His thrusts into her pussy were much more forceful, possibly even bordering on rough, compared to when he had been in her ass. He couldn't help it. Not with every sensation—the sights, the sounds, the textures—that had overwhelmed him since they began. Turning her face to the side so she wouldn't suffocate, he shoved her head down more. He lifted her back end, and she hooked her legs tightly behind his knees as his fingers and claws dug into her thighs once more. His thrusts grew increasingly forceful and rapid, making her body tremble with each impact. The metallic echoes of rattling chains that bounced off the walls punctuated her loud moans and sharp cries.

He wrapped one arm around her waist as the other hand went straight to her pussy. Finding her nub, he gave it a hard pinch before rubbing it in rhythm with his thrusts. The noises that continually left her mouth, not to mention the way her thighs quivered and her sex clenched around his cock, told him just how close she was to another release. Not that she would get one easily. He wouldn't let her come this time until she was screaming as she begged.

A slight tremor ran through Nia's thighs. Through ragged breaths and moans, she pled, "Please, Sir, may I come? Please, Sir."

His thrusts held steady, a relentless and unchanging rhythm. He uttered just one word—"No."

Although her thighs quivered, Nia clamped the inner walls of her sex around his cock.

A thunderous growl came out of him. He drilled into her harder at that moment than he ever had before, making her gasp. The force of his thrusts could have shattered her core. The way her sex tightly embraced his cock, providing a perfect fit, captivated him. Holy fuck, when he came inside her again and allowed her to orgasm, too, it was going to be utterly explosive.

"Please, Sir," she whimpered. "Please, may I come?"

Not yet. Almost, but not yet. His release was right on the edge, too, but he could hold it back until he was ready for them to come at the same time. "No," Hunter growled. Slamming into her one last time, he stilled his hips, remaining buried deep inside. As his fingers kept working her nub vigorously, his cock pulsated within her.

The walls of her pussy constricted around his cock tighter. "Please, Sir," Nia cried out. "Please, Sir," she begged. "Please, Sir, let me come."

That wasn't screaming, which was what he wanted. That was the limit he intended to drive her to today, anyway. She was right there, just one more move, and that should seal the deal. He barely held back as it was. "No," Hunter rumbled. He gave her pussy a hard smack and then pinched her nub. With a swift motion, he retracted his hips and plunged deep inside her, pausing briefly as his fingers resumed their relentless exploration.

"Holy fuck," she hollered. "Please, Sir," she practically bellowed. "Please, Sir," she pled, her voice louder. Nia screamed, "Let me come, Sir."

And they were there. *Fuck. Yes.* Shifting his hands back to her hips, Hunter resumed his thrusts, pummeling her core repeatedly. While he hadn't meant to draw blood this session—at least, not much—he wasn't able to stop his claws from digging into her hips a little. With his jaw still clenched, all he got out was one word: "Come." His loud roar reverberated, and he pitched over the edge into an explosion of relentless pleasure. Holy fucking shit. How many firsts had that been? So many things he'd never, ever done with a female before, and she'd brought them out of him in one session.

Nia's scream echoed in the room as a powerful orgasm left his dick completely saturated, with moisture trickling down her thighs and wetting the bedding.

He experienced a release of unprecedented power and duration, dwarfing any orgasm he'd ever had. There was a significant overflow from her pussy, intermingling with her own wetness. Holy fuck. His roar trickled off into a growl that took its time to quiet into nothing. When his body finally stilled, he couldn't move. At least, not for a minute or two, until his ragged breathing finally calmed.

Withdrawing from her, he slowly removed his claws from her hips. Spent. His cock was fucking spent. After one session. Utterly mind-blowing.

Usually, it took a few sessions for him to be sure how things would go with a submissive. Not this one. Not Nia. At this moment, he was absolutely certain, without a single hesitation—she was perfect. Exactly what he needed. His favorite submissive.

Hunter released her wrists from the leather straps, catching her before her body collapsed. He gently lifted her and carried her to a dry part of the bed, carefully arranging her on her back before he settled between her legs. He didn't use rags or cloths to clean the females up. Nope. He used his tongue. Nothing hurried or voracious; just slow, deliberate brushes as cleaned off the cum that coated her thighs and her sex. The blood on her hips made his taste buds practically sing.

A soft purr left her mouth.

His tongue never stopped moving, but his eyes quickly rose to meet hers. The noise was barely audible, but it hardened his cock a little all the same. Shit. His tongue traced the claw punctures on her right hip before circling back to her pussy and inner thighs.

The more he cleaned her, the more she purred, a low rumble that matched the increasing hardness of his erection. Not that he would give it any more attention. Not right now, anyway. They'd had their session. Their next one would come soon enough. As would the warning light; it should go off in about five minutes if he'd gauged right, giving them about twenty minutes left together. Ten minutes per hour was his norm.

Hunter shifted to her left hip, cleaning off the blood there too after finishing with her sex and thighs. He lingered, savoring the metallic tang of blood on his tongue before he sat up, then settled beside her. Only then—when anything remotely sexual had finished—did he say, "You have permission to touch me now. And you can use my name now if you would like." Adjusting his weight, he lowered himself to sit with his legs crossed. Draping her leg across his lap, he massaged her thigh in slow circles.

"You are strange," Nia uttered

A tiny smirk played at one corner of his lips. It wasn't the first time someone had called him strange. He was curious. "Why do you say that?"

"Instead of using the washcloths to clean me, you used your tongue. I can see that you are hard again, and while there is certainly time, you opt not to do anything about it."

"To the first,"—he cocked an eyebrow at her—"why ever would I waste something so sweet? To the second,"—his fingers moved nimbly from her thigh down to her knee—"I always use the last bit of my time to take care of the female I am with. You already took care of me—very well, I might add—now, I reciprocate."

"If you weren't well taken care of, would you have used the last of that time differently?"

"Yes." The light on the wall went off, sending a soft red glow around the room. Hunter spent little time below her knee. With the positions she'd been in, there shouldn't be much tension there. He massaged her calf a little, though, before moving to her other leg. "I pay for my time here, and because of how I need to fuck, I pay well. If I am not satisfied, what am I paying for?"

He didn't pay for dissatisfaction or disappointment. His irritation with the first woman he'd ever been with here, however many years it had been, had caused her to last only fifteen minutes. That had more to do with the fact that she was faking enjoyment. She had always wanted to be submissive and had expertly feigned pleasure until she was with him. She hadn't truly been ready for what that had entailed. At least, not with him as her master. By the time he'd left the room at the end of the hour, the female couldn't move.

"Is there something more or an alternative you'd like ready for our next session?"

Hunter gently kneaded the slight bruising from the restraints, his touch starting at her knee and working its way up her thigh. Flicking his gaze to her, he just stared at her for a minute. Once he finished with her leg, he shifted, positioning his knees on either side of her body. She flipped over onto her stomach. He massaged her hips, skipping where he'd punctured her skin and along her waist. "Tell me what you like. Position, whatever. What is your favorite?"

Her eyebrows furrowed as she glanced back at him, her gaze sharp. "Why?"

Her confusion didn't surprise him. When he'd asked the other two females the same question, their reactions were strikingly similar. Except he'd never offered that in the first session before. Not once. He'd offered it to Ivory at the completion of their third session. The other female when they were done with their fifth or sixth.

He knew he was a novelty, even among those with his proclivities, but it didn't bother him. Submissive or not, the more one cared for, thought about, and considered the female, the more she desired to take care of him. As desire grew, the pleasure intensified, felt equally by both parties. He despised any falseness, particularly if it was the slightest bit manufactured. As their desire to please him grew, the sessions escalated in brutality, drawing more blood and inflicting greater pain until the safe words were inevitably spoken.

"Because I asked. And because I like to give little rewards to those that please me the most." He smirked. "Ask Ivory. I am sure she would tell you." Ivory had pleased him. A lot. She just hadn't quite been enough for what he needed. "Besides, I am going to be back..." Hunter leaned in close and nipped lightly at her ear, "soon." A slight growl permeated the word. Sitting back up, he massaged her lower back. "You may get paid for this, but that does not mean I should be the only one getting what I want. I want to ensure you are fully enjoying yourself as well."

Nia's jade gaze focused on him. "I'm uncertain. I've given no consideration to my desires here before."

A small smirk crept across his face as his hands moved up her spine, leaving her lower back. Was he going to be the first one to give her what she truly desired? She'd enjoyed every moment of their session. He fully believed that, but it wasn't the same thing. Silence briefly stretched between them. His hand cradled her left wrist, his fingers brushing carefully around the purple and yellow bruises. "Think about it. Next time, we will start with what you like. You can tell me what you decide before we begin. The position is not what matters to me."

She was still peering over her shoulder at him. He couldn't quite decipher the expression in her eyes, but he didn't break her gaze. "I would like to show you exactly how much you pleased me today. So, put some thought into it." Hunter, unable to hold her gaze any longer, shifted his attention to her other wrist. "I am probably breaking protocol by telling you this, but you pleased me more than any other female has. Not that you should read anything into that. It just means I would like to continue coming to see you. Regularly." Which meant weekly. At least.

"Ensure you advise Shalla on your way out so she can adjust my schedule accordingly. In the meantime, I will think about it and give you an answer the next time we come together."

Oh, he would tell her. And he would watch while Shalla placed him on the schedule. He stared down at Nia for a moment. Three days from now. No. Two. His cock twitched. "Good." His fingers danced up the length of her arm, then gently caressed her shoulders. He took a little more time here. The positions she'd been in were less strenuous on her shoulder than others, but he knew soreness was inevitable without proper care. He'd give the back of her neck the same treatment. "Have you been doing this for a long time?" Why did he ask that? He never asked questions like that.

"I've been with the brothel for over twenty years."

"That is about how long I have been coming here. It is a wonder we have not met yet." Which was really too bad. So many disappointments over the years that he could've avoided. Oh, well; they couldn't change it, but going forward, he would be a permanent part of her schedule.

"I don't meet clients at the front. It was only recently that an opening in my schedule occurred."

"I meant that they had not paired us together yet. Though after today..." Hunter licked his lips. "I was just thinking I can completely understand why you have not been available." He didn't need, nor want, to know anything about her other clients. Obviously, she had them, but it wasn't his concern. He was glad that an opening had appeared in her schedule. He'd finally found what he'd searched for sexually. They'd just had one session, but he could already tell he'd never need another. No other female came close to comparing, and he'd been having sex for over thirty years. Nia wasn't his, and he would never get attached to her. Even if it wasn't against the rules, it would still be a dumb decision. If the brothel's rules weren't in place, and if she were with him often, he would utterly destroy her. It was just the type of person he was.

"Do you ever desire to meet them out front? Or do you prefer how we did things today?" It was one of the few concessions he'd allowed Ivory. He'd been with her the longest because she'd pleased him the most. So, she got special rewards that other females hadn't. Like kissing—something he'd never been particularly interested in—it was far too personal. But she'd enjoyed it, so they'd done it. At least until they entered her playroom.

"I prefer we do things the same as today. Though at some point, they won't escort you back. Shalla will simply advise you it's alright to come to my room."

That was how it had gone with the others, too. This worked perfectly for him. This way, she would always be ready for him when he arrived. Except for the next session, where they had something to discuss first. The red light on the wall blinked twice before illuminating again. Five-minute warning.

Hunter moved off of her and sat down next to her on the bed. "As do I." He glanced at her and gently touched the puncture wounds on her ass cheek, his finger tracing the small, red marks. Gods, he loved the way they looked. There was probably something wrong with his head, but if that was the case, he wasn't the only one with the ailment. Nor did it bother him in the least. "Wear red next time."

Nia bowed her head to him in deference. "As you wish."

His finger lifted her chin, forcing her to look at him. He had the strangest sensation to praise her again. Something he'd already done. More than once. It made no sense. He'd never felt the need to over-praise. Dropping his hand, he got up off the bed. He had a couple of minutes left in his session, but as the scent of them both lingered, the flush of her skin, the pouty look of her lips, her taste on his tongue, he knew he had to leave if he wanted to keep it together. "I will see you in two days, Nia."

When their gazes met, she stared at him for a long moment. "Two days," she echoed.

He nodded once, turned his gaze away from hers, and left the room.

Two

Nia tapped her chin, the sound echoing softly, as she walked up and down both sides of her closet. Choosing something to wear for dinner shouldn't be this difficult, but she had a certain standard to meet. One that clearly designated her elevated status within the den. Given the new client she'd taken today, it had to be something spectacular. Stopping in front of the row of dresses, she dropped a hand to her hip. The lace material of her midnight-blue thong brushed against her palm.

Grace sat on the floor, her back against the door jamb, feet tucked and tail heavy in her lap. A small smile played on the feline shape shifter's face as she lazily perused the book in her hand. "I would help you if I could, but clothing is something that will always be completely unfamiliar to me."

Silva had already slipped his feet into a pair of her stiletto pumps, clicking them on the floor. "Oh, I don't know, Gracie," he crooned. "You shouldn't sell yourself short, love." As he secured the newly gained pumps, he playfully waved a hand at her. "I've heard leopard is in this season. Especially with those kitty-cuddling trolls." He eyeballed Nia. "You don't need to change; just go as you are and gain a few more admirers."

A subtle smirk curved at the edges of Grace's lips. "If leopard is *in* this season, I am probably ready, yes? Besides, as fabulous as those look on you, Silva, I would break my ankles trying to walk around in those things. As I utilize those often in my performances, I think I am going to have to pass."

A petulant expression settled on his face as he pouted. "Well, that's no fun. We could always get Mr. Ibras to glam you up with some fierce new claws." With a sexy smile, he curled mock talons at her, his teeth gleaming as he emphasized her natural features.

Rolling her eyes at the two of them, Nia scowled. "One, I don't need more admirers." Nor did she want someone up her ass looking for guidance. "Two, those had better end up back where you found them." She pointed at the stilettos he'd donned. "Don't make me flood your room again." Grabbing a blue-velvet dress, she walked to her mirror. Might be too much. "I'm sure he'd love that. Mistress may not, but he's never really followed her rules."

"Too short," Silva retorted. "A little raunchy for our *finest* dining establishment."

Shaking her head, Grace closed the book in her lap. "I would suggest just buying your own shoes, but I know you get all your enjoyment from the thievery," she teased. A slow grin spread across her face. "Hmm. I *like* that idea." She spread her fingers, examining the smooth skin where her claws had once been. "Do you think I could get bling on them? Might spice up my numbers a little."

"Anything is possible. Because the designer is a bit of a diva, they conveniently craft all their merchandise with a price tag but no clear specs. All part of the mystical nuances."

"Thievery? I thought he did it because he enjoys annoying the fuck out of me." Nia let out a soft snicker. Over the years, how many times had he made off with a pair of her shoes? Too many to count. With a rustle of fabric, she strode back to the dresses, returning the one in her hand to its appropriate place on the rack. "Have you seen half the stuff in our closets, Gracie? I'm sure he could add some bling if you wanted."

"I do *not!*" Silva protested. "Okay, maybe just a teensy-weensy bit. But we're family. What's yours is mine." The eyebrow waggle made his performance even more laughable, but he spoke with a confidence that revealed a distinct absence of constraints. "As long as I return them, it's not stealing," Silva corrected, his voice echoing slightly as he shrugged. "Otherwise, it's just borrowing."

"Really? Only a bit?" Nia mocked as she skimmed over the other dresses hanging in her closet.

"Do you *really* have any intention of returning them when you take them, though?" Grace teased, her eyes twinkling with mischief and a smirk gracing her lips. With a playful wag of her finger, she feigned disapproval. "*That* makes it thievery, you know."

With a finger pressed to his lips, Silva winked at Grace before he quietly slipped off the set. "But of course! Nothing, not even in Nia's infinite shoe-dom, is ever worth wearing more than once. That's so faux pas."

Nia stopped, pretending she hadn't seen their quick glances, and stared at her friends. "Wait a second. When have you *not* returned my shoes? I know where everything is here. I'd know if something were missing." That was the truth. It was just like her cleaning routine after each client. She followed it to the letter, never missing a single step.

Grace shifted her gaze back to Nia. "What look exactly are you going for here?"

"Something that speaks to my status. We all know that Ivory is going to do her usual. You know, since she can't keep Hunter as a client, she has to do whatever possible to act as if she'll one day measure up to those of us at the end of the hall. Whether it's this end or over by Ipsy and Mae." Her gaze settled on another dress. Picking up the hanger, she held up a white number with a crisscrossed black pattern mixed in and straps across the chest. "What about this? Slutty, but classy."

Toning her smirk down, Grace tapped on her chin as she considered the outfit. "Hmm. I do like how the colors go together. And it shows some, but not too much, of your boobs off, which is sexy. I do not know, though. You could just go with Silva's suggestion. Pull a Mona and just go in your thong."

"I'm seriously thinking the two of you just like staring at my tits," Nia retorted, barely containing a chuckle.

"Too white." Silva yawned. "It's no secret you're not perfect, and we certainly hope you aren't trying to take over Shalla's job at reception."

Nia scoffed. "Definitely not."

He reclined on the palms of his hands. "If you wanted us to focus on your ass, you'd have to lean forward a fraction."

"Alright, so something that speaks to my sinful ways and offers a peek at all my assets."

"Yes, and let's not reveal our most valuable piece so readily," Silva interjected, rising from the floor to inspect the jewelry.

Nia put the dress back, then searched through her wardrobe, giving them a clear view of her backside. "Oh. What about this one?" She retrieved a crimson-colored dress. From the lace top, the skirt descended, each leg revealed by two slits that reached upward.

"Definitely that color," Grace commented. "But maybe something a tad shorter. So, it is not so easy for her bitchiness to step on the hem."

Something to save for later. Nia returned the dress in her hands to its rightful place. "I have something that fits that bill." After a few steps to the right, she picked up the crimson silk dress, noting the soft feel of the backless dress with a V-neck halter and slits.

"Gracie," he reprimanded. "We know better than to consider cheap drag whores when deciding what to wear. Besides, Nia's bloodlust is one of her best features." Silva flashed a dazzling smile. "The longer the dress, the less we'll have to clean up before Mother and her beasts find out."

Grace chuckled. "That is true. Well, if you do not care about the length, then go with the other one. They are both slutty, as you say, but the second is more so than the first. And the first is classier, but still shows off your *ass*-ets." She offered Nia a sweet smile. "Besides, we both know Silva would trip her and make sure she busts her nose again before she ever got close to stepping on your hem and ruining your dress."

"Here I was thinking it showed off my domineering side." Nia hung the sluttier dress up and retrieved the one before it. "Although my bloodlust settled earlier, who knows what kind of damage I could do with the right pair of heels? Maybe just accidentally step on one of her toes." From the hanger, she took the dress, then undid the buttons on the back before carefully stepping into the soft fabric. "Could you?" Nia glanced at Grace and gestured toward the buttons.

Before nodding and rising, Grace stifled a laugh, the corners of her lips twitching. She moved behind Nia to adjust the final delicate stitch of the dress.

Silva's eyes narrowed, and his lips curled up into a smirk. "You're so sweet. We know I'd do so much worse. It's no sweat off my brow if she suddenly perishes."

Nia sneered. "No one would miss Ivory. Not even her own sister." Her gaze flicked to Silva. "You and I desperately need a shopping trip. Maybe Mr. Ibras will send us some clothes soon." Since they couldn't exactly go to the marketplace yet. Gods, she missed shopping.

He perked up, a smile spreading across his face. "I'm sure between now and then there will be many unplanned, exciting surprises."

True. The shop owner loved his games. Nia collected a pair of six-inch, velvet stilettos to match the dress. With effortless grace, she slipped them on, securing each buckle around her ankles. "Did you find anything in there to work with the dress?"

"Who, me?" Silva asked, startled by the question. He peered down at the pieces in his hands, then back at the velvet displays, the rich fabric catching the light. "How about this?" He held the dangles, the ruby drops at the ends reflecting the lantern light like drops of blood.

Really? He could do much better. Unless he was just shopping through her stuff. Something he'd done once or twice. "Might be a bit too much on the crimson. And the shades aren't an exact match." She strode over to the dresser, her fingers tracing the smooth surface, and opened the top drawer where her collection sat. Diamonds filled this section entirely, and their facets caught the light.

"You should go on the more subtle side if you are going to go with diamonds," Grace suggested. "Something that is still flashy, but not so much that it detracts from the dress." She tilted her head a bit as she considered the outfit Nia wore. "Maybe just some posts?"

"That's what I was thinking. Maybe some studs and a tennis bracelet. Or would the bracelet be too much?"

"Hmm. Maybe try both first and see. If the bracelet is too much, you can just take it off."

Valid point. With a slight dip of her chin, Nia skimmed her collection of diamond pieces. She retrieved a pair of studs, put those on first, and then selected a bracelet with some width, though nothing thick. She wasn't going for gaudiness. Not that any of her jewels would fall into that category. With the bracelet secured, she propped her hands on her hips and glanced between her friends. "Well?"

"Perfect. You look great, Nia," Grace said.

"A knockout as always," Silva tacked on.

"Mission accomplished." Nia shut the drawer. She scanned the jewelry on top of the dresser. Although she noticed a few missing pieces, she decided that bringing them up would be more trouble than it was worth. Silva usually returned anything he swiped from her. Eventually. As always, she retrieved a pair of shades to wear. She kept the light in her bedroom low for a reason. Too much bothered her eyes. It's why everything in her room was black. "Let's go eat."

"Thank gods, I am starving," Grace remarked as she rose lithely from the floor. "Though not looking forward to dinner at the same time."

"Oh, come on. I love a good trash-talking session." Nia slipped the shades on as she headed toward her bedroom door.

"Oh, me, too. I would just like to go to one dinner without getting the insane urge to commit bodily harm by perhaps shoving my napkin down a certain person's throat. Maybe with my knife wrapped up inside."

"Well, that would certainly do the job." And then some. Not that she didn't think Ivory deserved it. The female gave a bad name to all of them. It didn't even make sense why Averine kept Ivory on the staff. Or at least bothered to give the woman a position. It wasn't like Averine cared all that much about what happened to them. At least not those who didn't make as much money as the top tiers. Maybe she let Ivory stay for pure entertainment.

Silva trailed behind them. They'd never made their way downstairs to the dining hall in such silence. Or even headed to the buffet in the same way. Maybe it had something to do with the tension in Grace. Which was pretty common whenever Ivory called for bets on Hunter. Not that she ever understood it. Grace didn't have shifters as clients. Something to do with being a shape shifter herself. At least she believed that was the case. It wasn't something they ever really talked about. One of the many things off-limits in this place. Her gaze swept over the buffet, considering each plate and its contents. Not that it mattered. She was on a restricted diet. It hadn't changed in her contract in the last ten years. A small side salad, two vegetables, and fish. That should do it. "Maybe we should see if Damari will make us some popcorn to go with all of this goodness."

"I'll pass." Silva frowned, his lips pressed tightly together as he trailed behind, barely glancing at the food on the table. He grabbed a single apple, its sweet smell filling the air, and playfully hip-bumped Grace. "You doing alright, Gracie?"

"Of course." She cocked an eyebrow at him. "You are going to waste away if you do not eat more than that," she teased.

He tossed the apple, caught it effortlessly behind him, bowed slightly in response to her smile, and then bit into it with a loud, crisp crunch.

"Nothing more than a fleeting murmur in the air. Wouldn't that be a shame?"

"We both know he's watching his figure." Had Grace purposely changed the subject? Or simply moved on? This was highly unusual for them. No matter the time of day, they always had something to talk about. After loading her plate, Nia reached for a glass of water and silverware. "Are we taking our usual corner table?"

"Of course!" Silva exclaimed.

There were a few familiar faces in the mix. A few less so. The newbies came and went so quickly. Made it a challenge to get to know anyone beyond their trio. Not that it bothered her any. Nia guided them towards the corner table, where the soft light illuminated the setting and gave them the best view of the dining hall. She could simply watch, choosing not to get involved in the chaos. Gracie could pick her company carefully, whereas Silva could encounter and talk to anyone who was nearby.

The three of them sat side-by-side. Nia, flanked by Grace and Silva, resisted the urge to roll her eyes while scrutinizing the other patrons. Obviously, Ivory had already started her charade. From a few tables over, half-naked Mona's overly enthusiastic look contrasted with her brother, Sin's, bored expression. Despite not chitchatting or getting friendly with everyone, Nia still knew each of them. *Great*, she thought. *We were the last to arrive.*

Ivory stood up. "Alright, ladies and gents. Now that our honored guest has arrived, I believe we can get started with the Fastidious Hunter betting pool. He's had one session with Nia. So, make sure that when you place your bet, you keep that in mind. Before we dive in, let's find out how it went. Shall we?"

"Fuck off, Ivory. What happens between me and the client stays between us." Like she'd share any bit of information with that bitch. Not to protect Hunter, but simply because she despised the female. And she had high standards to uphold.

"I believe that says it all, folks," Ivory stated.

Nia saw Grace's jaw clench, and then Grace slowly opened her mouth to take another bite.

Silva mumbled into his palm, the sound of his yawn echoing, "I figured we were more 'hooligans and tramps.'" Though he perked up as one of the younger workers passed, the scent of their sweet perfume lingered in the air. "Hello there, Miss Stormy," he offered, catching the preoccupied Seelie by the hand.

The female simply stopped and smiled, her gaze moving from Ivory's dramatic presentation to the inviting spread on the table. Stormy offered a shy greeting, her hand softly clasping his. Silva kissed the tops of her knuckles. "Hello, white one. Miss Grace, Miss Nia." With her hands clasped together, her dusty-blue-silk robe rustled at her waist, and lace edged the pink teddy beneath. Her gaze focused on Nia. "I love your dress. It suits you."

Nia offered Stormy an acknowledgment and thank you regarding the compliment. While she appreciated it, Silva usually took more of an interest in the newcomers. Still, it amused her the way he deferred to her before welcoming anyone to their table. Not that she cared.

Silva ushered Stormy to join them, and the female settled on his lap, visibly uncomfortable as she nestled against him, moving gingerly. His arms found their way around her waist while he rested his chin in the crook of her neck, breathing in the scent of her perfume. "Sweet as pie!" he whispered.

Grace met the female with a pleasant smile. "Hello, Stormy. How are you today?"

"I'm well, thanks." Despite its brevity, the acknowledgement led Stormy to slide a small vial across the table to Grace. After removing her hand, the light-purple liquid inside, shimmering slightly, became still. "Orchid," she stated.

Grace's eyes brightened. She reached for the bottle and, with a clatter, set down her fork before delicately pulling the cork. Her eyes closed as she inhaled. "Thank you very much. This is perfect."

Now, this was typical. Her friends interacted with others, while she remained quiet. It was how she preferred to keep things. No one in the den knew her history. Not even their so-called mother. When she'd arrived, she'd kept information about her past simple, yet truthful, omitting certain facts that would only offer one power over her. While she'd shared that she was a submissive, she'd also clarified that despite the low number of sexual partners, she was well-trained in the value of entertainment. And she'd strived to become a top-tier worker within a year. Something she'd accomplished.

Things from her past had given her a bit of an upper hand for reading people. Stormy hadn't needed to share her history. The female had a distinct tag on her ear, denoting her slave status; something she easily recognized from her time with her former dominant. Although Deacan was a nymph of noble blood, he'd often entertained Seelie nobility. As his partner, she had as well. Thankfully, she hadn't crossed paths with anyone from that period of her life. Not since she'd joined the den over thirty years ago.

"I have it on good authority that Hunter has scheduled a second session," Ivory declared, "so that is where we'll start the bidding. The rules haven't changed. The highest bidder for each number gets that pick. As always, Tamara will collect your funds for the pot. And I will announce the winner after Hunter has left Nia and returned to me, and we have a final tally of his sessions."

"*Good authority*," Grace mumbled, barely containing the venom in her tone. "Bitch probably stole a peek at Shalla's appointment book." She stabbed at a bite of fish, then calmly brought it to her mouth.

"Do you think she's considered that I've only ever had one client leave? Or that I currently have a waiting list of potential clients?" Nia placed a glazed carrot between her teeth and pulled it from the fork.

"Let's open up the bidding. Who's calling for a max of two sessions with Nia?" Ivory offered to the crowd.

As Grace bit into her salad, a small smirk played on her lips, and the scent of the vinaigrette filled the air. "Of course not. The only thing she can count is the number of dicks that make it between her legs or into her mouth. Why do you think she has someone else keep track of the funds?"

"I bet that you'll outlast Ivory in all things, Miss Nia." Stormy offered a quick look towards Nia, a tiny smile dancing on her lips.

Silva patted Stormy's thigh. "Not if Nia kills her first."

All three females shifted their gazes in his direction. Nia cocked an eyebrow. It was like he didn't know her at all. "I was thinking of a slow-forming water ball, maybe excessive sweating. Much better than death. That would be far too easy on her. And nothing compared to what she deserves. Besides, I'd never waste the breath it would take." She scoffed. Embarrassment went much further than death.

"We need to make her stink so badly that no client wants to go anywhere near her," Grace suggested. "But it would have to be something that would not wash off or go away easily. Otherwise, that would defeat the purpose."

"Hmm, I'm sure there's a way, Gracie." Nia spared a glance toward the timid female, who was nestled for comfort in Silva's lap. "And you're absolutely right, Stormy. I don't take one-offs any longer." Instead, she went through a careful selection process with each potential client before making her ultimate choice on the waiting list. This was the first time she'd taken on a new client in over twenty-five years.

"Your sense of smell is far superior to ours, Gracie. Be careful what you wish for," Silva cautioned. "Don't want her foul odor polluting the upper halls. Namely *ours*."

"Hmm, that is true. Maybe if we switched out her soap with something that made boils pop up all over her skin. Or something of that nature. I wonder if she is allergic to anything."

Although Ivory shared a room with others on the first floor, she still worked on the second. And if they stunk up the female properly, that odor could carry. "That would require either talking to her or her sister." At least with Red she could deal. Not that she had reason to speak with the woman.

"Two sessions go to Kami! Up for bid, three sessions," Ivory called out.

"Goltak slime soap," Silva offered, his smirk barely hidden.

Stormy turned to him, her eyes wide with a look of shocked inquiry. "I don't know what that is, but it sounds dreadful."

Grace visibly shuddered. "Please, Silva, I am trying to eat. I would prefer not to lose my appetite."

Nia scrunched up her nose, wrinkling it in distaste. "You had to bring him up."

"Oh, trust me, darling. It is," Silva said, focusing briefly on Stormy. "Hey, you never know. It could be a way to pawn him off. Seems like the type to enjoy his own filth."

"Are you referring to a client?" Stormy asked.

"One of Gracie's," Nia replied with a grimace, clutching her stomach.

"Yes, unfortunately," Grace responded, temporarily putting her fork down.

"I'm so sorry," Stormy said. "It sounds awful. I didn't mean to ruin your appetite."

Grace gave the female a reassuring smile. "It is all right. There is no need to apologize." Really, she didn't. Silva was the one who had brought him up. With a smile, Grace forked some vegetables and ate them, washing them down with water. "See? I am perfectly fine. He is definitely my most unpleasant client, that is all."

"At least you have me and Silva looking out for you," Nia commented. Especially on those days. "One way we all take care of each other." They'd each had their turn. The two of them had even saved her life once after a bad one-off she'd taken.

"Definitely," Grace replied.

"You are powerful as three," Stormy said, as if that explained everything.

Nia tilted her head. Who had Goltak before Grace? Or was Grace the only worker he'd ever seen? Not that she'd ask. The female didn't need her appetite ruined further, especially as it had bounced back so quickly. Better than thinking about the ongoing betting pool. "Do you think she'll offer an option that doesn't include his returning?"

Taking a deep breath, Silva exhaled and burrowed his chin into the hollow of Stormy's neck. "And what about you? I hear you're fond of wolfy companions lately." With a subtle adjustment, the female's body went still, like a statue. Her grip on his forearm tightened as she straightened, her knuckles turning white.

"You can smack him, Stormy. We don't mind. We've both done it before." A mischievous grin spread across Nia's face. Obviously, he'd made the female uncomfortable. Though she probably didn't help matters.

"I hold no desire to strike him." A weak grin appeared on Stormy's face, and she let go of Silva. Turning toward him, she cut off his question with a sharp dismissal. "That topic is closed."

"To each their own," Nia muttered. It would've amused her if the female had done so, not that she expected it. She'd offer to do it for her, but where would the fun in that be? Perhaps instead she could stir up some trouble. Her gaze flicked briefly to Ivory as she bit into a crisp snap pea. Just the way she liked them.

"Three sessions. Ten gold coins. Going once! Twice! Sold to Red!" Ivory exclaimed.

"Hey, Ivory. I've got a question," Nia called out over the din. The room fell silent, as if in awe of her presence. Not that it would last long.

"I noticed at the beginning of your tirade that you failed to mention what happened if Hunter never left me. Would that mean you'd keep the pot?"

"That is how it works. Except he's never stayed with one person long enough for that to happen."

"So, you remain perfectly neutral and don't place a bet? Or have anyone do it on your behalf? I mean, he has left you once again. It shouldn't surprise anyone, really. You're washed up, after all. And the male has needs. Of course, he'd leave you for greener pastures." She could have held her tongue and kept her cutting remarks to herself, but she wanted to provoke a reaction. Ivory had questioned her integrity as a sex worker in the den. For Hunter to leave would mean she'd have to leave him sexually unsatisfied. And that affected her reputation. One of the many things she prided herself on maintaining.

Grace picked up a bite of her salad, but didn't eat it just yet. Her voice, clear as a bell, cut through the chatter while her gaze remained intently on her food. "Seems to me as though he is just biding his time with someone *less than* until he discovers the one who can *truly* satisfy him. Obviously, that person is not you. Otherwise, he would not continue searching, leaving you to grovel as he walks away again and again and again."

Shit. Nia couldn't suppress the slight tilt of her mouth, especially as a multitude of eyes snapped in Grace's direction. This was the only place most people saw her, and those who did rarely spoke to her.

"He isn't searching, and I don't grovel," Ivory retorted. "I don't have to. See, if either of you really knew him, then you'd realize he comes back because he can't find anyone better than me."

"Are you sure that's the case? I mean, Gracie has a valid point here. If you actually satisfied him, what reason would he have to leave?" Watching Ivory's face flush a bright red brought a smile to Nia's face. The female positively fumed with anger. She could see it clear as day—they'd ruined her moment. "What's the matter, Ivory? Not sure what to say? That's okay. How about we get back to my last question? I noticed you didn't answer. Do you remain neutral in the betting pool? Or has someone bet on your behalf?" Her gaze flicked to Red. "Like, perhaps, your sister?"

"Fine! Yes, she bets for me. And I don't think you'll make it past three sessions with him. I'm shocked you survived one. Wait until he has a terrible day."

Did the female really think she'd take the bait? She looked forward to Hunter using her harder. They'd barely scratched the surface of how much further they could take things. "That sounds an awful lot like taking advantage of your first-hand knowledge, if you ask me. It would only be fair that you didn't take part in the betting. Don't you all agree?" Nia offered to the dinner crowd.

"Sounds a lot like *cheating* to me," Grace said, a small smirk playing on her lips. "You can say *whatever* you want, Ivory. Everyone here knows that every time he sees someone new that you practically beg him to spend time with you instead. And before you respond to that, do not forget—I have been here far longer than he has been coming here. Honestly, your obsession with him is nauseating. It is supposed to be the other way around. The clients should be the ones who are so desperate to spend time with us. But what else could one expect from someone like *you?*" Grace's eyes narrowed as she met Ivory's challenging gaze. The tension in the room was palpable. "Do you know what I think? He returns to you only because time with you costs *so much less* than it does with others of a much superior station. You are so *cheap.*" Grace's tone held layers of interpretation beyond the price of the woman's company. "But as both Nia and I said, if you *truly* could satisfy him, well, what reason would he have to look elsewhere for companionship?"

The shock on Silva's face was plain for all to see. Not that Nia blamed him. Typically, they were the ones spouting off, earning as much admiration from their companions as they did scowls and complaints from the irritated guards tasked with watching over them. Grace had rarely spoken up so harshly and so publicly. It made her beam with pride. Maybe she and Silva had rubbed off on the female more so than they thought. They had silenced Ivory, and the evidence was clear in her stunned expression. They'd taken control of the situation. Oh, how they'd turned the tide.

Silva buried his face in Stormy's neck. "I'm sorry," he muttered. Stormy patted his arm. His eyes, bright with amusement, returned his attention forward. "You gonna place a bet, love?"

"I may," she whispered as her gaze drifted sideways. "If Miss Nia doesn't do what we both know she's about to do."

His smile widened.

Nia finished the last bite of her fish. Oh, she was definitely about to take the cake. "You serve as the house, right, Ivory? And can match any wager?"

"Of course," the female answered.

"So, if I placed a bet for a thousand gold coins that he'll never leave, you could match that?" Over the years, she'd refused to take part in these things, but this time around she'd risk it. They'd had an excellent session. She truly believed he wasn't going anywhere.

"A t-thousand?" Ivory stammered. "Um, yes. I can. But how would we determine something like that?"

"Well, I imagine you have a cut-off point with the number of sessions." Nia stacked her dirty dishes, the clatter echoing in the quiet room, and then she finished the last drop of her water. If she didn't already have the pest right where she wanted her, then she would've upped the ante.

"Yes."

"Seven? Eight? Or higher?" She tilted her head, observing the woman's face as it displayed a progression of annoyance, frustration, and possibly anger. No one had ever bested Ivory at her own game. It was time that changed. "Higher, it is. Let's say... ten. That's a nice, round number."

"Ten sessions to mean that he'll never leave you?"

"Oh, darling, I took him with one. He's not going anywhere, but if you feel the need for a number... ten should suffice." And it offered plenty of opportunities for others to place their bets.

Grace's lips curved into a wider smirk, her eyes sparkling with amusement. She leaned into Silva and lowered her voice. "I was totally going to do that, too. So much better coming from her. I think I still may place one, though."

"Is it rude to bet he'll second-guess himself, leave only to realize his mistake and return?" Stormy asked in a hushed whisper.

"Whether it is rude, that was exactly what I planned to bet," Grace responded.

"If you don't feel that's a good number, double it or even triple it. No matter how high you go, he's not leaving. Your other option is to concede defeat and simply cancel this. Though I doubt that's the route you'll take." Ivory was too egotistical and dim. She would have no choice but to accept, or suffer and lose face in front of the entire brothel.

Ivory steeled her shoulders. "Ten sessions is adequate."

"Excellent." Nia waved her hand toward her friends. "I believe my companions have an alternate theory they'd like to explore. Once they've made their bets, retake bets on three sessions and forward."

With her gaze fixed on Ivory's eyes, Grace savored the last morsel of fish. She held up a finger, signaling a brief delay, before she chewed her food slowly and swallowed it. "I would like to bet that he will leave Nia at some point, but for one session only. And he will immediately return to her."

"You want to bet that he'll leave her, but only for one session." Ivory sneered. "And how much would you like to wager?"

"Hmm, let me think." Grace tapped her chin in mock-thoughtfulness. "What do you think would be a fair wager?"

"Well, you could go with a thousand gold coins as I did," Nia suggested. Oh, but she wanted to hurt Ivory a little more. The female hadn't seemed all that thrilled with that amount. "Or maybe double down."

"Double down?" Ivory squeaked. "Uh, yeah. Sure."

"Doubling down sounds perfect. As long as you are sure you are okay with that, Ivory? I mean, you look nervous over there."

"I'm not nervous. Not at all. I can cover that."

"Wonderful." Without another word, Grace returned to her food. She still had her salad and vegetables to finish.

Stormy settled back against Silva. "I'll buy the winner a day off."

"Way to make it more enticing, sweetheart," Silva chimed in.

"That sounds like an excellent idea," Nia said as she rose to her feet. "I believe you have a round of betting to start over." She shifted her gaze to her friends. "If you'll excuse me, I'm done here."

With a visible effort, Ivory relaxed her jaw and clasped her hands. "Well, I guess the pot has gotten even better. As recommended, let's start the bets for three sessions again."

Grace looked over at Nia. "I am going to finish my food, but I will not be long."

"I'll see you both soon." Nia disposed of her trash and got her dirty dishes in the bin before taking her leave from the dining hall, the lingering smell of the meal fading with her exit. The last time she had eaten something so good felt like a lifetime ago. Who knew how much fun dinner with a show could be?

Hunter arrived at the marketplace, bustling with activity, some hours before his second session with Nia was scheduled to begin. Although the area had been devastated less than fourteen days prior, most of the rubble had been cleared away. Large expanses of open ground were visible, though partially obscured by the debris of existing buildings. The crowds remained, though, as many of the vendors worked out of carts. Right in front of where their shops had once stood, by the looks of it. It had been some time since he'd gone to the jewelry store, but he remembered exactly where it had stood, as well as the female who had owned it.

He expertly weaved through the mass of bodies, ensuring he didn't touch a single person. Although that wasn't an issue, most people who saw him would scramble to get out of his way. He had a permanent scowl, a thunderous look that made it clear to all that he was not to be crossed, ever. While he didn't look straight at any of them, he noticed every single one tracking their exact location in his periphery.

He'd never really put much thought into why he chose jewelry for these special gifts over all other options. Maybe it had something to do with his upbringing and what had and hadn't been allowed. Clothing and toys would have been normal gifts in the den's environment. But a *normal* gift simply wouldn't do. He sought something special. Something to express just how much Nia had pleased him in just one session. Besides, clothing never survived with him. It definitely wasn't something he would have picked for this gift. As for toys, he required little for playtime. If the female didn't have the toys he preferred to use, she wasn't the right female for him, anyway.

He'd gifted jewelry to a female at the den only twice before. And only to the females who pleased him the absolute most. It was a onetime thing, too. Not something he ever repeated with the same person. Not that he'd ever gifted it this early, though—in the second session. But Nia was different, better, than any submissive he'd ever had before.

The first female he'd gifted jewelry to had fawned over the piece, practically begging him to bring her another. It had been incredibly annoying. He'd punished her for that conversation. And he'd never told her to wear it. Ivory had been the second female he'd brought jewelry to, and he hadn't done that until about their fifteenth time together. A rare, spectacular session with the female. He'd instructed her to wear it three times over all their years together. Not that it had done anything to *spice* up their time. What exactly did he see in her? Besides their familiarity, she could handle a basic session with him. Nothing more.

It wasn't something he wished to consider just then.

Right now, he was on a mission.

He quickly arrived at the jewelry store's former location. As expected, there was a cart set up with wares on display. But the female working it wasn't the one he'd bought from on his two previous occasions. Despite the obvious family resemblance, there were differences. Though it wasn't something he'd mention. Hunter gave her a polite nod, his eyes then drifting slowly across the display cases, examining the pieces carefully.

"Hello. Welcome. Is there something in particular you're looking for? Perhaps something special," the female said.

He flicked his gaze to hers for a moment, then returned his attention to the sparkling jewelry. "I am not sure yet. I believe I will know it when I see it." That was how it'd happened the other two times, anyway. And this piece had to be perfect. Not that he could explain exactly why. "Something blue, I think. Dark blue," he clarified. Why *dark* blue? He'd thought of the color because of Nia's safe word. But he'd yet to specify a hue, even in his mind.

"Hmm. A necklace, perhaps?" She slid aside a hidden partition and retrieved three unique pieces, laying them side-by-side. "Each comprises a variety of sapphires and diamonds. Does one of these speak to your liking?"

Hunter examined each piece with a critical eye, his fingers tracing the contours as he spent at least several minutes on each. The first was rather simple. Only one decently sized sapphire, oval, surrounded by diamonds positioned in eight different curlicues. He pictured what it would look like on Nia, but almost immediately decided against that necklace. Though undeniably elegant, it was not what he had in mind. Not extravagant enough. Hunter pushed the box containing it just slightly toward the female before moving to the next one.

This one was a bit more detailed. Again, just one sapphire, about the same size as the first, though in a teardrop shape. The diamonds that framed the gem almost formed the bottom of an hourglass, with more diamonds intricately placed on the top and bottom. Hmm. Almost looked like a perfume bottle of sorts. He envisioned how the piece would look on Nia's neck, its intricate details complementing her features. It was exquisite. But no. Not what he was looking for, either. Hunter pushed the box forward until it sat next to the first one. Then he moved on to the third.

His head tilted just the slightest bit to the right as he scrutinized every detail. This one had four circular sapphires that would adorn the neckline, each one ringed by diamonds. Diamond vines shaped like leaves continued, with a brief space between each sapphire. Sixteen leaves in all. Ah. The circular sapphires were to represent flowers. In the center, a larger, round diamond glittered, connected to a teardrop sapphire, which was encircled by smaller diamonds. Hunter briefly stroked his chin. Maybe. He summoned Nia's image into his mind. The sapphires and diamonds would shimmer, resting against her skin, with the largest gem nestled in the hollow of her chest. His head tilted slightly in the other direction. No, it was lovely. But no. Close, but not quite. He pushed the third piece forward to join its sisters, feeling the smooth surface beneath his fingertips before lifting his gaze to the female.

"The third piece"—he dipped his chin toward it—"I believe is close to what I am looking for. But not there yet. No, I need something more. Something even more extravagant." Why was he putting so much effort into this? It didn't make any sense. He hadn't put nearly this much thought into the other two pieces of jewelry he'd bought. Then again, neither female had come anywhere close to comparing with Nia. The things she did to him. For him. Just in that one session alone. The calm that had settled over him as their time together the other day came to a close. That calm meant more to him than he could—or would—put into words. He had to be sure she grasped the significance of that point.

"Closest, huh?" She returned the pieces to where they belonged. "You used to be a customer of my mother's, right? I mean, the previous owner?"

"Yes. I purchased from her on two occasions."

"Alright. I might have something. It's a piece she finished a few days—well, before everything happened." The female reached into another hidden compartment, retrieved another box, opened it, and presented it to him. "What about this?"

Hunter didn't speak as she opened the box, the soft click of the latch echoing, and presented it to him. He leaned in closer, his eyes scanning every minute detail. This piece was certainly more extravagant than the rest, with a bold design. A multitude of diamonds encased and separated seven midnight blue sapphires, with one larger oval sapphire dangling from the cluster. Hunter brought Nia's face up in his mind, imagining just what this piece would look like on her. The seven sapphires, each a brilliant jewel, would look perfect around her neck. The dangling piece sat right at the top of her cleavage. An image of her, bound to the bed, flashed into his thoughts. The piece seemed heavy just by looking at it. When he fucked her, it would bounce freely on her chest without flying up to hit her face or getting tangled in her hair.

Hunter flicked his gaze up to the female. "May I hold it?"

"Yes." She held the box out closer.

He gently lifted the necklace from the box with both hands. Oh, yes. There was definitely weight to it. But not so much that it would be uncomfortable. The way it felt in his hands revealed how skillfully it was made. The clasp, cold and metallic, felt strong to the touch. He could wrap his hand around the front or back of it without breaking it. Pull it tight against her throat while he fucked her. *Mmm.* He nearly licked his lips just thinking about it. *Nope.* Definitely didn't want to do that right now. Hunter returned it to the box just as carefully as he'd removed it. "I will take it."

With a slight nod, the female returned the lid to the box. "It's three hundred gold coins."

Hunter didn't even blink at the price. Which was utterly insane. Three hundred gold coins was a fortune. And more than he'd ever spent on any one thing. Ever. But it was worth every coin. He expected his sessions to be with Nia for the foreseeable future. This business transaction with Nia was going to be utterly perfect. And she had already made him feel and do so many things no other female ever had before. He could already tell he wasn't ever going to need another, and he wouldn't need to—or be forced to—move on from her. He'd searched for this kind of sexual connection for decades. Someone who could truly handle him and everything his body demanded he bring to the table. The full depths of his depravity and brutality.

And he hadn't even gotten there with Nia yet. But he would. Soon.

He almost wished the piece of jewelry cost more.

Hunter pulled a pouch of coins from the bag around his hip. Once opened, he counted three hundred, pocketed the surplus, and filled the pouch with the heavy coins. He tugged the drawstring closed and placed the pouch on the cart in front of the female, the scent of leather filling the air.

"It must be for someone truly special, as my mother intended," the female said. She handed him the box and collected the pouch from the top of the cart.

"You could say that." Not that he meant it in *quite* the same way she did. It was obvious the female indicated a romantic relationship. But one didn't have to have feelings for a person to recognize that they were special. The truth wasn't her business, though. Hunter carefully tucked the box into his bag, closing it up tightly. "Thank you." With a dip of his chin, he turned to leave.

"You're welcome."

Without a word, he pushed past the throng of people to find a way out of the crowded marketplace. He had just enough time to get something to eat before he had to head to the den for his session with Nia. It was going to be another that would be absolutely perfect. He could feel it.

Three

Nia perched on the end of her bed as she awaited Hunter's arrival. As she rested on her palms, her breasts were prominently displayed. With the brief discussion they planned to have, she'd opted out of starting in the submissive pose. The lingerie she'd selected for her session today with Hunter was one of her more recent acquisitions. As one of the top-earning females in the brothel, the owner often gave her special privileges, which included time to shop in the marketplace. This piece was all lace and string. A pair of lace panties molded to her form, the red silk strings a sensual touch. That didn't include the bow right above her pussy. Then the matching bra that just covered her nipples. Three bows adorned the garment: one nestled in the crevice between her breasts, and the remaining two sat where the straps gathered around each breast.

Hunter let himself inside, the door opening with a groan before he closed it quietly behind him. He took in every detail of her outfit, his eyes lingering as he gazed at her from head to toe, and he licked his lips.

"Welcome back, Sir," Nia said as she undraped one leg from the other. Hunter didn't return the greeting as she pushed up off the bed, rising to a height that put her right around six-foot. Still just over three-and-a-half feet shorter than him. Without the red velvet fuck-me six-inch heels she had on, she stood just over five-six. She'd always been on the shorter side for a nymph, but it didn't hinder her.

She took careful, calculated, and slow steps as she closed most of the distance between them. Nia noticed the slender black box in his hand, but she didn't mention it. Nor did she inquire if he appreciated what she'd selected for him. The look on his face said it all. "I have an answer to your previous question—my favorite position. Would you like to hear it in detail, Sir?"

Hunter silently placed the black box on a nearby table and then sat in a wooden chair pressed against the wall. With his forearms casually resting on his thighs and elbows on the chair's arms, he gestured to her. "Proceed."

Circumnavigating the bed, she grasped the bar at the foot of the mattress, its cold metal a stark contrast to the warmth of the sheets. This was what he had attached the leather straps to just the other day; because of their location, he could tie her to either end of the bed. "My favorite position is when I'm on all fours, my wrists bound to the bar, restricting my movements further with my ankles bound, too. I like to be blindfolded." Nia returned to the spot where she usually took her repose position. "So that spanking may be mixed in intermittently during the session."

The more she spoke, the darker his eyes got. "What do you like to be spanked with, Nia?"

While there were straps in various places attached to her bed, there were several items that hung on her wall, including paddles of different sizes, several sets of cuffs, and three floggers. That didn't include the additional pieces she had in the dresser below it. She longed to see him making his way through all of it. "Hand. Paddle. Flogger." Even though she remained impassive, just describing her desires and picturing him acting on them excited her. Hunter's expression didn't change, either. His cock stiffened noticeably at the mere mention of the flogger.

"Good." He stood slowly from the chair. "Get on your knees." Turning toward the dresser, he surveyed the blindfolds that were laid out on top.

His reaction and their brief conversation in the few minutes they spoke validated her initial thoughts, even if she hadn't been sure at the end of their last session. Hunter would become a permanent addition to her schedule. As he instructed, Nia kneeled. She bowed her head and rested her hands atop her thighs; the silence broken only by the gentle drumming of her heartbeat against her ribs. Out of her periphery, she watched him pick a blindfold out.

Most of the garment was red, from the flowery lace to the ribbon, but the inside lining was a deep black. His footsteps made no sound as he closed the distance between them. Pausing behind her, he lingered, then gently gathered all her hair, cascading it over her shoulders. His fingertips just barely grazed her collarbones. Placing the blindfold over her eyes, he tied the ribbon tightly behind her head. "Can you see anything? Do not lie to me."

She looked left, right, down, and then up. He'd gotten it tight enough that it completely blocked her view. "No, Sir." As Hunter circled her, the air crackled with an unspoken energy before he stood in front of her. With a tight hold, he gathered all of her hair in one hand.

Her lips parted instinctively as the blunt tip of his cock pressed against them. Nia swirled her tongue around the head. Hunter's grip on her hair tightened slightly as he tugged her head further back, pulling a more audible moan out of her. She extended her tongue so she could lick further up his length. His grasp of her hair was so firm that any attempt to move her head was futile. Not that she truly required it—for now, anyway. Though she wouldn't mind if he tugged a little harder on her locks. As she slathered his cock up, she let out a soft groan. His grasp on her hair constricted with more force. Goddess, she loved the slight burn against her scalp.

Retracting her tongue, Nia took advantage of where she could feel the length of his shaft and licked the backside of his cock. Her fingers pressed a little harder against her legs, and her thighs clenched as she focused on the tip of his dick. Her tongue stretched, and with it, the slickness of her saliva coated the head.

As a groan resonated from his throat, Hunter gave her hair a firmer tug and shifted his hips further back, but she adapted, needing only a touch more exertion to maintain their connection. She clenched her fists against her thighs, moaning at the electric jolts that surged down her spine. Nia retracted her tongue and licked her lips. "More, Sir." The words came out of their own volition. She didn't know if she wanted the playful pain of her hair being pulled or the teasing of his hips farther from her.

Hunter jerked her head back, her face tilted up toward the ceiling, and moved back so his cock wasn't anywhere near her mouth. "I did not hear you say 'please.' Are you demanding of me, or asking me?"

Holy fuck. If he hadn't turned her on before, she definitely was now. Shit, she'd need to get a fan for when they were together in her room. "Asking, Sir. More, please, Sir." Goddess, she definitely wanted his cock buried deep in her mouth and harder tugs on her tresses.

"Better."

Nia stroked her tongue across her lips as if she were enjoying her meal. Even though she hadn't gotten it yet, the pleasure humming through her body was already more than what she'd experienced with him a couple of days earlier. Every time a beautiful rumble resonated in his throat, tingles shot down her spine. The touch of his cock against her lips intensified the sensation, especially as he jerked her mouth from his shaft once more. Her fingers tightened against her thighs at just the image and the musky, intoxicating scent of his arousal. "More, please, Sir." She wanted all of his cock. "Please, Sir," Nia pled.

This time, he let her take a bit more, but not all of him. About a quarter of the way down. Even as he gripped her hair, he didn't immediately jerk her head back, a slight delay. Nor did he thrust home just yet. A growl rose in his chest. As she whimpered around his dick, Hunter yanked her mouth away from his shaft.

Her nails bit into her thighs. The tiny pinpricks sent small jolts of lightning coursing through her veins. Fuck, she was so hot for him already. Not that she was the only one hungry for more. They'd only just started, and his potent scent filled her nostrils. "More, please, Sir," she groaned. "May I have more of your cock? Please, Sir... please, Sir, I need more," Nia begged.

Without a word, Hunter forcefully guided her head back and rammed his cock deep into her mouth until it reached the back of her throat. And then he thrust it in and out.

Goddess, yes! This was *exactly* what she needed—him fucking her mouth with his cock, so damn deep. Nia extended her tongue, determined to slather as much of his dick as possible with every thrust he made into her mouth. Fuck, the heat rolling through her body was off the charts. Clutching her thighs, she alternated between licking each ball sac as he picked up the pace of his thrusts. She withdrew her tongue and ran it along the underside of his shaft while tightening her mouth around his cock. He moaned. His grip on the back of her head constricted. The speed and force of his thrusts increased.

It took every ounce of restraint she had not to grab his ass. Not a desire she'd ever had with her other clients. Not that she dared examine where the yearning came from. Nia scraped her nails against her thighs, teased the base of his cock with her teeth, and resumed sucking it, her mouth now clamped tighter around his shaft. She didn't just *want* him to come; she needed him to come. It was a primal desire that burned deep inside of her—the need to taste him as she swallowed every drop he had to give her.

The room filled with a growl, fierce and untamed, reverberated through the room. Though his claws scraped against the back of her skull, she only felt a sharp graze, not the sting of blood. Hunter slammed his cock into her mouth repeatedly. His orgasm exploded down the back of her throat. With the grip on her head, keeping her mouth wrapped around his cock, his growl morphed into a roar that damn near shook the walls.

As she gulped down his cum, Nia had to clamp the inner walls of her pussy to hold her own release back. Fuck, that sound was like a current that shot straight to her core and burned her from the inside out. While she fully intended to break the rules within the next two sessions, it was still too soon to do so. Something she'd already come close to doing earlier. Even if it had been an accident, it didn't mean she wanted to do it on purpose... yet.

Goddess, she remembered why the blindfold was one of her favorite things. The rest of her senses were so alive. The intense throbbing, the rise of goosebumps, the rumble of his growls, and the single moan from his lips—she felt it all with a consuming passion. No wonder she was on the verge of an orgasm.

Hunter wasted no time, right after the last drop went down her throat. He pulled his cock from her mouth and strode off, leaving her with the taste of him. A slight rattle indicated he had removed something from her wall. Hunter returned to where she kneeled, gripped a handful of hair, and lifted her to her feet before leading her to the bed. With a hand on her hip for balance, he lifted her onto the edge of the mattress. "Arms up. Now."

He secured her wrists and ankles, the brush of his fur against her skin sending a wave of awareness through her. Nia let out a small gasp with each touch. Then all she had was the air lightly caressing her pussy. She licked her lips, the taste of anticipation heavy on her tongue, as she longed for Hunter.

When she'd put the heels on earlier, readying herself for their time together, she didn't imagine she'd be standing on the bed while wearing them. Even though she had noticed his height before, the difference between their heights struck her now. Though she couldn't see, she sensed his height, even as she teetered in her high heels.

After a few moments, something wooden scraped the floor as Hunter reappeared before her. His hands went to her waist, his grip firm. Nuzzling at her sex, he let out a rumble that reverberated through her, reaching deep into her soul. With a savage grip, he tore her panties from her body with his fangs. "Come for me, Nia," he growled out before taking her clit in his mouth and sucking hard.

The vibrations from him that pitched her over the edge were so strong, she strained against the cuffs around her wrists. This release wasn't the most powerful he'd given her, but it hit close to the line.

Hunter shoved his tongue deep inside her pussy and likely swallowed every drop of her release. After withdrawing his tongue from her sex, he leisurely licked up her slit, nibbled on her clit, and then traced back up her slit. "I want you to continue with the begging. Until I stop to take a breath, you have permission to come when you need to."

Had she heard him right? Not that he gave her time to ask. As he drove his tongue back into her pussy, it was a good thing she didn't need clarification. She could beg in whatever way he wanted. The sensation of his tongue inside her brought to mind the vivid image of her hanging from the four posters. "Harder, please, Sir," Nia implored with a groan. The idea's origin was a mystery, yet it amplified the sensations coursing through her. "Harder, please, Sir... harder, please, Sir..."

His grip changed, moving from her hips to cup her ass. He drove at her harder and faster, his claws digging into her flesh. There wasn't a single inch of the inner walls of her sex that his tongue didn't taste and explore. Hunter growled against her, sending another vibration through her pussy.

Oh, gods. That did her in. "Sir, please let me come. Please let me come. Please let me come, Sir." The words slipped out automatically. They were far different from their first time together. Despite Hunter's permission, Nia took a breath between her cries before succumbing to the approaching orgasm.

Hunter sucked on her sex, getting every single drop. Not that he stopped there. He used his tongue to explore and stimulate her, sliding it up and down her slit, flicking gently at her pleasure point, and grazing his fangs against her outer lips. With a firmer grip on her ass, he pushed her sex against his mouth, increasing the pressure.

If it hadn't been for the straps around her wrists and his hold, she was pretty sure she wouldn't have been able to stand. His growls mixed with the dampness of his tongue sent her spiraling over the edge repeatedly. Each time, Nia begged him to intensify, squeezing her ass, quickening his pace, and she pleaded for release before she climaxed.

She'd lost count of the number of times she'd come. Not that the number mattered. Hunter completely devoured her, lapping up every burst of pleasure that ripped through her body as if he needed her juices just to stay alive. His tongue kept working its magic on her, as his claws clung to her. The pinpricks were a pleasurable torment. "Please let me come, please let me come, please let me come, please let me come, Sir," Nia prattled, the words coming out so rapidly, they practically ran together in one sentence.

Unlike before, she didn't bother with the breath; the blanket permission still held. She screamed, her voice now hoarse, as a colossal orgasm slammed through her body, and gushed out into his mouth.

Hunter's roar against her pussy caused a ripple of sensations, leading to an immediate follow-up orgasm. As her climax ended, he drew his mouth away, taking a moment to control his heavy, ragged breaths.

A loud clatter signaled the stool had fallen to the floor. Nia gasped when he tore her bra in half, freeing her breasts from their confines. Her skin was so sensitive, she swore she could feel the ridges and contours of his muscles as his arm came around her waist. His fur against her flesh sparked sensations that intensified as he released her and placed her in the middle of the bed.

Her hands and knees trembled, a feeling that escalated as he cuffed her to the bed, with her ankles held firmly in place. A low moan left her mouth as each strap got buckled. Gods, her core had already heated back up. Nia bit her bottom lip when the last of the restraints were in place.

He didn't join her right away. She couldn't see what he was doing, but she heard the soft creak of the mattress as he climbed onto it. Hunter's claws grazed her ribcage as he leaned in, the scent of his fur filling her senses as he bent over her. Goddess, she loved that. He meticulously licked up each stray drop of blood from where his claws had pierced her skin on her ass cheeks. He gripped her ass, pulling it closer, and then he made wet trails over the slight wound with slow, deliberate strokes of his tongue. A low growl vibrated out of him.

Her neck arched with a loud groan. Lightning's energy surged through her, sending shivers down her spine. Fuck, that felt amazing. And that noise... fuck. Her toes curled at the currents running across her flesh. "More, please, Sir," Nia urged.

Hunter spread her legs a little wider, pulling her body just a touch closer to him, so her wrists strained a bit more against their bindings. Gripping her hips, his claws dug in slightly as he penetrated her with just the tip of his dick. He lingered in the position, a subtle shift of weight preceding the moment he drew his hips back.

A low moan escaped her as her back curved, her backside lifting slightly. Fuck, how was it possible she felt as if she might explode if she didn't have more of him? Nia clamped the inner walls of her pussy down. With the number of orgasms she already had, it was on fire, but she had to have more. So much more. "More, please, Sir. I need more, please, Sir," she pled.

"Not yet." Hunter's palm connected with her rear, the sound echoing in the room. Nia cried out in ecstasy. With a firm grasp on her hip, he teased her entrance with his length while giving her another stinging slap on her buttocks.

Her neck and back bent, thrusting her backside out and pushing her pussy into closer contact with his cock. Holy fuck—she didn't know how, but she kept the inner walls of her pussy closed tight. Despite the other dominants she had, it was different with Hunter. He reminded her more of her first, except Hunter was better. No one had ever read her body or turned her on so much in just two sessions.

Hunter tightened his grip on her hip and pushed his cock inside her, a little further than before. Holding the position, he reached beneath and pinched her nub hard, then removed both his cock and his fingers.

Oh, gods. Letting out a moan, she was on the verge of asking him permission to come. But no, not yet. Nia kept her desire to orgasm in check, her bottom lip caught between her teeth. Just a little longer and then she'd ask. Although with how this session and the one previous had gone, she might bump up her timeline on disobeying him. She couldn't wait to see what punishments he doled out.

He slid his cock back inside her pussy, barely entering. Retracting his hand, Hunter landed a forceful slap on her ass before thrusting his cock deeper into her. They both groaned as the walls of her pussy clenched around his shaft.

The release that had built inside of her intensified more. Requesting permission to come sat right there on the tip of her tongue, but something stopped her. Whether she asked now or waited another moment or two, it was going to be a massive release. However, if she held out a little longer, something she was absolutely capable of, it might be so powerful she saw stars. Her fingers curled against the soft mattress, clutching the familiar weight of the duvet. One more moment, but no longer. She had that much in her.

A trickle of blood slid down her skin as his claws dug into her hip. As he withdrew from her, he pressed his erection against her entrance once more while reaching around to caress her clitoris.

Nia barely kept her body locked down. "Please let me come. Please, let me come, Sir," she begged, her words rushing together.

Hunter leaned over until his mouth was right next to her ear. "No."

Fuck, fuck, fuck... Nia groaned, the restraints biting into her flesh as she tugged against her bonds. She didn't think any had seeped out, but the vibrations from the growl in her ear coupled with the sensations riding up her pussy had her panting. Gods, he couldn't let her come soon enough. "Please let me come, Sir."

He pulled his hips back, positioning the head of his shaft at her entrance. "Come," Hunter growled out at the same moment he slammed his cock deep inside of her. A loud moan echoed around the room.

Waves of pleasure hit them both simultaneously. Nia cried out at the explosive release. The force was so intense that she saw tiny sparks of light behind her blindfold.

Moving his other hand back to her hip, his claws dug in deeper as he fucked her; his thrusts hard, fast, and unrelenting.

The jolts flooding her drew more moans out of her. Each time he drilled into her; the inner walls of her pussy clamped around his cock. The blindfold heightened her senses, already sensitized by the orgasms he'd given her. That was the point. At this rate, it wouldn't be long before he geared her body up for another release. "Harder, please, Sir."

Already, his cock swelled inside of her. As he moved his hand from her hip to her belly, his claws scraped against her skin, a sensation both painful and thrilling. His other hand moved from her hip and came to rest at the base of her neck. Her ass lifted higher as he shoved her head down closer to the bed, ensuring he didn't dislodge her blindfold. Hunter intensified his thrusts, increasing both the speed and force as he penetrated her.

Oh, gods. Nia moaned loudly. She squeezed and relaxed the muscles inside her vagina around his shaft. It wasn't just staving off an orgasm, but it was intensifying the pressure building inside of each of them.

Hunter let out a hiss as he drove his cock into her core again and again. "Come for me, Nia."

His aggressive thrusts and urgent demands brought her to the point of no return. As her body clenched, a scream escaped her lips, and her orgasm poured over Hunter's erection. An endless, torrential wave of wetness streamed down her thighs. His release exploded out of him and overflowed her pussy. A massive growl echoed around the room. As his hold around her waist shifted to her shoulder, his claws' painful grip dug into her skin. Shifting his hand from the back of her neck to the bar on the bed, he spread her thighs wider, his thrusts becoming more primal. The depth and volume of his growl drowned out the noise of their pelvises repeatedly slamming into one another.

"Oh, gods," Nia cried out. Her neck arched as she pressed her body closer to him, eliciting another moan from him. As his cock slid in and out, her pussy tightened around him, sending waves of sensation straight to her core. His thrusts became downright raw and extreme. Not that she'd change any of it.

His claws curled more around her shoulder, pricking her flesh, and he gave another massive growl as a rivulet of blood slid down her back. Bursts of pleasure shot through her veins. Fuck, she was so ramped up; she was ready to come again. "Please let me come, Sir." She didn't know how it was possible to have so many orgasms; then again, Hunter had called things out of her that hadn't occurred in over thirty years.

"Yes," was all he got out before he came on a roar.

A wave of ecstasy pulsed through her, spilling over his cock as their climaxes blended. Nia screamed as it saturated both her pussy and thighs. She believed a second release might've followed right behind the first. Either that or it had been rather continuous. Holy fuck, and it didn't seem like he was done.

Hunter fucked her through their mutual orgasms, barely stilling the swing of his hips even then. The bar he'd cuffed her wrists to locked into notches built into the bedposts. He released her ankles, the rough leather of the bindings against her skin, lifted the bar, the click of the lock echoing in the silence, and with a grunt, flipped it over as he turned her onto her back. After securing the bar back into place, he positioned himself over her body and fisted a handful of her hair. Grabbing the bar with his other hand, he shoved his cock into her mouth, and fucked it.

She didn't care about the wet spot beneath her back. It didn't bother her in the least. The taste of their cum together on his erection was the sweetest treat she'd ever had before. With her tongue moving sensually along his cock, Nia skimmed her teeth across the base of his shaft. As he penetrated her mouth, she extended her tongue to caress each testicle before withdrawing it.

His grip on her hair tightened as he hissed. The head of his cock rammed into the back of her throat again and again. *Yes, gods, fuck yes.* Nia swirled her tongue around his cock, from the head to the base, and then returned to sucking it as he pounded into her mouth. She fully slathered his dick, straining against the straps around her wrists as she got it good and clean. The whole time, she rubbed her thighs together, currents consistently sweeping through her body as their mixed cum went down the back of her throat.

Hunter slapped her inner thigh. The abrupt sound cut through the silence and stopped the friction on her legs. He increased the speed at which he fucked her mouth. A deep moan left him as his orgasm punched out of him. As he held her mouth on his cock, the grip on her hair tightened even more.

Shit. She totally wanted him to smack her thigh again. Not that she could truly respond at the moment. Nia focused solely on swallowing every drop of his release. Once the last of it had gone down the back of her throat, she purred, sending vibrations up the length of his cock.

His grip on her hair became even tighter as a guttural hiss, louder than before, escaped his lips. After her purr had faded away, he swiftly withdrew and positioned himself between her legs. He smacked first one thigh, then the other—his silent instruction for her to spread her legs. Something between a mix of a purr and a groan left her mouth. She couldn't quite identify the sound, but she *really* liked his hand on her thighs.

Using the leather straps on chains, Hunter bound her ankles again, but this time to the bedposts, forcing her legs wider, and angled back a little. It was a good thing the chains were long. Remnants of their last climaxes continued to seep out of her pussy, completely coating it as well as her thighs. Leaning down, he fused his mouth to her sex with a deep growl and sucked hard. Nia moaned and arched her back. Fuck—her body thrummed with all the stimuli, the slight stings, and their deliciously sweet taste.

Hunter smacked her thigh again, the sting a familiar sensation. "Lie still," he growled, then fused his mouth to her sex. He sucked and licked with growing urgency, his tongue driving deep while flicking and biting at her nub.

Oh, gods. His actions really pushed forward the idea of disobeying him and doing it anyway. No, no; she had a timeline for a reason. The fourth session was when she would purposely disobey him. Though with the way he devoured her pussy, it made it harder to keep that in mind. Nia groaned. Fuck, she was close to an orgasm, even almost to the point of begging. Given how hypersensitive her body had become since the beginning of their session, it made perfect sense.

Growling softly, Hunter sucked on her nub with fervor. Suddenly, he plunged three fingers into her wetness and teased her clit with his tongue. *Holy fucking shit.* Her thighs trembled at the way she clenched to hold the orgasm back. This wasn't something she could keep up for long at all. "Please let me come, Sir. Please, please, let me come, Sir."

Curling his fingers up to rub over her G-spot, Hunter sucked on her clit once more before sitting up and removing his fingers from her sex. Positioning himself at her entrance, he wrapped his arms around her legs and penetrated her with a powerful thrust until he was fully inside her. He groaned as their pelvises met, the head of his cock pushing up against her core. "Now you can come."

"Oh, gods!" Her orgasm gushed out over his cock. That was the second time she'd uttered words other than requests. Not something that was normal for her. Even with her first dominant, she'd never been like that. Somehow, Hunter drew things out of her that didn't occur with anyone else.

Hunter didn't hold back, and with a groan, he thrust his hips forward, colliding forcefully with her center. Then, he did it again. It took seconds for his speed to pick up. The growl reverberated around the room, and his grip on her legs became even more constricting.

At least twice before, she'd asked him to go at her harder. It seemed highly unnecessary at that point in time. His speed continued to increase as he pounded into her repeatedly. Nia clenched the inner walls of her pussy, tightening them around his cock as their mutual noises echoed around the room. Fuck, he was gearing her up for another release. Between his growls, the restraints on her wrists and ankles, and the sensitivity of her body—it was impossible for it not to be powerful.

Another moan left him. Leaning forward, Hunter planted his palms on the bed, leaving her legs to rest on his shoulders. As he delved deeper into her pussy, her toes curled up inside her shoes. His speed picked up even more as his cock begged her body for that one last release. *Fuck, fuck, fuck*... she was right there. "Please, please, please, can I come, Sir?"

Hunter growled as he slammed a little harder inside her. "Is that what you need, Nia? Do you need to come?"

There were a few things she needed, but he was already doing two of them, which just made the implosion that much more inevitable. Nia clenched her core around his cock. "Yes, Sir," she whimpered.

"Then come for me, Nia." He uttered her name before a huge, all-consuming orgasm burst forth, unlike before in their time together. His fingers clenched around the bedding, his claws ripping through it, and the roar that left him was enough to shake the walls.

His release tipped the scale and set her own off. Nia clutched the bar tightly, moaning with ecstasy as waves of orgasm swept through her, drenching his cock and flowing down her thighs onto his fur and the bedding. Another wave gushed out of him as well. Holy fucking shit. She panted as their mutual releases slowly ended.

Even when their bodies stilled, just like the other day at the completion of their first session, Hunter didn't move. Not right away, anyway. He stayed right where he was, buried deep inside her. As his breathing steadied, he gently grazed his claws up and down her legs, a soft rasp against her skin, when he could sit up. He pulled out of her after a minute, then began working on her bindings. Right leg, then left, and then her wrists. After taking off her heels and placing them gently to the side, he turned his attention to her blindfold. It joined the heels before he lifted her from the soaked bedding.

Hunter carefully carried her to the other side of the bed, gently placing her on her back before sitting back on his heels. Cum completely drenched the lower half of her body, her pussy still dripping. His tongue slowly swept across his lips as his gaze devoured her. As he gazed at her left shoulder, a storm of emotion seemed to darken his blue eyes. He obviously wanted to start there.

It was a good thing her bed was so big. At the end of her first year with the brothel, Averine had given her a look of confusion at the requests she made regarding her room. It hadn't lasted long, though. The female's expression had quickly changed. Not that she'd known then exactly what she'd been signing on for, but the money was necessary. It was the same reason she kept her room dark, with only the soft glow of the flickering candles that lined every floating shelf along each wall. It had nothing to do with creating a certain... ambiance.

Slowly turning her over onto her stomach, he straddled her body and swept her long locks aside. His cock pressed against her buttocks, oozing more semen between her cheeks. Nia watched from her periphery as Hunter licked the beads of crimson from her shoulder. Never once taking her gaze from his darkened gaze. Not that she quite understood why. Not anymore than she understood her desire to tell him her real name. Those moments when he'd used the name she'd given him... there was something about the way it rolled out of his mouth; it made her wonder what it would sound like if he used *her* name. Only a handful of people knew it.

It wasn't the only thing she couldn't explain. There were so many. Why he stilled at the end—as far as she knew, if what she'd heard was accurate, he hadn't done that with the other girls. Why did she want to know more about him? Something she absolutely could *not* do. It made things too personal. Yes, she had steady clients, and often they talked in the end, but she didn't initiate conversation. With Hunter... she *wanted* to know about him, but she wouldn't ask.

Once he finished cleaning her shoulder off, he tore his gaze from hers and moved down to work on her ass. He slowly and methodically cleaned her, relishing the salty tang of blood and the thickness of the semen that clung to her skin after their orgasms. Something had crossed his eyes, but she couldn't say what. Or even what had passed between them in that moment. Not once in thirty years had she ever become attached to a client, and that wouldn't start now. Nia closed her eyes. A low purr left her mouth. She couldn't quite help it. Her skin still tingled from the deprivation of her eyesight over the past hour and a half or so.

Hunter took his time finishing with her behind before he moved to her hips. Once he was done with her right hip, he moved to her left. His eyes locked on hers as his tongue caressed her skin. This time, her purr got a little louder. Really, she needed to stop it, but she couldn't, no matter how hard she tried. No one had ever made her purr since her first. It just meant Hunter was that good.

He traced the marks on her hip with his tongue, savoring the taste of her skin, before closing his mouth over them and giving a delicate suck. Watching that drew out a soft moan, which quickly returned to a purr as he trailed his tongue across the small of her back. None of her current clients did anything like what Hunter did. Some cleaned her up, though not in the same manner.

But she refused to question any of it. She lumped it up to the fact that he was simply like her first dominant. And she'd served that male for over a hundred years. Maybe that's what this was... why Hunter reminded her of her old dominant. That was exactly it. She remembered doing the same with her first as she watched Hunter cleaning her. Yes, she was simply equating the relationship. This thing with Hunter was nothing more than a business transaction. One they both fully enjoyed. Nothing more, nothing less.

Once he'd licked fully across her lower back, he made his way up her spine. As he did so, he slid his hands up her arms. Gripping her wrists, he ground his stone-hard cock into her ass. "If you do not stop making that noise," he growled in her ear, "I am going to go up front and pay for another hour. Or two." He pressed his erection firmly between her buttocks, intensifying the sensation against her backside. "I will bind you up so tight you cannot move an inch... and then I will fuck *this*,"—Hunter pressed his dick harder into her ass, the tip slipping in—"until you are begging me with tears in your eyes to please let you come."

Holy fuck. Good gods, she wanted that so badly. Nia couldn't stop the moan that slipped free. Somewhere in that, she completely overlooked that he didn't specify which noise. And it was definitely something she needed to know. It offered her insight into how to break rules so she could earn punishments. Although she tried, she couldn't get the image of what he'd described out of her head. If he wanted more time, he certainly could have it. Her next client didn't come in for a couple of hours. They had plenty of time to play a little more. Biting back a groan, she peered over her shoulder at Hunter. "To which sound are you referring, Sir?"

Hunter's eyes darkened a little further. As he moved his erection in and out of her ass, his grip on her wrists became tighter. "That *purr*," he growled out. "That fucking purr. I like it too much."

Nia's green eyes sparkled. Oh, he *liked* it, did he? "This *purr*, Sir?" she inquired and purred loudly.

His jaw dropped a bit. Their gazes locked onto one another. With a gentle rocking motion, he slid the blunt head of his cock in and out of her ass. Hunter's lips curled back and his fangs extended. This time, he didn't so much growl; he snarled—"Yes. *That purr.*" A fresh wave of wetness hit the juncture between her thighs. His grip on her wrists became crushing. She'd likely be bruised by the time he let her go.

Her desire to disobey him just went up a notch. There were so *many* ways he could punish her. With a more emphatic purr, she arched her back and lifted her head, pressing her ass a little closer to him.

Hunter withdrew his dick from her ass and forcefully brought her arms down to her sides. Then, he forced her knees beneath her, and she could feel them pressing hard against her chest. Grabbing the blindfold from the opposite end of the bed, he wasn't gentle as he retied it around her eyes, then shoved her head back down so her cheek pressed into the bed. It left her ass fully and completely accessible, but her pussy displayed as well. He bent down close, so his mouth was right next to her ear. "Stay."

Nia tracked every footstep as he stalked across the room. The door opened and practically slammed behind him. Here she'd thought that everything he'd done before had gotten her hot and bothered. Nope, not even close. She remained perfectly still. Even during the few minutes he was gone, she didn't move a single inch. How much additional time might he pay for? Could it end up pushing him into another client's time? Maybe. Not that she gave a shit. And she wouldn't examine that *at all.*

Fuck, who *was* her next client? Her thoughts silenced the second she heard Hunter. Though the door had opened without a sound, the subtle sound of his breathing filled the room. Her hearing was a little better than a shape shifter, but not as good as a dragon shifter. Nia remained perfectly still. Did he realize she'd sensed his arrival? How much time had he paid for? Despite her curiosity, she wouldn't ask.

Nia focused on each quiet, slight sound as he plucked items off her wall. Once he returned to the bed, he adjusted her position a little. Although she couldn't see anything, she paid particular attention to how he tied her up, especially when he readjusted her body. Before securing her wrists, he guided her to the edge, and the sharp scent of leather filled the air as the cuffs tightened. Next, he attached a spreader bar to her ankles, extending it so her thighs spread as wide as they could go without being overly uncomfortable, and keeping her ass raised in the air. He secured her arms between her knees and bound her wrists tightly to the spreader. Holy fuck. Each new restraint got her more and more turned on.

Hunter didn't utter a single word as he moved his body behind hers. With a hand on each side of her, on the bed, she felt the head of his cock brush against her ass. He grazed his fangs gently down her neck, shoulder, and spine. Reaching her ass, he bit down on her right cheek. It was enough to cause a slight sting, but not enough to actually break her skin.

Nia moaned, causing him to bite down harder until he drew a little blood. *Holy fucking shit.* She was *so* going to enjoy disobeying him. Not just in the punishment he currently intended to deliver, but in future sessions as well. Pain was pleasure. Goddess, it had been a long time since she'd disobeyed a dominant and earned a punishment. It rarely occurred this soon in the relationship, but she hadn't been able to stop herself.

Sitting up behind her, Hunter dug his claws into her left hip. He positioned himself behind her, ready to penetrate. Their cum still covered her ass, so lubrication wasn't necessary. During their first session, he gave her a split-second warning, his voice a low rumble, before thrusting into her. Not this time. He buried his cock as deep as he could until his pelvis pressed against her ass. A loud, vibrating growl echoed around the room. Reaching around, he played with her pussy, pinching and rubbing her clit before slipping three fingers deep inside her. His fingers plunged in and out, stroking her G-spot. He withdrew his hips, teasingly almost pulling his cock out of her ass, before plunging it back in. He got a swift rhythm going quickly, fucking her ass as his fingers fucked her pussy in perfect rhythm.

Good gods, she should've disobeyed him sooner. With a moan, she tested the restraints on her wrists, the coarse material digging into her skin. The little bites of pain only intensified the sensations as Hunter filled her ass repeatedly with his cock and the strokes of his fingers as he used them to fuck her pussy. Both in rhythm with one another. Oh yes, she'd thoroughly enjoy disobeying him. Provided he truly pushed her limits and denied her orgasm until it became painful. Fuck, she hoped he did. It had been *way* too long since that had happened.

Removing his hand from her hip, he drew it back and gave her ass a hard smack. Without pausing, he delivered another stinging slap. "Did I say you could try to move?" His fingers found her hip again, and his touch sent a jolt through her. The force of his thrusts, both with his cock and his fingers, intensified as he picked up his speed.

Nia groaned. It hadn't been intentional, but if he was going to smack her ass like that, she might have to do it on purpose. With the bindings, her movements were severely limited. Fuck, he felt so good.

With each thrust of his cock, a deep moan escaped him as his fingers pushed deeper into her wetness. With his claws digging into her hip, he snarled, the scent of blood thick in the air as it ran down her backside.

As she clenched the inner walls of her pussy, a moan mixed with a whimper left her lips. Something like a purred moan. A powerful orgasm built deep inside her core. The fire coursing through her veins was like a small blaze, and she suspected by the time they reached her breaking point, it would be a bonfire. It had been so long that she might need to rebuild to volcano. She believed he was just the male who'd get her there.

Hunter retracted his hand before delivering another, more forceful slap to her backside. Then again. Then again. His hand went to the back of her neck, and he pushed her face roughly into the mattress as he quickened his rhythm.

Not only did she clamp the inner walls of her pussy, but she also clenched her asshole, too. A full-on snarl resounded from him. *Holy fucking shit.* The blaze within her synapses grew hotter, consuming her with each passing moment. It wasn't quite at the bonfire level, but it wasn't too far off, either. Her usual timeline had gone out the window with Hunter. With nearly every other male she submitted to, they had gone months and had never even come close to this level before. They hadn't even gone through two sessions, and they were already there. Definitely her favorite. She'd have to bring out more toys for their next session together. Maybe even offer options other than the bed.

From her neck, his hand moved to her shoulder, his claws scraping down her back, leaving a trail of burning pain and a few drops of blood, and then gripped her hip. He snarled. Hunter shifted his touch from her pussy to her clitoris, applying strong and rapid pressure, while intensifying the pace of his thrusts into her ass.

Nia cried out in utter bliss. Fuck, it hadn't been like this with anyone in over a century. Their next sessions would have to be adjusted as they'd surpassed her normal expectations. Which meant they hadn't even approached hard limits. "Please, may I come, Sir?" Nia asked. Her core was only tight, so minor discomfort. But she expected he'd read both her body and the way she voiced the request, declining it.

Leaning over her body, Hunter removed his claws from her hip and flattened his palm on the bed. Not only did this allow him to fuck her ass deeper, but it changed the angle up, too. He moaned as her rectal walls squeezed each rigid length of his cock, especially when she clenched them again. Rubbing her clit harder and faster, he put his mouth right up next to her ear. "Absolutely *not*."

The powerful vibration coursed through her, reaching every part of her body and tingling her toes. Holy fuck, all of it pushed her closer to her breaking point. In fact, holding back her orgasm had certainly gone past minor discomfort and into slight pain. Nia groaned loudly.

Hunter slowed down his speed, but not the force of his thrusts, grinding into her each time his pelvis met her ass cheeks. He gave her pussy a firm smack before plunging his fingers back inside her deeply. She contracted her vaginal walls and clamped her cheeks around his dick. Motherfucker, he'd quickly pushed her into pleasured pain, right into bonfire territory. It was going to become more difficult to hold out. "Please, please, please may I come, Sir?" Nia pled.

He withdrew his fingers from her vagina and moved his hips back, leaving only the tip of his penis inside her asshole. "Hmm... I do not think I can hear you. You are going to have to be a little louder, Nia." He delved his fingers back into her warmth and drove his cock back into her backside, transitioning swiftly to the forceful, unhurried penetrations.

Fuck, fuck, fuck. Nia let out a powerful moan. Gods, she didn't think she could keep her orgasm back much longer. Behind the blindfold, stars exploded into her vision as a pleasurable pain coursed through her. "Please, please, please, please may I come, Sir?"

"Hmm, let me think about it." He stilled his hips, his throbbing cock buried deep, but his fingers kept their rhythm. "I think not." Hunter's fingers slowly withdrew from her warm, wet folds. His growl and a slight sucking noise told her he was cleaning her juices off of them. "I do not smell tears yet behind that blindfold of yours. I do not want to go back on my word." Hunter pulled his hips back and then slowly pushed back inside her. "But perhaps if you beg me a little more, I will allow you to come, anyway." Sitting up on his knees, he brought both hands to her waist and dug his claws in with a groan.

Holy motherfucking shit. To get tears, he'd need to provoke her to the point of almost erupting, like a volcano. It would be a feat no male had ever accomplished. Not that she didn't suspect he wouldn't get her there, just not in this session. With his claws digging into her waist, the burning erotic agony that coursed through her veins threatened to erupt. She definitely couldn't wait anymore. "Please, please, please, please, please, let me come, Sir," Nia pled in a moaned whimper. "Please, please, please, let me come, Sir. Sir, please let me come. Please, let me come, Sir."

Hunter's thighs trembled. With his claws digging in firmly, he removed his cock from her ass and settled onto the bed, positioning himself with his head nestled between her thighs and his mouth waiting beneath her pussy. "Yes, Nia, now you can come." He melded his mouth to her sex, exploring with his tongue.

As Nia plunged over the edge, a scream ripped from her throat, and her release flooded into Hunter's mouth. She strained against the ropes. She couldn't pinpoint how long the relief from the pressure remained. It was unlike anything she'd experienced in years. It felt like it had no end, as if it was one continuous stream.

A moan escaped him as his hands found her, his fingers sinking into the flesh of her ass. Hunter held her to his mouth as he drove his tongue in deeper. He eagerly devoured her sex, capturing every drop of her passion within his mouth. The more he plunged his tongue inside her, the more cum erupted out of her, filling his mouth all over again.

After the last drop flowed from her sex into his mouth, he licked her pussy one last time before repositioning himself behind her. He grabbed Nia's hips tightly as he pushed his cock into her pussy. His forceful thrusts were quick and intense as he drove deep inside her. It didn't take more than a few strokes for his release to shoot up the length of his cock and explode out of him on a roar.

Nia moaned. Her pussy's inner walls rhythmically clenched and released around his cock, prolonging his orgasm. She might've had another climax of her own if she hadn't just sent every drop into his mouth before he came inside of her. Though she couldn't see a thing, her heart hammered in her chest. Had he really pushed the burn inside her body until it was almost volcanic? She didn't think it had been possible for her to hold a release to that point since it had been so long. It couldn't just be something Hunter drew out of her. No, it was likely because of her age and the time she'd been in a D/s relationship. Yeah. That made the most sense.

As his cock jerked inside of her repeatedly, another wave spurting out of him, Hunter cried out. Something he hadn't done with her before. Or anyone else that she knew of. He dug his claws into her skin once more, and the coppery scent of blood filled the air. With a few more jerks of his cock inside her, his release trailed off. Hunter panted out ragged breaths, once again remaining buried inside her for a minute, utterly still.

As she lay there, cheek pressed against the bedding, she could feel her chest rise and fall as she struggled to catch her breath. New puncture wounds and likely some bruising around her wrists, possibly her ankles and waist. Not that she was complaining in the least. *That* had been explosive. Though she refused to analyze the effect something as simple as purring had on Hunter. She tucked the information away, along with all the other little details that had arisen in her mind during their session. She needed to stow every single one of them because *she* was a professional. This was nothing more than a business transaction.

An untold amount of time passed before Hunter pulled out of her and began undoing her restraints. With not a word spoken, he methodically put the ropes, the spreader bar, and the blindfold aside as he removed them. After he was done, he eased her to a dry spot on the bed, which was scarce, and gently placed her on her stomach.

Hunter hovered over her, his weight a physical pressure, with one leg and arm on either side of her. He swept his tongue along the metallic tang of blood drawn from her skin, a slight shudder running through him. He inhaled and exhaled a deep breath. "That was the most freeing session I have ever had in my life," he whispered.

The first time he'd cleaned her up, silence had stretched between them. A rather comfortable one at that. She'd never required much in the way of conversation. At least not with her current clientele. She had started at the brothel for a reason, and it still applied. But that was all information she kept close to her heart.

When they had spoken, and he commented on her purring, she knew how to handle that. This statement... What was she supposed to do with it? She couldn't just not say something, but what did she say? Nia hid her confused expression, but she observed him as she had before, casting a look over her shoulder. There was something about it she found relaxing. Not that she'd ever admit as much. "That's good." She almost tacked on how it made her glad, but she opted to keep that to herself.

Hunter looked up at her with a glint in his eyes, his tongue tracing a line down her back. He was thorough, carefully extracting every drop of her blood that had been spilled, savoring the metallic scent. When he finished, he switched to her left hip.

It didn't unnerve her that their gazes connected, though it should. She didn't normally watch her clients as they cleaned her up. Even when they took her to the bathtub or shower to handle the remnants of their session, she didn't watch. With Hunter... she just couldn't look away. Just not with their eyes locked together like this. It transformed it from business to something personal. "The box you brought with you. Is it for me?" She rarely questioned it, but she had to fill the space somehow.

"Yes." After working on her left hip, he paused before moving to the right, the rhythmic sound of his breath the only noise.

Somewhere in the back of her mind, she chastised herself for not tearing her gaze away from him, but how could she not continue to admire those blue eyes of his? It wasn't the exact shade of her favorite color, but it was a hue. That had to be why she continued staring at him. Though if she continued to pose questions about the box, it wouldn't feel as foreign. "May I ask what it is?"

"A necklace. Just a little something to show my appreciation. For how much you have pleased me already." His eyes never left hers as he moved downward. There wasn't much left to clean up down there, but he took his time along her inner thighs anyway, finishing it up with a few gentle licks along the outer walls of her pussy.

Jewelry? While a gift wasn't unheard of, most of her clientele brought her toys or clothing they wanted her to wear. Jewelry was personal. Nor was it something she'd received from anyone except her last Dom, but that *had* been a personal relationship. Not that she would ever say she loved him, but she had cared for him. A small part of her considered telling Hunter to take it back, except she couldn't. Instead, Nia responded graciously, "Thank you."

All he did was nod. As he sat up to massage her, he said, "You have permission to touch me now. And you can use my name now, if you would like." He crossed his legs and sat next to her, massaging her feet, mindful of the bruising on her ankles. His gaze still didn't leave hers. "You seem confused again." The tiniest lift appeared at one corner of his mouth.

Damn. She always prided herself on not giving anything away with her feelings. Somehow, he'd seen it. How did she explain it without giving him any details? Though it seemed less about her desire to keep her past and present life private and more in consideration of her contract. Vague but honest worked. "I haven't received jewelry in a very long time."

"I do not gift it very often. You are only the third female I have done so with."

Okay, well, that made it a little less personal. Though that truly depended on the necklace. If it was extravagant, well, she'd stick with a gracious response. There wasn't anything else she could do. Hunter had seen the rules enough to know them by heart, to understand that they were magically binding from the moment he made payment. She couldn't tell him they had their own binding contracts with a whole other set of rules. Things the clients knew nothing of—and that's how the owner preferred it.

"Well, thank you," Nia said. She hadn't meant to repeat the senti-ment, but she was still trying to convince herself it *wasn't* personal. Maybe if she redirected the conversation a little. "Did you have a preference of when I should wear it?"

He moved his hands slowly up her calves toward her knees, his touch light, making sure he left no spot untouched. "The next time I return to see you. In three days. And I want you to be wearing an outfit that matches."

Something that matched. Well, if she had nothing in her closet, she had a day off between now and then. Not that she required an excuse to shop. Even with her sensitivity to light, she still liked to go to the marketplace and buy clothes. It was one of the few things that made her life feel normal. "I'm certain that can be arranged."

"Good." After another moment of gazing at her, he looked away and moved higher on her, past her ass, and began massaging her back, carefully avoiding the deep gouges left by his claws. "I know I do things differently than most, in several ways. Even those with my proclivities. Needs. I have never been very conventional in any aspect of my life. If anything I ever do, or offer, bothers you or makes you uncomfortable, tell me. Nothing you could ever say is going to hurt my feelings. Honesty is essential. Dishonesty with me, in *any* capacity, will not elicit a pleasant response." His gaze quickly returned to meet her stare. "Despite the specific nature of our sexual relationship, I do not want you to feel you have to do anything you do not want to do. Understood?"

"Of course," Nia responded. Their relationship required honesty. Though keeping her thoughts to herself regarding the gift, even though she hadn't seen it yet, wouldn't be in either of their interests. "In the future, any gifts you bring me should comprise either clothing or toys. Jewelry can be perceived as personal, even when it isn't intended that way. Regardless of how things are kept private, workers around here have a way of finding out." Not that she'd ever utter a word about anything she ever received from him. Or what occurred between them. That was no one's business. "It's been a long time since I had a Dom who met my needs. I'd hate to see you banned for a misperception." That was the most she'd ever said to him. This was only their second session. But it was also something that needed to be put out there. She didn't want to lose a Dominant who understood her desires any more than she could afford to lose her job. Her family depended on her.

"I will not bring you any more," he said simply as he moved up to rub her shoulders. "Considering how quickly things are escalating, do you have any hard limits you feel you should tell me about?"

Good. Nothing further needed to be said on that matter. Or so she hoped. In all her thirty years with the brothel, only one male had to be reminded. And they had banned him. If she hadn't declined the item, who knew how the proprietress would've punished her? Personal relationships were forbidden. She could answer his other question easily. It usually wasn't a conversation that occurred until the third session, but he had a point. They'd escalated quicker than most. "No ball gags or any binding around my mouth. No hoods or full-face masks. Something over the eyes, like a blindfold, is acceptable. Nothing spiked, including spiked whips or anything that would leave a permanent mark. No cages. Nothing involving vomit, urine, or feces. No fire play. Kissing is acceptable, should you desire it.”

“None of that is unacceptable. With kissing, is that something you enjoy?”

The question wasn’t something she could answer vaguely. A good D/s relationship required complete honesty. While she preferred to keep information about herself out of conversations, it didn’t seem there was any way she could do that with this question. “Before I came here, it was something I enjoyed. In this environment, I believe it fosters a personal relationship, so it isn’t something I do unless it’s desired by my Dom.”

Hunter nodded as he moved his hands slowly down her left arm. “I agree. I only asked because I do not particularly enjoy it myself; it feels too personal, too. However, if a submissive really pleases me, I occasionally give them concessions. Like allowing them to pick the position. I have been with one other female who desired kissing. She was not submissive, but we spent quite a lot of time together, and she pleased me as well as she could have. So, I would allow it from time to time, sometimes more than others, depending on my mood.”

That certainly made sense. A relationship between a dominant and submissive was an exchange of power. One relinquished control, while the other took it. In a personal relationship, they would draw a contract covering everything they’d spoken of. A faint tilt of her mouth crossed her face. No, Ivory wasn’t submissive, but she was flexible in many situations. “Concessions are a natural part of the relationship. Play often alters depending on one’s mood.” Nia flicked her eyes to his. It made sense, as she knew little about him. “I’ve been a submissive for over a hundred years. The relationship I was in prior to coming here... it was a personal one. I understand that play will be impacted by your day-to-day life.”

“I have never had a personal relationship. I was with a few females prior to coming here, but never more than once.” Once he’d finished with her left arm, he moved to her right. “My day-to-day life does impact things. Sometimes my mood can get rather dark. My darkest moods... no one else has ever handled those. It has forced me to move on from more than one submissive because of them.”

“You’ll find I’m not like others.” There was a reason she was in such high demand. It had taken her less than a year to build her clientele and become among the highest-paid workers at the brothel. Over her time here, she'd even worked with a few of the submissives to take them to the next level. None of them compared to her, though. While they all had their reasons for being here, their pasts affected what they could handle. "I don't break easily."

"I did not expect you would." Hunter's blue gaze leveled on her. "When I am in a really dark mood, I will give you no warning, nor will I show you any mercy. My eyes will be black like they have been previously, but there will be an obvious difference in the lust you have seen in them, and the anger that will be present then. In those moments, I need you to understand that I am very dangerous. It takes every ounce of willpower I have not to go too far. I will push limits beyond what I have pushed in any other session. In those moments, I have teetered on the edge of doing things I cannot come back from. I also prefer no spoken words, unless it is to utter your safe word. You will need to come up with a hand gesture for if you absolutely need to come and cannot hold back. Those kinds of sessions are hard enough, so I prefer not to add punishments to that."

Nia didn't flinch at his words. In fact, she had almost no reaction. So much of what she'd experienced and just this conversation alone, Hunter reminded her more and more of her first Dom. Except there were differences, too. Not just in their species, but in other ways, as well. There had been sessions like that with her previous Dom. They even had a hand signal, as well as an additional code word, in case her wrists were bound. She shifted her left hand and brought her forefinger and thumb together, creating a circle. "Hand signal. As a backup, the word is rhino."

"Good." Having finished working on her right arm, Hunter sat up, and immediately his eyes flickered to the door. The red light had come on at some point. "I am going to go." He rose from the bed's edge and strode to the door, his steps echoing in the quiet room. He picked up the black box and carried it to the bed, offering it to her as she sat up. For a minute, his hand still rested on it as she closed her hand around it, their eyes meeting and holding. "Do not forget to wear this when I return. With a matching outfit. And you will be in a submissive position. I will see you in three days, Nia." Without another word, Hunter left before she could even open the box.

Four

Hunter opened the door to Nia's room, stepped inside, and closed it behind him. His eyes immediately snapped to the center of the room, where she kneeled on the floor in front of a bondage horse. Her head bowed, her hands resting on her thighs—the perfect submissive pose. Even those who had met him in the reception area before their session had to get into position before anything would happen. He liked to look at them that way. Completely obedient to him. At his mercy.

The bondage horse had four straps attached to it—one that would go across her chest, one for across her hips, and one for each of her thighs—along with four padded leather cuffs for her wrists and ankles. It had been on his mind to move things away from the bed. To take things up a notch further. This was one of his favorite pieces of furniture to use. Nia had once again anticipated his desires.

No, he refused to look further into that. They were fully compatible in the bedroom, and she was extremely adept at her job. Absolutely nothing more.

Hunter moved across the room, his body reacting to her presence as he stood before her, aroused. He took a moment, his eyes drinking in the sight of her as he gazed down. Her cinnamon-brown hair splayed out across her back, leaving her shoulders bare. He couldn't see all of her outfit, but the color perfectly matched the necklace he'd bought her. Even down to the heels on her feet. The jewelry hung around her neck and, just as he'd suspected when he'd picked it out, the larger diamond nestled perfectly in the valley of her breasts. During the first two sessions, he'd resisted the urge to lick his lips as more of her scent invaded his nostrils. He didn't this time. "Get up."

Without hesitating, Nia rose to her feet. As he hadn't given permission to lift her eyes, they remained lowered and focused on the ground. The negligee, a 'barely there' garment, molded to her form, emphasizing her every curve. The thin straps over her shoulders, a delicate design, crisscrossed at her back. It was midnight-blue with silver sparkles adorning it. She wore a matching pair of thongs and a pair of six-inch midnight blue heels with silver curlicues along the sides and toe, plus silver leaves that wrapped up the stiletto.

Hunter strolled around her, his fingers dancing lightly across her skin. When he stopped in front of her again, he slid one hand between her thighs and cupped her pussy. A small gasp left her mouth. Heat already bloomed in the juncture between her thighs. With a lingering touch, he used his other hand to raise her chin, meeting her gaze before tracing his finger along her skin, stopping at the gem nestled between her breasts. He liked the way the color looked on her. A lot. He almost opened his mouth to say so, but decided against it.

Withdrawing his hand, Hunter grabbed her hips, backing her to the bondage horse and lifting her to sit on it. "Get in position." It had been three days since he'd seen her. Three days since he'd fucked. His tongue had missed the taste of her pussy, and his cock had been begging to be put to use. He wouldn't deny them any longer.

The negligee lifted slightly as Nia moved into place, ready to be secured by him. There was a growl on the tip of his tongue. Whether that was because of the way her body arched as she got herself into position, the way her legs spread as she tucked them back alongside the frame revealing more of the thong that covered her sex, or the way her breasts pushed out as she raised her arms above her head, or maybe it was the way her eyes never left his once as she laid herself out before him, he couldn't say. Or maybe he just refused to.

Hunter left her lingerie right where it was for now and got to work on the straps. The first one went across her ribcage, right beneath her breasts. The next across her hips, right above her thong, after he'd raised her negligee up to settle around her waist. One strap went around each thigh and ankle, keeping her legs spread wide apart. Moving around to where her head was, he jogged his claws down her arms, feeling the texture of her skin. A soft moan slipped free from Nia's lips. Reaching her wrists, he got them in the padded leather cuffs.

After she was fully bound, Hunter fetched the familiar stool and placed it at the foot of the bondage horse. He sat, his eyes darkening as he inhaled deeply. Fuck, he'd missed her scent. And the taste of her cum that would flood his mouth soon. A louder moan came out of her as he grazed his claws from her knees up to her waist. Hunter leaned in and licked her slit through her panties. A low rumble immediately vibrated up his chest, pulling a rather audible groan from her.

Fuck. He absolutely loved her sounds. Hunter growled, a deep sound that vibrated against her, and grazed his fangs along her outer lips before biting her clit through the thin fabric. He grazed his claws over her stomach and over her hip bones, though just a little harder this time. He ran his tongue along her slit, trying to reach as deeply as possible through the fabric, while dragging his claws down her body. Dragging them down her inner thighs, causing the tiniest droplets of blood to appear, he enveloped her clit in his mouth and sucked vigorously. A deep groan rolled out of him as the coppery scent tinged his nostrils.

Nia let out a purred moan. "More, please, Sir."

Holy fuck, that noise. He growled against her pussy. Oh, he was going to give her more... *a lot* more. And her panties wouldn't last much longer. Nuzzling deeper into her sex, he raked his claws down her inner thighs again as he sucked hard at her nub. Fuck, she tasted so good, and he hadn't even made her come yet. Just doing this, even through her thong, made every one of his synapses light up.

The more noise she made, the more growls came out of him. Just the slightest bit muted, with his mouth pressed up against the sheer fabric covering her pussy. Fuck, he'd rarely made any noise during sex before, certainly *nothing* like all the sounds he'd made during sessions with Nia. But he didn't want to stop making them, either.

Hunter slipped his right hand beneath the fabric of her thong and slid three fingers inside her. This time, the claws of his other hand scraped across her outer thigh, and tiny beads of blood welled up. He bit hard on her clit through her thong, then sucked on it again. His tongue snaked out, stroking over it again and again, as his fingers curled up to stroke the inner walls of her pussy.

"Please, may I come, sir?" Nia urged.

Not with her fucking panties on. Not this time. He wanted every single drop to end up in his mouth when she came. *Holy shit,* the heat pouring off of her pussy. "Not yet." After taking his fingers away, he sunk his claws into her inner thighs and sank his teeth into the edge of her thong. Raising his eyes to meet hers, he ripped her panties off her. A loud moan left her. *Oh, fuck yes!* Spreading the sweet, swollen lips of her pussy, he extended his tongue and flicked at her nub repeatedly.

A groan escaped Nia, followed by a subtle scraping as her toes curled inside her shoes. The scent of arousal flared, too. A mixture of a growl and a snarl ripped out of him. Teasing more—later. Right now, he needed to taste her cum. "I want you to come on my tongue, Nia, now." Keeping his eyes on hers, he shoved his tongue deep inside her.

Nia cried out in ecstasy as a climax immediately slammed through her body, exploding onto his tongue. Her eyes didn't leave his... *the entire time she was coming on his tongue.* Holy shit. Had his cock ever been this hard? Had to have been, but he couldn't remember a time it had felt like *this.* The intensity of the throbbing and pounding was so overwhelming that he nearly came onto the floor. His growl continued, intensifying in volume. Holy fuck, he needed her to come again. Now.

"Again." His arms wrapped around her knees, claws digging into her thighs, as he shoved his tongue back inside and drove at her even harder. Another orgasm punched through her, exploding into his mouth. Still, Nia didn't look away as a purred moan slipped free.

A few drops of cum oozed out of his cock and landed with a soft plop on the floor. Despite that, he continued to pleasure her by using his tongue on her. Holy fuck... so good... she tasted so good. As he drove his tongue deep, a strangled moan escaped him, consumed by his relentless devouring of her. It wasn't a sound he'd ever made with anyone before, but that was far from what he wanted to focus on right now. He couldn't fathom taking his mouth away from her sex. Not yet. He needed more. So much more. Reaching one hand further around her leg, he rubbed her clit with hard and fast strokes.

Her nipples pebbled beneath the sheer material of the negligee. Endless moans and groans left her mouth, with a few purrs mixed in. To the point, he couldn't tell where one began and the other ended. The harder he went at her, the hotter and wetter she got, until he pushed her to that point again. "Please may I come, Sir?"

His body was a fucking live wire. Every inch of his skin electrified. His claws clenched, sinking further into her thigh, as continuous rivulets of crimson blood ran down her leg and pooled near her knee. He didn't ejaculate fully onto the floor, but droplets of semen continued to escape from his penis, impossible to control. The sounds of her moans, groans, and purrs filled the air, a symphony of pleasure, as he continued to devour her. Her pussy was so blazing hot, so wet against his tongue and his lips. *Fuck yes,* she could come. "*Now,*" he snarled out and fused his mouth to her sex.

Nia let out a piercing scream as a powerful climax surged through her body and into his mouth. One might think from the way her body contorted on the bondage horse she might have difficulty seeing him, even as she came, but she didn't have a single issue. Her gaze stayed with his just fine.

That strangled moan came out of him again as he lapped and sucked at her pussy, not letting a single fucking drop of her cum go anywhere but down his throat. No one else had ever brought that sound out of him. It was untamed, primal. That their eyes didn't stray from one another once just intensified everything that much more. He'd never had the desire to meet a female's eyes when they came. Not once. Never. But Nia... he couldn't have torn his gaze away from hers if he were literally on fire.

Once the climax passed, he slowly withdrew his tongue from her body. Without breaking eye contact, he sensually licked and sucked along the length of her leg, from the knee up to her hip, relishing every drop of blood his tongue collected from her skin. He continued up her body after taking in a fair amount, his eyes following the smooth curve of her skin. As his hands found her breasts, he tugged the material downward, unveiling their smoothness. The lingerie wouldn't last much longer on her body, but for right now, he couldn't wait one moment longer to be inside her.

A hand clasped her hip, and at the same moment, another hand grabbed her hair, giving it a brutal tug. With no warning, he slammed his cock deep inside her pussy. As his orgasm immediately punched out of him, a powerful roar echoing around the room, Nia cried out in pure, unadulterated pleasure. He didn't wait for his release to cease before he moved in and out of her, with rapid, powerful motions.

Nia's back arched slightly, pushing against the strap beneath her breasts. "Harder, please, Sir."

Those three words sent a jolt of lightning straight through to his cock. When she said 'sir,' a strange part of his brain bristled, wishing she'd spoken his name instead. Hunter shoved the errant thought as far away from the forefront of his mind as he could. Wherever the fuck that had come from, it wasn't allowed. Not in this place, during their sessions, while he dominated her, and she submitted to every single one of his commands. Using his name during a session would make things *way* too personal. She hadn't uttered it once. But he felt that if she ever did it, she would irrevocably change his life.

Gods, she was so fucking gorgeous. Hunter tightened his hold on her hair, jerking it back harder. Not that it took their eyes away from one another, even a little. His claws curled deeper into her hip. Blood slid between his fingers, dampening his fur. He felt completely unhinged; out of control. With increasing force and speed, he drove his cock into her core. "Come. Now."

Her body convulsed with a powerful climax, coating his cock completely, overflowing and running down her ass and his thighs. Nia let out a raucous scream that echoed around the room. She'd never cried out so loudly with him before.

Hunter bared his fangs and hissed. Holy fuck, he couldn't stop. Not that he wanted to. He needed more. He needed everything. At that moment, there wasn't a single part of her that his body wasn't demanding to control. Possess. Own. Her orgasm had barely trickled away when his own flared up. His cock thickened and his balls tightened. Holy fuck, he wanted to *come with her* at the same time. Something else he had never truly desired before. Not with anyone.

His thrusts intensified, his cock penetrating her deeply, while he gripped her hair even tighter. Hunter lowered his head closer to hers. Their gazes were barely an inch apart. "Again. Come for me, Nia, now."

Another orgasm exploded out of her, as if Hunter had completely owned her body. Her voice filled the room as her muscles contracted around him, unleashing a sensation they had never felt before. As the walls of her sex clenched, more of her cum surged out, completely drenching them both. His dick twitched forcefully inside her, releasing more of his seed and filling her completely. His body didn't just tremble; it *shook*. He pressed his forehead to hers. Her jade-green eyes with those flecks of yellow were all he could see. Neither of them looked away, their breaths coming in ragged gasps as they fought to regain control.

Hunter had no clue how long it lasted. It could have been moments, minutes, hours, or days. He had no clue. Nothing else existed at that moment. Not the piece of furniture beneath her. Neither the room nor the flickering candles along the walls. Just her.

And he refused to acknowledge that. Those feelings were forbidden, like a dangerous, thrilling desire. They had no place here. And he couldn't even think about entertaining them. This wasn't supposed to be personal. *None of this* could be personal. Even without the rules of the brothel, *he* didn't do personal. They might be compatible in the bedroom, but that was it. That was where it ended. Business transaction. That was all it was and all it would ever be.

His heart pounded in his chest. His grip on her hair and hip remained as firm as ever. Neither of them looked away from each other. *Holy fucking shit...* He was far, *far* from done with her for the evening.

He wasn't sure how long they stayed like that, staring into one another's eyes. They couldn't remain like this. He had to break their gazes. It was... too much. It was all too much. The urge to do something he'd never had the urge to do in his entire life threatened to overwhelm him. He'd never desired to kiss anyone, not even to know what it would feel like. Not even when he'd been young and had first become sexually aware. He'd done it with Ivory because *she* had enjoyed it, and she had pleased him, so he'd allowed it. This... no. This was different. He *wanted* to kiss Nia. But he couldn't do that. Not now. Never. Doing so would push them past that line they weren't supposed to cross, right into 'personal' territory. A place they could never allow themselves to go.

Hunter, with a swift motion, pulled away as he tore his gaze from hers. Not that he moved away from her body, though. His cock still throbbed, as if he'd never had an orgasm at all—how the fuck was that possible? He wasn't about to end this session early. He just couldn't stare into those exquisite eyes of hers another moment longer.

Lowering his head to her exposed chest, he greedily indulged in the sensation of her supple skin against his lips and the sensation of her blood rushing into his mouth as he sucked. With careful attention, he swirled and flicked his tongue against her nipple, savoring the feel of her skin.

Once they both puckered, he stepped away and headed to her dresser. Nia had laid out a few additional toys, including a variety of nipple clamps. Coincidentally, there was a set that almost matched the outfit she wore. Well, that was just too perfect. They even had slight weights at the end of them.

Bringing them back to where she was bound, Hunter gently slid the clamps onto the base of her nipples before giving them each a slow, deliberate tug with his teeth. A moan left her mouth mere moments before he resumed his position between her legs. There was no heads-up before he pinched her clit and delved his tongue deeply into the cleft between her thighs.

Nia groaned and arched her neck. Thank the gods. She didn't look back down at him. With his face buried in her pussy, it wasn't difficult to keep his eyes away from hers. *Lies.* But it didn't matter how difficult it was; he absolutely couldn't meet her gaze again. Especially the next time she came.

Grazing his claws up her legs, her stomach, and ribcage, Hunter gave the nipple clamps another tug. The negligee was still intact. That wouldn't last much longer. After running his claws along her sides, he firmly held onto her thigh with one hand and inserted three fingers inside her. His mouth closed around her clit, a soft bite preceding a deep, satisfying suck.

"Please let me come, Sir," Nia cried out.

His claws curled harder into her thigh. "No," he growled against her. With his fingers curled up inside her, Hunter skillfully stroked the inner walls of her pussy, feeling them grip his fingers tightly, while his tongue expertly flicked over her clit. The forceful grip of her sex elicited another guttural sound from him. Holy fuck, that felt good. Hunter drove his fingers deeper, plunging them in and out as he flicked his tongue repeatedly over her swollen bud.

Each groan that left Nia's mouth hardened his cock all over again. Her struggles against the restraints made his eyes linger, desperate for another glimpse of her face, flushed with the heat of passion. But he resisted. That was the last thing he needed. He still wasn't fully down from the high of meeting her gaze while she'd come multiple times. Hunter dragged his claws slowly down her thigh, all the way to her knee. His eyes snapped over, and he released a low growl at the metallic scent of the blood droplets. While his fingers were still inside her, he traced a path from her leg to her clit with his mouth, savoring the taste of her crimson essence with his tongue and gently grazing his fangs along her skin. The taste of her cum, mingled with the coppery tang of her blood, ignited a fire in his mouth.

With a loud moan, Nia contracted the inner walls of her pussy around his fingers. "Please, please, please, may I come, Sir?" she whimpered.

That noise damn near threw him over the edge. His cock didn't just throb now; it pounded with a force that shook him. Fuck, he needed to be buried back inside her. Which was exactly what would happen as soon as he swallowed every drop she was about to give him. He sucked on her clit as he pulled his fingers from her sex, the sounds of their pleasure echoing in the room. Hunter grazed his claws up her body until he reached her breasts. He gave the nipple clamps one last tug as he licked her from end to end. "Come," he growled and removed the clips as he drove his tongue inside her.

Her cries of pleasure echoed as she reached a climax that surged out of her like a relentless, unexpected storm. As the release pulsed through her, Nia's body arched, pushing against the restraints.

He covered her breasts with his hands, pinching and stroking her overly sensitive nipples. Hunter swallowed every bit of her cum, not letting a single drop spill. As the final, sweet traces of her climax lingered on his tongue and slid down his throat, he savored her essence one last time before rising to his feet. He slid his hands up her sides, the lace of her negligee cool against his skin, until he had it bunched in his hands. Though he tried not to meet her gaze again, his eyes gravitated straight to hers. At the moment he ripped the fabric in half, straight down the middle, he buried his cock inside her. Nia moaned as he filled her all the way to her core.

Holy fuck, she felt so good. Something else he'd refused to acknowledge in any of their sessions so far—how absolutely perfectly she fit him. More perfect than any other female ever had. Her pussy hugged each rigid length of his cock like they were made for one another—Hunter shut those thoughts down immediately. He needed to *stop*. His thoughts needed to stop. Derail. Something. That, too, was forbidden territory. The kinds of thoughts that weren't allowed. That could *never* be allowed. With a firm grip on her waist, he drove his claws in slightly as he picked up the pace and force of his thrusts, pressing firmly into her with each stroke.

Nia moaned. Her physical response was immediate, her pussy clenching tightly around his cock. "More, please, Sir."

It just geared him up more and more. *Holy fuck...* Oh, yes, he could give her more. Hunter undid the strap around her right leg, stretching her limb up against his torso. Despite their positions and height gap, the sharp heel of her shoe jabbed into his shoulder, but he seemed utterly unfazed. It felt fantastic. Hunter tightened his grip on her thigh and increased the intensity and speed of his movements, thrusting in and out more vigorously. He dug his claws deeper into her waist. To avoid looking at her face, he gazed at the jewelry he had bought for her, which sparkled around her neck. The gems jumped and shifted with each slam of his cock into her pussy. The color looked magnificent against her skin. She had said her safe word was 'blue.' While he hadn't asked her why, he'd gathered it was because that was a color she liked. The particular shade of the gems—a deep, alluring blue—had inexplicably drawn him. No other would do.

One ass cheek lifted just a little off the leather padding of the bondage horse. The impact altered the angle of his thrusts, enabling him to increase the force and speed of his movements. That heady mixture of a purred moan left her mouth. Each time he heard it, it pushed him closer to blissful sexual insanity. Hunter wanted to take her in every way, shape, and form that it was possible to fuck a female. And he would.

As his growl shifted closer to a snarl, his claws dug deeper into her waist and her thigh. His thrusts were powerful, but the desire for more remained. So much more. With each thrust, a primal sound escaped him as he felt her walls tightening around him. *Holy fuck, yes.*

"Oh, gods," she cried out. "Please let me come. Please let me come... Sir," Nia begged in a way she never had before.

It was the way she said 'sir.' Just something about it. It snapped his eyes straight back to hers. His cock jerked inside her and he damn near lost it. Not that he was sure how he held back. But something inside him told him if they came at the same time again, their eyes on one another, there wouldn't be any going back for him. And that would be *bad*, so *terrible.* It was just the sexual charge they brought out of each other. The insane perfection of their compatibility. The connection that existed just in this space. That was all it was. Nothing else. He refused to believe it was anything else. And he couldn't indulge these feelings. Never.

Hunter tore his gaze away from hers and clamped down on the orgasm threatening to punch out of him. He pulled his cock out of her, then unstrapped her left leg, and grasped both her ankles. Stretching both of her legs in the air and spreading them wide, he leaned his head down until his mouth hovered over her pussy. Her thighs quivered as he leisurely ran his tongue along the outer edges of her sex before sliding it up the length of her slit. He couldn't hold back a moan. Holy fuck, he didn't think he'd *ever* get enough of her sweet taste.

"Come for me," he snarled out, before fusing his mouth to her sex and driving his tongue as deep inside her as he could. His words elicited an immediate physical response in her body. A wave of pleasure crashed over her, culminating in a powerful climax that coated his tongue, flooding his mouth.

Hunter couldn't stop the growling moan that had started up. His hold on her ankles tightened as he drove at her as hard and as fast as he could. The moan continued, unending, completely untamed, as his tongue penetrated her sex again and again. No matter how much of her cum filled his mouth, it wasn't enough. He didn't just want more... he *needed* more.

Even when her orgasm finally ended, Hunter didn't stop fucking her pussy with his tongue. Her back arched easier, with only two straps in place across her body. A deep groan left her mouth and filled the room. The more noise she made, the more of her he had to have. His tongue and mouth devoured her relentlessly, desperate to get every single bit of her he could. As his orgasm was seconds away from erupting onto the floor, Hunter pulled his mouth away and stood up, unable to contain himself any longer. He reveled in the feeling of her heels pressing into his back as she wrapped her legs around his waist. Fuck, that was utter perfection. Leaning over her body, he grabbed onto the top of the bondage horse. "Come again for me, Nia," he growled out and slammed his cock inside her, causing her body to bow off the bondage horse. A roar left him as his orgasm immediately exploded out of him, so powerful his brain flickered and his vision momentarily blurred. *Holy fuck...*

Nia screamed at the orgasm that burst out of her, pulsating all over his rigid length. He moaned as her heels bit more into his back. All he could think of at that moment was the burning desire to feel her heels dig in deeper. As much as he enjoyed drawing blood on her... he wanted her to draw blood on him as well. He gripped the horse's edge, his knuckles tense, worried his claws had damaged the wood despite his restraint. "Harder," he moaned out as he rammed his cock in and out of her.

Nia complied with his request, her heels digging more firmly into his back. As she continued, a soft purred moan emerged, and her inner walls pulsed rhythmically around his cock. The heat between them rose a notch.

Holy fucking shit... Hunter couldn't hold back any longer. With a powerful tug of her hair, he climaxed, feeling the powerful sensation travel up his cock and erupt inside her. "Fuck!" The movements of his hips didn't stop for a moment as he fucked her through his release.

With each thrust, Nia dug her heels into his back, and the smells of arousal and iron filled the air. She contracted the muscles inside her pussy, drawing out his pleasure. Her back arched, straining against the straps until the tips of her nipples brushed against his fur. "Don't stop. I need to come, Sir," Nia said, the intonation in her words somewhere between demanding and begging.

If anyone else—*anyone*—had told him what to do, told him not to stop something, it would have pissed him off. Even when the queen gave him orders, he followed them—mostly without hesitation—but it was annoying. But Nia... with her, it just seemed to turn him on more. Just like during their last session, when she'd come so close to demanding, when she'd asked for more of his cock. Every nerve in his body sparked with energy as his erection throbbed inside her, increasing in intensity with each spasm that released more ejaculate into her vagina.

Hunter gave her hair another harsh tug, making her neck arch further back. It took him a moment to speak, with his orgasm still going on—how the *fuck* was that possible? After the last drop emptied into her, he thrust his cock into her one last time and pressed their pelvises together. Leaning down further, he tilted her head to the side. Licking up the length of her neck, he tried—and failed—to ignore the massive shudder that went through him, between the way her intoxicating scent consumed him and the taste of her skin. "You did not say please. You only come when I say you can come."

Her pussy clenched and relaxed around his dick. "Please, may I come, Sir?" Nia purred.

Another growl vibrated deep in his chest. With a quick movement, he pulled his hips back and then plunged his cock back inside her, gripping her hair tighter. "You know what that sound does to me." She'd made it several times already, and it drove him absolutely nuts. Maybe she was trying to get punished again. If that was the case, he could *absolutely* indulge her.

Hunter playfully nipped at her earlobe, then gently licked it. "I do not think I should let you come."

Nia moaned. Arching her back ever so slightly, she let out a deeper purr. *Holy shit, that noise.* A wave of tingles spread across his body, from his ears to the tip of his tail. Despite the straps on her torso, the proximity of his body pushed her breasts closer against his chest. He bit down on her earlobe, drawing a moan out of her as the throbbing in his cock intensified. *Holy fuck,* she was *trying* to drive him to insanity. Hunter pulled his hips back, but this time when he thrust back inside her, it was slow. Unhurried. When the head of his cock reached her core, he ground into it, his pelvis rocking against hers. "Do you want to be punished again, Nia?"

"I believe you should... *Sir,*" Nia replied, her voice deep and sultry.

He almost came right then. How was that even possible? Especially as soon as it was after the massive explosion he'd just had. It wasn't the particular words per se, but the way she spoke them that damn near set him off. The way they rolled off her tongue. Like she was begging him to punish her. "Are you sure, Nia? I thought you *needed* to come." His cock drove into her, and as he nibbled on her earlobe, he could feel her shuddering. "Are you sure you want me to punish you before you come... All. Over. My. Dick?" he punctuated his words by pressing his cock into her core repeatedly.

"I do, Sir," Nia purred. She dug her heels into his back, then lifted her hips and tightened her pussy around him.

A groan he couldn't control ripped out of him. His grip tightened on her hair, the wood groaning beneath his claws as he curled them more around the edge of the bondage horse. Oh, she was in for it now. She'd gone beyond naughty and downright into disobedient territory. It didn't help that, with his mouth still at her ear, each noise she made went right into his. *Holy fuck,* everything she'd just done felt so fantastic.

With a guttural growl, Hunter shifted her legs, breaking their connection and pulling away. He undid the two restraints still around her body, picked her up, and turned her over. After he'd secured the two straps, one across her upper back and the other around her hips, he walked over to the wall that held the toys he could use on her. Hunter gazed across the whips and floggers displayed. Though his cock was throbbing, desperate to return to the warmth of her pussy, he lingered, taking his time to make his selection.

He had two favorites with floggers. The one he chose was just one of them. It was basically a mini bullwhip. Black, like all the whips and floggers on her wall. The color he preferred. It had a single tail, which made it much harder to control, but he wasn't inexperienced with these in the least. And he had never once missed his mark, even in the beginning stages of using them. The tip of the tail was thin, perfect for delivering that sharp sting, and often leaving the beautiful red marks that he craved.

He'd drawn blood with it on one female. She'd warned him that if it happened again, he would have to move on. It had happened the next time he'd used it on her. He hadn't been able to help it. Once the first red mark appeared across her ass… that color always did him in. Next time he'd come to the brothel, they had paired him with another female.

With a firm grip on the handle, Hunter walked back to stand behind her, feeling the cool leather against his palm. Beginning at her neck, the tip of the flogger danced across her back, finally resting on her backside. He took aim, and with a stinging impact, the tip connected with her backside. A red mark immediately appeared. One that had him practically salivating.

The moan she made just got him that much harder. Hunter administered three more lashes to her buttocks with the whip before sliding his hand between her thighs to caress her. Fuck, she was so wet. He slid three fingers inside her, stroked the inner walls of her pussy, then snapped the whip across her ass before removing his digits. Bringing them to his mouth, he growled as he sucked every drop of her juices off.

Nia peered over her shoulder at him and purred.

Something halfway between a growl and a snarl rolled out of him. That throbbing pulse began in his cock again. She was definitely playing with fire now. And while he was going to have to punish her for it, he didn't want her to stop. What that fucking purr of hers did to him—it was exquisite torture; in a way he never could have imagined.

He raised the whip high, and with a sharp crack, brought it down on her shoulder while simultaneously smacking her bottom. He needed to come, likely as much as she did, but he could hold it back for a little while. If she didn't start behaving herself, his cum wouldn't go anywhere except all over the floor in front of her, denying her a single drop.

Nia moaned as her back arched, her breasts pressing against the padding of the bondage horse. The strap closer to her hips limited how high her ass could go. "More, please, Sir."

Oh, he was going to give her more. By the time he was done, he expected her entire back and ass would be a blanket of red. Just the thought had him licking his lips. Hunter's whip cracked repeatedly across the back of her shoulders and upper arms, each strike followed by a sharp smack on her buttocks. After at least a dozen hits, though he hadn't drawn blood—yet—he leaned over her and licked up her spine, from the top of her ass all the way to her neck. With his fangs, he took the back of her necklace and pulled it taut, positioning the front against her throat. Not enough to really hurt, but enough to bite into her flesh. She hadn't said choking was a hard limit, but he never dove right into that, either. That was always something he eased into slowly. And he never did it hard enough so they couldn't breathe. Releasing the chain from his fangs, he straightened and began anew.

Each new red streak across her back and arms, not to mention the reddening of her ass, and those magnificent noises she made, just amped him up higher and higher. His cock didn't just pulsate now; it pounded. *Fuck*, he needed to be back inside her. He needed to fuck her as hard as he could until he filled her pussy with his cum all over again. He needed to increase the intensity of his whipping until he drew blood from her. That would come in time, though. This time, the whip cracked on her thigh, a sharp sound that echoed as he spanked her. His whip struck her outer thigh, then her buttocks, alternating between the two, while his hand landed on her other cheek with each impact.

With every lash of the whip and his hand, a cacophony of sounds escaped her. A heady mixture of moans, groans, and purred moans. Her thighs tensed with tremors. "Please, please, please, please, please, please, may I come, Sir?" Nia whimpered.

Fuck, that whimper. With another growl suppressed, Hunter circled the bondage horse cautiously. He grazed his claws over her ass, spine, and shoulder. When he stopped in front of her, he lifted her chin up so their eyes met. His cock was right in front of her mouth, but if she wanted to touch it, she'd have to *really* extend that tongue of hers. "I need to come, too, though." As he set the whip on her back, he held his cock and started slow, deliberate strokes, his gaze fixed on her. "Do not let that fall to the ground."

Nia licked her lips as she opened her mouth and extended her tongue. It hit the blunt head of his cock first. Her gaze didn't leave his as she twirled it around his dick, flicked it over his fingers, and continued to stretch the length of her tongue until she reached his balls. She sensually explored each sac with her tongue before caressing the back of his shaft.

Hunter didn't stop the slow strokes up and down his length. While every single bit of what she did felt beyond fantastic, it was the last thing she did. It damn near did him in. A deep moan left him as his eyes rolled back in his head. He couldn't help it. It was the same reaction he'd had every single time she'd done that. But the first time she would see it.

Nia didn't break the connection of their gazes. Extending her tongue, she repeatedly licked along the underside of his cock.

Oh, shit... oh, shit... OH, SHIT... It wouldn't take her long *at all* to make him come. Even if he hadn't been close already when he got in front of her. He dropped his hand from his cock, then grabbed a fistful of her hair, giving her a clear path to continue unimpeded. "Do not stop doing that," he commanded as he picked the whip back up. All his previous plans had gone straight out the window. His entire focus was on her making him come and swallowing every single ounce of it before he would do the same to her. With a flick of his wrist, he brought the whip's end down on her ass.

Her tongue retracted as she let out a moan. With a purr, Nia's tongue darted out as she licked the base of his cock before withdrawing. "May I suck your *cock*, please, Sir?"

Shit... He nearly lost control, his orgasm on the verge of erupting and splattering across the ground. *Holy fuck.* The scent of her arousal—a potent and intoxicating fragrance—had nearly completely consumed him. "You had better hold your orgasm back just a little longer, Nia. You do not get to come first, but I promise when you do... it will be worth the wait." As he slid his cock into her mouth, Hunter let out a deep groan, savoring the sensation as it touched the back of her throat. "Now, make me come."

Nia tantalized him by running her tongue along his erect penis and delicately grazing her teeth on the base, repeating the movements in sync. His hands fell to the smooth, chilly edge of the bondage horse. His eyes rolled back into his head all over again. An insane urge rose suddenly with no warning—an urge to unbind her hands so she could grab onto him. Any part of him. But he shoved that thought away so quickly it damn near made his brain rattle. What was he thinking? He couldn't handle anybody's hands on him during sex. He—and a couple of females—had learned that the hard way.

Hunter tightened his grip on the bondage horse's edge as he thrust into her mouth. "Do not stop," he growled out, his jaw clenched. His orgasm was right on the edge. Any moment now—another stroke along the back of his cock, and it was over. The loudest roar he'd ever uttered in her presence left him as a massive orgasm erupted out of him.

No sooner had the last drop left him, and he was already moving. Hunter abruptly withdrew his cock from her mouth and swiftly made his way to the foot of the bondage horse, gripping her thighs as he kneeled down. "Come." He fused his mouth to her sex. He wouldn't let a single drop of her delicious nectar go anywhere but down his throat.

Nia screamed louder than she ever had before. The sound echoed off the walls as a powerful orgasm slammed through her body, pulsating out of her in nonstop waves. It gushed into his mouth like a raging river that only had one place to go. Holy fuck, she tasted so sweet. Utter perfection. He would always crave the sweetness that flowed from her thighs.

And... he needed to stop those thoughts. Immediately.

When it seemed like her orgasm might trickle off, he drove at her even harder. His tongue ventured as far as it could into her, tasting every inch of her warmth and flicking over her most sensitive area. He didn't want her release to end. He could stay down here, devouring her sex for hours and never even tire of it.

Moans and groans repeatedly left her mouth. Her back arched, causing the straps to bite into her flesh as her climax continued. *Holy fuck, yes... Keep coming, sweetheart.* Hunter bit down on her nub, sucking forcefully, before thrusting his tongue back into her pussy. He smacked her ass. He needed more. So much more of her sweet cum.

He couldn't tell if this was just one really long-ass orgasm, or if a new one followed immediately behind. Either way, he didn't give a shit. Hunter moaned when her pussy pressed a little harder against his tongue. Fuck, yes... *YES. Keep coming on my tongue, sweetheart.* Holy fuck, he'd never *needed* someone to keep coming. Certainly not to this degree. If she stopped right now, he'd go insane. He reached up and released the strap around her hips, giving her a bit more freedom of movement. With another loud smack, he thrust at her with increasing intensity.

Her hips writhed, intensifying the pressure of her pussy against his tongue. "Fuck," Nia cried out.

His erection returned, throbbing with ferocity. Not that he'd ever *not* been hard since he'd walked through the door. It had never been like that with any other female. Part of him wasn't surprised in the least. Nia had brought so much out of him that no other female had achieved. None of them had ever even come close to the level of sexual satisfaction she gave him. He refused to think about why that would be. They were perfectly compatible in the bedroom. That was all. Nothing else. Absolutely nothing else.

As he pushed his fingers deep inside her asshole, he grasped her left ass cheek tightly with his claws, moving with a forceful and rapid rhythm. He kept licking her pussy, not ceasing his intimate ministrations. *Holy fucking shit,* he needed more. He just couldn't get enough. Her cum was like a drug, one he was wholly and fully addicted to.

Her ass cheeks clenched around his fingers as her sex ground against his tongue. "Fuck. Please don't stop. Please don't stop... Hu—Sir."

She'd almost said his name. He was sure of it. Though Nia had covered it up quickly, switching almost immediately to the title he demanded to be used with him during sessions, he was absolutely certain she had nearly said his name. He wanted his full name to leave her lips.

Absolutely not. Nope. *Bad idea.*

Hunter shoved the unwelcome desire away, digging his claws into her ass and growling as he felt the warm blood trickle. The coppery tinge of her blood mixed with the scent of her cum was the sweetest perfume. Biting down on her clit, he sucked on it hard, and then flicked his tongue over it repeatedly. *Not stopping soon, sweetheart.* Holy fuck, he hoped she just kept on coming. He could happily get drunk on her taste alone.

Nia moaned.

Holy fuck, she was so close to yet another release. He could sense it in the shudders that swept throughout her, the tremble through her thighs. *That is right, sweetheart. Just a little further. Give me that cum.* Pulling his hand back, Hunter's palm connected with her rear. His fingers quickened their pace, eliciting a deep growl against her sensitive spot, causing intense sensations to course through her entire body and coaxing out another climax.

He certainly realized that she had disobeyed him, even as he devoured her, sucking at her pussy to get every delicious drop of this newest release. Once the orgasm trailed off, he slowly licked her clean, and then stood back up. Trailing the tail of the whip from her ass up to her back again, he stopped in front of her and stared down at her for a moment. "I gave you permission to come only *once*. You came… how many times… five? Six? No, I think it might have even been more than that." A slow smirk spread over his face. "I wonder what I should do about this. I have already punished you once today. But now I am going to have to punish you all over again." Bringing the whip over his head, he brought the tail down on one ass cheek, then the other.

It elicited a groan from her. A mischievous glint danced in her eyes as Nia flicked her gaze to his. "Harder, please, Sir."

At that moment, it took all his willpower to suppress the threatening growl building in his chest. This disobedient little minx was going to be his undoing. Hands down. The first thing he did was remove the strap from around her back, move her up onto all fours, and put the padded leather cuffs around her ankles. Without a word, he walked over to her dresser and picked up the first blindfold he came to. But it wasn't all he grabbed, either. He collected a couple of other things as well. Hunter returned to her, set the other pieces on the edge of the bondage horse, and got the blindfold in place. "Can you see anything, Nia?"

"No, Sir." Her tongue snaked out across her lower lip.

"Good." It was the last thing he said before he began getting the rest of the items in place. First, he placed a padded leather collar around her neck attached to a chain that he hooked to a loop on the front of the bondage horse. Next, a belt of the same nature went around her waist, right above her hip bones, the chains attaching to either side of the horse. She'd be able to move her body some, but not much at all. The restraints on her neck, waist, ankles, and wrists drastically curtailed her ability to move. Which was exactly what he wanted.

Moving around the table until he stood behind her, he picked up the dildo and slid it as far into her pussy as it would go. Straps encircled both her thighs, tightening to hold it securely. Next, he slid the butt plug into her ass. It wasn't the largest she'd had on display, but it was close. Both pieces vibrated. He switched them both on simultaneously, picked up the whip, and cracked it across her ass.

A multitude of sounds immediately came out of her mouth.

Holy fucking shit, she was beyond gorgeous. "You have been *very* naughty, Nia," Hunter growled out as he snapped the whip across each ass cheek. With a slow caress, he pinched her nub before dragging his claws across her left shoulder. Streaks of blood immediately welled up. As he leaned over, he tasted the faint metallic tang of blood as he soothed the claw marks with his tongue. He stood up, and the crack of the whip reverberated through the air as it struck her rear.

The sound of her fingers against the leather of the bondage horse with each strike made a wicked smirk spread across his face. He refused to look at the fact that he'd also… never smirked in sessions before. He had always stayed fully, 100% serious the entire time. It was just yet another thing that Nia brought out of him. That perfect compatibility they had in the playroom.

Nothing more.

The noises she made drove him absolutely insane. Not that he was going to say that out loud. He increased the vibrators' intensity, then simultaneously cracked the whip against her right shoulder and delivered a resounding smack to her rear. He repeated it several times before delivering the whip across her buttocks and thigh, each strike followed by a sharp smack from his other hand.

Nia moaned as her back and neck arched, the chains attached to the collar around her throat and waist rattling. Each limited her movement, but not so much that she couldn't press her breasts forward a bit. Hunter growled, picked up the nipple clamps, walked around in front of her, and attached them both to her nipples. Giving them each a tug, he snapped the whip across her ass. Grasping the base of his still-hard cock, he tantalizingly moved the tip near her mouth before pulling it back out of her grasp.

Nia licked her lips, making her tongue the primary focus, and then purred loudly. *Fuck,* that sound made it feel like bolts of lightning went straight to his balls, electrifying his nerve endings further. She was testing him, and while he absolutely loved what it did to him, it certainly made him curious about which of them would break first. Everything they did was blessedly tortuous. Suppressing a growl, he tried to ignore the insistent rhythm pulsing through him. Hunter stroked the head of his dick across her lips again, then returned to between her legs. The vibrator in her pussy had three more settings; the butt plug just one more. With no warning, he turned them both up to full volume, snapped the whip across her ass, and rubbed her clit hard and fast.

This time, he barely stopped the growl that threatened to escape as she purred again. *Fuck...* He firmly pushed the vibrator deeper into her core with his heel, simultaneously increasing the speed and intensity of rubbing her clit as he struck her back with the whip. His hand lingered on her sex as he continued to strike her back with the whip. Red mark after red mark appeared. He wanted nothing more than to fuck the shit out of her right now. Use his cock to take possession of her in every way, shape, and form. But he wouldn't break first. Not this time.

Each crack of the whip against her skin intensified with every strike. As soon as the first streak of crimson blood appeared, trickling along her skin, something snapped within him. A massive snarl and a loud moan reverberated around the room, the sounds bouncing from wall to wall. The two together sounded utterly divine. Drawing blood had always turned him on. He'd never given a thought to why. But this... drawing blood this way... it did things to him that using his claws to draw blood didn't do. Not that he could explain that, either. His hand lingered at her core as he leaned over her, tracing his tongue up the expanse of her back, his fangs skimming her skin as he consumed the blood he had drawn.

Nia arched her back, the chains rattling a little more. She let out another groan. "Will you fuck me, please, Sir?"

Holy shit, he wanted to fuck her. He *absolutely* wanted to fuck her. This was the first time she had ever pleaded with him for that, her voice laced with desperation. She'd begged him for a lot of things, but that was the first time she had used those particular words. And he absolutely loved it. He *needed* to be inside her just as much as she needed the same thing, though he wasn't *quite* ready to give in just yet. Not that it would likely take more than another moment or two before he wouldn't be able to wait any longer.

The whip cracked across her back, and as the blow landed harder than the last, his control frayed, a snarl escaping him as a fresh line of crimson bloomed. He allowed it to trickle down to her waist, right above the belt, before he swept his tongue across it, capturing every drop. Licking up her neck, he bit down on her earlobe. "How badly do you need me to fuck you, Nia?"

She purred. "Intensely, Sir," Nia replied, with a pleading tone to her voice.

Holy fuck, what those two sounds did to him. As his other hand tugged at the nipple clamps, he stroked her clit, feeling the heat of her body. "Have you learned your lesson today?"

"Yes, Sir."

"And how would you like me to *fuck* you, Nia? In your *pussy*?" He pressed hard on her nub. "Or in your ass?" He dragged his claws up her hip before sinking them into her flesh.

"Will you fuck me in my pussy, please, Sir?"

A low growl left him. He left that to be his answer before he removed the restraints, one by one. He took off the blindfold and nipple clamps as well, but kept both vibrators inside her, set to the highest setting. After he'd helped her off the bondage horse, he spun her around, positioning her with her back to him and her wrists restrained behind her. Hunter brought his hand down hard on her ass, leaving it there and digging his claws in once more. He leaned in close and growled in her ear, "Get on the bed. Lie on your back. Arms above your head. Then I will *fuck* your *pussy*."

A groan left her mouth before she crossed the small distance from the bondage horse to her bed. Nia climbed up onto the bed using both her knees, so her ass shook before she rolled over onto her back. Stretching her arms above her head, she spread her legs wide. She moaned with each individual movement as the dildo and butt plug vibrated; the sounds filling the room.

Hunter watched every single moment. But it was more than that. He couldn't look away. Nor did he want to. Every noise she made with each solitary movement made him salivate more. He took his time joining her on the bed. As he moved to straddle her, he locked eyes with her and lifted her wrists, drawing her further up the bed. Hunter secured her wrists to the bar at the end of the mattress, but her ankles remained unbound. With his gaze on hers, he turned off the vibrator that was in her pussy, slid it out of her, and slowly licked it clean. With a moan, Nia licked her lips as she watched him getting every drop from the dildo.

The look in her eyes had a tiny smirk crossing his face. Mind blowing. Not that he was going to explore why she could continue to make him react like this. It was best not to think about it. Better to clamp down on any thoughts that might threaten to go through his head, and just enjoy the sensations and his time with her. The way her pink tongue swept across her lips, like she was just begging for a taste... but a taste of what? Something else he wouldn't question, not even in his head. Going down that pathway of thoughts was far too dangerous.

Hunter, with one last, languid sweep of his tongue, made sure he collected all the sweet residue from the vibrating toy. He was secure enough in his manhood to lick something with cum on it, even if it looked like a cock. There was no way he would ever waste something so sweet. After placing the vibrator to the side, he lifted her legs over his, took hold of her thighs, and pushed into her with a deep groan. He held her as he wrapped her legs around his waist, supporting himself as he carried out his plan—he fucked her. And he fucked her hard. Though he took his time. With each deliberate thrust, he pushed his hardness deep inside her, maintaining a slow and forceful rhythm. Even through the walls of her pussy, he could feel the vibrations of the butt plug still going strong. *Holy fuck,* she felt so good. Too good...

Nia gripped the bar he'd attached her wrists to and arched her neck as she moaned. As he thrust harder, the vibrations from the butt plug became more pronounced, making her inner walls grip his erection firmly. Her legs even tightened ever so slightly around his waist. "May I dig my heels into your *ass*, please, Sir?"

All of it brought his orgasm closer to the surface with each hard stroke. He could hold it back until he'd fucked her well, though. "Yes. As hard as you can." He cupped her rear with his hand and hoisted her into his lap. He kept his grip on her ass, feeling the soft flesh give way under his touch, as he slammed into her core again and again. *Holy fuck,* he couldn't get enough. He didn't think he ever would. No one had ever made him feel this way. Never—Hunter slammed a steel mental door down on those thoughts. Things like that were too dangerous to consider, and he knew he had to push them away. *Far* away. They meant nothing, but even thinking about them... it was something he could never do.

With an endless stream of moans, Nia did as requested. With a minor shift of her legs, she secured the hook and then jammed her heels into his backside with maximum force. The aroma of his blood filled the air. Not only that, but her heels digging in so hard also lifted her hips closer to his. Another purred moan slipped from between her lips.

Hunter's growl was a low, guttural sound as he snapped a hand to her throat. He squeezed, not enough to cut off her airway, but enough to send her heart rate skyrocketing. His claws dug deeper into her buttocks, crimson droplets seeping between his fingers, while the intensity of his thrusts grew. "Look at me." Where had those words come from? His mouth. They'd left his mouth... and he couldn't take them back.

Nia immediately complied. The arch of her neck lowered until their eyes met.

Bad idea. BAD IDEA. Stop this. Stop this now. Look away. Look away... But he didn't. He couldn't. He was going to regret this later. As soon as he stepped foot outside that door. He could feel it in the marrow of his bones. But his body had a mind of its own, and he couldn't have torn his gaze away from hers if he had tried. Four days. He wouldn't see her for another four days. That would be enough to get himself under control. Enough time to bury these feelings that kept rising. Feelings he didn't understand, didn't need, and didn't *want*. It would be enough time to bury them and lock them so far away they never saw the light of day again. But for now... For now... Hunter's gaze didn't leave hers. "Come for me, Nia," he whispered. His commands had never been so soft.

An earth-shattering orgasm burst from her, her body arching against him.

Hunter gave a deep moan as his balls tightened. Her orgasm was so powerful, engulfing his cock completely, that it almost felt as if it was pulling his own out of him. Holy fuck, he was so close. Right on the edge. His vigorous thrusts intensified, almost causing the bed to tremble, as he relentlessly penetrated her over and over. There was something different this time. Even outside of when they'd been using the bondage horse and their eyes had met and held. Something more powerful. More passionate. Something he couldn't explain. Something he refused to do.

His eyes came close to squeezing shut with how incredible it felt, but he forced them to remain open. He didn't want to look away from those mesmerizing green eyes. As much as he needed to... as much as he should... he just couldn't. "Keep coming, Nia. Fuck... do not stop... I am going to come." He'd said nothing like that to her. To anyone.

Gripping the bar tighter, Nia pressed her heels into his ass while her inner muscles tightened around his cock. Her gaze didn't leave his as another release, just as shattering as the last, burst out of her, forcing her throbbing pussy to contract and release repeatedly around his rigid shaft until they were both coming. The climax that punched up the length of his cock and poured out of him was so forceful, so powerful, so all-consuming... for a moment, he wasn't able to draw breath. His lungs fought for air, his mouth agape, before a desperate moan escaped. That same strangled moan that had come out of him for the first time when he'd had her on the bondage horse, gazing into her eyes as he devoured her pussy relentlessly. He didn't allow himself time to think about the fact that he'd never made that sound with anyone else or that *she* was the only one that had ever pulled that out of him. He couldn't think of that.

So, he shoved that thought away too. They were just compatible *here*. In this room. Between these four walls. Doing this—fucking. That was it. That was all. It had to be. *This* was all it could ever be. Not just because of the rules of the brothel. But because of him. There was a reason he had come here. A reason he'd been coming here for over twenty-five years. He needed to remember that and stop letting his brain malfunction and acting like a fucking fool. He had four days to ensure that happened. If he couldn't... well, he would just have to find someone else to see. Someone else to share *this* with. Not that he would ever find someone he enjoyed *nearly* so much. No one in existence could come close to comparing with her.

Hunter wasn't sure how long their mutual release went on. Their cum flowed together, gushing out of her pussy, coating both of their thighs and soaking into the bed. He didn't care. She didn't seem to care, either. He just knew he needed more, as much as he could pull out of her, and she could pull out of him. His hands left her ass and her throat and wrapped around her thighs. Gripping them so hard, rivers of blood flowed down her skin to mix with their cum. He intensified his thrusts, determined to elicit at least one more climax from her. Or ensure it went on just a little longer.

"Fuck—" Her words cut off and a beat of silence passed. "Please, don't stop, Sir. Never stop." Nia dug the stilettos of her heels deeper into his ass cheeks. Her vaginal walls clenched tight around his cock. "Please, may I come, Sir?"

Oh, holy fuck, YES! He certainly would not stop if he didn't have to. With his claws digging into her thighs, Hunter thrust his cock into her, driving deep and fast. *Holy fuck...* he was going to come all over again. How was that possible? He didn't know, but he didn't care. He just wanted it... with her. "Yes... fuck... yes... Come for me, Nia. Come with me," he demanded.

Nia cried out in absolute euphoria as a colossal orgasm raged through her body and burst out of her like an unexpected torrential downpour. Her heels dug into his ass, and her fingers clutched the bar, the only things keeping her grounded.

The release that exploded out of him simultaneously with hers... he couldn't explain it. His entire body became electrified beyond belief, and he felt like he was floating. Never had he felt so utterly calm, despite the internal sensation that his body was detonating. Every nerve ending was on fire, every inch of him hypersensitive.

Wave after wave consumed him, yet another orgasm that seemed to go on with no end. So enormous, so phenomenal. He wasn't sure how he found enough air for the roar to expel from deep within. It mixed with Nia's cry, making the most beautiful music he never wanted to stop listening to. He withdrew his claws from her thighs, spreading her legs wider, and gripped her hair with both hands as he leaned over. Tilting her head back, their gazes locked, and for a moment, the world seemed to stop.

Holy fuck, he'd never come this much. Not in one orgasm. Not in his entire life. He didn't know how long it was before his body stilled. Just like every time he'd fucked her, he couldn't move. Whether it was unwilling-ness, inability, or both, he stayed right there, buried so deep inside her, it felt like their bodies were one entity instead of two. Completely and utterly joined. And *that* was exactly why he needed to pull the fuck out of her *right now*. Not that he did. Though he reached beneath her to her ass, flipped off the butt plug, and slid it out of her. No other part of him moved.

As he gazed into her jade-green eyes, the desire to kiss her, to possess her, became overwhelming. The sensation of her tongue encircling him was an unparalleled feeling. But the thought of what it might feel like intertwining with his tongue—he damn near dropped his head closer to hers. He came *very close*. Hunter squeezed his eyes shut. It was the only way to force himself to realize how absolutely unintelligent he was being. *What the fuck was he thinking?* He could absolutely *NOT* do that. Kissing... *no*. Too personal. *WAY* too personal. He didn't do personal. He fucked. That was as far as it went. Ever. And for good reason.

The last thing he wanted to do was pull out of her. Break the connection between them. Whatever the fuck it was that made him feel things he never had before—this calm. This... peace. He felt so fucking peaceful with her. No matter how hard the sessions got. No matter how much pain he caused and how much blood he drew. Nia took it all. Beyond that, she asked for more. Like it would never be enough. As if she was utterly desperate for him and the things he could do to her body. It was as though she wanted to consume him, to be consumed by him, just as he desired the same from her. She *challenged* him. And he loved every single moment of it. He wouldn't have tolerated it from anyone else. But with her... Nia made him come alive in ways he hadn't thought were possible.

But it was *IMPOSSIBLE*. And he needed to get that through his fucking head. Now. None of this mattered in the least. Beyond her *job*, beyond that, he was her client, and he paid her for sex. He wasn't good for anyone. He would ruin her. That was what he did—he ruined people. He'd ruined himself—with a shit-eating grin on his face the entire fucking time, at that. Even if a relationship were anywhere close to possible, she deserved so much more than someone who would utterly destroy her mind, body, and soul. Whatever this was, whatever he was feeling... he had four days to shut it away and lock it up for eternity. That was all there was to it.

Hunter separated from her, then with a swift movement, he unlocked the restraints from her wrists. With his gaze averted, he lifted her and transported her to a dry space on the bed, positioning her carefully on her stomach. Then he got comfortable beside her so he could begin cleaning her up. Before he began, he said, "No purring." And for once, he actually hoped she would not disobey him. The punishments were absolutely glorious. Mind blowing. His eyes couldn't get enough of watching how she responded to every single thing he did to her. But if the intensity, the passion... if any more of it occurred today... he knew without a doubt he'd do something he couldn't come back from. It was just too much. Everything he'd felt today, here with her... it was just too much.

"No purring," Nia echoed.

Hunter avoided her eyes while his tongue traced a path along her skin. Never had he cleaned her with such speed, the metallic tang of blood barely fading. He worked quickly, taking only the time needed to rid her skin of every drop of blood and the slick residue of his release. He could have easily gotten a washcloth and cleaned her that way, but he just couldn't bear wasting it. Shutting everything else down, he focused purely on his task. Once he was done with that, he massaged her legs. His gaze remained on the blanket that covered her bed, black like so much else in here. He didn't say a word. If he opened his mouth right now, he feared the wrong things would come tumbling out. For probably the first time in his life, he recognized the necessity of keeping his mouth shut.

After he finished with her legs, he continued to examine the rest of her body, mindful of every scratch from his claws or the sting of the whip. He'd never thought to ask how quickly she healed, but outside of the tiny scar on her hip, she didn't have a single mark on her body. The marks he inflicted on her were always gone when he returned. And he knew he wasn't her only client. A crushing weight settled on his chest, momentarily stealing his breath.

Fuck this. No, this wasn't him. He *did not* get attached. He didn't deserve to get attached. And Nia was the last person it would ever be possible with. He would force his mind to realize that if it killed him.

Stop it, Hunter, now. This is just sex. Just sex. You are not her only client and you never will be. It doesn't matter how compatible you are. How much you both enjoy it. How different every single fucking thing has been with her since the moment you walked through her door for the first time. It will be nothing but just sex. You make her cum like a fucking fountain, and she satisfies you better than anyone else ever has. End of. You will not fuck that up.

Indeed, he never wanted to be banned from this place, never. That wouldn't just suck; it would be dangerous. Where would that leave him? With his own hand and no pussy to stick his dick into. Nowhere to go to get his more savage urges out.

Definitely not something he was interested in.

He'd never massaged her so fast, his heart pounding, as he urgently needed to escape. The red light wasn't even on yet. How much time had even passed? It didn't matter. She could keep the rest as a tip. He had to go. "Wear white next time," Hunter said as he got off the bed, his eyes studiously landing on *anything* but her.

"Of course," Nia said, the word barely a whisper as she rose from the bed. Her footsteps echoed as she crossed the room to a sliding door painted black so it blended in well with the wall. Unless anyone noted the dark metal of the handle, it would go completely unnoticed. "Until next time," she called over her shoulder.

It took every ounce of willpower he had not to turn around and follow her. That was the opposite of what needed to happen right now. He had four days to get back to *normal*. Get back to sanity. As much sanity as he possessed, anyway. "Next time," he responded. He almost told her goodbye, but left it at just those two words. Crossing the floor, Hunter opened the door, closed it behind him, and left.

Five

As Nia cleaned herself up in the bathroom, the rhythmic sound of the water helped her as she replayed everything in her mind from their last few sessions. She'd been ready to get back to her routine, but something about Hunter made it impossible. Maybe if she complied a bit more, things wouldn't escalate further.

Too much had churned too close to the surface for her liking in today's session. Distance needed to start immediately. She had nothing to offer him. Her life had ended thirty years ago—the day she joined the brothel and signed a contract that offered no way out. Back then, she didn't care. All she had left was her mother and brother. They depended on her too much for her to indulge in something that couldn't be anything more than a fantasy.

It didn't matter that she had things with Hunter that she'd never had with another. Not even her first. Hunter awakened echoes within her that had been muted for years. Even Deacan had only reached those parts of her once or twice in all the years they'd had together. But in just three sessions, Hunter pulled them out of her. None she'd ever been with ever came as close as Hunter to Deacan.

She *had* to stop comparing them. They were nothing alike. But that was the point, wasn't it? Deacan had encouraged and supported her. Their relationship had been as fulfilling as it could be. While the male had cared for her and her family for over a hundred years, there had been things she'd never been able to provide for him. The one thing he truly wanted—children. Deacan had always desired a family of his own, a legacy that he'd leave behind. And she hadn't been able to give it to him. Although she took the daily supplements required here in the sanctum, she knew they weren't even necessary.

It was for that very reason she didn't blink twice at what the proprietress presented to her the day she arrived at the sanctum. At least, a life where she could be herself was something. And it gave her the chance to ensure she took care of the people who mattered most to her. Even if she had to be secretive about it and cut all ties. Truly, she had nothing to offer anyone.

As Nia stepped out of the shower and dried off, she heard a loud, swift knock somewhere out in the hall. Followed by a male voice.

"Grace. Grace, are you alright?"

What in the gods? Nia grabbed her bathrobe and tied the string tight. The familiar scent of lavender from the fabric calmed her before she headed toward her bedroom door.

The loud, hasty knock sounded again. "Grace!"

Nia poked her head out of her door. It was Einarr. Her gaze flicked from him to Grace's door. She noted the mixture of lights shining from beneath it—one red, the other purple. They all had a red light that showed the end of a session, but there were only a select few who had the purple light. It indicated that the self-locking mechanism on the door had gotten triggered. It was something that happened anytime a shape shifter was near Grace's door.

Shit. If the male waited outside... then that could only mean one client had gone over. Wait. Why was he out here? Shouldn't he be in the waiting room? Something to worry about later. Hunter had just left, so the purple light should go off momentarily. Still... "How long have you been standing there?"

"Ah..." Einarr's eyes darted towards her, and as he raked a hand through his flaming-red hair, he seemed to struggle for words, creating a ruffled mess. "I'm unsure... I just—" His voice abruptly ceased, as if the thoughts swirling in his mind had struck him speechless. "Something isn't right. Can you please, *please* open the door?" he pled with her.

Not that she could do much. What powers she had access to wouldn't unlock the door. Though it should occur momentarily. Hunter was well out of range by now. "Why don't you sit in my room while I see what I can do?" Cracking her door wider, Nia stepped into the hallway, the dim light of the hallway immediately visible. "Just not on the bed," she tacked on. She had cleaned nothing yet.

Einarr, with a nervous glance, considered both doors. His arm, poised between knocking and retreating, was stiff with indecision. As if changing his mind, he shook his head, brows furrowed with worry after opening his mouth to speak. "Um, no, thank you. I..."

Was the male always like this? Did she intimidate him or something? For crying out loud, she was in a bathrobe. Fuck, Grace got some weird ones. As if Goltak wasn't bad enough. "Then maybe you should go back to the waiting room. She shouldn't be too much longer. But she'll need a few minutes to... clean up." Yeah, because that damn toad was sick as fuck. And this kid didn't need to barge in on that shit when the door unlocked, which should happen any second.

Instead of doing either of the things she'd suggested, the male didn't budge. Instead, he returned to knocking on her door and calling out to her.

Holy fuck. Nia groaned, containing her exasperation and holding back an insult. "You're not helping. Trust me. If you want to help, then Go. Sit. Down."

"You aren't, either!" Einarr snapped. "My apologies. I didn't mean..."

Grace's door flung open and there stood the nasty fucking toad himself. Einarr jumped. The silence washed over him as he stood stunned.

"You are too noisy, little tadpole," Goltak grumbled, his voice echoing slightly.

Before things got worse, Nia grabbed Einarr's arm and yanked him away from the door. Best to give that *thing* a wide berth. Many of the amphibious or reptilians of the isle were toxic or poisonous. Not that it was the only reason that staying out of the male's path was an intelligent decision.

The moment Goltak was out of sight, the kid wriggled free and dashed across the hall, disappearing into Grace's room. Leaving the door ajar, he raced to Grace's side. Soaking his clothes as he went down, he sank to his knees in the water before scooping her up in his arms. She wasn't sitting, but propped up enough that the water could clear her lungs without issue. "Are you well?"

Grace practically slumped in Einarr's hold, her head landing on his shoulder. She purred and arched against them, running her nose up the kid's throat. "Mmm…" Her eyes widened as she stared up at him. "Your head… Is that your head? It is… fire… on fire… Your head is on fire."

Einarr's face and ears quickly flushed, revealing his embarrassment. "What? My head isn't on fire."

With purpose, Nia strode over to Silva's door and knocked twice, the sound of her knuckles echoing in the stillness. The code they'd created years ago for when Grace had a *rough* visit with Goltak.

Silva's door swung inward. He'd obviously thrown on the closest clothes and given his hair a quick, disheveled styling. He leaned against the doorjamb. "What's that bulbous fuck done to her now?"

"From the sound of it, I'd say she's high right now. You know… on top of the *normal* shit." Nia rolled her eyes. "Come on. Let's find where the fuck he hid the damn thing this time." She took a step and stopped. "Oh, and the idiot out in the hall is in her room."

"You know…" Silva blew out a heavy breath. "Somehow, I'm not in the least bit shocked."

Together, they headed into Grace's room. Neither uttered a word as they began searching for the vial that contained the antidote Grace needed to consume as soon as possible. Though she monitored her friend, too. The Seelie idiot could unintentionally make the situation worse.

"Are you injured? Sick?" Einarr asked. At his hip, he fumbled for his pouch, retrieving fresh, leafy herbs that smelled of the earth. "Here." He placed the aromatic herbs gently against Grace's lips. "It's sweet, but it'll help."

"Uh-uh. Nopey. I am… floating… floating *away*." Grace giggled as she arched against him with another purr. Her tongue darted out to taste the leaves. "Mmm… yummy." She licked them again. "Mmm. I bet *you* taste *better*, though. Can I taste you?"

Nia stifled a snicker. Oh, she had so many questions. Not that it would be right to tease Grace at a moment like this. But what were friends for? She glanced over her shoulder at Silva, who'd started on one side of the room, while she searched the other.

"I'd prefer you didn't." Einarr shifted his gaze to her and Silva, the sound of his cough masking his visible discomfort. "Are you searching for something?"

As he ran his hands beneath the crevice, Silva called out, "Antidote," his voice echoing around the room. "The bastard likes to play a little sadistic game of hide and seek with the cure for his toxin."

Einarr knit his brow, a frown forming on his face. "Averine *allows* him to do this to her—without curating her own antidote?! Does she realize what might happen if you don't find it?"

Nia shot the male an incredulous look. Did he really think their so-called *mother* cared? "Just keep her up the best you can. It won't take us long to find it." How many times had they done this already? Too many to fucking count. She scoured every crevice. Even used the only ability she could access, provided it would aid in the search.

"What about fresh water? Is there a way to get that for her?" Einarr asked, sounding less than hopeful.

Grace groaned, attempting to curl up, but her limbs were stiff and wouldn't budge. "Feel... yucky," she mumbled, trying to squirm out of Einarr's arms.

Yep, this was one of the really fucking bad ones. "I got it," Nia hollered as she rushed over to the spring. "I'd heft her out a bit more, and carefully." She'd seen the signs. Grace probably wasn't far off from vomiting. Best that happened in the muck rather than all over the floor. "I can rinse her off so we can get her in the shower."

Grace's gaze snapped to the bottle in Nia's hands. She immediately hissed, her fangs gleaming menacingly. "NO!" Scrambling harder against Einarr's hold, her violent thrashing sent them both backwards and nearly into the water. "NO! GET... GET AWAY WITH... WITH THAT!"

"Please, Grace, stop." Einarr's grip around her briefly relaxed as he attempted to draw Grace's gaze. Her struggle, along with the slick water, sent them both sprawling. "You must calm yourself. It's medicine. It will help."

Ah, fuck. Oh, her friend *so* owed her. "Sorry, Grace," Nia muttered and set the vial aside. With a surge, she called upon her water control to bind around the female's arms and lift her from the mire, washing away some of the poison at the same time. It was the only power she could access, but it would help in some small way. Though her friend might have a bruise or two later, considering how she thrashed about.

"NO! NOT... medicine... Poison. You... trying to... poison me. Leave me... 'lone." A half-hiss trailed off into a groan. "Ow... Hurts... Hurts...

Gonna…" Grace couldn't get any other words out before she vomited all down her front.

Yep, there it went. Just as she suspected. Whatever the Seelie had attempted, she didn't know, but it hadn't done shit from what she could tell. Nia ran more clean water through her friend's fur, washing away some of the vomit. The Seelie kid recoiled from the stench of vomit and desperately scrambled to regain his balance.

"Silva, get over here!" Nia yelled over her shoulder. It would take both of them to get the antidote down Grace's throat. They'd done this before.

Following her ability effortlessly, their friend got into position, using his wind to reinforce her water tunnel. "Taking charge as usual, *Mistress*?" Silva teased, his power visibly guiding the cool water towards Grace's parted lips. Before things got worse, a mouthwash could give them a fighting chance to save her.

Grace jerked her head in the other direction, causing it to fall back on her neck, as if it was too heavy for her to hold up any longer. Which just resulted in some of the water going down the back of her throat. Grace started coughing, bringing up more vomit and stomach bile. Tears sprang to her eyes as she trembled. "Lemme … go … Lemme go!"

Nia flicked her gaze to Einarr. "Grab that bottle there." With her head, she gestured to where she'd set it. "We'll hold her down; you give it to her."

The male, panting, almost lost his footing twice before he got to where she had indicated. He clutched the vial tightly, his knuckles white with the effort, trying to prevent it from breaking. That was the last thing they needed.

"No… No…" Grace shook her head back and forth as much as she was able. "Do not… want it… Do not… want…" she moaned, though her words came out much more fragile.

Yeah, sometimes it was the only way they got anywhere. "Fuck," Nia snapped. Grace's struggle only exacerbated the already dire situation. That fucking bulbous pile of shit. This was all on him. "We're going to have to do this the hard way." Not something she wanted to do, but they had no choice. Summoning her power, she redirected a bit of fresh water to hold Grace's head in place. It would make it a little easier to get the antidote down her throat.

"Grace... dear. We truly don't want to do this the unconscious way." Silva forced a smile. He stabilized his stance, continuing to reinforce Nia's hold as he turned to Einarr. "Any time now, kid."

Einarr got as close as he could to Grace. Even on tiptoe, she remained taller than him. "I can't reach."

"NO! NO! LEAVE ME ALONE! LEAVE ME ALONE! LET ME GO!"

It took every ounce of control she had to keep from lifting the damn Seelie into the air to make him useful. Nia flicked her gaze to Silva. "Two options. Either we lower her toward the ground since he's so damn short, or we lift him." Doubtless he knew which one she preferred.

"Three, technically," Silva corrected, steadying their current setup with one hand. With the other hand, he skillfully maneuvered the other with little effort, and the sweet smell of the liquid filled the air as Einarr generously popped open the vial and extracted the liquid. Silva hastened the yellow antidote, its surface shimmering, into Grace's mouth, trapping the surrounding air to keep it from escaping before she could react.

Grace nearly gagged. As soon as she had control over her airways again, she wheezed, squeezing her eyes shut.

Yeah. That would work. They hadn't used that option for a few months. She'd forgotten about it. Nia glanced at Silva. "How long did it take to work last time? Minutes? Might give us time to move her into the shower."

"Should work soon enough. Maybe we can set her down and carry her the rest of the way?"

"Sounds good," she said as Einarr stepped back, giving them more room to work. Yeah. They didn't need to draw things out, or risk drawing any attention to themselves. Or Grace. Hadn't this idiot done this once already? Nia and Silva worked together to set their friend on the floor. Grace groaned and immediately curled in on herself. The nausea might be gone, but severe pain undoubtedly wracked her stomach. Like daggers were getting buried repeatedly in her abdomen, as Grace had once described it. Nia's gaze flicked to Einarr. "Why were you out in the hall, anyway?"

"Um, I...ah... I was drafting up another poster... and thought it'd be okay to stop by." The male's cheeks flushed a bright red as he blushed. "Just for a moment."

"Uh huh." Silva's gaze landed on Nia, and his tone of voice made his feelings clear. He hooked an arm under Grace's, taking half her weight, while Nia did the same on the side opposite him.

Grace whimpered a bit. Her head lolled forward, her chin resting against her chest. She opened her mouth, but quickly closed it. Likely still nauseous.

"Right," Nia muttered. Oh, this kid needed a pleasant reminder of the rules. Pop by... unannounced? Gods, what the fuck was he thinking?

"If there is anything I can do to help..." Einarr suggested.

Silva and Nia exchanged another glance. This was setting up to be a long evening. "Sure." Although he smiled, the hollowness of his words revealed his insincerity. "How about you make sure her bed's all nice and fluffed while we get her cleaned up?" He dipped his chin toward Grace's concealed bed. At the very least, the kid could hopefully pull down a few blankets without getting into any trouble. Not that any of this was his fault. Still, he was an easy target for their frustrations. One who wasn't likely to fight back. So why the fuck not?

With a decisive nod, the man moved quickly and carefully, his eyes fixed on the path ahead.

Nia rolled her eyes. More regarding the way Silva admired the kid's ass. Seriously? Nia would fucking break the kid. Though it certainly amused her how Silva got the little twat out of their hair while they handled what the Seelie couldn't. And she thought Seelie were supposed to be useful.

Silva waited, watching the male disappear, before he started the faucet, the rush of water filling the quiet. "If your face contained any more *bitch*, you'd be out of a job." Her friend shook his head as they got Grace into the shower.

"Me? My bitch hasn't even shown." Nia yanked off her robe, the cool air hitting her skin as she climbed into the shower with Grace. Easier to hold her up this way. Not like they hadn't done this dance before.

As soon as the water began hitting her face, Grace's whole body trembled. As if, despite the fever and the warmth of the water, she was freezing cold. She curled up on the shower floor with her head in Nia's lap, clenching her jaw to keep her teeth from chattering.

Silva laughed. He helped her get Grace good and under, but once she was stable, he pulled away, flicking the water from his hand, unwilling to get drenched by the icy spray like Nia. "You're letting Grace's little pointy-eared floof get you all kinda riled," he stated, crossing his arms.

"He's doing stupid shit. I think he just needs a little reminder of how *not* to act." Not like she intended to hurt him. Her gaze flicked from Silva to Grace. At least, it appeared the antidote was working.

"Wh-who?" Grace's body jerked as a larger tremor swept through her. Each time she went through this, her body had to readjust to the temperature. "Who... else's here?"

"The kid," Silva replied. "The redhead who thinks you're a privileged house cat. Brings you... books." With his foot, he nudged a ruined book, stained with a dark, viscous sludge, back into the room. "Uh ... you wanna do something about that, Red?" he asked Nia.

Damn. Did she still have blood on her? Nia peered over her body as best she could, but noticed nothing. Nope. Just Silva being his usual self. She glanced back at their friend. "You good in here, Gracie? If so, I'm gonna go clean up the mess."

"I w-will b-be... f-f-fine. Soon." Grace inhaled deeply, the crisp air filling her lungs, then exhaled slowly, attempting to calm her trembling. "S-s-steam... T-turn on... the st-steam, please." She gently eased her head off of Nia's lap. "E-Einarr...? Wh-why is... why is h-he here?"

"He thought he'd *pop* by," Nia said as she got to her feet. She adjusted the heat of the water, ensuring it was warm, but not scalding, for Grace. Enough that the bathroom would steam, and then she climbed out of the shower to dry off and tug her robe back on.

"Nobility always believes they're privileged—no means yes," Silva tacked on, his words sharp and biting. "The shy, artsy Seelie is no different."

Grace tried to shake her head, but stopped quickly. She rested her head back on the shower floor and wrapped her arms as much around herself as she could. "N-no. Einarr... is not l-like that. I am—" She clenched her jaw and inhaled a breath, exhaling slowly. "—probably g-gonna n-need help again th-this time. Wash-shing up."

Nia wrapped the robe around herself, then knotted the sash tightly. Yeah, she knew the type well. She dealt with a few clients like that, but they always adhered to the guidelines without complaint. She poked her head in the shower and, with a flick of her wrist, commanded her magic to heat the water, transforming the shower into a sauna. "It's all I can do for now, Gracie." She glanced at Silva. "Looks like you got wash duty."

"Th-thank you, N-Nia."

"No offense, Gracie. But if he 'isn't like that'... then Mommy Dearest must *really* like those drawings." Silva eyed the bedroom where Einarr had disappeared to. With a weary sigh, he began his hunt for the scrub brush. "Where we startin' tonight?"

"Wherever is... ea-easiest for you. Do you need me to... to move closer?"

"Whichever position is most comfortable for you, sweetheart," Silva teased with a wink. "You know I'm flexible."

"Don't worry. I'll deal with lover boy," Nia called over her shoulder. She glanced at Einarr as she exited the bathroom. The male had made Gracie's bed. "Look at that. You *can* follow orders. Color me shocked." With a smirk, she surveyed the chaos and the chore it represented. Ugh. Disgusting-ass pile of shit. That damn toad was like a walking turd.

The male glanced at her and cleared his throat, a nervous sound in the quiet room. "My apologies if I cause you any issues. I didn't mean—I simply wished to help."

"If you want to help, then I suggest you leave. As you can tell, Grace is well taken care of." Using her power, Nia gathered the scattered water and guided it back to the spring. Thankfully, it didn't take much effort at all. She closed some of the distance between her and the kid. "And next time you get a hair-brained idea to drop by, remind yourself about the rules listed at the front. They aren't there, so you can decide which one to follow."

Einarr recoiled from the disgusting, slimy water. "My apologies. I didn't mean to cause trouble," he muttered. "Your boss said it was okay. Is Grace alright?"

Nia raised an eyebrow. Averine had agreed to it? That didn't make a damn bit of sense. But why would this kid lie about something like that? Curious. "Grace is fine. You're free to check in on her. She's showering." Shrugging him off, Nia turned her attention back to the spring, finding the button to shut it off and drain it.

With a nod of gratitude, the male quickly descended the ladder. He crossed the space, the scent of soap and water drifting from the bathroom, but stayed outside, resting his back against the wall. "Are you feeling better?"

"Yes, actually. You can come in."

Nia snickered. Yeah. Cuz he was going to come in. A hoity-toity like that? Not fucking likely. She watched as the last of the water drained and used her power one last time to wash the spring out thoroughly. Once it was all set, she put the plug back in place and reactivated the spring.

"Um... I... I'm good, thank you."

"Alright," Grace responded. "Suit yourself." A brief pause followed, interrupted only by a slight sloshing. Likely Grace turning over so Silva could wash her from another angle. "I hope you can excuse my... behavior earlier. I am never quite myself after I see that client."

That was an understatement of the century. Though Grace hadn't attempted to nuzzle her or Silva in quite some time. And not to the degree the female had done it with Einarr. It kind of amused her. Having finished with the spring, Nia went to the bathroom, navigating around Einarr as she went. "Alright, Gracie. Your spring is clean." Her gaze flicked from Silva to Grace. "If you need nothing else, I've got my own cleaning to attend to."

"Oh, the torture chamber requires a good scrubbing, does it?" Silva's voice dripped with a spooky inflection of mock horror. "Muahahaha!"

"After the use, it just got..." Nia grinned widely. "And you know how my room freaks out the staff," she tacked on.

"No, I need nothing else. Thank you, Nia."

"I'll see you both later, then." Nia strode back around Einarr. She started toward the door, but paused before she got too far. Her gaze flicked to him. "I'm curious. Is the shyness just part of your shtick, or are you still learning to fill your britches?" She definitely derived pleasure from making him fidget.

Einarr pulled his knees up to his chest, hugging them tightly. "My 'schtick'? I'm afraid I don't understand."

"She's asking if you're fronting, kid," Silva said. "Putting on an act. Taking on a persona that's not your usual."

"Do people actually do that?"

"Yes, they do. In so many, many ways," Nia purred. "But if this is really you... well, I promise not to bite unless asked." Not that she expected he ever would. Yeah, her initial assessment was right. She'd eat him alive.

"I... No, I am not. I don't believe in such things," Einarr admitted honestly.

Silva laughed. "It's funny *you* bite, and Gracie doesn't."

"Oh, I bite." Grace smirked. "It is just reserved for... specific clientele. Just because I do not have claws, does not mean my fangs are any less sharp."

"Touché, Gracie." Nia snickered. "I'll see you both later." As fun as it was to poke at Einarr, she had better things to do. She headed for the door.

"Thanks for your help, Nia," Grace called.

"Don't worry, kid," Silva assured. Someone shut off the water. "She's never bitten me, either."

"What happened to your claws?" With a confused frown, Einarr finally asked, his brow furrowed.

"I lost them *solaris* ago," Grace replied. The female stopped in the bathroom doorway with a towel wrapped around her body. She shifted her attention to Silva and Nia. "Thanks for your help. Again."

Yeah, no way Grace could tell him the truth regarding that. Silva joined her at the door. It was definitely time for them both to skedaddle. "Nice meeting you, Einarr," Nia called over her shoulder.

"Pleasure to make your acquaintance, Miss Nia," Einarr replied. He turned to Silva. "And you as well."

"You'll have to schedule a session to get the full experience," Silva shot back with a playful wink.

Nia paused in the doorway, turning to look back at them. "Just Nia. I'm nowhere near the age of 'Miss' yet. Still have a few hundred years before that happens." As she and Silva left Grace's room, she quietly snickered before shutting the door. Pausing halfway to her room, she flicked her gaze to him. "Did you hear what he said about... *mother*?"

Silva leaned against the wall, his gaze fixed on her. "And this surprises you?" His eyes dropped briefly to the floor. "Mother has her claws in him. Remember, he's nobility, and while I doubt those little posters are drawing business equally among performers, they are drawing new revenue. I don't imagine it's easily missed that he's more passionate regarding Gracie." He crossed his arms, his gaze subtly drifting toward Nia. "She wishes to break him of that."

Yeah, breaking him would make sense. Just not in the way Averine approached it. Nia's eyebrows furrowed. "By giving him permission to come and see Grace... unscheduled. Without paying for it." Even as a noble, she couldn't fathom how that would *break* him in any sense of the word. It was more like the female gave him exactly what he wanted.

Silva gave a half-hearted smile. "Come now, Nia. Mother knows our schedules. Einarr *only* sees Grace. Giving him the opportunity to see her at her worst... do you not see how that might *shatter* that singular delusion?"

That made even less sense. Nia shook her head. "I feel it might've backfired. He looked rather determined to..." Her words trailed off. Not like she really had to finish the direction of her thoughts. Einarr struck her as the rescuing type. Very unlike the cold-hearted nobility she'd entertained over the years. "Well, I guess we'll see what happens from here."

"I don't disagree. Merely stating it wouldn't surprise me if she thought to encourage him to sample other wares, hoping to further control him for the den's benefit." He shrugged. "He's likely paying more than average rates without complaint. Plus, the arrangement with the promotional products. Mother's collecting more at a faster rate than she would have otherwise. I'm sure it doesn't help that she knows he's a partner in some capacity with one of my clients. All the same... be careful."

He didn't need to tell her why. Mother's sudden interest meant not only higher security, but more eyes and ears, whispers from those workers devoted to rising among their ranks, or earning a little extra coin. "Don't most of our clients pay more than they probably should?" That didn't even include the little extra trinkets many of them brought. As for his warning... Nia rolled her eyes. "I'm a professional. Like I have anything to fret over. Just because I made a mockery of Ivory a week ago... that was just fun." A lot of fun. It amused her to torture the female publicly. And she'd only used words. A slow grin spread across her face.

"Yes, though I suspect even in Mother's initial plan backfiring, the house still stands to profit. Placing the Seelie boy in competition with the toad might start a wage war among all Grace's clients, who face losing privilege if one—or both—were to demand exclusivity." He pushed off the wall, ready to head to his room. "I wasn't referring to Ivory," he said. "Though I suspect you already knew that."

"I don't know what you're talking about." Just because she talked to a couple of her clients, it didn't mean she had anything to worry about. The important stuff remained private. It always would. Indeed, her session with Hunter had shifted their dynamic, yet she could clear her mind before he came back. "Well, I've got a room to clean." She wiggled her fingers at him. "I'll see you at dinner."

With a limp wrist, he offered a feeble wave. "Think I'll pass." Silva pushed aside the beaded curtain that clattered just inside his doorway. "My appetite departed with the warty abomination on flappy flippers."

"Alright, but you get to explain it to Gracie." If any of the three of them kept their little group together, it was that female. Nia strode across the hall to her bedroom, her footsteps echoing in the quiet space. She had things to handle.

Nia stood in her closet as if she were searching for something. She awaited Fallon's arrival. As the years went by, his craving for rape fantasy became a way for her to express her aggression and indulge in her masochistic desires. She liked to draw blood as much as she liked to have it drawn. Of all her clients, Hunter seemed to be the only one who enjoyed both. *Damn it.* There he went again, invading her fucking thoughts.

Three days had passed since their last session. She couldn't stop thinking about him, no matter how hard she tried to focus on other things. It was something she absolutely needed to do—a burning necessity in her soul. Her teeth sank into her cheek as she smoothed the ivory lace of her shorts, finally resting a hand on her hip. While she'd picked this outfit for Fallon, she hadn't been able to stop questioning whether Hunter would like it. Why the fuck did it matter what he thought? She wasn't even seeing him today. Even if she was, his opinion only counted in her servicing him. That was it. End of the fucking story.

It was a good thing the shorts and matching bralette wouldn't last past this session with Fallon. Then she could stop thinking about stupid shit. The stilettos always remained on since he liked it as much as she did when she dug her heels into him. This pair was among her favorites—cream-colored six-inch stilettos with gold studs lining the straps that went across her foot and buckled around her ankle. As she fought against Fallon, the straps might painfully bite into her skin. Gods, she really hoped they did this time.

Before she could process another presence, a forceful grip seized her wrists, pinning her against the wall as she felt a hard erection.

"I am back. Did you miss me?" Fallon growled out in a near-whisper, right next to her ear.

Fuck. Normally, she noticed when he entered her room. She was so preoccupied with thoughts of Hunter she didn't notice Fallon until he was right behind her. Sometimes, she ignored his arrival on purpose, but this wasn't one of them. At least it made their playtime a little more natural. "No," she whimpered and struggled to free her wrists from his grip. "Let me go!"

As this was a rape fantasy, the more she fought back, the more pleasurable sex was between them. Everything was consensual. In their very first session nearly thirty years ago, they'd gone over hard limits, soft limits, what kind of fantasy he had, and established safe words for both of them. Words and phrases like 'no,' 'please stop,' and 'get off me' weren't good options. She'd chosen the same safe word she used with all of her clients—blue. Unless she uttered that for any reason, they were still in playtime. They always talked afterward, something she quickly learned he needed, which helped them develop a friendship. So much of which she hadn't realized she needed, too, especially since she didn't form relationships with the workers here at the den—Grace and Silva not included.

Fallon's cock thickened against her as he removed his camouflage. "You know that will not happen." As he pushed his cock harder against her ass, his hold on her wrists became more intense. His hand moved from her hip, giving it a squeeze, then inched to between her legs. "You are going to give me *exactly* what I want."

"No!" Nia yelled, her voice echoing as she fought to contain the moan that threatened to escape her lips because of his tightened grip. Her years with Deacan had come in handy with Fallon. He never really hurt her, but whenever his hold on her increased in pressure, she always had to keep from showing that she enjoyed it. His hand found its way between her legs, and she clamped her thighs tight. While she could keep her noise in check, stopping herself from getting wet was an impossibility. His cock pressing against her ass was often the culprit. Fallon hadn't ever been into anal, though, something she rather enjoyed.

His chest rumbled. He forced her legs apart with his knee, and then quickly shoved his hand beneath her lacy shorts. He growled, the sound echoing in the room as his fingers finally found their destination. "You know you want it. I can feel it. Fuck, you are already wet." As he pushed two fingers inside her, he pressed his cock against her ass and let out a moan.

Well yes, she wanted it, but she couldn't *act* as though she did. It would kill the whole mood. Nia clenched her thighs tighter. "No! Stop!" Of course, she liked that as much as when he fisted her hair and tugged it back. Something she enjoyed with Hunter, too. *No! Damn it!* That motherfucker wasn't welcome in the space between her and Fallon. Hunter needed to get the fuck out of her head. Nia slapped and scratched at Fallon's arms, wrestling against the hold he had on her.

"Fuck yes, *fight me,* bitch!" he snarled out. As he let go of her hair, Fallon used his hand to cover her mouth and thrust his fingers deeper into her sex, curling them against the inner walls of her pussy. "I am going to make you come even if you do not want to."

Had she drawn blood? *Shit.* That never happened this early in a session with Fallon. It rarely happened until they'd at least made it to the bed. Fucking Hunter. Why the fuck did he keep popping up? He'd done it for three fucking days already. It hadn't just been in sessions with other clients. It had been during her downtime, too. Her fucking personal time and his smug-ass face appeared in her mind! The more he got in her headspace, the angrier she got. She needed to get him out of her head. Even if she had to rip him out.

Nia screamed against the hand over her mouth, fighting harder against Fallon. Despite her struggles and despite her physical resistance, her vaginal walls tightened around his fingers. A wave of pleasure, poised to break, already sat close to the edge.

Fallon moaned. He thrust his fingers deeper into her, curling them up harder. "Fuck, yes. Fucking give me that cum," he growled. "Then I am going to take what I really want."

While none of her other clients noticed any kind of difference in her demeanor, Fallon would see it. Not that she knew what she'd tell him. There shouldn't be anything to tell. If only she'd been able to pass Hunter on to another submissive. The idea of it tied her insides in knots, despite her previous investigation. He should not be affecting her like this. He was nothing more than another client.

The more pissed off she got about Hunter, the harder she fought Fallon. This only heightened her arousal, to where she could have accidentally stepped on Fallon's foot or kicked him in the shin with her heel. She couldn't quite tell which. Just as much as she continued to rake her nails across his arm and shoulder. Between that and his fingers' exploration, a wave of pleasure surged through her body. Her vaginal walls clenched as she came hard.

Fallon let out a growl in her ear as his hand closed over the front of her throat. He didn't really squeeze, just applied a little pressure. His thumb pressed into her jugular. "Oh... fuck... *yes*... You feel that?" He still stroked the inner walls of her sex. "Do you feel how much you want me? You just gave me all of this." Taking his fingers out of her pussy and shorts, he licked them clean with his mouth. "You are just a dirty little slut." He growled when her hand swung back at his face, her nails raking across his cheek.

The words and phrases came out of Fallon with ease, although she knew how much he hated they did. And he always felt bad afterward. She'd always accepted it, but never degraded him in return. It just wasn't something she'd been able to do. Even at the moment, with the anger coursing through her, she still couldn't. But she could glower at him in disgust. "Let me go," Nia whimpered.

His eyes darkened further, a storm brewing in his gaze. A slow smirk spread over Fallon's face as he took his time sliding the hand from her throat.

Fortunately, no one monitored these sessions. If anyone saw something like this without understanding she played a role, they might *almost* believe it was real. This was where things got fun. Not that she couldn't have moved more anytime he held her, even in the beginning. Again, all part of the role. Now... Nia, with a burst of energy, zipped around him, making a beeline for the door. Not that she'd make it there, but that was part of their playtime, too.

His speed was greater than hers, but even if it wasn't, he still would have caught her. Fallon paused for a heartbeat, then dashed after her, their footsteps echoing as he closed the distance. He grabbed her, pinning her arms, and lifted her off the ground, pulling her close. "Did you really think you could get away from me, you little bitch?"

"Let me go!" Nia screamed as she struggled, lashing out in any way she could. With her feet free the most, she kicked at him and scratched at his arms. Fuck, she really enjoyed causing Fallon pain with the stiletto of her heels. There had been a reason she'd opted for these shoes today. They hurt the most. With each stabbing push of her heels, Fallon let out a moan. Her body was already physically responding not just to the nip of her ear as he carried her toward the bed, but to the impacts of her hits on him as well.

Reaching the bed, he tossed her down on it. She rolled onto her back and scrambled away backward, but he grabbed her ankle and jerked her toward him. "Oh, no you don't." As she fought him, he got between her legs, but could only grip one of her wrists.

Fighting Fallon had always been a part of their playtime. Yes, she'd drawn blood from him multiple times over their years together. Her jaw clenched, a simmering rage building within her. Her desire to cause Fallon pain had never run this deep. It wasn't really what she wanted, but he could take whatever she dished out. Whether she clawed at him with her nails, stabbed at him with her heels, or hit him—he took it all. Nia raked her nails across his face again as she attempted to get her legs in front of her body. "Stop! Get off of me!"

Fallon let out a snarl. A drop of blood, metallic and warm, fell on his lip, and he tasted it as he grabbed her other wrist. "Fuck yes! Fight me, bitch! You know you want it!" He pinned her wrists with a single hand and pushed down, then he pulled the top of her bralette down to show her breasts. With a growl, he palmed one, his fingers massaging and kneading, before leaning down to kiss her.

Oh, she was going to fight him alright. Nia bit his bottom lip until a fresh wave of crimson trickled. Beneath him, she squirmed and struggled, her breath coming in ragged gasps. She even got one of her knees close enough to her body that she could kick at his thigh. The stiletto missed its mark slightly, but he would certainly feel the impact later. Her pleasure intensified as she resisted more, the pain a key to her arousal. No way he wouldn't feel the heat radiating from her pussy. Fuck, she really hoped he fucked her hard because she needed hard at the moment.

Fallon groaned. His eyes darkened close to black. He shifted upward on the bed, and her leg was no longer entangled with his. His body pinned her to the mattress as he ground his cock into her, the friction against her skin noticeable through her shorts. A snarl escaped him, and he pushed further into her, feeling the slick, wet fabric of her shorts. "Do you feel how hard you make me? Fuck, I am already close to coming. I am gonna fuck that tight little pussy until you are screaming."

Grabbing onto the front of her bralette, between her breasts, his claws ripped right through the thin material. Only the straps remained of the nearly decimated fabric. As his grip tightened painfully on her wrists, his other hand pressed and massaged her breast, and he forced his tongue into her mouth. A deep moan vibrated out of his chest as she bit down on his tongue.

"Fuck you!" Nia spat out. Where had that come from? Like she really needed to ask. Stupid Hunter and his ability to encroach on her thoughts and interfere with her normal, everyday life. Even the way he manipulated her body and triggered parts she'd kept control of for years. It just fueled her rage and made her fight more against Fallon, which only turned her and him on more.

She was close enough to him to bite any part of his body. Nia bit his forearm, tasting the metallic tang of blood as it welled up. A deep growl escaped his throat, swiftly morphing into a euphoric cry when she bit his lower lip, hard enough to draw blood once more. She used the stiletto of one heel to dig into his ass, and the other to dig into the back of his thigh. Which just caused him to grind harder against her. Fuck, she was so damn hot. Another orgasm, its arrival a breathless, tantalizing possibility. Her breasts responded to the hard touch of his hands, her nipples pebbling beneath his palms.

Fallon flipped her over onto her stomach, shifting his hold on her wrists, so he held them behind her back. Shoving her knees up underneath her, he grabbed onto the waistband of her shorts and jerked them down over her ass, to around her knees. "You are going to come for me again, you little slut. Then you are going to be a good girl and take my cock." He shoved her thighs apart with his arm, letting out a deep moan as he tasted her sweetness.

In this position, it was a bit more difficult to fight back, though not impossible. "No! Please stop!" Nia pleaded, her voice strained, as she scratched frantically at the hand that held her wrists captive. With his body positioned in that way, she could have used her heels to dig into his shoulders. Not as hard as she wanted to, but it didn't keep her from jutting out with her ankle as much as possible.

His moans and growls got louder. Fallon let go of her wrists, freeing her hands as he wrapped his fingers around the nape, and then pressed her cheek into the soft bedding. His right arm coiled around her leg, and his hand tightened on her other thigh, holding her legs open. He let out a ferocious growl against her pussy as he drove his tongue deeper into her.

Fuck, she was right on the edge of an orgasm. All it would take was one more push. With Fallon having her pinned, she couldn't do much with her heels, but that didn't mean she had no options. With a loud grunt, Nia clawed at the hand on her neck, the scratch of her nails echoing in the room. "Please stop!" Her screams echoed through the air as she clawed and scratched at the hand, her nails scraping against the skin, drawing more blood. The more she fought, the harder he fucked her pussy with his tongue. She dug her nails into his flesh, and she could feel the blood, warm and wet, beading beneath her fingers.

His growl against her pussy intensified. "Give it to me, bitch! Come on!" Fallon growled, his warm breath against her skin, then drove his tongue back inside her.

A wave of sensation crashed over her as she climaxed, the release mirroring his delight. Fallon moaned against her as he lapped and sucked at her pussy, swallowing every single bit of it. Once the last of it had poured down his throat, he got both of her wrists back in one hand and turned her over onto her side. He jerked at her shorts, half shredding them as he made quick work of getting them the rest of the way off of her. He took every single one of her glorious kicks to the chest and the face, only answering them with a snarl in return. "You see how hard I can make you come? Such a dirty little slut. You like being my dirty little slut?"

Getting her back on her stomach, he moved up onto his knees behind her, his grip still on her wrists; they'd be so horribly bruised by the time he finished fucking her, but right now, she didn't care. She just needed his dick inside her. Which was exactly what he did. Fallon held onto her waist with one hand and tightened his grip on her wrists with the other, driving his cock as deep inside her as possible. His moan echoed around the room as he immediately came inside her.

Nia bit back a moan. It was perfectly acceptable for her body to physically respond to everything Fallon did to it, but any noises she made or words she spoke all had to be a part of the fantasy. She didn't waste time and dug her stilettos into his ass, hard enough to break the skin. "Get off me! Get the fuck off me!"

While some of her rage had dissipated, not all of it had. By the time this session with Fallon was over, she needed it gone just as much as she needed to toss Hunter out of her head. She could *not* under any circumstances allow him further access. Maybe she couldn't cut him off sexually, but she could regain control of their playtime together.

Fallon's moan echoed, growing even more intense. "Fuck yes! Harder, bitch! Fucking fight me! You know how much I love it when you fight me." He gripped her waist tighter while retracting his hips and thrusting forcefully back into her. "Oh... *fuck... ye...* your pussy feels so fucking good! So fucking tight!" It took him next to no time to get a steady, quick rhythm going. His primal sounds of pleasure filled the room as he penetrated her deeply.

Harder. He wanted harder? She could fucking give it to him harder. Nia dug her stilettos into his ass more and bit the arm closest to her face. She didn't just bite; she clenched her jaw to lock her teeth around it. The fury she believed had settled hadn't gone too far.

Fallon cried out in ecstasy. Blood continued to seep through the thick fur on his backside and dripped down his arm. Intensifying what she was dishing out, Nia attempted to buck against Fallon, which did little given the tight hold he had on her waist. His hold changed, his fingers digging into her shoulder with enough force to cause a bruise after he let go, instead of her waist. The speed and force of his thrusts intensified as she gripped him tighter, the muscles in her pussy clenching around his cock. He moaned as he slammed even harder inside her. "Fuck *yes!* You may not want me, bitch, but your pussy fucking does."

Damn, she was on the verge of another orgasm, her body tingling. It had to be from the way she fought against him. Every kick, every slap, and every bite she had delivered to his body flashed before her. As much as it turned him on, it turned her on, too. She didn't release the hold on his arm. Nia bit down harder on his arm, the metallic tang of blood filling her mouth, before moving a stiletto from his backside to pierce his thigh.

A deep growl rolled out of him. "You want to take a piece out of me, you little slut?" he snarled in her ear. "Do it. Fucking do it. Bite harder." Fallon bit the tip of her ear as his knees shifted, widening her thighs more.

His grip tightened as he drilled his cock into her core. "Take it! Fucking take my cock!"

Normally, she wouldn't have responded to Fallon's encouragement to rip a chunk out of his arm. Then again, she rarely bit him this hard, either. But her self-directed anger turned into a torrent that she unleashed on him. It felt good to release some of her pent-up rage. Hunter was a constant presence in her thoughts, and she'd been trying to get rid of him for days. The harder she pushed, the more he seemed to invade her every waking thought. Even when she serviced her other clients! Just like he was now, while she was here with Fallon. Without a second thought, Nia sank her teeth in, feeling the give of flesh, and yanked back, ripping a tiny chunk of skin from his arm. She spat it out, the wet substance splattering onto the bedding right before her hands.

"*Fuck!*" Fallon snarled out.

Blood, still warm, dripped slowly down her chin. As she came, her vaginal walls constricted around his cock, causing her climax to cascade down her thighs and into his fur. Simultaneously, his orgasm jerked out of him. He slammed deep inside her one last time and stayed buried in her pussy until he'd completely emptied inside her.

"*Holy fuck, yes!*" After their releases had both ended, Fallon tore off the remaining pieces of her bralette, withdrew from her, and swiftly flipped her onto her back. His grip on her wrists was so tight that she could feel the bones pressing against her skin, as if they might snap at any moment. Fallon pinned her legs, his knees pressing into her, and as he covered her body he tasted the warm, coppery blood from her chin. "I am not done fucking you yet." He fused their lips together and drove his tongue deep inside her mouth.

Nia chomped down on his tongue, filling his mouth with blood, and head-butted him. It might not have been the wisest decision, yet she acted impulsively, fueled by the residual fury. "Get off me!" She pivoted her head and bit his biceps with conviction, and a sharp cry of pleasure escaped him. She bucked her hips fiercely, trying to fling him off.

She couldn't recall one time where she'd ever fought him this hard or drawn this much blood from him. Yes, it happened because it got them both off, but not to this degree. But it didn't appear she could help herself. Though if it became too much for him, Fallon knew to use his safe word.

Other than the session coming to its end, that would be the only thing that would make her stop.

Fallon ripped his arm away from her mouth, the coppery tang of blood filling the air as she tore another piece from his flesh. His hand recoiled, and with a resounding crack, he backhanded her, the force of the blow snapping her head to the side. The impact wasn't severe enough to cut her lip, but her cheek quickly darkened with a bruise. "I am not going anywhere, you fucking bitch." As Fallon grabbed her ass, his fingers dug in, and she could feel the ache beneath. After releasing her hands, he yanked her hair back, causing her head to tilt as he penetrated her once more. The primal nature of his snarl became more pronounced as he started fucking her.

Nothing he did slowed her down. In fact, it pushed her to get him to slap her again. Maybe if he did it enough, it would knock some sense into her. She was no helpless female waiting for a hero. The last thing she should do was give Hunter any room in her head. Nia wrapped her legs around Fallon's back, digging in her heels while scratching at his shoulders, head, and face. She needed to hurt him as much as she needed him to hurt her.

Fallon's snarls and growls filled the room. Blood splattered her blanket, the sticky liquid coating her face and chest, finally disappearing into her hair. Her nails raked across his cheek, and he quickly removed his hand from her ass before delivering another stinging backhand. A tiny split appeared on her lower lip. Fuck, that was the sting she needed, not that it accomplished what she wanted. Amidst their shared hurt, her body responded, ready to experience another peak of pleasure.

"You love it rough, huh, bitch?" He gave her hair a hard jerk as the speed and force of his thrusts increased. "Come on! Fight me harder! Make me bleed some more! Then maybe I will stop." Fallon bit down on her lip and moaned as he kissed her. He squeezed her neck, his hand tightening, the pressure mounting, though he stopped short of blocking her airway. Sitting up just a little on his knees, it widened her thighs further but also bared more of his chest to her as he fucked her even harder. "You know you love it. Come on, tell me. I want to hear how much you love it."

"Fuck you!" Nia spat out.

A wicked smirk spread over Fallon's face. "You are fucking me."

His repositioning caused her stilettos to shift from his back to his ass once more. She dug in with substantial force, grabbed his nipples between her fingers, and twisted hard. Something halfway between a moan and a cry left him. The inner walls of her pussy clenched around his cock. "You are going to come for me one more time, you fucking slut." Adding a bit more pressure to her neck, his hand tangled in her hair, pulled her head back further while he thrust into her deeply.

Just a little more pain. She needed to cause him a little more pain. Nia adjusted one of her legs so it hooked beneath his arm. She plunged the stiletto into his back, finding the space just below his shoulder blade, and raked her nails across the arm that was holding her neck. The welling of blood beneath her hands pushed her over the edge. She felt a massive orgasm course through her, sending waves of pleasure around his shaft. It was more powerful than any she'd ever had before with Fallon.

In the throes of his orgasm, he tightened his hold, his fingers digging into her hair and throat. His growl damn near shook the bed as wave after wave of cum spurted out of his cock and into her, practically flooding her pussy. His hips continued to jerk, slamming into her repeatedly through every single moment of it.

When their mutual release ended—however long it was before they finally trailed off—Fallon quickly released her throat and her hair. Both of his hands shook. No, that wasn't right. His entire body shook with an intense and palpable tremor. With a sudden jerk, he pulled out of her and fell away, landing on the floor with a thud. Sitting up, he leaned against the post, knees to his chest, and put his head in his hands. His chest heaved as if he'd been running for hundreds of miles without stopping. "Fuck... I am sorry... I am so sorry..."

Ragged breaths left her. It took her a while to return to reality, the adrenaline still coursing through her veins after all she had dealt him. Nia's gaze flicked to Fallon, scanning over the wounds she'd inflicted. The chunks she'd actually taken out of him. *Holy shit!* Slowly, she sat up and really inspected his wounds. "Gods, Fallon... did I?" As if she really needed confirmation that she had done all of that to him. Who else could've done it? It wasn't like anyone else was in the room. "I'm so sorry. I didn't mean..."

Fallon shook his head and winced. "Do not apologize. I am okay." The blood continued to leak from his open wounds, each drop leaving a warm, wet trail. His whole body was still trembling uncontrollably. To stop the tremors, his hands clenched into fists. "I did not mean to do that... to hurt you... like that. I am so very sorry, Nia. Are you okay?"

"I'm fine, Fallon. Just... stay here. I'm gonna get some washcloths and a bowl of water." Nia hopped off the bed and strode across the room toward her bathroom, the sound of her heels echoing in the silent space. Sliding the door back with a soft click, she disappeared inside. Gods, she'd never fought him like that. Their sessions had always been rough, but not to this degree. She always stayed in control. Not this time. Not only had she lost it, but she also didn't remember doing half of the damage she'd inflicted. With a bowl of water and a washcloth in hand, Nia returned to Fallon's side. "This is my fault."

"No," he insisted. Removing his hands from his face, Fallon gazed over her and winced. "This was *not* your fault. This was mine. All mine." He slumped forward, his chin against his chest, elbows on his knees, and held the back of his skull. Tears pricked at the edges of his vision. "Gods, what is wrong with me?" he muttered under his breath. He didn't get emotional every session, just every once in a while. Some hit him harder than others.

Nia sat in front of him, carefully cleaning around the ragged tear in his forearm. She'd lost control once before with him twenty years ago, but it hadn't been this bad. "This one's on me. I lost control, and I know that just pushes you." Which was always what she wanted. The more she hurt him, the more he hurt her.

Fallon glanced up at her, his eyes meeting hers for a moment. "Maybe I, uh... maybe I should not come back."

After a brief pause, Nia shifted the damp washcloth to her left hand. She cupped the water in her hand, then let it trickle down her face and around her neck. She'd half-noticed the marks in the mirror when she filled the bowl. The split in her lip. The black, purple, and red bruising that covered about half of her face. Her neck held a perfect imprint of his fingers from when they'd wrapped around her throat. At least this way, those injuries would heal and disappear, so Fallon had one less thing to focus on. It didn't have to be said; she knew what had gone through his mind. "Not over this. I let my emotions get the better of me and lost control of my anger." Nia returned to cleaning his wound. "It was consensual."

"I know," he whispered. Fallon watched her face heal, and yet, the guilt etched onto his features remained. "Are you sure? You are really okay? And okay with... still having me as a client?"

"Yes, I'm okay. I promise." As much as he needed her, she needed him, too. He was the only one she could release some of her tension on, and it helped keep her in check. Nia continued to work on cleaning his wounds. Not that it would assuage her own guilt. This was probably how he felt every single time afterward.

"I just... I do not know what I would do without... this." Fallon's voice cracked a little, and he blinked a tear back from his eye.

How he felt afterward hadn't changed over the years. Fallon always felt guilty and sick afterwards. Apologies always tumbled from his lips, and he'd watch her, waiting for her to reassure him. She gave it to him every single time. "You'll always have me, Fallon. I'll always be here." It was a promise she felt confident in making. Regardless of Hunter's influence, the situation remained unchanged. She was in a contract with no way out. "Besides... you're the only one I can let the masochist out with." He never minded how much she hurt him. In fact, he craved it as much as she did.

"I know. Thank you, Nia." He cleared his throat, the sound echoing slightly, then winced as he touched his tender face. "I am sorry. Staying on the bed would have been better. I hope I did not get blood on your floor."

"It's fine. I have a cleaning regimen I follow, which includes the floors... just in case." Nia half shrugged and reached up to clean around the chunk missing from his biceps. "You never know." Especially since she used toys and furniture with some of her other clients. It wasn't something she and Fallon really required. He didn't care to use restraints on her, so those things just hung on the wall, along with her blindfolds, whips, and floggers. They'd tried some of them in their first few years together, but they didn't quite work out.

"Right." He nodded softly, barely holding back another wince. He watched, his eyes fixed on her, as she carefully washed the wound. "You do not have to clean me up if you do not want to. I can do it."

It seemed like they had the same conversation—or some variation of it—after every session. Once he'd calmed down some, settled his nerves, buried at least some of his guilt... then they talked about other things. He showed her what he'd brought her. Gave her any news if there was anything new to share.

"I need to do this... please." Normally she did it as part of the after-care of their session. This time... this time, she had to do it for herself. To help just a little in his healing. She'd never taken chunks out of him like this before. Their session had started normally, but her thoughts had continuously referred to Hunter. Every time she clawed or struck Fallon, it had been to push Hunter out of her mind. To silence him and the chaotic thoughts that swirled within her.

"Okay." Silence hung heavy in the air as Fallon watched her for a few minutes. "Are you sure you are alright, Nia? And I am not talking about... what I did. Unless that is bothering you? You were just... you were different today."

His comment didn't surprise her. Of all those she saw, Fallon knew her best. At least, what she allowed him to know. There hadn't been a doubt in her mind he'd noticed the difference in her. She couldn't confess that a client was stuck in her gray matter, but she needed to speak and had to tell him something. "I'm just going a little stir crazy. It's been a long time since I've been cooped up in here for so long." Twenty-one days and counting. She'd been shopping in the marketplace once a week for twenty-nine years. Then it explodes... so to speak, and they went on full lockdown.

Fallon's eyes didn't leave her face as she spoke. "That is a load of crap." A small smile played on his lips. "But it is okay. I will not push you for information you cannot give me." He moved a bit, which gave her better access as she continued cleaning him. "Is there anything I can do to help? Or bring you? I know it must be rough being stuck in here for so long. They are still rebuilding the marketplace, but a few places have stands up, keeping revenue up."

Nia snickered. He knew her too well. "Um, yeah. I could shop by proxy. Give you some funds to spend and a bag with an extension charm to bring it all back." Getting out helped her a lot. It made her feel... normal. "I'm just trying to adjust to some changes." And remember her place. She didn't talk about clients with other clients, but she knew if she ever needed to talk to someone, Fallon would be there for her. "I really think some new clothes and shoes will just remind me that this isn't the entirety of my world." Even if it was.

"I can understand that. You know I would not mind at all." He gave her hand a small squeeze. "Anything in particular, or would you like me to just go with my gut?"

Tilting her head, she fixed him with a look of disbelief. "I think you know me well enough by now to go with your gut." She had a particular style of clothing and shoes. It had simply grown over the years as times changed. With as short as she stood, she preferred high heels with a four to six-inch stiletto. She didn't care for the wider heels. As for clothing, things that accentuated her curves.

"Well, you just said 'clothes.' I did not know if you meant comfy, off-duty clothes or lingerie. Or both; I can do both." He gave her another small smile, but it didn't linger on his face very long.

"Both would be good. I mean off-duty and lingerie." She'd never really done comfy. To her, that meant loose, and she just couldn't do it.

"I can do that. Before our next session, I will go there and look for something. I brought a few things for you, too."

"Oh? What'd you bring?"

Fallon glanced over at his bag, then back at her. "Have you ever had mangoes? One stand in front of the shops was selling this candy. I swear it tasted like that, but... not at the same time. I cannot remember what they called it, but it was great, so I brought some of that. And some chocolate, because it has been a while since I could bring you any. And that book you lent me a while back. I finally brought that back. I found another one at the market, too. It is not one we have talked about yet, so I do not know if you have it or not. But I liked it, so I thought you might, too." She continued to clean him up while he talked, his voice a low hum in the quiet room. He wouldn't need stitches; even the chunks she'd bitten out of him would heal before their next session.

"It's been some time since I had mangoes. I don't know if I've ever had candy that tasted like it, though." Nia got up and disappeared into the bathroom. Having finished with the bowl, she headed back to the bedroom, and on the way she grabbed her soft, silk bathrobe. "Chocolate is always a delightful treat when I get it. A new book—I can't thank you enough for that. I've gone through nearly everything on my shelves. Is it another art book? Or a story like the last one?"

He pushed himself up; the floorboards creaking beneath him and went to grab his bag. "It is no big deal. I am just hoping it is not one you have read yet." With a small smile, he glanced back at her before grabbing his bag and returning to bed. "It is a story. I cannot pronounce the author's last name. But it is about a man who gets falsely accused of a crime. He goes to this horrible prison for thirteen years, but he escapes and sets out to exact revenge on the people who stole his family and ruined his life. I do not want to spoil the ending, but I really liked it." He sat down next to her on the bed, and pulled out the brightly wrapped candy and chocolate, then got both books.

"That sounds quite interesting." Nia scooted back a little on the bed, the scent of the candy and chocolate filling the air, as she set them aside to remove her high heels and settle in. The two of them could spend a good hour just chit-chatting back and forth. Some of it was nonsensical, and some of it was news around the isle. Either way, she liked to get a little more comfortable. Nia crossed her legs and leaned back, excited to try the candy, her shoes discarded to the side. She let out a moan. "This is fantastic."

"Told you. But, see, it does not taste quite like mango. I do not know how else to describe it, though."

"You're right. Not quite like mango. There's a flavor I'm picking up hints of, but I can't discern what it is yet." She popped another one in her mouth, chewing on it for a good minute. It was superb, but it would drive her nuts if she couldn't figure out the flavor.

"Yeah, I could not figure it out, either."

"What did you think of the book I loaned you?"

He lay on his side, supporting himself with his elbow, and gazed at the pages of the book he had borrowed from her. "It was good. A lot of it was pretty amusing. The harder words are getting easier to understand; I do not have to look them up so much anymore. That dictionary you gave me a while back has really helped." Fallon glanced up at her and shook his head. "The main character is a... bit of an idiot." He chuckled. "I liked his attendant, though. I felt bad for the poor guy."

"Oh, my gods, yes. Pavlo was constantly apologizing for him and doing what little he could to rectify Efrain's screw-ups. I don't know why he stuck around so long."

Fallon chuckled. "Maybe he felt sorry for him. Efrain seemed like one of those people who would find a quick, accidental death if he did not have someone looking out for him. I cannot say I would have been able to do the same. Or perhaps he was just bored. If I can say one thing about all of it, there was never a dull moment."

"That's quite true. It was rather entertaining." Eating one more piece of candy, Nia tilted her head. "I don't know if I'd say Pavlo felt sorry for him, though. I wonder if it's more that he got something out of their relationship. Though he associated with someone who inevitably always appeared an ass, maybe he simply believed in his ability enough to rectify the errors made, eventually."

"That could be true, too. Mutually beneficial. I wonder if maybe he was just lonely, though. Or over time he just grew to care about the guy. I mean, Efrain promised him some really off-the-wall things. There is no way Pavlo could really have believed him; he seemed too intelligent for that. But he kept going along with it all, anyway. He stood by Efrain through everything he did, no matter how many punishments he received over it. He was not even the one screwing up, but he still paid for it without batting an eye." Fallon grinned. "If you figure out the extra kick in the flavor, let me know. It has been driving me nuts, too."

"It's tart. Maybe a little citrusy. Like a lemon or grapefruit." Though she leaned more toward the latter option than the first. "Pavlo was married, though. And with everything we discovered about him, he seemed happy with his wife. I suppose it's possible, although he could've been bored, and Efrain offered him continuous entertainment with his wild ideas."

"I did not get lemon from it. But I have never had grapefruit before, so that could be what it is." A subtle shrug escaped him. "You can care about someone and not be in love with them. You have to wonder, though... if he was so happy with his wife, why did he continue to follow Efrain through all his outlandish escapades? I mean... he went through *a lot* of crap for the guy, cleaning up mess after mess the best that he could. If that were me, and I had a mate waiting for me at home that I loved, continuous entertainment would not be enough to keep me away. I would have to really care about the person I kept chasing after, more than the one I had left behind."

Hmm, he had a point about that. She cared about Fallon, but they weren't in love. Maybe that's what it was with Hunter. *Seriously?!* He even had to interrupt a pleasant conversation with Fallon? For fuck's sake. Maybe if she stabbed herself in the head, she'd get that male out of her brain. Or if she pointed to her temple and had Fallon dig with his claw, then Hunter would go the fuck away.

Nia popped another piece of candy in her mouth and chewed it with a bit of ferocity. What had they been talking about? Right—the book. "Um... maybe it isn't so much Efrain himself, but what he represented.

Freedom from the regularity of his everyday life. An unknown journey that offered a multitude of opportunities.”

“That could be true, too. Although he could have found that without Efrain. Unless he was not adventurous or imaginative on his own and needed someone to follow. But if he truly loved his mate, he would not have needed that. When you are in love with someone, every day with them is an adventure, even if you are doing nothing. At least, so I have heard.” Fallon shrugged. “But he specifically followed Efrain. If he was craving adventure, he surely could have found someone else to chase after, where he would not end up being punished for so many things the guy did. I mean, look at how many people they met along the way. But he still stuck with the guy.” An eyebrow lifted, a subtle expression of his curiosity. “So, what was that look about? And the candy… you looked like you were trying to murder it instead of eating it,” he teased.

“A stupid, annoying thought that keeps popping into my brain,” Nia muttered. She hadn’t meant to say anything, but it was kind of out there now. Not that she had to elaborate on the details of the ‘thought.’

“Oh? Feel free to elaborate, but do not feel you have to.” He gave her an encouraging smile.

No, she didn’t, but part of her wanted to, just so she didn’t feel like she was losing her mind so much. And maybe by talking to him about it, she could talk herself through it. “It’s just a change that I’m not handling as well as I would like. Something I’m finding that’s rather challenging. Normal patterns don’t seem to apply, which just frustrates me more, and makes it so I can’t stop thinking about it.”

“And probably makes you push and poke and prod where you would rather not do so?” He chuckled softly. “Stop fighting it. Whatever it is, if it is bothering you *this* much… it is obviously something important. The gods are trying to get you to pay attention to something. Otherwise, it would not be getting under your skin so badly. Embrace the challenge, accept the differences, and find a new wavelength. Something shook your routine; now you have to figure out how to deal with that. But—” he gave her a look, “—you cannot let it make you go crazy. Especially not with you being on lockdown like this. I know that is not helping anything. So, adapt.”

It took every ounce not to let her jaw fall open. *Don’t fight it. Ha! Yeah, Fallon’s lost his fucking mind if he thinks I can do that.* That wasn’t something she could do with Hunter. Nor could she embrace the new wavelength. But she had to figure out how to deal with his impact on her normal routine. Their next session was tomorrow, and she typically started with something that warranted punishment. Except she already knew what punishment was like with him. At the conclusion of their last session, it popped into her head the possibility of getting closer to full submissive. It seemed the best option. "You might have a point about Efrain. I've never been in love, so I don't really have anything for comparison."

"Nor do I. I have never been in love myself. My mother was, though not to my father." He stilled, the words hanging in the air for a moment. "She would wait until my father had gone on some scouting mission. Then she would pull up this board in the floor underneath her pallet. She did not sleep with him because he always had... company, so she had her own bedding. But, anyway. She would pull out parchment and charcoal, and write letters to her dead mate. She was not delusional or anything; she just... missed him. I guess it made her feel close to him. I read them when I got older after she had passed away. They spoke of so many things I did not understand."

As she closed up the candy, Nia bobbed her head, her nod barely perceptible. Fallon hadn't spoken to her about his parents in quite some time. "My mother and father had an arranged marriage. Definitely no love there. As far as I know, she met no one as your mother had. What did her letters talk about?"

He smiled at her, then his gaze followed the movement of his claw as it tapped gently. "My father killed my mother's first mate. Then got permission to mate her. I found all of that out later. She died right after I turned six. She just went to sleep one night and did not wake back up." A brief pause settled over him. "Her letters talked about how, every time he left the village, it felt like her soul left with him. She would see something so simple as a specific shade of grass and it reminded her of something they had experienced together. The sound of a certain bird's tweet made her think of a song he had sung to her. How his voice could bring a story to life so vividly. All she had to do was close her eyes and *be there* wherever he was speaking about in the story. She talked about how she missed taking adventures that way. Missed lying in bed with him at night with his arms around her and just... listening to his words. How it felt like she died a little more every day that he was gone." Silence stretched between them.

"Every single word she wrote to him just... *bled* love... in ways I have never witnessed before."

"I can definitely say I've seen nothing like that. I can't even imagine loving someone so much you think about them just by seeing a certain color." Growing up, her home hadn't even resembled anything like that. Not that she'd been as young as he had been when he lost his mother. From what she knew about his father, that explained things a lot. "Seems like a fantasy, if you ask me."

"To me as well. I still do not understand many of the things she spoke about. But I think that is something one would have to experience themselves before they could truly understand it. Maybe that is why I live vicariously through the written word. Certain things will never be my reality."

"Makes two of us." Well, every worker in this place. Not that she could share that information. Nia narrowed her gaze at Fallon. "You really don't think you might find a female? I mean, I know how things are, but if something like the love your mother spoke of really existed... is it possible it could alter your needs? We change as we grow older."

"I know we do." Fallon shrugged, a subtle movement. "I do not have hope for that anymore. That my needs will change. Nothing I have tried, or we have tried, has ever worked. I cannot bring myself to..."

Risk hurting someone for real. Hurting someone he didn't just care about, but loved. She knew he hated how the sessions between them had to go. The one time he'd really hurt her had put her down for two days. Fallon had choked her so badly she'd blacked out. At her behest, they'd given him a warning and banned him for a short period. Even her ability to heal herself with water never assuaged his guilt.

Fallon shook his head a little. "I know I give you something you need, too, but this is not the only sex you have. Not that I know details. But, you know, this is all that works for me. Can you imagine me going out there, spending time with a female, courting them, getting to know them... then telling them the only way I can have sex is if she convincingly pretends she is being raped? Not to mention the things that come out of my mouth during?" He cringed slightly. "What female could want that? People like me... are outcasts. We do not get happy endings. That is just all there is to it."

A submissive who desired degradation and rape fantasies all the time. Not to mention everything they'd tried over the years. And being who she was, she'd been the perfect person. Dominant, submissive, she went both ways. As well as enjoying both giving and receiving pain. Nia shrugged. "You never know what females you might come across."

A small smile touched his face. "I already hate... so much that I put you through what I do. Even knowing you enjoy it. Doing the things that I have done, saying the things that have come out of my mouth to someone I do not just care about, but someone I loved..." Fallon frowned. "I stay away from females as much as possible when I am not here. It is necessary. The responsible thing to do. Finding a female that would want to be in a relationship with me despite how I am... *that* is a fantasy." He gave her a look. "Just like you believe, it is a fantasy that it is in the cards for you. Despite that, you deserve no less."

Every once in a while over the years, they'd had a discussion like this. Both of them continued to be very firm on the fact that neither of them would have a relationship with anyone in the future. Not a personal one, anyway. "I can't afford to think about what I may or may not deserve. I have nothing outside of this room to offer someone." That was the truth. The day she signed that contract, she signed her life away. Not that she'd ever mentioned anything about it. Aside from the fact that she literally couldn't talk about it. They forbade emotional connections for a reason. That was why she kept everything about her mother and brother a secret. They were her only emotional connection. It was just that simple.

"You know my thoughts on that already." Fallon tilted his head a bit as he stared at her. "So. You did not respond before. That must mean you agree with me." He paused for a beat, then grinned. "Pavlo had a hard-on for Efrain."

Nia burst out laughing. If the workers saw her like this, they'd think she'd lost her mind. It was just the type of friendship she and Fallon had developed over the years. "It's very possible. He put up with a lot of shit for that male. Maybe there was some underlying secret love between them."

"There had to be. I mean, would *you* put up with that much shit for someone if you did not love them? No, that had to be it. It just never made it onto the page, but you know they had to be banging."

"Fuck no. But I don't put up with shit from people I *don't* like, so I'm not a good comparison there." Nia picked up the box of chocolates and ate a single piece with a low moan. Her favorite candy. It was so damn sweet. The strangest question entered her head, but this was on point with how most of their conversations went. It had always been like this between them, even from the beginning. They could switch from sex to serious talk, to playful banter, to silly conversations, without batting an eye. "If they were, in fact, fucking... who do you think bottomed? I can't really see Efrain bottoming for Pavlo; he liked to be in control too much."

"That is true. He really did. I think you are probably right. I cannot see Efrain bottoming, either. He screwed Pavlo metaphorically during just about every other aspect of their journey; it would make sense he would be the one doing the actual screwing in the bedroom too, while Pavlo continued to just... take it." Fallon snickered. "Then again... that could be an argument for why Efrain might bottom. In charge everywhere else; secretly, in the bedroom could be the only place he relinquished control."

She didn't know how to respond to that suggestion. It almost sounded like her. Except she wasn't in control of the den by any means. The only aspects of her life she controlled were the number of clients she took on and which clients she accepted. The schedule her clients chose determined the days she worked, though she took one day off per week for herself. And she didn't entirely relinquish control in the bedroom. "Hmm. I suppose I could see that. Maybe it was the only place where he could truly free himself of the burdens of his life."

"Exactly. And if that was the case, the only person who would know about it was Pavlo. And that guy wasn't going anywhere, obviously; he was as loyal as they come. Maybe that offered Efrain a chance to be the person he didn't feel comfortable showing to anyone else. And it would have offered Pavlo a chance to let loose and take charge for a bit."

Nia tapped her chin with her forefinger. As crazy as it sounded, it could be true. Nothing like that was included in the book. Still, with how those two characters were portrayed, could she really see Pavlo topping Efrain? "I'm sorry. I'm trying to imagine this as a possibility in my head, but I'm not sure I really see it. There was a lot of bending over backward for Efrain. Could you really see him as a top?"

"You are trying to imagine it in your head?" Fallon's eyebrow rose, a subtle curve of surprise. "I did not peg you for someone who enjoyed watching male-on-male," he teased. "But, no. No, I cannot. Not at all, actually." He chuckled. "I do not think he would have had it in him to top.

Well... he would have had to have *it* inside him being on the bottom, but you know what I mean."

With another burst of laughter, it took a moment for her to compose herself and regain control. Nia cleared her throat. "I enjoy being with males and females. However, if I'm in the room and two males are together, I expect to be fully involved." Fallon had been the client she'd been with the longest, but when she first began getting regular clients, she had two females and seven males. While she never strayed from the number nine over the years, it often varied between the number of females and males. Currently, she had all males.

"I dislike males. Just females for me." Fallon chuckled a bit. "Why does that not surprise me?" he teased. "Of course, you would have to be involved. Much more enjoyable than just sitting back and watching." He tilted his head. "Have you been with two other people at the same time?"

"Yes, a few times. Only once since I arrived here." Most of them had been at Deacan's behest. He was a bit of a voyeur, and she did whatever he wanted to please him. That had been closer to the beginning of their relationship. As her proclivities during playtime grew and changed, his desire to share her lessened.

"Seems like there would be a lot of hands to keep track of."

"You get so caught up in the moment that you don't really focus on whose hand or mouth is where. As long as everyone is enjoying themselves, the rest doesn't really matter." It had certainly taught her things about her sexual desires. She much preferred one-on-one rather than three or more parties involved. The biggest issue she'd discovered could arise from a situation like that—jealousy. When someone felt slighted, like they weren't getting as much as they gave, or getting enough attention, it often stirred up trouble.

"Well, at least I know what that is like. Getting caught up in the moment." Fallon chuckled lightly. "Oh, hey, did you figure out what book you wanted to loan me this time? You said you wanted to surprise me."

"I did!" Nia jumped off the bed and crossed the room to her closet. The closet door remained open, as it often did in front of Fallon. She located the book, its worn cover familiar to her touch, plucked it from the shelf, and pivoted, the scent of old paper following her back to him. "It's about pirates."

Fallon scanned the cover. "I have only read a couple of books about pirates, but not this one." He sat up on the bed, a smile on his face. "I take it from your enthusiasm it is good?"

"Yes. It's got a bit of a slow start, but once you get into the action, it doesn't stop." She held the book out to him.

"Thank you. I promise to be careful with it."

She knew he would, but he still told her the same thing every time he borrowed a different one from her. Fallon took the book from her and tucked it into his bag. "Is there any type of book you want me to see if I can find for you?"

Nia considered a couple of options as she collected the boxes of candy he'd brought her, plus the two books. He liked the stories, though given his history, it didn't come as much of a surprise. They were often good, but she also liked to learn about different things, too. She crossed the room, her footsteps silent as she headed toward her closet. The items in her hands went to their appropriate places before she scanned over what lined her shelves. "Maybe some more art books," she called out over her shoulder. "I really enjoy seeing what various artists have come up with."

"I will definitely see what I can find. A lot of the businesses' stock was destroyed, but the lady that runs the bookstore mentioned something about some kind of protection over her back room. So, she saved a lot of the books there. I should be able to find some art ones. She had a book about building things I purchased. I am going to build an actual home. Nothing big, obviously. I do not know how much I will get done before winter hits, but I have shelter, so I will be okay. What about food requests? Besides sweets, is there anything you would like me to bring you?"

"That's good. The shelter, I mean." Nia grabbed a small velvet pouch from her bookcase, its soft texture contrasting with the wood, then got another from her dresser, and went back to the bed. "I worry about you. I know you're not in the village anymore, but a safe place is still necessary." Not that she didn't understand his reasoning, but still. Certain things were required to survive. "Um, maybe a couple of apples. Sweets are the easiest to keep in here." She didn't really like sharing those things, and if she ended up with too much, it would bring unwanted attention her way. Nia held the two pouches in her hands. "Here. The blue one has the extension charm, and the black one has money in it for any clothes or shoes you buy me."

"I promise I am okay. I am safe enough, and I know how to hunt for food. Living alone... away from other people is the best choice for me, now that it is a possibility. I just do not know how to actually build a home from the ground up yet. My grandfather built the hut in Métamorphe where I lived. After he and my father passed, I just repaired it as I needed to." Taking both pouches from her, he tucked them carefully into his bag. "That is easy enough to remember. Is there anything else you would like me to bring you?"

On most of her shopping trips, she purchased clothes and shoes. Nia glanced over at her closet. Was there anything else that she *really* wanted? She pondered a single thing, and its sudden appearance in her thoughts was puzzling. Her mind whirled, a desperate attempt to ignore the reality that threatened to shatter her. Nia cleared her throat before turning her attention to Fallon. "A pair of sapphire studs, if you can find them."

"Sure thing. You know I do not mind getting you whatever you need. Hopefully, you will not be stuck inside here too much longer, though." Fallon rose from the bed, stretching his arms toward her.

Without a word, Nia wrapped her arms around his waist, feeling the warmth of his body. She loved the way he would hug her. "Just depends on how tension across the isle goes." If it rose, then who knew how long they'd be on lockdown. If it settled... maybe those who'd previously had access could go out soon.

He wrapped his arms around her, too, ensuring he didn't squeeze too hard. "So far, things seem to be cooling down, but I know that could always change. Until then, I am happy to play errand male for you."

"Just be prepared for me to grill you for details as I try everything on." Nia snickered. "I may have to live vicariously through you until I'm allowed to go out again."

Fallon chuckled as he released the hug. "Grill me as much as you want. Hopefully, I will have some noteworthy news to bring back to you next time." He leaned down, his breath warm against her skin, and kissed her on the forehead. "Thank you, Nia."

"You're welcome." She'd told him a long time ago he didn't have to thank her afterward every time, but it hadn't ever changed. It made sense, too. What he had to put her through so he could get off. The corners of her mouth upturned. "Thank you for shopping for me."

"You are welcome, too. I will see you in about a week. Take care, Nia."

"You, too, Fallon." He really had become her only friend over the years. The only person she could trust implicitly. The workers around here gossiped too much. It served her better to keep to herself as much as possible. Though Silva and Grace would forever be the exception. At least in most ways.

With his bag secured over his shoulder and across his chest, Fallon gave her hand a brief squeeze before leaving, the door closing with a soft thud.

Hunter, eager to see Nia again, ambled down the hallway to her room. After their last session, he'd spent the entire next day completely drunk and hadn't left his home. The day after, he'd woken up with a pounding headache, feeling like a complete idiot. His mind wasn't fragile. He wouldn't give in to a moment of weakness, just because only one female in his almost forty-eight years had made him feel something other than self-hatred and malevolence.

Having pried himself from bed, he showered and did whatever was necessary to stop thinking about the female—helped rebuild the market-place, staying on the outskirts, or offered aid through the village. Anything to stay busy, to keep his mind from wandering. All the while repeating the mantra in the back of his mind that *sex* with Nia was all it was *ever* going to be. She was a means to an end, just like all the rest of them. Hunter repeated it religiously until he could ignore the agony those words brought.

Stepping inside her room, he shut the door silently behind him. His eyes went immediately to her, where she kneeled in a spot on the floor between the bed and the horse. He gazed at her, appreciating the outfit she'd chosen for today's session. She had on white lace-trimmed, low-cut body lingerie. It had a gemstone G-string, which really emphasized her ass. On her feet were a pair of white peep-toe stiletto heels with a platform mesh design and studded straps around her ankles. Once he finished gazing over her appearance—for now—Hunter walked over to her dresser. He ran his fingers across the fresh pieces of equipment she'd laid out, which included a variety of spreaders and cuffs. Most of them would put her on her stomach—less of a chance their gazes would meet—but there was one exception that would basically put her on display.

He selected the blindfold first. It didn't matter if she was on her stomach. It was best to avoid any risk of catching her eye. Though he regained his composure, the moment he was back in the room with her, her alluring fragrance filling his senses, the primal, fiery intensity stirred within him. Closing the distance between them, he stood behind her. This session would be different. But how much?

Hunter tied the blindfold tightly behind her head, the rough fabric a stark contrast against her skin. "Can you see anything?" He'd nearly tacked her name on the end, but it was also better he refrained from that, too. Each time he'd said her name in other sessions, regardless that it wasn't her *true* name, it just seemed to ramp up both of them even more. At least for this session, to be on the safe side, he would resist uttering it.

"No," Nia replied.

She had forgotten a very important word at the end. Gathering her hair in one hand, he gave it a tug. "No, what?"

She let out a gasp. "No, Sir."

Hunter refrained from the 'good' he normally uttered after. Instead, he chose silence. While she'd given him a blow job before without being restrained, he didn't plan to test her this session. That could open up that can of worms again that he'd fought tooth and nail to close. This session would be distinct from the others. He could just taste it in the air. Something he could sense.

Heading back over to the dresser, he picked up a black leather neck-to-wrist restraint. It buckled, so it was adjustable to whatever height he wanted her arms. Hunter, returning to his position behind her, kneeled down, his fingers brushing against her skin as he fixed the collar around her neck. He buckled it tight, but not enough to cut off her air supply. The belt stretched down her spine, to a couple of inches above her ass. Binding her wrists in the cuffs, he readjusted the buckle so her hands settled about midway down her back. Once he had it secured, he stood and circled around in front of her.

The desire to caress her hair, or even her cheek, rose like a blazing inferno. Slamming that urge away as quickly as he could, Hunter stroked the head of his cock along her lips once before sheathing himself fully in her mouth. He bit back the threatening moan with so much force his jaw cracked. Nia swirled her tongue around the head of his cock. His eyes closed as her teeth grazed along the base. Mostly because she wouldn't be able to see the way they'd squeezed shut. He allowed himself that indulgence rather than noises coming out of his mouth. It would be easier. Noises affected them both.

As soon as her tongue stroked along the underside of his cock, his eyes rolled back into his head. His grip on her hair became more forceful; his mouth parted slightly, but he suppressed a groan, almost. She sucked up to the head, and then wrapped her mouth around it, starting all over again. Keeping a tight hold on her hair, Hunter drew his hips back and thrust into her mouth. *Holy fuck*, how could her mouth possibly feel *better* than it had just four days earlier?

Skimming her teeth along the base of his rigid length, Nia zigzagged her tongue along the underside of his cock. *Holy fucking shit.* That was new... and absolutely incredible. That little motion sent lightning bolts straight into his balls. It took every ounce of willpower not to let out the moan that was on the tip of his tongue. Nia stroked and sucked his dick repeatedly. His hold on her hair tightened further as he fucked her mouth a little harder, the head of his cock hitting the back of her throat again and again. Fuck... it wouldn't take him long to come. Then again, it never had with her. She could always bring about his release in the most glorious of ways.

His brain flickered out for a moment. What she was doing with her tongue ... *holy fucking shit*, it felt fantastic... beyond fantastic... utterly mind-blowing. They weren't near any furniture he could grab onto, so he clenched his free hand into a fist, his claws digging into his palm. His head fell back, his jaw ground together, as he fisted her hair harder and put more force behind his thrusts. *Fuck yes, fuck yes, FUCK YES, take my dick, sweet—NO.* He couldn't use that term this time, not even in his head. Holy fuck, he needed her to make him come and swallow every fucking drop. Each harsh breath that left him seemed to echo around the room. Half of a moan rose to his throat before he swallowed it. *Oh, fuck... Hades yes, get my cum.* He wouldn't say the words out loud, but he could say them in his head. *Do not stop... Fuck, do not stop.* He pushed his cock deeper into the back of her throat, gripping her hair so tightly that he feared he might pull out a few strands. In that moment, she boldly moved her tongue to explore the intimate space between his balls and rear, nearly driving him wild with desire. He was so close.

Upon reaching the tip of his arousal, she twirled her tongue around it and created suction with her cheeks; it felt like his dick was in her pussy, not her mouth. His hips jerked as an orgasm shot out of him without warning. His thighs trembled, his claws dug deeper into his palm, and another half-moan made it out of his mouth. *Oh, fuck, fuck, fuck...* the first orgasm he'd had since he'd last been here and it was fucking amazing.

Nia sucked and licked, swallowing everything he had to give her. The moment she swallowed the last drop, Hunter removed himself and walked back to the dresser, where he picked up another set of restraints. He helped her up and brought her to the bed. He had plenty of plans for her today, but for right now, he just needed to taste her pussy. Tossing the second set of restraints on the bed, he picked her up and put her on the bedding on her stomach, so her knees were on the edge and her chest pressed against the blanket. Kneeling down behind her, Hunter licked slowly over her slit, then used his fangs to snap the G-string. He wrapped his arms around her thighs and drove his tongue inside her. *Holy fuck,* the explosion that immediately went off against his tongue...

Not that she made a single sound, which partially disappointed him. The other part took it as a challenge. He would milk those glorious moans, groans, cries, and screams out of her if it took everything he had. As Hunter growled near her, the sensation resonated through her body, intensifying as he raised his hand and struck her buttock forcefully. Despite spanking her three more times, thrusting his tongue deep inside her, and devouring her with intensity, she remained silent.

Hunter dug his claws deeper into her ass, a new growl *almost* making an appearance as the scent of her blood tinged the air. Still, she gave him nothing. His other hand suddenly withdrew from her thigh, while he inserted two fingers into her rear end and simultaneously spanked her other cheek. He stroked up her slit with his tongue and latched onto her nub, biting down and sucking hard.

Nia's chest heaved, and he could hear her heart pounding inside her chest as her pussy got hotter. She turned her cheek, pressing it against the mattress. "If you intend to hold your own noises back, then I suggest you try harder to claim mine, *Sir.*"

Oh... so *that* was how she wanted to play it. Well, he could certainly play that game, too. "Is that so?" He smacked her, and his claws sank into her flesh as he turned her and sat her up on the bed. "Perhaps I should try something completely different, then." Rising, his cock presented itself before her, and he ensured a gap remained, just out of reach of her tempting tongue. After removing her blindfold and placing it on the bed, he took hold of his own erection. Meeting her gaze, he fell silent, the only sound being the gentle rasp of his hand as he stroked it.

Shaking her hair back, Nia spread her thighs a little wider so her wet pussy brushed against the covers. Without her gaze leaving his, she dipped her chin and extended her tongue to lick the top of one of her own breasts, letting out a half-moan.

His jaw clenched. *Holy shit.* That was hot as fuck. "I do not recall giving you permission to do that." Hunter let go of his cock and closed the distance between them, lifting her up and placing her back in the position he had chosen. With one hand firmly on her ass, he cupped her pussy, shoved three fingers inside her, and stroked her G-spot. "Keep that tongue in your mouth or I will waste every drop of my cum by letting it spill all over the floor."

She licked her lips and clenched her vaginal walls around his fingers. "I'd be happy to waste every drop of cum on the bed..." Nia paused. "... Sir."

Oh... she knew just how to push every single fucking button he had. All of his intentions... If he wasn't careful, he'd happily forget every single one. He'd broken first before. That would not be the case today. Hunter continued stroking the inner walls of her sex, swallowing a growl. "If you are truly content, letting me go home without an excellent taste... I guess I will just have to figure out how to survive until next time." After withdrawing his fingers from her, he cleaned them by licking each one slowly. Resuming his position, he kept his gaze on hers as he went back to stroking his cock.

A purr slipped free from Nia's lips, right before she ground her jaw. That fucking sound had his cock hardening even more. But he clamped down hard on every sensation it brought him. He didn't want to be this way. With other females, absolutely. But not with her. Never with her. But it was necessary. If he allowed the things that had occurred in their previous sessions, he'd have to move on from her and be with someone else before he did something that he couldn't come back from. He'd come very close on more than one occasion. And that could never happen, for both of their sakes.

Moving on from Nia... it was unfathomable. Yet another thing that no one else had ever made him feel—he didn't want to be with anyone else but her. Even if that meant things were a bit more... muted than normal. He could keep his composure, dull down the passion, not allow her to see so much of the reaction that her sounds, expressions, body, and taste brought him. He could keep full and total control over himself, keep from losing it around her, and from becoming that unhinged savage that she loved so much, if it meant he got to continue spending these small windows of time with her.

Hunter didn't break his gaze from hers once—a horrible idea, for sure, but one he couldn't help—as he continued stroking his cock. As she settled back on her heels, her eyes fluttered shut, and he felt a wave of disappointment crash over him. He didn't want her to stop challenging him, pushing him, disobeying him. He didn't want any of that. It was everything he'd wanted with all the other females. And the last thing he needed with Nia. But again... it was necessary.

In their first session, she'd been fully submissive. Giving him exactly what he asked for and paid for. It seemed she was going back to that. So, he would go back to that, too. Their first session had been two hours long. The stark contrast between the two sessions made him think this one might be brief. It would still be enjoyable. They would both still find a release. But it would not *be as* enjoyable as things had been before. Maybe they just needed to find a happy medium. Right. They could do that.

"Good girl," Hunter said, still stroking along his rigid length. "Do you want my cock, Nia?" Though he asked that question, what he really wanted was to devour her pussy. He hadn't had his mouth at her sex *nearly* long enough. But he needed her noises with that, too. Those glorious gasps, moans, and cries. For her to beg him for more and beg him to come.

Nia opened her eyes but didn't meet his gaze. Instead, her eyes flicked to his cock and the way his hand stroked it. "Yes, Sir."

That her eyes didn't meet his was perfectly fine. Those gorgeous, mesmerizing green eyes of hers—*stop it.* Instead, he focused lower on her breasts. The lace of her lingerie barely held in those perfect swells, just barely containing her nipples. The two ribbons in the front trailed into a vee of gemstones matching the G-string he'd already snapped. It reached all the way to the dip between her breasts, just like the necklace did that he'd bought her. He gazed down at the two lace halves that framed her belly button. The lace of her panties barely covered her waist and the front of her sweet pussy. His cock hardened further.

If she was going to be fully submissive now, he would just order her to come. Because, while he wouldn't say it out loud, if her cum didn't fill his mouth at least a few times before he left today... he would go absolutely fucking nuts. Hunter closed the gap between them, his fingers finding the curve of her neck as he pulled her closer, guiding her mouth to meet his arousal. "Suck my cock and make me come. Do a good job and I *might* return the favor." *Lies.* He was *absolutely* going to return the favor.

Nia wrapped her mouth around his shaft. She took him deep, swirling her tongue from the head to the base. His eyes immediately closed. A low growl vibrated up his chest, one he couldn't hold back, but that was all he allowed. With his dick all the way in her mouth, she let out a low moan. A slight vibration went straight to his balls. Holy fuck, that felt so good. Nia grazed her teeth to the head of his shaft, and then went back down to the base, skimming the tip of her tongue along the underbelly of his length as she did.

Holy fuck, yes... keep doing that... Hunter clenched his jaw even harder than before. He wanted to say those words out loud, not in his head. Use her name. But he didn't. Sliding his hand up into her hair, he gripped it firmly and urged her to keep going. Once she reached the base of his cock, she started all over again. The feel of her teeth grazing along his dick laid a blanket of electric tingles over the entirety of his body. It took every ounce of willpower not to fuck her mouth. Not that he thought he could hold out forever if she kept doing that. The volume of his growl increased just slightly.

She scraped her teeth up his shaft to the head of his cock, popping it out of her mouth. She twirled her tongue around the head and started back toward the base. Zigzagging her tongue along the belly of his dick, she extended her tongue once she reached the base and drove it between his balls to lick the small skin behind them. Then she retracted her tongue, folding it around the underside of his cock, and wiggled it side-to-side.

He almost came right then. His hand balled into a fist again, his claws digging into his palm. The scent of his blood filled the air. It only flared up his arousal that much more. A louder, deeper growl vibrated out of him as he drew his hips back and slammed his cock into her mouth until the head hit the back of her throat. He couldn't stop the swing of his hips. No matter how much his brain screamed at his body to calm down, he couldn't stop.

Her tongue kept going, relentless in its maneuvers. *Holy fucking shit...* if she kept that up, it wouldn't take long at all for her to pull another orgasm out of him. Fuck yes, her mouth... her tongue... utter perfection. *Just a little more... Fuck, do not stop.* Nia folded her tongue around the belly of his cock and purred, sending vibrations up his shaft. It fucking did him in. Just like it had every single time. His head jerked back on his neck. A long, drawn-out moan came out of him as a massive orgasm shot out of his cock, pouring down her throat. He held her head down on his shaft, ensuring she got every drop. The vibrations along his length were so intense, they just amplified the release tenfold. *Holy fuck... keep purring... keep purring...*

And she did.

His moan continued right along with the release pouring out of him. *Holy fuck,* he just kept coming. He tightened his hand on her head. His thighs trembled as he slammed his hips forward with each jerk of his cock. He didn't know how long it lasted. Once the last bit of cum shot out of the head of his shaft, Hunter pulled out of her mouth and turned her around on the bed. He swiftly removed the restraints and grabbed the other set. There was a padded U-shaped pillow-type thing that went either in front of or behind the neck, depending on if the female was on her back or stomach; restraints for the ankles, and more for the wrists. This time, as he used it, he would put her on her back. But the blindfold had to go back on first. Although he would bury his face in her pussy, he didn't want to take any chances.

Hunter shut those thoughts off as quickly as possible. Picking her up, he placed Nia in the center of the bed, secured the blindfold over her eyes, and got the cuffs in place. Fucking perfect. His tongue practically begged to be buried in her sex. He slid his hands up the length of her body. Taking the two lace halves in his fingers, he ripped the flimsy lingerie straight in half. Tossing the pieces off the bed, he moved between her legs and leaned over her. His claws brushed her inner thigh, causing her to gasp. At that moment, he closed his mouth over her breast while his fingers plunged deep inside her.

Nia moaned, her voice sending a shiver down his spine as his dick throbbed. As her back arched, her breast met his mouth. A groan escaped Hunter as he latched onto her, his fangs sinking in just a touch as his tongue danced across her nipple. He curled his fingers inside her pussy, thrusting them in and out rhythmically and deliberately. He rubbed his thumb over her clit, slowly at first, but quickly picked up speed.

She groaned as her vaginal walls contracted around his fingers.

That is right. Keep going. Come for me. Hunter increased the intensity and speed of his movements, pressing his fingers deeper against her G-spot as he pleasured her. Though his teeth sank into her flesh, he controlled himself, and his fangs did not puncture her skin. If he got even one taste of her blood... he wouldn't be able to control himself.

"May I come please, Sir?" Nia asked.

Good gods, he missed the begging. The strain in her voice as she cried out. Hunter pulled his mouth away from her breast just far enough to talk. The urge to flick his gaze up to her face was overwhelming, but he ignored it. It wasn't a good idea. "Yes. Come for me." Latching onto her other breast, he increased the speed and pressure of his fingers in her pussy and against her nub.

With a groan, her body convulsed as pleasure exploded within her, finally spilling out. While it was a decent release, it wasn't nearly as powerful as any of the last ones he'd given her. Not even like the first ones she had around him. Part of him didn't even want to continue, but he couldn't bring himself to stop. Gods, this wasn't right. None of this was. It didn't feel right. Because it wasn't *them*...

But they couldn't have *them*. *It* was forbidden. *It* could get them both in a world of trouble. And while he didn't give a shit what came down on his own head—he never had, but especially since things in the village had changed and he didn't have to worry about Hayden as much—he cared about what repercussions came down on Nia's head. This was her job. Her livelihood. Her life. One he would never truly be a part of. He still understood nothing about what she'd made him feel—things no one else had ever come close to. But he would never be special to her. He had to keep reminding himself of that. No matter what went on in this room between them; he would never be special to her.

He would be nothing more than *this* to her. Someone who gave her coin for the privilege of fucking her. He paid her for the service she provided, and she provided well. That was all it could, and would, ever be. It was better this way, anyway. If she ever knew who he *really* was—beneath the black and orange fur, and the blue eyes; beneath the scars he'd never allowed even her to touch; beneath the Dom who gave orders and punished her when she disobeyed—she would run away screaming. At least this way... he had this much. This time, with her. However muted it had to be now.

Once he'd worked her through her release, Hunter moved further down on the bed and got comfortable between her legs. He cleaned off his fingers, ensuring he got every drop of that sweet nectar he'd pulled from her sex, then slid his hands beneath her. Gripping her ass, he licked slowly up her slit, barely holding back the growl as her taste exploded on his tongue all over again. A small gasp left her mouth, and her back arched with a soft moan.

Hades, yes. He needed more of those. They'd been too quiet. He needed them louder... more intense. That was a horrible idea. He wanted to bring her as much pleasure as he could. Even though it didn't seem like a good idea. With a low growl that pulled a soft purr out of her, Hunter slid his tongue deep inside her. He tightened his hold on her. He delved his tongue deep inside her, licking slowly up her slit, teasing and nibbling on her sensitive nub, before starting the process anew.

Gripping her ass tighter, he kept his claws in check. The scent of her blood right now would throw him over the edge. It took everything he had to keep control. It was better this way. Right. *Better.* The words were spat out with clenched teeth, a futile attempt to grasp at control as his mind fought back, screaming in defiance. Hunter lifted her backside off the bed, his claws barely touching her ass cheek as he kept one hand on her. He retracted his claws before gently sliding two fingers into her backside. Growling against her pussy, he drove at her harder.

"May I come please, Sir?"

Again, she just asked. Her tone didn't hold the pleading and begging she'd given before. Not even any yearning in her tone of voice. Hunter almost stopped right there. But he couldn't bring himself to move even a fraction of an inch away from her. No matter how much this session... hurt. "Yes. Come for me." Fucking her ass harder with his fingers, he drove his tongue back inside her. Despite her moans and the orgasm, nothing about this felt right. Or even comfortable. He sensed it was the same for her. As much as she was getting half of him, he was getting half of her.

They'd gone from no-holds-barred, unbridled, passionate savagery to... *this*. Whatever the fuck *this* even was. He couldn't even put a name to it. Except he'd never felt pain like this before. Not anything he'd ever been through as a child. None of his punishments. Not even when he'd received the Informant brand. Nothing had ever hurt this much.

Hunter took every drop of her orgasm—because, despite *this,* he couldn't bear to waste any of it—then sat up on his knees. He almost continued, but he just couldn't. His dick was hard and throbbing, almost painfully, triggered by the scent and taste of her. But he couldn't go on. Not like this. He just sat there on his knees, staring down at her body. It wasn't flushed. She wasn't straining at her bindings. The orgasm, while it had been natural, had been nothing compared to the many he'd given her in their last few sessions. Even in their first session. Her nipples weren't even erect. Her chest wasn't heaving. Nothing like any of their sessions. She'd done none of the things that burned a fire through every inch of his body, every synapse in his brain. No more than he had with her. With any other female, he wouldn't have cared. He would have taken what he paid for and left. And he would have felt nothing about it. They were all... nothing to him. A means to an end.

But Nia... It was different with her. It had always been different with her.

Hunter, without a second thought, shed her restraints and blindfold, then moved away, and sat at the edge of the bed. His feet hit the cold floor, and he leaned over, feeling the strain in his back as he rested his forearms on his knees. Had he ever shown his back to her? He wasn't sure, but he didn't think so. True, the darkness of his fur hid most of his scars, and the darkness of the room helped a lot, too. Just the way he liked it. But the scars on his back—from whips peeling away his skin, claws and fangs digging into his back and sides and ripping out chunks during fights—were certainly some of the more prominent ones. Then again... Nia had done everything she could today not to meet his gaze, just like he'd done with her. So, he didn't think she'd see, anyway. He didn't even know why he cared. He never cared, so long as no one touched them during sex.

This time, he did. And he couldn't even say why.

Nia shifted on the bed. Her breath hitched. Then he felt and heard her crawling toward him. "I'm going to sit behind you," she stated outright.

"Okay." He hesitated before the words spilled out, the sound of them barely audible. "I kind of feel like we should... maybe cut this session short. This is just... it is not really working. For either of us. So, if you want to touch me, I will not get mad." It wasn't an invitation, just reassurance. Permission, if she so desired. He didn't know how he would react to her touching him. More than once, amid their sessions, he'd desired her touch, while refusing to acknowledge that desire at the same time. They were still in the playroom, but this session had been emotionally brutal.

She moved behind him. Her thighs pressed against his hips as she scooted closer, stretching her legs. "Maybe... we start the next session... anew."

He'd allowed no one to sit behind him like this. Never. Even Hayden. If his twin had sat behind him to deal with some injury or another, it hadn't been quite like this. More often than not, Hayden had sat sideways to ensure he didn't feel too uncomfortable, or closed in. But it didn't bother him to have Nia sitting right behind him like this. The strangest urge to slip his hands to his sides and stroke her legs hit, but he kept his arms right where they were. Hunter gave a slight nod. "That sounds like... it would probably be a good idea."

Nia reached up to his shoulders, her fingers sinking into his thick, soft fur. "Maybe we, uh, set some ground rules."

Tingles, edging on tension, rippled across his shoulders and down his spine. The tension wasn't because she was touching him—because her fingers felt *way more* fantastic than he could allow himself to acknowledge—but at least partially because a random flash went through his head. What had happened the last time someone touched his scars without his permission? A female he'd been with before he'd come here. She'd been curious about them and kept wanting to touch them like he was some kind of sideshow freak or something to gawk at. He'd told her no. That it made him uncomfortable for them to be touched. She hadn't listened. Her curiosity had gotten the better of her, and she'd run her hand across his shoulders as soon as he'd turned his back. He'd spun around so quickly she hadn't had time to blink. Instinct had his hand snapping forward before he could stop it. He'd backhanded her, leaving her with a bloody lip and a bruised cheek. He'd felt horrible later, but at the moment, he'd only been pissed.

It didn't feel uncomfortable when Nia ran her fingers along his shoulders. Not at all. The feel as they sifted through his fur sent an unfamiliar warmth throughout his body. His eyes drifted closed. It was the only part of him that moved. "What kind of ground rules did you have in mind?" He'd spent four days trying to get over... *this.* These feelings she brought out of him. He didn't do feelings, emotions, but just being with Nia brought them to the surface like a flood demanding to break free. Four days should have been enough time to move past it. It wasn't.

"Well, we can start by identifying what seems to intensify everything and decide between those we would be okay without and those we simply must-have."

As her fingers drifted from his shoulders to his shoulder blades, he dipped his head, his chin nearly touching his chest. He thought about what she said, the things that really got him going, not replying for a minute. Could he go without any of it? No, but they had to figure something out or he wouldn't be able to come back at all. That was just... no, he didn't want that. Not at all. But he couldn't go through another session like this. Nor did he think she could, either.

"The noises you make. All of them. The scent and taste of your blood. And your cum... when you *really* come. You disobeying me—not one I would have expected. That has never turned me on before. When you dig your heels into me." Hunter paused. "Looking into your eyes when you release." Oh, yes. That one had... He didn't think he needed to put an explanation for that. Their last session... A shudder rolled through him. "And you?"

"Every single sound you make, but especially your growls. The pain you inflict. The harder you dig your claws and fangs into me, the more I want. Inflicting it in return. Like digging my heels into you. Disobeying you and being punished. The taste of your cum... sensing the slight shifts in your body when you *really* come. Looking into your eyes when you release."

Hearing every single one of those turned him on more and more. His blood pumped faster, his heart pounded harder, and his erection intensified. The mere thought of him inflicting pain, his claws and fangs digging into her, sent a thrill through him as he barely held back a growl. Gods, there was something seriously wrong with him. For years, he'd straddled that thin line between being right on the edge, falling over the cliff and ending up exactly where more than a few of Markham's Informants had been. The only thing that had kept him from fully crossing over that line had been Hayden. If it hadn't been for his twin...

He never hurt or killed people for sport. Not like some. But those things had brought him to a high that nothing else had ever come close to matching—until he'd met Nia. Nothing even came close to comparing to her. Nothing else had *ever* brought him the calm that being with her—*really* being with her—brought him. Which was why he had to do whatever he could so he wouldn't have to give this up.

"Hu—" Nia cut herself off.

Fuck. He really. *really* wanted her to say his name. She'd come so close. He was desperate to hear his full name leave her lips.

"There's a reason I'm not like other submissives you've *actually* been with here. I'm not a submissive. At least, not entirely." She paused. "I'm a switch."

Silence stretched between them. The words themselves didn't surprise him, but the sound of them being spoken was more jarring than the knowledge itself. Every time she'd challenged or defied him—even without the things he felt about her—she certainly wasn't like any other submissive. She wasn't like anyone else. "Makes sense. A lot of sense. I cannot be... submissive. Being told what to do, following orders—I tolerate it from my queen because I stayed in the village and that was the price that had to be paid. But honestly... I hate it. Not being in charge, especially during sex, makes my skin crawl. Perhaps that is because of the way I grew up. I do not know."

"That's understandable. For most of my life, I was the one in charge of the household. I had subordinates to maintain control over, and I liked things to run smoothly. Relinquishing control during sex... I prefer that. Decisions I don't have to make. Over my time here, I've learned to balance both the desire to control the situation and the desire to submit simultaneously. I rarely have such... difficulty. But something about you... just triggers both sides."

He definitely could understand that. All of that. Something about her triggered something in him, too. His back tingled as her fingers danced gently across it, and some of the tension melted away. It was something he'd never felt before. And something he only just realized he craved. A soft purr came from him. "You are the only one that does not piss me off when you challenge me. Disobey me. Instead, it turns me on. It is not something I am familiar with. Nothing about our sessions is familiar to me. But none of it is anything I want to go away." Hunter briefly bit down on his lip, savoring the metallic tang of the blood. He'd been close—too close—to saying things he absolutely should not say. Things that would ruin all of this. Things he couldn't even understand. He just needed more time to bury them. Get rid of them. Get back to normal. His version of normal, anyway. Yeah, he really didn't believe that. But it also didn't matter in the least. "I think if we can find a happy medium, we could both probably work with that. Somewhere in between that allows both of us to be fully satisfied... but does not push us over that edge." Yeah, but where was *that*?

Nia's forehead dropped against his back, pressing close as her thighs clenched tighter against his hips. His brow furrowed. No one had ever done that to him before, either. Right now, it intensified what he felt. It wasn't uncomfortable at all. It felt... nice, actually.

"I'm over two hundred *solaris*, and no one has ever challenged me the way you do," Nia muttered. "I don't want it to go away, either." She slowly lifted her head from his back, and with a lingering touch, she began her exploration of his muscles. "A happy medium would be good. We know what our triggers are... What if we assign some as hard limits?"

The difference in their ages didn't even faze him. It was just a number, and sometimes, he felt like he'd lived ten times the number of years he actually had. "I am almost fifty. I learned quickly what kind of sex I need to have to get the release I need. The females in my village... most of them are as submissive as it is possible to be. But most of them are afraid of me, and I am not a rapist. It is part of the reason I started coming here. Not to mention... here, I cannot get anyone pregnant. That is not the case elsewhere. Without rules, like this place offers... people cannot be trusted. And the last thing anyone needs is for me to become a father."

What the fuck was he doing? Saying? He had meant to say none of that. But the words had come out, anyway. Not that he could take them back now. Gods, even with how their session had gone, she could make him more comfortable than he'd ever been. Vulnerable, almost, and it didn't even bother him. Shaking the thoughts away, he focused on the rest of her words. Assign some as hard limits. That was an idea, but which did they choose? What things that she did should he set as a hard limit? It was a good thing their playtime hadn't lasted long. They had plenty of time to discuss this. "Maybe... what if you always wore a blindfold? Since you like it... and looking into each other's eyes... it triggers both of us."

"You don't want children? I'm sorry. That's a really personal question." Nia's hands stilled. "Blindfold. Uh, yeah, I think that's a good idea."

"It is okay. I started it." He hadn't meant to say it, but it didn't change what happened. "To answer your question, no. I absolutely do not want children. I know what young need. It is nothing they would find with me. I am not nurturing or loving. Quite the opposite. The version of me you see in this room... there is a lot more to me. But I am sure that is true with every client." That needed to be the end. Personal stuff needed to stay the fuck out of this. They weren't supposed to be doing anything to bring them *closer*. That wouldn't help anything. "Okay. Good deal. One down. How badly do you need the pain and drawing blood? Maybe if I just... do not do it as much... more like our first session? A little without going over the top? It would give us both a taste without pushing us over. Maybe. Our last two sessions... differed from our first. Maybe if we go back to more like that one?" Except they had used none of her toys during that session. Only the bed restraints, no other furniture. He liked those things. too. A lot. He didn't really want to stop using those, either. Hunter let out a quiet sigh.

"I can't have children, so you definitely don't have to worry about that with me." A moment of hesitation passed before Nia's fingers resumed their curious exploration of his fur. "Something more in between the first and second with pain and blood. I don't exactly want to go back to the first in whole. I enjoy being able to pull out my toys."

"Did you ever want them?" Hunter cursed. Hades, he really needed to stop. But he hadn't been able to stop the question from coming out of his mouth. "You do not have to answer that." Even though part of him hoped she did. His back involuntarily arched at her touch. Gods, he *really* liked her touching him. It didn't make a single bit of sense, and... it made all the sense in the world. Now, to get this fucking conversation back on track.

"Alright. Something in between. I was hoping you would say that about the toys. I really enjoy using them, too. But how much should we use? Which ones?" He didn't think any of the restraints would cause them issues. Or the vibrators. But the whips... He loved using those. They were among his absolute favorite toys. And he was very skilled with them. He could cause pain without drawing blood. Leave that to his claws and fangs. "How much blood should I draw? Our first session did not throw me over the edge. The other ones..." Where he'd literally gouged his claws across her skin in parts... He didn't really want to leave figuring out a medium for that until they were in the middle of a session. That seemed unwise.

"My ex wanted them. So, we tried... until eventually, we discovered I was infertile. Um, the restraints, whether cuffs or spreaders, don't seem to be an issue. With the whips, as long as you stick to the snakeskin one or something similar or with less of a sting, I think we should be okay. The vibrators... maybe we set a limit on the butt plugs. As for the amount of blood... perhaps a little more than the first session, but not to the point of the second."

"So, you tried for kids even though you did not want them?" Seemed a strange concept. Then again, he'd never cared about anyone like that. Even if he did personal relationships, and he'd been with someone who wanted kids... no, he still wouldn't want to have them. And he would do anything in his power to ensure that didn't happen. Hunter's back arched again as her fingers continued to sift through his fur. Another purr came out of him. "How come you did not want them? Before you knew you could not have them?" Hades, why couldn't he stop with the fucking questions? Their relationship was supposed to be solely about physical gratification. Hunter rubbed his forehead wearily, then settled back into his position, forearms braced. "Um, yeah. All that... I think that sounds doable. The blood... dig my claws in, but no gouging? And the vibrators..." A tiny smirk lifted one corner of his mouth. "Pussy ones are good, ass ones and butt plugs limited?"

"Deacan and I had a complicated relationship." A heavy silence hung between them, thick with unspoken words. "Like you, this is only a small portion of who I am. Um, gouging... minimal should be okay. And yes, ass vibrators and butt plugs limited."

Yeah, that made sense, too. Here in this room... you could be whatever you wanted, whoever you wanted. You didn't have to show your true self. Too many people judged, their words dripping with venom, hating for no reason, and stared as if what you enjoyed was a grotesque spectacle. Desired. Needed. That was another reason he'd started coming here. He'd barely turned nineteen when he'd tagged along with Clay. His brother had just given him a sideways look, and then shrugged. Neither of them had said a damn word the entire way here. Then, when they arrived, Clay had only asked if he had money. Which he had. He'd stolen some from Azazel when the male had been gone on a scouting mission. Two satchels worth, just in case.

Hunter just nodded. He wanted to ask more questions. Why was the relationship complicated? Who was she outside this room when she wasn't in a session? What did she do with her free time? What things did she enjoy? He refused to indulge that urge, though. With just a few back-and-forth questions, they'd already gotten too personal. Best to put a stop to it before it went too far. "That sounds good. I think that should probably work better than this one did." He paused for a moment. He didn't really feel like leaving yet, but he also didn't really feel in the mood for sex any longer. "So, when I come back... we will see how things go. I think if we stick to all that, we should be good." Hunter peered over his shoulder at her. "But you have *got* to give me your noises. I almost went fucking nuts not hearing them."

One side of her mouth tilted up. "I felt the same regarding yours." Nia narrowed her eyes at him.

Whoa... That look—a threat and a dare all rolled into one. And... his cock was immediately hard. *Really* fucking hard. Hunter swallowed a growl. "The effort was there. The execution... not great, I will admit. I think next time will be better." His eyes smoldered as his gaze remained on hers. "Provided you let me hear how much you enjoy it when I make you come... I will let you hear how much I enjoy it when I eat your pussy."

Nia's jade-green eyes sparkled with mischief. "Oh, I'll let you hear *every* single sound. Just know I expect *every* single one of yours. I want to hear how much you enjoy me sucking your cock, how much you love my pussy, and how much you enjoy fucking me. Understood?" She leaned in, her breasts pressed against his back and her hands tracing the curve of his hips.

Holy fucking shit, she could turn him on in ways no one else had ever been able to. The things she did, said... if anyone else had used that tone of voice with him, it would have been bad news for them. But not her. Nope. She was different. Hunter let out a low growl. His eyes remained fixed on hers as he lowered his head. Right now, all he wanted was to overpower her, forcing her onto her stomach with her hands restrained, and assert his dominance. He slowly flicked his tongue out, the taste of the air lingering on his lips. "Yes, Ma'am." Not that he meant it seriously. He'd never submit, not even to her. He just wanted to see what those two words would do to her.

With a contented purr, Nia bent her knees, her legs now intertwined with his in a slow, sensual slide. "Good boy." Her nails danced a quick rhythm along the top of his thighs as she finished her sentence.

A deep, guttural growl rumbled from his chest. He liked what she'd said to him, not to mention the way she'd said it. A lot. Not that he was going to admit that out loud. Hunter spun, fangs displayed, and secured her wrists with one hand, while his other hand forced her chin up. His cock was still fully erect. "You like saying things like that to me, Nia?"

Her heated gaze met his. "Among other things. Would you like an example?" Her tongue snaked out across her lips. "If you're a *really* good boy, I'll give you a reward."

As he pushed her back onto the bed, a growl emanated from him, vibrating the very air around them. Raising her arms, he held her wrists, the pressure a stark contrast to the soft mattress beneath them, as he straddled her, his knees a vise. "And what kind of *reward* would you give me for being a *really good boy*?"

"Given how much you like having your mouth on my pussy, an hour before your next session, I'll insert vaginal beads and even have a couple of clit vibrators out for your use." She tilted her head. "I'll even let you pick them out before you leave today. How does that sound as a *reward*?"

Oh, she knew *exactly* how much he enjoyed having his mouth on her pussy. With a growl, Hunter seized a handful of her hair, pulling her head back sharply. As he used his knees to spread her, he lightly teased her slit with the head of his cock. *Fuck*, she was wet. "And how am I supposed to earn this *reward*?" He leaned in, tilting her head back to give his tongue access to the sensitive skin of her neck. "I am not very good at being a *good boy*. I am much better at being *bad*." He bit her earlobe, then licked her neck again.

A loud moan left her mouth. Nia's legs found purchase on his thighs as she wrapped them around his hips. "I want you to fuck me hard while I dig my heels into your ass. So, it isn't *too easy*. While I may have multiple orgasms, you cannot have more than two to fully please me." The same tilt to one side of her mouth reappeared with a glint in her eyes. "I suggest you make them count," she purred.

A shudder went straight down his spine. *Fuck, that purr of hers.* He kept the head of his cock from doing more than a delicate dance against her opening. Hunter's tongue traced a path along her neck as his grip on her wrists grew firmer. "No one... has *ever* told me how many times I can come. What makes you think you get to tell me that?"

With a groan of anticipation, Nia leaned in, her breath tickling his ear. "Because..." she purred. "I know how *badly* you want that reward. Only *good boys* get rewards." She nipped his ear.

A powerful shiver ran down his spine, all the way to his groin, causing his cock to give a small twitch. Hunter sucked in a breath. *Holy fuck,* that felt good. He growled against her neck as he brushed his erection a little harder against her pussy. "You are not playing fair."

She ever-so-slightly increased the pressure of her hold on his hips. "I never said I would." Nia's tongue darted out, briefly touching the sensitive skin of his ear. "Now, are you going to be a good boy?"

Oh, she definitely wasn't playing fair. He pinned her wrists to the mattress on either side of her head, trapping her. Staring down at her, he licked his lips. He *really* enjoyed holding her down like this. Restraint without *restraints*. "I do not know, Nia. Perhaps we should find out." Without uttering a single word, he forcefully penetrated her, releasing a guttural moan as he entered her deeply. "Fuck..." he growled out. He started doing exactly what she wanted.

Nia groaned loudly. *Gods...* Fuck yes, that was *exactly* what he wanted to hear. She tightened her grip on him, digging her heels in, and moans and groans echoed in the air. His fangs extended at the way she arched her back, bringing her breasts nearer. Fuck, he wanted to bite them. Difficult at this angle, though. He widened his thighs and pressed her wrists down, escalating the intensity and rhythm of his thrusts. "Come for me."

As she dug her stilettos further into his ass, Nia's cry echoed through the room as a powerful orgasm surged through her, covering his cock with her release. "Fuck!"

"Fuck *yes,* just like that, Nia," he groaned. "Fucking come all over me." With growing intensity, his thrusts became even more forceful. Her body jerked each time he rammed his cock into her core. Oh, he was going to pull as many fucking orgasms out of her as he could before he finished. The session may not have started off great, but it would certainly end that way.

With her wrists pinned down, he couldn't hoist her up, no matter how hard he tried. But she took care of that. With a firmer grip, Nia pressed her stilettos into his backside and subtly shifted her hips, increasing the depth of his penetration. "Holy fucking shit. Fuck, don't stop!"

Hunter let out another moan. The pressure from her heels intensified, almost breaking the skin. The depth of his cock inside her pussy had him damn near gasping. Holy fuck, it felt incredible. His cock throbbed painfully inside her. But he could hold back his orgasm a little longer. Fuck no, he wasn't stopping. He intensified his speed, driving his shaft into her core with relentless vigor. "Oh, *FUCK!* Get your ass up higher!"

Adjusting her grip on his hips for better leverage, her stilettos sank into his flesh as she lifted her hips, reaching the ultimate angle. A loud, drawn-out moan escaped his lips as her heels, with a sickening squelch, drew blood. Her eyes rolled back in ecstasy as her vaginal walls squeezed around him. "Fuck... I'm gonna..." Nia screamed. An immense climax erupted within her, a geyser of pleasure engulfing his shaft before she could speak the last word.

Fuck yes. The intense clenching of her pussy around his dick pitched him over the edge. Hunter let out a massive roar as he came right along with Nia. *Holy motherfucking shit.* His orgasm matched hers in magnitude, bursting out of him and saturating her to the brim and more. He didn't stop fucking her for a single moment of it. Their thighs were so slick with their cum. The slap of his pelvis against hers resounded throughout the room like a booming drum, matching their passionate cries. Without altering his position, Hunter intensified his movements, driving deeper into her with rapid, forceful thrusts, preventing either of them from recovering from the high. "Holy fucking SHIT! Gods, yes! Keep coming, Nia! Holy fuck!"

"Holy fuck!" Nia echoed. Her vaginal walls contracted and released repeatedly. "Oh, gods! Fuck!"

The things she did intensified everything even further. The speed and force of his thrusts didn't subside even a little. "Fuck... YES!" he snarled. "Keep coming all over my dick! Holy fuck!" Hunter didn't stop. When it was over, he withdrew and turned her onto her stomach. With her knees raised, he spread her legs apart. Grabbing her wrists, he pushed them onto the mattress and let out a cry as he entered her once more. He hadn't been able to stop himself from changing the position. But he'd given her what she wanted. He wasn't finished yet, far from it. And while she might not dig her heels into his ass, she could dig them into his legs, at least. And he'd only come once so far. He still had another one left. Hunter leaned in, the scent of her perfume intoxicating him, and brushed his tongue up her neck before biting down on her earlobe, more forcefully than he had. The drop of blood that hit his tongue ignited a fiery explosion of taste. He moaned. "You are going to keep coming all over my dick until you have nothing left," he growled in her ear. He resumed his pace, thrusting into her core repeatedly.

"Fuck... yes!" Nia pushed her bottom upward, folded her legs, and found a grip by driving her heels into his thighs. A surge of delightful agony rocketed up his legs and into his cock, which caused his fangs to grow. His hiss was desperate and needy. The room filled with the sounds of her moans and groans as he thrust his cock deep inside her.

"Fuck, yes. Gods, Nia... you feel so fucking good." He marveled at his strength as he drove his cock into her with greater force. The feel of her body, every noise coming out of her mouth... She had him crazed with lust. He couldn't even fathom stopping. He needed so much more.

"Fuck, yes... so do you," Nia cried out. "Oh, gods!" Her vaginal walls clenched tighter around his cock. She dug her stilettos deeper into his thighs as a powerful climax spilled over his erection. The screamed moan that left her mouth echoed around the room.

"Fuck, yes! That is what I want to hear! Scream for me, Nia! Fucking scream for me!" Hunter thrust his cock deep inside her and maintained the position. Shifting both her wrists to one hand, he held them firmly on the bed while sliding his other hand beneath her. He rubbed her clit, the friction building, and a primal sound rumbled from his chest. He yearned to prolong the sensation of pleasure as much as his body allowed. And then he would fuck her all over again until she rewarded him with another one.

"Holy fuck!"

Hunter groaned as each wave crashed over him, soaking their thighs and the sheets below. "Fuck... yes... that is it. I love the noises you make. Every... single... fucking... one." He punctuated his words with smacks to her pussy. Hunter pulled back, thrusting hard inside her as his fingers reconnected with her clit. "You have fucking drenched my cock. You had better clean it off when I am done fucking this pussy."

"Oh, gods... yes..." Nia glanced over her shoulder, her eyes meeting his. "A treat I could never turn down." A groan escaped her lips as her vaginal walls clenched, and a wave of heat washed over her.

Holy fuck, that look in her gaze sent shivers down his spine. "You can have as much of that treat as you want." Hunter stretched their joined hands out further on the bed, and the soft mattress yielded to the pressure of her breasts. He spread her hands out, palms down. "Stay." Hunter shifted, rose to his knees, and clasped her hips, drawing her close. He raked his claws across the flesh, and though it didn't draw blood yet, he knew that with more pressure, it might. A loud, primal growl reverberated throughout the room as he took her once more. This time, he didn't let her adjust to the relentless rhythm and power of his movements.

Clutching the bedspread tightly, Nia cried out as he rammed his cock relentlessly into her. With each thrust of his shaft, her vaginal walls clenched tightly. "Fuck... don't stop... never stop..." she hollered. As her eyes remained fixed on his face, her heels sank deeper into his thighs.

Gods, he would never tire of hearing every single one of those noises out of her beautiful mouth. It was a bad idea for their gazes to remain locked on one another as she came for him. But he found himself unable to break the gaze of those captivating green eyes. Nor did he want to. A surge of energy coursed through him, making him feel alive. His blood pounded through his veins. Heat poured off of him as he plunged his cock into the depths of her pussy repeatedly. Each stroke of her walls against his shaft, along with the delicious bite of pain from her heels, took his arousal to new heights. "I am not stopping until you soak this bed through with your cum." As he penetrated her, Hunter delivered a sharp smack to her rear before plunging back into her.

"Oh, gods... fuck..." A screamed moan left Nia's mouth, reverberating off the walls.

Holy fucking shit. Hunter cried out as the inner walls of her sex squeezed his dick so hard he almost saw stars. Another ocean of cum poured out of her, soaking their thighs and the bed beneath them all over again. He didn't slow down his thrusts even a little. If anything, he fucked her harder. "Fuck, yes! That is what I need!" His claws sank into her hip, and as blood welled, a lustful snarl escaped his lips. He brought his other hand back and then brought it down hard on her ass. "Again! I want every drop of your fucking cum, Nia!"

"Fuck... harder... all of it... harder." A provocative purr escaped Nia, resonating from deep within her chest and seeming to vibrate the surrounding air. It wasn't like anything she'd ever made before.

It almost drove him completely insane. *Holy fucking shit.* Her purrs ignited an uncontrollable fire in his soul. But this one... A louder snarl than he'd yet uttered practically shook the bed. Hunter withdrew, then seized her thigh, turning her onto her back with a swift motion. He gripped her ankles, pulled her in close, and hoisted her legs up onto his shoulders. With his knees straddling her body, he held her wrists high above her head and thrust into her. Her jade-green eyes were the only thing he could focus on as he thrust harder, deeper, and faster than ever before. Every nerve ending in his body screamed for her—more of her sounds, more of her body, more of her cum. Unhinged didn't come close to describing him any longer.

Nia screamed. The sound ripped through the air, and her fingers tightened, grasping the bedding beneath her. A wave of ecstasy more powerful than before ripped through her. Her cum gushed out of her body like a burst dam.

Even with that magnificent release of hers, he couldn't stop. Nothing could have stopped him right now. A fire could have swept through here, turning them to ash, and he would have gone down fucking. Her body kept releasing cum in continuous waves, blurring the distinction between multiple orgasms and one never-ending climax. When he was done with her, her wrists would bear the purple marks of his actions. So would her thighs and pelvic region. Her entire body was going to be consumed by a stinging ache, at the very least, from the ferocity of the way he fucked her. He didn't care. It made him sick, an absolute animal, but he didn't care. On the contrary. It only made him want to fuck her harder.

He pounded into her pussy until he could no longer resist releasing his own pleasure. His fangs extended to the length they were when he was in his animal form. A feral snarl, a low growl that seemed to shake the very foundations, escaped his chest, the echo reverberating through the space. As his orgasm ripped through him and burst forth, he let out a primal roar. With each forceful thrust, he pushed her wrists down harder onto the mattress, driving into her with unyielding intensity. *Holy fuck,* it made his head spin. Just like hers, there didn't seem to be an end to it. His cum just kept pouring into her pussy, drenching their thighs, soaking the bed.

Hades... it was glorious.

As everything finally slowed, Nia remained unmoving, her gaze fixed on him. His chin fell to his chest, but his gaze remained locked on hers, unwavering. Holy shit, his lungs practically burned from the exertion. Had he ever fucked anyone like that before? He certainly couldn't recall it *ever* being like that with *anyone*. It took him a couple of minutes before he could release her wrists, as well as let her legs down. Hunter went slowly as he lowered them onto the bed. His fangs shrank back to their normal humanoid size. They'd never extended so much during sex, either. It had taken every ounce of control he could muster not to bite her... somewhere, anywhere, during his crazed carnality.

After slipping his cock from her, he lingered, his tongue darting out to moisten his lips as he gazed at her. "When you can breathe normally, and regain the ability to move," he smirked. "I believe you promised me a cleanup."

"Yes, I did," Nia replied through ragged breaths, her voice soft and slightly hoarse.

Gazing over her body—and how she didn't move immediately—a rumble of satisfaction vibrated out of him. Not to mention the slight rasp of her voice. *He* had done that to her. Didn't that just make him feel something special? "If you would like, we can clean each other up at the same time." That had been *a lot* of fun during their first session. They hadn't been cleaning each other up then, just part of their playtime, but still.

The corners of Nia's mouth tilted upward. "Mmm... I like that idea *a lot.*"

"You just tell me when. Because as soon as you are ready, I am going to shove this dick in your mouth."

As she purred, Nia bent one leg, then the other, her stilettos making a slight indent in the bed, as if giving him an answer. A guttural growl, fueled by lust, escaped his lips as she presented herself to him. Oh, *fuck yes*, he was about to be *all* over that. He shifted, positioning his knees on either side of her head before sliding his hands under her legs, grabbing her ankles. She could fuck his tongue, but he was going to keep her firmly in place while she did. Without hesitating, he released a growl while plunging his tongue deep into her core. A moan resonated as the flavors burst onto his tongue, a complete transformation. *Oh, fuck yes...* her taste was perfection.

The moment her hands grazed the backs of his thighs, Hunter's body stiffened with a sudden jolt. No one had touched him during sex in almost three decades. The tension dissipated as she gripped his ass, took him deep in her throat, and let out a moan while pleasuring him. He tightened his grip on her ankles, releasing a deep, primal groan against her core. *Holy fuck.* He thoroughly explored every pleasurable part of her intimate area with his tongue, savoring and consuming every bit of her arousal. Teasingly, he ran his fangs along her outer lips, nipped her clit, and then thrust his tongue back inside her.

The heat and scent of her arousal became stronger, making his cock grow harder. And that was nothing compared to what her mouth and tongue did. A groan left her mouth, sending vibrations up his length as she dug her nails harder into his ass. Tingles shot straight to his balls. As she licked up his shaft, Hunter released another guttural moan against her pussy, while she cleaned off the mixture of their cum. The way her tongue curled around it sent shivers down his spine, like a sudden burst of energy.

After swirling her tongue around the tip of his cock, she cleaned the cum off one of his thighs, and then the other. As soon as she finished, she pressed her nails into his backside and skillfully took his cock into her throat, twirling her tongue around it. A low growl, like the rumble of distant thunder, escaped him. *Holy fuck,* that felt *fantastic.* Bolts of lightning shot straight to his balls. His fucking cock throbbed already. Her touch ignited a fire within him, leaving him in a heightened state. He just wanted to consume every part of her even more.

Hunter slid his hands higher on her thighs, feeling the soft flesh before digging in his claws. He delved deeper, relishing the sensation of her damp, heated center embracing his tongue. Unlike his usual rush, this time he moved slowly, savoring each gentle step. He intended to take his time, even if she had nothing left for him to take.

Holy shit, it wouldn't be long before she pulled another orgasm out of him. With the way they were teasing one another, it wouldn't surprise him if this one was just as explosive—if not more so—than their other ones.

After popping his length out of her mouth, she focused her attention on sucking on each of his balls. Then, she raked her nails across his ass, and a deep purr rumbled in her chest. A raging inferno of desire consumed him, scorching every inch of his body once more. As he continued, Hunter intensified the pressure of his mouth on her pussy, increasing the depth and forcefulness of his tongue movements while moving at a steady pace.

He would have let no one do that to him. He knew she was the cause, yet he wouldn't admit the truth. Why things were so very different with her. He broke all his rules with Nia, something he hadn't done with others. Maybe it was because, even given the opportunity to touch him, she hadn't focused on his scars. Only expressed her desire to touch more of him. The comfort of her touch was like nothing he had ever known, a feeling he hadn't experienced even when his sister Elisa had been alive. Perhaps this was because he had let no one get close to him. Not even as a nestling. Nia made him *want* that. But only with her.

Hunter kept her legs spread out as he inserted two fingers into her ass with one hand and three fingers into her pussy with his other hand. His hips swayed, moving in a slow rhythm as he slid in and out of her mouth, igniting sparks along his nerve endings with her lips and tongue. It seemed they'd both at least momentarily forgotten about cleaning up. Now they were just focused on making a mess all over again.

Nia's nails dug deeper into his ass, a sharp contrast to the slick, wet sensation of blood welling up beneath them. A throaty moan left him, not quite a noise he'd ever yet uttered before, even with her. Holy fucking shit... doing it with her heels was one thing, but with her nails... was a *whole* other thing entirely. He didn't need her to say the words out loud to know what she wanted. Hunter stilled his hips, but his thighs shook with the immense effort of remaining motionless. He wasn't familiar with it, nor did it feel right, yet the way she used her mouth, and the pain from her nails, completely overshadowed the confines of the space.

"Fuck, yes, suck my cock!" he snarled out. Taking his fingers out of her pussy, Hunter moved his hand beneath her and firmly grabbed her buttocks. He dug his claws in, the metallic scent of blood already in the air as he held her against his mouth. Hunter devoured her with an intense new passion, burying his tongue deep inside her. If their timing was perfect, they would arrive simultaneously, which would be enormous for them both.

Holy shit, she was about to fill his mouth with her cum. Each glorious act was met with his throaty moans, muffled by their closeness. His grip on her ass tightened further. He struggled to restrain himself from thrusting his cock into the back of her throat, feeling an overwhelming sense of pleasure. Hunter let out a massive growl against her pussy as he drove at her even harder. *Holy fuck,* he was about to come. Nia did something she'd never done before. She took the head of his cock into her mouth, lightly nibbled the tip with her teeth, and sensually moved her tongue around the tip.

Oh, holy motherfucking shit... Hunter's brain shorted out. His *fucking toes curled.* What the actual fuck? That had *never* happened before. *Fuck,* he needed her to come into his mouth. He fucked her ass harder with his fingers as he devoured her pussy with even greater ferocity. *Come on, sweetheart, give me everything you have got.*

Nia deep-throated him, buried her nails deeper into his ass cheek, squeezed his balls, and purred. Firebolts shot through every single inch of him, not just pushing him over the edge, but *shoving* him. A primal roar escaped Hunter as he experienced a powerful orgasm. Her toes curled so tightly in her peep-toe heels they seemed to vanish. An orgasm ripped out of her. She eagerly consumed every drop of his cum, letting none spill out of her mouth as she screamed around his cock.

Hunter didn't let a single drop of her delicious nectar go anywhere but down his throat. His roar continued until he'd taken every single bit of it. *Holy fucking shit.* Once he had ingested the last drops of her orgasm, he withdrew his tongue from her pussy, swept it along her slit, and nuzzled her inner thigh. No fucking idea why he did that... but he hadn't been able to stop himself. He sensed the way her blood pounded through her veins, the thrumming of her heartbeat through her femoral artery. Hunter licked along her inner thigh, his fangs grazing along in sequence. "Mmm..."

Wow... that had been... the most unique session he had ever had in his life. So different from any he'd ever had, wanted, or allowed. And he had loved every single moment of it. Nia had touched him during sex—just the oral part, but still sex—and he had loved it. He hadn't wanted her to stop touching him. He'd wanted her to grab on tighter and not let go.

After moving off her, he rested on his side, and gazed at her face for a moment. His brow furrowed in obvious confusion, and then he just shook his head. He couldn't think about the whys. Doing that would take him down a path he couldn't allow himself to go down.

Nia flicked her eyes over to Hunter. No words passed between them. Just silence.

With a final shake of his head, Hunter pushed up onto his knees. He tenderly lifted her and moved her, then settled her on her stomach in a dry spot on the bed. He'd been right. She definitely had bruises. There wasn't really any cleanup to do, though. He might have drawn a bit of blood here and there, but between all the fucking, it had rubbed off on the blanket. He'd licked her pussy and her thighs clean already. Hunter carefully massaged her shoulders as he straddled her hips, feeling the tension melt away.

Nia rested her cheek against the bed. "When you're done, I'll show you the vaginal beads and clit vibrators for you to pick out for our next session."

A small lift graced one corner of his mouth, a subtle hint of a smile. Oh, yeah. She was *definitely* holding up her end of the bargain. "Okay." Hunter glanced at her, then focused on her, gently massaging her, making certain not to hurt her. "Do you have any favorites?"

"Stainless steel Ben Wa balls, the one and a quarter inch. I also have a couple of different clitoral jewelry I prefer over any of the other stimulators."

"Good choices. I figured you had favorites." Hunter's shoulders rose and fell with the barest of movements. "But you never know." He hadn't even known that things like sex toys existed before he came here. The first female here who had asked him if he enjoyed using them... he'd only been able to give her a blank stare. It had made him feel like a clueless virgin.

"What about you? Do you have favorites?"

"Out of the clit vibrators?" He hadn't really ever thought about it specifically. Honestly, he liked them all, depending on the session and the female he was with. But he supposed there were some he'd had more fun with than others. "I like the finger ones, especially the ones where you can get the clit and the G-spot all at once. I think they are easier to control and have a little more of a natural feel for them. Sometimes the bullets can get slippery."

"That's why I like the jewelry. Kind of like a good nipple clamp. It's not going anywhere until you want to remove it," Nia replied. "No preference on the beads then? Or have you not been with someone who used them?"

"Not really. Few females I have been with liked anything up the ass, and the ones that did, I leaned toward that being my dick. There was one female here who liked the vaginal beads, but I could not fuck her the way I like to fuck while they were in. It got too uncomfortable for her. She would use them when I gave her oral, though. Mostly, the submissives I have been with have not been very... adventurous. I ended up getting annoyed. More often than not; too restricted because of their limits."

"Ben Wa balls are great during anal sex," Nia purred. "That's why they're my favorite."

That fucking purr. If she wasn't careful, she was going to rev him up all over again. With his gaze fixed on hers, Hunter eased his hands away from her shoulders, kneading the knots in her back. "Then I guess we know what position I am going to fuck you in first next time."

"Have you decided what color you'd like me to wear next time?"

Hunter considered for a moment, running through the colors he'd seen her in so far, and the other options he could choose. "Purple."

She leaned on her elbow, and her cheek rested on her hand as she focused on him. "I'm just curious. What would you do if you picked a color I *didn't* have in my repertoire?"

What almost immediately came out of his mouth was that, for *her*, he'd go buy something. But... *nope*, he really didn't need to utter that out loud. They were trying to get *away* from personal, not get closer to it. He also didn't want to examine the answer that had sprung into his mind so fast.

He'd never been able to explain it, not even to himself. Shape shifters didn't wear clothing—fabric shaped into tops, bottoms, lingerie. Since he had slept with other species, garments were nothing new, though he'd worn none himself. Some made the female more appealing; others didn't. Some aroused him more; others he didn't bat an eye at. He'd started giving the females just a color, curious to see what they created, because it offered him a glimpse into their thought process. In the playroom, their true personalities were hidden, held back by a feeling of constraint. One female, he'd told her to wear red. Her entire outfit had been white except for the tiny polka dots on her stiletto heels. She hadn't disobeyed, not *really*. But she'd known that wasn't what he meant. That punishment had been pleasurable for both of them.

But choosing the *specific* pieces they would wear, even straight out of their closet... Envisioning it on their body, like he'd envisioned the pieces of jewelry he'd gifted three females now. The way it would emphasize the curve of their breasts or ass. The curves of their hips. Watching their backs arch as he fucked them or satisfied their desires was a captivating image. He considered which parts of them he would grasp or sink his teeth into while tearing them away. *That* seemed too intimate. *That* would bring him too close to crossing the line into the personal. At least, in his mind.

"In the past, if they did not think they could make a trade with anyone else, I just chose a different color."

Nia's nose wrinkled ever so slightly. "That's highly unsanitary. I wouldn't ever trade my clothes with another. Not that it's typically necessary for me. I have an array of attire in my closet."

"Well, I would hope the ones that trade at least clean them first." In one corner of his mouth, a small lift appeared, a subtle expression of something he was feeling. An array, huh? It certainly made him curious. Not that he was going to ask. She'd had no problem fulfilling each one of his clothing demands so far, and he'd told her to wear a different color each session. "What is your favorite color?" Hunter hadn't meant to ask that question. It had just come out all on its own. What the fuck was this female doing to him? He absolutely could *not* put any thought into that question. He moved his hands lower and massaged her ass. All it made him do was want to lean down and bite it.

"Midnight blue, like the color of the night sky. What about yours?"

That confirmed his suspicions about her safe word. And filled his mind with the need to ignore... the *precise* color he'd gravitated to when he'd picked out her necklace. In answer to her question, he almost responded with green. Why the fuck did he almost say green? He'd never had a particular draw toward that color. Until recently. *Shut the fuck up, Hunter.* He knew *exactly* why he'd almost said green. Just like he knew *exactly* why he'd gone down into the caves inside the boundaries a couple of days ago, when he hadn't been able to sleep, to this one particular cove where the color of the rock made the water appear almost the same color as her eyes. The only natural thing he'd seen on the isle that came *that* close to the shade of the gaze that stared at him right now. As soon as he realized why he'd returned to that spot, he'd left and vowed not to return.

His favorite color wasn't green. It had never been green. It had always been—"Red. Crimson, to be exact." It was the color he'd asked her to wear during their second session. Not that he'd specified the hue.

"Have you ever asked a female to wear that shade? Or do you always keep it general?"

"General is best, especially with red. If I ever told anyone to wear crimson..." His eyes hooded. "There is just something about that color that triggers something in me." He flicked his gaze up to hers, a flicker of something unreadable passing through his expression. "You have seen how I react to blood. It is not just the smell and the taste that get to me. Seeing that shade on the female form..." He shifted his gaze downward, and his hands worked, kneading her legs. "It happened once here. About a year ago. I told the female I was with to wear red. She chose that shade. It was only our fourth session. But... it became our last. I did not blame her one bit." That female had always been desperate to please him. She'd held out as long as she could before saying her safe word, but they hadn't even made it through an hour.

"Is that the longest you've ever been with one female here? Four sessions? Outside of Ivory, I mean."

It made sense that she knew who he'd been with before her. People talked, especially females. How much Ivory had revealed about what sessions with him could entail prior to him and Nia being paired together? Or if any of the other females had said anything. Not that any rumors, true or false, would bother him in the least. He'd come here so long, though, been with so many females, he'd almost given up on having a *truly* utterly mind-blowing, 100% totally and completely satisfying session. And then they'd paired him with Nia. That *had* to be what all these lingering feelings were about. As much fun as he'd had with other females, she had been the only one to *fully* satisfy him. His sessions with her—even this one that had started out like it had—had all been incredible. This was his and Nia's fourth session. He wanted to have so many more with her.

"Out of the submissives, yes. The others that I have been with here, like Ivory, have not been submissives. I have been with several one-offs, but I reached five sessions—technically four and a half—with one of them before I had to move on. Or, had to move back to Ivory, I should say. She has sort of been my go-between. Not submissive, like I prefer, but able to handle my harder sessions. Though... not my hardest. There was a period—about four or five months, I want to say—where I was just seeing one-offs or randoms, whoever could fit me in and agreed to have a session with me, but I could not come in to see her." The corner of his mouth tilted a little. "She called it 'putting me on probation.'" That had been a dark period, even for him. Ivory had completely understood, given the circumstances, but the fact remained that he'd gone beyond losing control in that session with her. He had even stayed away from the brothel for a few weeks until he was sure he'd felt like he'd regained control of himself. After those few months, it had been business as usual.

"I take it that it resulted from the mood you forewarned me about?"

"Um... yes." He'd mentioned it at the end of their second session, when they'd gone over hard limits, the hand signal, and the additional safe word. Hunter sat down, then gently flipped her onto her back before draping her leg over his knee. He began at her thigh, cautiously avoiding the bruised areas. His brow furrowed. Why the fuck... did he *want* to tell her? He couldn't explain it, but he did. Not that he should. He straddled that line again, between 'personal' and 'just sex.' The words seemed to come out all on their own, too.

"My father is a genuine piece of work, is all. Some things he does—or did, before we got new leadership—used to get to me. But it was not so much what he did that put me in a mood that day. I did something because of his actions... that did not sit well with me. It still does not. Even though I know it was the right thing to do." Despite the urges, the scent of blood within the hut roared through him, but he ignored them. He'd done what he felt was right. Licked his fingers clean afterward, but that was an insignificant detail. He really needed to shut his fucking mouth. He felt the line he was straddling beginning to give way, growing ever more fragile. Maybe she wouldn't ask, but with the way this session had gone down, he didn't see that happening.

"What did you do?"

"I did a mercy kill of a female." Without the slightest pause, the words tumbled effortlessly from his mouth. Well, no taking them back now. Nia didn't seem like the type of person who would let a statement like that go without details. Or at least some kind of explanation. Which he would give to her if she asked. It just wasn't something he'd ever spoken about to anyone. He didn't talk to anyone about anything, really. Not even to Hayden. Something he just couldn't explain had him *wanting* to talk to Nia. Any time she asked him a question, something uncontrollable kept forcing answers out of his mouth. He couldn't help but respond.

Hunter moved his hands to her other leg, the scent of wax filling the air as he stared at the candle burning across the room. He was far from unfamiliar with death. He'd taken dozens of lives himself, at least. But those deaths hadn't bothered him; they'd deserved what they got. And he had enjoyed giving it to them. Immensely. The one he was talking about now... it had been different. The sight of the hut when he'd stepped foot inside... he would never forget it.

"Was it a brutal rape?" Nia asked. "I'm not unfamiliar with what things were like before the change in leadership in your village. I know rape was pretty common around there."

Her words surprised him, though he kept his composure. While plenty around the isle knew how things used to be in Métamorphe, he didn't think that extended to the females here. Then again, several of his species frequented this place. Okay... yeah, he *really* didn't want to think about anyone he knew having sessions with Nia. Nope. Not a single bit. At all. Right, those thoughts were *done.* "Yeah, it was. One of the most brutal things I have ever seen. But that is my father for you." That last sentence came out laced with venom. With his back to her, Hunter moved back slightly, pulling her legs around his waist, her feet settling comfortably in his lap. Starting on her left side, he unfastened the strap, removed the heel, set it down, and then repeated the motion with the other shoe. This wasn't something he should talk about. He should go, but he just didn't want to.

"My father threw a party in his hut. Not uncommon by any means. He and his friends and my oldest brother often came up with... unique reasons to celebrate. They would spend the night getting their fill of spirits and women. I want to say they had five, maybe six females inside that time. A few of them barely lasted the night. But the one my father had... Her fur had been light gray before. By the time I walked into the hut, I hardly recognized her. Her fur was dark red, almost completely maroon. She'd bled so much. Just from all the wounds on her. She was not making any noise, but her eyes were just... filled with pain. Shit being what it was there... I knew nothing could have saved her. She had maybe an hour left, tops. But... *dear old dad* would not have stopped until her heart quit beating. So, I sped it up a little. Pretended I was going to join in, got close enough, and then used my claw to slit her throat. My father made it... well-known how upset that made him." That part had been fun. They'd both been a bloody mess by the time Markham returned to the village and put a stop to the fight.

Nia rested her cheek against his back. "Taking a life is never a simple choice, even when you're sparing someone further agony. Sometimes we're left with no alternative but to make the hard decisions in the worst of circumstances."

Hunter said nothing for a minute. He liked the way her cheek felt pressed against him. Not that he should—or would—say that out loud. A whisper of a purr vibrated gently out of him as he continued rubbing her feet. "That has never been an issue for me. Taking a life. It is not a hard decision for me to make. Killing when it is justified or necessary has never bothered me. I enjoy it. It gives me a high that almost nothing else can. I have always been that way. Just a part of my father's genes made their way into me, I suppose. But I do not kill unless there is a legitimate reason."

He paused, the weight of the decision still heavy on his shoulders. "She had a three-month-old son. I think what angered me so much about it at the time was my father wasting another innocent life just so he could get his dick wet. And creating an orphan. Orphans in the village... back then, more often than not, they would have been better off dead, too. Without family or someone close to protect them, they became targets. His father never claimed him, even after his mother's death. Seeing him grow up, I realized he is a lot like my twin, who is the exact opposite of me. I suppose what continued to bother me so much about it over the years were the parallels. It was like watching my twin go through that all over again."

With a slow, rhythmic motion, Nia began stroking his sides, her fingers sinking into his fur. "Watching the people we care about suffer... I don't think there is a greater pain, especially when it seems there is little we can do to stop it. Maybe, since things have changed in your village now, you can help the young. Something to alter the course and separate it from what your twin went through. Even if you do it in secret."

"My twin suffered as little as possible. I made sure of that. He has always craved things that would be like poison to him. But I took care of him. And he is still good because of it. He is the only one in my family who is truly good." Hunter didn't even plan or mean to do it. One moment, she was there, and the next he was reaching, grabbing her thighs, and they were rolling onto his stomach. She straddled his back now, with his tail wrapped firmly around her ankle. For a moment, the sudden urge to shove her away and escape through the door consumed him. Except... the feel of her perched upon him utterly captivated him, a comforting, secure embrace. Despite the turmoil of his thoughts, Hunter kept speaking, his voice steady, as if nothing had happened. "As for the young, that is not my place. He has an older brother. They were just not allowed to live together before. His brother's mother takes care of him now. She and the female were close, from what I have gathered. So, he is doing just fine now." He paused. "I have always hated that it bothered me so much."

"He was innocent. So was she. While you weren't responsible for her death, you were the one who dealt the final blow. It was right, but that doesn't mean it takes any less of a toll."

"Killing is fun for me. But not like that. The after with my father was fun, though." With his arms crossed, Hunter laid his cheek against them as he turned his head, peering at her over his shoulder. *Why the fuck* did he keep talking? Why couldn't he just shut the fuck up? He didn't even know how long he'd been here. The *intelligent* thing to do would be to get up, go straight for the door, and get the fuck out of here. But, *apparently*, intelligence had momentarily escaped him. "Have you ever fought a drunk person before? They do not know when to stay down. They just get up again and again and keep swinging. He started bragging the next day that he had won the fight. Until a couple of other males set him straight. He blamed it on the spirits, but they really had nothing to do with it." A small smirk played at the corners of his lips. "He has always hated me because I chose Hayden over all of them."

"No, they don't," Nia muttered. "From what you've told me, I can't say it surprises me. I'd be willing to bet your father considers Hayden weaker than him, right?"

It was only three small words, but it was in the way she said them. She knew exactly what he was talking about... just differently. An icy wave crashed over him, leaving a chilling hollowness in its wake. "It sounds like you have your own experience with that." Not that he expected she would elaborate. But the offer was there to listen, if she chose. He needed to grab his tongue, rip it straight out of his mouth, and shut himself the fuck up. But he just couldn't seem to stop talking to her. Not helped along by the feel of her fingers running through his fur. He tried not to reveal his emotions, but his eyelids fluttered shut for just a second. Hades, that felt incredible. "He does. Hayden is a very skilled fighter; he just hates it. Causing pain to someone else causes him pain. He is very soft-hearted, emotional, kind, nurturing, and loving. Everything I am not. We have always differed from one another. My father groomed me to be everything he wanted in a son. He just did not realize how much I would enjoy it—though he never got me to rape anyone. I just fed that dark part of myself any way that I could, and then I used it to my advantage."

"Some things, no matter how hard they push, it's just not something you truly have inside you to do." Nia's eyebrows furrowed. "My father was a drunk and a mean one at that. Not that anyone could ever tell. I suppose that's what happens when you drink every day. As long as he didn't leave permanent marks and I still had my virtue, I was valuable to him."

Hunter didn't move. As her fingers explored slowly, he kept his cheek against his arms, his gaze fixed on hers. His expression didn't change. Right now, his eyes probably resembled two dark voids, devoid of light or life. "He beat you." Not a statement he felt needed to be a question. The rest of what she said... for a moment, the image of a female came into his head. One with Hayden's coloring, but her eyes were a different shade of blue than theirs. Azazel had no qualms about casting aside virtue to make a profit. Hunter slammed the door shut hard. "Was he planning on selling you?"

"Yes." Nia averted her gaze. "No male wants a female who can't fully submit."

I do. The words were ready to burst forth, and to stop them, he bit down on his tongue, the urge a physical pressure. Hunter swallowed the metallic-tasting blood that had gathered, and then he licked his lips. Reaching back, his fingers brushed softly against the warm skin of her thigh and knee. "That is exactly what they taught in my village, too." His father had been one male who had drilled it into his children's heads with everything he had. Verbally, and with physical examples, too. Kind of made him wonder. Was the sex he needed really a natural proclivity? Or was *that* the real reason? His father's *lessons*? Even if he hadn't grown up in Azazel's home, the male's teachings had certainly made a lasting impact. Hunter's sadistic tendencies had been an enjoyable revelation—at least to him. There wasn't much of anything his father had done to him personally that hadn't brought a smile to his face. Regardless of the amount of his blood Azazel spilled, bones broken, or the concussions he suffered. That Azazel couldn't break him had only added fuel to the fire with his father. Azazel took it as a challenge. One that Hunter had never allowed him to win.

"I wonder if that is part of why things never worked out for me with the other submissives," he muttered to himself. He hadn't even meant to say the words out loud, but really, it made him curious. None of them had ever truly challenged him. They all had certain limits he couldn't push. They'd... bored him. He gave a slight shrug. He really needed to go. Now. So, why couldn't he make himself tell her to get off of him so he could get up off the bed?

"Maybe," Nia said.

"You survived. That is the important thing."

"You survived, too."

"Only for Hayden. Not for myself." It wasn't something he'd ever admitted out loud to anyone. Not that Hayden didn't know purely because of their connection. "Life has never brought me joy." However, the time in this room with her had forged a bond unlike any other. Something it was too dangerous to think about. The strangest urge to move his caresses from her leg to her cheek instead—no, he couldn't do that. Absolutely not. What the fuck was he thinking? That was the last thing he should do. Gods, he really needed to leave.

Her fingers stroked along his tail, where it curled around her ankle. "My father died a long time ago, so he can't hurt me now."

His eyes drift closed for another moment. The soft, gentle purring coming out of him—*when the fuck had that started?!* He hadn't even realized... That wasn't a sound he'd ever made before. It was a minute longer, at least, before he spoke. Yup, he really needed to go. "Good. That is good." Hunter gave her leg a light squeeze, then continued his soothing caresses. "I bet you have to remind yourself of that from time to time. Even being in here."

"When he first died, I did. Here... only once."

"Good." He didn't know what else to say. This was a first—the urge to ask more questions, learn more about her, and just listen to her talk overwhelmed him. But they'd already left that line in the distance—that line between personal and professional. It was way past time for him to go. Hunter forced his tail to unwind from her ankle. "I should be going."

Nia climbed off of him and got down off the bed. She walked across the room; the floorboards groaning beneath her feet, and stopped in front of the ornate dresser, then opened the small drawer. "Vaginal beads."

It took him a minute to force himself off the bed. Another moment to step away from it. Hunter cleared his mind of foolish thoughts, steeled himself, and crossed the room, halting only when he stood directly behind her. The drawer she'd opened comprised two rows, with five sets of beads in each row, each set atop linen. Of those, she had three different sizes of Ben Wa balls. Hunter didn't miss the barely contained shudder as he reached forward, purposely brushing his arm against her shoulder, and pointed to the one and a quarter inch. "I think those will do."

Nia gave a small dip of her chin and shut the drawer. She opened the one directly below it. "Clitoral stimulators."

This drawer comprised two rows, four in each row, each stimulator set atop linen. Everything was in its exact spot, creating a perfectly symmetrical pattern. Just like the drawer above it. Hunter flicked his gaze down to the top of her head. Interesting. Shifting his gaze to what was in the drawer, he took his time looking over what choices she had. Lots of different choices. Each fun and pleasurable in its own right. "I think..." He brushed his arm against her shoulder again and leaned in slightly, his pelvis grazing her ass briefly. "... this one." He pointed to one of the finger vibrators, his favorite type. It was black and would fit over his thumb and forefinger. "And ..." Shifting his finger over to the second row, he pointed to one piece of clitoral jewelry. It was gold with a couple of faux-diamond gems on the end. "... that one." Hunter leaned down closer, so his breath tickled her ear as he spoke. "That is... if I was *good* enough to pick two?"

"Yes," Nia replied, her voice low and sultry. "I believe you were *good* enough to choose two."

He bit back a growl and licked his lips. His mouth was so close to her, the tip of his tongue grazed her earlobe. "I am already looking forward to it."

With a final click, she shut the drawer and turned, her fingertips gently tracing his pelvis as she met his gaze. "Makes two of us."

A low growl left him as a shudder went down his spine. Her touch, even as slight as it was, immediately hardened his cock. As close as they were to one another, she'd definitely feel it. With a possessive grip on her hips, he pressed her against the dresser. She gasped, sending a ripple of lust through him. "I will see you in four days. Wear purple. And *those*." Hunter nodded down at the drawers. "And I expect you to be a *very good girl*." A small smirk appeared on his face.

"The Ben Wa balls as agreed. And the stimulators will be out for your use, Sir." Nia smirked. "Wouldn't want the jewelry to snag."

His grip on her hips tightened. "No, we would not." He slipped his hand between her thighs, cupping her most sensitive spot and inserting a finger as deeply as possible. "Then next time... I would be *so* happy... to put it in myself," he said, punctuating his words with slow thrusts. Removing his finger, he brought it to his mouth and slowly licked it clean with a growl. *Fuck*, he had to get out of here. Right now. Before he didn't leave. After giving her hip one last squeeze, he released her and turned toward the door.

"At least you'll get to take out the Ben Wa balls," Nia replied.

He clenched his jaw, his teeth grinding together before he could respond. If this back-and-forth continued, he really wouldn't leave. The moment he shut the door, the realization washed over him. After they'd talked, and then let loose... she hadn't asked permission to come one time. And she hadn't called him 'Sir'—at least, not until they'd been at her dresser. He hadn't noticed once. A slow smirk spread, the corners of his mouth tilting upwards. He wouldn't go back inside now, but next time... he would give her a punishment she'd never forget.

Seven

Nia didn't assume her customary submissive pose as she waited for Hunter to arrive for their session, a change in her usual demeanor. Instead, she sat on her queening bench at the end of her bed. It was mostly black, with a red base and red padding that felt soft, and a couple of restraints across the top. With her elbows braced on the mattress and feet on the floor, she spread her legs as she leaned backward. The attire she'd chosen was a halter made completely of purple lace. The hem stopped about mid-thigh, and there was a slit down the middle that reached from the top all the way to her belly button. There was no back, and the two halves barely covered her breasts. Her panties coordinated with her ensemble, and instead of standard heels, she'd selected black, knee-high boots with strips of fabric up the back that barely revealed glimpses of her skin. She'd also braided her hair and, as an added touch, painted her lips with a crimson gloss that would make them plumper.

When the door finally opened, she watched Hunter step inside and close it behind him. He stopped right inside the door, clasping his hands behind his back as he stared at her. His eyes immediately zeroed in on her lips and darkened to pitch black. His cock became erect, and his fangs extended rapidly, causing a slight cut on his bottom lip. Hunter kept his eyes trained on her as he reached out with his tongue to gather the crimson beads, remaining still inside the door. "You were very naughty last session, Nia. When I fucked you the second time… you did not address me correctly. Nor did you ask for my permission to come." He took a few steps closer to her. "I thought you were going to be a good girl. Instead..." Hunter gazed over her from head to toe before settling back on her lips. "... it seems I may have to give you a bigger punishment than what I already had in mind."

"I couldn't seem to help myself, Sir. The Ben Wa balls and our previous departure gave me so many ideas, Sir." Nia draped one leg over the other. "Shall I choose a fitting punishment, Sir?" she asked, a mischievous spark in her eyes. Every word that had come out of her mouth had been nothing but the truth. He'd previously punctuated his words with his finger in her pussy when they last parted ways. As a result, a cascade of ideas flooded her mind. Despite her best efforts over the past four days, she couldn't stop herself from carrying them out.

Just as she promised, she had inserted the Ben Wa balls an hour ago. That had been after her shower. Then she cleaned things up and prepared the room and herself for his arrival. The lipstick had been the final touch, simply because she wanted to see his reaction. And oh, it was *so* worth it. Yes, she had been *very* naughty.

A low growl rumbled in his chest, and his hands balled into tight fists. "What exactly did you have in mind that you think would be... *appropriate* for your disobedience, Nia?"

While she mulled over ways to punish him, she also considered how he could punish her. Having moved around the room for the last hour with the Ben Wa balls, a pleasant warmth had already spread through her. "Once strapped to the bondage horse, I'd begin with a spanking using one paddle on the wall, Sir. I suggest the paddle as it is my least favorite, Sir. However, given the time the Ben Wa balls have been inserted, if you wished to further enhance my stimulation while denying an orgasm, I'd recommend the flogger, Sir. While continuing to deny an orgasm, I'd follow this up with a blowjob, Sir. Provided I did a good job, then you might allow me one orgasm, Sir. To ensure I remembered only good girls get rewarded, you could fuck me in the ass, declining my orgasm again, Sir."

Even though she had more ideas, they had already executed a few. There were, of course, other ways he could use the agreed-upon items to punish her. For some, he'd have to remove the Ben Wa balls, but where would the fun in that be? Nia uncrossed her legs and leaned forward on the bench. "Another option, Sir, would be to begin right here. With the restraints in place, I could give you a blowjob while you deny my orgasm, Sir.”

“I do like the way you think, but do you know what I think, Nia?” Hunter walked toward her, his approach as quiet as a whisper as he strolled across the floor. “I think you just want a taste of my *cock*. But that would not *quite* be a punishment for you, would it? Because I know *just* how much you love to suck my cock until you swallow *every single drop* of my cum.” Stopping in front of her, he lifted her chin until their eyes met. He swept his thumb slowly across her lower lip. Licking his own again, he secured her wrists with his left hand and lifted her arms above her head. He leaned in close to her, and his right hand brushed the bench, then landed near her as his voice dropped to a whisper. “I have a few ideas of my own. Would you like to hear them?”

Nia gasped. Fuck, she really enjoyed his closeness. None of his statements were inaccurate. She was confident that by the end of the session, she would pleasure him with her seductively painted lips, as he wouldn’t be able to resist. She was definitely curious about his plan. Almost as much as she couldn’t wait until he saw the back of her boots. She didn’t think he’d quite noticed them yet. “Yes, Sir.”

“I do like many of your suggestions, Nia. So, I think I will weave ours together a bit. We are going to begin right here. I will not restrain you—yet—but you may not touch. Or taste. Instead, I am going to finish something I started during our last session.” The corners of his lips upturned into a smirk. “My cock is going to be just out of your reach, and you are going to watch me pleasure myself. If you are a *good girl* while I do so, I *might* allow you a taste when I come. After we are through with that, we are going to move to the bondage horse. Once strapped down, I will begin your spanking. However, I am going to use my hand. The paddle is also my least favorite, and I know *just how much* you enjoy the flogger. While I am spanking you, I am going to use the finger vibrator on you as well. You *cannot* come. If you are a *good girl* and make it through that portion of the punishment without coming *all over* my fingers, I will follow that up with you giving me a blowjob and allow you *one* release while you are sucking on my cock. Provided you do a good job with that, I will allow you to swallow *all* of my cum. And then, as you suggested, to ensure you remember that only *good girls* get rewarded, I am going to fuck you in the ass while denying your orgasm.” Hunter stood back up, then slowly took a few steps back from her. "Get on your knees, Nia. I want your face level with my cock. You may pick where you put your hands. On your knees, beside you, behind you, wherever you would prefer. Provided they do not move during this portion of your punishment."

Fuck, she was *absolutely* going to enjoy this. And if he hadn't noticed the back of her boots yet, he would the second she got down on her knees. She was going to ensure it. Hunter watched as she eased down from the queening bench, her descent graceful like a feather in the breeze. His eyes trailed down to the back of her boots as she spread her knees, revealing the intricate ladder-patterned straps. A low growl rolled out of him. *Yes, give me your growls, Hunter. I need them all.* Even if she hadn't heard the noise, the look on his face told her everything she needed to know. It might have been impossible to determine the direction of a session with him, but she could say one thing—it would be *exactly* what they both needed. Nia rested her hands on the bench behind her. Any of the rest would've been too easy and could've kept the back of the boots hidden longer. She wanted Hunter to see it *all*, to note every choice she'd made when dressing for him. With her body in this position, it put her breasts more on display, too. They practically strained against the thin, lace material covering them, her nipples right at the edge of the fabric now.

Meeting her gaze again, Hunter wrapped his hand around the base of his erection. "Shall we begin?"

"Yes, Sir," Nia replied. Not being able to move would be difficult to a degree. Only because the Ben Wa balls would move a little less, depending on how much her pelvic muscles responded to Hunter's masturbation.

Her lips pulled his gaze, an unseen force compelling him to look again. His fangs elongated a little further, the tips digging into his lower lip. A couple of trickles of blood slid through his fur and dripped onto his chin. As he stroked his shaft, he did not wipe them away, letting them run down his face. He groaned, his grip tightening as he increased the tempo slightly.

A deep moan left her mouth. Not that she could say what turned her on more. Considering all that had occurred in their previous meeting, staying still might be harder than she thought. She was familiar with the sensation of his cock in her mouth, though she had not yet held it in her hands. Her fingers had glided through his fur, and it felt softer than the finest silk she'd ever touched. Nia couldn't take her eyes off anything he did. The way his lips parted as his breathing got heavier. His moan reverberated through the room as he quickened the pace and force of his movements, electrifying her. Fuck. Despite her lack of movement, her pelvic muscles reacted to his actions, causing the Ben Wa balls to shift and generate vibrations in her pelvis.

Fuck, she wanted to feel his claws in her body as much as she yearned to have his fangs in it. Her toes curled in her boots. The vibrations of the balls against her pelvis intensified, making her even more aroused. Gods, she needed him to come in her mouth. She craved his sweet taste, a sensation that would flow down the back of her throat. The more ferocious his snarls became, the more she craved the sound. She held herself back from reaching for him as he moved faster and pressed forward. Blood trickled through his fur as his fangs pierced his lower lip, and his claws dug deeper into his thigh. Goddess, she wanted to sweep her tongue across his body. Her nails made a scraping sound against the queening bench as he climaxed, spilling onto the floor.

His eyes lingered on her lips before quickly darting up to meet her gaze. A grin spread across his face, the blood on his fangs reflecting the light. "You were a very *good girl,* Nia." Releasing his cock and his thigh, Hunter strolled leisurely around the puddle of his cum on the floor before extending his hand in front of her face. "I told you I might allow you a taste when I came. I did not tell you how I would offer it."

Oh, if—no, *when*—she got her mouth around his cock later in this session, she would take her sweet, sweet time making him come. If he was only offering his hand, she could ensure he'd regret this meager gesture. She remained still as her tongue contacted his pinky finger. She could easily clean it without opening her mouth completely. In fact, she didn't have to do that for a single part of his hand. No, she could get every bit of his sweet cum with her tongue. Which was *exactly* how she proceeded. He'd have to wait to have her mouth around something until she got his cock.

The way his fangs continuously dug into his lips made her crave the taste of blood as she wanted to wipe it off with her tongue. It probably tasted just as sweet as his cum. Her gaze flicked to his as she ensured that she'd fully cleaned his hand. "I believe I've got everything, Sir."

"I believe you did." Hunter leaned down closer to her, one arm on either side of her body as he covered her hands with his own. His tongue snaked out across his lower lip. His grip on her wrists tightened, yanking her up, and the rapid movement made the Ben Wa balls inside her shift and click. Then he drew her closer, his hands firmly gripping her ass, until she could feel the heat radiating from his body. As their eyes met, Hunter's gaze was intense, fueled by a potent lust. "Where did you put the toys for your pussy that I get to use?"

Nia moaned before she answered him. Her body was on fire. No doubt the stimulation from the balls reflected on her face. Through each session, she'd lost more and more control of her expressions. "On the dresser, Sir," she replied in a husky voice.

Hunter bowed her body back to the point she would have lost her balance if he hadn't held onto her so tightly. His nose brushed softly against her cheek and then lingered on her neck. Nia groaned, a sound that only got louder as he licked up to her ear and nipped her earlobe with his fang. "Go over to the bondage horse. Lean backward against it as far as you can. Put your arms above your head, and spread your legs." Setting her upright, he let go of her and headed over to the dresser.

Fuck—yeah, they'd agreed on a blindfold. But she really liked the way his eyes looked at the moment. Especially his facial expressions. The slight nuances as he became more aroused. The various tics on his face just before he came. Among so many other things, she noticed. Still, she wanted to see it all. Not that she could say any of that.

"Yes, Sir." Obediently, Nia approached the bondage horse, which was positioned in front of her makeup table, moving with a subtle sway of her hips. The thong already put her ass on display; this just made it stand out a little more. She felt his eyes on her, and the sensation sent a shiver down her spine. The bondage horse almost came up to the middle of her back. As Hunter instructed, she leaned against it, spread her legs, and bent back with her arms above her head. Not only did this showcase her flexibility a bit, but it pushed her breasts out as well. The purple lace rose as she splayed her body out for his use.

He selected a blindfold made of black silk, with its smooth texture, and a subtle hint of purple trim. From atop the dresser, he took the finger vibrator and clitoral jewelry he had picked at the end of their last session. Hunter crossed the floor to stand behind her, and the smell of leather and anticipation hung in the air as he placed the vibrator and jewelry on the bondage horse, then tied the blindfold around her head. His fangs grazed over her shoulder and up her neck. Her body shook with a shudder, and a groan rumbled from her throat.

"Can you see anything, Nia?" he whispered in her ear.

She angled her head ever so slightly before she answered, "No, Sir." She couldn't tell how close her mouth was to his ear, but she could feel the warmth of his fur. Hunter's breaths became ragged. His claws scraped against the leather of the bondage horse. She felt his presence as he moved, a subtle rustle before he stilled again. He trailed his claws down the lace of her lingerie, starting at the halter that encircled her neck, brushing across her breasts and the peaks of her nipples, and finally, down to the valley of her vee. He slid his hands inside, the warmth of his touch spreading as his fingers danced across her stomach, finally clasping around her waist. A light squeeze to her waist, a fleeting touch of his claws across her stomach, and then his hands were gone from her lingerie.

The noises that escaped her grew more frantic as his claws scraped along her until they brushed against the fabric of her lingerie. A claw brushed the thin, purple fabric, then curled beneath each delicate strap of her thong. With a single cut, her underwear fell away, landing softly on the floor. Her moans and groans cut off when Hunter attempted to place the clit jewelry.

"I have never put one of these in myself," he said, his voice tinged with a growl. Hunter leaned in close, his lips gently touching her, then flicking the tip of his tongue across her clit just once. "Does it feel like it is correct?"

That didn't really surprise her. It wasn't situated correctly, which amused her a bit. She'd have to cleanse it after their session concluded. When she'd pulled the clitoral jewelry out of the drawer earlier, it had occurred to her to offer a second option... just in case. She had the foresight to set out a clit clamp, believing it would be more appropriate for his planned activities. "It's not on correctly, Sir."

"Show me."

Adjusting her stance a little, she first carefully removed the jewelry from her clit. Starting from the part that protected the clit, Nia pinched her labia together and gently nudged the clit out to insert the jewelry carefully. It went over the labia, not inside of it, but she didn't state that. "It's intended to restrict circulation during foreplay so that when it is removed, all the blood comes rushing back to the clit. Which makes it hypersensitive, Sir." Even in a short duration, it had already worked. Though it wouldn't work at all with the stimulator that she suspected he'd picked up. "This is how you would take it off, Sir." With the same ease, she slowly withdrew the jewelry from her labia and held it out, the metal cool against her skin. It hadn't been necessary to remove the blindfold. Though she would've killed to see the way his face contorted as he watched her place and remove the jewelry. "There is an alternative atop the dresser, Sir." The device didn't clamp onto the clit, but focused on the outer skin. Unlike the jewelry, it didn't extend all the way over the labia, allowing for flexibility while in use.

If the fresh scent of copper was anything to go by, he'd enjoyed watching her demonstration. The points of her ears twitched as he took the adornment, the metallic tang of the jewelry momentarily filling her senses, then he stepped away, and after a minute, placed the cold, smooth clit clamp in her hand. It was much smaller and lighter.

"Put it on," Hunter ordered.

Without taking the blindfold off, Nia picked up the three-inch clit clamp between her fingers and lifted it to her mouth. As she licked the silicone prongs, the taste of metal filled her mouth until they were dripping with saliva. His growl sent a jolt of arousal through her. She let out a soft moan as she placed the clamp on either side of her clit, making sure the jewel rested against her pelvis before adjusting the pressure by sliding the metal loop down. Contented that the object was secure, Nia leaned back, stretching her arms above her head.

Another growl vibrated out of his chest. Hunter's hands went to her hips, his fingers getting a tight grip. "This one will work better for using the vibrator at the same time?"

"Yes, Sir. I didn't set the pressure too tight, so it can still stimulate the clitoris." And she would feel it. Not as much without the clamp unless he loosened the metal loop. Then it would be a rush, and she might not stop the orgasm. Should she warn him of that? This was supposed to be a punishment. Well, it might end up as punishment for him. Then again, it wasn't like he didn't know how clamps worked altogether. She didn't need to tell him what he should already know.

"Good." His claws, sharp and cold, trailed slowly up and down her body. He traced her thighs beneath the delicate lace of her lingerie, his touch lingering before moving to her collarbone, and then restarting. "Tell me, Nia. How many spankings do you think would be appropriate for this portion of your punishment?"

That depended on how much value he assigned to the punishment he had delivered not that long ago. Except he intended to use his hand.

Oh, so how many times should his palm come across her ass? That was a good question. Maybe one for each orgasm she had in the second half of their last session. Not that she'd counted. Then another for the color she'd painted on her mouth and three more for not being in the right pose when he arrived. All of that added up to... "Ten, Sir."

"*Only* ten? Hm." Another growl vibrated in his chest. "How about we make it... twelve?" Hunter gently tugged the lace aside and held it, his eyes fixed on her as he took each nipple into his mouth. "You knew *exactly* what you were doing when you put that color on your lips, Nia."

Hearing those words coming from him made her want to hear *her* name tacked at the end. Not what she went by around the den. He yanked the fabric; the material tore with a harsh sound as it gave way, and she was suddenly nude before him. He dropped the pieces on the floor at her feet. In that instant, every thought evaporated, and the feel of his warm palm captivated her, inching up her skin to her neck. With his fingers curled around her nape, he hauled her up before moving them to her waist, where they tightened their hold. Before she realized it, she was sitting on the cold leather of the bondage horse.

"Get on your knees, Nia," he demanded, his voice husky.

Nia shifted back a little, then turned slowly, her legs swiveling to the right. The position allowed her body to align perfectly with the straps attached to the equipment. Last time she'd been on it, well... the situation had been a little different with him. She'd started with her legs tucked under and eventually ended up on her stomach. This time, she was practically beginning that way. Though it felt a little different with the boots over her knees.

Once she was on her hands and knees, Hunter got to work on the restraints. He didn't use all of them, though. Just the straps that went around her hips and upper thighs, and the leather cuffs around her wrists. "I want you to count each spanking as you receive them, Nia. And count them loudly. We do not want to lose count."

His finger slipped inside her, finding her G-spot while his thumb teased her clit. It was a good thing she'd opted to have the jeweled part of the clit clamp toward her pelvis. She already had to clench. Without warning, Hunter turned the vibrator to its highest setting and delivered a hard smack on her ass. A deep moan escaped her lips, vibrating in the silent air, before she could even bother with counting. Nia swallowed to wet her parched throat. "One, Sir."

"I thought I said to count *loudly*, Nia." His finger pressed harder against her G-spot. "You have been such a *good girl* during your punishment so far. Do not ruin that now." He removed his hand from her ass and then brought it back with a sharper smack.

Holy fuck. The lower half of her body was so damn stimulated she could feel it in her nipples. It wasn't just jolts running up her spine; it was fire raging across her nerves, and electricity shooting to her core all in one. She dug her nails into the leather padding of the bondage horse. "Two!" she yelled. "Sir." Next time, crimson top-to-fucking bottom.

"Good girl." Hunter's hand recoiled before smacking her ass cheek again, and then he stroked the reddening skin.

"Oh, gods," she groaned. Oh, he'd have to be a *great* boy to earn any more rewards. Her nails scraped harder against the leather. The Ben Wa balls hadn't gotten her *that* stimulated beforehand, had they? She didn't think so, though there was a lot going on in the lower half of her body. "Three, Sir!" Nia hollered. *Nine left.*

Hunter's hand came down, and with a resounding thwack, he struck her other ass cheek. Without taking his fingers away from her pussy, he leaned down and licked across her flesh, right where his hand had just connected.

"Fuck." Each new strike heightened the vibrations of the stimulator and the pressure of the clamp on her clit. Not to mention the way the Ben Wa balls shifted as well. Nia licked her lips. "Four, Sir!" she exclaimed. Recalling the order in which he intended to punish her, a thought popped into her head. When she'd painted crimson on her lips, she knew he wouldn't be able to resist the desire to see her mouth wrapped around his cock. A little torture went a long way.

Hunter's hand landed on her ass cheek with a resounding slap. A stinging sensation washed over her skin as his claws grazed it before he retracted his hand. "Turn your head, Nia."

As her nails dug into the leather, she squeezed her vaginal walls tighter. Holy shit. Sensations assailed her core from all sides. When she did finally come, it was going to be fucking massive. "Five, Sir!" Nia called out as she turned her head.

This time, Hunter let out a low snarl. His touch—a tantalizing dance of finger, thumb, and palm—edged her nearer to the threshold of pure ecstasy. More sounds left her mouth. It wouldn't surprise her if the heat in her body became volcanic. "Six, Sir!" she called out. *Six more and it's my turn to tease you.*

"Halfway through." Hunter returned to her first ass cheek, the sound of the smack echoing slightly this time. At the contact of his palm against her skin, a half-growl, half-snarl ripped out of him.

"Holy fuck," Nia hollered. That blissful sting shot straight to her core. Both her vaginal walls and thighs clenched tight. "Seven, Sir."

"Mmm... five more left." He gave her ass cheek a gentle bite, then trailed his claws along her lower back. "One... two... three... four..." The smack of his hand against her ass cheek reverberated around the room. "... five." Hunter massaged the spot he'd delivered the blow for a moment before removing his hand.

"Eight, Sir," Nia moaned loudly.

This time, when his hand met her ass cheek, the familiar touch became a sharp, tiny scrape. His claws hadn't connected enough to pierce her skin yet. "What number are we on now, Nia?"

"Nine, Sir," she replied with a deep groan. Fuck, her body was on fire.

"Three more to go." He slowly and carefully slid the metal loop of the clamp up, releasing the pressure while she felt the scrape of his claws.

Holy motherfucking shit. Nia clenched her teeth on the leather padding of the bondage horse, feeling a surge of blood and sensation return to her clit as Hunter smacked her ass once more. It muffled the sound of her moan. Her toes curled, and her fingers scraped hard against the leather, while her muscles clenched from her vaginal walls to her thighs. It took every ounce of willpower she had to keep from coming. Oh, she was going to enjoy torturing the shit out of him and keeping her mouth off his cock. Her chest heaved, the rise and fall likely noticeable in her back. Nia let go of the padding, her teeth leaving an imprint on the soft material. "Ten, Sir."

"Is it getting a little too *hard* for you to handle, Nia?" He grazed his claws over her ass cheek. "There are only two more to go. I know you can handle it." His palm landed another blow on her ass.

Nia let out a purred moan. This male didn't know how badly she was going to tease him. Nor did he seem to recall that *he* had submitted to her in the second half of their last session. He had worked to please her and earn a reward that he no longer seemed to deserve. Her tongue moved slowly and deliberately across her lips. "Eleven, *Sir.*"

Hunter let out a loud growl as he increased the pressure on her G-spot and sensually rubbed her clit with his thumb. He retracted his hand and delivered the most forceful slap yet to her rear. A deep guttural moan escaped her, a sound she didn't recognize as her own. She refused to look too much into it. After all, her core had endured *a lot* of stimulation. Still, she clenched tight and held her orgasm back. "Twelve, *Sir.*" Nia punctuated the two words with another purred moan. This was only the beginning of how she planned to tease the shit out of him.

Hunter's hand dug into her hip, breaking the skin, and a monstrous growl filled the air. "You have been a *very* good girl, Nia. But you have been a little naughty, too. You know what that fucking purr does to me." With the stimulator still inside her, snug against her G-spot, he repositioned his thumb to reach her clit. As he delicately ran the tip of his tongue over her clit, a deep moan escaped his lips.

He didn't know how naughty she could be. All she'd given him was a *small* taste. Despite his naughtiness, bad boys didn't receive rewards. "Yes, Sir," she purred. To emphasize the words, Nia contracted and released her vaginal walls, working the muscles against his finger as she let out a moan.

Pressing his thumb back against her clit, Hunter bit down on her ass cheek. "Do not forget, you have to continue to be a *good girl* to be allowed to swallow my cum, Nia."

Oh, he'd dished out a good chunk of his punishment. Perhaps he needed to be reminded of *exactly* what she expected he'd been looking forward to for the last four days. "And only *good boys* get rewards, *Sir.*" Nia punctuated the last word with a deep moan. Besides contracting and releasing her vaginal walls around his finger, she also tensed her thighs and buttocks.

A deep growl emanated from his chest. "Maybe I do not feel like being a *good boy* today, Nia. Besides, I am already getting my reward." Once again, he moved his thumb aside and playfully teased her clit with his tongue while inserting two fingers into her ass.

He seemed rather sure of himself. However, the purpose of the heightened sensation was for him to bring her to climax. His further attempts felt fantastic, especially with her clit so sensitive. "Mmm, are you sure you're getting your reward, Sir?" Nia kept going with the contract and release, feeling the strain in her thighs and ass cheeks. He'd decreed that as part of her punishment, he'd allow her *one* orgasm. Maybe he needed to beg for it. Then he needed to beg for her lips around his cock.

"My mouth on your pussy is *always* a reward. But if you would prefer we do something else instead of you getting that orgasm I promised to allow you..." After biting down on her clit, he stood back up. His fingers moved in a slow rhythm, exploring her body, with his thumb resting on her sensitive spot and his forefinger stimulating a deeper pleasure. "... we can proceed with the next part of your punishment. Perhaps you would prefer we wait until *after* you swallow my cum before finding your own release."

While she didn't hold back her noises, she held onto the orgasm that was ready and waiting. No matter how much she struggled to control herself, the satisfaction of hearing him say 'please' would make it all worthwhile. Oh yes, he enjoyed eating her pussy. But he wanted her cum just as much as he wanted that blowjob. "Here, I thought my *cum* was your reward, Sir. Or do you just want my mouth around your *cock* that badly, Sir?" Nia purred.

"Both. And you fucking know it." His fingers moved in and out of her buttocks with more force. "My question is... which one do *you* need more?"

Oh, that wasn't the question. The question was which of them could hold out longer. He'd seen her full-submissive side. Over their sessions, he'd triggered her dominant side. What if that was *all* he got? "I believe you should *earn them... Sir,*" Nia punctuated the last three words, her voice husky with a soft moan. At the end of their last session, he'd asked for an example of her dominance. Perhaps he deserved another. The muscles in her ass cheeks clenched his fingers so tightly, their movement restricted.

With a deep snarl, Hunter removed his hand from her pussy and his fingers from her ass. He walked around the bondage horse until he was in front of her, clenching her hair in his fist, pulling her head back, and carefully adjusting her blindfold so their eyes met. His own were pitch black, and showed clearly *exactly* how much he needed her. He leaned down close, their breaths mingling, his free hand gliding down her skin to cup and caress her breast. "This is *your* punishment, Nia. I do not need to *earn* anything. Perhaps when we are through with this... I will throw you on the bed and *earn a reward.* But that does not happen right now." His tongue snaked out and licked her bottom lip. A visible shudder swept over him from head to toe, a blaze of heat pouring off of him.

For a split second, her mind went entirely blank as tingles blasted down her spine, straight to her core. A bit of cum seeped out before she recognized what was happening and quickly cut that shit off. His words flooded her senses, offering an alternative path for her thoughts to follow. Her green gaze narrowed at him. "A punishment that was only *partially* warranted. In case you forgot..." She bit her tongue as she nearly spat out his name. "... *you* asked in our last session what *I,* as a dominant, would've done. You did not *ask* me to call you Sir; therefore, as a dominant, I wouldn't have. Or did that slip your mind, *Sir*?"

She might consider him punished enough. Not that they'd placed kissing off limits, but they were attempting to keep it from crossing into personal. He'd fucking licked her bottom lip. To make matters worse, she wanted him to do it again. *Holy fuck.* She needed to get *that* out of her head right now. Fuck... with the amount of heat pouring off the both of them at that moment, they could've started a fire in her bedroom. She didn't know what she wanted most right now. His cock in her mouth, in her ass, or in her pussy.

"Nothing *ever* slips my mind about the time I spend with you, Nia." Hunter squeezed his eyes shut for a moment, then opened them again. "But I think our perception of that conversation is a little off. I never asked you what you would do as a *dominant.* I asked you about *rewards. After* you asked me if I would like an example of the things you like to say to me. I believe I *fully* earned my reward last session. Or was I wrong about how many times I made you *come*? I told you when our first session started, when we are playing, you will call me 'sir'. That has never changed, Nia."

Oh, it was skewered all right. Hadn't she fully admitted to him she was a switch? Hadn't they completely discussed that neither of them cared for *just* her as a submissive in their playtime? "You earned it. But tell me..." She bit her tongue again, her eyes narrowing with a flash of annoyance. For the second time, she almost spat out his name. "What submissive gives a dominant *rewards*? Or have those before me completely fucked up your understanding of a D/s relationship?"

Fuck, she'd never struggled so much with the desire to use his name. Nor had she wanted him to fuck her so damn bad... in positions that they'd never attempted before. It had to be because he'd licked her lip. That made perfect sense. No, it didn't. It was a bloody load of crap. Though it had a few more images of things they *shouldn't* do popping into her head. All of which needed to go.

"No. What I think has fucked up my understanding of *everything* is spending time with you. I have never been with a switch. Things I have allowed with you, I have allowed with *no one* else. If *anyone* pulled half the shit with me you do..." He growled. "I would have walked out their door and not looked back. I have done so before. But with you... I cannot do that with you. I love it too much." He ran his thumb across her bottom lip. His lips parted, and he panted. She could hear the pounding of his heart in his chest. Hunter's fingers remained tangled in her hair as he tilted her head, and his fangs brushed against her neck, accompanied by a soft hiss. "I am trying not to completely lose it here... and you are *not* helping."

The same guttural moan that had escaped her earlier now slipped free, and he hissed in response. "Well, that fucking makes two of us," Nia spat out before she could stop herself. She didn't mean to admit that. Too late to take it back now.

Hunter trailed his nose along the length of her neck. He sucked on her throat with a moan, his grip on her hair tightening until she felt his fingers against her scalp. "So, let us lose it," he whispered, his voice gravelly.

This was a bad idea on so many levels. But, fuck... she needed him in a way that she'd never needed another. That wasn't accurate. It went much deeper than that. She yearned for what she'd only been able to get from him. And she couldn't wait a second longer. "Yes... please..." Nia bit her tongue to keep from saying his name, the effort visible in her clenched jaw. "... Sir." Even if she lost every other piece of control, she had to maintain that.

Hunter didn't say a single word as he undid every single one of her restraints, picked her up, and threw her over his shoulder. He carried her over to the bed, tossed her down on it, then flipped her around so her head partially hung off the bed. Any idea she'd previously had was gone. Nia completely enveloped him with her mouth, eliciting a loud moan of ecstasy from Hunter as he released. He spread her legs wide, his fingers tracing a path along her inner thighs. He let out his most thunderous growl yet as he pressed his mouth against her pussy and delved his tongue as far as possible.

As she swallowed every drop of cum that came out of him, the orgasm she'd been holding exploded out of her in a massive wave. A deep, guttural moan fell from her mouth, sending vibrations up his dick. Not that she wanted him to go anywhere. Nia grabbed hold of his ass, digging in with her nails. Oh no, they were far from done. She twirled her tongue around the head of his cock and skimmed her teeth along the base.

He began fucking her mouth before he finished swallowing every drop of her first release. A powerful, throaty moan came out of him, a noise he'd uttered for the first time during their last session. His claws sank into her thighs as he explored every part of her pussy with his mouth. His tongue plunged deep, tasting her, consuming her. He gently licked from her entrance to her sensitive spot before delving deep inside once more.

Holy fuck. Although she'd just had a massive release, every nerve ending in her pussy was still hypersensitive. It wouldn't take long before she came again. Which was perfectly fine. It wouldn't deter her from keeping her mouth around his hardened shaft. She needed to draw as many orgasms out of him as she could. And she knew exactly how to do it.

As Nia moaned with increasing intensity, her nails dug into his ass with more force. She sucked her cheeks inward, her teeth gently scraping against the skin, and her tongue then wrapped around him. Parting her lips slightly, she slid her tongue between his balls to taste the skin behind them, then moved on to each ball sac before repeating the sensual act. Hunter's claws dug into her flesh, an ecstatic pain coursing through her. Blood trickled across her skin, and he let out a guttural yell as he came at her with renewed ferocity.

So many unfamiliar noises came out of her she couldn't tell where any of them began and ended. Harder? He wanted her nails harder? Fuck, yes, she could absolutely do that. Nia dug her nails into his ass until she felt a warm, wet sensation beneath her fingertips.

A guttural sound, impossible to place, seemed to rumble from within him. As Hunter quickened his movements and intensified his actions, he let out a primal roar when she pitched over the edge, her climax pouring into his mouth. It just drew more noise out of her. Not that it stopped her from lathering his cock with attention. She couldn't stop. She needed more. With a single, powerful action, she had him reeling, the taste of him sweet on her tongue as pleasure took hold.

There was no telling when either of them would feel as if they'd satiated their hunger for one another, at least in this manner. Their bodies continuously begged for more. Before anything concluded, she needed his cock in her ass and in her pussy. Hunter lifted her off the bed suddenly, but with enough care to prevent her from losing her grasp on his ass or his shaft. As he turned them around, his tongue continued to pleasure her as he sat on the bed and leaned back. With deliberate movements, he carefully raised one foot onto the bed, then the other, and finally scooted back a bit. His claws sank deeper into her ass while he licked her from end to end. "Fuck my tongue, Nia."

Nia carefully arranged her legs and then spread her thighs wide. She moved her hips rhythmically, guiding his tongue to match the pace of her sucking his cock. Holy fuck, if she didn't know better, she'd swear she could feel his tongue deeper in her pussy than ever before. And being at this angle, it allowed her to switch the placement of her hands on his body as well. His mouth closed over her clit, sucking hard as his tongue fucked her. His mouth eagerly explored every part of her pussy, craving another release. Keeping his feet flat on the bed, he continued to thrust harder into her mouth, hitting the back of her throat over and over. A deep purr, vibrating in her chest, escaped her lips.

His moans, groans, and growls persisted as she ran her nails along the inside of his thigh, tugged and squeezed his balls, and deep-throated him. Gripping another section of his attractive round backside, she traced her teeth up his penis, then engulfed him completely, running her tongue along his shaft. As she quickened the movements of her mouth and intensified her actions on his tongue, he pushed her pussy harder against his mouth while increasing his own movements.

Oh, gods, she was about to come again. But she wanted to pull another one out of him at the same time. Rocking her hips quicker, she squeezed his balls, traced her thumb along the skin behind them, and dug her nails into his flesh on his thighs. His hips intensified their movements, driving his cock deeper into her mouth. She kept her orgasm at bay, anticipating his release to climax in her mouth before surrendering to her own pleasure. With the way both of their hips swung, it wasn't far off.

Hunter tore his mouth away from her sex for just a moment. "*Fuck,* come with me!" Before delving back inside with his tongue, his fangs skimmed her outer lips, and he growled as he fervently pleasured her.

Holy fuck. The image that popped into her head sent a shockwave rolling through her body. Immediately after, an enormous orgasm surged within her, erupting and flooding into his mouth like a burst dam. His cock twitched repeatedly, releasing spurts of his cum into her throat. A moan echoed from him, mirroring her own as he suckled at her pussy. Neither of them wasted a single drop.

They barely caught their breaths after their mutual orgasms concluded, and then Hunter tossed her over on the bed. He was instantly on his knees, his fingers digging into her hips, and pulled her body to his. The sound of his growl reverberated throughout the room as he forcefully penetrated her from behind. With each thrust, the Ben Wa balls remained deep inside her, shifting and creating sensations that traveled along her G-spot and vaginal walls. Nia gripped the bedding with a soft moan and moved her hips against him. It did little to impact the way his claws scored her flesh, which was a good thing. She craved to experience each thrust of his cock, every sensation from the sharpness of his claws, and every shift of the balls within her. She wanted all of it. "Fuck... harder..."

A powerful growl vibrated from him. Hunter dug his claws into her hips, and blood trickled down her thighs, staining her skin red. Maintaining a firm hold on her, he thrust his cock into her ass with increased intensity and speed.

"Oh, gods... yes..." She didn't care about the blood as it trickled down her thighs. She felt nothing but pure sexual bliss behind it all. Her body was already poised on the edge of another climax. The greater the force of each stroke, the more the balls moved around. Nia, her breath catching, held the comforter tightly while she arched her hips back against him.

Sliding his hands down to her thighs, Hunter widened her legs, and the soft material of the bedspread brushed her cheek as he shoved her head down closer. He firmly gripped her hips once more, emitting a steady growl as he increased the intensity of his thrusts into her rear. The new position allowed him to penetrate much deeper. The movements of the Ben Wa balls grew stronger, generating ripples of sensation throughout her core. Something he likely felt as much as she did. Fuck, she was so close to another release. "Fuck, gods... yes..." Nia bit her tongue, the metallic tang of blood a harsh reminder to keep his name unspoken. "... harder ..."

She hooked her legs behind his knees while his fingers found purchase on her thighs. He held her so tightly that she knew there would be bruises, increasing the intensity of each forceful thrust without pause. His claws sank deeper into her flesh, an ecstatic pain coursing through her. "Fuck... come... come with me," he whispered before a deafening roar escaped him as he came.

Nia's stilettos dug into his thighs, and she squeezed the bedding with a loud, husky moan. Her release burst forth. *Holy fucking shit.* Waves of pure, ecstatic sensation washed over her, making her gasp with an overwhelming sensation of joyous surprise.

Even when both of their releases had ended, Hunter didn't stop fucking her. The speed and force of his thrusts didn't wane even a little. The constant slapping of her buttocks against his pelvis resonated throughout the room, mingling with the other noises. "Harder."

A blast of heat, like a sudden fever, pulsed through her body at the utterance of that word. She happily complied. Nia dug her stilettos into Hunter's thighs with more force, drawing exquisite noises out of him. He wrapped his arm around her thigh and slipped his hand between her legs, his growl intensifying as he explored her. His fingers found her clit, and as he rubbed it in sync with his thrusts, she felt her breasts brush lightly against the duvet. As she turned her face, their eyes met, creating a spark in the air. With her cheek against the mattress, Nia shifted her hand from the comforter to pinch one of her nipples before massaging and kneading her breast.

The last thing she expected was for Hunter to flip her over. That was exactly what he did. He then positioned her legs over his thighs and drove his cock forcefully back into her ass. "Oh, fuck!" With her hand still at her breast, he seized her other hand and guided it down to her pussy. She had never experienced anal sex like this before, despite having done it many times. Holy fuck, it felt amazing. And the way he moved her hand... holy shit, he wanted to watch. Nia felt his grip on her waist tighten as she dug her stilettos into the back of his thighs and played with her nipple between her fingers while kneading her breast. Hunter watched intently as she pleasured herself by stimulating her clit with two fingers before inserting them back into her pussy, repeating the motion. The combination of it all just intensified the fire burning through her body, which made her noises grow louder.

A sound that defied description emerged from Hunter as he pushed his cock into her ass with increased speed and intensity. "Holy fuck, yes. Do not stop, Nia."

Not that she wanted to. But even if she did, she couldn't. Not with the sounds coming out of him. She needed them too much. The lengthening of his fangs made her pulse quicken as the desire to be bitten intensified. His hands kept her in place as his cock pistoned in and out of her, their conjoined noises echoing around the room. Hunter's claws plunged into her flesh, and crimson trickles of blood slid down her skin, vanishing into the soft blanket below. Nia increased the pressure as she kneaded her breast, then lifted her head to flick her tongue across her nipple. Adding to the pleasure building between them, she withdrew her fingers from her clit and pushed three fingers into her vagina, moving them in and out rhythmically. "Oh, gods!" Tense energy vibrated within her body, ready to burst forth.

"Oh... fuck, yes... make yourself come, Nia. Then I am going to taste that pussy all over again."

She dug her stilettos deeper into his thighs while quickening the pace of her fingers to synchronize with his movements inside her. A metallic, coppery scent assailed her nostrils, originating not only from her hip where blood trickled but also from the blood that was running down his thighs. With a sharp pinch to her nipple, Nia let out a cry of pleasure. A powerful climax surged through her, spilling out from her core and running down her ass onto his shaft.

A deep growl rumbled out of him. After pulling his cock out of her, Hunter removed her fingers and then slid them into her mouth. With their eyes locked, he forced her legs apart, his claws piercing her inner thighs once more. Just the look in his eyes sent a jolt of electricity through her body. As she wrapped her lips around her fingers and licked the cum from her hand, she felt the warmth intensify. Hunter leaned over and ran his tongue from her backside to her core before enclosing her sex with his lips. He let out a feral growl as he eagerly devoured her, savoring every drop of her essence. As he completed cleaning everything from her ass and pussy, Nia diligently cleaned everything from her hand. Fuck, all of that nearly had her coming all over again.

As he sat on his knees, Hunter pulled her legs over his, his knuckles brushing against her skin. "Do you want to take those out, or would you like me to?" he murmured, his thumb gently circling her clit.

That was a good question. Either way, she was certain they'd both enjoy it. Though when she had suggested them, she had imagined him removing them. Hmm, they didn't feel like they were too far up inside her. As she liked the stainless-steel ones, there wasn't a string to remove them. Nia squeezed his legs with hers, the warmth of the touch lingering before she spread her legs. "I believe you should," she purred, "Sir."

Hunter's bright-blue gaze remained fixed on her as his fangs dug into his lower lip. It required immense self-control not to clench her vaginal muscles as he slid two fingers in and out of her. Then a little further inside her, then out again. He kept going, repeating the motion until his fingertips brushed against the first Ben Wa ball.

Throughout the entire process, Nia never looked away as he extracted it from her vagina and popped it into his mouth. A small smile played on his lips as he meticulously licked up all traces of her release. Then he repeated the process with the second. *Holy fuck, that's hot.* She didn't think she'd seen anything so damn sexy.

Having licked both of them completely clean, and his fingers, too, Hunter put them over on the nightstand then settled back, drawing her legs atop his. His grip tightened as he wrapped his fingers around her wrists, pushing them above her head against the soft, yielding mattress. "Now. Where were we?" Slowly, he caressed her with the tip of his hard shaft before penetrating her. "Right here."

Nia let out a deep, guttural moan at the same time he did. As he continued pumping in and out of her, she drove her stilettos into his ass, the force of each thrust growing stronger and faster. The urge to have him bite her returned. Her body seemed to have a mind of its own as her back arched, pushing her breasts up. Hunter's fangs extended slightly further, and with a hiss-growl, he slammed harder inside her, increasing his pace.

She dug her stilettos in more and lifted her hips, meeting each of his thrusts. The heat coiling inside her core got hotter and hotter. She was so sensitive from the Ben Wa balls. The urge to feel his teeth sink into her flesh became an undeniable craving. "Bite me... please," Nia pled in a whisper. As she rocked her hips against his, she pushed her breasts out more. It wasn't where she wanted, but she couldn't ever allow him to bite her there.

As they teetered on the edge, her own control felt fragile, like a spider's silk. If she ever uttered his name or told him hers... or if he ever marked her, there would be no turning back. Those were lines they could never cross. "Bite me, please, Sir."

Their gazes remained locked as a guttural hiss escaped him. Hunter's fangs were now fully visible as he lowered his head to her, sinking them into her breast. His bite was sharp and immediate. His thrusts grew more intense, accompanied by a passionate moan, as he repeatedly entered her.

A wave of pleasure, unlike anything she'd ever known, erupted from her. A sound unlike anything she'd ever produced erupted from her mouth. It was some kind of erotic, purred moan that came from deep within her throat. There didn't seem to be any other way to describe it.

His fangs stayed embedded in her flesh as he brought her to completion with each thrust. Her stilettos dug into his ass even more forcefully as her hips continued to move in rhythm with his thrusts. Hunter pulled his mouth away as a guttural hiss resonated from his throat. "*Fuck* harder. As hard as you can."

"Oh, fuck." His fangs pierced her flesh as he latched onto her other breast, and an erotic, purred moan escaped her lips. It became easier for her to dig her heels into his backside, even though she knew she could still increase the pressure. Though it was close. Almost as close as another climax. With a rough jerk, Hunter freed her wrists, tore the tie from her braid, then plunged his fingers through her hair, finally grasping a fistful of her cinnamon-brown locks.

Fuck, she liked how that felt. With every session, it was something that became more and more common. Which had been why she'd worn it back in the first place—to mark the line. Not that it worked. She just pushed against it in other ways. Unfamiliar urges, impossible to understand, swirled through her mind. That wasn't true. She *could* explain them. The control they'd agreed to relinquish. At that moment, she was merely stopping herself from speaking his name aloud. Though she'd come close so many times because she wanted to scream it at the top of her lungs so badly. With him, everything felt extraordinary, as if the world was painted in vibrant colors. The way they connected sexually, the way he responded to all she threw at him, and then demanded more. Though she would likely wonder about it later, right then, she was a spectator, not the driver.

Nia's hands came around his back, her nails boring into his shoulder blades. A sound, like a blend of a moan, groan, growl, and snarl, rumbled from deep within him. As she pressed her stilettos into his ass with great intensity, she didn't let up, tightening her thighs around his sides to adjust their position slightly. She nipped at his ear, eliciting a guttural groan, then traced the side of his face and throat with her tongue, causing him to shiver. Hunter's head tilted to the side right before Nia sunk her teeth into his shoulder.

Hunter cried out against her, his voice echoing, as his grip on her hair tightened. "Harder... *holy fucking shit* harder!" He embraced her tightly, his claws digging into her side, as he buried his face in the curve of her neck, moving with increasing speed and intensity. He cried out again, the sound reverberating through the room, as she bit down harder on his shoulder. Nia intensified the pressure of her nails on his shoulders and gripped her thighs tighter, causing her stilettos to sink deeper into his ass cheeks. A wave of ecstasy barreled forward. Her vaginal walls clenched tight around his cock. The second they released, she was going to come hard.

"Fucking come for me, Nia! Come all over me!" His bared fangs and hiss accompanied a powerful release that momentarily left him breathless.

Her vaginal muscles released the tight hold on his cock. A massive surge of pleasure erupted within her. Its potency shredded her last bit of control. Nia bit down on his shoulder, the coppery tang of blood flooding her mouth as she screamed. Not that she'd done it to muffle the sound of her scream, but to bury the sound of his name in her mouth. *Holy fucking shit... holy fucking shit.*

Their hips didn't stop swinging. Nor did she let go of him as they continued to fuck. As much as she *should*, she simply couldn't. She didn't want to let go. Nor did she want him to let go of her. When his claws transitioned from her waist to her backside, digging in again, she craved a more intense sensation against her flesh. He grazed his fangs across her skin, sucking on her throat. As Hunter moaned, his grasp on her ass and hair intensified, and she felt a stinging sensation as a few strands of hair separated from her scalp. Her entire being vibrated with a raw, desperate need, the air itself heavy with her desire.

As Nia swept her tongue across the place she'd bitten, his deep moans echoed, and she held him closer. "Fuck, yes," he moaned against her.

Fuck, she needed more of him—all of him. After savoring the metallic tang of the blood, she bit down with more force, and her mouth filled again. But she didn't stop there. Her nails penetrated deeper into his shoulder blades.

"Nia... fuck... yes... you feel so good..." His fangs scraped over her neck. "Turn around, Nia," he panted out.

Holy fuck... yes, they needed to change positions. If they didn't, one or both of them would do something they'd never be able to turn back from. Even if she screamed his name or he cried out her real name, the way his fangs scraped across her neck, sending a sharp pain—that was the one thing she couldn't ever let him do. She couldn't ever let him mark her. Nia's grip loosened, Hunter's hands left her skin, and he withdrew from her. They both let out a noise. One she just couldn't control. Her breath came in ragged gasps, and she moved to a more stable position on her hands and knees.

Hunter kneeled behind her and softly caressed her ass before trailing his claws up her spine and down once more, his hands settling on her hips. Without hesitation, he thrust his hard shaft deep into her wet core. "Holy fuck, yes!"

"Oh, gods!" Nia cried out as she threw her head back. He gripped her hair, and as he raked his claws into her hip, a guttural moan ripped from her. She hooked her feet over his calves and with each thrust, their bodies collided in a rhythm of passion. It felt as though his cock delved further into her pussy as he widened their legs. No matter how glorious it all felt, she needed more. Her voice was full of desperation, as if her very survival depended on having all of him. She couldn't acknowledge that feeling. If she did that, it would take her completely away from every incredible sensation flooding her body. Nia focused on nothing else as she tightened her grip on his calves, her hips moving against him with a sudden, increased intensity. "Fuck... harder..."

Hunter's cock plowed into her core with more force than ever before. He clenched his fist tighter in her hair. His claws tore into her hip, and crimson rivers cascaded down her leg. "It is not enough," he moaned. "Fuck... I need more."

She agreed completely with his assessment. It wouldn't ever feel like enough, but this time in her room, here at the den, was all they could ever have. Giving her hair a hard jerk, Hunter pulled her body up against his. A deep, guttural moan left her mouth. Even though she swore it originated from deep inside, she couldn't allow herself to acknowledge the feeling. As he moved faster, one arm encircled her upper body, caressing her breast, while the other hand found its way between her thighs, stroking her clit in time with his thrusts.

Reaching back, Nia grabbed hold of one of his rear cheeks with a firm grip. With the other hand, she went in the opposite direction and grasped tight to his back. Given their height difference, it was as high as she could reach. Hunter's growl-moan echoed through the room as she pierced the soft flesh of his ass and back. But she wasn't done. Not in the least. Her hips ground back into his. As much as he needed more, so did she. Somehow, she swallowed his name before she spoke. "When you come... bite my shoulder... bite hard... please."

As Hunter's touch intensified, he massaged her breast and increased the pace on her clit. His erection hardened, his cock swelling within her. A long, drawn-out groan rolled out of him. "Holy fuck... yes... I am going to come..." He bent his head down until his mouth was level with her ear. "Come with me, Nia. Come all over me."

She knew *exactly* what she'd asked him for—a desire that was close to where she truly wanted and far away at the same time. It was better this way. As he came, he did as she requested. He bit her shoulder with a loud roar. His entire body jerked as wave after wave of cum spurted out of him and into her. As he sank his fangs in deep, blood flooded his mouth. His growling-moans filled the air as he devoured it bit by bit. His fingers closed around her throat as his fangs sank into her neck, the coppery scent of blood filling the air.

A scream of delight erupted from Nia as a wave of euphoria coursed through her. As an earth-shattering orgasm burst, her walls convulsed and opened, releasing everything within her. It seemed to have no end. It seemed his release didn't either. As they both reached their peaks, their fluids soaked his cock, spilled from her pussy, and drenched their thighs and the bedding. The aroma in her bedroom—a strong fusion of their cum, his sweat, their blood—was a novel olfactory sensation for her. It was like a perfect combination of the forest, the river, and the night sky. And she didn't want it to go away... not yet. Never.

Hunter's hand, which had been between her thighs, fell to the bed as he leaned over, shifting their bodies, so she moved her hand from his rear and placed it on the bed, next to his. Her pinky grazed his thumb, a sudden jolt of electricity. His hand shifted and settled atop hers, and the contact sent a jolt of awareness through her, especially as he threaded their fingers together. As strange as it should've felt, it didn't. It just felt... right. Even more so as her fingers curled over his. She perfectly realized what she was doing. She just couldn't stop herself. The line that they had been so desperately clinging to was becoming more and more blurred.

His hand around her throat tightened, his movements became savage, and as his fangs sank deeper into her shoulder, she craved more. She desperately clung to him, her fingers digging in, knowing this was a true refuge. Fuck, she needed more of him. So much more.

And it appeared he required just as much of her. The whimpering sounds he made while his jaw clenched on her flesh and he thrust into her with no hesitation confirmed it. An unspoken need sparked between them, their desires igniting with an electric charge of a connection neither had known they needed. Neither of them could've stopped what transpired as their bodies came together, even if they'd tried.

Gasping for air, he reluctantly pulled his jaw away from her skin, still thrusting into her while blood trickled from his fangs and dripped down his chin. "Nia... Fuck... Come... Come for me."

The noise that escaped her mouth was indescribable as a soul-shattering orgasm overtook her. Nor could she describe the force behind her release. She could have sworn she had become a volcano with how powerful it all felt, as if the earth was rumbling within her. That if she didn't hold on to him, she might fly away. As Nia dug her nails into his back, more blood welled beneath her fingers, and she squeezed his hand until her nails bit into his palm.

Hunter's thumb pressed over her jugular. Their hearts beat in sync, the pounding echoing in the abrupt silence. As sweat dripped off him, it mingled with their cum, saturating the bed underneath. He licked her shoulder, the warm, wet sensation of his tongue lapping up the blood that was still flowing. His tongue traced a path up her neck before reaching her ear. He gently bit her earlobe, his teeth grazing the sensitive skin, and gave a low growl. "I need you to come again," he whispered. "Come again for me... fuck... come all over me."

She didn't know how, but her body complied. Although she'd learned to come on command years ago, the climax that burst out of her wasn't anything like that. Her muscles clenched tightly around his cock, the sensation intense and volcanic. She came in a wave that flowed with great magnitude. The sounds that slipped through her mouth matched everything she gave him.

None of what she experienced with Hunter was like anything she had ever experienced before. It was magnificent and powerful. A driving force that required no explanation and demanded one at the same time. The more time they spent together, the more she desired, and the more of him she yearned to have. The noises he made and his body wouldn't be enough. She wanted things from him she didn't feel she deserved. Things she didn't believe she could ever have—warmth, love, intimacy.

He groaned as he pulled out of her, the final tremors of her orgasm still echoing in the air. He turned her beneath him, his fingers tracing the curve of her spine as he wrapped her legs around his waist, before he slowly slid back inside her. A growling moan vibrated out of him. His gaze met hers, and Hunter's body tensed, the stillness broken only by a shallow breath. Not that it lasted. Each thrust slammed his cock into her core anew. Each stroke was slow, unhurried. There was a brand-new passionate heat rising between them. "Hold on to me, Nia," he whispered.

Just once, she wanted to hear him call her name—*Narcissa*—not the name she used there at the den. She opened her mouth and snapped it shut. What was she doing? She couldn't tell him her name. It didn't matter how much she wanted to or how much she yearned to call his out. Except it was so much more than that. The feelings he stirred inside of her were taking root. Desires she'd buried long ago were surfacing. She felt the wall she hadn't realized she'd erected crumble, like sand in the wind. So much so that she wanted everything he was trying to give her. Things she couldn't accept. They had these few hours together. Nothing more. Just a few hours every few days.

With the way those blue orbs sparkled above her, she relented. "Okay," Nia mumbled. As she adjusted her position, lifting one leg, his eyes never strayed, watching her pull him in closer. She slowly slid her hands up his arms, enjoying the sensation of his soft fur against her fingertips, before grasping his broad shoulders. Her hips arched to receive each slow, deliberate push. It was unlike any other time they'd come together. As if they were both desperately clinging to those last few minutes. Simultaneously, something new was igniting between them.

Hunter's hands slid beneath her head, cradling it, his fingers tangling securely in her hair. Angling her head back just a touch, he sucked on her neck, right at her pulse point. "I need you... to come with me. Come with me."

She couldn't say what had made her do it. The heated gaze in those bright-blue eyes of his, the way his forehead pressed against hers, the multiple times he licked her neck, the length of his fangs, the way he said 'I need you,' or those beautiful, plump lips of his. No—it wasn't any of that. It was a desire so deep that she had thought about it several times since their second session. A desire that had risen closer and closer to the surface, especially after what had happened earlier.

While she shouldn't have given in to that yearning, she hadn't been able to stop herself, either. A deep snarl rumbled from his chest as her vaginal muscles clenched tightly around him. Nia's grip on him became a vise, her nails and stilettos slicing into his flesh. She swept her tongue along his upper lip, savoring the subtle taste before ending the kiss with a whisper of a touch. A deep, guttural moan slipped through her mouth, the sound fusing with the one that echoed out of him. A full-bodied orgasm detonated inside of her, gushing all around his cock. At the same moment, one exploded out of him. The explosion was so potent she felt it in every nerve-ending of her body.

Hunter jerked her head back and bit down on her bottom lip. His entire body shook. Every feeling in her body surged and intensified with his bite. She wanted to drive her tongue into his mouth, but she suppressed the urge. The two of them rode out their mutual releases together until the quaking of their bodies stilled. Nia unwrapped her legs from his body and removed her hands from his back. In the quiet room, with only their labored breaths audible, she was jolted back into reality.

What had she done? While she had broken no rules of the den, she had broken several of her own. That line that they'd clearly drawn. Somewhere in their agreement to lose control, they'd nearly obliterated that line. They hadn't just gone into a personal connection—it had become intimate. It wasn't something she ever allowed. Not just a conversation where they exchanged information about their past, but something more. Something that never ended well.

He withdrew his fangs and hands, then Hunter gently touched her lower lip, absorbing the tiny droplets of blood with a soft suck. His eyes locked onto hers, as if something held them. Time ticked away as the silence stretched between them. At some point, he finally pushed himself up onto his hands and knees, then sat back on his heels.

She knew what came next. His eyes traced over her body, and she couldn't allow him to clean her up. It would only strengthen the intimacy that they'd shared in this session. Before Hunter could move, Nia climbed off the bed and strode toward her bathroom. She slid the door open, disappeared inside, and shut it behind her. It didn't matter that she hadn't gotten information on what color he wanted for their next session. That was something she couldn't think about or even fret over. What they needed at that moment—distance. And a lot.

Closing her eyes, she pressed her forehead against the wooden door. "Fuck," she muttered under her breath. *Fuck, fuck, fuck, fuck.* If she thought for one second it might do any damn good, she'd hit her head against the door. But it wouldn't. She didn't know what would help. Or if anything could undo what they'd just done. Either way, leaving this bathroom while Hunter remained in her bedroom wasn't an option.

It was at least a couple of minutes before she heard his voice. Right outside her bathroom door. "We should pretend this session never happened, Nia."

With her head against the door, she could feel the sobs wracking her body as tears streamed down her cheeks. She had heard a multitude of words spoken to her over the course of her life. Many that had been hurtful, some that had been comforting, and others that had been informative. None of them had ever caused her such immense pain. Nor could she remember the last time she cried because of something uttered to her. *Pretend this session never happened.* Her throat constricted, each shallow breath a desperate plea against the crushing weight. It didn't matter that he was right—which just made it that much worse.

Nia spun, her breath hitching, the cold wood of the door pressing against her back as she sank to the floor. She brushed her hair back, then curled up, burying her face against her knees and inhaling the scent of her own skin. Tears streamed down her face, a silent scream escaping her lips as she felt herself crumbling. It felt as if her very soul had shattered into a million pieces. None of which she understood. How could she feel so empty and so broken at the same time?

The moment the door clicked shut, she allowed herself, after almost thirty years, to feel the weight of her emotions. The sobs wracked her body, tears flowing freely for the first time in her life, stinging like a fresh wound.

Eight

Hunter hadn't given himself a chance to second-guess his decision the entire way home. This wasn't *his* idea, but dinner with his twin and Hayden's new female was as far away from a *good* idea as it was possible to get right now. With a storm brewing inside him, this was going to be a disaster.

Reaching the hut, he opened the door and stepped inside. Some of Hayden's books sat in the far-right corner with a lap tray next to it containing shit for tea, a book of matches, and an unlit lantern. Though his bedroom door was shut, the lingering scent of stale alcohol still permeated the air. Hayden's door was open, but only his bedding was visible.

As Hunter closed the door behind him, he ignored the drawings tacked next to it—one of their mother and one of Elisa—as his eyes immediately went to the female standing beside Hayden. Rainbow. Merfolk—something that would have been obvious even if Hayden hadn't told him, because of the multicolored scales over her shoulders and down the backs of her arms. Her hair was pinned up, and it was a perfect match for her formal appearance. Sapphire-blue eyes. A pale-blue dress, shorter in the front and longer in the back, with an ocean design on it. Upper class without trying to look too upper class. Interesting. Standing nearly four feet shorter than Hayden.

Behave, Hunter. I mean it. Hayden reached over and took the female's hand. "Rainbow, this is my brother, Hunter. Hunter, this is Rainbow."

Hunter gave her the once-over, a subtle smirk flickering across his face.

"Do not do that," Hayden said.

"What? I am... admiring. I did not know you had it in you."

"What is that supposed to mean?"

"Just that you have expressed no kind of interest in females before. And Rainbow is..." Hunter looked her up and down again.

"Stop it, Hunter."

"I just mean she is obviously attractive. I did not know you had it in you to snag a female like this."

Rainbow squeezed Hayden's hand. "If you are attempting to insinuate there is some kind of defect with him that would prevent him from, as you so blatantly put it, *snag a female* with my appeal. I fail to see your rationale behind it."

Hunter almost laughed. Or he would have, if he did that sort of thing. This female had spunk, that was for sure. And the protective instinct she felt over his brother was so glaring it practically smacked him in the face. Something he liked. Very much. "No defect. I was just making an observation. Looks do not ultimately matter. Which is a good thing. If they did, I would never get laid."

Hayden gripped the back of his neck, his fingers tightening as he squeezed the female's hand back. Hunter stood a couple of inches taller than him, had more muscle, and had a bit more weight on him, too. *Please behave... please,* his twin thought to him.

With the mood I am in this evening, feel lucky things are going this well.

"Should we eat?" Hayden asked, his words edged with the unmistakable sound of annoyance.

Without a word to his brother, Hunter sat down on the floor near the blanket, the aroma filling his senses. "You met in the marketplace?" He reached for the plate of steak and pulled it to him, the weight of it in his hands. There was only one, and it was rare—just how he liked it. Hayden preferred fish, of which there were two. Along with some type of rolls that were probably sushi that smelled really unappetizing. And some kind of apple thing. Flavored water to drink. Quite a spread. He was interested in only one thing.

Hayden kept his hand on Rainbow's until she'd sat down, waiting until she'd gotten situated before joining her and pouring drinks.

Rainbow didn't offer an answer to his question until they nestled on the floor. With her legs tucked behind her, she crossed one ankle over the other as she settled in. "Yes, we did. He has been helping with the rebuilding of my club."

There weren't many in the marketplace, even before it had gotten destroyed. "You own a club. Nice. Which one?" Hunter used his claw to slice into the steak, the sharp sound echoing, and brought a bite up to his mouth.

Hayden silently crossed his legs, placing a fragrant plate of fish before Rainbow, another before himself, and the delicate sushi between them.

"The Mystical Moon. I had barely been open a month when everything occurred." Rainbow focused on Hayden. "I believe I saw you grab utensils, correct?"

Before Hayden could respond, Hunter swallowed the bite in his mouth and said, "I know some people who went in there. You must have gotten hit on *a lot*." No way she could still be a virgin. She was going to eat Hayden alive. The corners of his lips curled up into a smirk, almost a sneer, when he met his brother's gaze. He'd never seen them darken quite like that before. Yes, he was being a dick, showing his ass, all that jazz. And yeah, it was hurting Hayden's feelings, too. He would hate himself a little more for it later. He just didn't care right now.

He hadn't seen Nia in two days, but the feeling of emptiness in his chest had yet to subside. Normally, he liked pain. But not of this kind. *"We should pretend this session never happened, Nia."* Right... *great fucking idea, Hunter.* They should have done this little dinner thing another night. He was in a shit mood, and nothing had improved it. But Hayden had come across him this morning when he still reeked of spirits, surrounded by empty jars down by the river. He hadn't brought up rescheduling. Just begged him to behave himself. Like that ever happened when he got like this. He was actually doing well, a feat rarely seen when he was in a foul mood.

There are other places you can eat that steak, Hunter. If you cannot stop with the comments, perhaps you should go find one of those. I just wanted one night... one night, where I could introduce you to someone important to me. If you cannot give me that, you should not have come. I know you are going through something, but that is no reason to be rude and disrespectful to Rainbow.

Doing the best I can, little bro.

Well, the 'best you can' is crap.

Per usual. You seem surprised.

I am not. I suppose that is part of the problem. You are the only other person who I really care about, Hunter. I suppose I was just hoping we could have one decent dinner where we actually act like a family, instead of you acting almost like Sam.

Hunter, his face etched with anger, jabbed a finger in Hayden's direction across the blanket. *I am not like Sam.*

Well, your attitude and your comments come pretty close. I did not even think about introducing Rainbow to them. But I wanted to introduce her to you. Now... I am starting to regret that.

Hunter lowered his hand, the savory scent of the steak filling the air as he sliced another bite and ate it. *I will stop.*

"Thank you," Hayden said out loud before focusing on Rainbow. "My apologies for... *that*. Yes, I brought utensils." Taking them from the tray, he passed them out. "I hope the fish turned out okay. You can tell me if it did not. I think I am going to try one of these first," he said, gesturing to the sushi.

Hunter ignored the fork and knife his twin had laid next to his plate. He looked over at Rainbow across the blanket after swallowing his food. "If my twin did not warn you of my mood this evening, that is on him. But I will make a better effort of... *behaving* myself." He took a long, cool drink of water from his cup. "What is it like owning a club? That has got to keep you busy. Or... did, I am sure."

Before she answered, Rainbow tilted her head back and took a long sip of her water. She offered Hayden a soft smile. "Thank you. I'm certain it's wonderful." Rainbow sliced the fish, her eyes flickering to Hunter before settling on the food before her. "In response to your initial statement, it is quite possible. If my bouncers didn't handle the situation, then my only acknowledgment would be exactly what my older brother taught me." She met his gaze, lifting her eyes with a proud tilt of her head. "Lean in, grab their balls, yank, and twist."

Hayden visibly winced. Something that amused him, not that he opened his mouth just yet.

"If it's done appropriately, even a male who might typically find that pleasurable will scream and think twice before he opens his mouth again.

I don't tolerate lewd behavior of any kind in my establishment. People come to drink, eat, dance, and have a good time." Rainbow, as if she'd said nothing, popped a piece of fish into her mouth, delighting in each slow, deliberate chew. "To answer your second question, it kept me busy. The building initially appeared abandoned; however, it required some repair and a lot of cleaning. One of my sisters helped me with that. Even afterwards, I still had to vet and hire a lot of staff. Servers, bartenders, bouncers, DJs, and a team of cooks. That didn't include establishing food and drink menus, decor, advertising, and more. With rebuilds currently underway, I'm still quite busy. I have the chance to improve the building."

Using his fork, Hayden picked up a piece of sushi. He put it carefully in his mouth and chewed slowly, his eyes widening a little at the 'explosion of flavor' as he described it in his head. Little bro liked it. Big surprise. He had been delving into all kinds of culinary experiments lately, some that had boggled even Hunter's mind when he'd come across Hayden in the kitchen house.

As Rainbow spoke, Hunter listened intently, barely registering the food in his mouth. "Who the fuck would find that pleasurable?" He spared a glance over at his twin. "Maybe you *should* introduce her to Sam and our demon spawn father. I mean, if she knows how to do something like *that*... That would probably be the best thing I have ever seen in my entire life."

His brother shot him a look as he picked up a different sushi. "Do not joke about that."

He had meant nothing by it, but he knew how Hayden felt. Not just about harm coming to another—even if they deserved it, or worse—but he knew how much his brother wished that their brothers and father were the type of people he could actually feel comfortable introducing a female to. Or spending time with at all. People who actually wanted any kind of relationship with him. They just weren't the type, though. And thank the gods for that.

Despite all that, Hunter rolled his eyes. *Did not mean it like that. Lighten the fuck up.* "Just saying, more than a few around here could use treatment like that to knock them down a peg or two." He took another bite of the juicy steak, chewed it thoughtfully, swallowed, and then cut off another slice. "Sounds like a lot of work just to give people some entertainment." Hunter shrugged a little. "I would say I will come check it out sometime, when the rebuild is complete, but clubs are not my scene. I prefer other methods of... entertainment. But I have been helping sporadically in the marketplace. If you need more assistance, holler. I could at least make an attempt at leaving my shitty attitude at home. Unless any of your crew has a thing for that." The words were empty. He was far from interested in *anything* like that. But he had to forget about this *thing* he had with Nia somehow; these *feelings* that were so fucking dangerous for both of them. He had yet to figure out exactly how to do that. They had another session in two days. He had to figure this shit out or stay the fuck away from her. For good.

Hayden put the third type of sushi roll in his mouth. "I am sure it is going to be wonderful, more so than it was before."

"I'd welcome any help. There's still a lot of work to do and somewhere amidst the rebuild, I need to find a replacement DJ. Most of my crew are friendly. Some use more profanity than I would like, but I won't fault them for that. Besides, I prefer my bouncers to be tough. Keeps the riff-raff out." Rainbow smiled at Hayden, her eyes sparkling with joy. "I believe so, too." Using her fork, she picked up a piece of sushi. "You're welcome to try any of the sushi here if you'd like, Hunter."

"I cannot help you with the DJ," Hunter said. "Cannot say I know any." He'd fucked one at some point way back in the day, but couldn't have remembered her name if his life depended on it. That had been one of the first females he'd ever been with... for all of fifteen minutes before she'd been unable to take anymore. He met her at a club he shouldn't have been at, fueled by alcohol at an age he shouldn't have been drinking, and left her bleeding before her threat echoed in his ears, promising castration if he ever dared to look her way again. Back then, it was the most amusing thing he'd ever heard in his life.

The mere thought of a past sexual encounter caused a sharp pain to lance through his sternum. Could sleeping with someone new actually erase the complicated emotions he'd developed for Nia? He was out of his gods-damn mind. Maybe if he quit drinking in the evenings long enough to string two coherent thoughts together, he'd come up with something. Not likely to happen. Not soon.

Hunter's claw scraped against the plate as he cut another piece of his steak. He felt his tail start to twitch, so he stilled it by wrapping it around his leg. "I am good on the sushi. Never had it, but it never appealed to me."

He brought the bite of food to his mouth and ate it, chewing harder than was probably necessary.

"You are missing out, Hunter. It is great." Hayden put a piece of sushi into his mouth. He glanced at Hunter out of the corner of his eye, concealing his confusion and worry as he turned his attention back to Rainbow. With the last of the roll gone, he took a quick drink of water to wash it down. "So far, the Rainbow roll is my favorite, too." A small grin touched his lips as his cheeks flushed with a little heat. Hayden picked up another of the rolls with his fork. "How does the fish taste?"

Rainbow beamed. "A lot of flavor, right?"

"Definitely a lot of flavor. I like the way they mix. The others are good, too, though."

Seriously? There was a sushi roll called the *Rainbow roll*? The only reason it was Hayden's *favorite* was because of this female. Hopefully, the reason it was Rainbow's favorite was because of the taste.

"It's good. Soft, moist, not overly cooked, and it has just the right hint of lemon."

Hayden's grin widened. "I am glad you like it. I was really hoping it would turn out okay."

If you two want to get a room, there is one right behind you, Hunter thought to his twin.

Hayden's hand stopped halfway to his mouth. *Stop it, Hunter!* He thought back. *Just because she did not hear that, does not make it any less rude. Besides, we have not... done anything... yet. We have not even kissed yet.* Hayden put the sushi roll in his mouth and chewed slowly.

Really? Hunter thought back. Gods, give him a fucking break from the mushy-gushy bullshit going through his brother's head right now. *Interesting. And... why not? She is hot; you two are obviously attracted to each other. What is the hold-up?* The flush that covered Hayden's face now was amusing.

That is none of your business, but if you must know... we just met. I do not want to rush anything.

Why the fuck not?

Because. Now, stop it. Please. Hayden focused back on Rainbow as he swallowed the roll. "Mmm. That... there is almost a... nutty flavor? What is that? Is that the avocado?"

Right. Change the subject. That wasn't obvious *at all*. Hunter cut off another piece of his steak, its tender texture a delight, and chewed it slowly.

"Yes, that's right. You have a very good palate, Hayden." Rainbow procured another bite of fish.

"Thank you." Hayden smiled. "We never had much variety here, so everything just tastes... new. Even with the ingredients I have tried before, I have been noticing more of the little nuances in the flavor I did not pay as much attention to before. This is the first time I have had avocado, though." He took a drink of his water. "The Lunar roll is fantastic, too. I think it might be my second favorite. I like the way the cucumber gives it a little crunch."

"That's expected. The more you try different flavors, the more you notice how they explode on your tongue or hit your taste buds in various manners. For most sushi eaters, the seaweed is the biggest conflict. It's something you either like or you don't. Sushi can be made without it, but I think it adds a little something to the texture of the roll."

"I do not mind the seaweed. It is not my favorite part of the roll, but I agree with you. I think it adds something to the texture."

Rainbow turned her attention back to Hunter, the scent of the roll still lingering as she chewed and swallowed before speaking. "Is building things something that interests you, Hunter?"

Now that they'd finally stopped prattling on about food. Hunter swallowed the steak, the savory taste still lingering, and looked over at Rainbow. "Not in the least. I just do my part to help, like everyone else. The queen wants us involved in the marketplace rebuild, and so, we are. She has sent me a few times because..." A small smirk lifted the corners of his mouth. "... I am good with my hands."

I am going to hit you, Hayden thought to him.

Fat fucking chance. You could not even think about hitting a fly if it was buzzing incessantly in your ear.

Behave!

I do not know how to.

Yes, you do. You are just being a jerk.

Rainbow took a sip of water. "That's good to know. Then what interests you?"

Hayden silently looked at Hunter, then lifted his utensils to cut into his fish and eat a bite. Gross. Sure, he'd eat it if he had to, but Hunter couldn't understand how anyone would want to eat the shit that came out of the river. Maybe it was just the fact that fish blood tasted exceedingly different from deer or people's blood.

He put another piece of steak in his mouth, chewed slowly, then took a drink of his water. Before he answered the female, he flicked his gaze back to his brother. *Should I tell her exactly what I like to do with my free time? Or keep it vague?* Without waiting for Hayden to answer, he looked back at Rainbow. "Two things, mostly. Neither is suitable for dinner conversation. Or so my brother has informed me."

Not that Hayden knew *everything* he did in his downtime. He'd never told his twin *exactly* what he did that lined his pockets, so to speak, more than any other Informant. What had the floorboards under their home filled with more coin than anyone else in the village—except, maybe, the queen herself—had ever seen at one time in their life. His twin knew he went to the brothel—though Hayden definitely didn't have any desire to hear what went on during those visits—but details of his other... hobby... not to mention how much pleasure it brought him to carry those acts out, would likely give Hayden nightmares. He might be a bastard of a person, but he didn't want that. His twin wasn't ignorant of the darkness that lay within his soul, but that didn't mean he needed more images attributed to it in his head than were already there. "However, if you are *really* curious, I would be happy to tell you."

"Unnecessary. I trust Hayden's judgment."

An amused expression crossed Hunter's face. "That is probably a good idea. What about you, Rainbow? What do you do when you are not putting your club back together? And spending time with Hayden, but not—" He stopped mid-sentence, a small smile playing on his lips, as he felt his twin's emotions and let the words sink in. "Nevermind. I probably should not finish that sentence either." Not that he didn't want to. *Really* want to. Hayden was blushing so hard, it surprised him steam wasn't rising out of his twin.

No, you really should not. Do not even think about it, Hayden thought to him as he put another bite of fish carefully into his mouth. His free hand found Rainbow's, and he gave it a gentle squeeze.

What? I am really just curious about what the hold-up is. If the situation were reversed, I would have fucked her fifteen times over by now. At least. Wow, your eyes are really dark. That is amusing.

I am telling you—again—that it is none of your business. Stop it. Right now. Or I am locking you out of our hut tonight.

Yeah, right. Even if you did, I—unlike you—could easily find someone willing to keep me warm. You know, if there is something wrong, if you cannot get it up or something, they have herbs for that.

Hayden's jaw clenched. *I am warning you, Hunter.*

Ooh, now I am terrified.

"What is your problem?"

Though his brother hadn't meant to say the words out loud, they'd come out, anyway. His twin could not hold them back or even send them through their mindlink. Fuck, if the conversation continued this way, he might actually get a chuckle tonight. Gods, he was such a bastard.

Hunter chewed slowly, his eyes locked onto his brother, as the savory scent of steak filled the air. "Not a damn thing, Hayden." That was a lie. He knew *exactly* what his problem was. At least, part of it. He'd spent his life knowing without a doubt he would never have what was obviously growing between his brother and this female. He'd been okay with that. Fully at peace with the fact that he would always be alone, except for when he paid females for sex. Fully aware of why that was for the best. No female in existence deserved the level of darkness, malice, and depravity that came as a packaged deal with him.

And then he'd met Nia. Feelings and desires had grown—not just on his end, but hers as well. He had to grapple with the reality that she was the last person he could share such intimate experiences with. He could never share his life with her. Only a few hours every few days in the room they fucked in. Both of them pretending they still held their control; both of them pretending they hadn't grown attached to one another. Hunter flicked his gaze back to his twin's female. "Anyway. What interests you, Rainbow?"

Rainbow squeezed Hayden's hand. "Oh, please continue your statement. I'm certain it has more to do with your desire to focus on that and less with the internal struggle that seems to weigh on you. Or would you prefer we continue with your question about my interests?"

His eyes narrowed a little. She probably couldn't know the first thing about struggles, internal or external. *Especially* not with his. She might be with his brother, not him, but if he told her even a fraction of the shit in his head, she'd run for the fucking hills. "Oh, I am good with either. This dinner was supposed to be so we could get to know one another, though, yes? So, tell me *all* about your interests. But if you truly want to know what was about to come out of my mouth... I was merely wondering if you were going to be the female he finally allowed to take his virginity."

Even through the look on his twin's face, what Hunter could feel radiating out of him in waves—hurt, anger, embarrassment—he didn't stop talking. He knew he'd hate himself later, but right now, with the dull ache in his chest stubbornly refusing to fade despite his efforts and the alcohol he consumed, he was indifferent to the consequences of his actions. Even if that person was Hayden. "I mean, we are almost fifty years old. I have been fucking since we were in adolescence. But Hayden has never looked twice at a female, had no interest in them. You know, for a little while there, I thought he might be gay, but that is obviously incorrect. But *you*... there has to be something *special* about you, Rainbow. I would say something special about what is between your thighs, but he has not gotten that far yet. You caught his attention, and I am merely curious if you will be the lucky winner to cure the massive case of blue balls he *has* to have going on down there between his legs."

Rainbow glowered at Hunter. He could tell she was absolutely livid, and that just amused him all the more. She tightened her grip on Hayden's hand before she spoke. "*That* is *none* of your fucking business. Unlike you, who will stick his dick in anything that has two legs, some people not only have respect for their bodies, but they also value the bond and intimacy associated with a physical connection. Regardless of when that decision is made, it's none of your damn concern. The audacity to think otherwise is outrageous. It makes me question whether you are the male Hayden described to me, because I don't see a protector in front of me. I see a male whose own courage is faltering to the point he'd rather inflict pain on another than address his own."

Once again, if he had laughed, he'd have done so right then. He suspected that if he hadn't been Hayden's twin brother, whom he cared so much about, Rainbow would have done that thing she'd spoken about earlier and ensured a certain part of his anatomy no longer functioned correctly. Which would just be tragic. "You got a couple of things wrong there. One, my courage never falters. Two, I do not fuck *anything* on two legs, just females. And another—"

"Get out." Hayden's words came out barely audible, but Hunter didn't have any trouble hearing him. His gaze had dropped to the floor. Humiliation poured out of him in waves. Right along with an overload of embarrassment, anger, and hurt. He was even on the verge of tears, fighting to maintain composure.

Hunter raised his hands in a posture of surrender, but his sneer gave away his deception. "I did not mean to offend. Really was just curious. But I have obviously hurt your feelings. Never hard to do, I know." He ate one more bite of his steak and finished his water. "Maybe you will get lucky and she will give you a pity fuck to make you feel better."

"I said get out, Hunter. Now. If you plan on sleeping here tonight, I will sleep elsewhere, but I would like to finish dinner with Rainbow. So please just leave."

"That was the plan. I definitely need a drink. I hope the two of you enjoy the rest of your meal. It would be more enjoyable without me, I know." Hunter rose from the floor, cracked his stiff shoulders, and turned to leave the room.

Rainbow opened her mouth and snapped it shut. Not that it lasted long. "You're a selfish jerk, Hunter. I hope you find whatever answer you're looking for at the bottom of whatever bottle you intend to drown yourself in, though I highly doubt you'll succeed."

"I am going to do my very damndest." Selfish jerk was putting it *really* lightly. Maybe she could finally help Hayden see that. After his little... whatever the fuck this could be called, it shouldn't be too hard. "You have the hut tonight, Hayden. I will lay my head elsewhere." It was the last thing he said before he walked out the door. The breeze caused the parchment with the images to flutter as Hunter closed the door behind him, one of them tilting out of place.

Nia stared at her reflection a moment longer. Though her skin held a rosy hue, it couldn't capture the melancholy she felt inside. She had a just-out-of-the-shower look; her damp hair hanging down her back. She and Fallon had done this fantasy before. Like all the others, she always wore high heels. Which didn't really make sense for having just showered, but he liked it. She glanced at the stiletto heels, which stood silently by the makeup table just outside her bathroom. Gods, she just didn't have the energy to wear them today.

It had been two days since the session she was supposed to pretend hadn't happened. Not something she had any idea how to do. It just drained her emotionally. Which worked out great for a submissive. Not so much for the dominant she usually pulled on for her sessions with Fallon. Maybe this would help. She could push aside whatever she believed might have developed between her and Hunter and... let it go.

Adjusting the towel, Nia inhaled deeply, then steeled her shoulders and strode out of the bathroom, leaving a trail of dampness behind. She glanced one last time at the stilettos as she paused by her makeup table. Nope, still didn't have the energy. She slid the bathroom door shut and started toward her bed.

She felt the pressure of his fingers as they wrapped around her wrists, her arms now raised above her head. Fallon's body pressed her face-first up against the corner post of her bed, his cock grinding against her ass. "You always smell so delicious right when you get out of the shower."

Nia's eyes widened. Holy fuck. Was she *that* out of it? She knew he often camouflaged, but her bathroom had been ajar this entire time. She should have heard the door or the soft pad of his feet on the floor, but there was no sound at all. Not that it mattered, it just made their playtime a bit more natural. She struggled against his hold, as she normally would. "Get the fuck off of me!"

The more she tried to break free, the more her backside contacted his groin. Fallon groaned as an erection quickly formed, and shoved a knee between her thighs. "That will not happen. Not until I get what I want." With a quick motion, he slid his hand under the top of her towel, gently massaging and kneading her breast.

"Which is what exactly? Do you even know?" She couldn't say where the words had come from, aside from, obviously, her mouth, but they made no sense. Why would she even ask them in a fantasy rape scenario? With a shake of her head to dismiss the thoughts, Nia sank her teeth into Fallon's palm, tugging fiercely to loosen her bonds.

A deep growl left him. His hand left her breast, and then with a swift movement, he snatched the towel away, and it landed with a soft thud on the floor. "Yes, I know exactly what I want." With his knee still pressed between her thighs, it gave him plenty of access to her sex. Pushing two fingers deep inside her, he groaned as she arched her back, pressing her rear closer to him.

Nia barely bit back a moan. Yes, she knew what Fallon wanted. At that moment, what *she* wanted was for him to fuck her pussy with his fingers harder. Unlike Hunter, whom she just asked to go harder, she had to fight Fallon harder. What in the good gods was she doing? She didn't compare them! She didn't think about their differences. It was bad enough that Hunter had invaded her dreams. He had to interfere with this, too?

Nia pushed all thoughts of Hunter as far back into the recesses of her mind as she could. She had to focus on this moment with Fallon. With a desperate attempt to break free, she sank her teeth into his arm and stomped down on his foot. Given the position of his hand and knee, the stomp lacked any real impact.

As he intensified his grinding against her rear, he pushed his fingers further into her pussy, curving them against her inner walls. Her juices were already beginning to flow. "Fuck yes, you know how much I love it when you fight me."

Yes, she did. And the more she fought him, the more turned on she got. It was just how it was with Hunter, except he liked to cause her pain just as much as she liked to cause him pain. Holy fuck! "Get out!" Nia screamed. Shit! Shit! Shit! "Get out, get out, get out." She repeated like a mantra. Despite the distraction of her thoughts, her body remained in the moment, squeezing tightly around Fallon's fingers. Nia sunk her teeth into his arm once more, this time with a ferocity that drew blood.

"Fuck yes!" Releasing her wrists, he seized her hair and arched her head back against him while his fingers moved with increased speed and intensity inside her. "Give me that cum, slut. You know you want to."

For a split second, she didn't see Fallon; she saw Hunter. As a result, a soft moan slipped past her lips. His fingers stilled for only a moment. "You can't be here!" Nia blinked, and the image vanished as quickly as it had appeared. Fallon's face flooded her view. What the fuck happened? Was she losing her damn mind? As she scratched his arms, blood bloomed beneath her nails and splattered the bedpost. An orgasm surged forward, gushing all over Fallon's fingers.

"Fuck yes! Give it to me, bitch!" Fallon's fingers ravaged her pussy with a fierce snarl as she reached her climax. "You can pretend all you want to that you do not want me. This proves otherwise." With a cruel grip on her hair, he dragged her around the bed, shoving his fingers into her mouth.

Nia bit the fingers inside of her mouth until blood's coppery taste exploded on her tongue, and scratched harder at his hands. Yes, this was what she needed—pain, more pain. She had to deliver it as much as receive it. Although she knew how much he would be upset with himself afterward, she had to push Fallon to the point of slapping her again. She'd do anything to get outside of her own head, which was where Hunter seemed to linger.

Fallon shoved her over the side of the bed, forcing her body to bend and her head to hang low. One hand firmly clasped her neck, while the other tightly held her hip. Pushing her thighs apart with his knee, he let out a deep moan as he forcefully penetrated her. "Holy fuck, *yes*! Take my cock! Every fucking inch of it!"

The position he had her in made it a little more difficult to claw at him. At this angle, she could only reach the hand around the back of her neck. And she would make it hurt as much as she could. Now, if only Fallon would dig his claws into her hip like Hunter did—"Fuck! Get out! This doesn't work that way!"

More blood dripped off his hand—some landing on her skin, some on the blanket—as he drilled harder into her core. "Holy fuck, yes!"

If nothing else, regardless of how crazy she probably sounded, it didn't seem to impact how Fallon's body or hers responded physically. It seemed the harder she tried to keep it together, the worse it got. Fuck, she needed pain. That was the only thing that made her feel normal... like herself. Would it take Fallon out of the moment if she inflicted pain on herself? The probability was high. Okay. Then she just had to fight him harder to get him to cause her pain. Nia's nails scraped across his hand as she dug in deep. Even though their position was restrictive, she attempted to stomp on his foot or kick him.

"Is that the best you have got, bitch?" He laughed as he leaned in closer to her ear, his hips slamming into hers over and over. "Maybe you *do* want it. You want this cock. I can feel it. You are about to fucking drench it."

Fallon pulled out his cock and flipped her onto her back, positioning her with her ass at the edge of the bed, then spread her legs wider than ever. As he pushed her legs into the bed, his fingers dug into her, causing a sharp pain. This was good, but it wasn't enough. Then a primal growl left him as he rammed his cock into her pussy as deep as he could. With a growling moan that shook the room, an immediate orgasm seized his body. His fingers squeezed her thighs even harder as his hips jerked, his release pouring into her. Nia's second release followed right after.

Not that it stopped him. Even before his body fully relaxed from the peak, his movements became more forceful. But even this wasn't enough. She needed more pain. Nia clawed at any part she could reach—his arms, chest, and face. She didn't enjoy having to push Fallon's buttons, knowing how it made him feel, but she had no choice. It was the only way to get Hunter out of her head. To stop seeing him in places he shouldn't be. To stop comparing him to the person she was with right now. "You fucking bastard! Get out!"

"Never. I am not done fucking you yet." His fangs elongated as a deeper growl rolled out of him. Fallon reached up, his fingers tangling in her hair as he jerked her head back. His other hand grabbed her side, his fingers sinking into her flesh, making her shift from the intensity of the grip. Each time he slammed his cock back into her, it shook her body to its core. The growl rumbled from his chest, nearly shaking the bed, and his teeth broke the skin of her lip.

Nia's hands completely stilled. The line hadn't become blurred—they had obliterated it. Beyond physical intimacy, they connected with each other. For the second time, Hunter's face replaced Fallon's. It wasn't Fallon who had sunk his fangs into her lower lip. It was Hunter. Then, the last words he spoke to her replayed in her head. *We should pretend this session never happened, Nia.* Her vision blurring with tears, she balled her fist and punched the face in front of her.

"You want it rough, bitch? We can do this rough." His jaw cracked as he removed his hand, then his palm connected with her cheek. Not once, but three times. First his palm, then his knuckles, each tap echoing in the silent room, then his palm again. The coppery scent of new blood merging with the taste of what his fangs had already drawn.

Nia's tongue darted out, tracing the stinging line of her split lip. Surely, her face had bruised. For a moment, through her ragged breaths,

Fallon's face swam in her vision. Then the hold he had in her hair tightened, hard enough to pull a few strands loose... just like Hunter had done the other day. "Why won't you leave me ALONE?!" she screamed and fought back harder than she had been. Although his position hindered her, she could still maneuver a little. Nia bit the wrist closest to her mouth and clawed at his forearm.

The strong, coppery scent of his blood intensified, the crimson staining more of his light-colored fur. "Fuck yes! Fight me, bitch! Harder! Fucking bite me harder!" As he pounded into her, his fingers dug into her side, adding to the intensity of the moment. His claws extended and tore into her skin, accompanied by a sharp ripping sound.

That was exactly what she needed. Just like Hunter buried his claws in her flesh. "No!" Nia screamed. This wasn't happening. She wasn't consistently thinking about *everything* he did to her. All the ways he pleasured her body. The way they connected. They connected not merely through physical intimacy, but also through their intimate conversations. It wasn't happening! Her legs moved, drawing them up close before launching into a powerful kick.

"Yes! Fuck yes!" The rumble shifted to a moan as his cock swelled. "Fuck, I am going to come again!" No matter how much she moved her legs—pulling them in close or shoving against him—it didn't impact his ability to keep on fucking her. His grip on her side tightened, causing more blood to well up and slide over her skin.

Nia's body automatically responded to the increased pain. That beautiful sting brought her nothing but immense pleasure. Her vaginal muscles tightened and relaxed, an orgasm bursting forth, enveloping Fallon's cock. He raised one leg, placing his knee up on the bed. With the change, he could thrust himself further within her. As his claws tore down her side to her hip, digging in repeatedly, he released a deep, guttural moan.

Hunter's face materialized in her mind's eye, overshadowing the scene before her and distorting her vision. It fueled her determination, pushing her to work harder to pull her legs in, then extend them in a kicking motion.

Fallon's eyes were practically black with lust. The heat radiating off him was so intense it shimmered, as if it would pull steam from his body. Despite the orgasms he'd already had, his pulsing erection stirred within her once more. Just as he jerked back even harder on the fistful of hair he had in his grasp, Nia's foot connected with his face. A crack echoed, and suddenly blood, warm and thick, gushed from his nose, poured into his mouth, and dripped down his chin. Fallon roared, backhanding her so hard that the impact sent her sprawling onto her stomach. The burning sensation across her cheek knocked Hunter's face from her vision.

As he got onto the bed with her, his claws dug into her hip while he flipped her back over, positioning himself above her with one leg on each side, prepared to thrust his cock into her once more. The constant sting in her flesh didn't seem to help her keep anything straight. Or maybe all she could see was Hunter because, no matter how hard she pushed, she couldn't get him out of her head. "You are a selfish bastard," Nia said, her voice rising with each word. "How can I forget when you keep appearing?!"

"Maybe because I do not want to leave," Fallon snarled out. His claws left deep gouges down her sides and back, spilling blood across her skin as he jerked her body towards him, thrusting deep inside her once more. "*Fuck!* Your pussy feels so fucking good! Always so tight! Take it, you fucking slut! Take my cock!"

"That's all you care about. How good my pussy feels." Nia spat some of the blood in her mouth at him; he just licked it off his face.

It was one of the many reasons he kept coming back. Among so many others. Deep down she knew that, just as much as she knew she wanted him to come back. She didn't want to forget. But she had to; otherwise, it would ruin everything she'd built over the last thirty years. She had to stop these budding emotions. They couldn't go any further.

Despite the number of bruises covering her face, her sight hadn't been too badly affected. Nothing she'd done had stalled her feelings. If anything, she swore she just saw flashes of Hunter more. The only way she knew to stop them, to quiet her mind, was to receive more pain. To do that, she had to push harder. Nia punched Fallon in the chest. "Get out!"

"Why would I care about anything else but your sweet pussy?" Fallon smacked her hand and landed another blow to her cheek. One of his hands went to her throat, and the feel of his touch was like a viper's strike as the other curled over her shoulder, his claws disappearing into her skin. As he thrust his cock vigorously into her, his thighs spread hers even wider.

Yes. More pain. That's what she needed. Hunter wasn't gone yet. She could still see him, still feel him. The physical differences between Fallon and Hunter didn't matter. She couldn't reconcile them. All she felt was Hunter's grip on her throat, Hunter's claws in her shoulder. It wasn't Fallon fucking her; it was Hunter's cock drilling into her pussy. If she could quiet her mind or cut the emotional connection, then she'd stop seeing him.

Nia slapped at the arm curled over her shoulder and punched Fallon repeatedly in the chest. All she needed was the right opening. Then she could headbutt him. "You wouldn't. It's why you have to be in control. That way, no one knows that deep down, you're nothing but a pussy. A coward that feeds on pain."

"Only yours, you stupid bitch. I want your pain, your pussy, your cum. I want every fucking thing."

"You can't have it!" Nia screamed and used every limb that she could to fight him off. She clawed at both of his arms, across his face, and even started thrashing around with her legs.

"Yes, I can. And you are going to fucking give it to me." Fallon almost roared, the release from his cock erupting like a scalding geyser. With her body held tight, he ignored her struggle until his release emptied completely into her. As he flipped her onto her stomach and prepared to thrust back inside her, she retaliated by driving her heel into his stomach, narrowly missing his groin.

Fallon wordlessly grabbed her shoulders and plunged her upper body into the yielding mattress. His claws remained embedded in her shoulders as he leaned in, his hot breath against her ear, and snarled, "If you *ever* do that to me again... I will kill you, you fucking cunt." He raked his claws down her back, the sharp pain intensifying as he reached her hips. Nia screamed. The sensation normally registered as pleasure, but not this time. Her back burned. Her mind split in two. No matter how she pushed, Hunter would never have threatened her or hurt her that way.

Fallon shoved her knees beneath her body, and she winced as her thighs and knees got scratched. His cock pounded into her ass, intensifying the chaos in her head. Hunter had fucked her in the ass multiple times. Confusion weighed heavily on her. Nothing made sense. Her addled mind made it difficult to track exactly what her body was doing, other than fighting back.

"This... *this*... is all... you are good for," he growled out, punctuating his words with powerful thrusts.

A surge of adrenaline coursed through her, the fight blooming inside, a desperate dance against the encroaching euphoria. With one of her legs, Nia kicked out behind her over and over until her foot connected with something.

Fallon's leg jerked to the side, pulling his cock half out of her and yanking his claws from her hip. A ferocious snarl echoed around the room as he swiped his claws across her back. They gouged deep, splattering her blood back against his chest. "What did I just fucking tell you, bitch?!" With a firm hold on her hip, he forcefully pushed her back against him, plunging his cock deep inside her as another immense orgasm overtook him. Every muscle in his body seized. His hips pounded against hers repeatedly, releasing his climax into her backside, the warm sensation spilling out around his shaft and soaking the duvet below.

Each sound, each strike, each word created more of a divide in her mind, dragging her back to reality. Despite how bloody her back was at the moment, she wasn't completely there. Regardless of what he stated, it didn't stop her from kicking out at him again as she inched forward in the opposite direction.

Her foot connected with his leg, right above his knee. Fallon's claws gouged a path across her shoulder blades. More blood, smelling metallic, gushed down her back. "Did I say we were done fucking?!" He grabbed onto her hair and dug his claws into her thigh, pulling her back onto his cock. Despite all his orgasms, he was still as hard as a rock. Fallon shoved her ass down until her inner thighs pressed into the bed. He pinned her hips down as he thrust his shaft into her rear repeatedly. His growls and snarls filled the room, and she felt the searing pain as his fangs pierced her neck.

The split in her mind snapped. Every agonizing wound in her body registered at once. The deep gouges on her back and shoulder blades, the bruised and swollen face, and the marks on her thigh and hips bore silent witness to the ordeal. A warm, wet sensation traveled down her breasts, sides, and hips as she felt the blood trickling. Even how it had collected in her hair. The realization that it was Fallon atop her, fucking her in the ass—some place he never fucked her—completely settled in, along with the many injuries. *Oh, gods...* Everything hurt. "Blue," Nia said as loud as she could muster.

But the use of her safe word didn't seem to stop him. Not only had she lost complete control, but it also seemed Fallon had lost it, too. Hot tears coursed down her cheeks, blurring her vision. Uncertain of what else to do, she called her safe word out again. "Blue!" *Gods, please let it get through, please let it get through.*

She uttered her safe word one last time, Fallon's erection went limp, and his body stilled, a sudden silence falling over them. His body shook with a quiet tremor as he climbed off of her and scooted toward the edge of the bed.

Nia's ragged breaths continued. Her chest constricted, each sob a suffocating wave threatening to drown her in the abyss of dread. Her ears twitched, picking up every creak and groan as he stumbled around her bedroom. The soft clink of the wheel echoed as the sliding door to her bathroom shifted. The distinct sound of water filling her clawfoot tub followed. Something else occurred after that, but she couldn't tell for sure if it was what she thought. Not that it would surprise her if Fallon had vomited. He always hated it anytime he hurt her, and this... it was pretty bad.

One of her eyes had already swollen shut. She didn't need to look; the throbbing confirmed this was more severe than before. But she had pushed and pushed so she could get a reaction. Hunter had invaded her thoughts so deeply that she couldn't even think straight anymore. She had to get up and heal her wounds. In a second, when she could find the strength and her breathing got a little easier.

No matter how hard she tried, she couldn't move her body. Not even to shift her hands so they were beneath her chest. Her gaze flicked back to Fallon when he re-entered her bedroom and made his way to the bed. The mattress dipped slightly.

"I am going to pick you up." His voice was strained, and every word quivered, sounding slightly choked. "I will be careful."

She couldn't quite nod at his words, but she could acknowledge them. "Okay," Nia said, her voice hoarse.

She couldn't stop the groan as Fallon slid his hands beneath her and lifted her into his arms. He gently cradled her against his chest, the bed creaking as he scooted his way back off. Once he'd made it into the bathroom, he carried her to the tub and stepped into the water. Slowly, he eased down.

As soon as her thigh hit the water, she felt the burning sensation where his claws had pierced her flesh. A hiss escaped Nia as warm tears streamed down her cheeks. Immediately, she knew there was a problem and just what it was, too. "No salt. Out. Need out." The words came out in a less than coherent thought, but she had to stop him before he got too far. Otherwise, she would end up with scars that couldn't be covered. They would both suffer the consequences if that happened. Nia swallowed to wet her parched throat. "Salt in the tub. I'll scar. Take me to the shower."

Fallon jerked immediately back onto his feet. He wouldn't intentionally have put salt in the water. The only thing she could think of—her jar of bath salts. It had to be in the water. The lid must have been loose. Stepping out of the tub, he trembled violently as he carried her to the shower. There wasn't a seat or anything in here, but it was large, more than big enough for both of them standing or sitting. He eased her onto the floor and tried to lean her against the wall in a way that wouldn't aggravate any of her injuries. After moving away from her, Fallon turned on the water and stood under it, briefly scrubbing his fur to remove the lingering salt. He sat, then gently cradled her back into his embrace, her chest softly pressed against him as she rested in his lap. He didn't scrub; just sat there, letting the water cascade over both of them. The silence stretched between them as it plastered her hair and his fur to their skin, slowly rinsed the blood from her flesh, and healed her injuries.

As her body healed, the skin mended, the discoloration disappeared, and she took a deep breath. Not that any of it stopped her quiet sobs. He was crying, too. His fur hid the tears sliding down his cheeks well, but she still saw them. How could she have lost control so badly? She hadn't missed the crimson that stained his fur, the scratches on his face, and other parts of his body. Had she broken his nose?

Oh, gods... She hadn't just lost it; her control had disappeared, which impacted his control. Fallon would blame himself, but it all lay with her. All because she couldn't deal with the emotions rising inside of her from the short time that she and Hunter had together. The thoughts running through her head just made her sob harder. "I'm so sorry, Fallon," Nia hiccupped.

"No," he whispered. More tears spilled down Fallon's cheeks. "Just... stop it, Nia... please," he croaked out. "This was... me... this was on... me... Me..."

"This was my fault. I know your limits, and I lost control. I needed you to hurt me... just to get out of my head." It went beyond that. So much more than that. How did she even explain? He deserved to know the truth. If she lost him as a client, then so be it. That was a consequence she'd deal with because of her actions. She just didn't want to lose him as a friend. He was the only one she had.

During their session, her mind seemed to separate from the present, and she mixed Fallon up with Hunter. They didn't look like each other, but that didn't alter where her brain had wandered. Nothing like that had happened since her last session with Hunter. Was it because with every session they continued to grow closer? Or was it something else?

Fallon reached up and turned the hot water up a little more. He stared through the open shower door in silence. Tears heavy with emotion spilled down his face. "Why?" he whispered, his voice cracking with just that one word.

No matter how she explained it, the bottom line was that she took advantage of everything it took to anger him and get him to hurt her. So that she could get Hunter out of her head. To feel less of the emotional pain that had filled her since their last session. Nia swallowed hard, the silence amplifying the sound, and dropped her gaze to the cold tile. "That thing I told you I couldn't get out of my head... it's a new client I took on not too long ago. I broke some of my own rules. Things got personal."

As if that explained everything. It explained nothing. Despite how long Fallon had been with her, no way he understood everything, regardless of how little she'd actually said. "Our last session... things got really emotional. Things I can't allow myself to feel. To regain control, I didn't allow our normal aftercare routine. So, I got up and hid in here." Her vision blurred, each blink a fresh wave of agony. It hurt just as much to say it now as it had when those words left Hunter's mouth. Even if it was the right thing to do. "Before he left... he told me to forget the session happened."

Fallon tightened his hold around her. "Can you?"

"I've tried. I've tried so much. Pain helps, but it doesn't last. The memory just comes back... Gods, I'm so sorry, Fallon. I'm so sorry," her voice cracked. She didn't care how hard she sobbed. She deserved them just as much as she deserved the tightness in her chest. If she had been stronger, or addressed her emotions better, or canceled this session with Fallon—there were several other choices she could've made, and she hadn't made a single one of them. Instead, she'd convinced herself that this session with Fallon wouldn't be worse than the last.

Except she broke. Her mental constitution fractured, and as a result, she lost control and hurt the one person she called a friend. She wouldn't blame him if he never forgave her. Thirty years together. The two of them had nearly thirty years together and she knew the power that she held in her hands. Today, she had abused that in the worst way possible. "I'm so sorry, Fallon. I thought I was in control enough, but I wasn't. Everything just got mixed up."

Fallon tightened his hold on her even more. He cleared his throat a little. "Can you let him go? Pass him off to somebody else?"

"I tried once, but I couldn't do it." Instead, she'd stood there staring at Shalla for a minute, only to end up walking away. That had been after her fourth session with Hunter. While that had been where it really seemed like the personal started, if she was honest with herself—and given what she'd just put Fallon through, she needed to be brutal—it had started with their first session.

Her eyes remained fixed elsewhere as she spoke, never meeting Fallon's gaze. She'd seen the damage she'd done to his face. It was more than that. Despite her repeated apologies and insistence that she was to blame, Fallon would still take the fault upon himself. He always did. "I'm so sorry, Fallon. I should be able to pass him off. He's just so much in my head... the thought alone... it makes my skin crawl." Like she would lose a part of herself.

"Please stop apologizing," he whispered. He cleared his throat again. "I think you need to talk to him about it. The next time you... see him, or whatever. If you want to continue working here without getting in trouble, and the two of you cannot come up with a solution that allows you to stay professional... you are going to have to force yourself to stop having sessions with him, deal with your skin crawling... or force yourself to lie to rest what he makes you feel. Bury it. Never dig it up again. You cannot have it both ways." He'd always been blunt with her. This time, though... the words had just seemed to come out differently. With a bare hint of harshness he'd never used with her before.

As much as she had struggled with it, Fallon was right. She and Hunter had attempted to set boundaries, and they didn't just cross them; they completely trashed them. What she wanted didn't matter. She'd signed a contract thirty years ago, understanding that the owner would get value out of her. She didn't know what would happen if she ever out-served her sexual value. This was the life she'd chosen.

And she would never do this to Fallon again. She couldn't. His friendship meant too much to her. There was no doubt in her mind about what she needed to do. Not just for her own sanity, but for the life she'd created here. It wasn't much, but it was still hers. "You're right," Nia replied, her voice low. "I'll talk with Shalla and get him assigned to someone else." No matter how much it hurt, it was the right thing to do.

"I hope it works out for you, Nia. I am sorry. It is a choice you have to make."

Easing her off of his lap, Fallon stood up and used her soap to wash off. Once he finished, he left the water running, reached out of the shower's warmth, and grabbed the fluffy towel from the cabinet beside him. After roughly drying off his fur, he disposed of the towel in her hamper, then unplugged the tub so it could drain and headed into her room.

Nia waited until he had left the bathroom before she got to her feet. As she shut the water off, her eyes passed over the three fresh scars, perfectly distanced apart at an angle, midway up her left thigh. They would serve as a constant reminder of this day for both of them. Gods, she wished she could wipe their memories away. Just so she could lift the weight of what Fallon had to be feeling. Thirty years and not once had she done anything like this. Even the one time that had been the hardest session before... wasn't something that had been on purpose.

After she dried herself off, Nia slipped on her bathrobe, tugging it down to cover the fresh scars as much as possible. She crossed her bathroom and stopped in the doorway. Her gaze flicked to her bed, which Fallon had completely stripped. Then she turned her attention to the floor. Despite the black coloring, one couldn't miss the crimson that coated it. "Please let me clean this," she said. She had to do it, even though it wasn't something she usually did.

Her eyes flipped briefly to Fallon. Maybe when she talked to Shalla about Hunter, she should also talk to her about assigning Fallon to someone else. He deserved better. Someone who could help him past his self-hatred. She certainly had never been the one to help him. Not that she hadn't tried; it just never worked.

Fallon said nothing as he disappeared back into the bathroom. He returned with a bucket of soapy water and a stack of cloths. Kneeling on the floor, he kept his gaze lowered. "No, I need to... I cannot let you... I have to..." His voice trailed off. He wiped his eyes with the back of his hand. "No." It was all he said as he put a damp cloth to the floor and scrubbed.

Nia's ears twitched. She hated watching him clean up the mess on the floor. Clasping her hands together tightly, she sat on the black velvet chaise in the corner. What other choice did she have? At the moment, her normal routine didn't matter. Nothing about their session had been *normal*, even for them. Why should cleanup be any different? It didn't matter that she'd go behind him and clean it all again. Not any more than it mattered that she accepted the blame. Fallon still blamed himself, which meant *this* mess was his responsibility, not hers. That made her feel even shittier. Fresh tears streamed down her face, and she quickly wiped them away.

Footprints, splatters, and stray droplets marked the path from the bed, too. Not to mention what had splattered on one of the corner posts of her bed, the bloody handprints, and what had dripped onto the frame. Fallon's breathing sped up with each inch he cleaned. Fighting back tears, he blinked furiously, the muscles in his face tensing with each blink.

All she'd been able to do was sit there and watch. Not to mention the number of times she rubbed up and down her arms to stave off her compulsive need to jump in and take over. The cleanliness didn't matter, no matter how it looked. It wasn't done *her* way. It wasn't the way she would've done it. She'd lost track of how many times she'd stood up and paced, staring at her closet to keep from getting involved. She didn't even know how long it all took him, but finally, he finished the bedroom. Then he moved to the bathroom, which led to more rubbing up and down her arms and pacing.

Fallon cleaned the floor, thoroughly scrubbing the tub and shower down as well. With a clatter, he dumped the bucket full of crimson liquid into the toilet and flushed, then rinsed the now-ruined rags, stained dark, in the sink and placed them into the hamper, and finally put the bucket away. Even with everything completed, Nia couldn't quell the urge to clean everything immediately, using the right amount of soap and water in a specific sequence.

The cold, smooth porcelain of the sink welcomed Fallon's palms as he leaned his head against the mirror. Watching him this way brought new tears to the corners of her eyes. She had to do *something*. He was freaking out because of her.

As she walked over to the sink, he turned the cold water on and splashed it onto his face. Nia filled a glass with water and set it down, then placed a hand atop one of his. At her touch, his fingers clenched the sink's rim. "Fallon," she said firmly to get his attention. His eyes flew open. They'd been through this before, and he needed to calm down to keep from having a panic attack. "Inhale through your nose and exhale through your mouth. Slow and shallow breaths."

His face in the mirror reflected the scratches that covered his face, neck, arms, and chest. His obviously broken nose and busted lip. The darkening beneath the white fur around his eyes showed two black eyes.

"Nose hurts. Chest hurts, too," he mumbled.

"I, uh, I think your nose is broken. Should probably set it." It would hurt, but it would be easier to breathe. As for his chest... shit, had she cracked one of his ribs? Nia swallowed to wet her throat. Nothing about this was easy—not what she'd done to him, nor what he'd done to her. If she'd been smart, she would've canceled their session until her headspace improved, but she'd been confident it would be alright. They'd been okay at the end of their last session. Though she hadn't considered the two sessions she'd had with Hunter since then.

Her gaze flicked from Fallon to the sink. She had to take care of him. Provided he would allow her to do so. "Maybe check your ribs, too. Make sure it's nothing more than a fracture. Please, Fallon. Please... let me... at least do that." It wouldn't ease any of her guilt, but she wanted to make sure he was physically all right. Mentally, emotionally... that was a whole other story.

Fallon shook his head. He didn't look at Nia as he spoke. "I should go. I am going to go ahead and... go. I need... I have to get to ... the marketplace... before the vendors go home. See if I can find something... to help me sleep. I have not been sleeping well lately. Bad dreams. I left your bag... the stuff I brought you..." He gestured vaguely out of the bathroom, toward the table next to the door.

"Thank you," she replied. What else could she say? She wanted to help, but the likelihood that he'd allow her to do that was slim. Nia gripped the back of her neck. "I have some herbs I can give you... to help with sleep. If you need to go, I understand. Please let me set your nose and check your ribs before you leave." Things had never been easy afterward, but this wasn't like that. No, this... Tears slipped free, trickling down her face. Thirty years and in one session, everything changed.

Fallon just shook his head again. "It is okay. I can do it when I get home. But if you have some herbs... I would appreciate that. I will replace them the next time I return."

"Okay," Nia said. Her voice reflected how small she felt at the moment. It didn't feel like enough, but it was something. She left her bathroom and retrieved a sheer lavender pouch of herbs. He needed them more than she did. Making her way back to the bathroom, she offered them to him with a slight tremor in her hands. "There's no need to replace them."

"Yes, there is." Taking the pouch, he gave a nod of thanks, and as he closed his hand around it, he saw the glass of water that sat on the sink. He picked it up and gulped the whole glass down. He coughed twice, winced, and set the glass back on the sink. Silence stretched between them for what felt like longer than the minute or two it probably actually was. "Take care, Nia."

Fallon left the bathroom, exiting into the bedroom. Nia stood in the doorway as the sound of the door closing faded behind him.

Nia returned the book she'd finished reading to the top shelf on the bookcase. It was her day off, and she still had a rather important conversation to have with Shalla. Regardless of what she'd told Fallon the day before, she struggled to walk out of her bedroom and discuss Hunter's reassignment with Shalla. Nia gripped the back of her neck. She had delayed this long enough. Putting it off wouldn't change what needed to be done. Her session with Fallon the day before proved that.

With a weary sigh, she wiped her face and steeled herself; her resolve hardened for the challenge to come. As prepared as she would ever be, Nia left her bedroom and with a deep breath made the long trip to the front desk. Her stilettos clicked against the hardwood floor with every step she took. There were five hallways in total. The main hallway had unassigned bedrooms on each side, used mostly by the workers who waited in the front. From there, one hallway diverted to the left, and the other diverted to the right. Another hallway connected to each of those.

Those identified as submissives and dominants had rooms at the end of the left hallway. Farther back were the top earners. Although she was among them, her bedroom was on the opposite side of the building. A couple of other top earners occupied the bedrooms across from hers, but seeing as they had their bedrooms before her, she couldn't complain about it. Within her first year, she'd earned one of the larger bedrooms with its own bathroom. It worked out better for her clients, who required more discretion given their proclivities.

No matter how much it hurt, this was the right thing to do. Her time with Hunter hadn't just impacted the two of them; it had bled over into someone she cared about. She couldn't lose control like that again. Her family depended too much on her income. Not to mention the way she'd hurt Fallon. By the time he left, she could see their relationship would never be the same.

Nia's pace slowed the closer she got to the reception area. Her only saving grace. At this time of day, there wouldn't be anyone in the waiting room. Walking the last few steps, she paused by the front desk and knocked lightly on the wall. "Hey, uh, Shalla, can I talk to you for a second?"

The female looked at her. "Of course, Nia. What can I do for you?"

I need to do this for my family and for Fallon. They deserved nothing but the best from her. "I need Hunter assigned to another worker." A cold sweat slicked her skin as the words clawed their way out, each syllable a struggle against an invisible force.

Shalla turned her chair and draped one leg over the other. "Are you sure? He seems satisfied with you, if that's what you're concerned about."

"No, it's nothing like that." Shit. It hadn't occurred to her to come up with a reason. Something she had always done when she requested a client to be moved to another worker. And she usually knew who would serve them best. But she hadn't thoroughly vetted Hunter as she'd done in the past with others. "I just don't think we're a good fit any longer. It would better suit him to be with... someone else." It took every ounce of willpower she had not to say 'her.' Hunter belonged with her.

"Alright." Shalla stood and went to the filing cabinet. "Do you have someone else in mind for him?"

"Unfortunately, I don't. I know he's been with Nina, Kandy, and Ivory. I don't know if he's been with Diamond, though considering how new she is, I also don't think she'd live up to his expectations." Gods, she didn't want to think about him with another female. Each breath felt like a weight crushing her chest, the words echoing in her ears like a mournful dirge. But this was best for everyone involved.

Peering over her shoulder, Shalla raised an eyebrow. "You don't have a suggestion?"

Did that need to be repeated? Obviously, a lack of recommendation wasn't like her at all. Something Shalla knew better than anyone. She'd even been able to come up with the right person for Clay after just one session. "No, I don't."

With a slight dip of her chin, Shalla closed the drawer she'd gone into and faced Nia. The female folded her arms across her chest. "Something going on? Something I should know about?"

That definitely wasn't a question she could answer. It wasn't even something she could admit to herself. Not to mention the number of ways it would impact her contract and livelihood. "Of course not. I'm a professional, Shalla. We're just not as compatible as I thought. I believe he'll be better suited to someone else."

For a second, the female didn't look as if she'd bought it. Shalla's eyebrows furrowed. "You're certain this is what you want, Nia?"

"Yes. It needs to be done." Of that, she didn't have any doubt. Her feelings didn't matter. Did she want to do this? No, of course not. She'd never been with anyone like Hunter. But they had gotten personal, and that couldn't continue. It wasn't good for either of them. But this had to be handled with finesse, which meant she needed to tell Hunter of her decision herself. "I know he has a session scheduled for tomorrow. I'll keep that and, at the end, I'll advise him of the change."

"Alright. I'll see who we haven't paired him with and go from there." She opened the top drawer of the filing cabinet again.

"Thank you, Shalla." Without waiting for a response, Nia walked away. The stilettos of her heels clicked against the floor. Her breath hitched; a chilling shadow seemed to consume her from the inside out. She'd made the request. And it left her broken in two.

Nine

Hunter took his time going to Nia's room. The last few days had gutted him. He'd spent most of it drunk, made a horrible impression at dinner when he'd met his twin's female, and had gone back and forth on his decision to even return at all. He squeezed his eyes shut, a silent scream building in his throat, imagining life without her—a desolate wasteland or a self-inflicted, agonizing wound. All the more reason he should *not* have returned to see her. Yet... here he was. Taking the path down the hall to her room for the sixth time.

It hadn't even crossed his mind to apologize for how he'd left the last session. He didn't apologize. He'd made no decision lightly. And it had been the right thing to say to her before he'd left. Forgetting that session had ever happened... forgetting how close they had gotten... how personal... how intimate... it would be better for both of them. Definitely the intelligent decision to make. Even if he couldn't, he hoped to all the gods that she had. Not that he had a lot of faith in that.

It had been his reason for deciding on things for their session today. Yes, he'd already done so much with her he'd never allowed with any other female—and loved every single moment of it. Wanted, craved, and desired more. But maybe this... maybe getting a little more out of his comfort zone would help.

Or it could just end up making things worse.

Hunter stood at her door, breathing deeply, making sure his emotions were in check. Outwardly, he was the epitome of calm. Inside, he was already half-crazed, ready to rip the door apart to get at her. Oh, yes. This session was going to go *much* better than the last.

He opened the door, slipped inside, and closed it with a soft click behind him. Nia stood in a small room off of her bedroom, one he'd not seen before. Had to be her closet, with what he could see of it. Her back was to him as she stood before a wooden dresser. Like a curious serpent, his tongue flicked out over his lips. Hades, she looked good. *Really* fucking good. Her attire consisted solely of silver, lacy panties and stiletto heels, the straps of which gracefully encircled her ankles. Her hair was down, the waves flowing freely, swaying gently against her back. She held something in her hands, her fingers tracing its contours. Nia shifted her stance just slightly, and he realized what it was.

The necklace he'd given her. It hadn't crossed his mind, but with what she was wearing... he definitely wanted her to put it on. Several more silent steps into her bedroom, and Hunter came to a stop at the foot of the bed. His eyes didn't stray from her once as he clasped his hands behind his back. "Whenever you are ready, Nia," he said calmly. "Put the necklace on. And I want you naked." He loved ripping clothing off. One thing he'd decided on today—maybe, if he took that away, it would help.

Her fingers curled a little tighter around the necklace. She cast a glance over her shoulder, a small smile gracing her face. "May I leave the high heels on, Sir?" Nia purred.

His cock hardened and thickened. *Fuck,* why did she have to do that? Not just the way she was looking at him right now, but that *fucking purr.* Holy shit, he was in trouble. The word '*Absolutely*' almost flew out of his mouth, but he bit it back. "Yes, you may."

Hunter watched as she swept her hair, and the surrounding air seemed to thicken as she wrapped the necklace around her throat, the clasp clicking softly as she fastened it. Then, with a gentle push, she closed the drawer of her dresser before proceeding, the faint scent of sandalwood lingering in the air. Taking her time, she hooked her thumbs in the sides of her lace panties and slowly peeled them down her legs, then placed them on the dresser.

He did his best not to show anything on his face. Not to let the growl rise in his chest. Not to let it be so apparent that he was salivating already. His fingers clenched together behind his back, his traitorous tongue licking over his lips again.

She turned to face him; the world seemed to slow as she met his gaze. He zeroed in on her thighs, not because he was looking at her pussy. His lip curled back, exposing his fangs, and a snarl escaped his lips before he regained control. His breath quickened with each passing moment.

Three scars. Three scars that *absolutely had not* been there four days ago when he'd left her. Perfectly distanced apart at an angle, midway up her left thigh. He could have been a complete moron, and he still would have known what species had given those to her. And what form. Claw marks of a feline shape shifter looked different from those of a canine. It could be difficult to tell unless you paid attention to that kind of thing and knew what to look for.

He knew Nia had other clients. He'd always known she had other clients. It would have been stupid to think otherwise. She'd never told him anything about them, and she wouldn't tell him now. She wouldn't tell him what had happened, wouldn't give him details about it, and wouldn't tell him who had done that to her. That crossed a line between client and worker confidentiality.

But someone had *marred* her skin—those marks certainly hadn't come from him because he'd left nothing permanent on her—and she hadn't been able to heal the injury in time before it had scarred. It wasn't so much the scar that bothered him, though; it would have been incredibly hypocritical if it had. That one of her other *clients* obviously enjoyed doing at least one thing that he enjoyed. And they'd left their mark *there*. In a place that came *extremely* close to a very significant part of the body for feline shape shifters. Like him.

A torrent of thoughts rushed through his mind, unstoppable before he could even process them. A mental checklist formed of every canine shape shifter he knew that came to the brothel. Some he'd seen here in passing over the years; others he'd just heard frequented the place. It wasn't a very long list. One in particular he would have previously sworn didn't come to see Nia—before she'd told him she was a switch, anyway. Now, he couldn't say.

Hunter squeezed his eyes shut, imagining the echoing sound of a steel door slamming shut to halt his train of thought. A sharp pain had stabbed through his chest, stealing his breath. This was definitely *not* what he needed to be thinking about. Not now. Not during their session. Maybe later, if he felt like driving himself further into insanity. The murderous impulses surging within him were a silent, unseen storm, impossible to unleash. Not unless he wanted his throat ripped out by the queen. Digging his claws into his palms until he drew blood, he focused on the sensation to force himself to take deep breaths and to calm down. With each inhale and exhale, he mentally talked himself down until his breathing evened out, his heart calmed, and the roar of rage subsided.

Hunter swallowed hard, trying to hide the desire to pry for more information. A name. It would be pointless. She wouldn't tell him. And it wasn't something he had any right to ask. He was just her client—one of many. Those scars should mean absolutely nothing. His eyes opened, and he turned his gaze back to her, with a silent question in his stare. He rolled his shoulders and neck, the pops and cracks echoing as he stretched, and then deeply inhaled and exhaled. "Are you ready to begin?"

It took Nia a second to respond. She shut her eyes, paused for a minute, and then she lifted her gaze to his. "Yes, Sir."

"Good." Any feelings about the mark on her thigh that arose needed to be ignored until it held no significance for him. Or at least until he could pretend it didn't. Until he left this session, anyway. While he was here, all he was going to focus on was his time with her. Nothing else. "Get on the bed, in the center, but stay standing." Hunter turned and headed to the wall that housed her toys. So many possibilities. But he would not get too in-depth today. Too many toys just got them into trouble. He chose a plain, black-silk blindfold, metal cuffs meant to fasten to the chains hanging from her bed, and several chain extenders. Nothing else. At least, not right now. That could change as the session went on, but this was enough for now. With everything in hand, he turned and ambled back to the bed.

Nia already stood in the center of the bed. The tips of her fingers curled around the bars, barely reaching, but just enough to grip them. He could feel the heat radiating from her body, and he could smell the sweet, heady scent of her perfume. Before climbing up to join her, Hunter set the extender chains on her bedside table with a clink. He reached behind her and gently placed the cool, silken blindfold over her eyes. "Can you see anything, Nia?" He secured her wrists, first with the left cuff, then the right, as he waited for her response. Remembering the way her fingers had gripped the bars, he cautiously loosened the chains and secured them to the cuffs. He wanted her arms straight above her head, and tight to allow little movement. For this portion anyway. He wasn't planning on binding her ankles.

"No, Sir," Nia replied.

"Good." Before he truly began, he planned to savor her, both in taste and in touch. Hunter's palms glided over her arms, across her shoulders, and finally, he cupped her breasts. A soft moan, like a whisper, left her mouth. A soft caress of fingers preceded his lips and tongue as they brushed down her neck, resisting the urge to tug on the chain of the necklace with his fangs. His fingers drifted downward, while his lips and tongue trailed down her back. "I want to do things just a little differently today. First, I am going to devour your pussy until you come. Many, *many* times. You must ask my permission to do so." As he moved in front of her, he continued tracing a trail of licks and soft strokes with his lips along her hipbone. His hands followed suit, caressing her ass. Hunter's tongue grazed along her pelvic bone, then his lips brushed her slit, eliciting a sharp intake of breath. "Once we are finished with that, I have some more plans for us this session."

"Yes, Sir," Nia groaned.

Fuck. Those sounds of hers. *Give me every single one, sweetheart. I want them all.* Hunter's tongue danced up her belly, pausing at the cool metal of her belly button ring. She had never worn something like that in his presence before. But he liked it. *A lot.* He hadn't noticed it when she'd originally turned around. The scars on her thigh had completely stolen his focus. He certainly noticed it now.

The silver jewelry held three sapphires: a tiny one on top, a larger one in the middle, and a star-shaped gem set in a silver crescent, accented by small diamonds. Hunter gently tugged with his fangs, a low growl rumbling in his chest, before licking around her navel. "I like this. You should wear one more often."

Nia gasped, and the metallic sound of the cuffs scraping against each other filled the air as she moaned and pulled. "As you wish, Sir."

He gave the jewelry another gentle tug with his fangs as he licked around her navel once more. "Spread your legs for me, Nia."

Once she'd done so, Hunter sat down on his ass and situated himself, so just one of his legs was between both of hers. He held her ass gently with one hand while the other slipped between her thighs. Hunter parted her pussy lips and softly drew her clit into his mouth with a deep rumble. *Holy fuck*, he had missed her taste with epic ferocity. His tongue moved leisurely across her nub while his fingers traced up and down her entrance.

"Oh, gods," Nia groaned.

He took his time teasing her already swollen bud, more so than he ever had before. With tender touches, his fingers gently caressed her opening, only grazing the surface, not pushing too far. While he maintained a firm hold, his fingers skillfully massaged and kneaded her buttocks instead of digging his claws into her.

The noises coming out of her mouth didn't stop; they only increased and got louder the more he teased her clit. "More, please, Sir," Nia pled.

The corners of his lips upturned in a smirk. Fuck yes, that's what he wanted to hear. He craved her begging and pleading; he craved her utter desperation. Every sound that escaped her lovely lips made his cock ache with desire, but in that moment, it was the least of his concerns. He was far from done teasing her. Hunter swept his tongue fully up her slit and growled against her nub. He gently bit down on it, then returned to teasing her clit. Simultaneously, he penetrated both of her entrances with his fingers—three in her pussy, two in her ass—but stopped at the second knuckle. Enough to bring her a fleeting moment of pleasure, yet leave her craving an abundance.

"More, please, Sir."

"How much more, Nia?" His words held a teasing quality, a new sound that had never been directed toward her. Hunter took her clit between his fangs once more, emitting a more intense growl against it.

"A lot more, please, Sir."

"Is this enough, Nia?" he asked, a playful lilt in his voice. The growl grew deeper as Hunter slowly stroked his tongue over her nub. His fingers delved deeper into her pussy and her ass before retreating, then plunged back in, this time passing the second knuckle. With every touch from him, the heat radiating from her intensified, amplifying the scent of her arousal.

"Oh, gods." Her neck arched back a little. "No, Sir. More, please, Sir. Much, much more, please, Sir."

Even though the blindfold obscured her face, just staring at her in her aroused state was enough to make him feel close to climax. Not that he would. He wouldn't come until he was fully inside her. "What about this?" Hunter pushed his fingers into her ass and pussy with force, exploring their depths. He skillfully stimulated her G-spot with one hand while the other hand pleasured her ass in a rapid, rhythmic motion. He eagerly sucked her clit with quick, strong motions.

"Yes, Sir," she said, her voice catching in her throat with a gasp.

Holy fucking shit, yes! Gods, he needed every single one of her moans and gasps. Hunter skillfully synchronized his movements, intensifying the pressure on her ass as he entered her, providing dual pleasure while also orally stimulating her clitoris.

"Please, don't stop, Sir."

He didn't plan to stop soon. He intended to give her many orgasms before they proceeded further. His plan for the day was to be on the receiving end, so he wanted to extract as much as possible from her before anything else happened. Gods, she tasted so fucking good. And she hadn't even come yet.

"Please, may I come, Sir?"

Against her pussy, Hunter let out a lengthy, lingering growl before responding to her. He pulled his fingers from her and reached around to deliver a sharp smack to her rear. "Yes, Nia, you may come." He let out a resounding growl as he plunged his tongue deep inside her.

"Oh, gods!" she cried out. Nia's head fell back as she tugged on the cuffs, an orgasm exploding through her, its culmination a moment of sweetness on his tongue.

Holy fuck, yes... he'd missed her taste. The chains rattled furiously as he drove at her repeatedly. Even after her body stilled, his tongue continued to tease her swollen pussy. His sharp claws pressed into her ass, not drawing blood at that moment, as his fingers resumed their movements inside her. The moans and groans coming from her mouth didn't stop. Each sound she made intensified the growl rolling out of him. He needed more. More of her noises, her pussy, her taste. More of her everything. Sliding his hand down to her knee, Hunter felt the warmth of her skin as he hooked one leg over his shoulder. After another hard smack to her ass, he tightened his grip, his claws now digging slightly into her skin. As his tongue plunged deeper into her pussy, his fingers increased their pace and pressure in her ass. *Holy fuck,* he needed her to come again. He needed her sweet nectar to fill his mouth and flow down his throat. Four days had been *far* too long. He'd been starving for her. And he fully planned to satiate his hunger before he even got close to leaving today.

Nia's leg gripped his shoulder, her muscles tensing slightly. "Harder, please, Sir."

Fuck, he wanted her stiletto digging into his back. Not something he should encourage, all things considered. He was going to encourage it anyway, even though he knew the risks. As much as she wanted him to go harder, he wanted her to do the same. His claws sank into her flesh again, his fingers delving deep inside her, as he released an even louder growl against her clit.

A deep moan left her mouth. Her leg tightened its grip, the stiletto heel digging into his back with added pressure. Not enough to puncture his flesh, though it likely wouldn't be long before it happened. "Oh, gods. May I come please, Sir?"

One taste hadn't been nearly enough. Hunter just didn't have it in him to tease her right now. With his mouth reluctantly leaving her pussy, he grunted out a single word—"Yes"—before diving back in with his tongue. With a tight grasp on her ass, he stimulated her with his tongue and fingers.

A strangled moan escaped him as Nia strained against her bonds, pressing the stiletto deeper into his back. With a cry of pure bliss, her waves of pleasure, hot and pulsing, exploded into his mouth. Hunter drank down every single delicious drop she gave him, his growl never-ending. Though he slowed down, he didn't stop.

Her sounds never relented at any moment. Though it seemed impossible, her cries of pleasure grew louder as her stiletto sank further into his back, pulling them closer. "Please don't stop, Sir. Please don't stop."

Hades himself couldn't pull him away from her sex right now. Gods, he'd never needed someone so much. It went beyond sexual desire. Far, far past. If he were honest with himself, it had been that way since their first session. No one had ever reacted to him the way Nia had. Made him feel or want things like she had. No one had ever fully and completely accepted what he needed and then begged for more. No, that was only Nia, too. They were perfect for one another. And they could never have more than this.

Shifting his hold, Hunter moved her other leg over his shoulder and let go of her buttocks before grabbing onto her other cheek. With a slight grip from both sets of claws, he raised her off the bed, aligning her pussy with his mouth. A deep, guttural moan left her mouth. Nia crossed her ankles, the sharp points of her stilettos digging into his back. The delicious bite of pain wasn't intense enough.

"Fuck harder ..." Her words temporarily trailed off. "... please, Sir."

A small smirk lifted the corners of his lips. Nuzzling her thighs, Hunter moved his head from side to side, flicking his tongue over her slit and teasing her nub. "Not yet." He resumed his slow pace. He could have stayed down here for hours and still not gotten enough of her pussy. Just as he'd predicted, a fiery inferno roared within him, and his need intensified. His hands slid from her ass to beneath her knees. Hunter gripped tightly as he spread her legs wide, feeling the warmth against him as she pressed her heels into his shoulders. With each passing moment, the sting of her stilettos intensified, sending a sharp pain down his back. Holy fuck, that felt *fantastic*. Still, he needed them harder.

The new angle also opened her pussy up even more to his tongue and fangs. This wouldn't last long. He just wanted her arousal at an extreme high before he allowed her to fuck his tongue. Only when her voice reached a high-pitched scream as she begged for a release would he let her come. His claws sank with each bite, while her body flushed hot, her heels responding by sinking into his flesh. Pressing harder, she finally drew blood, and the metallic tang filled the air as she moaned again.

Hunter's claws sunk in deeper, the sound of tearing flesh as crimson trails streaked through his fingers and down her legs. A monstrous hiss tore from his lips as he broke away from her. His gaze fixed on the visible pulse of the femoral artery in her inner thigh. His hiss became more pronounced. In that moment, it took all of his willpower to override the sudden instinct that roared through him. Something he absolutely could never even think about indulging. Perhaps this position had been a bad idea. Not that he was going to stop soon. He didn't want to be anywhere right now but between her thighs, sucking and licking at the sweet nectar she gave him. With a deep growl, he intensified his grip on her legs while thrusting his tongue back into her core.

"Oh, gods," Nia cried out. Her thighs tensed for a split second. "May I come please, Sir?"

Hunter didn't answer her right away. He just continued devouring her sex, letting her anticipation and arousal intensify for a couple of minutes. He needed her to come in his mouth too badly to draw it out for too long, though. Not that he could fathom taking his mouth away from her pussy, even to answer her question. He softly murmured his approval against her, indicating his eagerness to savor her wetness. Holy fucking shit, she tasted and felt so good. *Come for me, sweetheart. Come hard.*

Nia screamed, her body convulsing as she climaxed, her release flowing into his mouth. Hunter let out a guttural growl-moan. His lips and tongue didn't part from her sex for even a moment. The savage way he feasted on her left her on his chin, but he could worry about the mess afterward. His shoulders bore the brunt of her weight as her stilettos dug in while her hips moved against his mouth. Holy fucking shit. It just made her come more. *Fuck yes, sweetheart, fuck my tongue.* He snarled menacingly as he delved deep into her core with his tongue repeatedly.

"Fuck, yes," Nia moaned. As his claws dug into her flesh, she shifted, widening her thighs to accommodate the position. Utilizing his height to her advantage, she gripped the bar and adjusted her hips for a more pleasurable experience with his tongue. "Holy fucking shit. Fuck, don't stop. Please don't stop... Sir."

Holy fucking shit was right. Hades, he'd felt nothing like this. So much more openness came with the new angle. The way she moved on his tongue made his cock pulse with an almost unbearable intensity. Drops of pre-cum glistened on the tip of his dick. But it wasn't time to move on. He didn't have any plans to stop just yet.

His mouth stayed pressed up against her pussy as it begged her body for another release. Then another. Then another still. Her cum was dripping off of his chin, but still, he didn't stop. One more. One more earth-shattering release before they moved on. But she was going to have to really beg for this one. It was going to be an orgasm like no other. *One more, sweetheart. Give me one more dose of that cum. Then you get to fuck me.*

Nothing had ever been quite like this between them. While there weren't any *glaring* differences between this session and their others—at least, not yet—everything about this session was different. Not just in this position, but in the way they were toward each other. Maybe it had something to do with the decisions he'd made for their time together today, but he didn't think that was it. No, it was something else altogether. They had gotten closer and closer over sessions, and the line they were forbidden to cross became more and more blurred. Was it even there any longer? He couldn't say with any certainty that it was. Nor could he say that he cared. Not in the least.

Hunter couldn't stop the strangled moan that vibrated out of him, not that he had any desire to stop it, either. With a slight lean and change of her legs, Nia widened her thighs. She drew him closer, and the coppery scent of his blood filled the air as she pressed her heels harder into his back. Still, it wasn't close enough. Neither of their noises ceased, mixing and echoing around the room. He buried his face deeper between her thighs, pushing his tongue as far into her pussy as possible. It didn't matter how much of her he got; none of it was enough. All of it just made him desperate for more.

A deep groan left her mouth as Nia unhurriedly rocked her hips against his tongue. "Fuck, don't stop, Hun—" Her words cut off, and she quickly corrected herself, "Please, don't stop, Sir."

She almost said his name. It should have stopped him in his tracks, immediately putting an end to this session without blinking an eye. That was crossing a line. He didn't allow his name to be used during sex. It made everything too personal. Another reason he enjoyed coming here—none of the females used their real names. Her saying even half of his name right now should have pissed him off.

It didn't.

Hunter's gaze snapped up to her face. His breathing sped up. His heart hammered against his ribs. Between his thighs, his cock throbbed and pulsated, with a few more drops of pre-cum escaping and sliding down his erection. His growls and snarls became louder, each amplifying the intense vibrations. As he moved his hands from her rear to her spine, he let her lean back further while his tongue increased its pace and intensity inside her. More ... *holy fucking shit*, he needed more...

And not just more of what he was getting from her already—he needed more of his name. More than just those three letters. He needed to hear her say the full thing. *Bad idea... Bad, bad idea...* He just didn't care.

With a shift, Nia pushed the sharp heels of her stilettos further into his back. Her movements on his tongue became more forceful and rapid. A deep, guttural moan left her mouth, followed by a strangled moan from him, slightly muffled by his mouth pressed against her sex. *Holy fucking* **shit**... *fuck yes, sweetheart, fucking ride my tongue.* That noise she made nearly had him shooting his load all over the bed. He'd hold it until he got inside her, though. Probably not a single moment longer, though. Harder... he still needed it harder. With one arm supporting her spine, Hunter slid his other hand under her thighs and pushed three fingers deep inside her. He thrust vigorously and rapidly, repeatedly delving into her deepest center, while his tongue stimulated her clitoris.

"Oh, gods," Nia moaned. "Harder, please, Sir."

Oh, fuck. She dug her heels in harder, sending them even deeper into his back. He could feel his blood coursing through his fur, creating a gentle tickling sensation on his skin. Hunter let out a thunderous growl. "You, too." As he intensified his movements with his fingers, his tongue rapidly teased her clit.

Nia gave a deep, purred moan. Matching his pace, she pressed her hips against his fingers and dug her heels in deeper. "May I please come, Sir?"

Hunter couldn't answer her at first. All of that made it impossible to do anything but continue tasting her pussy. Breaking his mouth away from her sex for just a moment, he growled out one word—"No." *Not just yet, sweetheart.* He increased the pressure and speed while sucking on her clit, his fingers penetrating deeper before curling to stimulate her G-spot. Holy shit, she was a fucking inferno at his mouth. Her scent completely enveloped him; her taste permanently etched on his tongue. And it still wasn't enough. It would never be enough.

Nia responded by riding his fingers, the rhythm of their movements now faster, digging her heels into his back with more pressure, gripping the bar above her head so tightly that her knuckles turned white, and moaning louder, the sound echoing through the space.

Another guttural growled moan left him. *Oh, holy fucking shit...* Just a little more. Then he wouldn't be able to wait any longer to indulge his need for her sweet, delectable cum filling his mouth and flowing down his throat. Taking his fingers away from her pussy, Hunter ran his fangs gently along the outer folds of her sex before reinserting his tongue. Another moan left him. Never enough. *Holy shit,* it was never enough. His tongue delved into her pussy while his thumb resumed its attention on her clit. *Give it to me, sweetheart. Give me every single bit of it.*

"Oh, gods! Please let me come, Hunt—" Nia barely cut his name off before finishing it. Not that he knew why she bothered. It would've been so damn easy to add the *-er* and cry out his name. "Please, please, let me come, Sir."

Holy fuck, yes... Not much more than the first time, but still a bit more. What it did to him; the sensations it sent roaring through him. The world burst into a symphony of color, a boundless exhilaration coursing through his veins. But he needed more... so much more... He never would have guessed how much he would crave hearing his name screamed from her lips. He'd never been so desperate for anyone or anything in his entire life. With a surge of self-control, he pulled his mouth from her sex, and granted her permission. "Fucking, come in my mouth *right now!*" As Hunter pushed her pussy towards his mouth, his claws dug into her, and he plunged his tongue deep inside her.

Nia screamed as she came, wave after wave gushing out and flowing down his throat. Hunter couldn't identify the noise that came out of him, nor did he care to put a name to it. All he cared about was swallowing every wave of her cum that filled his mouth. His claws left fresh blood marks on her ass cheeks, and her stilettos left similar marks on his back as he repeatedly delved into her sex with his tongue. *Holy fucking shit*, this orgasm was on an entirely new level. Not just more powerful than any she'd had this session, but more powerful than any she'd had with him, period. At least, it seemed like that on his end. The way her body jerked and writhed, her hips bucking against him, her thighs trembling. A surge of energy coursed through him, every part of him buzzing with a strange, electrical sensation. Hunter continued to eagerly suck and lick her pussy, ensuring his greedy mouth left not a single drop untouched.

He didn't know how long it lasted before the last wave surged out of her. After swallowing every bit with a deep growling moan, he leisurely removed his tongue from her sex and licked her pussy and thighs clean. "Do you have *any* idea how fucking delicious you are?" Hunter nuzzled her sex with care before sliding his tongue along her entrance once more.

Nia licked her lips. "If your sounds are anything to go by, Sir... delectable." She purred.

His jaw clenched, and he growled, the sound a low rumble in his chest, as her purr made his cock jerk. Hard. *No,* he was *not* going to orgasm all over the bed. Absolutely not. Though he was so damn close, it was a miracle he'd held it in so far. *Delectable* didn't even cover it. Not even close. The way she licked her lips just made him want that tongue somewhere else. Even more than he already did.

"As I stated earlier, Nia, I want to do things just a little differently today." Hunter eased her legs down slowly, then stroked his tongue up her inner thigh, her slit, and her pelvic region. He nipped at her hips, and then he delicately tugged at her belly button piercing with his fangs. "There are times I will need to be in control—*fully* in control—and I will need you to embrace that." With his tongue, he followed a path up her stomach and along her ribcage, before moving on to suck on her breasts and tease her nipples. "But I recognize the dominant in you as well. And you know how much I enjoy that part of you, too." Hunter licked her collarbone, then her neck, and finally, gave a tiny, playful bite to her ear. "Even though it is... extremely difficult for me to relinquish any control whatsoever. But I thought that today, we could do a bit of both."

Minus the noises that came out of her mouth as he'd trailed his tongue up her body, Nia didn't utter a word. Reaching over to the bedside table, he grabbed the extenders. After releasing her cuffs from the chains, he attached the extenders, then attached those to the chains at the top of her bed. Hunter lowered her to her knees, the clang of the chains echoing in the silent room as he checked the restraints. She could move as much as she needed to, but her arms would remain above her head. No touching. That was important for this session. He absolutely craved it, but that had become part of the problem. "Your arms will remain restrained above your head. But today, you are going to be a bit more in control than I have ever allowed before."

Hunter lay down on the bed, his muscles tensing as he allowed himself a moment of hesitation before pulling her close. He had never been in this position before. Not once. Never. His cock was angled upwards, firmly pressed against his stomach as he moved her pussy along the length of his pulsating erection. He couldn't stop the groan that escaped him. Holy fuck, she felt good. Even like this, it felt ...*fuck;* it felt *good* to have her on top of him.

"Today, Nia... I want you to fuck me. And you had better make it good."

"I'm going to fuck you so good, you won't want it any other way," Nia said, following it up with a purr.

Those words, not to mention that *fucking mouthwatering purr* that followed, just about did him in.

With a slight stretch, she adjusted her legs and hips, positioning her feet under his backside. "Sir," she punctuated as she swayed back, his cock head brushing against the entrance to her pussy. One thrust would bury him deep inside her.

Hunter let out a deep groan. Holy fucking shit, he couldn't wait. He'd never wanted this from anyone. But right now, it was all he wanted from her. Definitely *not* how this plan was supposed to go.

But there was no turning back now.

"I am going to come as soon as I get inside you." Grabbing onto her hips, Hunter buried his cock deep inside her. As promised, a massive orgasm erupted from him, shaking his entire body. "Oh, *fuck!*" he cried out in unison with her. He let out the loudest moan yet, his head immediately pressing back into the bed, and his body arching with the strain. With each jerk of his cock, his claws dug further into her flesh. *Holy fuck, holy fuck, holy fucking shit!* Before it had even ended, he thrust his hips up into hers as hard as he could. "Fuck me, Nia."

She hooked her shoes tighter, her stilettos digging into his thighs, and moved her hips. A long, drawn-out growl rolled out of him. *Oh... fuck.* Her movements were completely unhurried as she rolled her hips against his. Holy shit, he went *so* much deeper inside her. It took another minute before his climax concluded. As it did, he tightened his hold on her hips and met her thrusts, keeping his pace just as slow as hers.

Fuck. Fuck. Fuck. He should hate this. Not being fully in control. Having a female on top of him. Being in a vulnerable position like this. He should absolutely hate all of this. But that was *far* from the truth. Nope. Not even close. Not even a little. It couldn't possibly be just because he enjoyed the position. Nope. He wasn't stupid enough to believe that. It was because *she* was on top of him. *Nia* rocked her hips against his, rode him, fucked him.

Bad... this was bad... This was *so bad.* But... oh fuck, it was *so good.*

Each thrust sent shockwaves down his spine, straight to his dick and into his balls. Hunter pulled his claws from her hips and brought his hands up to her waist, mirroring her movements and pace, while still letting her lead. With as good as this felt, it wouldn't be long before he'd need to pick up the pace. But they could stick with this. For now.

Even though he was giving up control to her, it didn't feel like that. At least, not like he would normally feel at even just the thought. The weight of obedience pressed on him as he recalled every order he had to follow, every time he had to defer to another, each time he wasn't in charge. This didn't feel overbearing, stifling, constricting, suffocating. This didn't make his skin crawl. No—it felt *fucking fantastic. Looked* fucking fantastic. Even if he couldn't feel her weight on top of him, just watching her as she slowly rode his cock was utterly intoxicating. Hades, he *really* should not have chosen this position for today. This had been a *horrible* idea.

But there was no going back now. Not even if his life depended on it.

Nia used the chains, making a slight adjustment to her angle, leaning back ever so slightly with her back and hips. "Holy fuck," she moaned.

A choked moan resonated from him as he penetrated deeper, his movements stimulating her G-spot consistently. "Holy fuck is right." Hunter thrust even harder up into her, their bodies moving in a slow rhythm. As his growls intensified, his cock pressed against her core, stroking her inner walls with increased vigor. "*Fuck!* Fucking ride my cock, Nia. Gods, you feel fantastic." He hadn't meant to say the last words out loud. He'd never said those words to a female before. But he couldn't take them back. Besides, they were true.

As Nia changed the angle again, a guttural growl rumbled from his chest. She leaned forward, spread her thighs wider, and tucked her heels more against his ass. He felt a slight disappointment that the angle didn't allow her to use her stilettos on him, but the other sensations more than made up for it. Not to mention, it put her breasts more on display. Holy fucking shit, how was it possible for him to go even deeper inside her? He didn't know. All he knew was that nothing had ever come close to feeling like this.

"Holy fucking shit," Nia moaned.

Hunter, unable to restrain himself, leaned in and took her breast into his mouth, savoring the moment. His fangs pierced her skin, his tongue caressing her nipple as he sucked. With a loud moan, Nia clenched her vaginal walls. Her hips rocked faster against him. That was good because the new angle required them to quicken their pace. It was all he could do not to tighten his hold on her waist. He couldn't explain—and had no desire to look into why right now—he didn't *want* to take the control away from her. He wanted to give her more. Laying back fully, Hunter gave her waist a squeeze, the sound of their breathing filling the room as he matched her pace. "Harder... *fuck*... fuck me harder, Nia."

The way her pussy squeezed his cock was so intense, he was on the brink of climaxing for the second time. Hunter hadn't even realized he was that close already. Holy fucking shit. Her noises quickened his pulse, and the blood rushed to his groin. Made that saying all the clearer—that males could only think with one head at a time. That was certainly the case now. Before pulling her on top of him, whatever had been on his mind had vanished. The urgent need consumed him for her to ride him harder and faster, fueling their passion until they reached a mutual climax.

She widened her thighs as she shifted her feet to apply more pressure to the mattress. A guttural moan left him as her heels dug into his ass. *Fuck... yes!* Within the confines of the cuffs, she leaned forward to the maximum and upped her pace as she intensified her actions.

"Oh, gods!" she cried out.

Her intense heat surrounded his cock like a blazing fire, her inner muscles pulsating around him. He synced his movements with hers, driving deep into her over and over, his hands gripping her firmly. "Fucking come for me, Nia. Soak my dick with your cum." He bit down on her breast, feeling the soft flesh give way as he sucked hard.

Nia's emphatic scream sent shivers down his spine and heightened his arousal further. Hunter's growl joined her scream as a colossal orgasm surged through her body, completely drenching every inch of his shaft. He didn't know if one release followed another, or it was all one orgasm. Either way, it gushed out of her in one long-ass wave.

"Oh, fuck!" Nia groaned.

As she increased her speed and rode him more intensely, her stilettos pressed deeper into his ass, but they still didn't feel deep enough. He needed more. So much more of everything. "Oh, fuck yes, sweetheart, give me every fucking bit of it!" Hunter latched onto her breast, sinking his fangs into her flesh while flicking his tongue repeatedly against her nipple. Nia let out a deep, rumbling, purred moan. *Holy fucking shit,* she felt fantastic. He craved another scream, more of her moans, and the sensation of her hips moving against his. Fuck, he wouldn't be able to hold this orgasm back much longer. He thrust up into her, matching her rhythm as she rode him, battling the instinct to restrain her.

"Harder, please, Sir." Nia subtly shifted her hips, the chains above her head rattling faintly as she pulled at them. With a firmer grasp on his ass, she increased the pressure of her stilettos and widened her leg position. After settling in, she quickened her pace and pressed her pelvis more firmly against his erection.

"Oh, *fuck!* Nia! Holy *shit!*" Hunter growled out. *Fuck... yes...* He was on the very edge of an explosive orgasm like no other. Just a little more. He needed her to make his blood run until it soaked the bedding beneath him. But he wasn't the only one who wanted it harder; she did, too. And he was more than willing to give it to her.

Hunter planted his feet flat on the bed, his knees bent, and slammed his cock up into her. His fangs sank further as he eagerly sucked on her breast, his tongue lavishing it with thorough care. His grip on her ass intensified as his arms moved in sync with her, allowing her full range of motion as she took control. How was it not enough? That he *needed more* of this? How did he *like* this position? How was he already on the edge of another orgasm? He'd given up his control—at least, a good amount of it. Besides her wrists being restrained, she was in control of all of this. How the fuck was that okay with him?

Nia leaned back, leaving a little space between her back and his legs. Her thighs spread wider, her stilettos sinking as she increased the intensity of her movements against him. His dick stroked against her G-spot with each thrust, jolts of electricity shooting straight to his balls.

"Fuck..." Nia let out a soft moan.

Every inch of him was hypersensitive, in a way he'd never experienced before. The only thing he could concentrate on was the sensation of her warmth surrounding him. How he needed her to fuck him harder, faster, dig her heels more into his ass. Hunter lay back against the bed, his claws digging into her ass cheeks as she swung her hips against his repeatedly, causing his back to arch slightly. "Fuck ... fuck, Nia ... holy shit, do not fucking stop. I am going to come."

"Fuck! Please let me come, too, Sir," she cried out, digging her stilettos in for more leverage.

"Holy fuck! Fuck yes! Fucking come all over me—" A jolt of pure energy went down Hunter's spine as the words left his mouth. He felt a sharp tightening in his groin as his orgasm erupted through him like an internal explosion. A savage roar ripped out of him, echoing around the room. As his orgasm flooded into her, Hunter held her close, his release untamed and frantic, like a beast struggling to escape. It was so fucking powerful his vision blurred. His thighs gave an unexpected, violent twitch. *Holy. Fucking. Shit. YES!* "Fuck! Keep going... holy shit!"

Her vaginal muscles tightened, and she climaxed, releasing all over his erection and dripping down onto his fur. Nia's scream of orgasmic euphoria was so loud, it vibrated the air in the room. He didn't give a fuck if anyone heard it. He could listen to that fucking scream of hers all day long. Repeatedly and never even get enough of it.

The moment their mutual release had trailed off, Hunter did something he *really* shouldn't have done. He didn't even think about doing it. His body moved without his control, as if guided by an unseen force, far removed from thought. Hunter, his breath ragged, sat up, one hand anchoring him as he cupped her waist with the other. The new angle of penetration sent him reeling with pleasure, almost pushing him to the brink of climax as he relished the intimate connection. *Holy fucking shit...*

Hunter buried his face in the crook of her neck as his hips heaved up to meet hers. Her captivating scent, like a sweet perfume, embraced him and permeated his entire being. A predatory growl vibrated out of him against her throat. Reaching up blindly, he released the restraints around her wrists, then practically ripped off her blindfold. He tossed it somewhere, not giving a fuck where it actually went.

What the fuck are you doing, Hunter? What. The. Fuck. Are. You. Doing?!

Exactly what he wanted to do. And damn the consequences.

"Do not stop," he growled. "Fuck, Nia, do not stop." He needed to move his head and his mouth away from her pulse point. Away from where his fangs were itching—*begging*—to sink in. He couldn't do it. He couldn't force his body to move that way. Maybe she'd push him back on the bed and do it for him. That would be good. That would be *really* fucking good right now.

Fuck, he should *not* want that. He really should *not* want that. But, fuck him, he did.

Nia's hands came down on his shoulders. "Not stopping." As she continued to swing her hips, her fingers brushed against his fur as she shifted her hands from his shoulders to his chest and pushed him down against the bedding.

He should *not* have liked the maneuver that much, though it completely diverted his attention. Hunter let out an aggressive hiss. His fangs *did not* want to move away from the warm pulse of her throat. But his mind screamed that it was necessary. He'd bitten her on her shoulder, but there—no, absolutely not. Bad idea on so many levels.

Changing the angle again, Nia brought her body closer to him. Hunter moaned as her nails scraped across his shoulder, drawing a small amount of blood near his biceps. She nipped at his collarbone and then bit his nipple hard. His fangs grew, and a hiss, wild and untamed, escaped him. Her eyes met his as she dragged her nails across his chest and teased his nipple with her tongue. Hades, that felt phenomenal. A deep, throaty moan left him as she sat up slightly.

"Holy fuck..." Nia groaned.

'Holy fuck' was right. Holy fucking shit. Their bodies created new, heated friction when they assumed the new position. The movement of her hips dictated the tempo and the profound sensation of his cock inside her. Hunter's grip on her tightened, his claws sinking into her flesh. His hips moved to meet hers, carefully staying in sync with her rhythm. Hades, he needed more. So much more. "Harder! *Fuck!*"

Splitting her thighs as wide as they'd go, Nia dug her stilettos into his ass cheeks. The scent of copper, sharp and metallic, hung in the air, but she pressed onward. Another aggressive, but more drawn-out hiss left him. They just weren't deep enough. None of it was enough. He craved more of the punctures, the metallic tang of his blood, the mingling scent of their arousal, the musk of their releases, and every exquisite sound she produced. The depth of his cock inside her, the grinding of their hips together, left him more sexually charged than ever before. His overloaded synapses felt like they were about to explode, and his nerve endings were on overdrive. His mind was completely blank; nothing mattered but the feel of her on top of him, giving him an experience that nothing else even came close to.

The position, or even how incredible all of this felt, had nothing to do with it. It was because it was her. Because somehow, during all of their sessions, he had become comfortable enough with her to even consider something like this. Somewhere along the way—from their very first session, if he were honest with himself—he'd opened up to her. And not just that; he'd wanted to open up to her, something he didn't even do with his twin. He thought about almost nothing but her when they were apart.

Wanted to be nowhere but right back here with her. He trusted her when he didn't trust anyone. Not even himself.

No matter how idiotic, dangerous, pointless, and forbidden indulging any feelings with her was... nothing could make him care. Nothing could keep him away. He'd kept coming back, time and time again, even when he'd admitted to himself that he shouldn't. They'd gotten far too close. That things needed to end before they went even further—to a point neither of them could come back from. A point that was coming quicker and quicker each time he returned to see her.

Nia drove her nails into his chest until blood beaded beneath her fingertips. Her hips moved faster, and as she increased the intensity, a husky moan escaped her lips, which Hunter then returned. "Fuck! Harder, Hunter, harder!"

As soon as his full name left her lips—on a scream that echoed around the room—an orgasm he hadn't even known was on the edge exploded out of him. It was incredibly strong, filling her so much that it spilled out, soaking their thighs and the bed beneath him. Each syllable struck him like a blow, the impact vibrating through his very being. It stirred something within him, a feeling he wasn't even aware he possessed. Immense pride and satisfaction blasted through him. His lust, desire, and need for her intensified, crashing over him in a wave he couldn't control.

Hunter roared as he dug his claws even further into her backside. His other hand shot up and gripped her hair, clenching it. He forcefully drove his cock into her, matching each of her movements with a forceful one of his own. "Say it again, Nia," he snarled out, giving her hair a hard jerk. "Fucking say it again."

"Hunter," Nia purred. She emphasized each syllable by digging her nails into his chest more.

A savage growl practically shook the bed beneath him. *Holy fucking shit.* The sound resonated within him, vibrating with an intensity he had never felt before. "Fuck *yes!* Again!"

Her vaginal walls tightened and then loosened around his shaft. The rhythm intensified, and Nia's moan echoed in the air as her hips moved faster against him. Hunter thrust his cock deeper into her pussy, keeping pace with her movements. His tail looped around her ankle, and his hand quickly moved from her backside to her wrist. His black gaze, filled with intensity, could have ignited a spark as he locked eyes with her. "I need it harder, sweetheart. Like this." Putting her hand back against his flesh, he gouged her nails down his collarbone with a husky moan.

"Oh, fuck," she groaned. With her other hand, Nia plunged her nails into his flesh, letting the crimson blood pool before pulling them down his chest. Hunter arched his back and cried out. As he gave her hair another tug, his claws dug even further into her ass cheek. A ferocious growl rumbled from his chest as ecstasy exploded from her, soaking his cock and their entwined thighs.

"Fuck, Hunter! Harder!" Nia screamed, her voice echoing in the room as she increased the intensity of her hips.

Holy fucking shit, he was going to come again. "Fuck *yes,* sweetheart. Fucking *scream* my name." He couldn't get enough of it. Didn't think he ever could.

If she wanted harder, he could *definitely* give her harder. His grip on her hair remained firm as he pulled her chest against his. With a firm grasp on her hair and rear, Hunter kept her close to him while thrusting force-fully into her. "Like this, Nia? Is this hard enough for you?" he growled in her ear. "Or do you need this, too?" He shifted his hand to her rear, pushing three fingers into her backside and starting penetration.

Nia let out a deep, guttural moan. She turned her head slightly. Her eyes flicked to his mouth and then to his eyes. "All of it. I need all of it, Hunter." She bit his bottom lip hard and plunged her tongue into his mouth.

Hunter let out a deep, strangled moan against her lips. Sparks explod-ed through every single inch of him—mind, body, and soul. Not a single thought entered his mind about how bad this was. How dangerous. How they *absolutely, one hundred percent, should not* be doing this right now. Kissing was bad. Very bad. But how could something so bad feel so utterly and completely perfect? Like every fractured piece inside of him—at least, for right now—had been stitched back together? If they broke away from one another, he would crumble into pieces.

His hand left her hair, and he gently cupped the back of her head as the kiss intensified. Another choked moan escaped him, his tongue dancing with hers in a kiss so deep and passionate that it felt like they were sharing air. With each breath she inhaled, she was breathing it for him. *HOLY. FUCKING. SHIT.* Hunter thrust his hips forcefully, increasing the intensity as he penetrated her ass more vigorously with his fingers. Oh, fuck, he was going to come.

Throughout their kiss, Hunter's cry mingled with the sensation of her nails running along his shoulder blades and her stilettos piercing his ass cheeks. Holy fuck, that felt so good. *She* felt so good. *Everything* about her felt amazing. The delicious bites of pain were so incredible, they didn't just pull but *jerked* his orgasm out of him the same moment she exploded all over his cock. It had barely trickled off when he slid his fingers out of her, grabbed onto her ass, and rolled them over on the bed so he was on his knees. Her legs wrapped tightly around him, her backside nestled into his lap, and his elbows were digging into the soft mattress.

"It is not enough. I need more," he breathed out as his hips slammed into her repeatedly. "Fuck, Nia," Hunter moaned against her mouth. "Give it all to me, sweetheart. Give me everything." As he fused their lips again, a predatory growl emanated from his chest, and his tongue took possession of hers. All his senses focused on her totally and completely. She was all he saw, smelled, heard, felt, and tasted. The air crackled with the sexual energy that poured off of them. But it was so much more than that... so much deeper.

For the first time in his life, being with her like this—all their walls down, nothing hidden, nothing shielded—at least, in this moment... he felt whole. No longer ruined. His black heart had no cracks. His soul knew no shadow. Like it might even be possible for something *good* to exist in him. Like he wasn't just made for death and destruction, only capable of malice and acts of evil. Nia made him feel things he'd never even considered he might deserve. But right now... he felt like he did.

Nia crossed her ankles as their hips continued to meet thrust for thrust. Fuck, yes. It just brought them closer together. Still, it wasn't close enough. A moan escaped his lips as she playfully nipped his tongue, their tongues tangling again, creating a symphony of sensations. A deep growl started and persisted as her stilettos pressed into his back, and her nails raked across his skin, down his shoulder, and the back of his arm. Holy fucking shit, he couldn't even put into words how all of this felt. How alive she was making him feel. How she was making him soar. He just knew that if they stopped, he would lose his fucking mind. And not in a good way.

"I need more, Nia. Fucking make me bleed for you." His hands left her neck and her ass, sliding up into her hair. Roughly, his fingers tangled, getting a tight hold. His tongue swept along the inside of her mouth, over her teeth, then fused back together with hers. He didn't know how it was possible to fuck her any harder than he already was, but he managed it. Each powerful thrust made her body tremble as her back and neck arched, her head snapping back from the grip on her hair.

Readjusting her legs, she hooked one beneath his tail and dug her stiletto in until the coppery scent of blood filled the air, then bore in more. But she didn't stop there. With her other leg remaining locked around his waist, her stiletto pierced his back. Just above her leg, she clawed her nails into his back and raked them upwards. She adjusted her hands, driving her nails into his shoulders before pulling them down to join the existing marks.

With each sharp sting and fresh surge of blood soaking through his fur, he inched closer to another orgasm. Hunter's noises didn't cease anymore than hers did. His cock plunged into the depths of her pussy, as deep as he could go, shattering her core with every thrust. None of it was enough. It was like 'enough' was an impossible summit they just couldn't reach. Not that the both of them wouldn't continue trying.

Hunter sat up, bringing her with him, so she sat more in his lap. He leaned her back, ducking his head to sink his fangs into her breast, a low growl rumbling as she moaned, her blood a metallic tang on his tongue. A strangled moan escaped him as the sharp heels of her stilettos plunged further. As her nails raked down his arms to his elbows, his expression shifted from a growl to a snarl. Holy fucking shit, that felt magnificent. But each delicious bite of pain just made him crave even more.

The blood pooling beneath her hands and heels had no bearing on the rhythm and force of their hip motions. "Bite me harder, Hunter," she pled.

"You, too, Nia. Harder," he growled against her before sinking his fangs deeper into her breast. He shifted his grip from her ass to her hip, sinking his claws in deeply and pulling her hair forcefully.

"Oh, gods," Nia cried out in ecstasy. One stiletto punctured his ass cheek with more ferocity, and the other drove harder into his back. Her fingers danced through his fur before gouging her nails into his shoulders and scratching down his arms.

Releasing her breast, Hunter threw his head back and let out a savage hiss. "Fuck!" Holy fucking shit, that felt fantastic. Even with each fresh wound she gave him, each new wave of blood that spilled out of him, it still wasn't enough. He needed more. The delicious swirl of pleasure and pain, perfectly combined. Jerking her head closer, Hunter nipped her bottom lip with his fang, growling at the thin trickle of blood that slid down her chin. "When you come... I want you to come so hard for me I could fucking drown in it." His tongue swept across her lips, tasting the coppery tang of blood as he kissed her deeply. He increased the speed and strength of his thrusts, plunging deeper into her with a more aggressive rhythm.

Nia moaned deep in the kiss. Their tongues continued to entangle as if it symbolized the connection forged between them. Their pelvises slapped against one another with great vigor, giving each other exactly what the other desired.

With a careful shift, placing one leg atop the other, her stilettos pierced the flesh of his back. She bit down on his tongue, the coppery tang of blood flooding their mouths, and she traced her tongue across his fangs, letting out a soft purr. Words completely failed him. All he could do was let the noises fly free. Nothing existed except for Nia and the sensations running rampant through his body. A jolt of electricity shot straight to his cock. A strangled moan escaped Hunter, growing louder as Nia's nails dug into his skin, leaving bloody trails. Holy fucking shit, nothing had ever felt like this. Nothing had ever sent him soaring this way. His mind emptied, yet his body burned with heat, adrenaline, and a growing arousal fueled by her every touch.

With a shift, she found herself on her back on the bed as he kneeled above her, bringing her legs up to rest on his shoulders. With his palms planted firmly on the bed, he granted her unrestricted access to his arms and chest while penetrating her core. As Nia's fingers sifted through his fur, the sensation sent a wave of shivers down his spine. She clawed her nails down his arms, and then dragged them down his chest, leaving streaks of blood in their wake. Each slice of her nails into his flesh, drawing blood and sending jolts of pain, made his possessive growl rumble even deeper. The inferno in his body matched hers. Their heartbeats echoed in perfect time with each other, a rapid, insistent rhythm. Holy Hades, how was none of it enough? It would never be enough. He needed to own every single part of her—mind, body, and soul. And he needed her to own every single part of him. In this moment, it truly felt like they did. Like there wasn't a single part of his essence that she didn't have control of. Her body pulled responses out of him that he'd never given to anyone else.

Her pussy tightly gripped his cock, her vaginal muscles contracting rhythmically, signaling his impending orgasm. He needed to release with her, the two of them coming simultaneously, their bodies shattering and coming back together as one. "Come for me, Nia. Come all over me."

Immediately, as if her body obeyed his very command, Nia came so massively, there just weren't any words to describe it. She screamed his name, and the echo of it was enough to trigger his own release. As the most intense orgasm he'd ever felt consumed him, every muscle in his body contracted. The roar that left his body shook the walls with its intensity. His hands clenched hard, his claws ripping the bedding and slicing into his palms. His fangs throbbed with the overwhelming need to bite something. Anything.

Somehow, Hunter held back from the savage urge to bite into her throat while his instincts surged, craving what he couldn't deny. His fangs extended, his roar intensified, as he bit down on the first part of her he reached. Crimson stained her shoulder as he released the bedding, and his arms wrapped around her, his claws digging into her flesh as he held her tightly against his chest. Time didn't exist as his cum spurted out of him, filling her sex and pouring out of her, mixing with her cum and completely soaking their thighs, her ass, and the bed beneath them. No matter how many waves passed through them, none of it stopped. *Holy fucking shit.* At some point, she was sure as fuck going to come on his face this way. And if he drowned in it, so be it. He'd die the happiest motherfucker ever.

Nia cried out in pure bliss. She bit into his shoulder so hard that blood welled up, and she suckled, letting out a deep purr. It set another wave of pleasure gushing out of her body.

Hunter cried out against her. Another wave of thunderous passion exploded out of him. He bit down harder on her shoulder, the coppery tang of blood suddenly flooding his mouth. He needed her to do the same. The need was so overwhelming; it was a visceral ache that consumed him. He couldn't fathom taking his mouth away from her to utter the words, though. Hunter tightened his hold on her, feeling the warm, sticky flow of blood as his claws dug into her flesh. He stroked his tongue over her shoulder, the taste of her blood rich on his tongue, and he sucked hard. Their hips crashed together repeatedly, the fucking continuing without end.

As Nia bit down harder on his shoulder and stroked her tongue across his fur, he couldn't help but cry out again. *Holy fucking shit.* The sensation of her body, the depth of his cock inside her, every action she took, every sound she made exclusively for him, the flavor of her skin, her essence, her blood had him so intoxicated. She was like his own personal drug, able to get him higher than any substance in existence. It was so much more than that, though. He'd never felt so utterly weightless as he did right now; never had a single moment in his life where he had no worries or cares about a single thing. He'd never felt so free. All the things he'd told himself repeatedly—that it was foolish to feel for her, and not just foolish, but idiotic and dangerous—none of them seemed insane any longer. It felt insane *not* to indulge them, *not* to give in to them.

Everything she was making him feel right now... he never wanted it to go away.

Hunter couldn't fathom how they could have anything left, considering the circumstances. But somehow his body wasn't fully sated just yet. He gently lowered her legs, the cool air touching them as he removed his arms, then encircled her once more. With their bodies joined, he rolled them over on the bed, the movement gentle. He was unconcerned by the soggy, clinging feel of the bedding against his fur. He wanted to breathe in her scent, as though it were a balm, and he gloried in the marks that adorned his body, each one a testament to their connection.

Nia nestled her legs closer, pressing the sharp point of her stilettos into his backside as she moved her hips rhythmically. Because of their height difference, she tilted her head a little, but her teeth met his skin quickly. They sank back in, just centimeters from where his shoulder connected to his neck.

Hunter couldn't stop an audible gasp from leaving his mouth. While it wasn't the feline marking spot, it was *very* close. He couldn't even describe how it felt to be bitten there. How it felt to be bitten by *her* there. Even more so as she let out a purred moan against him, sending vibrations through every inch of his body. That all-consuming weightlessness renewed tenfold, his entire being drifted in a sea of utter ecstasy. As his head fell back, fangs dislodged, his eyes shut, and a long, guttural moan echoed from him.

Oh, fuck... he needed her mouth just a little further over. Needed her teeth to sink so deep into his throat, right where his pulse throbbed, that blood soaked his fur. It didn't matter what it would mean. That was precisely why he wanted it. Why he wanted—*needed* that—from *her*. Nothing about that seemed insane any longer.

Her hips began rocking against his harder and faster. Even though Hunter's fangs ached to sink into her flesh, he was frozen, only able to match each of her movements. He couldn't think. Could hardly breathe. "Nia ..." he breathed out on a moan. Her teeth left his shoulder. Hunter's eyes drifted open, and he met her gaze, a silent understanding passing between them. Possibilities instantly filled his mind. Nothing else existed but the two of them. Everything around them melted away. Their surroundings fell silent, leaving only the synchronized pounding of their heartbeats, their labored breaths, and the sound of their bodies meeting with each thrust. All he could feel was her.

"Narcissa," she said on a husky breath. It wasn't the name she'd given him when they'd first met two-and-a-half weeks ago. This was her real one.

Narcissa. Her name alone filled him with a comforting warmth, a tender affection, a feeling he'd never encountered before. He didn't know what to make of it. But he didn't fight it, either. On an instinct he had no desire to ignore, Hunter tilted his head to the side, just moments before her face closed the small distance and she bit the side of his neck—right over where his pulse point throbbed. His head fell back once more, eyes tightly closed, as he called out her name, "Narcissa," while his hold on her grew stronger. As her tongue swept over his fur, he held her mouth against his throat, and she purred as she swallowed the metallic-tasting blood. Despite having just orgasmed, he was hit with a surge of adrenaline and arousal that sent jolts of electricity through his body, culminating in a powerful climax he hadn't anticipated. As he let out a roar that resonated in the surrounding air, Hunter intensified his thrusts, drilling his cock up into her. Despite his closed eyes, an intense spark ignited within him, a feeling of ecstasy washing over him, though any visible glow remained undetectable at that moment. Without letting go of his throat, Narcissa screamed his name against his neck, her teeth sinking more into his flesh.

Holy fuck, every new orgasm he had this session was more powerful, more overwhelming, more all-consuming than the last. He didn't know how it was possible to have a single bit left, but each time he thought the release might be close to ending, a brand new wave spurted out of him, and her as well. He couldn't describe the sensations that had overtaken him.

The knowledge of what she'd just done. She had staked a claim on him. It should have surprised him that he was fully, totally, and completely okay with that. But it didn't. The intensity, strength, and depth of everything she made him feel should have frightened him where nothing else did. But he didn't feel that, either. He'd never had feelings like this before, not for anyone, but it didn't feel foreign or uncomfortable. Nothing about any of this—not this session, not her marking him—seemed anything but utterly natural.

Even after their mutual releases eventually trailed off, neither of them stopped moving their hips, though their movements became unhurried. Hunter growled her name as his claws bit just slightly into her flesh. *Holy. Fucking. Shit.* Narcissa stroked her tongue across his fur, cleaning the blood from his throat as much as possible, and bringing a low moan out of him. Fuck, that felt fantastic. Then she trailed her tongue up the side of his neck, along his jawline, and crushed her lips to his. As he tasted his blood on his tongue while entwining it with hers, his growl became more intense, matched by her soft moan that sent ripples of sensation through them. *Holy fucking shit,* nothing had ever felt this dominating. The strangest part of it was how little that bothered him. How little it bothered him too, that this female could have told him to do many things, could have told him to sprout wings and fly to the fucking moon, and he would have figured out a way to make it happen. The ramifications of what they were doing didn't matter to him in the least; they didn't even appear in his mind. He just didn't want any of it to stop. Not for the rest of his life.

He wanted to say her name out loud again and again, hear it echo around the room each time their hips ground against each other. But he couldn't fathom taking his lips away from hers. So, he said it in his mind. *Narcissa. Narcissa. Narcissa. MINE.*

A deeply-passionate, purred moan escaped her, and it evoked the deepest, most-frenzied growl he'd yet uttered. With each forceful move-ment, she clenched and relaxed her vaginal muscles around his shaft, dri-ving him closer to the edge. Holy fucking shit, he didn't have any words for how any of this felt. A strange sensation swept across his skin, like a thousand tiny needles, as if lightning had struck him. His body was a raging inferno. Hunter's teeth sank into her lip, and he growled, savoring the metallic tang of blood as he licked it away. In that instant, their eyes met, and the world seemed to fade away, leaving only the perfect clarity of the moment. "Come for me, Narcissa. Come for me now."

The deepest, most-guttural moan she'd ever uttered for him vibrated in the air as he claimed her mouth once more. It pushed another release right to the edge for him. Simultaneously, their bodies erupted in an explosion of pleasure. It was so colossal, so powerful, so overwhelming, it took over every single part of him. An ocean's worth of fluid burst free, as if a dam had broken. It was akin to a cleansing, ridding him of the darkness and evil that resided within. Their connection—a vibrant passion and an unbreakable bond—which had taken root during their very first session, had blossomed, their roots running deeper than ever. He no longer felt like himself, the male who had walked through that door for the first time two-and-a-half weeks ago. He no longer felt alone... even in his very soul. Like his spirit had merged with hers to become one. Holding her in his arms, Hunter felt like he'd finally found something he hadn't even known he was searching for.

Their chests rose and fell with ragged breaths, a rhythmic push and pull, pressing into each other. The pounding of his heartbeat still matched up perfectly in sync with hers. His cock remained buried deep inside her. The sensual kiss continued, their lips and tongues locked in a passionate embrace. Hunter slid his hand up her spine to the nape and wrapped his tail around her waist, the deep purr vibrating against her. Narcissa purred in return. He'd never felt this wholly and completely sated. His thirst was utterly quenched. His hunger fully satiated. He'd never felt this relaxed or this free. As if just holding her in his arms laid the most blissful blanket of calm over him. He couldn't give her up—ever. Narcissa belonged to him, just as he belonged to her.

Even thinking about getting off this bed and heading toward the door, let alone leaving the room, was unfathomable. He felt complete for the very first time in his life. He'd never experienced a moment of such absolute perfection. Years could have passed and he wouldn't have noticed. Nothing existed but her. He wanted to be nowhere but with her. With Narcissa—*his* Narcissa.

With the kiss done, Hunter held her close, forehead to forehead, staring deeply into her eyes. Those beautiful orbs of jade green with flecks of yellow. He didn't want this feeling to go away. For the first time in his life, he prayed to the gods that reality wouldn't seep in. That they could just stay like this, just the two of them.

Forever.

As Narcissa settled more against his chest, her magnificent purring still continuing, Hunter's only intensified. It wasn't a noise he'd ever made before. Not outside of this room, anyway. The back of her knuckles brushed against his cheek, and he couldn't help but lean into her touch. Not that he had any desire to fight the urge. The all-encompassing peace that had taken over wasn't diminishing in the least. While he was loath to shatter this illusion they'd created between them... as much as he might pray it never ended, he knew he couldn't stay here forever. At least, not today.

Hunter reached up, his rough thumb tracing the curve of her cheek in a slow, soothing motion. "We made quite a mess for me to clean up. Makes up for my missing out last time." It wasn't what was really on his mind. Not in the least. But he wasn't sure he wanted to hear the answers to the 'What now?' questions in his head. He wasn't sure it was something he'd be able to handle hearing right now.

"Yes, we did."

He gently traced the curve of her spine, the pads of his fingers following the subtle dips and swells. Never had he ever been so gentle with a female, either. It didn't feel strange, though. Because it was *her.* "I have never had a female on top of me before." Even during their last session—when he'd turned them over so she'd straddled his face, the taste of her filling his mouth as she fucked his tongue while she sucked his dick—he had never allowed a female in that position with him before, either. And this... *fuck no,* never. He was always the one in control. No one was *ever* allowed to dominate him. No one but *this* female. He hadn't felt uncomfortable or weak in allowing this. Instead, it had just made him feel powerful. Mighty. Like a god with his goddess on top of him. Like he was the pedestal holding up her perfection.

"I've never been on top of a male like this before."

With whom she was here with most people—always the submissive—that didn't surprise him. Not that she'd told him that she'd shared with anyone else she was a switch. It was just a feeling he had. If she had told everyone, it likely would have come up immediately. "You make me forget... everything. All the darkness, the bad stuff, the evil in me. When I am with you, it is like none of it exists. And when you touch me, you make me forget what covers me. It has never been like that with anyone else."

"For the first time in my life, I feel like I can see myself. Like I'm not broken or damaged. When I'm with you, it's like we're the only two in existence. You touch me, and I feel like I'm more than just a warm body. I've never had that before."

Oh yeah, he definitely understood that. And more than just in this session. When he was in this room with her, nothing and no one else existed. They were in their own little world where they were the only inhabitants. He understood the broken and damaged parts, too. It was exactly how he felt with her. "You are more than that to me, Narcissa. So much more. I have never wanted to be with anyone. Not that way. Not for more than sex. I am too damaged, broken, scarred, both inside and out. I have never been with a female who could not see past that. But you do. What I have grown to feel for you, there is nothing I would not do to keep these feelings from going away. I would break every rule, take any consequence to be with you."

Narcissa laid her head down on his chest. "I don't want what I feel for you to go away, either. We can have that..." She opened her mouth and snapped it shut. Hunter felt the separation before she even moved, his cock sliding free from her. As she sat on the bed and pulled her knees up against her, he felt a chilling wave of dread wash over him. She didn't have to say the words for him to know he'd been right. He definitely did not want to hear the answer to the unspoken question.

"You mean a lot to me, Hunter. The things I feel for you... I didn't think any of it was possible. But this is the only place we can have that. None of it can show out there."

Right... *in here* was the only place they could have this. Not out there. Not in front of anyone. Never anything but secret. He knew the rules of the den like the back of his paw. Had never once forgotten them since he first came here twenty-eight years ago. So, it wasn't as if he didn't understand. He'd known all along that what was growing between them was forbidden and would create a mess of shit that would bring an enormous amount of backlash and consequences for both of them.

He didn't care.

She obviously did.

It wasn't like he didn't have things to lose. Maybe not much, but he did. Still, he would risk that. Risk everything. Fight for something he'd never even thought would be possible for him.

Her... not so much.

Hunter's gut twisted, a surge of fiery acid burning its way up his throat. His chest constricted, as if a vise was squeezing the air from his lungs. That icy dread grew, and it felt as though he had been plunged into the biting cold of an icy river. This pain... this... *rejection* ... no, this was definitely not a pain that was enjoyable.

"I see," he muttered. He sat up slowly on the bed, his fingers gently touching the puncture wounds she'd left at his pulse point. She'd fucking marked him. Even without that, a fragile hope flickered within him for things he'd never imagined he was worthy of. Gods, he'd been so fucking stupid. *Really* fucking stupid. Of course, this *thing* between them wouldn't go beyond this room. How could it? He was who he was, and she was who she was. Apparently, not even something as extraordinary as what they'd just shared could change that. But the fucking mark... How fucking selfish of her had *that* been? "So... you get to claim me, but I do not get to claim you. You *marked* me—which I can only assume you have knowledge of what that means for my species—but I do not get to do the same. Despite what the both of us freely admit we feel for one another, what we have brought out of one another, the parts of ourselves we have given to one another... I have to continue to share you with..." A grimace, tight and angry, twisted his mouth. "How many clients do you have?"

Her jaw clenched. His eyes tracked her as she got off the bed, crossed to the closet, removed her heels and put them away, then covered herself with a black robe. Ah. So, *that* was how it was going to be. Not that he could really blame her. The tone of their conversation had shifted in the blink of an eye. Unable to sit on the bed any longer, Hunter stood up off of it and leaned against the nearest post, his arms crossed as she turned to face him.

"You think this is easy for me? You think I don't want to just run off with you? It's not that simple. You come in, pick who you plan to screw, pay, fuck, and leave. That's the extent of your involvement. Little different for those of us who are here. You can't even imagine what it's like. They even get a hint that we feel anything for each other, they'll put as much separation between us as possible. That doesn't even consider why I'm even here. Why I have spent the last thirty *solaris* of my life letting a string of endless people use my body."

"I never once said this was easy for you. Or that you did not want to leave with me. But you obviously will not, so that is a moot point. Whatever consequences or punishments would rain down on you because of this"—he gestured back and forth between them—"obviously overshadows anything you might feel. If they have *that* strong a hold on you, control you *that* much, to the point you will not even attempt to fight for something you so clearly want as much as I do—which is a phenomenon all on its own, by the way, that I would even want this for a single moment—then fine. It is what it is. But do not act as if I do not understand. Whatever reason you came here and stayed... I am sure it was a good one, whatever it is. I started coming here for a multitude of reasons, just one of which for what this place can offer that I could get nowhere else. Because that is all I deserve, Nia, a quick fuck that I have to pay for. I am no good to a female for anything else." And she proved that a bit more right now. Her job was more important and more necessary to keep, the punishments and consequences too much to bear, to fight for what they obviously had. Even after all their declarations. Even after what she'd done.

That she wouldn't leave with him, that she'd stay and continue to work here, insist that they could only ever have a relationship in secret while she continued to screw however many others... *that* wasn't even what he was the most pissed off about right now. "Even knowing *all* of that, knowing how this was going to end up, how this was going to have to be... you still did *this*." Hunter tapped the side of his throat harshly. "You still claimed me *as yours*. There are some in my species who take marking lightly, but *not* me. *Not* in this spot. When I am with a female, I am exclusive with them by choice, but *this*... You obviously have *no* idea what this meant to me. You did this knowing I would never get the same exclusivity from you. There was *no* chance of it ever happening. That was *cruel*, Nia. It was cruel, and it was selfish."

Nia flicked her gaze to him. "I didn't intend to mark you. I'm sorry that I lost complete control. But don't act like you're completely blameless in this. Or that you weren't close to doing the same damn thing yourself. I've done everything—*everything*—in my power to keep the wall between us, but you just barreled that shit down. So much to where I asked Shalla to assign you to someone else after this. Only to end up realizing that I couldn't follow through with it. No matter how hard I try, I can't seem to give you up."

Oh, she was *sorry*. *That* made it all better. "Never said I was blameless. Never said I was far from doing the same thing, either. But that is the difference here, Nia. I did not. You did." If he marked her, or things went even further and his eyes glowed... fuck, it would all be over then. He *couldn't* have her to himself. She made that abundantly clear. It would always be an impossibility, a pipe dream, something that could *never* become reality. If either of those things ever happened on his end... he'd essentially have no choice but to rip his own throat out before he went utterly insane.

That she'd asked Shalla to assign him to someone else after this... Hunter ground his jaw. He didn't fucking want anyone else. Could he even bring himself to think about sleeping with another female at this point? "I am not altogether interested in anyone else. But thank you for the heads up." His voice dripped with sarcasm, yet he remained utterly indifferent. "But, hey, since you cannot bring yourself to give me up, that certainly makes the marking make sense. You cannot give me up, but you do not want anyone else to have me, either. I suppose it is just too bad I do not get the same courtesy." He was being a dick, but he didn't care about that, either.

"I have tried, too, Nia. I have tried every-fucking-thing I can think of, too. Even the way this session went today. I thought, hey, if I forced myself out of my comfort zone, it would force some common sense back into my head, too. We see how well that went." Fucking horribly. Backfired in the *worst* fucking way. "You are the *only* one who has ever come close to breaking my walls down. But you did not just break them down; you fucking shattered them." He paused for a moment. This was the last thing he wanted to fucking say to her... but it was the truth, regardless. Nothing could change that, either. "I cannot keep coming to see you... knowing that things will never change... unless my walls get put back in place. So, perhaps... it would be better for the both of us if I see someone else." *Holy fucking shit,* that hurt. The words felt like a physical blow, as if someone had reached inside him and torn his heart and soul apart.

"We both know that won't go over well, and you'll just end up coming back to me. So, I have a suggestion. Something that might work for us both. We reverse roles."

Hunter said nothing for a long moment. His skin crawled at the implication of her words. "To the extent of?"

Nia gripped the back of her neck. "Complete reversal. You're the submissive; I'm the dominant. It's the only way."

Well, if that wouldn't break him out of this... *Fuck*, he'd never done that before. Never even *thought* about doing that before. For a multitude of reasons. Her challenging him didn't piss him off like it did when others had done the same. But what she was suggesting was *far* from the same thing. She wouldn't just be challenging him during their next session—she was going to have to break him completely. Something no one had ever accomplished with him before. Not that Azazel hadn't tried on multiple occasions. It was the only way this correction was going to work, though. The only way to remove the personal and restore the professionalism in their relationship. Rebuild the barrier and recreate a divide between them. The only way for both of them to regain control of themselves. The only way he could continue coming to see her at all.

Today had changed everything. And not just because of what they felt for one another, but what she'd done, too. *Marking* him. *Claiming* him. The puncture wounds would fade, but he suspected he would never stop feeling them. He could still feel her teeth, a sharp sting as blood gushed down his throat and gathered in a crimson pool on his collarbone. What that had meant for him... She could never offer herself to him in the same way.

Outwardly, he was a total jerk, supremely confident, irritating, sarcastic, and always seemed to brush off any insult with a smirk.

He truly was sadomasochistic in every way. Pain had always turned him on, whether he was causing it or receiving it. But that didn't mean he hadn't internally screamed until his lungs practically shattered over what was being done to him. That didn't mean he'd enjoyed being whipped and stabbed and fucked by his father. If he had control, then he could push all of his demons away and bury them. The need to be in control of his surroundings, of any situation, helped him to forget those moments when he felt powerless. Where he was at the mercy of another. Where he was truly vulnerable. If he had control, everything was great. Everything was perfect. If he wasn't...

Even today, he'd chosen how the session went; he'd chosen to have her on top. If he agreed to what Nia was proposing... he wouldn't get to choose a damn thing. He would be completely and totally at her mercy. Even though he trusted her implicitly, the thought of it churned his stomach.

The silence had stretched between them for long enough, but he still didn't know how to answer her. She was right; this way would be the only way. If *that* didn't work... Without a word, Hunter headed for the bathroom, slid the door back, and stepped inside. Leaving the door ajar, he went to the shower, turned the water on, and then, without waiting, stepped into the icy spray. He wasn't saying no; he just needed at least a few minutes to wrap his head around exactly what she was proposing. Since Nia was wearing a robe, his usual aftercare routine was off the table. Not that it would really be the best idea, either. He was practically dripping with sweat and other unknown fluids, the air thick with the smell of exertion from both of them. For once, he didn't want to leave here with all of it still on him.

He stood there, lost in the spray, when she entered, the wet silk of her robe pooling in the hamper as she climbed into the shower. "Move over."

Without a word, he shifted over to give her space, resuming his position with his palms flat against the shower wall, head down, the water drumming on his head. Gods, he'd never felt so defeated. What she'd suggested would work. He knew that. How could it not? The idea of having no control twisted in his gut, bringing a wave of sickness. Brought memories to the forefront of his mind that he'd buried a long time ago out of necessity. "I know I should have asked to come in here. Use the shower. I just..." Hunter let his words trail off.

"It's fine." There was no heat in her words. Perhaps their conversation had left her with a heavy heart, just like it had him. Getting under the spray, Nia closed her eyes and allowed the water to wash over her. The water streamed over her, and the marks on her hips and buttocks mended, vanishing completely as if they had never been. With the way he was standing, if it hadn't been for their height difference, he likely wouldn't have seen what effect the water had on her. Ah, so that was how it happened. He hadn't actually thought about her having an extra ability; had just figured she healed exceptionally fast. It wasn't like he knew a ton about her species as it was. But how convenient. No wonder she retained none of the marks she received. Well, except for the new ones from sometime between his last session and this one. Something he hadn't wanted to think about.

Every mark he'd put on her—every bruise, every claw mark, every bite mark—all of it disappeared as if it had never existed. Like it had never happened at all. His gut twisted violently, and with a grimace, he had to avert his gaze. It was one thing to know they disappeared, to see her each time without scars from their previous session. But watching them disappear was another thing entirely. It wasn't something he could do.

"I'm sorry, Hunter. I wish I could offer you more, give you what we both seem to want, be... different. Marking you was something I shouldn't have done. There's no excuse for that."

He wouldn't tell her it was okay, because it wasn't. He'd fought so fucking hard to keep from biting her neck *specifically* because of the implications, because of what it would mean to him. How sacred something like that was. His neck would heal, but the emotional marks would remain etched on his soul. Not that he planned on saying that out loud. He didn't have to be staring at her right now to know she felt bad. It wasn't his goal to guilt-trip her. He'd just keep his pain to himself, as much as possible. It was one thing he was very good at. What he'd become a pro at before he'd even reached adolescence. Something he didn't even openly share with his twin. "I wish I could be different, too." At this moment, he desperately wished he was anyone but himself. That he *didn't* need the type of sex that he did. That he hadn't *ever* had to come here. To find what he'd found in Narcissa—*Nia*—he needed to keep calling her by her den name, not her real one. To find what he'd found in Nia, and now this... he'd take anything over *this* pain.

Fucking Hades, that wall needed to go back up strong. Now.

Well... she'd certainly presented what had to be the solution. The only way things could go back to the way they needed to be. No matter what it was doing to him, just thinking about it. But he didn't have a choice. "I consent to what you proposed. For our next session."

"Confirm your appointment with Shalla like normal. When you come in next time, you'll knock on the door and wait for permission to enter. Once it's given, you'll come in, close the door and wait for instructions."

If the daggers could miraculously leave his chest, it would be a tremendous relief. Hunter reached up and pinched the bridge of his nose. *Permission. Instructions.* He placed his hand back against the damp wall. There was no other choice. He didn't even consider coming up with a safe word.

He couldn't include one. The only way this would work was if every limit he had was utterly pulverized. He ground his jaw before the next question left his mouth. "What should I call you?"

She steeled her shoulders as she reached for her loofah and body wash. "You will call me Ma'am. Hard limits—will they remain as previously discussed?"

Ma'am. Had he ever called *anyone* that? Nope. Not that he could recall. Not except for that one time in that one session with Nia, and that had just been playful. *Ma'am.* Even in his mind, it sounded unnatural. "No," he said simply. "I will need to get... as far out of my comfort zone as it is possible to get."

"Then tell me your hard limits."

"For this?" *Oh, fuck. Oh, fuck. Oh fuck.* "None." Half of him thought he might not know what he was saying. The other half knew that this was the only way. The only way to break this hold she had on him. And if she utterly and completely broke him... maybe that would break the hold he had on her as well.

"Are you sure?"

No, he wasn't sure about *any* of this. Not in the least. But that still couldn't change his answer. He felt the weight of her gaze, even though he hadn't shifted an inch. Her stare was so piercing, it was like she was making a tunnel straight into his soul. "Yes. For this... to do that during our next session... it is the way it has to be. Otherwise, it will not work. But... I need to warn you of something."

Several moments of silence hung heavy in the air between them. "Okay."

"Depending on what you plan to do... while you have full control... there are things that could trigger me. Because of the things that have happened to me in the past. I do not know how that would manifest."

"Alright. Then, you need to pick a safe word. Before you argue with me on this, you know as well as I do why we have safety measures in place."

Yes, he very much did. How many times over the years had a female used their safe word with him? This *plan,* or whatever they should call it, was to put a divide between them. If she pushed him *too* hard... there was the potential she wouldn't be able to get him back from it. While he trusted her instincts, as well as her ability to read him, it wasn't unintelligent to have a backup plan. "Alright. I will not use it, but if you insist. Red."

His favorite color would work just fine; and 'red' was easier to say than 'crimson.' Easy to remember, too. Not that he would need to remember it. And after this session... no, this would be the only time a safe word for him would even be in the picture. This would be the *only* time he would have a session like this. If the circumstances didn't demand it, it wouldn't even be on the table. Because if *this* didn't work, he wouldn't be able to return to see Nia. If this didn't work... he couldn't risk them getting even closer. He couldn't risk marking her; he'd already come too close. And he *certainly* couldn't risk his eyes glowing. Not when things would never change with her. Not when there could never truly be an 'us' for them.

"Okay."

Having a safe word was definitely the intelligent thing to do. It wasn't something he'd ever even needed to think of before. Just the thought of what might occur that could lead him to use it... no, he couldn't think about those things right now. What their next session would entail was something they had to do for both of them. They would never have what he'd dreamed of for one short, blissful... foolish moment. The illusory dream in his mind, the feelings that had grown between them... They didn't need to just be shattered—they needed to be wiped away. There was no other way to do it.

With a slight nod, Hunter stood up fully and washed up as quickly as he could. He had to get the fuck out of here. He felt like he couldn't breathe in here. It wasn't a feeling he liked. Without adding further to the tension, Nia turned back around to finish washing up as well.

Hunter finished before she did. Avoiding any physical contact, he circled her and reached for a warm towel as he stepped out of the shower. He dried off quickly, his back still to her, the air thick with the smell of soap. After drying off and cleaning the water he'd tracked onto her floor, he walked across the room and dropped the wet towel into the hamper.

"I am going to go," he said without turning around. The last thing he wanted to do was leave. He wished to avoid this session in the future, never forgetting their connection, preserving the mark on his neck, and keeping her away from other clients, possessing her entirely. But what he wanted wasn't ever going to be a possibility. So, time to get those foolish notions out of his head. "I will see you in four days, Nia."

"Four days," she echoed.

Hunter offered a subtle nod before exiting the bathroom, traversing the bedroom, and reaching for the door handle. His body wanted to hesitate, but he didn't allow himself to. As he walked out into the hallway and closed the door behind him, the pain inside him roared, and he finally understood what it was. Heartbreak. His fucking heart was broken. He didn't think he had the capacity for that emotion. Nor was it one he enjoyed. The sooner it hit the road, the better. Hades, their next session... Hunter ran a hand roughly down his face before heading down the hall. What the fuck was he getting himself into?

Ten

Nia knocked on Aniya's door. As much as she didn't want to be here, she needed advice. Thirty years had passed since she last dominated a submissive. And this had to be done. If this didn't work, then she and Hunter would only end up biding time until things progressed too far. Not that Aniya was her only option with dominants. She could've gone across the hall to Irina, but they'd never spoken all that much. At least, nothing beyond their initial meeting. Something had told her it was best to keep her distance from the female. One of the many reasons she ended up with a room on the other side of the floor, near Silva and Grace.

Aniya propped a shoulder against the doorjamb as the door swung open with a creak. "Nia. To what do I owe the pleasure of this visit?"

Yeah, some time had passed since the last time she truly spoke to the female. It seemed the best way to keep things to herself. Even the conversations she shared with Grace and Silva revolved around clients or shopping or general interests. "I was hoping we could speak privately regarding a client of mine." Not that she'd mention Hunter's name. "One I need to..." With a quick look around, Nia made sure the only person present was the guard stationed near the back door. She lowered her voice. "... break."

"You've come to the right place." With a smirk, Aniya pushed the door, and the hinges groaned in protest. "Come on in."

While she didn't expect the guard to say anything, this conversation had to be discreet. Nia entered the female's bedroom, a place she'd never fully ventured into before. Surveying the room, she noticed how similar to her own it appeared. Like her, the female had chosen dark-colored furniture. Unlike her black, dark red coated the walls. Most of the differences came from the equipment. Full facial masks, along with collars, leashes, and ball gags, lined one wall. Not something she could ever imagine using.

"I take it you've both already agreed upon limitations," the female stated as she shut the door.

"Yes." Her attention drifted to Aniya. "But I think that's part of the problem. He's given me a wide berth, with no limits, hard or soft. However, I have some lines that I just can't cross." Not again, anyway. Nia glanced at the various ball gags. She hadn't used them for quite some time. For a good reason, too.

Narcissa struck Tiza's thigh with the crop. A slight moan passed her lips as his pale skin reddened, a beautiful welt developing from the sweet pain she'd delivered. Especially as his back arched against the restraints holding him against the bondage horse. She rather enjoyed watching the leather straps dig a touch into his flesh as she brought him closer and closer to an orgasm. "Do not come yet," she said as she dragged the crop across his chest. "Hold it back a little longer. I promise it'll be like nothing you've ever experienced before."

Tiza nodded. The ball gag did its job, preventing him from speaking. Not that it impacted his sound in the slightest. Which was good, because she wanted those more than his words. Narcissa circled the bondage horse, her eyes focused, before striking his other thigh. Oh, gods. The new mark looked just as beautiful as the first. She repeated the process, flipping back and forth between his thighs. As she watched his back arch repeatedly, her gaze flickered toward him, catching glimpses of his focused face. His groans drove her to strike harder with the crop.

"We're almost there," she promised, bringing the edge of the crop's head down with a loud crack. The sound bounced off the walls. She barely bit back a moan. Her eyes lifted to her submissive's face. His nostrils flared, and his eyes widened. Shit. Were those tears in his eyes?

"Tiza?" No response. Dropping the crop, Narcissa rushed to his side. With deft movements, she removed the gag and straps, and then rubbed his chest in a slow, rhythmic pattern. "Come on, Tiza. Come back to me."

"Hey!" Aniya snapped.

Nia focused her attention on the female. "Sorry. I got distracted." That time in her life was a closed book she didn't want to revisit, the pages filled with shadows. Maybe it was best if she didn't eye all the various pieces on the female's walls. Especially the things she refused to have in her room.

"I take it the ball gags are a line you won't cross," the female suggested.

"Correct. Among other things. Like the leash and collar." She had to break Hunter, not degrade him. This was just to realign their professional boundaries.

"They aren't for everyone. Besides, you said you need to break him, right?" Aniya crossed the room and sat on the chaise in the corner, her silk dress rustling as she draped one leg over the other, and gestured to the chair across from her.

"Yes." Nia joined the female and claimed the velvet chair. Surprisingly, it was much more comfortable than it appeared. She tucked a high-heeled foot under her opposite leg. "I have served as a dominant in the past, but many *solaris* have passed since that time in my life. While I'm familiar with what's needed, I have to push every button of his possible."

"He typically serves as the dominant, correct?"

"Yes." Which was true for most of her clients. It had been that way since her arrival at the den. Mostly. She had honed some of her dominant skills in the downstairs club, but now they felt distant and unreachable.

"Well, there are all kinds of things you can do without crossing your hard limits. Humiliation can be done without a leash and collar. You can have him kneel before you, even crawl on all fours. That is certainly a way to push a person's buttons. Then, of course, there are the more common things like caning, bondage, cock and ball torture, just to name a few. If you want to take things up a notch from there, you can try knife or fire play. Maybe even sensory deprivation."

Hmm, Aniya had a point. She could easily deprive Hunter of his senses just by facing him in certain directions on the bondage cross. Using bondage in their play would also break him down as well. "I wouldn't go for knife or fire, but perhaps... wax play. It's not something I've done in quite a while. Do you have any candles for that purpose?"

"I do, and I have a few oils I used to aid in healing for the submissive. Presuming you intend to bathe him before the entire session concludes?"

"Absolutely. I may try to break him, but I take care of my submissive." It wasn't like she had much in mind for how this session with Hunter would go. No matter. Harming a submissive wasn't in her genes.

"Good." The female dipped her chin and folded her hands in her lap. "I don't imagine you need much from me. Come on, Nia. Just because I've never seen your room doesn't mean I'm unaware of your reputation. I'm certain you have enough equipment at your disposal to accomplish your task adequately."

"That I do. Though I certainly wouldn't have considered humiliation if you hadn't mentioned it." It offered her a few ideas of how to begin things with Hunter. He certainly wouldn't like any of it. While he might enjoy the pain she delivered, it might just do the trick if she took him somewhere dark.

"It sounds like you've got what you need. Unless you want any further suggestions?"

"No, thank you, though. I've definitely got the session formulating in my mind." Nia stood. Not that she could leave until she had what Aniya promised her. "Is there something I can give you for the candle and oils?"

"That's unnecessary." Aniya climbed off the chaise and rose to her feet. She crossed the room to the nightstand, where she picked up three vials that clinked softly and a candle, then went back to Nia. "We're sisters. What is family for if not to aid one another?"

Right. Family. How could she forget? They were all siblings in the den. So what if several of them fucked one another on the side? Averine didn't care about that, as long as they did their job. "I appreciate that." Nia accepted the items offered. "If you ever decide you need something, let me know." She'd put it out there. The last thing she wanted was to be in someone's debt.

"Of course."

"Thank you again, Aniya." Nia strode for the door, her footsteps echoing, and slipped away swiftly, her breath held tight. At least, she prayed it didn't appear hurried in any manner. She definitely didn't need that. No one needed to know about the direction her sessions with Hunter had taken. Especially after their last one. As she rounded the corner, she spotted Shalla. Damn it. She was one of the few people she'd hoped to avoid. She hadn't spoken with the female since their discussion regarding Hunter. Maybe she could slip by unnoticed. Continuing forward, she strolled past the female.

"Nia," Shalla called out. "We need to talk."

Fuck. No, they didn't. At least, in her book. She couldn't let anyone find out she'd marked Hunter. Or that they planned to reverse roles for their next session. Or why they'd decided on that. But if she didn't stop, it would bring up questions. Nia paused, then whirled around, the motion causing her hair to fly up. "Shalla. I didn't see you there."

"Of course not." The female clasped her hands together in front of her body. "As Hunter scheduled another session with you, I take it you changed your mind about releasing him as a client."

"Yes. I simply realized we were a good fit." In many, many ways. Not that she could openly admit that.

"Are you sure?"

"Absolutely. It was just a premature decision." Something that had happened more here lately than she cared to admit. Not that she could say that. Or really acknowledge it. The last thing she needed was to trigger accidentally the ancient, volatile magic bound within her contract with the den. Workers who did always disappeared. None of them ever came back. Except Shalla. Or so the rumors went.

"Alright. If you say so." With a slight dip of her chin, the female headed toward the second-floor waiting area.

Nia turned around and saw Ivory lingering at the corner. Why didn't that surprise her? This bitch had a knack for being in the way, especially regarding Hunter. Gods, if he only knew the shit she'd pulled over the years. Something else that her NDR prevented her from talking about—what went on behind closed doors. Tightening the grip she had on the vials in her hand, Nia hooked her thumbs into the front pockets of her jeans. It would make her appear less defensive. "What do you want, Ivory?"

"Nothing really. I just couldn't help but overhear your trouble with Hunter. You're what... five sessions in?"

"Six," she corrected. "So, just back off. He's mine... my client." Fuck. She needed to stop talking. Now. Best not to play the slut's game. All she had to do was leave. Nia strolled forward, continuing toward her bedroom. Just one hallway away.

"Not yet. We agreed on ten sessions. Remember? Ten full sessions, and *then* he'd be completely your client. Still four more to go. Not that I think you'll make it." Ivory smirked, a flash of white teeth, and then retreated a few steps. "Tick Tock, Nia. Tick Tock."

Do not respond. Do not respond. Nia clenched her jaw and kept walking. She swallowed hard, her chest tightening with each shallow breath, the weight of her actions suffocating her. She already felt the sting of guilt for marking Hunter, her conscience pricking her. The last thing she needed was to make things worse. And if she opened her mouth again, especially to Ivory, that's exactly what would happen.

Hunter took his time, more than he ever had before, as he made his way down the hallway to Nia's room. Hades, he couldn't get rid of the unease curling in his gut. This session would push him to his absolute limit, more than he had ever experienced. *Necessary. This was necessary.* The inner mantra did nothing to settle his nerves. Something else he didn't like. He didn't get nervous. Nothing shook him anymore.

Nothing except for this.

He didn't know what manner of things Narcissa had planned for today. The implications were as clear as a cloudless sky. *"No limits. I will need to get as far out of my comfort zone as it is possible to get."* Hunter had been nothing but dominant, both in and out of the bedroom. He didn't follow the same practices as other dominants, but he had experimented with a wide range of activities to figure out his preferences with his submissives. There were several things he enjoyed doing to them that he wouldn't be able to stand having done to himself. But this time, things were going to be different. So very different. *She* was the Domme. And *he* was the submissive.

She had to dismantle him utterly. Something no one had ever accomplished with him before. Not that Azazel hadn't tried on multiple occasions. It was the only way this correction would work. The only way to remove the personal and restore the professionalism in their relationship. Put a barrier, a divide, between them. The only way for them both to regain control of themselves. The only way he could continue coming to see her at all. Their last session had changed everything. And not just because of what they felt for one another. After she'd claimed him, marking him as hers... Though the puncture wounds on his neck had long since healed, he could still feel the phantom ache. What that had meant for him... And she could never offer herself to him in the same way.

Gods, this was going to be a nightmare

Hunter stood before her door, heart pounding, unsure how much time had passed before he could muster the courage to announce his presence. The hesitation was stupid. It was a weakness. This was something he'd agreed to. It was necessary. He needed to get this over with. Once it was done and behind them, things could get back to the way they were supposed to be. The personal shit would be gone, the professional relationship restored. Steeling himself, Hunter raised his hand and knocked firmly on the door.

Nothing. No sounds to indicate she walked toward the door. No word granted him entrance.

Hades, he wasn't *nearly* in the right headspace for this shit.

While Hunter waited for her to *grant him permission* to enter—one minute, then another... and another still—he tried to channel what he'd demanded from his submissives over the years. Not that he was altogether successful. He just didn't have it in him to be submissive. Not fully. Not like *this*. Nia was given some control during their last session, but this was different. He was going to have to pull it out of his ass for this session. He'd been having sex in his way for thirty-one, almost thirty-two years. Something like that. Just this once, he could do things differently. He had control over his mental state. He could keep the demons at bay for this session. *Surely,* he could do that. No matter what stops she pulled out.

Yeah, he wasn't sure he believed that.

Hunter rolled his shoulders. Resisted the urge to shift his stance. Cracked his neck. He clasped his hands behind his back, feeling the tension in his shoulders, then let them fall back to his sides. Holy fucking shit, he really needed to get a hold of himself. A few hours at most. That was all this would last. No longer than their other sessions. He could handle this switch for a few hours.

Because what did it say about *him* if he couldn't? *That* was a weakness all its own. And he was far from weak.

Finally, the door opened. "Enter," Narcissa stated. Without a word, she walked to her queening bench, the cool fabric of her clothes rustling with each step, sat down, and crossed her legs.

Hunter didn't say a word as he stepped inside and closed the door behind him. The scent of jasmine with a slight hint of sandalwood filled the room. Just inside the door, he reminded himself to wait for instructions, the sound of his own shallow breathing filling the otherwise quiet space. Nothing more. He could do this. Follow orders. He'd done it for almost thirty years under Markham. Even longer under Azazel. Now, he followed the orders that Devin gave him. He could follow orders from Nia now, too. Except he'd *followed no one's* orders in the bedroom. He *always* dominated in the bedroom.

Except now.

Shut up.

Hunter tried to ignore the irritating prickles that swept across his skin. With his legs apart, hands clasped, he stood, his gaze unwavering. Not that he couldn't see Nia out of the corner of his eye. Besides, looking at her allowed him not to pay attention to the new... additions to the room. They had put the bondage horse away. In its place stood a ten-foot metal bondage cross with big, comfortable rings for attachment. The rings at each corner held cuffs. A set of spreaders and restraints sat waiting on the chaise, plus additional restraints had been attached to the bed. The toys currently lining the top of the dresser comprised a couple of cock rings, nipple clamps, a cock ring and nipple clamp combo, a few dildos, anal beads, and butt plugs. A leather crop hung along the wall with the floggers and paddles, along with several additional blindfolds.

Forcing his attention away from all of that, he focused fully on Narcissa. Everything about her had changed from their previous sessions. All of her mannerisms. Her eyes, sparkling with amusement, mirrored the curve of her lips. She sat with perfect posture, exuding a sense of unwavering control. The surrounding air crackled with an unspoken authority that spoke volumes about her attitude. Both her hair and voice were different. Even her clothing was different. A V-neck, spaghetti-strap, stretchy black dress with straps lining the sides from the waist down hugged her body in *all* the right places. Her feet were in a pair of black peep-toe high heels with a red stiletto and strap around the ankle. Her lips were painted bright red.

Hunter had never seen her in anything but underwear during their first session, and lingerie during their other sessions. But the dress *definitely* suited her. He almost growled just looking at her in it. Was he *allowed*—his lip almost curled in distaste—to growl? Would it get him in trouble if he did? What would the punishment be if he did something she didn't want him to do?

That everything about her was so *different...* this was good. He could deal with the discomfort. They needed *different* to fix things.

"Kneel."

Hunter clasped his hands so tightly behind his back, his knuckles popped. With his hands behind his back, he slowly kneeled to the floor, the rough texture of the floor meeting his knees as he inhaled a deep breath.

Narcissa stood up from the bench. "You will hold nothing back. Every sound of yours belongs to me. Every growl, every moan, every groan—I expect all of them. Do you understand?"

With every word she spoke, the prickles intensified, making his skin crawl. He was unsure whether it was the words she chose or the cadence of her voice that he found so unsettling. Maybe both. "Yes." His jaw clenched. "Ma'am."

This was a stark contrast to the way she usually challenged him. He liked when she did; it turned him on. But *this...* he didn't like how *this* made him feel. He didn't like having *zero* control and the way it made him feel. He could throw in the towel, but that would make him weaker than he already felt. And it would accomplish nothing. So what if he *didn't like* it? That was the point. This session was *supposed* to be different. *Everything* about it had to be different for this to work. Their roles had to be *completely* reversed. She had to be *completely* dominant, and he had to be *completely* submissive. He'd known that going in and had accepted it. He could fight it every step of the way, make this more difficult on himself than it already was... or he could embrace it—as much as possible—and deal with the consequences after.

Best-case scenario—it did what they needed it to do. Created a divide between them. Removed the personal. Restored the professional. Allowed him to continue coming to see her and have sessions with her.

Worst-case scenario—it *didn't* work. It somehow brought them even closer. And he wouldn't ever be able to come back to see her again. That wasn't something he would ever be willing to accept.

It was time to welcome the role he had to play for tonight.

Just for tonight.

"Good boy," Narcissa purred.

Those two words momentarily brought him back to three sessions ago—how things had started, then shifted, then ended. But that she *purred* those words... Hunter's eyes immediately darkened. He growled, overcome by the heat radiating from her body and her increasingly potent scent.

Narcissa walked around him, purposely stepping over each of his legs as she ran her fingers along his shoulders. A slight tremor went through them. "On all fours," she stated, standing somewhat behind him and to the right.

Hunter's muscles tensed. The unease that had curled in his gut before he'd ever arrived here intensified. Though he didn't move his head, his eyes flicked over to the right. It took every ounce of willpower not to turn his head and look at her. He didn't like people standing behind him, out of his immediate line of sight. *Especially* those who were in charge when he wasn't. It made him uncomfortable. Vulnerable. A feeling he despised.

For a moment, all he could think about was the last time he'd been on all fours in his humanoid form. But he slammed the mental door back tightly on *those* things, not allowing them to fully surface. This *was not* the same thing. This was not *them.* It was Nia. He trusted Narcissa. He might not be comfortable with *any* of this, but he *trusted* her. Keeping his gaze fixed forward, Hunter took his hands from where they were clasped behind him. Each movement was slow and carefully controlled. As he did what she'd ordered, a knot of tension tightened in his stomach. When he unclenched his fists and planted his palms on the floor, they were slick with blood. He hadn't even realized he'd dug his claws in.

Narcissa closed the short distance between them, the clicks of her stilettos marking each step. Her hip brushed against his side as she planted her ass on his back. Draping one leg over the other, she rested her palms against his back, one close to his shoulder blades, the other close to the small of his back.

Hunter flinched. He couldn't explain the reaction. He knew it was *her* on top of him. Maybe it was what had just attempted to go through his mind. Hades, this was ridiculous. He'd barely made it inside the door. They'd done nothing yet. If he was going to lose it now—already—they would fail. As far out of his comfort zone as it was possible to get. *No limits.* That had been *his* decision. That was what was necessary for this to work. He had to follow through with this. He refused to give her up. And this was Nia; this was not—his muscles tensed again. No, this was his—this was Nia.

"Crawl to the bondage cross. Do not waste time and do not let me fall. Understood?"

Hunter's gaze flicked across the room to the piece of equipment. How many times had he restrained a female on one of those? When he'd been restrained, it hadn't been against anything like that. All the same. *Never would he have ever thought he would willingly—no limits. It is necessary. This is not the same as that. This is Narcissa. I trust Narcissa.*

Hunter steeled himself as he inhaled a deep breath. "Yes, Ma'am," he managed through clenched teeth. And then he crawled—yup... he was fucking crawling—across the floor. His pace was even. Not too slow, but not so quick it would jostle her atop him, either.

A purr escaped Narcissa, causing Hunter to feel a jolt of energy, and he responded with a low growl. Not that it stopped his movements or slowed his pace any. Even though all he wanted to do right now was push up off the floor and *run*. Right. Yeah. He really didn't need to *actually* be a pussy right now. This was absurd. Getting tense over *any* of this shit was fucking childish. How many times had he been in restraints? He hadn't freaked out at any of those times. Not outwardly anyway—internally had been a different story. Not getting a reaction out of him had gotten a better one out of Azazel. And it wasn't like the pain hadn't felt fantastic. It was the restraints that always got to him, without fail. Being chained or caged. Held down. Unable to escape or fight back. Unable to protect himself. Complete and total vulnerability. Entirely at the mercy of another.

Narcissa uncrossed her legs, holding her position as he closed the last of the distance to the cross. Once he stopped, she climbed off his back and retrieved a stepladder from behind her tall dresser. "Stand and face the bondage cross."

Hunter's hands clenched into fists again as he rose from the floor, the tension evident in his taut muscles. A futile attempt to stop the slight tremors that swept from his hands all the way up his arms. He felt his heart race, echoing in his ears. His stomach twisted into knots. It wasn't the *same* thing as a tree branch. Hadn't always been there either. His wrists had sometimes been bound around a tree trunk. Sometimes, it was the shackles and collar in the middle of the clearing. Sometimes, he just had to stand there and take it, and if he moved too much, even by accident, it had been worse. Forcibly shaking all of that from his mind—not that he was sure how long that would last—Hunter faced the cross.

Narcissa had gotten the ladder between her makeup table and the bondage cross. Given their height difference, it would be required to lock the restraints around his wrists. "Hands and feet toward each corner," she said as she climbed the ladder.

Each time she stepped on a rung, the sound reverberated like a thunderclap in his ears. His heart boomed, a deep and powerful echo, rather than simply thundering. So intense, it felt like it would break right through his chest. As Hunter forced himself to close the small distance, his breath hitched in the cold air as he neared the cross. He spread his legs—first his left, then his right. His palms slid up the cross, feeling the rough wood until they met the cold, metal rings. As he leaned his forehead against the top part's edge, his fingers curled around it, a familiar sensation. Only then did he feel the wetness. The sweat that had beaded across his forehead. *Deep breaths. Deep breaths. No limits. Necessary. This is necessary. I cannot lose her. This is not the same as that. This is Nia. I trust Nia.* Hunter squeezed his eyes shut for a moment, inhaled the deepest breath he could, then exhaled slowly as he opened his eyes again. Eyes needed to stay open through this as much as possible.

Hitting the top rung of the ladder, Narcissa paused for a moment. "Eyes on me."

Her voice cut through the noise of his racing heartbeat and the thrumming in his neck. Without taking his forehead off the metal, Hunter flicked his gaze over to hers. He focused on the jade green of her eyes, with their bright-yellow flecks, and traced the exact length and shade of her eyelashes. Narcissa reached toward his left wrist. The cuff locking around his furred flesh had his fist clenching harder. His claws dug into his palms so hard that the metallic scent of blood filled the air as it soaked his fur. Hunter didn't take his eyes off of hers as she did the same to his right. Blood slid down that palm as well. His lips parted slightly as he tried to draw air into his lungs. It wasn't *too* difficult... Not until she started heading down the ladder. Further out of his sight...

Narcissa closed the ladder and propped it up against the side of her makeup table. Now standing back at the rear of the bondage cross, his eyes still hadn't left hers. She wrapped a hand around his waist, brushing her fingers along the small of his back. A jolt went through him, jerking his entire body, before he trembled uncontrollably. A low growl left him. It was as if the two halves of his brain were warring for supremacy. With a simple touch from her, his desire flared like a wildfire. Hades, she could just look at him a certain way and he was raring to go. But the other half of his brain was fighting for dominance, too. That part of him had not awakened in years. Hunter would never openly admit it, but he was afraid. No, not just afraid—terrified. But the only way it *wouldn't* be apparent at this moment was if Nia had zero senses. All she had to do was look at him. On top of that, it was a tangible scent, thickening the surrounding air. It just intensified Hunter's discomfort. How vulnerable he felt.

It wasn't so much what she might do to him. It was *this*. Being restrained. Held down. Caged in. Nowhere to go. Nowhere to run. Completely vulnerable. Completely at her mercy. She could kill him if she wanted to—not that Nia would ever want to do such a thing, but it was the principle—and he wouldn't be able to stop her. The equipment could hold any species, large or small. He had his safe word, and that would stop all of this if it got to be too much, but he didn't want to use it. No matter what. If he used it to stop this, this session wouldn't do what they both needed it to do. It wouldn't fix anything between them. It would all be for nothing.

"Listen to my voice, Hunter. I'm going to talk while I get your ankle cuffs in place, and as I move around. You'll just focus on that sound when you can't see me. Understood?"

Clenching his fists, Hunter inhaled her scent mingled with his blood, which smelled like the sweetest air. Her voice. He could focus on her voice. He could do that. Without taking his forehead off the metal, he gave a slight nod. "Yes, Ma'am," he whispered.

"Good boy," Narcissa purred.

His fangs bared, and a growl rumbled from deep within his chest. That fucking purr *just about* overrode everything else. But the sensation didn't last.

She kneeled down to get one ankle strap in place. "Today, we'll be in three locations, though the positions on the first will alter. I won't tell you what I have planned, as I don't want you to anticipate anything."

Try as he might to focus on her voice, Hunter barely tracked the words that came out of her mouth. A cold sweat broke out across every inch of him. The tremble in his body intensified. He tried to move his leg, but couldn't. Jerked at the bindings around his wrists with no success.

Narcissa stood and moved around to the other side. The sound of her every movement echoed loudly in his ears. The sensation of the buckle clasping around his ankle caused a dizzying effect to wash over him. He tried to draw in deeper breaths, but it felt like he was pulling air in through a narrow tube, his chest aching with the effort. He pressed his forehead harder into the metal until it stung.

Break him. She *had* to break him. That was the plan. It was necessary. The only way this would work. No limits. No limits had been *his* idea. This was *Narcissa. Narcissa.* He could do this. He could do this.

She moved away from him, and he heard a slight shift as she picked something up. Not that he could tell exactly what it was. Something leather maybe, by the sound of it, but he couldn't be sure.

Fuck, what had she just said? Hunter couldn't concentrate. Something about cum—not getting it on the floor. "Yes..." His voice was ragged, the sound of it like dry leaves skittering across the ground. Gods, he fucking hated this. "... Ma'am."

It was a leather crop. He knew it as soon as it struck his ass. Surely not as hard as she could swing it, but enough that it stung. A slight hum vibrated through his body, clearing his mind as if a weight had been lifted. A low moan left him.

He completely missed whatever words she spoke. The nails that raked across his inner thigh didn't belong to her. The room vanished, and he stared at the tall tree, its bark a textured wall. He couldn't smell her sweet perfume, or the metallic scent of his bloodied palms, or the stale sweat clinging to him. All he could smell was the foul stench of stale breath, the earthy aroma of dead earth, and the putrid scent of the festering tree trunk. The rope, not leather, bound his wrists, and the strain of it, looped over the tree branch, kept his arms suspended above his head. He couldn't hear Narcissa's voice; all he could hear was *his*, right in his ear, as Azazel's cock pressed up against his ass and a phantom hand grabbed onto his dick. *"Barely past your growth spurt, and this is already your favorite toy. Maybe I should take it away."*

His muscles were taut and rigid, making his body feel tense. Pain shot through his legs, back, arms, shoulders, and neck. Hunter recoiled, trying to escape the fetid stench that washed over him. He struggled against the hand on him, but his bonds were unyielding. His body shook so hard his teeth chattered. All the air closed in around him until he couldn't breathe. He couldn't breathe... *Not again. Not again.*

Footsteps he didn't recognize clicked on the outskirts of his hearing. He heard a small clatter, then a larger one, but he was too distracted to register what they were. Nor was the voice that spoke words he couldn't decipher.

"Hunter, come on, come back to me."

A hand wrapped around the back of his neck—*NO!* He didn't want it; he didn't want to do this; he didn't want it. His head whipped back and forth, as if trying to escape the unrelenting hold.

"Come back to me, Hunter. You're here with me, not there, but here. Right here where it's safe, and it's just us."

With the words, a female voice finally penetrated his thoughts, the weight of the moment heavy as he tried to grasp when and where they had arrived. When what was in front of him shifted until it was hazy, warped. The massive tree trunk dominated half of his vision. The other half was her—Narcissa—slowly coming more into focus the more her mouth moved. Hunter blinked rapidly as she swam in and out of his vision. The pain in his chest intensified with each thunderous beat of his heart. With every quick, fleeting breath, his nostrils filled with the sharp, clean air. His body didn't stop shaking. But he could see her more and more clearly every moment. Here. Not there. Here with *her*. Not there with *him*. Here. Nia. Just them. Safe. He was safe. His breathing settled just a little. Narcissa. It was Narcissa. Not him. Not *him*. Her room. He was in her room. Safe.

"That's it. You're right here with me." Narcissa's thumb brushed his neck in a slow, calming circle, her touch light and feather-soft. "There we go. Right here. No one but you and me. Try to take shallow breaths until you can take a deep one."

Neither of them took their eyes off one another as she spoke to him. Her jade green with flecks of yellow. Not brownish-gold flecked with black. Green. Those beautiful green eyes. A soft purr rumbled from his chest. Right here. Just them. Just him and Narcissa. Her room. Not *there*. Not *him*. Hunter kept his breath shallow until the constriction on his chest eased up a little. The shakes rolling through him settled a little, closer to trembles. Just him and Narcissa. His Narcissa. Safe. He was safe with her. He was always safe with her.

"Definitely better. Take a deep breath if you can."

Hunter couldn't respond, not with words. He felt as though his heart had been ripped from his chest, exposing his deepest secret to her. Totally exposed. Vulnerable. Powerless. Defenseless. Helpless. He didn't like it. He hated it. Feeling this way. If he didn't have his control, he had nothing. He fell apart. Became *weak*. A crumpled mess. Someone who couldn't function on a normal level. He *had* to have his control or he couldn't be *himself*.

With his eyes still upon her, Hunter followed her instruction and pulled in a bit of a deeper breath. It didn't hurt his chest so much. Felt easier to draw into his lungs. He took another. Then another. Then another.

"That's good. Much better." Narcissa offered him a small smile as she loosened her grip on the back of his neck. "Shall we get back to it then? I know you must really want to see what's underneath this dress."

Pressing his forehead more against the metal, Hunter allowed the slight sting to clear his head further before he gave a small nod. Then, he did what he could to steady himself the rest of the way. Not that the unease or dizziness completely left him, but they'd both settled somewhat. The fear wasn't going anywhere until all of this was over. But at least he could breathe *almost* normally. And he *wanted* to see what she had on under her dress. Hunter cleared his throat a little before speaking. "Yes, Ma'am."

"Good boy," she purred. Releasing her grip on his neck, Narcissa climbed down the ladder.

This time, she didn't use her voice. Didn't say a word. So, Hunter had nothing to focus on but his restraints and the slight shifts he could hear as she moved around out of his line of sight, then behind him again. The fur on the nape of his neck raised as a fresh sheen of sweat coated his skin, dampening his fur. His heartbeat sped up. Slight tremors started up along his shoulder and back muscles. His fingers tightened around the corner rings as he steeled himself, before the leather crop cracked against his ass, the sound echoing in the silent room. The sting was more intense than before, bringing a more pronounced moan out of him this time.

"Oh, yes, Hunter. I enjoy hearing those sounds come from you." Narcissa struck each ass cheek twice with the crop, and then across one of his thighs. She kept the same power behind it as she had with the previous crack.

Hunter couldn't hold back the hiss. The delicious sting seemed to travel through the full length of his cock. But then she bit one of his ass cheeks and moaned. Hunter's whole body jerked. His hands clenched so tightly around the rings that his knuckles cracked. His eyes flipped black—though not in a good way—and he let out a snarl. He fucking loved being bitten, especially when *she* did it. But *not* there. Not... *there.* Her moan kept him—just barely—grounded. Focusing on that sound had kept anything else from taking over his mind. For now. With his hands still gripping tightly, Hunter attempted to calm himself by focusing on his breath. He attempted to regulate his chest's frantic movements.

Narcissa brought the crop down again and again, the stinging strikes landing on his backside, then his thigh, before returning to his ass. Each blow to his ass drew out more guttural growls and whimpers, the one that landed on his opposite thigh, a sharp intake of breath. The tremors through his body didn't cease, though. His hands didn't unclench once. His ragged breaths, heavy with each inhale, seemed to remain the same. With his hands still wrapped around the rings, the sting of pain and the metallic scent of his blood, both sharp and present, helped Hunter stay grounded.

"I believe it's time we took things up a notch." Narcissa's heels echoed sharply across the polished floor. The perfume of jasmine and sandalwood grew stronger with each step. "I've been looking forward to using this on you, but don't worry, I plan to use it on myself, too." Narcissa took her place behind him once again. "Are you curious about what it is? This isn't something I've used in a long time since it can be too easily mishandled."

No, he wasn't curious. He'd known immediately what it was, and what its purpose was. When he'd gotten his introduction into D/s play and explored, really fine-tuned what he liked and what he didn't—something that had lasted about a year, as he hadn't been able to come here with any kind of regularity—he'd considered wax play. The submissive he'd gotten paired with at the time had even used it on herself, to show him how it worked. Explained the differences in candles, and how to do it safely, and what precautions to take. But that had not been something that went on his list of likes. He didn't enjoy playing with fire. Bad things had happened around him with fire. It wasn't a danger he enjoyed. It spread and destroyed too quickly.

Hunter moaned as the crop cracked against his rear, the sting of the leather lingering. A drop of hot wax landed on his skin, just above the curve of his buttock. His back slightly arched, and his moan grew into a deep, guttural sound, consuming Narcissa's soft groan. He liked the brief burst of pain. He *did not* like the feel of the flame so close to his body. Nor the things it conjured up in his mind. It was as if a floodgate had opened. The first trigger was like an undeniable invitation, beckoning every demon he desperately tried to keep locked away.

While his mouth opened, Hunter couldn't get his tongue to work. Not to form words. His mind was only half here. The rest of it had drifted somewhere else entirely. But he could still feel what was being done to his body. An alternating pattern of the crop against his ass and the wax on his thighs. With every strike of the crop and burst of wax, his moans echoed in the room. Before long, growls had replaced them. Then slight whimpers worked their way in, too. It wasn't any darker than usual in Narcissa's room, but he couldn't see anything around him. All he could see was what was in his head. The dirt walls of the tiny hiding spot in Azazel's floor. The bare hints of natural light above him.

The damp scent of earth surrounded him. His three-year-old body was tiny, but there was barely any room for him down here. Sam put him down here to be mean. He enjoyed being mean. He was going to put Hayden down here instead, but Hunter wouldn't ever let that happen. A plume of candle smoke, sharp and acrid, caused his nose to twitch.

Hunter's hands clenched tighter. His arms and legs were rigid. The tremors in his shoulder and back muscles grew with each passing second. Sweat rolled down his forehead, blurring his vision. A growling moan escaped him, and his back arched, the sound dissolving into a small whimper.

Samael reeked. He hardly ever bathed, and he was always drinking. His stench was so bad you could usually taste it on your tongue.

"Hey, Clay, Clay. How long do you think he would survive down there if we set this place on fire?"

"You are drunk."

"I am always drunk." Sam chuckled. "Hunter." His voice held a singsong tone. The floor creaked as the heat drew closer. The acrid scent of

the smoke grew, making his eyes water. Sam's voice was quieter this time, no longer teasing, a growl on the edge of every word. "I am gonna burn you alive." Wax oozed through cracks in the wood overhead, splattering his lower back and the outer part of his thigh.

Hunter let out a small yelp, but he clamped down on his tongue, silencing the noise.

It just encouraged his eldest brother when he showed any fear. A few burning embers singed his fur.

He whimpered again.

"Stop it, you idiot," Clay snapped. "You burn down the hut, Dad will kill you."

The bursts of pain felt so good, but he didn't like it. Hunter let out another whimpered moan as another drop of wax hit him.

The top of the hiding spot opened suddenly. "Here, dipshit, have a present." The candle, still lit, was thrown, and it landed in his lap with a soft thud. The flame ignited the fur on his outer thigh, and a scorching smell filled the air. Hunter let out a bloodcurdling scream, the sound of which was nearly unbearable as he scrambled to put out the fire.

Hunter strained against the restraints, groaning as the whip cracked against his skin, then felt the hot wax drip down his leg. His body shook harder when it landed directly on the scar, a stark reminder of the scent of burning fur when his brother burned him with that candle. Mostly on his leg, but partially on his hip. Somehow, his fur had grown back. You couldn't tell the scar was there unless you felt for it.

A scraping sound echoed across the floor before a hand seized his neck, a thumb tracing slow circles on his skin. "Eyes on me, Hunter."

Who was that? The female voice seemed so out of place with what was in his head. Hunter blinked rapidly. With each passing moment, the dirt cage on the floor and the cold, unlit candle became less distinct, and her face gradually became clearer in his sight. Narcissa. It was Narcissa. Narcissa was talking to him. It was *her* hand on the back of his neck. When had he started purring?

As his vision cleared, Hunter found himself drawn to her gaze. She had such beautiful eyes. Just looking into them calmed him. They'd always been able to see straight through to his soul. Had she seen any of this before? These dark, dirty things that were in his head? The nastiness that had attached itself to his soul?

There was more. *So* much more.

Please, gods, let them stay buried. Do not let them come out. I do not want to go back there. I do not want to go back again.

They wouldn't stay buried, though. The door had been flung wide open, as if inviting her to step through. The lock lay in pieces, twisted and broken. This session would do what it needed to do. He already felt so full of cracks. Fragile. Ready and waiting for just the right thing to shatter him completely. Would Narcissa help him put the pieces back together when he did?

"That's it. You just keep coming back to me." Narcissa didn't stop with the slow circles. "Shall we continue?"

A chill went down Hunter's spine. His stomach lurched with a nervous flutter, and his hands clenched into fists. *Continue.* Of course, they would continue. They were far from finished with this. He had only a few cracks in him. She hadn't broken him yet. Hadn't yet shattered him. He forced his hands to loosen, and as he did, Hunter took a deep breath, the air strangely still and heavy. Pressed his forehead harder against the metal. Let out a slight sigh at the sting of pain across his brow. And then he nodded. "Yes, Ma'am."

Narcissa immediately purred in response. It took her another minute to remove her hand from the back of his neck or even to ease up on the circles. She gave a nod. "Good boy." Descending the ladder, she set it aside and crossed to her dresser again. "We're going to take things up another notch."

The sensations running rampant through his body amped up once more. Even though he should have been dehydrated from sweating so much, a new thin coat of sweat beaded across his skin, bringing a chill. Prickles swept up and down his spine. The veins in his neck throbbed. His stomach clenched. Even his heart rate sped up. All of this was necessary. Narcissa not holding back—no matter how much he flashed back—was necessary, too. He had to shatter at her hand. They had yet to reach that point.

Hunter curled his fingers tighter around the rings as her stilettos clicked across the floor. From the subtle noises he could hear, she'd taken something down from her wall. His back and shoulders tensed.

Without warning, Narcissa struck out and didn't hold back. A slight rushing noise, like a swarm of angry bees, heralded dozens of sharp stings across his ass. She'd grabbed a flogger this time. As Hunter's head fell back, his hands clenched, his claws digging into his palms. Blood from his palms dripped to the floor, splattering with a wet thud as a deep moan reverberated through the silent room. The pain was exhilarating, and it seemed to swell in response, immediately making his dick even harder. But with that floodgate in his mind open, it took little. Especially with the way his eyes had immediately closed. The buried demon from three decades ago seized control of his sight, the experience as jarring as a sudden blow. He wasn't in the room with Narcissa any longer. He was back home again.

A low chuckle left him. "Is that all you have got?" Hunter sneered as blood oozed down his legs.

Azazel cracked the whip against his back, his ass, and the back of his legs repeatedly. Hunter would laugh, sneer, and utter a mocking sentence with each new strike he landed. Azazel had already been pissed off before he started this punishment. Hayden had been ordered to fight the other male in the ring. But his twin hated fighting. It made him uncomfortable and scared him. He'd been trembling from his head to the tip of his tail long before he ever made it to the ring. Not to mention, the other male was quite bigger than Hayden and way more skilled. It was an accident—or a horrible, irreparable injury—just waiting to happen. Unacceptable.

So, Hunter had taken over instead. He enjoyed fighting. And it didn't matter how much he got hurt. The pain worked better at getting him high than drugs or alcohol ever could. The other male's size, strength, and skill hadn't mattered. Hunter had still won. He'd completely ignored Azazel's yelling at him from the sidelines through every single moment of it. Ignored all of his demands to get out of the ring. Afterward, when they'd argued, he'd been even more defiant. So much so that by the time they'd gotten to this, Azazel was in a complete rage.

Good. Bring it on, Daddy.

His paws throbbed from the tight shackles, while the collar constricted his throat. But the smug smirk didn't leave his face for a single moment. It just made Azazel more and more pissed. His strikes with the whip got harder and harder.

Hunter's back arched at the brand new strike with the flogger. A sharp pain shot through his inner thigh as nails raked across it, and a touch stroked his cock. Everything in his mind shifted in the blink of an eye.

A rope bound his arms, suspending them above his head. His father's breath, damp earth, and a rotting tree trunk filled his nostrils. Hunter's claws elongated until they pierced straight through his palms as Azazel stroked his cock from behind. If he had cried, tears would have been streaming down his face. But he didn't. Crying was weakness. And they could not be weak.

"Maybe I should take it away. Hmm? No, I think not. I like what it does to you when I do this." The strokes of his cock got harder and faster.

Hunter whimpered, then bit down on his tongue so hard he could taste the metallic tang of blood filling his mouth.

Azazel laughed. "Yes. That is what I like. Everything you are feeling right now—that disgust, that self-loathing, that fear—I can smell it. And it smells so good."

His muscles spasmed, and a searing pain exploded within him. Hunter's body thrashed violently, his head whipping about as he fought against the constricting bonds. But he couldn't get away.

His eyes widened as Azazel's other hand came around and gripped the front of his throat.

Hunter's nostrils flared as his breathing got quick and shallow. The whimper escaped, a raw, emotional sound that was much more pronounced, and he couldn't hold it back. His cock received two more strokes before the flogger hit him multiple times with substantial force. This time, the strikes landed not just on his ass and cheeks, but also on his thighs, where the wax had hardened. As his cock was stroked, his struggles against the restraints intensified. Shooting pains erupted through his upper limbs and the back of his neck as his muscles in his arms and hands got pulled. His body shook. Sweat poured off of him. Hunter couldn't control the whimpers. He couldn't seem to get a single bit of air into his lungs.

Azazel squeezed his throat tighter, stroking his cock harder and faster. "I am going to make you come all over the fucking ground. Then I am going to watch while you lap it up... like the good little pussy you are."

The flogger would crack across his ass or thighs, and the sting would cause his vision to blur. The delicious bites of pain pulled moan after growling moan out of him.

Azazel hollered at someone that Hunter couldn't see. There was a brief lull in the whipping. He heard Azazel crack his joints, then a rush through the air as a different implement whistled toward him. The tails slammed into

Hunter's back, knocking every single inch of breath out of him. His claws dug deeper into the earth. Still, he didn't lose the smirk on his face.

His father had made this whip himself, and it had intrigued Markham the first time the bear king had seen it. Made of thick leather, each of the twenty-two tails had claws from feline shape shifters embedded into them. They faced every direction and reached about halfway up every tail. There was no way at least a few of them wouldn't find purchase with every single swing.

Which they certainly did. And not just on his back. From his shoulders, his sides, the full length of his back, his ass, even down his thighs. Strip after strip of skin was peeled off of him. Hunter's blood flowed freely, soaking the surrounding ground.

"Break, dammit! Fucking break!"

Hunter didn't move. His smirk didn't diminish in the least. Even as Hayden continued to holler plea after plea while Elwin held him back.

"You worthless... fucking... piece of... spourgiff shit! I said... fucking break!" Azazel laid into his back with even greater force, each strike coming faster and faster.

With each new strike of the flogger, his moans ceased. A malicious smirk spread over his face and held. Hunter didn't make a single noise. Not in those moments.

Back and forth. Back and forth.

Then a stroke along his cock. He thrashed at his bindings, fighting to get free. His body trembled as he became a complete whimpering mess, hysterical and frenzied.

The flogger cracked across the top of his ass, his ass cheeks, and his thighs. That cold, calculating calm came back over him, the malicious smirk returning to his face. He made no movement, no noise. It felt so good. He loved this pain. More. Give him more.

"You will never break me."

Hunter's back arched more than before. He let out a growling moan at the fresh scent of his blood. Reality didn't exist any longer. He felt completely crazy. More than half insane. The pain was exquisite. The sexual abuse was bad. There weren't any beats in between; he didn't have time to come down from either. Hunter let out another whimper as his body sagged slightly in his bindings.

Teeth dug into one of his ass cheeks. As he struggled against his bonds, Hunter's whole body tensed, the cuffs digging into his skin and restricting his movement. He couldn't hold the whimper back, even through the stroke of the tongue across his damp flesh. Then everything stopped. His head lolled forward, his forehead landing on something metal.

Click. Click. Click. Like someone in heels was walking across a hard floor. He sensed someone drawing nearer. Nothing made sense. The cacophony of smells, sounds and sights disoriented him, pushing him further into a state of confusion. Once more, his muscles began an involuntary struggle, flailing. When a grip wrapped around the back of his neck, it didn't help. Azazel always held him down by the back of the neck when he fucked him so it was harder to fight back. But this was a unique touch... a comforting touch... It made no sense... Nothing made sense.

"Come on, babe, come back to me," a low voice spoke, though he barely heard or registered the words. "Come back to me, Hunter."

Hunter didn't want it inside him. It was big, and Azazel was rough. It hurt, and he bled, but not in a way that he liked. He didn't like this. He didn't want this. His head thrashed, his muscles coiling tight as he fought against the coarse leather binding him. His eyes misted. Though he couldn't formulate words at the moment, his mouth moved continually, mouthing, *"No... please... no..."*

"Come on, Hunter, please come back to me." The soft kiss on his lips and the sudden sensation against his forehead made him stop. He heard the faint words as though they were carried on the wind from afar. They made little sense, either. "I need you to come back to me. Follow the sound of my voice. You're not there. We are here together. You're safe."

He could see the tree trunk's coarse bark, feel the scratchy ropes, and smell the stale smokiness of Azazel's breath. His father's cock pressed against his ass, and the male's hand wrapped around his dick. He was still there. He wasn't safe. Not safe. Hunter's body jerked and tugged at the bindings. A strangled whimper ripped its way out of his throat. *"No more... No more..."* He needed it to stop. He needed Azazel to stop. *Please... please, stop...*

"Come back to me, babe. You're here with me, Narcissa. You're safe. Hunter, you're not there. You're not there."

Though the tree remained in his sight, its form softened with each passing second. Hunter felt Azazel's touch less and less, too. He no longer smelled the stench of the male's breath saturated with liquor, or his sweat, or his cum. The bindings around his wrists didn't feel so much like rope. It was her name... His Narcissa...

Her lips found his, and a tongue traced along his lip. "Come back to me, babe. Come back to me."

The spoken words against his mouth preceded another sweep of a tongue across his lower lip. The circular motion never stopped on his neck. *Narcissa.* He smelled... her. He smelled her. "Narcissa," Hunter purred. His lips still touching hers, he blinked rapidly, as if trying to erase the memories that plagued him. Allow him back into the present. He didn't want to be there anymore. "Narcissa," he purred, the sound rumbling in his chest, before his tongue met hers in a soft, sensual moan.

Her tongue swept along the backs of his fangs. Tingles shot through them, sending a low, growling moan vibrating out of him. Hunter extended his tongue, wrapping it around hers as he deepened the kiss. A little difficult to do with his forehead pressed against the metal of the bondage cross, but it worked. Each moment, the more he tasted her, the more he smelled her, the less the bad things affected him. Azazel wasn't touching him any longer; he was gone. The tree in front of him disappeared, and he could see her. The bindings on his wrists weren't rope at all any longer; they were leather. He moaned into the kiss again as his purring intensified. *My Narcissa. Mine. Mine.*

Narcissa slowly ended the kiss, but she didn't move. Stroking along his neck, her eyes flicked to his. "I'm going to remove your restraints so you can turn around. Once I have them back in place..." She grinned. "... I'm going to show you what's under my dress."

A low rumble of satisfaction vibrated out of him. He *definitely* wanted to see what was under her dress. But he wouldn't get to tear her clothes off this time. That was unfortunate. Yet he knew he'd enjoy watching her undress for him. Keeping his eyes on hers, Hunter tilted his head to give her better access. His purr grew louder as she stroked further along his neck. "Mmm... yes, Ma'am." Extending his tongue, he licked her bottom lip. "My ankles are sore," he mumbled. It wasn't something he'd noticed until they'd gotten here, in this short, quiet moment. His wrists were really sore, too. Intermittent tremors traveled along his muscles. "May I hold on to the cross while I turn around?" He didn't want to fall down. That would be embarrassing. Like he should really worry about that right now, but still.

"Mmm, yes, you may." Narcissa unbuckled the straps around his wrists first, descended the ladder, and undid the straps around his ankles. She set the ladder aside and strode around to the front of the cross.

Hunter's grip on the rings tightened as the tremors in his leg muscles became increasingly pronounced. Once he'd turned around, he leaned back against the cross. His head tilted back slightly, feeling the cold, hard metal against his fur. His eyes flicked first to one ring, then the other, then back again. The tremors started up again. His stomach clenched. His heart hammered against his ribs as his breath hitched in his throat. He shut his eyes, took a breath, and then felt the coldness of the rings as he wrapped his fingers tightly around them. Maybe things wouldn't get so intense this way, with him facing her. Being able to see what she was doing. That it was *her* doing it. Maybe.

Opening his eyes, he focused his gaze intently on Narcissa.

She stood there and licked her lips as she popped a hip out. "If you can stay still, we'll forgo the restraints for a bit."

Visible relief washed over him. As his heart rate and breathing steadied, the tension in his stomach and the tremors in his body also vanished. Gripping tightly to the rings, Hunter kept his eyes on hers as he slowly nodded. "I can stay still," he whispered. "Am I allowed to move any part of me at all? So, I know? So, I do not get in trouble?" He didn't want the restraints. Without them... he might not get lost for a bit.

Narcissa closed the distance between them, purposely crossing one high-heeled foot in front of the other with each step. Stopping in front of him, she placed her hands on his hips and inched her hands back over his ass. His eyes darkened, and a low growl vibrated out of him. Gods, he loved her hands on him. "Your hips. You may move them. Now, I'm going to take off the dress, and then retrieve something I pulled out special for you."

"Yes, Ma'am." Hunter hesitated for a moment. "Thank you." This way... oh, yes, this way was good. He might not be allowed to move anything but his hips, but he could feel her, see her, and that was all that mattered. She still had to break him—and she would. He knew she would. But he needed at least a slight reprieve.

Narcissa purred. "Good boy."

Hunter growled as she raked her nails over his ass.

He watched, his gaze unwavering, as she took a few steps back, the silk of her dress rustling as she removed it. The urge to—rather forcefully—assist her in her dress removal was a pretty powerful one, but he overrode the desire with the thought of what he'd get if he moved. No moving. Moving equaled restraints. Not something he wanted. So, he just stood there, not moving a muscle, his eyes darkening as she slid first one strap then the other ever so slowly down her arms. The lingerie she had on underneath was black, too. It was a halter, by the looks of it. All he wanted to do was untie that ribbon with his fangs. *No moving. Have to be good. No moving.*

Fuck, she was *really* taking her time getting the dress off. He groaned as she slowly peeled the thin material down the length of her body. His hands clenched tighter around the rings. *No moving. Definitely not moving.* Once she had it off completely, she carefully tossed it on her bed. He couldn't stop the growl. Or the lick of his lips. The crotch barely covered her pussy. He wanted to run his tongue up the crisscrossed ribbons in the front. And then just bite straight through the thin strip between her breasts.

"Would you like to see the back, Hunter?"

Hunter licked his lips again. *"Yes, Ma'am.* Very much."

The deep growl began, and it followed Narcissa across the room, never ceasing as she made her way to the dresser. Holy fuck, he liked this one. The back was nothing but a thong and two ties, one at her hips and one around the middle of her back. Fuck, he really wanted to untie those with his teeth.

Having retrieved the object from her dresser, she turned and walked towards him, her footsteps echoing in the quiet room. As Narcissa stopped in front of him, she held up the combination toy she'd picked out. Not that he took his eyes off hers still. That didn't mean he didn't see it in his peripheral vision, though. It had probably been over twenty-five years since he'd used a cock ring, and the only time he'd worn nipple clamps had been in the beginning when he'd been exploring his likes and dislikes. But he couldn't recall ever using a combination before. This would be interesting. Especially considering that it appeared the cock ring vibrated. An adjustable leather strap and a chain connected the nipple clamps, so any shift would cause them to tighten.

"If you're a really good boy, I'll let you choose how it comes off."

Her words made him growl all over again. "I know how to be a *really good boy*," Hunter said with a smirk.

"Oh, I'm certain you can." Narcissa grinned and moved the cock ring combo to one hand. "Now, let's get this on. I'm quite thirsty."

Hunter let out a low moan as she stroked her hand along the length of his cock. "Well, we cannot have that, *Ma'am*." He was *fully* ready to *quench her thirst.* Hopefully, she would let him do the same soon. He wanted her pussy juices in his mouth.

Tilting his gaze down without moving his head—so he wouldn't get in trouble—Hunter watched what she was doing. First, she stretched the material of the ring before lowering it over his cock until she got it at the base of his shaft. It was tight, but not uncomfortable at all. He groaned when she gave a slight tug on the buckle and lifted the clamps. There was a burst of intense pain as she got each clamp in place. His eyes drifted closed, a soft purr-growl vibrating out of him, as she tightened the bolts. "Mmm..."

After getting them into a comfortable position, Narissa reached down to the cock ring and turned on the vibrator. A low rumble started up immediately in his chest. The vibrations made his shaft and testicles tingle, intensifying the throbbing that the cock ring had escalated. Already, his erection felt fuller and thicker.

"I believe we're ready to begin."

Narcissa ran her hands up his chest, a groan escaping him as she gently tugged the clamps, the sound amplifying as her nails scratched his sides. His grip on the rings tightened, any soreness completely and totally forgotten by now. His groan shifted to a growl as she dragged her nails hard over his hips and down his thighs. "Fuck..." Hunter hissed.

She crossed the room back to her dresser and retrieved another crop. It was similar to the first one, except this had a thin, braided nylon tassel at the end. His tongue snaked over his lips as he got a magnificent view of her ass. Holy fuck, he *really* wanted to bite her ass cheeks. While she'd been teasing him with her treks back and forth, she didn't take long to return to him this time. The renewed view of her front just made his fangs throb. *So many places* he wanted to sink his teeth into.

Narcissa struck his thigh with the crop, the string hitting his ass cheek at the same time. His growling moans, which had begun softly, quickly grew louder as she grasped his cock and stroked it twice. "Fuck..." Hunter groaned while pushing his hips forward, craving more of his dick in her grip. He reveled in the way the movement tugged on the chain, tightening the clamps around his nipples. As she continued her strokes, another moan escaped him as she struck his other thigh; however, her nails across his inner thigh elicited a raw hiss. *Holy fucking shit*, everything she did felt so good. It was more difficult not to move than he thought it would have been. His muscles trembled as he fought not to move anything but his hips. *No moving. Have to be good. No restraints.* Not that he stopped his hips; he could move those. He kept the rest of his body still, even his head.

"Once I get my mouth on your cock, you may come when I tug on your balls. Understood?"

"Yes, Ma'am." Oh, fuck yes, he wanted her mouth on his cock. He wanted her nails on him again, too. Another strike from the crop. Everything. He wanted more of everything. Hunter's eyes darkened and his tongue snaked over his lips. "Would you do that harder, please, Ma'am?"

Narcissa purred.

Fuck, he loved that.

"Which part would you like harder, Hunter? This?" The crop struck him with a stinging force. "Or this?" Her grip on his shaft tightened as she continued to strike him with the crop, escalating the strength behind each one. "Or this?" Between each lash of the crop, her nails dug sharply into his thighs. "All of it?"

Hunter's hands were clenched so tight that the tendons in his arms and shoulders bulged. It was just one thing to keep his body still, keep everything but his hips from moving. Those didn't stop thrusting in rhythm with her touch. His breaths became more ragged, his moans louder, and his growls more aggressive with each strike of the crop and stroke of his cock. His feral hisses grew with each press of her nails into his thighs. "All of it. Please. All of it."

Narcissa swung the crop, increasing the strength behind the impact. He moaned out loud at the contact. So good... so fucking good.

"All of it, *what*?" As if to emphasize exactly what she wanted to hear, her palm stilled on his shaft.

"*Ma'am*," he purred out. "All of it, Ma'am."

"Much better." She increased the force of the crop's impact as she alternated between each of his thighs and stroked his cock once more. Her touch lingered, then her nails raked hard, a stinging sensation across his inner thigh.

Holy fucking shit, he already needed to come. His claws dug into his palms until he was bleeding, but this time, the sting just added to the pleasure coursing through him. Between her actions, the tightening of the clamps as his hips strained against the chains, the vibrations from the cock ring, the heat radiating from her, and her increasingly potent scent... Hunter was about to climax. "I need to come," he moaned. *Shit.* "Ma'am... *oh, fuck...* please... I need to come."

He cried out the moment her lips touched him. Narcissa deep-throated him, taking his entire length into her mouth. His sensitivity was such that his entire body quivered in the struggle to hold back until she gave permission. The sting of the crop on his thigh brought forth yet another ecstatic cry. And then her hand tugged on his balls—his cue to let go.

A powerful roar emanated from him, so intense that it seemed to ignite every flame in the room and even rattle the walls, like a colossal release of energy. His hips didn't stop jerking forward, fucking her mouth, as a torrent of cum gushed out of him and down her throat. It felt like his claws punctured all the way through his palms as he fought to move nothing but his hips. *HOLY. FUCKING. SHIT.* He didn't think he'd *ever* had an orgasm like this in his life.

Her lips remained locked around his shaft as she swallowed every drop that filled her mouth. *Holy fucking Hades,* even when his orgasm finally ended, she didn't stop sucking his cock. Nor did he stop fucking her mouth. A strangled moan left him, his eyes rolling back in his head, as she swept her tongue along the underside of his cock. "Oh... holy... shit..." he groaned. "Fuck... fuck yes!" His palms slipped against the rings, but he tightened his hold and managed not to move his arms. As she dug her nails into his ass cheek, his moans transformed into a steady growl, while her other hand hammered his thighs with the end of the crop. "Oh, fuck... fuck... fuck... gods... please, do not stop! Fu—Ma'am... please, do not stop! Gods, please, make me come again!"

Though she didn't answer him verbally, the deep moan she let out was more than enough. His eyes remained rolled to the back of his head while Narcissa sensually explored his cock with her tongue, gently grazing her teeth along the base of his shaft as she continued to suck on it. He probably looked completely insane right now, but he couldn't have cared less. Everything just felt *so fucking good.* He could already feel the familiar warmth building within him, signaling another orgasm. The intensity of her actions drove him to increase the force and speed of his movements, synchronizing with her scratching and the crop hitting his thighs. "Harder! Please, Ma'am... harder... Everything, harder, please!" Hunter let out a massive snarl as his head fell back against the metal of the cross.

As Narcissa sucked and grazed harder, the pressure of her nails increased, and the crop hit his thighs with more force. Hunter gasped out moan after moan, no longer able to form any words. The part of his brain that allowed words to form and leave his mouth seemed to malfunction. His noises just got more guttural and savage. With his head pressed firmly against the metal surface, his movements were forceful as he continued to push his cock into her throat repeatedly. Blood, still warm, trickled down his palms and wrists, the crimson liquid beading before it dripped from his arms. Just one more strike to his thigh with the crop and that was all it took. An immense orgasm, so powerful it stole his breath, exploded from his cock. Every muscle in his body tensed up as she swallowed his release.

Narcissa didn't stop until she had thoroughly worked him through his climax. Once his release ended, she licked along the underside of his shaft as she sucked up to the tip of his cock. *Holy... fucking... shit...* he was actually dizzy.

She ran her fingers down his outer thighs before rising to her feet. "Mmm, yum." Her tongue swept out across her lips. "I believe you should receive a reward." With a smile on her face, Narcissa struck his thigh once with the crop, then strode back across the room. She set the crop atop the dresser, grabbed the edge of the queening bench, and made her way back toward him. "How would you like my lingerie to come off?"

She'd asked him a question. Her lingerie. It was time for it to come off. Fuck. "With—" Hunter gasped as his erection pulsed, the ripple causing the chains to tighten, thus increasing the pressure of the nipple clamps. Amid everything, he'd almost forgotten they were there, but they were *extremely* tight now. "—with my teeth. If that pleases you, Ma'am."

"Mmm, oh, yes, very much." Narcissa licked her lips as she got the queening bench set in front of him.

A low growl rumbled from Hunter's chest. He really wanted his tongue back in her mouth, too.

"How's the cock ring and clamps feel? Do we need to adjust them?"

"No, Ma'am. The cock ring is fine. The clamps are extremely tight, but I am okay." He wasn't ready to remove either, any more than it seemed like she wanted to. He waited for permission to move, his eyes locked on hers, while his fingers curled around the smooth, sticky rings.

"Good." Narcissa climbed onto the queening bench, giving him a perfect view of her ass. "You may move."

With permission given, Hunter immediately dropped to his knees. He crawled over until he was behind her and untied the ribbons with his fangs. He started by licking from her left ankle, tracing a path up her calf to her knee, then up her thigh until he reached just below her ass. Following the same pattern with her right leg, he delicately bit down on each cheek, savoring the explosion of her taste in his mouth. He slowly traced his tongue along her crevice before seizing the top tie with his teeth and tugging until it unraveled. A soft moan left Narcissa's mouth. His tongue danced up her spine, reaching the soft skin at the middle of her back. With the knot undone, he lowered his pace, a soft growl rumbling in his chest as he savored the taste of her, his fangs tracing the length of her spine, her shoulder, and the curve of her neck. The noises Narcissa let out intensified.

Hunter held the tie in his mouth and pulled it, the silky material unwinding from her neck at a snail's pace. The lingerie slipped off her body and pooled in her lap. Another low growl left him. The very air around them seemed charged with sexual energy. Holy fuck, she was so fucking sexy. Not to mention her incredible scent and her exquisite taste. He could happily worship her body for hours and still not get enough. Hunter crawled around the queening bench, his knuckles grazing the cold floor, as he kneeled before Narcissa, meeting her intense gaze with his own. "May I lick your pussy, please? *Ma'am?*" The 'ma'am' came out purred as a slight smirk lifted the corners of his lips. "I would really, *really* love to lick your pussy."

Narcissa carefully untucked one leg at a time and placed a high heel on either side of his knees before leaning back on her hands, the heels clicking on the floor. "Since you asked so nicely, you may."

"Thank you, Ma'am." Hunter set her lingerie aside, reveling because he'd actually managed not to rip it. That meant she could wear it another time. His hands landed on the bench, caging her between them. He could have used the headrest, but the journey would be more pleasurable without it. He would have much better access this way. Not to mention, she couldn't dig her heels into him if he used the headrest, nor could he grab her ass. "May I touch you with my hands?"

"Yes, you may," Narcissa purred.

His eyes darkened, a growl vibrating from deep within to meet her purr. Without a word, his hands began their ascent, gripping her tightly as they reached her ass. Hunter slowly trailed his fangs along her inner thighs, starting with one and then moving to the other. His chest rumbled as he got closer to the source of the blazing heat rolling off of her. Her scent, sweet as honeysuckle on a warm summer day, was enough to make him forget everything. Even as he reached her pussy and tasted her, his gaze never wavered from her eyes. His growl grew louder as he enveloped her clit in his mouth, flicking the tip of his tongue against it. Narcissa gasped, followed by a moan that jolted through every inch of him.

With a gentle bite, Hunter teased her clit, traced his tongue slowly up her slit, and then sucked on her nub. He began again, her arousal thickening in the air as he slid one hand from her ass. His claws swept across her hip, then over her thigh, touching her knee and finally tracing her inner thigh. He retracted his claws as he reached her pussy, sliding three fingers deep inside her.

Narcissa let out a husky moan and arched her back, her muscles already contracting around his fingers. "Harder, Hunter."

Hades, she was so sexy. He'd never tire of gazing at her, no matter if she was in the throes of ecstasy or not. Hunter didn't take his eyes off of her once as he followed her command. He gripped her ass harder, digging his claws in. He pushed his fingers into her, increasing the intensity and speed, curling them to stimulate her G-spot. The swipes of his tongue got deeper, the bites and sucks to her clit more intense. He desired her taste as much as he needed to breathe.

As she gripped the queening bench, a wave of pleasure coursed through her, leaving her breathless. Hunter quickly withdrew his fingers and pushed his tongue as far into her core as possible. Her pussy released a torrent of cum into his eager mouth, resembling molten lava cascading down a volcano. Hunter's growled moan continued uninterrupted, caught between the heavenly sound and the irresistible taste of her body. His eyes didn't leave her beautiful face once. Even as he stroked his tongue up her slit, lifted his head from between her thighs, and licked his lips.

"May I please keep going, Ma'am? I would love to make you come again."

It took her a second to respond as her gaze zeroed in on his mouth. Leaning forward, Narcissa fused their lips together and gripped the back of his head. A moan escaped him, and then it became a snarl as her tongue touched his fangs. Hunter's fingers found the curve of her neck as the kiss intensified, their tongues meeting and dancing for a full minute. Fuck, he loved kissing her. And the way they tasted together made his taste buds tingle.

Narcissa ended the kiss with a sharp bite on his lower lip. A shudder shot down his spine. "Yes, you may."

Hunter licked her bottom lip, then his. "Thank you, Ma'am." A slight smirk crossed his face. "May I put your legs over my shoulders?" He desired to feel her stilettos as they dug into his back. Preferably until they drew blood.

"Fuck yes." Narcissa scooted closer to the edge of the queening bench and leaned back. She spread her arms wide and wrapped her hands around the sides of the bench.

A low growl escaped him, and his tongue slowly snaked across his lips. *Fuck. Yes.* Hunter hooked her legs over his shoulders, his hands gliding from her heels to her knees. His tongue lazily explored the smoothness of her inner thigh as his hands roamed up the outside of her legs, across her hips, and upward to her stomach, finally cupping her breasts. "I am looking forward to you fucking my tongue, *Ma'am.*" Hunter murmured the last word before sliding his tongue deep into her.

Narcissa arched her back, pressing her breasts further into his hands while moving her hips in rhythm with his tongue. Her deep moan filled the air as she squeezed the bench, digging her stilettos into his shoulders. The pinpricks of her heels had him moaning against her. They weren't deep enough. Not yet. They would get there, though. He craved the feeling of them piercing his skin until blood dripped down his back. But he wouldn't ask. When Narcissa wanted to do it, she would. Hunter intensified his oral ministrations, pressing his mouth firmly against her core as his tongue delved deeper and quickened its pace. His hands moved rhythmically, massaging her breasts while his fingers teased and gently pinched her nipples.

As she rode his tongue with more force, her heels pressed harder into his back. He could sense another orgasm about to explode within her, but they were content to savor the moment. She let go of the bench and increased the pressure of his hands against her breasts, intensifying the massage. *Mmm, holy fucking shit.* Gods, he needed more. *Come for me, sweetheart. Give me every single drop.* Fuck, he would never get enough of the way this felt; the way she tasted.

"Don't stop, Hunter! Don't st—" Narcissa cried out in ecstasy. Like a torrential downpour, her sweet juices exploded into his mouth.

Hunter purred as he swallowed every drop, lapping at her pussy to ensure he didn't allow a single bit of it to go to waste. Even after her release ended and he'd taken every drop, her hips didn't stop lifting. Hunter moaned against her. *Fuck yes,* he was so hoping she wouldn't be ready to move on just yet. He hadn't had nearly enough of her yet. Her heels dug into his back, the metallic tang of blood mixing with the sweet scent of their climax and the flickering candle. The pleasure had him crying out against her. *Holy shit.* Fuck yes, that's what he wanted. Hunter spread her thighs wider using his shoulders, allowing his tongue to delve deeper into her, experiencing every part of her pleasure.

Narcissa arched her back with a husky moan. His moan answered hers, and she tightened her hands around his. After releasing her clitoris, he whisked his fangs along the outer lips of her pussy, while his tongue glided up her slit and flicked over her nub multiple times. As if reading his thoughts, she traced her nails from his hands to his forearms, then dragged them back, digging in as she reached his hands. A ravenous snarl left him. Narcissa's hips lifted over and over, rocking against his tongue. *Holy fucking shit,* he loved that. Each lift of her hips made it harder for him to continue what he was doing. He needed his tongue buried deep in her pussy once more. After giving one last stroke up her center, he plunged his tongue deep into her, releasing another low growl that reverberated throughout her core.

"Fuck yes." With renewed intensity, Narcissa dug her heels into his back, causing a more painful sensation, and quickened the pace of her hips. Another sharp cry left him. *Fuck yes ... so fucking good.* His deep rumbling snarl grew louder as he drove harder and faster at her pussy. As his claws pierced her breasts, the air filled with the coppery smell of her blood, blending with his primal scent. Hell yeah, he craved that aroma as intensely as he craved another taste of her release.

As her scream filled the room, Narcissa's hands clenched the bench, and she met Hunter's rhythm with untamed passion. Holy. Fucking. Shit. *That* noise amplified the already intense throbbing in his cock. Not that he could even figure out how that was possible.

Her climax erupted forcefully, gushing into his mouth as if a dam had burst open. "Fuck!"

Hunter swallowed every morsel, ensuring not a single bit escaped the journey down his throat. Shifting his hands from her breasts to her inner thighs, he widened her legs to the maximum extent and let out a powerful roar against her pussy. Despite the overtones of the entire session, he didn't think he'd ever felt more dominant than he did in this moment.

"Fuck!" Narcissa cried out. "Hunter, don't stop!"

No fucking way was that happening. His roar had barely faded when her pussy released another gush of cum, filling his mouth once more. Hunter lapped up every single glorious drop. Gods, he could fucking stay here between her thighs for all eternity and still not get enough. Once he'd swallowed the last, he raised his head and smirked up at her. "You always taste so fucking delicious, *Ma'am.*" Once again, he purred the last word out, then stroked his tongue slowly over her sex.

Narcissa muttered something akin to an agreement, bringing forth a slight chuckle from him. It was a moment or two before she unhooked her legs from his shoulders and sat up. "Yes, I do, Hunter." She leaned forward, her lips meeting his as her tongue invaded his mouth.

Fuck, she tasted so good. His moan intensified as she brushed her tongue against his fangs, sparking a shiver down his spine, before intertwining their tongues. *So, so good.* As he deepened the kiss, one hand found its way to her knee while the other gently cupped the nape of her neck. Narcissa groaned into the kiss. For a minute, their tongues danced before she pulled away, her forehead finding his. Slowly, her eyes met his.

As much as he wanted to protest—and nearly did—Hunter bit his tongue instead. He already missed the taste of her pussy, as well as her lips. But it was time... Time to move on to the next stage. The reprieve was officially over now. Despite his resistance, an icy dread consumed him, making his skin prickle with gooseflesh and his breath catch in his throat. Hunter slowly removed his hand from her knee and the back of her neck, clenching his own knees to regain composure. His shoulders and neck muscles became rigid, and he fought the urge to reach back and massage the knots away. Gods, he didn't fucking want to do this... But it was necessary.

There was no other way.

There were things he could suggest. Things he was almost certain would *absolutely* break him. Completely shatter him. But he was loath to utter a word. As much as he knew this was necessary... as much as he knew this was what *had* to happen between them... that didn't mean he wanted it to. So, he just sat there, hands on his knees, eyes on hers, and waited. If she wanted his help, she would ask. And he would answer. But it would have been impossible not to get some indications from his reactions to what she'd already done. So, unless she asked... he would just sit here quietly and wait for her instruction.

Narcissa sat up. "Crawl to the chaise and climb on it, face down."

Face down... Hunter squeezed his eyes shut. *Oh, gods...* His heart hammered against his ribs, and a tight band seemed to constrict his chest, making it difficult to draw a breath. *Face down... Face down... Face down... Stop it, Hunter.* This had to be done. He just needed to get it over with. Digging his claws into his palms, he attempted to take a deep breath, then gave up when it was obviously futile. His eyes lifted to hers. "Yes, Ma'am."

Placing his palms on the floor, he lowered his head and crawled. His legs and arms trembled every step of the way. Once he reached the chaise, he tried to sit up. Rise from the floor. Get on the chaise. Something, anything. But it was like he'd become frozen in place. As he flicked his gaze up to the furniture, a dizzying wave of nausea washed over him, knotting his stomach. It took every ounce of willpower he had to get up on it.

Hunter, struggling to catch his breath, stretched out on his stomach on the chaise. A groan escaped him as the vibrations intensified, the chains yanking again, and the nipple clamps tightened. The pressure of his stiff and throbbing cock, sandwiched between his body and the chaise, almost caused him to climax, if not for his overwhelming anxiety and trepidation. Hunter pressed his forehead to the cushioning, breathing in and out slowly, feeling the soft texture against his fur. Following her instructions would give him some breathing room, even though the weight of the situation felt like it was suffocating him.

He gripped the legs of the chaise and held on tight, letting his arms fall uselessly to either side. She'd likely move his arms, restrain them, but this would help keep him from moving too much until she did so. Oh, gods, he couldn't breathe. His lungs burned, a hollow echo resonating with each agonizing, failed attempt to breathe. He positioned his tail so that it wouldn't be in the way. And then he prayed. For what might have been the first time in his life. He prayed that all of this would be over quickly.

Even though he knew it wouldn't be. This portion, more than any of the others, would not be a swift thing. And when it finally ended... Hunter knew he would no longer be the same.

There was a slight shift as Narcissa rose to her feet. Each footfall echoed in the hollow space, a deafening drumbeat of impending doom in his mind. She strode across the floor, and while he could hear her gathering a few items, Hunter couldn't decipher what they were. Eventually, she moved toward the chaise where he was lying.

Though he made an attempt, against his better judgement, to see what the items were as she set them atop the dresser there, he couldn't focus. Narcissa leaned over him, and with a metallic clang, buckled the strap around his left wrist, pulling the chain until it was taut. Every ounce of breath Hunter had gathered in his lungs left him in an instant. Desperate, he dug his claws into his palms, but even the delicious sting couldn't stop the world from spinning, his stomach from churning, and his body from quivering.

When she did the same to his right wrist, it made every sensation assaulting him that much worse. Sweat broke out across his entire body. His heart hammered in his chest, as if trying to escape its confines. From atop the dresser, Narcissa retrieved the spreader, the metal clicking softly as she locked it around his ankles. Hunter's entire body went rigid. *Oh, gods... Oh, gods... Oh, gods...* It wasn't like he hadn't had some inkling when she'd had him lay face down. But the spreader bar made him want to vomit. Would she fuck him with something? Is that what she had planned? Or was this just a way to keep him spread the way she wanted him to be, moving as little as possible? Both?

"No limits. I will need to get as far out of my comfort zone as it is possible to get." That's what *he'd* said. That had been *his* decision. That was what was *necessary*. This wouldn't work otherwise, and all of this would be for nothing. He could do this. He could get through this.

Couldn't he...?

Hunter bit his tongue so hard, he could taste the metallic tang of blood. The taste and sting of pain failed to pacify him. The trembling in his body intensified tenfold. He couldn't stop the constant string of cursing in his mind as Narcissa placed the blindfold around his eyes and bound it at the back of his head.

"Can you see anything, Hunter?"

He barely heard her question. He didn't like the dark. Not the pitch dark. Never had. He'd even knocked a hole in his room back home, so the sunlight or moonlight could stream in. On nights when the moonlight didn't make it to his bedroom, he didn't sleep. Just paced until the light returned. He didn't want to be in the dark. He hated it. Bad things happened in the dark when he couldn't see.

Each breath burst in and out of his mouth. Despite the biting cold, he felt nothing. Unsure if he could get any words to come out, he would have shaken his head 'no' but he couldn't seem to move, either. "No—" The one word came out almost whispered. That wasn't good enough. Narcissa wouldn't accept that. He had to be louder to get his words out more clearly. Hunter tried again, but it wasn't any better than the first time. Clearing his throat as much as he could, he tried once more. "No, Ma'am." Still wasn't great, but it was the best it was going to get right now.

"Good," Narcissa stated.

Before he sensed her moving behind him, a small object tumbled from the dresser with a soft thud. Before Hunter could react, the whip sliced across his back; the sound was barely audible. His back arched, and he moaned, the sound muffled by the pressure of his claws against his palms. As the exquisite pain coursed through him, the room vanished, the chaise morphed away, and even Narcissa, with her familiar perfume, faded from view.

The whip cracked across his back again. Hunter's eyes squeezed shut. The coppery taste of blood filled his mouth as he bit down harder on his tongue. The muscles in his back tensed up as he fought not to move. He pressed his palms against the rough bark, feeling the sharp edges of the scratch marks his claws had made. He was just shy of eleven, so they weren't as sharp as they would be in a few years.

"Stop flinching," Azazel spoke from behind him. "If you flinch in a fight, you are dead."

Blood trickled down his back, leaving a cold, sticky trail that prickled his skin. Burning his open wounds. But he didn't dare move. If he moved, Azazel would whip him harder. He had to endure this. Get to where he didn't flinch at all. The goal being that, in a fight, if his opponent jumped on his back and dug his claws in, the pain wouldn't faze him and he could overtake his adversary without issue. Only then would Azazel be satisfied with this part of his training.

With each strike, Hunter moaned, the sound echoing through the air as his back arched. The whip struck first one ass cheek, then the other. Everything Hunter saw in his head shifted to something completely different. Now, he was five years younger—six years of age and in the orphans' hut. Doing everything he could to keep his father away from his brother.

Azazel's claws drew blood as they swiped across his back and his butt. Any closer and the asshole might have ripped his spinal cord. Elwin had warned him more than once never to leave his back exposed to any of the males here. Not that Hunter had needed the warning. He just hadn't been able to help it this time. He immediately spun around to face the male who was supposed to be his father. Azazel was no father, though. He was just a nasty jerk.

If his father wasn't drunk off his ass, Hunter would have absolutely been dead by now. He was already bloody on more than just his back and backside. His arms and legs had scratches and puncture wounds, and there were bumps on his head. Any time Azazel had gone for Hayden, Hunter had gotten in the way. He'd bitten and scratched with all his might. His teeth and claws weren't as sharp as they would get as he grew older, but with as much force as he was putting into each blow, he was at least irritating the crap out of Azazel.

Something Samael kept pointing out each time. The male was leaning against the doorjamb because he was too drunk to stand upright, drinking something clear out of a jar that stung Hunter's nose. His gigantic form blocked out the moonlight that otherwise would have shone in. He'd called Hunter everything from a 'dumb pussy' to a 'fucking idiot' along with several other things. Hunter couldn't pay him any attention, though. He had to stay focused on Azazel. Had to keep him away from the corner his twin was in, curled up in a tiny ball.

Azazel had gone for Hayden because Hayden wouldn't fight. Hayden hated fighting of any kind; it scared him. So, Hunter fought for him. He was older. It was his job to protect his younger twin. And he always would. No matter what punishments that brought him.

No matter how hard Hunter fought, it wasn't long before Azazel got a hold of the back of his neck and slammed him face down into the floor. Blood gushed from his nose as it broke.

A hard, rigid, and thick object pressed against the sensitive skin of his ass crack, followed by another stinging lash of the whip.

The hand at the back of his neck tightened. Rancid, spirit-filled breath sounded in his ear. "You wanna stand between me and the little pussy, you get to get it twice as bad."

Hunter gasped for breath as his claws scraped at the floor. He pulled and strained, but whatever held his wrists and ankles wouldn't budge. He couldn't move. Couldn't get away. No matter what he tried to do, he couldn't get away...

The whip cracked against his skin, a sharp sound repeating four times. The unforgiving object scraped across his sensitive skin and then pressed against his asshole.

His heart hammered against his ribs in a frantic rhythm. He felt a wave of dizziness wash over him. And nauseous. The sensation became increasingly unbearable as pressure mounted against his backside. Then the pressure left for just a moment.

While he couldn't feel the flame, Hunter could feel the wax that dripped onto his thighs. The teeth that bit into one of his ass cheeks. That hard, rigid thing that got close to his asshole again. All of that stayed at the back of his mind, though, barely there in his consciousness, completely overridden by what he could see, and the sensations only present in his head.

Hunter's eyes rolled back in his head and he let out a gasp—*as the greatest pain he'd ever felt in his life speared through his butt and up his spine. The intensity was so consuming; it was like his skin was ablaze. Split completely in two. Oh... ow... oh, gods... What... what was this...? It hurt... Oh, gods; it hurt...*

A bloodcurdling shriek erupted from his mouth, a sound so piercing it reverberated through the village. Every inch of his body shook. His eyes bulged. His nostrils flared. Pain speared through his chest as his lungs constricted. He jerked even harder at the bindings on his wrists, but it didn't do any good. His claws gouged into anything and everything they could reach. But he couldn't get away. Couldn't get free. Couldn't stop the pain... Oh, gods, the pain...

Hunter didn't know anything could hurt this much. Before his vision gave out completely, black spots danced before his eyes. Azazel's claws tore into his shoulders and arms, the agony intensifying with each passing moment. It was like his butt was literally burning. Like he'd sat right down in a fire. Every inch of his body felt like it was being ripped to shreds from the inside out. He lost the ability to breathe. Vomited all over the floor. He could hear Hayden whimpering and crying in the corner. His twin was speaking to him through their mindlink, but Hunter couldn't make out the words. It didn't stop him from trying to get his brother out of there.

A bone-chilling crack split the air as his pelvis fractured.

Hunter screamed so loudly, it felt like his eardrums would shatter. Tears poured down his cheeks.

Twin cracks reverberated off the walls of the hut as his thighs snapped.

Hunter's mouth fell open. He tried to scream again, but his vocal cords failed, and not a single sound emerged. Faint gasps, barely audible, escaped as he fought for the breath he couldn't grasp.

Azazel's claws dug in deeper. A wet, hot, and sticky sensation oozed through the fur on his arms and shoulder blades, and a pool formed between his thighs. It smelled of blood. Was he bleeding?

Even in his mind, Hunter could barely hear the words. But he had to keep saying them. He had to keep his twin safe. Even as the last vestiges of his awareness flickered, the darkness threatened to consume him.

His body was going numb. There was nothing visible to him as he struggled to make out his surroundings. His exhaustion was a heavy weight on his shoulders. He just wanted to go to sleep. But something kept slamming into him repeatedly. It wouldn't stop. Gods, please... please... stop...

Somewhere in the distance came a growl-grunt. Then, with a deafening crash, something slammed against the side of the hut. Hunter knew that only because everything around him shook. Then, the floor of the hut trembled. The immense weight on him and inside him was suddenly gone.

Hunter screamed as the unseen force tore something from his body. Hot tears relentlessly poured down his cheeks. His cry of agony faded, turning into soft, mewling whimpers. His lips trembled. He vaguely registered something clattering to the ground behind him. Nothing else came at him. Nothing else hit him.

Growls and snarls filled first the hut, then moved outside.

Suddenly, he could sense a new presence next to him. The blindfold fell away, but he kept his eyes closed, as if the light would hurt. He didn't want to see whatever, or whoever, was in front of him. A hand gently touched his face, wiping the tears from beneath his eyes. Hunter flinched, trying desperately to get away. No... No... No more... No more...

Lips pressed against his, then his forehead. Hunter struggled, but his head remained fixed in place. Gods, please, no more...

"Hunter? Can you hear me? Hunter? No, Hayden, you stay right there. Do not come over here, do you hear me? Oh, gods... Oh, gods... Do not move, buddy. Do not move. You are going to be okay. Just lie still, alright?"

The hand on his face moved to the back of his neck, rubbing slow circles along the nape. Hunter sobbed. His body shook even harder. Wasn't he gone? Wasn't Azazel gone? It had ended, right? It was all over... right? Please... please, let it be over...

"Hey! Get me something to move him! Now!"

No matter how hard he tried to jerk away, the gentle touches continued.

The growls and snarls outside ceased. He could hear Markham's roar. Hear bodies slamming up against trees... or huts... or something. He couldn't be sure.

Hunter cried out in pain again when they moved him onto something flat and lifted him off the ground. It felt like the pain was brand new all over again.

The scent of tears that weren't his own filled his senses, but it wasn't something he could track. Not just yet.

"We are going to get you help. You are going to be just fine, Hunter. Hayden, you stay here with Elijah, okay? You stay right here with him."

The hand, soft and warm, caressed the back of his head and across his ears before settling into gentle circles along the nape of his neck. Hunter tried to jerk his head away. His lips moved, but his words didn't have any volume. *"No more... please... no more,"* he mouthed. *"Please... stop, please... please..."*

They carried his tiny, broken body toward the doorway, where a dim light spilled from the hut. As they crossed over the threshold, Hunter couldn't hold out any longer. A chilling void engulfed him, and his breath hitched as the shadows tightened around him.

But even as the images in his head ceased, the sensations persisted. A wave of agony crashed over him, a sharp pain that lanced across his body. His very core screamed, a desperate plea for something, anything, to mend the gaping wounds that threatened to swallow him whole. The sensation of his skin crawling. The overwhelming fight-or-flight. But he couldn't get away. Couldn't get free. Still held down at the wrists and ankles, unable to break out of the restraints. So, he fought instead. Tugging, pulling, jerking. His head thrashing. His lungs screaming as he hollered out a wordless plea.

The voice right beside him continued to whisper words he couldn't make out. A touch on his head, ears, and neck continued, causing shivers to run down his spine and limbs.

He fought. Until something snapped in his mind. Shattering the illusion of the past. The force of the present slammed into him, making him gasp for air. The blindfold was gone. Not that it mattered. His vision was too blurry to actually see anything. But he could smell her now. He could hear that it was her voice. Narcissa.

Hunter tried to speak, but his voice box produced only a croak. All he could do was mouth the word *red* repeatedly, as he ignored the blinding pain that throbbed through his left wrist. "Take them off. Please, take them off, take them off, take them off," he sobbed.

"I'm taking them off." Narcissa rose to her feet and swiftly unbuckled the straps binding his wrists, followed by the ones securing his ankles.

The moment they were off of him, Hunter rolled away and onto the cold floor. He struggled with the nipple rings and cock ring before finally removing them and tossing them aside. He curled inward, drawing his knees to his chest and shielding his head with his arms, creating a tight, protective shell. With his chin tucked in, Hunter squeezed his eyes shut as tight as he could. The shakes still rolled through him as tears continued to pour down his face. He couldn't seem to get a hold of himself. He didn't even care how ridiculous he looked. How weak. The self-loathing, disgust, and embarrassment would set in later, he was sure. Right now, he just needed to breathe again. Needed the stabbing ache in his chest to go away. For his head to stop pounding. For his eyes to quit fucking leaking.

Narcissa pushed the chaise aside a little further and crawled over to him. She slid one of her hands beneath one of his, caressing his shoulders with her other hand.

Though Hunter flinched, the soothing touches brought forth a fresh wave of tears. He couldn't even say why. He *never* cried. Never even *felt* like crying. He couldn't actually remember if he ever had. Now, he couldn't seem to stop.

"Take shallow breaths. Squeeze my hand as hard as you need to."

Try as he might, breathing refused to come any easier to him just yet. His left wrist was swollen, throbbing with a dull ache that suggested a fracture. He didn't know for sure, nor did he care. Hunter gently removed his left hand from hers, then slowly moved his right hand over to cover the hand she had placed on his head. It was the only movement he could bring himself to make.

If this wasn't fucking broken—no, not broken, *shattered*—he didn't know what was.

He couldn't remember a time he'd ever been this... *raw*. He felt like a shell of his former self. No longer Hunter. No longer *him*. This session hadn't just fragmented him; it had stripped him of everything that made him who he was. Made him *Hunter*. It had released his demons from the prison he kept them locked in, set them free, and allowed them to run rampant on his mind. They had devoured his control, his self-confidence, his personality, his dominance, his poise. His very being. Turned him into someone who fell apart at the slightest touch.

He didn't like it. Not one bit. And he didn't know how to get himself back.

Eleven

"**G**ods, I'm so sorry, Hunter. I'm so sorry." The words didn't even feel like they would be enough. Nothing could be enough to repair the spiritual damage she'd inflicted. But she had to do something. Anything to help him steady his breathing and calm the tremors in his body. Once that happened, then she could handle his aftercare, and that would offer more aid. This was one of those moments where she envied the nymphs who could soothe someone. But that wasn't how she was made.

So, Narcissa did the only thing that came to her mind. She lay down on her side and curled around him, the scent of his skin filling her senses. Anything to comfort him. Not something she'd ever really done before. No, that wasn't true. She'd done it once before with him. In their third session, she'd sat behind him and wrapped her arms around him then. Gods, was that when everything had changed between them? Or had it been like that since day one?

"No. Not your fault," Hunter mumbled. Before she could track what he was doing, he changed positions. He turned over, facing her. He crossed his arms and inhaled her scent, nuzzling his face into the soft crook of her neck.

It seemed the most natural thing to have him tucked against her like this. Careful of his injuries, she held him closer, her arms wrapping gently around him. He didn't flinch this time, which was a good sign. Gently, Narcissa stroked the back of his head, up to his ears and back. A soft purr left him, a noise she craved in his absence.

She'd never felt agony like this before. Even when she'd bid her mother and brother goodbye, it didn't feel like this. Yes, the intention behind this session was to break him, to reset the line between them. But she hadn't expected her composure to shatter like glass. There was a difference between pleasurable pain and true pain. While they had certainly experienced the first, she believed they'd experienced the second as well. That was the last thing she ever wanted to cause him.

Narcissa was in love with him, a feeling that had crept up on her without her knowing when or how. It was why she'd marked him four days earlier. She didn't want to share him. Not anymore than she wanted to be shared. It wasn't their reality, though. A realization that split her soul in half. If this was what she had to deal with in order to keep seeing him, then she'd find a way. Maybe it wasn't like anything she'd ever known before, but she wasn't unfamiliar with emotional misery.

Right now, she needed to focus on Hunter. She kissed his forehead gently, then ran her fingers from the base of his neck, along his ears, and back down again. "When you're ready to move, I'll draw a bath."

Hunter offered the faintest nod, his face unmoved and eyes still closed as he inhaled her scent, over and over. His breath deepened slowly, and it seemed to become easier for him. The trembling subsided, and finally, the sobs that wracked his body calmed. With each passing moment of ease for him, her heart felt less constricted as his body found peace. This was good.

"I think I can move now," he muttered.

Narcissa kissed his forehead once more, the warmth of his skin lingering on her lips. "Okay." She stood up slowly, kicked off her heels, and padded barefoot into her bathroom. Leaving the door ajar, she made her way to the black clawfoot bathtub, and the scent of water filled the air as she turned it on.

After the incident with Fallon, she'd learned her lesson and moved her fragrant bath salts to the cabinet. A loofah hung on the shelf along with a couple of other things. Aside from a few personal items, the oils she'd obtained from Aniya lined the top of it. As instructed, she added three different oils to the water, the surface shimmering with each drop. One to aid healing, one to relax the muscles, and one to soothe the senses. While the tub continued to fill, she retrieved two large, fluffy towels from the stand by the door and set them on the small table by the tub.

Once she had the water at a good level, Narcissa turned it off. For a moment, she stood there, casting a glance back toward the door. Hunter sat there, his knees pressed against his chest, his arms wrapped tightly around them. He stared at the open bathroom door, his cheek resting against his knees, the silence broken only by his breathing. Without asking, there was no way to know what had gone through his head. Or even what was running through his mind at the moment. The one time she'd pushed Tiza, it hadn't ended like this. Yes, he had required some comfort, but nothing to this degree. Hunter looked so much more than broken. He appeared cracked. It was as if she'd yanked the plug, and every buried, painful memory flooded his mind. Such things were difficult to suppress. But that didn't mean she couldn't help him.

Narcissa emerged from the bathroom and walked toward him. She held out her hand. "Come with me."

Hunter glanced up and met her gaze. His right arm peeled away from his legs, and his fingers reached out and gently clasped her waiting hand. Pressing his palm to the floor, he pushed himself up and winced. He stood upright, his left arm wrapped around his midsection, as if he was trying to hold himself together. His shoulders hunched over a little, and his head lowered.

Narcissa wrapped her arm around his back, pulling him near so he could feel her warmth. Most of the time, their height difference could go completely unnoticed. Not in this instance. But it didn't matter. She could still wrap her arm around him and, feeling the silence, ran her fingers up and down his side as she led him toward the bathtub. From its depths, only a slight amount of steam rose, barely visible in the heavy air. Hunter's nose twitched. Stopping beside the tub, Narcissa gestured to it. "Get in. Then I'll get in."

Gripping the tub's edge, he lowered himself in, his muscles tensing against the cool, wet porcelain. He brought his legs up to his chest, crossed his arms around them, and then lowered his cheek to rest against his knees. She climbed in directly behind him. For now, she held him close, her lips gently meeting his back in a tender kiss. As she slid her legs alongside his, she scooped the clear water and let it cascade over his arm. "Lean back against me and place your wrists in the water. It'll help with the swelling."

He scooted forward without a word and leaned, finding the comfortable curve of her neck for his face. It was a good thing her tub was so huge. A slight groan escaped his lips as he submerged his arms in the water. "Think I fractured it."

As she wrapped her arm around him, Narcissa stroked his fur from the back of his head up to his ears. That beautiful soft purr came out of him. She should've stopped sooner. The second her own tears had started. Maybe even before that. "There's an oil in the water that will accelerate your natural healing ability." It was something, but it did little to lift her spirits. Nothing would likely do that. But this wasn't about her. It was about Hunter. Part of aftercare didn't just include addressing the physical issues, but the mental and emotional as well. "Do you want to talk about it?"

"I can," he whispered. "If you want to know any of it, I will tell you. But only today. Only now. Once I walk out that door... I never plan to speak about any of it ever again."

That didn't surprise her at all. Given her own secrets and the things she'd endured, she didn't blame him in the least. There were a lot of things she went through with Deacan that she preferred not to dredge up. Not to mention her father. Although she'd told Hunter some things, she hadn't told him everything. Narcissa thought back over different parts of the session. "When you were on the cross, you seemed to have two different reactions. As if you were being pulled between memories."

"I was. Back and forth between two of them." Hunter nuzzled a bit more into her throat. His purr deepened as she continued stroking his head. "I was in late adolescence in both of them. Sixteen and seventeen. When you used the whip on me that time, it took me back to when my twin was supposed to fight somebody. Very good at it, but he is, as they say, a lover and not a fighter. The opposite of me. His opponent would have severely injured or killed him. So, I took over."

Narcissa listened intently as he recounted the rest of his memory. Not that anything he said surprised her much. She'd witnessed his enjoyment of pain throughout their sessions. They had that in common. The way his father reacted, with a sharp tongue and beatings, bothered her. It reminded her far too much of her father and how he'd responded any time she defied his orders, argued with him, or fought back.

"The other flashback that time... when you raked your nails on my thigh and stroked my cock... it took me back to..." Hunter's words trailed off, and a long silence stretched between them. "It was the last time my father ever sexually abused me."

Oh, gods. From the way he'd reacted, she thought that had been the case. But to have confirmation of it. That wasn't something any person should have to go through, regardless of age. If that memory had appeared while he was on the cross, she could safely presume the one while she had him on the chaise... likely the first time his father sexually assaulted him. The more she heard, the more she wished for his father to meet a bloody end like her own father.

As she continued to caress the back of his head and ears, Narcissa rested her head against his, feeling the warmth of his fur. With the description he offered of his twin, it explained more of what she'd asserted based on what he'd told her a few sessions back. "You've always done whatever you could to protect him, haven't you? Your brother, that is."

"Yes. Always. No matter what. There is little good I have ever done in my life. But at least I have done that." Another stretch of silence, heavy with unspoken words, passed between them. "The first time..."

Something shifted in him. He tucked himself closer into her, shielding his eyes even more if that were possible. It was almost an unconscious motion. She hoped he wasn't feeling shame. Or, worse yet, reliving the experiences in his head all over again. She wouldn't let him feel guilty for all the wrongs that had been done to him. Despite the potential for his words to sadden her, she would never pity him. She would just do this. Hold him, stroke him, and listen. It was the best thing she could do for him right now.

Not once did her fingers still as Hunter spoke, continuing his story and recounting the first time his father assaulted him. Nor did she interrupt him. Talking about any of this couldn't be easy for him. To be so young and introduced to sex in the worst way possible. Six? Not to mention the broken pelvis and thighs. Hunter had suffered so much at the hands of his father. An icy dread coiled in her stomach, mirroring the agony he'd endured. Her heart broke for him. Good gods. If she hadn't been around her own monsters, she'd wonder how someone like that could exist in this world. If death hadn't yet come for his father, she prayed it came sooner rather than later.

"Not long after that... a couple of other males in the village came and put a stop to it. I am not really sure who all was there, but the ones who tried to kill Azazel and Sam paid dearly for it. Attacking Informants was not allowed under any circumstances unless sanctioned by Markham. And I was basically an orphan then. He did not care about little 'ole me. But they did. And Hayden did. The last thing I remember was his telling me he loved me. I was told later that I almost died. I had to be kept asleep for a while. Someone had to leave and get some supplies to cast me. We just did not have what was needed in the village. Then I had some issues... relieving myself... that took a couple of weeks to get under control. Even after I was healed, I did not talk out loud for four weeks. Hayden... he did not leave my side once."

"I'm glad you didn't die and that you have someone who cares for you. Even when we don't realize it, they're often the ones that help us survive, get us to push through the day." Her own family did that for her. It didn't matter that she hadn't seen them in thirty years. "The relationship you have with Hayden reminds me a lot of my brother." There were many similarities. "Dionele is forty *solaris* younger than me. I've cared for him since the day he was born. Something my father noticed fairly quickly. As my beatings had become ineffective... Dionele became his new target. A way for him to control me." Not that she ever allowed it. She fought her father every single time, her movements sharp, demanding his attention. Until the day she killed him. "Dion clung to me a lot. Even after my father died, Dion was afraid he would find us."

Closing her eyes, Narcissa laid her head atop his, and felt a connection that went beyond words. "There is a special place in the underworld for males like our fathers. One day, if he hasn't already, I believe your father will meet his maker and pray for mercy that will not come."

"Sometimes, I think as much as we know they need us... we need them just as much. Maybe even more. Whether we freely admit that to ourselves. It is because of Hayden that I never went over the line. I pushed the boundaries—most of the time, to be honest. Especially with my father. But I never went too far; did nothing that would get me killed. Never... seriously considered suicide. I had to be there for him. I could not leave him alone in the place." Hunter reached up, his fingers sinking into the soft ponytail as the strands effortlessly glided through his fingers. "It is good that your brother has you. They need to know they always have at least one person who will never leave. Never give up on them. No matter what."

Narcissa removed the tie from her hair, and it tumbled down her back like a silken waterfall. She'd always worn her hair up whenever she dominated in a session. This time was no different. It typically stayed that way until she finished with the aftercare. Not that she could explain what made her take it down. That wasn't true. She wanted Hunter to have full access to it. To feel his fingers through every strand.

He let out a rumble of satisfaction. He started at the top of her head and worked his way down, feeling the silky strands between his fingers until he reached the ends, then repeated the process. "I am glad that your father is deep in Hades's domain. A prison he can never escape. That he can never harm you or your brother ever again. And while my father is not there yet, I know that one day he will be. And I pray I will be there to watch when he breathes his last. Both of them deserve every bit of pain they have ever brought to another, though a thousand times more."

Truth be told, she didn't know if her brother knew he still had her. Despite the lack of a physical presence or frequent meetings, her unwavering support was always available to him. She took care of their living expenses and his medical care. It didn't seem like much, but it was all she could do to ensure their safety. Though she agreed with two things Hunter said. One, she hoped he got to see his father get what he deserved. Two, she had needed her family. Just as Hunter had done anything for Hayden, she'd done what needed to be done for Dion.

"You asked me once why I was willing to try to give Deacan the children he desired, even though I didn't want them." Narcissa paused. "Dion... he's the reason. He and my mother." Her eyebrows knitted together as if a storm was brewing. "Dion requires a lot of specialized care. He doesn't view the world the way we do. The way anyone does, really. He doesn't understand social cues. He doesn't recognize... evil. Callousness. Cruelty. He wants to talk to and hug everyone. He has little understanding and little control over his emotions. Even to where he can lose control of his temper." It had been such a long time since she'd spoken about her brother. Gods, she missed him. Both of them.

Narcissa swallowed, feeling the lump in her throat grow larger with each passing moment. "Deacan took all three of us in. He ensured that my brother had the best care. That my mother didn't have to handle the ins and outs of Dion's schedule, of his life, alone. The only thing he asked of me in exchange was a true D/s relationship. We drew up a contract, so we both knew exactly what the other expected. One thing he included was that after an appropriate amount of time... I would bear his children. No matter how many times we updated the contract to accommodate changes in our relationship, that request never altered. When we discovered I couldn't give him the one thing he wanted... he had a new contract drawn up. The support he provided us would continue as long as I acknowledged my failure and dealt with the humility of seeing him with another submissive who could give him children. That lasted for a few *solaris* until both she and the baby died in childbirth. After that... I know he had other relations, but it wasn't in my face, either. I started doing what I had to do to prepare for the day he no longer cared to provide for us. I suspect that if he hadn't died when he did..." She half-shrugged. "Not that it mattered. He had left his entire estate to his mistress and their children. So, I moved my mother and brother to somewhere safe, and I came here."

She hadn't meant to say all of that. It just didn't seem to stop once she'd started. All she'd intended to explain was why she'd tried to have children with Deacan. The rest really could've been left out. Not that she had any interest in taking it back.

"He sounds like a real selfish bastard." Slipping his other hand from the water, Hunter lifted her chin so their eyes met. "You listen to me, Narcissa. He did not deserve you. Not being able to bear a child is not a *failure.* Deeming it as such, shoving it down your throat, forcing you to bear humiliation and degradation because of it... that was *his* failure. *Not* yours. What you just described to me was deplorable behavior from someone who never should have called themselves a male, let alone someone who ever should have had the privilege to be in a relationship with someone like you. And then to leave you with nothing after all of that... The level of disrespect he showed you is appalling. You deserved better than someone who would prey on your heart just to ensure they got exactly what they wanted. That he forced you into that says everything about him. And that you accepted it to ensure your family was cared for says everything about you. If he ever truly cared for you at all, he *never* would have treated you that way."

Gods, why couldn't they have met sooner? Or under completely different circumstances? Despite what she did for a living, she could say Hunter never made her feel like anything but a person. Someone who had value. As she stared at him, listening intently, his words ignited a warmth that bloomed in her heart. It only made her love him more, if that was possible. This male, who had been through so much in his lifetime, deserved the world. Something Narcissa wished she could give him. Something she *wanted* to give him. Not that she was certain it was possible. At least, not at this point. Nor was she even positive he would want it.

This wasn't the time to give thought to any of that, though.

Narcissa replayed his words in her head. No matter how many phrases she considered, only one felt right on her tongue. She brushed a soft kiss across his lips. "I believe the same applies to your father. It's not a title he deserves. Nor does he deserve to have you and your brother as sons. What you've done, what you've endured and survived to protect your brother... says a lot about the type of male you are."

Hunter's brow furrowed slightly. As he kept his gaze fixed on hers, he slid his fingers from her chin, caressing her cheek. "No one has ever said things like that to me before."

From what little he'd told her of his family, it didn't surprise her in the least. His twin brother may not have known how, and the rest... they wouldn't have wanted his true strength to build. Instead, they would've done anything to tear it down. Not that they would have succeeded. A person with *true* strength always got back up. That was all she saw in him. A male who had true strength. A male who never gave up, who never stopped fighting. "You deserve more than you've been given." Narcissa leaned forward, her heart pounding, and pressed her lips to his. Not because she wanted to emphasize her words. Not because she wanted to show him what she meant. For no other reason than simply because she loved him.

He was the only thing that mattered to her right then. It had been a hard session. So much so that he'd used his safe word. While she hadn't expected him to respond to the kiss, she hadn't needed him to, either. Still, he did. And it was unlike anything they had shared before. Nothing deep or overly passionate. Just soft, slow, and sensual. As if it included everything they couldn't put into words. Somehow, through their short time together, they had slowly picked up the shattered pieces of their souls and stitched one another back together. Things she hadn't quite recognized in herself, Hunter naturally called out of her. There was no other way to explain it.

She didn't know if he would want to go any further at all. If he didn't, she was okay with that. Whatever he did or didn't want, she would respect. Her desire for him would never change. No matter what he'd been through, or even what the future held for them. As the kiss deepened, he nearly broke the contact. He repositioned her to sit sideways on his lap. An arm held her waist close as the other hand continued to comb gently through her hair. She cradled his head with one hand on his cheek and the other stroking the back of his head and his ears, feeling the texture of his fur. Hunter held her close, and she could feel their heartbeats sync, a steady rhythm against her chest.

However long he remained today, it was time that belonged to them. At this moment, they were simply Narcissa and Hunter. The rest of the world didn't exist. They weren't in the den, but someplace private between the two of them. Somewhere where he was hers, and she was his. That was the only place she wanted to be right now. With her arm across his shoulders, her fingertips traced the contours of his spine. The strokes and caresses intensified, causing him to arch deeper into her with each passing moment. Hunter purred, and she could feel his grip tighten around her waist as he pulled her closer. But the kiss stayed soft and slow. It was absolutely perfect.

Hunter's tongue was hesitant as it slid over the seam of her lips and asked for entrance. Although momentarily surprised, she would never refuse him entry. With a soft moan, Narcissa caressed his tongue with her own as she opened up to him. This felt new and familiar all at the same time. The last time she recalled feeling this way was when she'd lost her virginity. Something she'd given to Deacan, too. With everything she'd ever been through with him, it seemed as if all the weight she'd carried from that relationship had disappeared. In the time she and Hunter shared, they had wiped the slate clean.

Hunter had embraced Nia, a woman who had shut down emotionally and closed herself off, cutting herself off from the world. Just as he had Narcissa—the female who loved her family so much, she not only sacrificed for them, but she killed for them, too. The same female who, at one point, had been vulnerable enough to give her heart to a male whom she believed cared about her. A female who had been fragile enough to accept that was enough.

Maybe the walls had come down between them. If they hadn't, would Hunter have been able to fill the holes that she didn't even realize existed in her soul? Would she have pieced herself together without realizing she had fallen apart? Would she have been able to do the same for him? No, she didn't think it would've been possible. Not if they hadn't trusted one another enough to let their defenses down. It was what had needed to happen.

Each time she kissed Hunter, it was like kissing him for the first time. No two kisses had been alike. This one wasn't any different. Though their tongues entangled, neither of them moved to deepen it. The kiss remained as sensual as it had started. There wasn't any urgency or desperation behind it. Something that didn't change as his hand slid through her hair and caressed down her spine, returned to the top of her head, and drifted downward again. Or his fingertips traced random patterns on her hip and her thigh. Even when his tail wrapped around her waist, the moment felt suspended in time. Narcissa completely understood it. She felt it down to her bones. The only place she wanted to be was in that tub with him. For however long they could. She wasn't in a rush to get to the other side. Instead, she focused only on the present.

The second his lips left hers, she missed them. He was right here, their foreheads touching lightly with their gazes locked in a silent conversation. With as hard as she'd pushed him, it didn't surprise her in the least that things didn't go further. And she was okay with that. A comfortable silence hung in the air, thick with unspoken thoughts. She didn't want to break that. Not when there were things she was positive they both wished were a little different. Not the time they'd spent together thus far. She wouldn't trade a second of that. Nor did she believe he would, either. Especially with where it had led them. The only thing she'd change—the possibility of a future with him. That was something she wanted more than anything. But there was no way out of her contract. At least, as far as she knew. If the rumors she heard were true, Shalla was proof of that.

She needed the silence to go on just a little longer. Narcissa's eyes remained locked on Hunter while her hand moved to grab items to wash him. She wet the sponge and lathered it with soap, which had a cedar scent tinged with jasmine. Hunter's eyes held a serene peacefulness, even without them exchanging a single word. As she washed him, running the sponge first over his shoulders, his eyes drifted closed and a low groan came out of him.

"That feels... fantastic," Hunter whispered.

"No one's ever done this for you before, have they?"

"No, they have not," he breathed.

To get everywhere she needed to, she had to change her position. Narcissa readjusted and straddled his legs. It took little effort, just her left leg sliding over to the other side. She repeated the familiar motions with the wet sponge, scrubbing his left shoulder in the same pattern as the right. His purr grew louder. Hunter tilted his head first one way, then the other as she took the sponge along the sides of his neck. Her focus remained on the front until she got that finished. She wasn't in a hurry, savoring each pass of the loofah, enjoying the feel of the water and suds.

"I do not actually recall anyone ever bathing me. I assume my sister did so when I was a newling and nestling. But she died when Hayden and I were four. It would not have been like this, either." A barely perceptible twitch pulled at the corner of his mouth.

With what she knew of how his village had been, she didn't imagine it was anything like this. Even the baths she'd given her brother when he was a newborn didn't compare. The closest would be what she'd given Tiza at the end of their sessions, except they weren't as intimate. Nor did she linger over the task. She wanted to extend this for as long as possible. Things had irrevocably changed between them. Not that she knew how that would impact their future. "I'm sorry to hear that. It sounds like she cared about you."

"I do not really know. Perhaps she did, but I remember little about her. I did not let anyone in, even then. Hayden adored her, though. She was not supposed to spend time with us, but she would sneak into the orphans' hut when she could." He stayed in place, leaning against the tub, tail around her waist, an arm wrapped around her, idly drawing on her hip and thigh, and the other arm hanging over the edge. "He was devastated when she died. We still do not even know what happened."

Closed off at such a young age. Maybe he just instinctively knew he couldn't let anyone in on his inner thoughts or the things he felt. Not that she was any different. It had been necessary to keep things to herself. It only made her a bigger target for her father. She suspected Hunter had protected his twin even before the first time he was sexually assaulted. That his sister had snuck into the orphans' hut made her wonder if it wasn't as secret as the female believed. The last thing people like his father would've wanted was someone who would give them hope their lives could be better. "Do you think your father did something to her?"

He groaned again as he leaned his head back, the edge of the tub pressing into his neck. "Yes. It would not surprise me in the least. But she would have been a source of income to him. So, I am not sure what could have made him kill her. Not that it would have taken much, really. Females died all the time there. Usually when a male got too rough with them during sex. All we know is, one day she was there, the next she was gone. Hayden asked Sam where she was, and the only answer he got was that she was dead." A short beat of silence passed. "We will probably never know what happened to her."

"I imagine not knowing must be difficult." She didn't know if he'd ever gotten closure from the loss. Or if it was something that he might feel, given that he was no longer—at least temporarily—closed off emotionally. Even if he didn't think that at the current moment, it could change in the coming hours, even days. Thoroughly washing over his ribs and stomach, Narcissa focused on his left arm.

"I never really... thought about it before, to be honest." Hunter paused, his brow furrowed as his eyes remained closed. "I never allowed myself to get close to Elisa. So, when she was no longer there, it was not anything that really fazed me. Our mother died in childbirth. One brother did not care, and the other was just cruel. And my father..." He shrugged. "I always just focused on protecting Hayden. I did not care about anything else. There was no one I ever wanted to get close to, even then. Letting people in is too dangerous. And vulnerability can get you killed. It did not take me long at all to learn that you even had to protect yourself from family if you wanted to survive in that place. And showing that you cared about someone just put a target on their back. It was better—safer—for me to be that way."

"I can understand that." More than she suspected, most would. Narcissa moved over to his right arm. "About a cycle before I came here, I began emotionally distancing myself from my brother and mother. As far as most people know, they disappeared at the same time my father did, leaving me all alone. This is the first time I've spoken of them in thirty *solaris*. I haven't seen them since the day I left. It's the only way to keep them safe."

"What are they still in danger from that you have kept from even contacting them?" Hunter, with his eyes narrowed to slits, watched as the sponge moved down his left side and across his hip.

How did she explain it? She couldn't just come out and say they would be in danger if anyone here found out about them. Nor could she say that there was always a possibility of retaliation if anyone ever found out she had killed her father. Even when she could spend time outside of the den, she was never alone. It wasn't just her shopping partner, but guards, too. She couldn't tell Hunter any of that. Biting her bottom lip, Narcissa tossed different ideas around in her head. Maybe there was a way without revealing specifics regarding the den. "People here just can't know about them."

"I can understand that. Getting a message to them would be too risky, I presume?"

It was something she'd considered several times over the years. Yes, the payments arrived as scheduled, which should reassure them she was unharmed. Mostly. But that wasn't something they'd *know*. Or needed to. "I believe it is. My mother or the person they're living with might try to find me. They could ask questions that couldn't be answered. Or their scents could unintentionally end up being carried in here. With our added security..." Her words trailed off. The latest additions likely spoke for themselves.

Hunter's eyes darkened. "Right. Well. If you were ever to change your mind. I would do so for you. I am stealthy enough that no traces of them will follow me back here. And I am sure that if it were strongly expressed to them how dangerous it would be to seek you out, if they care about you, the message would suffice."

"I appreciate it." Part of her wanted to take him up on his offer. Not knowing anything about their well-being had been extremely difficult over the years. If she did, though, she'd have to give him something to prove to Tiza that Hunter could be trusted. It was something to think about.

"The new security. They do not bother you, do they?"

She didn't trust the new security, but that wasn't what he asked. "They don't mess with me." No, they got the females who made little or, like Cheshire, would screw them. A small smile crossed her face. "I'm... out of their price range." She would be one that would be off-limits. Her value to the proprietress far outweighed the value of the guards.

Hunter's eyes snapped open, and he met her gaze. "That will not matter. Not to those males. Not forever. Promise me you will be careful. Never be alone with any of them."

If Narcissa hadn't seen the genuine concern in those gorgeous blue pools of his, she might've cracked a joke. But at a moment like this, it wouldn't comfort him. Her thumb traced the line of his jaw as she cupped his face gently. "I promise I won't be alone with any of them." If she could help it. "But trust that I can take care of myself." If her father couldn't avoid a sharpened root through the chest, then neither could a shifter.

"Thank you. And I know you can." With a gentle touch, Hunter leaned in and covered her hand with his, his skin warm against hers. "I have just seen the things they have done. All they care about is getting what they want. You are the last female I would ever want them around."

Yeah, she didn't doubt that. If what she heard the other day was anything to go by, yeah, they totally gave her the creeps. But she definitely didn't want them around her for a multitude of reasons. At the top, she didn't need anyone realizing she'd fallen in love with Hunter. If it ever got noticed, it would be bad for both of them. "Do you know whether any of them have any special abilities?" Normally she wouldn't ask, but there was so much more at stake for the two of them.

"I know of a few, but under the previous leader's rule our forms rarely mixed. Some bragged; others did not. Most of those males no longer feel any pain. Alexi has an *extremely* keen sense of smell. Athos can see heat signatures, which means camouflage does not work on him. I believe Colt has some kind of special ability, though I do not know exactly what it is. Just that Markham utilized him often on scouting missions. Luke and Santiago are trackers, but Luke is better at it. I believe this may be a natural skill, though. With Santiago, I know he had to learn it."

She didn't anticipate any of those would be useful around here, but it was still good to know. Fallon was the only one she'd ever seen use camouflage, and he didn't do that until he was at her door. Colt would be who worried her the most, especially without knowing his ability. Trackers would only be worrisome if someone actually escaped. That was easier said than done.

Narcissa nodded and washed his armpits. "Supposedly, Santiago is interested in a dancer." Her hand paused for a moment. Damn it. She hadn't even thought about it before the words came out. Without moving her head, she glanced around the bathroom. Nothing happened. No shock, no debilitating pain, no static... nothing. That made little sense. Except, well, it had nothing to do with how things worked around here. Maybe it didn't fall under the NDA. Interesting. Shaking it off, she returned to washing him.

Hunter's brow furrowed a bit. "If that is true, she should be careful. He is not the worst of that group, but I still would not trust him with anyone I cared about." He leaned his head back against the tub, his eyes fluttering shut, as the water lapped gently. "Are you alright?"

"Yeah." Not that she could really explain anything further. The NDA kind of prevented that. She scooted back a little and cleaned over his pelvic region. His eyes flicked open to just slits again as he watched her hand. "Just some things we can't really talk about." It was the simple truth of the matter. It was a rule not to discuss personal information, but that didn't manifest in physical repercussions and alarms going off. Well, unless someone noticed personality changes, but she knew how to conduct herself outside of her bedroom.

"I see. That seems logical, I guess."

"I suppose so," she mumbled. It hadn't been her intention to bring anything up. It had just come out of her mouth. Adjusting to one side of his lap, Narcissa washed down his left leg. Yeah, not being able to talk about it made it more difficult for any of them to truly leave. Not to mention the rumors she'd heard about—what happened when someone tried. Maybe she'd said something because all she could think about was trying to figure out a way to get out. What other options did she and Hunter have?

Hunter, with his eyes half-open, watched her as the sponge scrubbed his fur. His gaze flickered up to her face, his eyes lingering on her features, and he simply stared. Drinking her in, as if he were seeing her for the first time. Or the last. "It does not, really. I was just attempting not to push you into something you obviously cannot talk about." He gave her hand a brief squeeze, and then he closed his eyes, resuming his relaxed pose. His tail stroked up and down her spine.

Narcissa glanced at him, her lips curving into a subtle smile. "Thank you, but you're right. It makes no sense. It's just a way to keep control and secrets." Lots of secrets.

"I know all about that. Well, unfortunately." Hunter slipped his hand back into the warm water and gently caressed her hip.

"I imagine you do." She leaned forward, and the water lapped against his fur, washing his leg and foot. His toes wiggled a bit. She peered over her shoulder. "Does it tickle?"

"I do not know what that means." A barely perceptible scoff, like a whisper of amusement, escaped his lips. "It just felt funny."

Grinning, Narcissa moved over to the bottom of his other foot. "It's a sensation that often has a tendency to make a person laugh. It can vary in degree."

"I see. I think." The toes of his other foot wiggled, too. "I have never laughed before. I am not sure that is something I know how to do."

"If you ever meet my brother, I imagine it'll happen before you even realize it. Or he'll annoy you. Either is possible."

"If you ever meet my brother, he will probably make you something to eat. Or annoy you. But probably both."

Narcissa snickered as she continued to clean up his leg, her fingertip tracing the smooth skin of his foot.

His whole lower leg twitched, and that slight noise came out of him again. "Ooh. I am not sure I like that."

"No? Is it too close to smiling?" she asked, running her finger across the bottom of his foot again.

Another half-chuckle left him, then Hunter jerked his foot back a little. "No. It is just... really tingly. But in a weird way. Not the tingles I get when you touch me in certain ways."

No, it probably felt nothing like that. "Someone who cooks for me is a good thing. I'm not allowed in the kitchen."

"I have only ever cooked anything over a fire. Why are you not allowed in the kitchen?"

With a practiced touch, Narcissa shifted away from his foot, washed his thigh, and slid her hand under his leg. How had Silva and Grace put it? "I've been told it's like watching fruit mold." She smirked. "I'm extremely precise in measurements, which means I can take three times the normal timeframe to make food."

His eyebrows raised a little as he bent his knees, giving her better access to the underside of his legs. "That is quite a long time. My brother would definitely annoy the shit out of you then. In the couple of times I have been around when he has cooked, he just tossed ingredients in and tasted frequently until he seemed to like how it came out. He keeps trying to make me try new things, too, which I have not been very receptive to. My tastes are fairly simple with food."

Narcissa stilled, and her eyes snapped to his face. "I'm sorry. Did you say he just *throws things together*?" Oh no. Just the thought of watching someone haphazardly toss ingredients into a dish sent a visible shiver down her spine. "That's just complete insanity."

"Wow, that really bothers you. Is cooking supposed to be precise? Or is that just how you prefer doing it? He could not cook before, so he is just learning how to do all of it. I almost bit his head off when he begged more than once to at least try my steak a different way. Why? I know how I like it, and it only takes a few minutes to cook."

"Everything is precise." She couldn't break from the expected order of things, held captive by her routine. Her jaw clenched, every muscle screaming in protest if she even tried to break free from the compulsory rule. "All of my clothes, shoes, books, and accessories have an exact location. I'm meticulous in how I clean my bedroom, my equipment, my toys, and even my body. It's not any different when I cook. If I'm given a recipe, I follow it explicitly. If popcorn calls for a cup of kernels, then there should be exactly 1,024 kernels."

Hunter's head tilted, his brow furrowing a little. "I have never had popcorn before. Do you... literally count out 1,024 kernels?"

"I did... once. After that, my neighbors forbade me from even making that." It had gone so far that she couldn't even get drinks. "Like I said. I'm not allowed in the kitchen any longer." They'd rather do it themselves so it wouldn't take twenty-plus minutes for something as simple as popcorn. Narcissa carefully climbed behind him, feeling the warmth of his body, and placed her legs on either side of his hips.

With his knees still drawn up, he rested his arms there, then laid his head atop his arms. His tail settled, a warm weight that wrapped loosely around her knee and calf. "I suppose... I can definitely see why. Standing between someone and their food, even out of necessity for preciseness, can put them in a terrible mood," he teased. A minuscule upturn of his lips hinted at amusement. "But at least that is one thing you no longer have to worry about, yes?"

"My neighbors like to tease me about it." They rarely ended up in a bad mood, though Silva was always more vocal than Grace regarding her issues. Others, they ended up... well, 'bad mood' put it lightly. "Valid point. Not that my diet has ever been overly complex, but it is nice not having to make my food." Now, if only she could get Silva to stop stealing her shoes.

That would be great. Narcissa washed the top of his shoulders, the soapy water cascading down his spine. His shoulders hunched as a low groan escaped his lips. She paused. His comment about how he liked his steak sank in. "Do you eat your steak raw?"

"Yes. Though, I dislike it cold. Just over the fire long enough to heat it up, while still leaving it bloody."

"I've never actually had steak." Though she'd been told there were various cuts that would fit within her diet, she opted not to take the chance. Bringing more water up to his shoulder blades, Narcissa let the water roll down his back, the scent of soap filling the air as she washed a little lower.

"It was always that or fish, which I have never much cared for. Herbs and spices were fairly scarce. We did not always have vegetables, and fruit was just about nonexistent. Our previous leader did not care if we ate or not, so most of the time, it fell upon the males of the village who could hunt and purchase things in the marketplace. Many of them only cared if they ate, and screw everyone else." Hunter shrugged. "Since people saw my twin and me as orphans, we ate last. Being picky would have meant starving to death. I always made sure Hayden ate before me and took whatever was left. Turned out I just liked my meat like that, so I never changed it. Hayden thinks it is disgusting. Not that he says it out loud."

Narcissa followed the same process and then inched a little lower on his back. While she was taking her time, she also didn't want to draw it out. Okay, maybe, but she enjoyed his company. There were some similarities in their worlds, but differences, too. "In the nymph kingdom, the queen ensured no one went without food. That didn't mean it wasn't controlled in personal homes. As looks were something my father valued, he limited what and how much I ate. Then with Deacan... and now... I guess you just get accustomed to what you've could do for so long, it becomes more of a habit than anything."

"I hate that you have ever had to deal with that. Are still dealing with." Hunter slid one hand down, squeezed her knee, then left it there, gently brushing his fingers up and down her leg. "The new shape shifter queen is the same way. She appears to prioritize taking care of everyone in every way. But I agree with you. I have lived so long a certain way, I am pretty set in my ways now."

It didn't bother her as much. Not that she didn't understand his perspective. But she ate enough to be content, and she had the treats that were often sneaked in for her. The chocolates she still had in her closet. She usually finished the fruit that someone brought her quickly. The chocolate and candy lasted a little longer. Besides, there were other things that had happened here to be far angrier about, but she couldn't mention any of those. "It's good that your queen wants to change how things have been done. Sometimes, change is necessary to thrive."

"Mmhm. I agree. We definitely needed change there. I think she is doing a good job so far, and she obviously cares about all of us and wants to make things better. But I think her naivete is going to catch up with us at some point. And who knows what the fallout from that will be."

Though she suspected she knew what he inferred, she wanted clarification. "What do you mean?" Fallon had told her some things about the village and the changes it had undergone. Not that he stayed there any longer. Something else she understood.

"She wiped the slate clean. Basically. For anyone who stayed in the village under her leadership, any acts committed under Markham's leadership are supposed to stay in the past. Murders. Abuse. Rape. All of it. Which, on one hand, I can understand her reasoning. Many were forced to do what they did, and hate themselves for it. But many were not. And she did not differentiate between them. She is giving everyone a chance to... I do not know if 'redeem themselves' is the right term. Acclimate, maybe." He paused as Narcissa drizzled more water over his back, and he arched slightly as the sponge followed. "A couple dozen males left, pretty much all canines, and I can gather why they did. All the new security here were in that group. My father stayed in the village, though. As well as several other felines who are just like him. If they harm another without cause, they will pay the ultimate price. But I doubt that would deter any of them at the moment. I think it was an unintelligent decision on her part, is all. And I am not the only one who thinks so."

Yeah, she could understand his point-of-view and his queen's. Without being able to truly differentiate between them, they'd all have to be treated equally. "If some of those who'd left hadn't ended up here, I'd say the concern should be more with those who stayed. At least, the ones with true darkness in them. If they remained in the village, it would be for a reason. Given the likelihood that they won't change their ways, this means they have to get better at concealing their actions. Otherwise, they'd face the consequences she laid out. If that's the case, why would they choose to stay?"

"Exactly. More than one have young there who they have nothing to do with. And Devin abolished the Informant position, as well as any unwilling matings, the day she took over, too. Nothing is truly keeping them there except for the promise of comfort and a home. Something that really means nothing to males like them. Hades, it means little to *me*. I have only stayed there because Hayden chose to. He is the only thing tying me to that place. I refuse to leave as long as he resides there, so close to a danger he cannot truly see." Hunter paused. "I believe the genuine concern should lie with the fact that those males stayed despite everything that was stripped away from them. Their females. Their position. It makes me think they may have stayed to plot something."

"Say that's true. Wouldn't it then be prudent to watch them more closely than normal? Spy from afar and see if any of them at any point unintentionally offer information or insight that could be useful for when they do?" He'd told her that he could check on her family without notice; give them word she was alright. Then he should be capable of watching those in his own village without them noticing.

"It would be, definitely. I monitor my father and brothers. Azazel and Sam seem to be attached at the hip anytime I see them. My other brother, Clay, has done nothing but keep to himself. I do not think anyone has anything to worry about with him. If Devin is monitoring the other males, or having them watched, that is not information I am privy to. She gave most of them guard duty around the perimeter. From what I have seen, except for one that was already put briefly under house arrest, they seem to toe the line so far."

As she continued to wash him, her hand slowed, the water softly cascading over his body. He had a brother named Clay. It couldn't be the same Clay she'd seen years ago, could it? The one who was *so* obviously gay? The one she'd referred to Jezzy? She couldn't divulge anything about clients, past or present, but that didn't mean she wasn't curious. "Sam and Clay are your half-brothers, I presume?"

"Mmhm. They are half-brothers to each other, too. Both of their mothers have passed as well, along with... I believe they each had a sister at one point, too. I do not know if my father had other females before our mothers, or how many of his children in total have died."

"Oh? Does that mean all of you have taken more after your mothers in looks, or your father? Or has it been a mix?" She didn't want to give away *why* she was asking, but she absolutely had to know if Clay, his brother, had been her client once.

"A mix. Azazel is mostly black in coloring. Sam looks like him, even down to the eye color, but he does not have any spots. I am going to guess that Clay took after his mother; he is more orange with some white, and his spots are almost brown. Had to have gotten his mother's eye color, too; he has these really light lavender eyes. Elisa looked exactly like our mother; I only know that because we have a picture now. Hayden has her coloring. I took more after our father, except for the eye color."

Holy fucking shit. His Clay and hers were the same. Fuck. That meant—Narcissa's eyes widened a bit. She'd screwed his half-brother. Good gods, how was it possible for the den to be that small? Yeah, well, she could confirm that Clay wouldn't be someone to worry over. Not that she knew if he'd accepted the truth of his desires yet. To find that out, she'd have to talk to Jezzy. Really, she didn't need to know. "Except for my skin tone, I mostly take after my mother. The only thing my brother got from our father is his eye color."

"I am sure that is nice. Not really looking like him. Most of the time, it is not something that is on my mind. But sometimes... I really hate that I look like mine."

"But your eye color and personality set you apart. Whether you share even a small part in looks, it doesn't matter because you're nothing like him." She didn't have to meet his father to know that.

"I am some," Hunter whispered. "I enjoy fighting, like he does. Drink too much, like he does. Enjoy causing pain, like he does, though not to the same degree. And I have his bloodlust, too, both with spilling it and tasting it. I am not... *quite* as ruthless as he is, and there are many things he has done that I would never do. But I am a little like him."

Narcissa scooted closer, her hands finding the curve of his hips as she leaned against him. A low rumble left him. "Being a little like him doesn't *make* you like him. Where you have lines you don't cross, he has none. That's all it takes to separate you from him."

"He is the last person I would ever want to be like. But I feel like that place... the way he was... made it nearly impossible not to be."

"I think you simply did what you had to do to survive. Not just for you, but for Hayden. Because surely, he wouldn't have made it without you. Not with what you've told me of him. You made the sacrifice so Hayden didn't have to. Azazel would never have done that. You're the one who took what he did and used it as fuel. It didn't tear you down. You used it to strengthen yourself, better than anything Azazel could ever hope to be. That's the simple truth." Narcissa wondered if he would ever believe the words that tumbled from her mouth. Maybe this was how Fallon felt trying to convince her she deserved to be happy. Not that Hunter had verbally stated he didn't believe her, but she could sense it. If he required more convincing, there were other things she could tack on, though some were better left unsaid. She was certain Azazel couldn't care about—or even love—another, but Hunter did. Even if he didn't believe he had it in him, the fact remained that he did. Otherwise, the emotions they had fought so hard against wouldn't exist.

"Not everything I did in that place was for survival, though. And I enjoyed much of it, as well as other acts I carried out outside of the village. Yes, I always took care of Hayden, but... I do not know how someone who enjoys the things that I do... could ever truly be a good person."

"I think that depends on how you define *good*." If they viewed it as pure, no, that definitely wasn't a term that could be attributed to either of them. "You know, sex workers often get a bad rap. We've been seen as drug addicts and home wreckers for *solaris*. People think there's something wrong with us just because of what we do. But that isn't always the case. We serve a purpose, and sometimes we can even prevent issues in a person's life from arising. We're not seen as good, but that doesn't mean we aren't, even if we enjoy what we do." It seemed like a horrible comparison given she didn't know what he did outside of his village. Nor did she want to paint that light on herself, given the emotions brewing between them. If she could leave the den, she would without hesitation, as long as she got to be with him.

"Informants received a bad rap as well, but they received that honestly. Regardless that there are some who were not ruthless murdering rapists, all anyone ever had to see was the brand and their opinion was formed. As for the poor reputation sex workers have received... if the clients were not receiving something they could not get elsewhere, they would have no reason to come. It is not like spending time here is cheap. I brought one male here *solaris* ago who has certain proclivities that could have gotten him killed in the village under Markham's rule. He could come here and get what he needed, and save face with the other Informants." Hunter leaned back slightly and turned his head, his cheek now softly pressed against her shoulder. He nuzzled back into her neck, and a soft sigh escaped his lips. "A lot of what you said sounds like me," he whispered. "Except I know there is something wrong with me. I have always known that. But I do not lie, and I help people... in unconventional ways. And I have lines I do not cross, unlike my father and brother. But... I have never felt *good*. I have never thought of myself as a good person. Quite the opposite."

Narcissa's fingers danced along his neck, and a low rumble of pleasure escaped him. Yeah, she knew a couple of males like that. "Just because you don't feel good, it doesn't mean you aren't. Just not in the conventional way that most people would assume." She tenderly pressed her lips to his forehead and then, a fleeting kiss upon his lips. "For the record, I don't think there's anything wrong with you."

As their eyes met, Hunter reached up and gently brushed his fingers across her cheek. "You are in the minority, then, if you believe that."

As far as she was concerned, her opinion was the only one that mattered regarding him. But she couldn't say that out loud. "I can accept that." Nothing would change her mind about him.

"Me, too." His thumb moved against the curve of her mouth. "Maybe you believing that... might one day help me believe it too."

"Maybe." It was a nice thought. One she hoped would come true. He deserved to believe that. And so much more.

He stroked her cheek once more, and then his lips brushed against hers, a whisper of a kiss. "So. What do we do now? You and me?"

It was a question that needed to be asked, so they could decide where to go from here. Staring at him, she wished she had a better answer. That while they'd been in the bathtub, she'd come up with something. Sadly, that wasn't the case. "I don't know."

"Me, either. I know I do not want to stop coming to see you. But... this session did not exactly do what we were hoping it would do."

"I don't want you to stop coming, either." And she certainly didn't want him to see anyone else. As for the session, it seemed to do the complete opposite of what they'd hoped. Trying to see if she could find a way out... she didn't want to get his hopes up. Asking questions about that would draw attention. That would separate them for sure. She wished she had something to suggest.

"What if I have to..."

Regardless that he hadn't finished the question, she knew what he was suggesting. She doubted her strength for that, as much as she'd like to believe, so long as he went to anyone else besides Ivory. Narcissa's jaw locked, and her knuckles turned white as the thought fueled a burning rage within. It ignited a murderous rage within her. She shook her head. It all came back to one thing. But she didn't know how to go about it without drawing unwanted attention to either of them. "I need to find a way out. That's our only option."

"What if you cannot find one? Is that even a possibility?"

There was no easy way to answer either of those questions. If she couldn't find a way out... fuck, she didn't want to think about those options. She'd been with the brothel for thirty years, and she knew nothing about her contract or exactly what it would take to get out of it. *If* it was even a possibility. All she had were rumors. And none of them had pleasant endings. Narcissa dropped her gaze and, with a subtle movement, made small circles in the water, watching the surface undulate. "I don't know. I just... I don't want you to get your hopes up."

Hunter gripped the bridge of his nose. With her settled back in his lap, he leaned against the tub's edge, embraced her, and rested his cheek on her head. It was a few minutes before he spoke. "I cannot stay... like this." His quiet voice was strained. "Not with what I feel for you. Not with... the way things are. It will end up killing me... and it is too dangerous. For both of us. I need my control back. I have to do... whatever it takes to get that back."

Clarification wasn't required. She understood exactly what he meant. And it sucked. Narcissa's breath hitched, an icy shiver crawling up her spine as she clutched at the invisible weight in her chest. Not that it helped the pain. At least, not any more than it stopped the tear from trickling down her cheek. "I won't pretend I like it. But I understand." If he was with someone else here... gods, she didn't know if she could handle that. No matter who it was. Unless she just didn't see it or hear about it. It wasn't like she could tell him who had big mouths or which ones to avoid. That seemed like it would fall under the NDA. Fuck. No suitable answer, no matter which direction they turned.

"I dislike it, too. Trust me. I just... I do not know what else to do. I thought this session... I thought it would work. That it would do what we needed it to do." Hunter tilted her head up, so their eyes locked, and with a soft touch, he brushed away the tear. "I do not want to be with anyone but you, Narcissa. But... I can feel it. Every time I come to see you, it gets stronger. My soul is dangerously close to claiming yours, and if that happens..." He didn't need to finish the sentence. "I do not know how much you know about when a shape shifter male finds their mate. But... it would not be good for either of us. Not with circumstances as they are."

They were in the privacy of her bedroom, even further in her bathroom. None of the windows were open. While she was certain he knew how she felt, she wanted to make it clear. "I don't want to be with anyone but you, either." With a soul claiming one another, she had more knowledge of how it impacted his people than her own. "I know a little. Mostly how to recognize it."

Hunter brushed a soft kiss over her lips, and then held her close, forehead to forehead. Neither of them wanted to be with anyone else. But they didn't seem to have any other choice. Meeting her gaze again, the gentle rasp of his thumb on her skin sent a shiver down her spine. "I have had few examples over the *solaris* of true matings between my species. They were very rare. If a shape shifter found a mate of another species, they had to go deep into hiding to avoid death. But what I have not seen firsthand, I have heard about. Unless I completely close off to you—which, from what I have heard, can become very painful, denying that connection—I would feel your emotions. Your pain. Your... arousal. Some mates of my species share a telepathic connection; sometimes words, sometimes images. Shape shifter males are very possessive and jealous by nature regarding their females. Truly bonded shifters will kill any male who dares to touch their female and not think twice about it. Which means... once my eyes glow for you..."

Everything he described didn't sound like anything she'd ever seen or even heard about in her kingdom. But nymphs were extremely sexual creatures. Not that it didn't seem implausible. Though it would explain some of what she was feeling. Did that mean it was possible in her own species as well? If so, had it been information that was hidden? That seemed highly unlikely. They had a queen who cared about her people. She wanted to know if her species possessed this trait and what it looked like when it was triggered. "There's no telling when that would happen, is there?"

"No. I just know it will probably be soon... if something does not change. That I have wanted to mark you more than once and during our last session, when you marked me, I felt something like an intense sparking in my eyes." He paused, the silence stretching out around him. "I just know it will probably be soon."

"An intense sparking? Like something was trying to take root?"

"Yes, exactly. If I had not been fighting it so hard out of necessity... I believe it would have already happened."

She had felt something like that, too. Not that it made any sense. Unless her species had something similar. If that was the case, would it only intensify what he felt when his eyes glowed? Would it intensify what *she* felt? As things tumbled around her brain, Narcissa placed her hand in the water and warmed it up a bit. They'd been in here so long it had cooled. She didn't warm it up to the point of steaming, but got it close to it. "I want to say I felt the same thing. Not my eyes, but something deep inside of me. I didn't recognize it, but the more I felt it, the harder it became to resist marking you. I don't know if my species even has something like yours does."

Hunter held her a little tighter. "It has definitely been difficult resisting doing the same. I think all species must have something similar, but I only know for sure of a couple."

At that moment, she wished she could explain everything to him. Tell him what things were really like here at the den. Maybe then, the two of them could figure something out together. But she couldn't tell him anything. Not the lack of information regarding her contract, the auction, her NDA, or even how they were all indebted to the proprietress. None of it. As she rested her hand against his chest, the slow circles drew a contented purr from him. "It's not something that ever came up in my education. Though, I suppose it would make sense if each species identified soulmates."

"We could not be educated about anything except for fighting. Fucking. Punishments. Anything else had to be learned in secret. Most of what I know of true mates or the mate connection in my species, I learned by observation." Hunter's forefinger left her cheek and slowly charted a course down her neck, brushed her collarbone, and paused between her breasts before circling one and repeating the journey. A soft moan escaped Narcissa, then turned into a purr that seemed to make his eyes darken.

"We spend most of our younger *solaris* learning the history of the different fae species. One *solaris* is devoted to other species of the isle. Then we learn various skills until we turn sixteen. From then until we hit our 18th *solaris* of birth, the sole focus is sex." Although her mother was a water nymph, she hadn't been among the warriors. "In my kingdom, people arrange many marriages."

"That is quite a lot of focus on sex. We started training to fight as young as five. Well, not really *fight*. We started learning how to kill. That is all Markham wanted us to be—killers. One of the other males in the village taught me and Hayden how to hunt. I taught him how to fish. We could not learn how to read or write—though it did not stop everyone—because education would have made us too intelligent, and Markham wanted to keep us stupid. Most times, as soon as a male left adolescence, they would become an Informant. Some were not large or strong enough to be considered, or he passed over them for some other unknown reason. Others were so large and strong, or had a special ability, they became Informants while they were still in adolescence. Refusing the position was stupid, so almost never happened. The females were the ones who had to cook, do the cleaning, and take care of the young until they no longer needed constant supervision. They were to be seen and used and never heard. We had our matings arranged, too. From what I saw over the *solaris*, it was very rare for there to be an actual connection between the couple. It was just a business transaction, and a display of ownership for the male. The ceremonies could get extremely brutal. Devin did away with all of that, too, though."

His touch, lingering around her breasts, caused her to purr with a rising intensity. Not that it deterred her concentration of what he was telling her. Her kingdom wasn't anything like his village. The differences extended beyond their treatment, encompassing the disparities in their education. "Nymphs are sexual creatures by nature. Our warriors train alongside the education provided. They begin at an early age. Though we don't discern by gender. It has more to do with the family, their station, and the physical attributes of the child. As for the marriage ceremonies, they're extravagant parties. More so if you're a member of the queen's court."

Hunter's face scrunched up for a moment. "I have never liked parties. Though, I am fairly certain the ones I have been around were probably completely opposite from what occurs in your kingdom." Circling her breast again, his finger brushed against her nipple, arousing her with the soft touch.

Narcissa moaned. She couldn't help the sounds that came out of her mouth. "I've never been a fan of them myself. Just seemed a recipe for people to get stupid." From his chest, her hand migrated, mapping the contours of his shoulder, the length of his arm, his side, and finally his back.

As his body warmed and his cock hardened, his purring transitioned into a low, guttural rumble. "That seems like an accurate description. Not that the males I have been around during parties needed an excuse to get stupider than they already were." He circled her nipple with a finger before cupping her breast, working his hand over it with care and softness. His other hand cupped her ass cheek, and his fingers tightened with a light squeeze.

Another moan, loud and desperate, escaped her lips. She hadn't expected they'd be together in that way. Not after what she'd put him through. Even if it didn't happen, that would be alright. Not that she didn't want him—she'd always want him. That would never change. Narcissa's hand slid up his neck, her fingers grazing his skin as she tilted her face up to meet his eyes. There was no doubt in her mind about how much she loved him.

His hand at her breast soon found its way to the delicate skin at the back of her neck. Without taking his gaze off hers, he gently pressed his forehead to hers. A hint of nerves appeared in his eyes. "I need to go slow," he whispered. "I just want to be... us... before I have to leave."

"Whatever you need, Hunter." It didn't seem like enough, but at least she could do that for him. Especially with what she knew had to be done. Meanwhile, she would seek the one person who might offer her some insight. They needed to do whatever it took to put some of those walls back in place. Delay their feelings growing stronger for as long as they could. "That's what I'll do."

"Thank you, Narcissa."

Before she could respond, Hunter leaned down and gently kissed her. A soft moan left them both. His tongue slowly emerged and brushed against the curve of her lips as his fingers tangled in her hair. This was the last time they could be together, fully open, no walls. Something they could never have with anyone else, and never have with each other again after today. Without hesitation, Narcissa opened up to him. Gently, she curled her hand around the nape of his neck, and her fingers moved rhythmically up and down the back of his head.

She'd never been able to be this open with anyone before. Someone who saw past the broken parts of her, the things she'd done, the scars—physical and emotional—and accepted every piece of her. He didn't see her as an object, but as a person. And treated her like one, too. The two of them were perfect for one another.

Hunter moaned softly, deepening the kiss, their tongues meeting and swirling together. The control was in his hands, even when he readjusted her so she straddled him. His hold on her ass tightened just slightly. Both of them let out a deeper, more passionate groan as her sex rubbed against his cock. *Oh gods.*

Her fingers moved up the back of his head and then down, lingering for a moment on his ears. His purring intensified, a rumbling vibration against her fingers, as her touch soothed his shivering. They were the only two who mattered in this moment. Every ounce of her being poured into this fragile, desperate emotion. Her heart swelled with a warmth she felt only for him. Her Hunter.

Hunter gently rocked her against his cock, eliciting another deep moan from her as his erection grew harder. *Holy fuck.* Even just that slight connection felt amazing. Not that it affected their kissing. As one of her hands skimmed along his shoulder and spine, his back arched, the touch sending a shiver through him. He tilted his head, and their kiss intensified. A moan, slightly tinged with a growl, came from him. Narcissa swallowed it as if it were a breath of fresh air. It didn't matter that it was low. Not anymore than how slowly they were going. Everything about this moment was utter perfection.

Beneath his touch, her body ignited, and each stroke of his cock against her sparked a fiery sensation. If they had to spend the next few minutes doing this, she didn't care. Though she desired to have him buried deep inside of her, she'd wait however long he needed. That had no bearing on how she felt about him. Nothing could ever change that. All she wanted was for him to feel her love and to let it wipe away all the dark stuff.

A few minutes passed before Hunter moved her pelvis up his erection once more, aligning the head of his shaft with her entrance. As he slid deep inside her, they both cried out at the same time. *Holy fucking shit.* That one stroke nearly threw her over the edge. It wouldn't take long before she came. Whatever transpired next between them—whether it was a single orgasm or their bodies demanded more, or he wanted her to take over—it was all okay.

Hunter's grip on her hair and ass tightened, a subtle, possessive squeeze. "I need you... please..." he whispered. He slid his tongue back into her mouth, a symphony of wetness, and ground his hips against hers with a moan.

Although she didn't think that was the entirety of his statement, he didn't have to finish it. Locking her arm around his shoulder, Narcissa ran her fingers up and down his spine. With her other hand, she skimmed along the back of his head to his ears. She rocked her hips against his, the water lapping gently as she tucked her feet beneath his thighs.

A louder groan came from him. Hunter detached his tongue from hers just long enough to moan four words—"Please, do not stop"—then fused their tongues together again. His hips pressed more forcefully against hers as he ran his fingers along her spine, from the back of her neck to her rear, and back up.

She had no intention of stopping. The slow rhythm, which she was not accustomed to, was perfect. Each thrust of his cock sent a jolt of pleasure through her. A wave of sensation coursed through her, igniting every synapse. Their tongues intertwined, and the sounds of moaning and purring filled the space. Everything was more intense, more passionate, than anything they'd ever shared. It was as though the slower pace gave their senses the opportunity to become fully immersed. She could almost feel the silent, intimate bond that connected their souls.

With each thrust, he tightened his grip on her as they moved together in perfect harmony. "Oh, gods... Come with me, Narcissa. Come with me."

This didn't sound like the requests or demands they often made of one another. It was a desire. She had no problem complying. As his orgasm exploded out of him, it set hers off. Her vaginal walls clenched, and fiery waves of pleasure burst forth. Her moan joined his, forming a symphony that bounced off the bathroom walls. Narcissa maintained the gentle sway of her hips against his as they rode out their shared climax. Something about this was different between them. She couldn't quite explain it, but the feeling resonated within her, deeper than she had ever experienced. Her spirit soared as warmth bloomed in her core, lifting her from within. Her heart and soul reacted as intensely as her physical body.

"Do not stop," Hunter whispered when the last of their release tapered off. His arm tightened, his other hand gripping her ass, and he thrust deeper. Some water spilled over the rim and onto the floor, splattering softly. Not that either of them cared.

If he didn't want her to stop, then she wouldn't stop. As she didn't know how long he'd be able to continue, she'd do whatever she could to make their next orgasm as powerful as possible. Sliding one arm beneath his, she trailed her fingers along his spine. His purring intensified even more. It seemed to vibrate the very air around them. Her other hand found his, and she threaded their fingers together, feeling the warmth of his skin against hers, over the hand he had around her waist. All the while she rocked her hips back, keeping the rhythm slow. With each movement, her vagina tightened around his cock, creating a sensation of increasing pressure. As their lips met, her tongue explored his mouth, tracing the contours of his fangs.

A guttural moan vibrated out of him. As their kiss deepened, Hunter's panting filled the air, his hold on her waist growing more possessive. As he thrust harder into her, his hand left her ass and gripped the tub's slick side. The noises he made only got louder, rougher, and huskier each time their bodies connected.

Jolts of electricity coursed through her entire body. They unfurled from her spine, extending to the very top of her head and the ends of her toes. Gods, things with him always felt incredible, but this seemed to just be so much more than anything she could've ever anticipated. Was this something that happened naturally when one fell in love? That, as the connection grew stronger, sex between them also got better and better? She didn't know how that was even possible. Yet she could feel his purring the way she felt his strokes—to her very core. Her slow hip movements contrasted with his forceful and deep thrusts, creating a harmonious blend. Not once did their mouths part. The kiss continued as if they breathed life into one another. It wouldn't be long before another explosion occurred between their joined bodies.

Hunter's grip on her waist tightened, matching the firmness of his grip on the tub's edge. Without quickening their pace, he drove his cock into her with more intensity. Their kiss deepened, their bodies moving closer together. At least, until a wave of pleasure crashed over him, filling her with a hot torrent. A monstrous release exploded from her body, echoing his own. As she threw her head back, they screamed out each other's names. The sounds blended into a cacophony, filling the room. Her vagina clenched and released rhythmically as she rode him to climax, coaxing out every drop of his seed.

Even when their mutual release had ended, Hunter didn't move. His arm stayed wrapped around her, their fingers laced together. He slowly released his grip on the side of the tub, the water gently lapping against the porcelain. His thumb stroked her cheek slowly, a gentle caress as their eyes met and held. Neither of them said a thing. In a moment like this, silence was the loudest language. They truly loved one another. It confirmed her resolve to contact the only person who might have the answers she sought. She just hoped they gave her options.

Hunter hadn't returned home the night before. Hadn't been able to. He didn't want to be anywhere near Azazel or Sam. Hades, even Clay or Hayden. Nor anyone else in the village. No one. If he couldn't be with Narcissa, he just wanted to be alone. Not that being alone was anything particularly unusual for him. He'd shot Hayden a message that he wasn't feeling like himself, so he wouldn't worry, as his twin was prone to doing. Then Hunter had shut down.

He'd spent the night in the caverns, mesmerized by the ethereal glow of the underwater rocks, lit by a sliver of moonlight. He'd stared into the water, trying his damndest not to think about anything. It had an exquisite color of jade green with flecks of gold.

Today he'd done his village duties and forced himself to eat, but spoken to no one. Then he'd literally forced himself to leave the village and head back here to the den. Exactly where he *didn't* want to be right now. Hades, this was the *last* fucking place he wanted to be right now. If he came to see Narcissa, it would be a completely different story. Unfortunately, he definitely wasn't. Nope, he was here to sleep with someone else. So that last tiny thread of control didn't get severed and put him and Narcissa in a world of trouble.

The whole point of their last session had been to rid them of their growing feelings for one another. Instead, it had only amplified the intensity of their emotions. Completely shattered, every fragment of the wall, the pieces now scattered on the ground. At least, on his end. If he couldn't follow through with this, with how close they'd grown... it would probably just make things so much worse for the both of them. But the longer he came to see her, the stronger their bond grew. The closer he came to that one final shred of self-control snapping. How much longer would his body, mind, and instincts disregard what she did here with other males when he wasn't with her? It was her occupation. Hunter didn't look down on her for it, and he would never think less of her, no matter what. But that didn't mean he liked the things she did with other males that he didn't want her doing with anyone but him. If he kept coming to see her, and his feelings for her got even deeper... at some point his eyes would glow. Once that happened, there wouldn't be any coming back.

He didn't think he could handle not seeing her at all, either. No, that would drive him just as insane, if not more so. There was no other choice but this. No matter how much he didn't want to think about it. Despite knowing that Narcissa understood the necessity just as much as he did. It felt like cheating on her. He had a personal rule: he would only be exclusive with a female until he had to move on, for his own private reasons. But this went so much deeper than that. Narcissa was the only female he wanted to be with. Ever. He knew that to the depth of his soul.

But life was unfair. He knew that better than anyone. Over the course of his life, he'd had to do things he didn't want to do an untold number of times. He could do this, too. There was no other choice.

With a deep breath, Hunter steeled himself, then slowly opened the door and entered, heading to the second floor. He walked to the reception area without glancing around, his footsteps echoing in the silence. Leaning just slightly against the counter, he kept his voice low. "I know I am not scheduled today, but I need a session with someone. But not N—" Hunter cleared his throat. He'd almost said 'Narcissa'. That would be *bad*. "Nia. Not with Nia, though."

He had put no thought into *whom* he should have a session with. Just that he would obviously need to be with a submissive. Though, it would have to be someone who could take a harder session with him. The choice was obvious. Not that he wanted to think about it. *Stop thinking, dammit.* Thinking about what he had to do wouldn't help anything. All he wanted to do was go down the hall to Narcissa's room and be with her. No one but her.

But Narcissa was 'off limits,' so to speak, tonight. So he needed to suck it up and get this done. Put more distance between him and Narcissa—*Nia.* Build those walls back up and make them strong again. That was the only option. Until—*if*—she could get free of this place. They didn't have any other options.

Shalla's eyes locked onto him for a long, silent moment. "No problem. Let me see who's available." She quickly scanned the schedule. "Diamond has something open. Nina should be available in an hour. Ivory should be finished any moment now."

Shit. Diamond *definitely* wouldn't work. Nina would be a slightly better option than her, but still not a good one. Ivory... he didn't want to be with her, either. He didn't want to be with *anyone* but Narcissa. But Ivory was, at least... familiar. And she could take a harder session. Not his *hardest* session; he had a feeling only his Narcissa could do that. *Fuck*, he *had* to stop thinking about her. For now... he had to stop thinking about her. Otherwise, he'd never be able to get through this.

Hunter quickly glanced back as Ivory stopped and leaned against the wall at the hall's end. All the female's attention shifted from her departing client and straight onto him.

"Hey, Hunter."

As much as he absolutely didn't want to use any fucking pet names with her... not with anyone but his Narcissa—*stop it stop it stop it*—if he let on that anything was wrong with him, it would just lead to questions. Questions he couldn't answer without getting both him and Narcissa in trouble. He'd called Ivory the same thing from the moment he laid eyes on her. Changing that now would make it obvious.

Hunter gave her a smirk, a brief upward curve of his lips. "Hey, sweetness." He faced Shalla and gave a slight nod, the gesture barely perceptible. "Ivory will work. Let us start with two hours." As he placed the bag of coins on the counter, he forced his hand not to stall, the weight of them heavy in his palm. Gods, his skin was fucking crawling just thinking about doing this. Which was *exactly* why it needed to be done.

"Alright." Shalla collected the payment, the sound of the coins clinking as she stashed it away.

Ivory swiftly moved to his side, her touch lingering as she wrapped an arm around his waist. "You know I'm always available to you." She winked.

Hunter allowed himself a moment. The silence amplified the weight of his decision. And then he forced the switch. He couldn't be the *new* Hunter. The one that Narcissa had discovered and brought out of him. The one who felt things; allowed himself to feel emotions other than lust and anger. Who didn't need control 100% of the time. The one who wanted Narcissa and *only* Narcissa. The one who knew without a doubt that she was his female. His perfect mate, handpicked by the gods. The other half of his soul.

He had to be the *old* Hunter. The one who didn't care with whom he screwed. Who didn't care what they looked like or felt like as long as they didn't fake it and got him off. As long as they listened and were *good girls* and allowed him to be the master of their bedroom and their bodies for a couple of hours. The switch might not be complete in his mind, but at least he'd succeeded with his body. His mind would follow. Hopefully. It was necessary for the time being. Hunter slid his hand over Ivory's ass and gave it a squeeze. "Oh, I know you are." He pulled her in, her body molding to his. "You act like you missed me or something," he said, his other hand securing her as he carried her away down the silent hallway.

"It has been quite some time since I had the pleasure of your company, *Sir.*"

In fact, it had been over a month. The last time she'd even spoken to him had been when she'd escorted him down the hall to Nia.

Though Hunter's eyes darkened and filled with satisfaction, that was as far as it went. The feeling wasn't internal in the least. He didn't like the way she said 'Sir.' Not anymore. It wasn't like the way Nia said it. It didn't sound the same in the least. But he kept his mind separate from his body. That's what he had to do. Until he could shut down what he felt for Nia completely—at least, bury it sufficiently enough for the time being—he had to keep it all separate.

As Hunter nipped at her bottom lip with his fang, she moaned softly. Something else he didn't want to do, but was normal for them. *Normal.* He had to pretend everything was *normal.* "Then I guess I should not keep you waiting any longer."

"I like the sound of that very much, *Sir.*"

He *didn't* like the sound of it—not that he gave any indication of that—but at least she did. Not that it honestly mattered to him whether she did. "Good."

Once they reached her room, Hunter set her down on her feet and opened the door. Though she immediately entered, he indulged in one more of those brief, fleeting moments. Once he stepped through that door, there wasn't any going back. That was how it had always been with him. Once they were in the female's room, the only way out was if she backed down, got overwhelmed, or he was completely satiated. He'd never pussied out. Not once. And he couldn't do that now. He had to reestablish dominance for himself. He had to get his control back. Because if he didn't, what he and Narcissa had would be revealed to all, and they'd both be in deep shit. If he didn't do what needed to be done to get his walls back up as firmly as possible, any chance he and Narcissa had for *anything* would no longer be a possibility.

With no further hesitation, Hunter crossed the threshold and closed the door behind him.

Twelve

Narcissa reached over to her nightstand, and with a slight tug, opened the top drawer. She checked the time on the pocket watch she kept there. Two hours. Fallon was two hours late. She suspected he wouldn't show up, which was highly unlike him. In thirty years, he'd rarely missed an appointment. Closing the drawer, she got to her feet and crossed her bedroom to the closet. Her stilettos clicked against the floor with each step. There wasn't a need to change, but with no one else scheduled for the day, she could put on a belly button ring.

Normally, she opted for shorts with Fallon. As their last session left her with a scar, she'd thought it better to wear a pair of dark blue, stretchy denim jeans that laced up the outside of each leg. A pink, off-the-shoulder crop top with long sleeves and a crisscross design barely covered her breasts. As dark as the jeans were, she opted to wear a pair of sparkly-pink, six-inch high heels with a gold strap and stiletto to complement the outfit. Not that it mattered too much what she wore.

Similar to Hunter—damn it, really, she shouldn't be thinking about him. Given everything that had occurred between them the day before, and the number of times they stalled his departure, he shouldn't be on her mind. Not that she could help it. After seeing two clients, she felt an unsettling sensation on her skin, like tiny insects were crawling beneath it. Thankfully, neither male seemed to notice that she didn't respond to either of them as much as usual. While she'd been with them, Hunter was all that had been on her mind.

As much as she'd tried *not* to think about him, like she'd done with Fallon in their last session, she'd compared everything her other clients did to what Hunter did. The differences in how much harder she and Hunter went at one another. The sounds the other males made just didn't really do it for her the way Hunter's did. That the things they each preferred didn't rise to the level of what she and Hunter liked. Gods, she didn't know how it would be possible to go on like this.

The reasons weren't difficult to identify, either. One, because she missed him; just twenty-four hours and she was beyond eager to see him again. Two, no matter how much she tried to push it as far away from her mind as possible, she knew that either today or tomorrow he'd screw some other female. Even though he'd restrain that female, her mouth and tongue would still be all over his body. His mouth and tongue would be all over hers. Plus, his dick would end up in her pussy, and even in her ass. Although she didn't know who the female was, it didn't stop her desire to murder the bitch.

With the 14-gauge dangle navel ring in, Narcissa shut the drawer that contained her jewelry. This piece was one of her favorites. It had a crescent moon and featured a double-heart mini-dangle inside of its metalwork curve. A clear gem rested at both ends of the curved barbell. She retrieved what remained of the box of chocolates Fallon had brought her a week ago. She'd gone through the whole thing in nearly a day. Typically, they lasted her a couple of weeks. The one before this box, she finished last night. Fuck, with as much chocolate as she'd shoved in her mouth, she was going to have to spend extra time in the rehearsal studio.

With the last morsel consumed, Narcissa tossed the box aside and entered her closet, where the soft whisper of silk suggested infinite possibilities. Fallon would've been her last client. As much as she wanted to apologize again for what happened between them last time, she was glad he didn't show up. Her heart just wouldn't have been in the scenario he required. At least this way, she didn't have to worry about the latter. Instead, she selected rehearsal attire and stilettos, then packed them in a small black bag. Plan for the evening—she'd check with Shalla and see if Fallon confirmed at all, then change in the communal bathroom downstairs, and spend an hour in the studio. Maybe she could work off some of this stress.

Perhaps it would silence her thoughts. Not that she had much hope of that.

Narcissa closed her closet doors, then left her bedroom, the quiet slam of the door echoing behind her. She didn't really need to check in with Shalla, but part of her wanted assurance that Hunter hadn't come by today. It was stupid. She shouldn't even be torturing herself like this, but she couldn't stop, either. Even if she could get her head to agree, to see reason, her feet had a mind of their own. As they carried her down the hall, the clicking of her heels seemed to ricochet off the walls as she rounded the first corner, passed the 'Personnel Only' door, and then turned into the main hallway.

With a weary sigh, Narcissa paused halfway down the hall, dragging a tired hand across her face. Good gods, what was she doing? Yes, she loved him. Yes, part of her wanted to know. But part of her didn't. They had both understood it had to be done. He had to sleep with someone else. Dammit! No matter how hard she tried to convince herself to stop this, she couldn't. She had to know.

Narcissa strode the rest of the way to the waiting room, the polished floor reflecting her determined face. She eyed the area surrounding the receptionist desk; it was completely empty except for the guards. Two of the most recent hires—Informants. Well, rogues, according to what Hunter had told her. Not that she gave them any attention. She'd been more interested in the workers that typically hung out here and were nowhere to be seen. Too soon to tell if it was a good thing or not.

"Can I help you with something, Nia?" Shalla asked.

Right. The reason she intended to use, anyway. Narcissa closed the distance between them and rested on the smooth edge of the desk. "Can you check my schedule? Fallon didn't show up. He's never missed an appointment."

"Sure."

The way she sat against the desk gave her the perfect angle to scan the appointment book, provided Shalla had it open. Instead, she watched as the female flipped to the tab for her schedule for the month. Fuck. Really, it would've been great if Shalla could've just done what she wanted. Except it wasn't her business. Two more days until she saw Hunter again. It felt like it would take forever to pass.

"Alright. So, I had him penciled in, but it wasn't inked. I don't think he confirmed his appointment the last time he was here." Shalla pointed out the information in the book she referenced.

Not that Narcissa would admit it verbally, but it made sense. Didn't that just make her feel like shit? Fallon was a friend—provided he still allowed her to call him that—and she'd taken advantage of what she knew about him. If she was a genuine friend, the next time he came in, she'd talk to him about assigning him to another worker. "That's strange," Narcissa said. Despite what was going through her head, she had to act like it confused her. "Do you remember anything about when he left here last week?"

Shalla closed the book with a soft thud and leaned back in the chair, clasping her hands. "He seemed a bit out of it, almost as if things weren't quite registering. If I remember correctly, I called his name twice, but he just kept walking."

Yeah, he'd zoned out even before he left her room. That happened somewhere amidst the mess he refused to let her clean up, even if she was technically at fault. Not that he ever blamed her for anything. "That's so unlike him."

"Well, he has another appointment in..." Shalla's words trailed off as she opened and consulted the appointment book again. "... six days. You know the rules, though, about missed appointments."

"I know." They were fine as long as they had prepaid. Once they ran out of those, their space opened up. Not that she'd ever fill his spot until she spoke with him first. The same was true for Hunter. Actually, that wasn't true. She'd hold his spot open indefinitely. Without hesitation and without question. As long as she was stuck here, he'd always have a place. Narcissa pushed off the desk. Maybe it was better that she didn't find out who Hunter could be with, if he was even here, or had already come by.

"Did you need something else, Nia?"

Yes, she did. But the female had already warned her not to talk about it again. Offering Shalla a half-hearted smile, Narcissa shook her head. "I'm good. Thank you." Without another word, she retraced her steps down the long, dimly lit hall toward the personnel door. Before she got halfway, the sound of a door creaking open made her stop in her tracks. Who should step out but Hunter. If he'd been alone, she might have been okay. Except he wasn't. The woman clinging to him was, to her utter dismay, Ivory, the only person she despised seeing him with.

Her gaze flicked from him to the skank, who had the smuggest look on her face. *Mother-fucking whore.* Narcissa's jaw tightened as she clenched her teeth and fixed her gaze on Hunter, her hand gripping the bag so hard her knuckles were white. Even though she wasn't certain, a spark, a new fiery blazed had ignited in her pupils.

Though a half-smirk flickered across his face, she could see the tension in his jaw. The expression didn't reach his eyes. "Hey, Nia," Hunter said.

Somehow Narcissa's jaw unclenched, and she saw the redhead practically draped all over him. Was she trying to fucking climb him? He wasn't a fucking tree. Honestly, it just made the skank appear extremely desperate. "Ivory."

"Nia." A smug look remained on the female's whorish face as her name left the bitch's mouth.

Narcissa turned her attention back to Hunter. He didn't even fucking see it, did he? No, she couldn't have told him to use *anyone* but Ivory. She couldn't utter a single word about the betting pool the female ran every single fucking time he jumped to someone new. Normally, it hadn't bothered her, but they had to fall in love with one another. Her grip tightened around the bag in her hand, anticipating the bragging that would come later. Though honestly, it should make her happy that, despite whatever he'd just finished with Ivory, he'd gotten hard. She could see it in her periphery.

As much as she thought she could handle this, she couldn't. "Hunter," Narcissa got out before she moved to step around them. Her fists clenched, nails biting into her palms, as the air crackled with a silent, simmering rage. Really, she had to get the fuck out of here before she did something stupid and bitch-slapped Ivory. Or broke the bitch's arm. Or worse.

Ivory tightened her grip on Hunter's waist, seemingly the only thing that had him heading further down the hallway.

Even with the disapproving glare Ivory sent her way, Narcissa knew Hunter was hers. Let the bitch have her moment. Not that she wouldn't make Ivory pay for it later. Once she figured out what to do, she would implement a plan. Continuing in the same direction, Narcissa sauntered away, her hips swaying with each step. Her teeth ground together, and a fiery heat surged through her veins, leaving a metallic taste on her tongue. Although she shouldn't have, Narcissa glanced over her shoulder once.

Hunter half-turned his head, his eyes on her as she retreated down the hallway. Yeah, she could see the sorrow in his eyes. The guilt on his face. Really, it wasn't his fault. She couldn't blame him for what she'd have to deal with later. It was this place, the rules, the things they couldn't talk about. Not that it entirely lessened the anger she felt. Although the heat in her eyes didn't dissipate, she loosened the hold on her bag. Pausing in front of the personnel door, Narcissa peered in both directions out of her periphery before she turned her eyes back to his and mouthed, *downstairs*. He'd been going there long enough that he should know his way around. At least, in the areas where clients were allowed. Without a word to Hunter, she flung open the door, and her footsteps echoed as she hurried down the stairs.

Once she got to the first floor, Narcissa checked the hallway in each direction, slipped her heels off, and then exited through the personnel door. Another quick scan told her the halls remained empty. As quietly as possible, she checked the performance room to the right. Also empty. Usually, the ones in the back stayed that way. She leaned against the side and slipped her shoes back on as she waited.

A few minutes later, Hunter joined her. He silently pushed open the door of the performance room next to her, ensuring no one was near. After confirming the room was empty, he gestured toward it before stepping inside. Once she entered, Hunter closed the door behind her.

Narcissa barely let the door close before she started in on him. "*Ivory?* Three other submissives here, Hunter, and you had to choose that non-submissive skank?!" It was impossible to miss the emotions swirling inside of her in those words. She walked over to the two chairs, their velvet upholstery catching the dim light, angled toward the stripper pole, dropped her bag onto one, and faced him. "Why her?"

"I take it the two of you... do not get along." Hunter leaned against the door, arms crossed, and a sigh filled with weariness slowly escaped his lips. "I did not actually put any thought into it before I showed up. I had been trying not to think about it at all. My arrival was completely unexpected. Shalla told me Diamond had an opening, that Nina would be free in about an hour, and that Ivory would be free any moment. I knew Diamond definitely would not work; Nina was a little better of an option, but not a great one; and Ivory..." He shrugged. "She is at least familiar. I have been seeing her on and off for over twenty-five *solaris*. She can take a harder session. Not the hardest, but a hard one. Had I known..." Hunter paused, the unspoken meaning of his words hanging between them. "... I would have gone with Nina or come back tomorrow."

"It has nothing to do with whether we get along, and *everything* to do with the person she is." Narcissa paced back and forth, the polished wood floor reflecting her movements as she stepped between the chairs. Hunter's eyes remained on her every step of the way. "And I know how long you've been seeing her. I checked you out before you were offered a session with me." That had been a fun conversation. Ivory was sugary sweet with the clients until they turned their backs. The female was the biggest gossip next to Tamara. Honestly, she didn't know who had the bigger mouth. Narcissa dragged a hand down her face. "I know it's not your fault. Trust me, if you knew the truth, well, you sure as shit wouldn't have gone to her."

Narcissa's fingers dug into her shoulders. "Seeing you with anyone else would bother me." As much as she tried to pretend it wouldn't, the gods' truth was that knowing exactly who he'd been with would kill her. The biggest difference, not all of them would brag about it afterward. That's exactly what Ivory would do. It would get rubbed in her face for days. She'd get to hear all the details regarding the different ways he fucked that whore because Ivory enjoyed describing her dalliances.

"All I know of her is what I have seen. I am not naïve enough to think that is who she really is, but I have never cared to get to know her. I have never cared about her. Just... what she could do for me." Hunter dropped his head and stared at the floor. "Just knowing that you are with other people bothers me," he whispered. He flicked his gaze back up to her. "If it makes you feel any better... I hated it. I spent the entire time comparing her to you, wishing I was with you, because you are the only person I ever want to be with. And no matter what... I will never do that again. I cannot." He gripped the back of his neck. "I did not... I just hated it. It did not do what it was supposed to do, anyway."

Narcissa paused, her breath catching as she slowly raised her eyes to meet his. "Knowing both of you, it's not surprising you hated it." That it didn't work bothered her, but only because it meant they had limited time left together. Fuck. There were no other options. She couldn't even tell him to buy her exclusivity. That would only go so far. With a slow stretch of her neck, she stepped between the chairs, the polished wood reflecting her movement as she shortened the space between them. "That you were comparing her to me... a little. I've been doing that for the last week." Not that she'd understood why until she recognized that she had developed feelings for him. "My skin crawled the whole time I was with my clients today. I've never been so grateful when one of them didn't show up. That's not any consolation. I'm sure nothing could make you feel better about it."

Her steps continued slowly, the anticipation building with each footfall, until she stood right in front of him. It was stupid, but she couldn't help herself. They were so similar. Despite the number of conversations she had with Fallon, not once had she ever let anyone in until Hunter. He was the only person she'd ever talked about her past with. The only one who had ever convinced her a future outside of this place *might* be possible. Not even her neighbors knew anything about her past. Narcissa reached behind him and locked the door with a decisive click, the sound echoing in the silent room. "Is it wrong that I want to do nothing more right now than wipe away everything about this day?"

"Maybe." He cupped her jaw, the pads of his fingers brushing against her skin, his thumb moving rhythmically along her cheek. "The question is..." His other hand reached for her hip, and his touch sent shivers down her spine as he drew her closer. "... do we let that stop us?" Leaning down, he licked over her bottom lip. "I say no. I say... we fuck each other here in this room. Wipe away every single thing we hate about our situation. Every single thing that makes our skin crawl. Every single other thing except me and you. Because that is all that truly matters."

That *was* all that mattered. Narcissa had only one response for him. Because fucking him sounded like the best idea she'd heard all damn day. She wrapped her arms around his neck, and their lips met as she leaped into his arms, her legs wrapping around his waist. She could feel his stiff member pressing against her core, the sensation vivid even through the barrier of her jeans. A deep moan poured out of both of them into the kiss. She couldn't care less if he tore her clothes to shreds, considering she had a spare set in her bag. Fuck, she needed him more than she thought she could need anyone.

His arms wrapped around her, his hands squeezing her, as his tongue plunged into her mouth, dancing with hers. Hunter brought her to the stage, where a single pole stood, and with a grunt, laid her down. He didn't break the kiss once. He gripped the top of her shirt and ripped it, the sound of the fabric tearing echoing as it freed her breasts. She quickly aided Hunter in removing her jeans. They needed to be gone *now*. The easiest way she could think of was to tear at the leather string that crisscrossed along each side. Unfortunately, it also meant she had to unwind her legs from his waist. It would only be temporary. Without question, Narcissa lifted her hips to help in any way she could to get the fuckers off. A moan escaped her, met with Hunter's low growl as their tongues tangled deeper, and the kiss intensified. Fuck, she'd missed him. It hadn't even been a full day, but that didn't seem to impact those feelings in the slightest.

With her hips lifted, he shoved the jeans over her ass, the rough denim scraping against her skin, and then he used his claws to rip at the leather string. Hunter broke the kiss and then sat up. His grip tightened as he raised her wrists above her head and secured her fingers around the cold metal pole. Lowering his gaze slightly, he met her eyes as he clutched at her jeans, pulling them down with a ripping sound. Hunter maintained eye contact as he positioned her legs on his shoulders, grasped her thighs, and delved his tongue inside her with a passionate moan.

In sync with his moans, Narcissa clasped the pole, pushed her heels against his shoulders, and swiveled her hips against his tongue. Fuck yes... This was what she needed. His growls, moans, his mouth on her pussy and hands on her thighs. Gods, she needed more, but she didn't want to rush this too much. Or at least as long as she could keep herself—maybe both of them—from rushing through it all. She just hungered so much for him. Her gaze didn't once leave his. At no point did she want to stop looking at him and staring into his eyes.

Hunter delved deeper and quicker with his tongue, savoring every part of her intimately as if he was insatiable. As he tightened his grip, the scrape of his claws pricked her thighs just slightly. It sent bolts of heat straight to her core. Everything he did took her higher. Fuck, yes. With a better grip, Narcissa dug in her heels and increased the pace of her hip movements. Still, it didn't feel like enough. She needed more. "Harder, please, Hunter, harder."

A massive growl rolled out of him. With a shift of his grip to her inner thighs, Hunter slowly widened her legs without letting her heels slip from his shoulders. He intensified the pressure against her sex, plunging his tongue into her with fervor. Her orgasm drew closer and closer as she rocked her hips in rhythm with his tongue. The first of however many they had in whatever time they spent together. With her heels digging into his shoulders, Narcissa arched her back, her chest thrusting forward. "Oh, fuck. Hunter, don't stop."

A snarl ripped its way out of him, vibrating through her sex. His claws pierced her flesh, and she felt the warm, wet slide of blood down her skin. It nearly sent her flying over the edge, but it was just a little too soon. Narcissa held it back, savoring the moment, for when it finally came, she wanted its impact to be breathtaking, a torrent.

After removing his tongue from her pussy, he licked up her slit and then sucked on her clit. Narcissa stilled her hips, her heels pressing harder into his shoulders. A continuous growl vibrated out of him. With her clit fully in his mouth, Hunter's tongue darted and played against it in a frenzy.

It became harder to restrain herself, particularly with their gazes fixed intently on each other. In her mind, this was the only thing she truly longed for. This time between the two of them, where it was just them. These would be the memories that carried her until they saw one another again in a few days' time. Those thoughts were the catalyst that pushed her over. Narcissa couldn't hold back. "Fuck, I'm gonna come."

"Fuck, yes," he growled against her. "Come for me, Narcissa, now." Stretching her thighs even wider, he joined his mouth to her sex and thrust his tongue as far as it could go.

He didn't have to tell her twice. Her body convulsed as a powerful orgasm surged out of her, pouring into his mouth. Narcissa rode his tongue vigorously and swiftly throughout the entire climax, persisting even after it was over. It didn't need to be stated that this wouldn't be enough for either of them.

Hunter moaned against her pussy, his intense focus unwavering as he continued his passionate exploration. Fuck, yes. His response told her just how much they were on the same wavelength. She craved one last peak, and then the sensation of his hardness against her was all she could think about. As she dug her heels in, he cried out, and a metallic smell of copper filled the air. Gripping his forearms tightly with her nails, she intensified the rhythm of her movements against his tongue. His claws, sharp and unrelenting, dug deeper into her thighs, causing blood to flow freely.

It didn't seem necessary to tell him not to stop as heat coiled deep in her core. With what he did, he knew *exactly* what she wanted. Needed. It was what he wanted and needed, too. Just like she knew he would clean up the blood from her thighs before they left the room. She could almost swear that the gods had woven their lives together. Their desires matched up so perfectly, she wasn't sure if there was any other explanation.

She could feel the intensity of his tongue as he pleasured her, matching the vigor with which she rode him, signaling that another orgasm was imminent. It was right there on the edge already. Narcissa's grip tightened, her nails biting into his forearms until tiny crimson beads surfaced. The wet sensation threw her over the edge. Her body convulsed as an orgasm exploded, and she cried out, the sound of her pleasure filling the air.

Once Hunter had swallowed every bit of her release, a low growl escaped his throat as he surged up until his body hovered over hers. He spread her thighs apart and immediately thrust his cock deep into her wet pussy. As he clenched her hair, her name escaped his lips in a guttural moan.

Narcissa barely got his name out before his lips fused to hers. Her legs wrapped around his waist as she let out a deep moan, her body arching into the kiss. Her hips rose to meet him, a rhythmic dance to match the forceful beat of his movements. Holy fuck, he felt incredible. Her hands moved up his arms, her nails finding purchase in his shoulders.

As the kiss deepened, his cock thrust in and out of her, relentlessly hitting her center. Hunter bit her lip hard and growled as he licked up the droplets of blood. "Fuck... come with me. Come with me, Narcissa."

Coming for him felt as natural as breathing. So natural that he didn't even have to command her—though she loved when he did. She dug her heels into his ass, feeling the rhythmic contractions of her vaginal walls around his cock. Narcissa cried out his name. Her body convulsed with ecstasy, spilling out onto him. *Holy motherfucking shit.*

"Fuck!" Hunter roared, and she felt the hot, pulsing surge as his release flooded her. "Oh, fuck!" His hand tightened on her hair, pulling so hard that it made her head throb. His hips maintained a relentless rhythm as he continued thrusting deeply inside her.

'Oh, fuck' was right. She didn't mind the dampness of their thighs and the stage beneath them, both soaked from their shared release. Narcissa matched his rhythm, her hips rising and falling with each thrust. They were so far from done. She needed more of him. A lot more of him, to carry her until they could be together again.

With no warning, Hunter reached beneath her and grabbed a handful of her ass, then flipped them over on the stage. "Fucking ride me, Narcissa." He tugged her head closer, his grip still tight in her hair, and then their lips met once more. With his knees bent and feet firmly planted on the floor, he thrust his hips upward repeatedly.

With a swipe of her tongue, she savored the taste of his fangs before hooking her feet to the back of his thighs and driving her stilettos in. But she didn't stop there. Narcissa splayed her legs and clawed the skin of his lower back with her nails. All she needed to ride him the way they both wanted was a good, firm hold. Which is exactly what she got. Her hips moved back and forth, grinding forcefully against his shaft as he penetrated her. The kiss swallowed every sound they made each time their pelvises connected.

Holy fuck. The way he felt was nothing short of amazing. She could already feel the emergence of another orgasm. It all made her feel a little lightheaded. Had it ever been *this* raw and intense between them? Had they ever gotten to *this* level of such inflamed passion? They'd come close, that was for damn sure, but there was something different about all of this. Something that took them to a whole new level. Not that she could quite explain it. Her hips swayed more urgently as she dug her stilettos in harder, and the kiss grew more passionate.

Hunter's noises got louder. Blood, warm and sticky, trickled from her ass cheek, coating his fur. It was as if he was offering her everything, his entire self in that moment. Allowing her to dominate him in a brand-new way. Something she wished she could reciprocate. But wanting to give herself fully to him and *being able to* were two different things. It wasn't something she could do. At least not yet. Maybe that was why this seemed so different between them. A gentle warmth bloomed in her chest, a quiet hope that painted a brighter future for them. But until that day, this was all they had.

Hunter cried out as the kiss intensified, her body suddenly wracked with pleasure. His claws dug into her, drawing blood that stained her skin before he raised his arms. He licked her blood from his claws, the crimson liquid glistening as his gaze remained fixed on hers. Narcissa purred. Then he grabbed onto the pole behind him with both hands. A guttural growl escaped him as she drove into him with a ferocity that shook the very ground beneath them. "Holy shit, yes! Fuck! Ride my cock, sweetheart."

He continuously slammed his hips up into her pussy in perfect synchronization with her motions.

She slid her hands from his shoulders to his chest, sinking her nails into his flesh until a crimson bloom appeared. Hunter let out a deep snarl. As he tightened his grip, his claws made a grating sound against the pole. He widened his legs slightly, causing her thighs to spread wider, as he thrust deeper and quicker into her, while she pressed against him.

"Oh, fuck," Narcissa moaned.

"Fuck yes! Do not stop... *Fuck, Narcissa, do not stop*," he groaned out.

"No stopping." That definitely wasn't in the cards. Narcissa buried her stilettos deeper, feeling the strain as she moved her hips with more force. Their bodies warmed with a flush, every nerve alight with thrilling anticipation, an electric current surging through them. It wouldn't be long before the two of them came together again.

His neck arched, and his ragged pants, moans, groans, and growls filled the room, a heavenly concerto of pleasure. Taking his hands from the pole, one landed firmly on her ass, and the other tightened around her throat. He pulled her closer, his warm breath on her neck, until their gazes met. As he continued thrusting into her, he bit down firmly on her lower lip, drawing blood with his fang, and then soothed it with a stroke of his tongue. "Come for me, Narcissa," he whispered. "Come all over my dick. I want every single bit of it. Give me every fucking drop."

Narcissa bit his tongue, merging their lips, and a scream of pure ecstasy escaped her as she kissed him. As she gripped his shaft tightly, wave after wave of ecstasy coursed through her, triggering his climax in an endless stream. A muted roar, almost swallowed by their kiss, tore from his body. Their bodies moved in sync as she rode him, feeling the repeated connection of their pelvises with each thrust of Hunter's hips.

Holy fucking shit. As she continued to ride him hard, the kiss never ending, the feeling was something beyond words. The day faded into a silent echo, like a lost, forgotten dream, replaced by a profound slate of limitless potential and radiant hope. The sensations of their orgasms seemed to stretch into the endlessness of time. Even once they finally ended, their hips still didn't still. They didn't stop kissing, either. If anything, the kiss only deepened further. Obviously, neither of them was in a hurry to go anywhere. But they couldn't stay in the performance room much longer. She didn't even know how long they'd already been in here, but it would never feel like long enough. If they allowed it, things could become all-consuming between them. And they couldn't do that. But Narcissa wasn't ready to vocalize that their time there needed to conclude.

A guttural moan escaped his lips as she swirled her tongue across his fangs, explored the inside of his mouth, and then intertwined with his once more. Narcissa increased the speed and force of her hip movements, tightening and releasing her vaginal muscles around his shaft to enhance each thrust. In order to prompt his claws to dig into her, she applied more pressure with her stilettos on the back of his thighs. She wanted more of him. And she wanted it now. Hunter returned the gesture, sinking his claws further into her flesh, tightening his hold on her neck while his lips consumed hers. His hips kept rising, driving his cock deep inside her.

Fuck, yes. Her synapses lit up like the night sky. Fire raged through her veins. Desire fueled the two of them forward. A purred moan escaped her lips as the rhythm of her hips intensified with each swing. She wanted to pull one more orgasm from him, one that was more intense than any others that had come before.

Taking his claws out of her ass cheek, Hunter retracted them before inserting two fingers into her backside. In sync with her movements, he rhythmically pushed them in and out of her. "Fuck... *Narcissa.*"

Holy fuck. Her orgasm drew closer to the edge. Narcissa sat up and slowly raked her nails down his chest before abruptly digging them into his abdominal muscles. Removing her stilettos from the back of his thighs, she readjusted them while spreading her thighs wider and settling back against his hips. "Oh, gods!"

Hunter remained silent, instead emitting a growling moan that vibrated in the air. As she continued to move up and down, she saw his eyes almost rolling back in his head from pleasure. "Fuck... come with me, Hunter," Narcissa demanded.

He intensified the force and speed of his movements, driving deeper into her while increasing the pace of his fingers and tightening his hold on her throat. The moment he climaxed, her body reacted in kind, their pleasure a synchronized explosion. A scream left her lips, mirroring his thunderous roar that filled the room when his head pressed against the stage. Both of their releases were so powerful that they soaked their thighs, the stage, and the floor with a slick sheen.

Narcissa didn't stop riding him until their mutual release had reached its end. Not that they immediately appeared to have one. She didn't know how long before it finally settled, but once it did, she released his abs as he released her throat and ass, and she collapsed onto his chest, gasping for air. Hunter wrapped his arms around her, and in that moment, he just held her, the world fading away. The only sounds echoing in the room were their ragged breaths and the urgent drumming of their heartbeats.

As much as she knew that everything about this had been different, she didn't want to explore any of the reasons. That would only lead them closer to danger. They already walked a fine line. The last thing they needed to do was make the situation worse. Not that it would change the experience at all. As she lay there, they both struggled to catch their breath; the only sound was the frantic pounding of his heart. Such a powerful organ, and so fragile at the same time. Afraid to disrupt the stillness with a word, Narcissa kissed his chest, then rested her head, as though the moment was ordinary.

Hunter's hold on her tightened. His fingers traced the line of her lower back, the smooth curve of her ass, and then climbed her spine. Still, neither of them said a word. As if speaking even one word would break the all-encompassing peace that had washed over them. Hunter kissed the top of her head, a light brush of his lips, and then acted as if the moment was insignificant.

Her eyes drifted shut. Not because she was falling asleep—though she suspected it was possible—but because a desperate, hollow ache filled her, the spreading warmth a lifeline in a frigid void. It was unlike anything she'd ever felt before. As a child, only her mother ever kissed the top of her head, a gesture of love. It only seemed to reaffirm what neither could openly acknowledge. It simply wasn't safe to do so. Narcissa opened her eyes. If she left them closed for too long, things could get even more complicated than they already were. And neither of them wanted that.

Time didn't exist as they continued lying there. But they really needed to go. It wasn't safe for them to stay like this, in this position. They would see one another in a few days. It wasn't soon enough, but it would have to do. It was all they had.

Hunter swept a hand up her back, and then tilted her head, meeting her eyes. "I have to go."

"I know." They shouldn't have stayed as long as they did. Not that she'd been able to help herself. Not anymore than she suspected he'd been able to. With brief hesitation, Narcissa climbed off of him, giving a small moan as his cock slipped free. She located the remnants of her clothes and called on some water to run over her body. It wasn't enough to fully clean herself. Just enough to heal the punctures left by his claws. She'd have to get dressed and clean the stage and floor before sneaking out of here.

Hunter rose from the floor. The fur on his lower body was soaked, heavy and clinging to his skin. "We need to do a quick cleanup."

"I can take care of that." As the water cascaded off her skin, Narcissa, with a delicate flick of her wrist, directed the flow onto his thigh. "It might be a little cold." Twisting her hand, the water trickled through his fur in a circular motion, from his thighs and up. While she took care of that, Narcissa called on another wave of water, and used that to clean up the mess on the floor. It didn't require her focus for those two things to take care of themselves and for the water to disperse. Narcissa took advantage of the moment to change into her studio clothes from her bag. A simple pair of black knee-length yoga pants and a black tank top with heels to match.

Hunter stood still as the water cleansed his fur, his eyes on her. Once it finished, he took her hand and drew her close. "Before we leave this room..." Lowering his head, Hunter captured her lips in a slow, deep kiss. Though he only allowed it to go on for a couple of minutes. He brushed one more kiss across her lips and then pressed his forehead briefly to hers. "Shall we?"

The languid kiss had thrown her off for only a split second. While she wished it lasted longer, she understood why it couldn't. They were risking everything to have even a small sliver of time together. Narcissa nodded. She strode to the door, the click of the lock echoing softly, before easing it open. The faint murmur of voices drifted from the waiting room. Shit. The guards. As silently as she opened the door, Narcissa shut it again. "We can't go out that way."

"Can we slip out the back way?"

Well, he knew about it. It wasn't something she'd revealed. "Follow me." She led him back to the stage. Narcissa hoisted herself aboard, using her knee rather than the stairs, and then she went to the back door. She cracked it open, and her eyes scanned the dimly lit space as she peeked down the hall. Completely empty. "Coast is clear."

Hunter followed behind her out into the hall and closed the door silently behind them.

With their leaving the room at the end, they didn't have far to go to get to the door that led into the side hallway. Once more, she cracked it open and cautiously peered out. Narcissa glanced back at him. "You leave first. I'll slip out in a few minutes." That way, it wouldn't appear they could've been together. Or rouse any suspicion.

"Okay. I will see you in a few days." Without another word, Hunter made his way nonchalantly to the exit and left.

Narcissa pushed open the door to the rehearsal studio, the scent of rosin and sweat hitting her, and stopped just inside. If anyone had to be the first person she ran into, she was happy it was one of the two people she actually liked to be around in this place. "Hey, Grace."

The female's nose twitched subtly, even though Grace's face revealed nothing. "Hey, Nia," she said as she continued stretching. "You look... flustered. Are you alright?"

Flustered? Flustered wasn't good. While Grace didn't know what Hunter smelled like, the scent of sex probably still hung on her. Shit, shit. Narcissa set the bag with her shredded clothes and other pair of shoes aside. "Um, yeah." *Just did something I shouldn't have. Not that I'd been able to stop myself.* Gods, what the fuck was wrong with her? Dumb question to ask. As if she didn't know the answer. Okay. Grace was a good person. The female always had her back, even though they knew little about each other. She, Grace, and Silva were like three peas in a very fucked-up pod. Narcissa crossed over to where Grace was stretching. "Actually, think you could do me a favor?"

"I probably could. What is it?"

Narcissa glanced nervously over her shoulder at the door and then focused back on Grace. No one was around. It was just the two of them. Still, she lowered her voice. "If it comes up, you and I were hanging out over the last hour... hour and a half." Estimated time frame, but it sounded accurate. It had been difficult to tell how long she and Hunter had been in that performance room. Narcissa's nails dug into the back of her neck, a sign of her unease. It couldn't have been longer, right? Right.

Grace raised her eyebrows. "Sure... What did you do?"

"Can we leave it at something I shouldn't have?" As if screwing a client wasn't bad enough. At least, when she wasn't sure if payment occurred or not. He could've dropped some money at the receptionist's desk for all she knew. It was completely out of her sight. Add the sneaking around to do it. Among a few other things.

"No problem, Nia. You were with me the whole time." Grace sent her a warm smile before she finished stretching out her muscles. "Hey... can I ask you something? Privately, just between us?"

The question was a first, but the female had done a solid for her, so she could definitely answer. As well as keeping it between the two of them. "Yeah. Sure."

Grace, without a glance, got up off the floor and walked to the wall, her hand brushing against it. She climbed the ladder onto the platform that would allow her to get on the aerial hoops. "I noticed Hunter has been your client for the last few weeks. I used to know him before I came here. Is he doing okay?"

Her eyes, and maybe even the way her face fell, gave away how much the female had taken her by surprise. Narcissa's hand instinctively went to the tense muscles at the back of her neck as she walked over to the wall and stretched at the ballet bar. How did she answer that? If she took their emotional connection out, then yeah, he was okay. But it felt half-assed, and that wasn't something she could do to Grace. "That's a complicated question." Balancing on the bar, she stretched one leg, and then the other. Even though she could see Grace in the mirror, it helped to give her back to the female. Her gaze dropped to the wooden floor. "Mostly yes, he's doing okay. Things aren't exactly how he would like, but he's doing the best he can under the circumstances."

Grace didn't immediately speak. After unhooking the hoop, which was attached to the ceiling, she steadied it before stepping onto the bottom. It was possible to adjust the equipment to any height. Grace took a tight hold of the hoop, hooked her knee, and then the air whooshed as she dropped. Silence stretched between them as the hoop eased to a standstill. "I will not ask for details. It is... none of my business. I used to ask Ivory every once in a while—discreetly, of course—but she never had much information. I just... think about him from time to time. Pray that he is doing okay."

"He's never talked to Ivory. Not like that." An excellent decision on his part. That whore was a blabbermouth. "Things have changed in Métamorphe. The old leader was killed. A female took over, last I heard. That's been a bit of an adjustment for Hunter. But he keeps Hayden at his forefront, like he always has, so he's made it work. Even though their father is still alive." Not that any of that made anything complicated. No, it was their relationship and her job. Those were the obstacles between them. They didn't have a way of solving it in the foreseeable future. All they could do was bide their time until his eyes glowed. That was it. The realization that their time was limited settled in her mind, and Narcissa stood still, the air around her thick with unspoken emotions. Her gaze flicked briefly as Grace got into her first position, moving gracefully as always.

"Does he talk about Hayden much? Or himself?"

Narcissa crossed the room and got some music going. Softly, but enough that she could feel the bass as she practiced some on the pole. As she did, the words exchanged between her and Hunter echoed in her mind. Although Hayden had come up in a couple of conversations, it had mostly been regarding the past. She knew little about what was happening in his twin's life recently. Well, except for one thing. A soft chuckle left her mouth. "Just that if I ever met Hayden, he'd likely try to feed me. I told him it would be a good thing as I've been banned from the kitchen."

Grace chuckled to herself. Likely remembering the very scenario she'd referenced to Hunter. Narcissa returned to one of the shiny stripper poles, gripped it, and spun around it before gracefully hooking her leg around it. As she executed a front hook spin, her mind drifted, and she could feel the ground beneath her feet as she spun. She began with a backbend, then effortlessly raised her legs overhead, maneuvering into an inside leg hang, the smooth metal of the pole cool against her palms. It was a brilliant move that displayed all the lines of the body. Lowering her stilettos back to the floor, she addressed the second part of Grace's question. "He talks about himself. Things he's been through, that he's done... Some about his family, even those who aren't with him anymore."

"I was not close to Hunter, but I was very close to Hayden. Hunter allowed no one to get close to him. Even back then. I have prayed that, over the *solaris*, that would change. It makes me happy that he has found someone he feels comfortable enough to talk to." Grace paused for a moment. "Does he ever talk about his sister?"

It was strange. Things she might have normally picked up on, and questions she wouldn't have typically answered, she responded to. Likely because of the subject. Growing up, friends didn't really exist for her. There were a few people she associated with, but not anyone she'd consider a friend. It had been rather easy to keep to when she first arrived at the den. Obviously, that had changed over the years, and she hadn't even realized it.

Narcissa paid little attention to her movements as she worked through them on the stripper pole. They weren't in any order. She simply allowed the music to guide the direction she took. It helped that they were talking about Hunter. She could imagine that she was dancing for him, the music flowing through her veins. As Narcissa spun in a front split on the pole, she replied to Grace, her words echoing in the air. "Actually, he has. They even have a picture of her now." Her words continued as she came out of the split and slid down the pole in a spin. "Did you know her, too?" The words exchanged with Hunter echoed in her thoughts, a troubling tune in relation to this, and Narcissa couldn't identify the source of her worry.

"Yes. I knew her." A brief silence stretched between them as Grace shifted her position on the hoop. "She died... a long time ago."

"That's what Hunter said." His sister died when he and his twin were young. Not that she knew how much time had passed. Of course, she didn't know how old he was, either. At least, not his exact age. Just that his sister's death had been a few decades before. Given how young he'd been at the time Elisa died, he remembered little from the few years he had with the female. Though she hadn't asked for too many details, either. They already knew more about one another than they should. "Would you believe through some of what he told me, I found out I've had one of his brothers as a client once?" Still not something she *ever* planned to tell Hunter.

"You survived, obviously, so that is a good thing," Grace said, her tone edged with a playful lilt. "Which one was it?"

"Clay. It took only one time to see the truth, though." The music pulsed as Narcissa smirked and climbed the stripper pole. "He's gay. At the time I saw him, things were still what they were in the village, so it made sense why he couldn't come out. Sent him to Jezzy after that. As far as I know, he's still with her." Maybe one day things would change for the male. They had some male workers here who serviced male clients.

Grace started another routine. "I have heard the rumors about what sessions he has here. That is not what I ever saw from him in the village. Though, I suppose that should not surprise me."

"Yeah, it didn't surprise me much, either. I've had a few males like that. Takes them time to really accept their truth. I found that if they work with Jezzy, she can usually transition them to a male after a bit of time." She didn't expect Clay would be any different. From what she learned from Hunter, Clay probably just required more reassurance than most. Maybe even something more.

"Well… hopefully that is the case with him as well. I did not particularly like him back then. But I suppose everyone deserves to find their happiness."

That seemed to be how Hunter felt. Well, the latter anyway. She had said nothing about sleeping with Clay. Nor would she, either. Just like she didn't go into any kind of detail regarding some things she and Hunter spoke of. That was between them. "I hope so, too."

As they practiced, the music swelled, the only sound in the otherwise silent room, and they spent a couple more quiet minutes. "I appreciate you telling me about Hunter and Hayden. If you do not mind… could I ask you about them from time to time?"

For the first time, she glanced at Grace. Her right ankle was hooked over the base of the hoop as she arched backward and began the next phase of her routine. The female offered her an opening. One where she could talk about Hunter if she so desired. Obviously, there were some things she'd never talk about. But there were some that she would. "Yeah. I guess that would be okay."

"Thank you, Nia. I really appreciate it. I am sure this goes without saying, but please mention nothing about me to Hunter. Or Clay, on the off chance you see him here. They do not know that this is where I ended up."

Halting mid-climb, Narcissa flicked her gaze to Grace. The female's statement replayed in her mind. If it hadn't been for those words, and the request before it, she might not have given any further thought to their conversation. The female was a shape shifter, so it stood with good reason that Grace knew Hunter. They appeared close in age, or so she assumed. Grace had already been here when she first joined the den.

As she went back through her conversation with Grace compared to her conversations with Hunter, some things lined up a little too much. Grace had been closer to Hayden than she had been to Hunter, which was the same thing Hunter had told her about Elisa. She hadn't gotten a description of Elisa. All Hunter had told her was that his sister looked exactly like their mother. But she knew a little of what Azazel looked like. Hunter had his father's coloring, but the eyes—those he got from his mother.

Aside from that one night when she, Grace, and Silva had a thing, she'd never paid much attention to the color of Grace's eyes. Narcissa studied them. They were blue like Hunter's, just a different shade. What had Hunter told her about Elisa's death? The clinking of the pole accompanied Narcissa as she slid down, trying to remember the jumble of conversations. *"Hayden asked Sam where she was, and the only answer he got was she was dead."* That was what he'd told her when she asked if Azazel had done something to Elisa. However, no one ever found her body. And Grace had supposedly known *all* of them. Otherwise, she wouldn't have pointed out not saying anything not only to Hunter, but to Clay as well. *Holy shit.*

Could Grace be Elisa?

None of them shared their real names. The only person who knew hers was Hunter. She crossed the floor, hearing the faint music and the rhythmic swish of the hoop as Grace continued her rehearsal. Narcissa folded her arms across her chest. "How did you know them again?"

Her lower back pressed against the hoop's base as she spread her legs wide, her upper body hanging down with her hands gripping her calves. She glanced at Nia quickly before contorting her body, keeping the hoop twirling. "I used to live in the shape shifter village," the female said casually. Grace, averting her eyes, hoisted herself back onto the hoop.

Narcissa narrowed her jade-green gaze. That wasn't really an answer, was it? More like how one might respond if they were attempting to deflect the question. Many people used to live in the village. But for someone who only *lived* there, and knowing how long Hunter had been going to the brothel, even seeing Ivory, Grace asked questions that someone who simply used to live there wouldn't have asked. Maybe she needed to approach this differently. "Why would it matter if Hunter or Clay knew you were here?"

"I cannot really answer that."

Almost sounded like an answer she'd given Hunter in the session before last. There were questions she couldn't really answer. Their contracts and NDAs prohibited them from speaking about certain things, even to one another. Which could only mean her suspicion was correct. Fuck. Narcissa's fingers tightened on the back of her neck. "Then I'm going to take a shot in the dark that you're the sister they all believe is dead. If that's the case, don't worry, I won't tell him." That would be the last thing she needed to add to Hunter's plate. They were already biding their time together before the clock ran out. "Or Clay," she tacked on.

Grace stood silently on the hoop's base, her hands gripping the rough rope as she set it swinging once more. Back on the platform, she rehung the hoop with a soft clink against the wall, and then stood, the silence between them echoing. "Thank you, Nia. I appreciate that."

Normally, she wouldn't do this. And it was probably stupid. But considering the number of things she'd already told Hunter, it would be minimal. "Narcissa. In private, Elisa, I'm Narcissa." Maybe she didn't know what led Grace here, but she could understand protecting one's family. That's exactly what the female was doing. And she could respect that.

Her friend's hand clenched around the ring. She gave a slight nod. "I will keep it to myself." She slowly released the hoop, then walked across the platform, before pausing at the ladder, not ready to descend. "I have not been called by my birth name in... almost forty-four *solaris*." Her words were so soft, they were almost inaudible. "They were only four... the last time I saw them. I miss them... very much."

"I know the feeling. We do whatever we must to protect our families."

Grace gave a barely perceptible nod before gripping the ladder's rungs, beginning her descent to the stage. Her friend stood there at the foot of the ladder, her back to Narcissa, not moving at all. "Thank you. And..." Grace flicked her gaze over her shoulder. "I know nothing. I promise."

"Thank you." It seemed her friend had finished rehearsing. Not that she blamed her. Things had taken a turn in their conversation. "You want to head back up together? I should shower and change before we grab Silva for dinner." While her species didn't sweat, Hunter's scent still lingered on her skin. Which meant that tonight, she'd definitely need her friends there.

Otherwise, she might end up strangling Ivory. Unless the female didn't brag, not that she saw that happening.

"Yeah, that sounds good. Do you mind if I sit in your room while you shower?"

"As long as you promise not to steal my shoes." Narcissa grinned. It wasn't a secret that Silva loved to screw with her by taking her stilettos. A new pair every week since she'd moved into that room. How many times had she yelled at him over the years? Or barged into his room to get her shoes back? Too many to count. "I don't mind at all."

"Thank you. And no worries on that front. I will leave the footwear theft to Silva. We both know he secretly enjoys donning heels."

Narcissa's nose scrunched up, which caused Grace to giggle. "Gods, I'm really going to pray that's a joke." She collected her bag and got the music turned off so they could head out. Hopefully, they could get back without crossing paths with anyone. A run-in with anyone who could get her in trouble wasn't what they needed. At all.

Thirteen

Hunter hadn't told Hayden where he was going. It wasn't an un-common thing. He rarely told Hayden anything, so he didn't think his twin would think anything of it. Well, anything more than usual. He'd snagged a jar of spirits from his home before leaving the village and taken his time heading to the marketplace. After the jar of spirits was empty, he shifted and journeyed the rest of the way there in his animal form.

A week and a half had passed since his introduction to Rainbow. And acted like a complete douchebag. A lot had happened between then and now. The last two sessions with Narcissa were brutal: she marked him in one and in the other, she'd left him feeling exposed and broken. That bullshit with Ivory—some lame attempt to fix things that he and Narcissa both had known wouldn't work. Sneaking off and making love to her.

Shaking his thoughts away, Hunter continued on. It was beyond time he apologized to Rainbow for his behavior during that dinner. He'd done so with Hayden already—and completely shocked the shit out of his twin. Even when he'd acted like that in the past, he hadn't apologized to Hayden for it. He'd never apologized for anything. But things were different now. While Hunter knew exactly where the change had come from, he also refused to acknowledge its origin. It wasn't something he could do right now. Not when it took everything he had not to pine after his female. He could have done this in the village; Rainbow had been planning and organizing Zagan and Alastor's mating ceremony. But he hadn't wanted his twin or anyone else to witness it. Not that he could say why.

Upon reaching the marketplace, Hunter shifted to his humanoid form, wandering amidst the sounds of hammering and sawing as he passed through the reconstructed buildings, alleys, bridges, and streets, eventually arriving at The Mystical Moon. That was what Rainbow had said her club was called. It didn't appear to have reopened just yet, but it looked like it was coming along nicely. She hadn't taken him up on his offer to help rebuild the place. Not that he blamed her in the least. If the situation had been reversed, he wouldn't have wanted to be anywhere near him, either.

Hunter pushed open the front door, his eyes scanning the space before he walked down a narrow hallway to the main floor. The strong, pungent smell of fresh paint caused his nose to twitch involuntarily. At the end of the passage, a staircase offered passage upwards to the second level, dimly lit. A swinging door toward the very back. The main floor featured a bar, flanked by high-top tables, with a dance floor and a DJ booth visible past the bar. Looking up, he could smell the faint aroma of stale ale, a hint of another bar on the second floor. He glanced once more around the room before focusing on the female who was polishing glasses behind the bar. Though she didn't pause in her work, she was giving him a wary stare.

He dipped his chin to her in greeting, his footsteps echoing as he walked toward her before halting at the bar. "Evening. Is Rainbow in tonight?" She hadn't been to the village to see Hayden today, and he was catching her scent, but that didn't mean she was here in the building *now*. Nor did it mean she'd be willing to talk to him.

The female raised an eyebrow at him. "You here for a job?"

"No, but she knows me. Name is Hunter. I need to speak with her if she has a few minutes."

Her wary stare didn't dissipate in the least. "I'll see if she's available." The female set down the glass she'd been drying. "Just stay here." Stepping out from behind the counter, she went toward the swinging doors.

A soft smirk settled on his face. No, he was going to run rampant while she went to check if Rainbow would see him, or wanted him to get the fuck out. "No problem. Is it cool if I take a seat?" Hunter gestured toward a table with a nod.

"No one's stopping you," she called out before she disappeared into the back.

She seemed fun. Crossing to the nearest table, he sat and leaned back, feeling the cool fabric of the chair against his back. His ears twitched as he picked up on the individual noises in this room, elsewhere in the club, as well as in the immediate vicinity outside. The marketplace itself wasn't very busy at this time of the evening. Things would pick up before too long; they just hadn't yet. He swept his gaze around the room, taking in the ornate details, as he waited for Rainbow or the other female to appear. His ears perked up, catching the snippets of the conversation between the female and Rainbow.

"Hey, Rainbow," the female said. "There's a shifter out there asking for you."

"Did they give you a name?"

"Hunter and he said you would know him."

"What?" Rainbow's voice registered complete shock. Hunter couldn't help but chuckle slightly to himself. "I'm sorry, did you say Hunter?"

"Yeah. That's the name he gave."

"Everything okay?" a male voice asked.

"Uh, yeah. I'll be back soon. This is good to add to the menu." From the back door, Rainbow emerged. The other female trailed behind her, returning to the bar as Rainbow made her way toward the table where he sat. "What can I do for you, Hunter?"

He hesitated for a moment before speaking. Not something he usually did. "Was kind of hoping we could talk. I owe you something." Hunter barely refrained from shifting in his seat. Yeah... apologizing to Hayden had been tough enough—not that he'd outwardly shown that. Apologizing to his twin's female... Unlike with his brother, this wouldn't be just a simple acceptance. Afterward, Hayden had been too shocked to say anything else, and then they simply went on with their lives. With Rainbow, he had a feeling the 'conversation' would go a lot differently.

Rainbow's face twisted as she scrutinized him, her brow furrowed in concentration. "Alright. But if you expect me to sit and listen, then you can start by asking me to do so."

Hunter raised an eyebrow, but just nodded once. "Would you sit? Please," he tacked on at the end. Shit, he wasn't good at this crap. He didn't think he'd ever get used to her... *formality.* "Are you by chance stocked enough that I could have something to drink?" The unsettling nature of his last two brothel visits still lingered, refusing to leave him alone. They had brought him and Narcissa closer together, but that calm didn't last long once he left the room he was in with her. And stuff like this really didn't help.

Rainbow clasped her hands, dipped her chin, and then sat in the chair across from him. "I have a lot of things in stock. Do you have a preference?"

"Something strong."

Rainbow's eyes fell upon the bar, a long wooden structure. "Hey Kal, can you bring him a double of 'The Shine' and me a glass of orange water?"

"Coming right up." It didn't take her very long to fulfill the request. The female carried a tray with two glasses—a tall one filled with water and orange slices, and a short glass filled about three-quarters with a clear liquid garnished with a lime. She set the water in front of Rainbow and the other before Hunter, then returned to the bar.

Hunter removed the unnecessary slice of fruit before taking a slow sip, then set his glass down. Yeah, he'd get on with it here in a minute. He flicked his gaze over to the other female at the bar, Kal. "When I finish with this, do me a favor, please. Bring me the best that you have and keep it coming." He'd pay for whatever he drank before he left; he never left home without coin. He glanced back at Rainbow as he took another sip. "I owe you an apology. And before you ask, I have already apologized to Hayden." For the first time in his entire life. From the look on his twin's face, Hayden had damn near keeled over from the shock.

Though Rainbow kept any shock off her face, Hunter could sense it in her. She peered over at the bar and gave Kal a nod of approval before the female went about doing as he'd requested. Rainbow leaned back in her chair a little. "For what?"

The female couldn't just take the apology, could she? No, of course not. Hunter took another sip of his drink. "For acting like a complete swine when Hayden introduced us. My personal... shit should not have influenced how that dinner went. And I could have acted much better. Or—as I do not believe you are going anywhere—rescheduled for another night."

"I won't disagree with you on either point. Though I suspect some of your... statements had little to do with your personal stuff, as you so kindly put it, and more with your protectiveness of him."

"I suppose you could say that." It wasn't an entirely inaccurate assessment. Rainbow wasn't wrong, but his attitude really *had* to do with his mood that day. Hunter finished his drink and raised his glass briefly in the barkeep's direction. "Hayden is... a special male. In a lot of ways. As such, he needs a special person to share his life with. Regardless of how sure I have come across to you so far, no one has ever looked out for him more than I have. His safety in every sense of the word is not something I have ever taken lightly."

Rainbow took a sip of her water, the condensation on the glass dampening her fingers, and then waited for Kal to replace Hunter's glass before she spoke. "I'm fully aware of that. Do you not think he told me everything you've done for him over the *solaris*? The way you protected him, especially from Sam and Azazel?"

"He does not know half of what I have protected him from." Hunter took a sip of his fresh drink. He hadn't meant to say that; the words had just come out. Really, he should just leave. She hadn't verbally accepted his apology, but no matter. He'd come here to apologize, and he'd done that already. Something kept him in his seat, though. Not that he could put a finger on what. Maybe he just wanted to assess her a little more.

"Oh?" she inquired, her brow furrowed with curiosity.

Hunter drank about half of his drink down in one swallow. That wasn't a question he wanted to answer. He'd opened a can of worms, though. It didn't seem right to leave it open. "What all does he think I have protected him from?" The question didn't need to be asked. He already knew the answer. But he needed a moment.

"Most of what I've heard are generalizations. That you would step in and take whatever cruelties they intended to bestow upon yourself. Not only that, but you also keep your mindlink closed often to protect him from you. If anything, prior to our dinner, with the way he spoke of you, I held you in higher regard than what matched your actions."

"It was a bad day. Not much of an excuse, but it is what it is." He shrugged. "I do not really have the capacity to be a nice person. I would say that I try, but I have never much seen the point." Hunter downed his drink and, with a subtle nod, held the glass up to the barkeep before setting the empty glass back on the table. "None of that is untrue. There is just a lot more to it than that. Things it would probably be good if he knew, if only so he'd change his mind about them. But things I would prefer he never find out about, because he does not need things like that in his head."

As Kal brought over another drink for him, Rainbow took a sip of water, the ice clinking against the glass. "I haven't known Hayden very long, and while I have seen Sam and Azazel only in passing, I don't disagree with you. They don't deserve for him to care about them. He's too good for them. However, he isn't the type of person *not* to care, even when it's obvious they don't care about him. One look was all I needed to tell him not to give them any of his time. While he may not try with them any longer, he will always care. That's just who he is."

Yeah, and therein lay the problem. "What kills me is, I think that even if he knew the full truth, he would still care just as much about them." Hunter shook his head, then took a long, slow sip of his drink. "They do not deserve anyone's love. Least of all, his. Azazel would have killed him... and raped him were it not for me." Hunter took another drink, the liquid burning his throat before he looked at her. "Again, not something I ever want him to know. Understood?"

Her face registered shock, her eyes widening. Slowly, Rainbow nodded. "You have my word. Anything we discuss here, it stays between you and me."

Hunter merely nodded in response. Gods, why the fuck had he said that? It was true. But that was the last thing he should have fucking said. One more sip and he'd be through this one, too. Hunter leaned back slightly in his chair, the wood creaking softly, and studied the female. "You said you have not known him very long. You really think you can be what he needs? In *every* sense of the word?"

"Yes, I do. Regardless of what you think you know about me or believe you see, I can promise you, it's likely wrong. Just because I look sweet and dainty, that doesn't make me weak. I'm much stronger than one might imagine. Yes, we've led very different lives up to this point, but I don't think that hinders us. It just makes us more perfect together."

"I never said you were weak. Nor did I ever think that. If I did, female or not, you would not still be around my brother. There is literally nothing I would not, and have not, done to protect him, in every way he needs protecting." Hunter swallowed the last sip, savoring the taste, and set his glass on the table's rough edge. "I just need to know that the female he spends his life with will protect him, too. Not just from those around him who would wish him harm, but from himself as well. I am not talking about physical protection either." Hunter nodded and took the glass, feeling the cold liquid slide down his throat, and waited for her to walk away.

"Hayden is strong, and one of the best fighters I know. He can be fierce when he wants to be, but he despises being pushed to that. No, that is not where he needs protecting. It is his *heart* that needs guarding, and he does not know how to do that on his own. He loves *hard*, often the wrong people, and his heart breaks easily. He needs someone who is going to put those pieces back together for him. I have tried in the past, but to be perfectly honest, I am pretty shit at it. I am not a nurturer, and I probably do more harm than good 99.9% of the time. But he also needs someone who is going to keep him from making stupid choices. Those 'wrong' people he loves... He needs someone that can keep him far away from them. I know he will never stop loving them, because that is just who he is. But they will never stop trying to shatter him, because that is just who they are. It is a game to them. One they are determined to win, and one that I do not think Hayden has ever realized he has been forced into playing. I have almost killed myself more times than I can count to keep him safe. He needs someone who will do the same." Hunter brought his glass up for another sip, but the empty glass made a hollow sound as it clinked against his teeth. Had he been drinking it while he spoke? He hadn't even realized.

"From the moment I met Hayden, I could tell he wore his heart on his arm. It's one of the many things I love about him. I would hurt anyone who dared to take advantage of that or cause him pain. I wouldn't allow that." Taking a sip of her water, Rainbow adjusted in her seat a little. "I can read auras. It doesn't take much for me to determine what kind of person someone is. For example, looking at your aura, that stuff you mentioned earlier, I can tell it has something to do with emotions you're not accustomed to feeling. Love, to be more specific. I may not discern the details; however, I can say without a doubt there's an issue surrounding it. Obviously, it's impacted you."

Rainbow paused, the silence broken only by the rustling of her dress as she folded her hands in her lap. As she did so, the female at the bar slid a fresh, cold drink across the table. Maybe she should have just left the bottle. He rarely drank this quickly, but he couldn't seem to help himself tonight. Auras... Hunter internally cursed, though nothing outwardly showed through in his body language or expression. Though it wouldn't—apparently—matter to her. He knew enough regarding reading auras. Even knew a couple of people who had the ability themselves. *Issue* was putting it mildly. They wouldn't talk about him and his shit, though. There was only one person he'd ever spoken to about himself, and she was not in this room.

"There's a reason I stated it only took one look at your father and half-brother to know what kind of males they are. With their auras, that doesn't lie. No matter what crap they spew, I judge them based on the truth of what I see. I told him they didn't deserve his affection. They'll never return it. They don't actually have the capacity to care for him in any manner whatsoever. If they even try coming at him—if anyone tries—it'll be the last thing they do. I won't let anyone hurt Hayden ever again. That includes you."

The female had a lot of spunk, that was for sure. Her ferocity regarding his twin was something Hunter liked. Whether she'd survive, he could tell that she would willingly go toe-to-toe with anyone that tried anything with Hayden. The look on her face made that abundantly clear. Just as she had at the failed dinner, all but getting up in his face when he'd been a complete prick.

"You may not be a nurturer in the complete sense of the word, but you're capable of something," Rainbow continued. "Otherwise, you wouldn't be here to apologize, nor would you have apologized to Hayden. The latter matters more to me than expressing your remorse to me. See, after you left, he apologized for your actions, as well as his. I told him the truth. Your actions were not his fault. Yet he was still concerned that you might have chased me away. You know what I told him? I don't scare easily."

With a last gulp, Hunter downed the drink in his hand and set the glass down on the table, the wood cool under his fingertips. "That is good. Being connected to our bloodline, not scaring easily is definitely a necessity." A small smirk lifted the corners of his lips. The barkeep brought another drink, and he savored the first taste of it. "They are incapable of caring about anything or anyone other than themselves. Hayden just craves a connection that has never existed, and will never exist. He thinks if he loves them enough, then *he* will be enough for *them*. All it is going to do is destroy him. They know that, and it just makes the game more fun for them. They do not deserve him or his love. Neither do I. He is better than all of us. He deserves better than this... shit family the gods threw him into. Not that I think he truly believes that, though I have tried my damndest. But he needs someone who will *make him* believe that. Someone who will take him away from all of it. Make him leave it behind. Forget it. I do not know whether I am making much sense. I am not good at—" Hunter gestured between them. "—this."

He took another sip. "I did not used to be the type of person I am. This is just what they wanted me to be—at least, mostly—so I made myself into this person... hoping they would stop chasing him. Unfortunately... I ended up enjoying it a lot more than I should have." He paused for a moment. "Would you believe this is the first time I have ever apologized for anything? And I cannot even say what changed to make me do it, either."

A smile spread across Rainbow's face as her eyes lit up. She took a drink of water, clasped her hands together, and propped them under her chin. "Yes, I would. I'd even say I could probably explain it to you. If you like." Her grin grew, stretching across her face.

Why did he feel like she was laughing at him? Hunter narrowed his eyes slightly as he took another drink, the ice clinking softly in the glass. "Oh, I am sure you could. Feel free. Though I cannot say I will like your answer."

"I can see that, despite whatever the complexities are, the emotions you're feeling for whoever this female is, she's pushed you to not only face your demons, but to grow as well. Love has a way of making you change. It isn't altering your personality; however, it is allowing you to see situations from another perspective. Become the male you could have been if circumstances had been different. Most of the time, it happens so subtly that you don't even notice it. Unless something like this occurs and the action you take is unexpected or uncommon for you."

With deliberate slowness, Hunter raised the glass, finally tilting it back to drink every drop. His gaze fixed on hers, he carefully set the glass back down on the edge of the table. "What do you know? I was right." Of course, she could tell all of that. It didn't matter what was on his face or in his body language. He could keep every ounce of emotion out of his outward exterior, and those who could read auras could still tell. She was right, too. For a while, he hadn't even realized what Narcissa was doing to him. How she was changing him. Until it had smacked him in the face.

The problem was that she was changing him in ways he didn't know how to deal with. And there was no way out for her. No escape from that place. Ever. Without her, he didn't know how to adapt to his new normal.

The way he'd lived before he met her was how he had survived. Forever closed off. Letting no one in. Not even his twin.

"Just because you don't like the answer doesn't make it less true."

Nope, sure didn't. But that wasn't really the point, either.

"I may not determine the issues surrounding the female you've fallen in love with, but I can see you're struggling with it," Rainbow started. "But that's not why you came here. You came to apologize—which you've done—and, I imagine, to finish the interrogation that began during that dinner. From my understanding, that is common when one introduces their significant other to family. You are the only one Hayden cares about. It's important to him that you and I get along. Therefore, it's important to me."

Hunter said nothing as the barkeep brought over another drink for him and exchanged it for the empty glass. "I will not talk about me and... all of that. Just so you know. It is something I would prefer not to discuss." Because it wasn't anyone's business. But, also because there wasn't anything anyone could do to help. And he didn't discuss his own feelings with anyone. Except Narcissa. She was the only one he'd discussed anything with regarding himself.

"I can respect that you don't wish to discuss that. It's your business."

"If interrogating a family member's significant other is common, I do not know. Hayden is the first"—outside of what he had with Narcissa—"in our family to have anything that could be called a significant other. Mates never meant the same thing in our village as they did elsewhere." Hunter took a sip of his fresh drink. "I had not particularly planned on continuing to interrogate you, but I suppose I could. This is as good a time as any. And I give you my word I will leave the more unsavory—" A slight smirk touched his lips. "—questions to myself." He took another sip of his drink. "You are wrong about one thing, though. He cares about them, a lot. For now, he is doing that from afar. I just hope it remains that way. Nothing good ever comes from his trying to connect with them."

"I'll concede that he cares about them from afar, but your opinion is the one that matters. He has no interest in introducing me to them. Not even Clay, who I don't think is anything like Sam or Azazel. But that's for another time. And that's good, because I won't answer those questions. That is between Hayden and me alone."

"No worries. I will never understand my brother in that regard anyway, but that goes both ways. I know he has never understood me there, either." Hunter took another sip, then the glass clinked softly as he set it on the table. "I do not know why he cares about my opinion. We are completely opposite people in every sense of the word. As for Clay..." Hunter shrugged. "He is who he is. A great pretender, but not inherently bad. Better than me, I think, if that tells you anything." With a smirk, he took another drink, savoring it before carefully considering what he would say next. Interrogating a significant other about his brother wasn't the type of interrogation he was used to doing. Hmm, what questions to ask?

"Just something to think about, and it might clarify a few things. Given your feelings toward your unnamed female, if you had a big decision to make, would you ask her opinion? And give weight to her thoughts? You don't have to answer that openly, but try applying that same thought process to Hayden, and why he'd value your opinion of me."

Hunter couldn't honestly say whether he would. He valued Narcissa's opinion and enjoyed talking to her. She was the only one he could talk to. But he'd never gone to anyone before deciding, big or small. He'd always made the best choice for the situation at hand, and that had been the end. It was a moot point, anyway. She was stuck there, and he lived out here. If they could truly be together, live together, perhaps he would think differently. Then again, perhaps not. That was something he would never find out. "Even then, it would not be the same thing. The opinion of someone you are in love with versus a sibling. Why should it matter whether I like you or not? I am not the one in a relationship with you. Hayden likes you. That should be all that matters." He finished his drink, the taste of the liquor still lingering, and raised the empty glass toward the barkeep before setting it down. "I suppose I just never understood the concept of caring about what someone else thought, no matter what it was. Seems like a pointless waste of mental energy to me."

"It matters because if he and I get married... mated, then we become family. You don't have to like me, but it does matter to him that we get along. For that reason alone. Plus..." Rainbow leaned forward again. "... whether you see it or not, you're the closest thing he has to an actual father figure."

Hunter's eyebrow arched, a silent query as a fresh drink was brought to him. Seriously? A father figure? Where in Hades's name did she get that?

If that's what he was, he was a pretty fucking horrible one. "If you say so." He took a sip of his drink. "I guess that is just a lost concept to me. I dislike, nor get along with, most of my family. But that is just how it is. The only one I care about in my family is Hayden. Perhaps if we had grown up differently, that would not be the case." Taking another sip, he tilted his head a bit. He still wasn't sure what he should ask her regarding his 'interrogation'. "So, when you and Hayden have a ceremony and whatnot, where do you plan on living? Do you stay elsewhere when you are not here working on all of this? Or running this place when it opens?"

"While we haven't discussed it, I imagine we would live somewhere near you. Hayden won't ever want to be too far, and I'm perfectly amenable to living on land."

He nodded slightly and took another drink. That was a lost concept to him, too. He'd never understood why Hayden cared about him and wanted to be near him so much. He wasn't anyone worth caring about. And he really was not good at this. "You want kids?" His face contorted, a subtle reaction to the word. "I only ask because I know he does." Yet another reason they were completely opposite. Him as a father was a frightening thought.

"I do."

"That is good. I know Hayden wants them. Though, I never understood the desire for that, either." Taking another sip, he considered his next question. Really, what all was he supposed to ask her? Hayden was in love with her, and she'd been good to him, and for him. That much was obvious. She treated him very well. Supported him. She made his twin happy, and he respected a lot about her. Not much else mattered than that. Leaning his elbows on the table, Hunter steepled his fingers together. "How are you going to react if, one day, he wishes to connect with them again, and nothing you say or do will change his mind?"

Rainbow clasped her hands together as she leaned back. "I'd go with him. Stand by his side and do whatever I could to protect him."

"Even knowing that someone of your size likely has little defense against two males of their size? And I mean no offense with that question. I am sure you have abilities because of your species, and you could probably kick someone's ass in a fair fight. But they do not fight fair." Leaning back in his chair once more, he picked up his drink, and the ice clinked against the glass as he drained it. "One time I did that, I ended up with a broken leg, a cut inches away from my carotid artery, and a really heartbroken twin. Another time, I ended up with a nearly broken neck, a spiral fracture in my arm, my first liver injury, and Hayden had a concussion. I could go on." Hunter waited until the female had dropped off drink number whatever-the-fuck it was and walked away before continuing. "Now, trust and believe, I do not give a shit what happens to me, honestly. And I am not telling you this to make you feel sorry for me. Fighting with them is fun for me. But it tore Hayden up in ways I have rarely seen for him to witness that. And he still loves them and cares about them. Unfortunately, nothing is going to change that. But with that comes serious danger. Dangers you are going to have to accept if you expect to spend your life with him."

"Let me break a few things down for you, because you offered little in the way of options with your question. It was very limiting. First off, Hayden wouldn't even introduce me to them, and they saw me. Do you know what he did? He put his arm around me and pulled me closer to his side. If he were completely adamant about going to see them, and I said I'd go with him, I guarantee he wouldn't go because he wouldn't endanger my life. Second off, if this happened in the future where we have children, I'd clarify that he had a choice. His children and me, or them. I don't want them anywhere near any children we have. Third off, if you honestly believe, after everything he has witnessed them do period, seen them do to you, and had done to him, he would risk my life, or any future children, then maybe you don't know your brother as well as you think you do. Yes, he still loves and cares about them, but that doesn't mean he's trying to have a relationship of any kind with them. He is accepting that is something that will never happen. Now, if for some asinine reason, Hayden tried, and I went with him, I have an older brother, and he has taught me well where you hit when someone is taller than you. I may be short, but I'm also at a fantastic height to punch the crap out of a male in the nads."

"Part of me wants to ask how many times you have wanted to do that to me, but I think I can guess the answer." Hunter smirked and took a sip of his drink. "I am not trying to irritate you, though I do like how defensive you get over him. I like it a lot." He took another drink. "I know him well. Better than anyone, though you are running a very close second already. Hayden goes through periods where he understands the necessity of keeping his distance; understands that they cannot help but hurt him, as well as those he cares about, just to get a rise out of him. Sometimes, those periods last a long time, and sometimes they do not. Then, he goes through periods where the urge and desire for that connection with them is so strong, he cannot stop himself from trying again. He always swears it is the last time, that he understands a relationship with them is impossible, but it has never stuck before." He took another drink. "That he did not want to introduce you to them is comforting. Maybe he will be different with you than he has been in the past. I hope that is the case." Hunter took another sip, savoring the cool liquid before finishing his drink. "I am not trying to put him down, either. Just telling the truth. As much as he loves you, and would love any future young you two have, I do not want you to be naïve in thinking it could never happen again. Or that he will never crave that again. How he handles that craving, and how they play him, will be on him, and I hope he does the right thing. But you need to be prepared for the possibilities, is all. Perhaps you will be the one who can finally make him see the light—permanently—with them." As the barkeep brought over another glass, he handed over his empty one.

Rainbow raised an eyebrow. "He craves a family connection, period. Has it ever occurred to you that if he had a better connection with you, then just maybe, he might not try with them? Granted, I know that hasn't been possible in the past. It would've just given them fodder to cause more pain. But things have changed in your village. And obviously, some things have changed with you as well. Maybe things that haven't been possible in the past could be now."

"You think he wants to know the shit that is in my head? The shit I have been through? Trust me, he is better off not knowing. There is nothing good about me to get to know. He sees things in me that no longer exist. Maybe they never did. But I came to terms with who I have become a long time ago. I am a psychotic, sadistic bastard, and I am perfectly okay with that. I know I am no good for anyone, especially him. Not even for myself." He wasn't good for Narcissa, either. But he was too selfish to stop returning to see her. It wasn't even a thought he could entertain. That much had already been proven. He was too greedy, craving the things only she could offer. For what he felt with her, and she with him. He would never understand why she felt the way she did about him, or why he felt the way he did about her, but it wasn't something he could discard. He knew what they were to each other, that the gods had created them for one another. But that wasn't something that could ever truly be their reality.

"Hayden is full of light, and I am full of darkness. But I have zero regrets because his heart is still pure, and he can still love someone like you. The best thing he could ever do is walk away from me and never look back." Fuck, his drink was empty again. How had that happened? "I do not know how to get close to people." And that was the truth. With Narcissa, it had just happened. Like a boulder speeding down a mountain, impossible to stop. "And before you come back with 'he would not have to know all the shit that I have been through,' that shit, my darkness, is everything about me. My hobbies, the things that I like, would give him nightmares. We have nothing in common except blood and who we are related to, and that will not change. I care about my brother, and I want the best for him, always, but the best for him is not me."

"You know, he told me you were the one who taught him how to fish."

So? Someone had to. "Yeah, I did. When we were ten. Though I should have taught him sooner." Another drink arrived, but Hunter, lost in thought, simply reached out and took it. "He had to know how to feed himself, and he prefers fish over venison or other forms of meat. Always has. We were considered orphans, so we could not rely on others to feed us there." Hunter took a long pull of the drink, savoring the cool liquid. "Sam beat the shit out of me later that night because I stayed in the village with Hayden instead of going to hang out with him and Clay." Why the fuck had he said that?

"It was something that you did together. If you could do that at ten, with the risks associated with it, why is it that you don't believe you could find any common ground with him now as an adult? Especially as things differ completely from what they used to be?"

"'Cause I am not the same person anymore. And neither is he. Hades, even then, I did not do it because I wanted to, or because I thought it would be fun, or some shit. It was not a brotherly outing. I taught him everything, and fishing was something he needed to know, so I taught him how." That wasn't entirely true. He could vaguely recall the words he'd spoken to Hayden all those years ago. Hayden had told him he shouldn't have stood up to Sam like that. That he knew what Sam was like when he was mad. He'd told Hayden, *"Of course, I should have. You are my brother. They are just a coupla jerks. I am always gonna look out for you, 'member?"* Later,

Sam had just reminded him once again exactly how his decisions with Hayden—the so-called weakest link of the family—would always impact him. And once again, Hunter hadn't cared. So long as Hayden didn't get hurt.

With the last of his drink gone, he placed the glass gently on the table. "We have literally nothing in common. He likes to read. Books bore the shit out of me." Not entirely true, either, he just couldn't read very well, so he never bothered. He'd been able to teach Hayden the alphabet and the basics, enough to get by, and he was pretty sure Elwin had taken over from there, though they'd never discussed it. Not to mention, his mind never stopped. His demons never truly left. Though buried, their lingering presence was like a persistent low hum. That was why he drank so much. Maybe the *only* reason. Being able to concentrate long enough to read a book, even if he read well, wasn't something he imagined he had the mental capacity to accomplish.

"He is a chef. I probably should not say what I have made a living doing for most of my life. And I do not even like to cook for myself. Just do so when necessary. He would not hurt a fly even if his life depended on it. Me, well, I think that goes without saying. He is optimistic about just about everything. I am pretty sure the gods hate me and regret putting me on this land. You want me to go on? I can." Another drink arrived, and Hunter immediately reached for it, relishing the icy touch of the glass before taking a sip. "Hayden does not even need me around anymore. He can take care of himself. He will just not tell me to stay away."

"Hunter, I don't think he'd ever tell you to stay away. Yes, he can take care of himself, but that doesn't mean he doesn't want you around. You're his brother, his twin. The one person he has counted on his entire life. So what if the two of you like or do different things? That doesn't mean you can't show interest or have a conversation with one another." Rainbow shook her head. "I have four siblings. None of us enjoys doing the same thing, but I still spend time with each of them. We still talk, and I ask questions, even if it's just to find out how their day is going. I listen when they need someone to lean on. I don't believe any of this is impossible for you. Yes, it might take a bit of effort, but it would mean the world to Hayden if you did."

Of course, Hayden wouldn't tell him to stay away. That was part of the fucking problem. Hayden didn't know what was good for him.

Not regarding him. Hunter took another sip of his drink. "So... I should get closer to him... so I can ruin him like I have ruined myself? Do not answer that; I can probably guess what you would say." That applied to Narcissa, too. An icy dread gripped him; he understood the situation's inescapable, terrible nature. One day, depending on how long they had left together, he would ruin her, too. With how much she cared about him, it was inevitable. And that he cared about her as much as he did meant he couldn't stay away from her. No matter how hard he might try. "I am not a good person to be around. I already told you that Hayden deserves better than what the gods gave him with blood. That includes me. There is nothing in my head that he needs in his head. Som what exactly am I supposed to talk about with him?"

Rainbow's sapphire eyes widened, and she stared at him in quiet disbelief. "Let me give you an example. My sister, Aqua, spends a lot of time in our library, engineering new technology, and working on our education system. Neither of these are things that interests me. Just yesterday, I asked her how her day was going. One simple question, and it led to something that one of her students did and a new project she'd started. I didn't understand half of what she was talking about, but that isn't the point. My interest isn't in what she did, but in her. You want something to ask Hayden? Ask him if he's tried any new recipes lately. It's a way for you to show interest in him. That's the bottom line."

Again, Hunter brought his glass to his mouth, tasting the familiar warmth before he took a swallow. "So... asking him about himself... shit he likes... and not offering anything in return... that is supposed to be sufficient?" Gods, he was annoying himself. She was annoying him, too. With that look she kept giving him. This was why he always fucking drank alone. He talked too much, and he got stupid. This conversation had really gone in a direction he hadn't planned, and didn't want to continue going. He didn't know how much he'd drunk, but he needed to go. Hunter brought his glass up to his mouth again, only to find it empty. Yeah. He really probably should go. That thought didn't stop him from signaling the barkeep again, though.

"Yes. Eventually, it may change, but it's a starting place. That's all that's needed right now."

"Alright. I guess I can... try that." That wasn't something he'd ever understand, either. He didn't need anyone, even those related to him, to be *interested in him*. It was never a desire he'd had inside himself. He knew his brother loved and cared about him. Even that Hayden wondered what he'd done all these years; how he'd maintained such a huge amount of coin. He'd asked a few times, but Hunter had never given him an answer, outside of it was something he didn't need to know or worry about. And he'd absolutely closed down their mindlink tightly when he'd been on a non-Informant job, even during the rare times he'd accepted a much smaller fee to play bodyguard. The female dropped off another drink, and he took a sip, the cold liquid soothing his parched throat. "I do not understand the need, but I can try to give it a shot. Does that work?"

Rainbow nodded. "That's all I ask."

"Okay." He took another sip of his strong drink. "All I ever cared about was protecting him. Making sure he was as safe as possible. And you know, he ate and everything, of course. Nothing else ever seemed important to me. Maybe I am just wired differently there, too."

"I don't think you're wired differently. It's natural for siblings to care about one another and ensure they're well. With twins, the connection is special all on its own. They aren't common in my species, so I have little to go on regarding that. But, from what I understand, the relationship between twins is stronger and more unique than just normal siblings."

"I just meant... wired differently because I have needed no one to be interested in me. And I do not really understand why that is so important to him. I have been like this for as long as I can remember. Even when we were nestlings, and our sister would sneak in to see us, I do not remember having any desire to get close to her, either. Did not have conversations with her, or ask how she was doing, or listen to the stories she told Hayden. I mean, I heard them; I was in the same room. But I never paid much attention." He couldn't remember ever being any other way. Narcissa was the first person he'd ever wanted to get close to... and that had happened without him even realizing it. The cravings, the desires—they'd snuck up on him until they were so overwhelming, it took everything not to stay at the brothel with her, or run back to her when he had to return to the village. "I did not always stay closed down to him, though. That happened more... after Elisa died. As we got a little older." He could pinpoint the exact time that had happened, though. When they were six. When he'd woken up in Aradia's hut. He'd immediately shut down to Hayden. He'd stayed open enough that they could converse telepathically, because he hadn't spoken out loud for about a month after, but that had been it.

"Maybe you're wired the way you are because it's what you and Hayden needed to survive. More so, maybe it's what your female needed. Just like she is likely what you need now. I know it's an incomplete explanation, but we can't always understand why things happen the way they do."

What they *needed* was for her to be free of that place. He couldn't think about that, though. Maybe survival was why the gods had made him the way he was. If that was the case, Hunter couldn't say for sure, but he'd definitely used it for his own advantage over the years. While his father had lined his pockets in other ways, he'd mostly lined his pockets taking lives. And enjoying every moment. Hayden never would have accepted a single coin from him, or a single item bought with that coin, if he'd known it was blood money. Maybe that was part of why he'd kept that truth from his twin.

"Perhaps." He shrugged. "I never tried to understand why I am the way I am. I just made it work for me and him, because I took care of him." With a last gulp, Hunter drained his drink, admired the empty glass, then placed it firmly on the table. It wasn't working for him now, though. The female he'd fallen for, that he needed, and who needed him... they could never truly have each other. He and Narcissa could never be together. "I have never understood the way I feel about anything. 'Specially now." Especially why the gods would choose someone for him that could never truly be his. Putting them both through unending agony. Hunter took a sip of the drink, tasting the sweetness, and set the glass down with a slight thud.

"I know it's not something that you're accustomed to, or have even done in the past, but you *have* those you can turn to for help," Rainbow stated. "In whatever you need. Your own queen or even me. I'm... more connected than one might think."

What the fuck was that supposed to mean? Gods, nothing made any fucking sense right now. "There is no one who can help," he mumbled before downing the drink in his hand. He almost waved down the barkeep or waitress or whatever again, but thought better of it. He didn't know how much he'd drunk so far, but it was probably enough. More than enough. Considering that, as he glanced across the table at Rainbow, she was pretty blurred around the edges. Yeah. Definitely more than enough. "I need to go."

"Straight home, right?"

Hunter nearly nodded, but he quickly realized that a nod would be a mistake in this moment. His head was a little sloshy. Perfect for passing out and sleeping through at least most of the night. If he was lucky. "Mmhm. Yeah, o'course." Setting the glass down on the rough wooden table, he slowly rose to his feet. "Thanks for the talk. I will pay on my way out." Swaying just slightly, he turned to leave but then pivoted and locked eyes with her. Or tried to. He wasn't sure whether he had succeeded. "We did not have this conversation."

"Drinks are on the house. And yes, I know we didn't. I'm having dinner with Hayden. If you give me half an hour, then we can head to the village together."

"Nice of you, but I always pay." He didn't think she'd accept that, though. The look he could make out in her eyes kind of confirmed that. But he wouldn't back down from paying, nor did he have the energy to go back and forth about it. He dropped the bag of coins on the table, the metallic clatter echoing in the room. It was probably enough to pay for triple the number of however many drinks he'd had tonight. Maybe. He wasn't exactly sure what was in there. It didn't leave him broke, though. He still had another bag of coins with him. "You can give the... whatever... the servers an extra tip tonight. And no thanks, I am good. Just gonna... weave my way home. I will be alright. See ya later, Rainbow." He turned around and stalled out. "Mind pointing me to the exit?"

"Yeah, sure. Follow me." Rainbow slowly led him back to the hallway.

"Right behind ya." Oh, good, she was meandering. Yup, he had this. He was good. Hunter followed her back to the hallway. Ah, right, yeah, this was the way out. "Thanks. And..." He paused, chewing on his tongue for a moment. "Thanks. For being good to my brother. He deserves it, ya know? He deserves someone who will be good to him."

Rainbow peered over her shoulder at him. "Thanks aren't necessary. I love him."

"Yeah." He nodded, and the motion made the contents of his head shift. "Alright, bye." He turned back to the door, and the chilly night air hit him as he stepped outside.

Out of the corner of her eye, Narcissa glanced at the dining room entrance for the third time. Maybe the fifth. She hadn't exactly counted. Though she certainly expected Cheshire to storm through the door any moment. Unless somehow news hadn't gotten back to the female, or even Diablo for that matter. Either of them worked. Sure enough, he'd go after Cheshire, who would attack Ivory as planned. Not that she hadn't tried to listen to her friends. She had... Their advice just hadn't worked out all that well.

Narcissa recalled their conversation.

A wide grin bloomed on Narcissa's face, revealing a flash of white teeth. "It's simple, really. All we have to do is get a rumor going that Ivory talked about Chesire going off her supplements to get knocked up by Diablo. To make it believable, we can throw in how she mentioned overhearing the two of them going at it like a couple of pigs in the courtyard. Diablo and Cheshire will take care of the rest."

"And when they discover we're responsible for it?" Silva asked, the weight of the question heavy in the air.

"I, for one, do not want to be on the receiving end of his wrath," Grace said warily.

"Who says they would discover we started it? The point is for it to sound as if we overheard it. It isn't as if Ivory hasn't already spoken about them." She flicked her gaze to Grace. *"Someone warned me to stay away from him."* But really, like the three of them couldn't conceal the fact that they started the rumor?

Not that either of them had supported her recommendation. Both Grace and Silva, despite wanting to witness the fallout as much as she did, listed all the things that could go wrong, including Averine's reaction. Something she couldn't care less about. Silva had referenced how close they were to freedom. They weren't on the same page regarding that.

Narcissa chewed on the inside of her cheek. Watching the door wouldn't do any good. She simply had to trust everything would roll downhill as she expected. Popping another piece of broccoli into her mouth, she peered at her friends. What were they talking about? She had paid little attention to the conversation. And they hadn't tried to ask her anything. At least, not that she'd noticed. Maybe they'd overlooked her lack of involvement. Maybe.

"—is great, so far. If you are up for story time later." Grace popped a berry into her mouth as she discreetly flicked her gaze from Silva over to Narcissa.

Oh, good. They were only discussing a book. It didn't sound as if she'd missed much of anything. Thankfully, Grace usually only read a certain type of book. None of which included romance. It made little sense for any of them to read about something none of them could ever have. At least she could count on that. "Sure," Narcissa replied. She didn't need to draw any unwanted attention to herself, especially with how often her gaze drifted toward the door.

"Gracie, you know I love to snuggle in your soft, cozy corner." Silva's face lit up as he beamed. "As long as I'm free." He glanced at Narcissa, his eyes meeting hers for a moment. "Are you doing alright, dear?" he questioned, his brow furrowed with concern. "You seem a bit... *impatient.*"

Her eyes darted between Silva and Grace, a silent question in her gaze. Shit. Had they both noticed? Or had she just been that uninvolved? Narcissa furrowed her brows, a gesture of confusion, and offered a slight shrug. "I'm good. Totally fine. Not... impatient."

Yes, she fucking was. After the stunt Ivory pulled, the female deserved whatever came at her next. Narcissa thought back to the shit last night that drew her down this path.

Ivory rose to her feet and strode over to their table, pausing in front of it. "Hey, Nia. I just wanted to make sure there weren't any hard feelings earlier. Hunter can be difficult to please. Really, you lasted longer than I truly expected."

"None whatsoever, Ivory." Since she wiped out what little he got from the bitch. If only the female knew the real reason he'd screwed her, the bitch wouldn't act so entitled.

With a curt nod to Ivory, Grace put a bite of fish in her mouth.

"Hey, Ivory, I know we're not friends, but if you have any sense, then take my advice and keep whatever you want to say to yourself, hold it, and—" Silva paused, drawing out the word as he held up a finger, the silence amplifying the moment. "Swallow." The grin he gave was a grimace as he chewed

and swallowed the rice. "See? Easy." Boredom painted his face as he listlessly looked back at the plate in front of him. "Now, off you fuck, sweetheart. You're ruining our dinner." He waved her off with a flick of his wrist, his expression condescending.

A snicker escaped Grace, nearly causing her to choke, and she faked a cough to hide her amusement. After a long swallow of water, she followed it up with a bite of salad.

"Oh, yes. We all know how good you are at swallowing." Ivory smirked at Silva. "Besides, I'm just having a little friendly chat. Nothing wrong with that, is there?"

Gods, she loved Silva. He always had a great comeback. It may not have worked, but he tried. Right then, she wished the bitch would just get on with it and walk the fuck away. Before the bitch got stabbed. The tines of the fork dug slightly into Narcissa's palm as she tightened her grip. "Of course not. But you'd have to know what's good and how to be friendly for that to happen. Honestly, Ivory, we've given you enough fashion tips to figure all of that out by now."

Ivory crossed her arms and narrowed her eyes, a storm brewing in their depths. "Here I thought this was just going to be a little one-on-one tête-à-tête." The female turned toward the crowd. "May I have everyone's attention, please? For those of you who participated in the Fastidious Hunter betting pool, we'll be crowning some winners today. Whoever had... what was it, Nia? Seven sessions? Before he crawled back to me?"

Several things followed that little showdown—her friends showing their support, several people whining over their losses—but none of it made her feel better regarding the situation. Hunter didn't deserve to be the butt of Ivory's joke. Despite Hunter knowing nothing about it, Narcissa was the only one who could take care of it, even though her friends disapproved of her choice. Her attention refocused on her companions.

"I hope your storybook characters can hide their feelings like a professional poker player," Silva said, chuckling. He nodded at Narcissa, his smirk widening as she shot him a look of annoyance.

"I have a decent poker face." She stuffed a piece of broccoli into her mouth. Not like he'd know any different. Even with all the years they'd hung out together, how much did they actually know about one another? Okay, that didn't entirely apply to Grace any longer. The two of them had recently shared way more information than they had in the past.

"You look like you are expecting someone to waltz through here in a bright-pink tutu and start singing a show tune," Grace said before taking a sip of water. A mischievous smirk played on her face. "Or is it better than that? What are you waiting to happen?"

Damn. These two were too smart for their own good sometimes. Narcissa's eyes rolled upward, a silent sigh of annoyance. "Fine, fine. I *might* have ignored your suggestions." And set something in motion. Not that she would openly admit that. But they could figure it all out for themselves.

Grace raised an eyebrow. "*Might* have? Or *did*?"

That was the question Grace posed? Really? Here, she'd expected differently. "Do you really need me to answer that?"

"Nope. Not at all." Grace briefly glanced at Ivory before her gaze shifted to the heavy oak door. "So... who are you waiting for *exactly*?"

Before Narcissa could answer, Cheshire burst through the door, the scent of anger practically radiating off of her. With a half-shrug, Narcissa gave Grace and Silva a sheepish look. "Hmm..." Not really an answer, but it no longer seemed necessary.

Cheshire strode through the bustling dining hall, her eyes locked onto Ivory. "You bitch!" she yelled, the venom in her voice as she shoved Ivory, sending her tumbling from the chair. Cheshire climbed atop her with a hiss, then punched her, a flurry of blows. Despite the difference between them, Ivory attempted to fight back.

Grace's eyes widened. She flicked her gaze from the scene unfolding over to Narcissa, then back again. A bit of blood had actually just splattered from Ivory's face onto a nearby table. "So. What *exactly* is the rumor floating around?"

Silva slurped his drink through the bamboo straw, the noise a deliberate attempt to draw attention. "You really don't want to know."

Grace glanced at him. "I probably really do not... but, at the same time, I really do."

"I'm surprised you haven't heard it already." Someone had mentioned it to her twice, shockingly enough. "From what I was told in passing... I believe it's something about Cheshire purposely trying to get pregnant by Diablo." Yeah, she'd technically started it, but no one could prove that. She just set things in motion. How long before the guards got involved?

"Cheshire!" Red hollered. She grabbed at the female's arms. "Let her go! That's enough!"

"Get off!" Cheshire screamed, sending Red tumbling to the ground, and then punched Ivory with a resounding thud. Blood splattered across the white shirt Cheshire wore, staining it crimson. A few of the other workers had gathered, crowding around the ongoing fight. Some even cheered Cheshire on.

Grace shook her head as she watched the lopsided fight unfold before her eyes. "You know I hardly speak to anyone, and keep to myself as much as possible." She raised a bite of food to her mouth as the sound of Diablo's thunderous entrance echoed throughout the dining hall.

Diablo spared Cheshire, Ivory, and the surrounding crowd a glance that lasted several seconds, then headed up to the buffet without a word. He grabbed a tray and practically slammed it down before loading it up with food. Yup. He'd definitely heard the rumor, too.

"Yeah." And with good reason. Narcissa watched Diablo for a tense moment. Maybe she should feel bad for using them to exact her revenge on Ivory, but she didn't. Not in the least. Narcissa took another bite of fish.

Red scrambled to her feet. "Cheshire! Let her go! You're going to kill her!" She grabbed at the female's arms again.

"Back off, Red!" Cheshire shrugged the redhead off. "It's time she learned that her words have consequences." Ivory's face met her fist with a sickening crunch. Not that it mattered much. The female no longer fought back.

Three hulking trolls, their heavy footsteps echoing, rushed into the dining room. Shalla trailed right behind them. One male, Druid, ran over and got a hold of Cheshire, yanking her off of Ivory.

"Get off me!" Cheshire screamed, and the force of her head hitting his face caused a sickening crack.

"Damn it, Chesh! Calm down!" Druid yelled.

Though her nostrils flared with a fiery glare, Cheshire stopped fighting him. With a gentle puff, she sent the stray strands of hair away from her eyes. "Bitch deserved it."

"Is she alive?" Shalla asked as she approached the scene.

"Yes, but barely," Zunabar replied. He scooped Ivory into his arms and headed for the door. "I'm taking her to the infirmary."

Narcissa's gaze followed Grace's subtle look at Diablo, who, having piled his plate, turned to find a seat. If possible, it seemed he was even more pissed off. The hushed whispers and furtive glances that swept through the dining hall likely explained a lot.

"I think I am just about finished here," Grace said. "I am not very hungry today." Half of her plate remained, which was unusual for her, but not unexpected considering the circumstances.

"I'm right behind you, Gracie." Silva stood poised and ready, as if expecting an immediate command. He bumped her playfully with a smile that crinkled his eyes. "I am always captivated by the tales you tell!"

"Well, I have a new one that is fantastic so far." Grace smiled at him and playfully bumped him, their laughter echoing in the space. "Are you coming along, Nia?"

"Yeah. I'm just going to pop into my room for something small to munch on." Narcissa savored the last morsel of fish, then pushed herself up from the table. She didn't need to see the rest of what happened. Surely, more rumors would fly around tomorrow about Cheshire. However, she found it strange to see how quickly the female calmed down from the two words uttered by Druid.

"Take her to the receiving room," Shalla said to Druid and turned to the crowd that still lingered around. "Disperse. Now! Unless you'd like to receive a punishment as well."

Druid escorted Cheshire from the dining hall.

Narcissa watched from her periphery as the group of onlookers returned to their seats and focused on their meals. As chatter filled the room, it was a stark contrast to the loud clamor when Cheshire had first arrived. Not that she and her friends planned to hang around or listen to any of it. Whatever happened from here on out, they'd likely hear all about it tomorrow. She glanced at Silva and Grace as they disposed of their trash and dealt with their dirty dishes.

Would either of them say anything to her regarding her actions? Not likely. Which was good, because she didn't want to hear it. Ivory had gotten everything she deserved. As for Cheshire and Diablo... well, she probably wouldn't hear any more of their grunts outside her bathroom window again. *Mission accomplished.* Narcissa grinned widely as she, Silva, and Grace left the dining room.

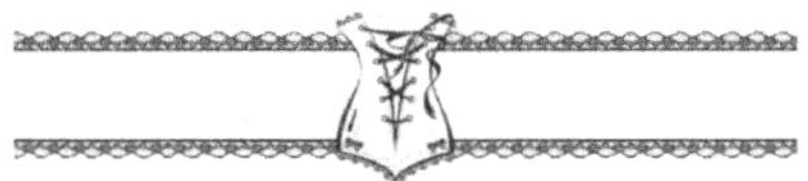

Hunter's head was pounding. As if something was banging against the walls of his skull, wanting to escape. Holy fuck, how much had he drunk last night? He kept his eyes closed, allowing his ears to pick up the surrounding sounds. It smelled damp in here, musty and earthy. Something was dripping. Something hard and gritty pressed against his back. It felt like the wall of a cave, not that he knew how he would have gotten to one. Why wasn't he at home? A heavy, metallic scent hung in the air, tinged with the sharp tang of sex and blood. His brain could sort of make out the sound of a male's grunts. *What the fuck?*

With eyes barely open, Hunter squinted and surveyed his surroundings. He could discern only blurry shapes because his vision was clouded. He squeezed his eyes shut and shook his head to clear it, the abrupt action sending a jolt through his skull. A sharp pain shot through his temples, jolting him awake and allowing his vision to clear.

"Are you fucking insane?!" The male voice that growled the words out belonged to Clay. Reaching forward, he grabbed hold of Samael and threw him across the room. Sam's back slammed into the cave wall. A massive snarl echoed around the cavern.

Well, if he hadn't been awake before, he certainly was now.

"I am a sick son of a bitch, but you two have always taken the cake," Clay growled, his jaw clenched.

As he stood back up, Sam threw his head back and let out a maniacal laugh. Awakened by the noise, Azazel, in his animal form, stretched and yawned. A wicked smirk spread across his face as he shifted into his humanoid form. "It was extremely enjoyable. You should have joined us, Clayton. I have been craving a release such as I received last night for quite some time."

Ignoring his brothers and father, and whatever the fuck was going on there, Hunter looked back over to where Samael had been—

He froze. Oh... *fuck*. This could *not* be happening ...

Against the far wall, three Seelie females were held captive. The thick chains, cold and rough to the touch, disappeared into the stone, ending in the locked shackles around their wrists. What was left of their clothing, torn to shreds, was identifiable by its quality as high-end, expensive and probably custom made. These females didn't just belong to one of the most dangerous species on the isle—by the looks of it, they were fucking royalty. Or very close to that. He could be wrong, but he didn't think he was. Just because his species didn't wear clothing, didn't mean he didn't notice those things.

And he'd been here with them. Likely, all night. While they were violated.

Everything about last night was a blur. He remembered talking to Rainbow at the club, but he couldn't for the life of him pull up a single thing he'd spoken to her about, outside of the fact that it had been about Hayden. No details. He remembered running into Sam and Azazel, tagging along with them. Why? Why had he done that? Were the females already with him then? Had he... assisted in the kidnapping...? No. Absolutely not. Even in a plastered state, that wasn't something he would do. He'd harmed females before, but not like that. Just as he knew without a doubt, he had violated none of those females. But he hadn't prevented it or stopped it—obviously. Which made him just as guilty.

Hunter didn't even have to check the females over. Just the fact that it had been Azazel and Sam gave him all the information he needed.

He leaped up, marched towards his father, who was still stretching, and yanked the key from the chain around the male's neck. He gave it a hard jerk, and the chain, with a metallic screech, snapped. Hunter had always wondered what this fucking thing went to. Seemed he'd finally found out. Azazel started growling, yelling useless shit that Hunter paid no attention to. The tips of his claws even grazed over the back of Hunter's shoulder as he attempted to grab hold. Especially insignificant, seeing as Clay grabbed onto Azazel's neck and slammed him against the wall to prevent him from interfering.

Sam made one move toward him. Hunter saw it just barely out of the corner of his eye. Before the male could react, Hunter swung, the impact of the punch reverberating through the air as the male hit the floor. Blood gushed from his mouth when his fang broke loose. Sam's face contorted as he spat it out, fury blazing in his eyes. Hunter's gaze was just as dark. "Do not fucking touch me."

That was the last bit of attention he paid to any of them as he stalked across the cave floor to the wall where the females were. Kneeling down, he did everything he could to ignore the recent stench of death. The female on the left had hair so light it looked almost white, and light-blue eyes that would have stopped his heart if looks could kill. She was completely naked, but Hunter didn't look at her any more than it took to assess how much blood was on her, and what he could see of her wounds. Bruises marked her body, and a split lip marred her face. Claw marks around her hips and waist, likely across her back, too. Her shoulders, waist, and stomach. Both of her breasts were bloodied, with bite marks marring their surface. The claw marks on her inner thighs were deep, purplish-black, the bruising a testament to the agony she had endured. And her neck... Fuck. She'd been marked.

With each glance, a murderous fury consumed him more and more. Hunter couldn't remember the last time he had ever been this angry. Before he could unlock them, he grabbed the female's ankle, averting a blow to the gut. "Stop it. I will not hurt you." He made quick work of her shackles and tossed a silvery-blue cloak at her. It was covered in blood, as well as other fluids, but at least she could cover herself. The rest of her clothing would no longer accomplish that.

Moving onto the next female, it took him only moments to assess that her injuries were much the same. The only noticeable difference was the series of deep claw marks on her inner thighs, which continued down to her knees. She had blonde hair highlighted with white, and a more angular jawline than the first female. Even if he hadn't nearly choked on the smell of her fear, her emerald-green eyes showed nothing but terror. Hunter met her gaze. "I hit back, so just sit still. I am only going to unchain you, just as I did her." The female didn't respond, but her petrified gaze didn't leave him for a moment. Once her restraints were removed, he tossed a white cloak to her. It wasn't in any better condition than the one he'd given the first female, but it would cover her as she made her way home.

Hunter didn't want to turn to the last female. He knew exactly what he was going to see when his eyes fell upon her. The overpowering stench of death assaulted his senses like a physical blow. Her injuries mirrored the other two, with the unsettling marks encircling her neck. There were just a few differences. Her hips bore claw marks, somewhat deeper, while blood soaked her thighs, and her broken neck was undeniably visible. What had ultimately killed her? Too much blood loss, or had her neck been broken first? She'd been marked. Had the bite just been too deep? It didn't matter. Either way, her dark-blue eyes were glassy and empty. They would never hold life again.

This time, as Hunter leaned in to unlock the restraints on her wrists, it wasn't the only thing he did. He brought his face in close and inhaled deeply. The cave air was thick with a mix of scents: his father and brother, mingled with the earthy smell of the females and everything else. But this female... She smelled like death. And Sam. Not a hint of Azazel was on her. Only Sam. Which meant Sam had been the one to kill her. Hunter sat back and just stared at her for a moment. The death was so senseless. So fucking senseless.

Something inside him snapped.

The assessment and release of the females had taken just a couple of minutes. What happened next took much less time. Hunter lunged up from the floor, his footfalls echoing in the cavern as he stalked across it and grabbed Sam by the throat. As he dragged the male to the cave's entrance, Azazel followed closely, only to have his face snapped at when he tried to touch Hunter. "Get in my way right now, and I will rip your throat out, too, when I am done with his," Hunter snarled. Then, he continued dragging Sam out into the open air.

He threw the male to the ground with a grunt, before the growl escaped his throat, as he let his claws and fangs extend. Hunter didn't fully shift into his animal form. He didn't need to. "Get up!"

"You have made your point, Hunter. You are *pissed*." As Azazel joined them outside the cave, his tone dripped with sarcasm, like venom. "You are letting your pussy show. Those females meant nothing. Go home and cool down and—" His words cut off as Hunter drilled his elbow back into the male's face. Azazel crashed against the cave's edge, a crimson tide erupting from his broken nose and splattering on the stone. A savage snarl ripped through the air, but Hunter's focus remained on Sam.

"Get up on your own. Now. Or die like the coward you are." He wouldn't give the male more than another moment or two to pick his ass up.

With a deep growl echoing in the air, Sam pushed up off the ground and went chest-to-chest with him, their faces inches apart. "What the fuck did you just call me?"

"A fucking coward. Because that is all you are. *Pathetic. Weak.* A lowlife piece of shit who has to kidnap and rape because no one would fuck you willingly even if you paid the—" The hit to his jaw made him grin. That reaction was exactly what he'd been looking for.

Hunter returned the blow with a swift punch and then slammed Sam into the closest tree, the impact echoing through the air. The trunk snapped, the sound echoing through the air as it nearly toppled from the force. Sam wasted no time in retaliating. While Hunter felt the impact of his fists, claws, and teeth, the pain just spurred him on, driving him higher and higher. He didn't make a single noise as blow after blow was traded. Blood flew, splattering crimson streaks against the rough bark of the trees and the cave entrance. He calculated each movement, executing it a split second before Sam could react. With each blow Sam landed, a retaliatory strike followed, two times the strength. Even with the blood stinging his eyes from the claws' diagonal slash across his face, he pressed on. He didn't need his sight; he could hear his opponent's movements and knew where he was. Azazel had made sure of that a long time ago. There was a reason Sam preferred not to fight him. He'd never won. Not once.

And he didn't win this time, either.

Once Hunter was done toying with him, he lunged. It was over in moments. Mid-leap, he shifted into his animal form, slammed Sam to the ground, and pinned him with a paw, the pressure cracking ribs. With a crunch, his claws curled in around his brother's ribcage, and the scent of blood filled his nostrils as his other paw pressed Sam's cheek into the dirt. The male's struggle was futile. Each continued blow with his claws against Hunter's flesh did nothing to dissuade his attack. It filled him with warmth. Malevolence bled through every inch of his expression. Blood dripped from his fangs, splattering on the male's face.

"Rest easy, Samael, knowing that no one is ever going to miss you." Hunter leaned in close and with those last words, he ripped out the male's throat, blood splattering everywhere. The taste of blood, rich and metallic, exploded in his mouth, a symphony of muscle and nerve endings. Swallowing everything that was in his mouth, Hunter licked his lips and fangs as he moved off what remained of Sam's limp body.

Out of Hunter's periphery at that moment, Clay let Azazel go. With a furious swipe, the male's claws raked over Clay's face and neck, drawing blood. Blood drizzled from the wounds on his face, but Clay remained still, not a muscle twitching.

Azazel then turned to Hunter. The rage permeating every inch of him shifted to amusement. "You are going to pay for this." He gave a menacing laugh. "She will rip your throat out for this."

"Good." Was he supposed to care? Not only that, but did the dumbass think he was going to escape punishment himself? His gaze fell upon Sam's broken body, riddled with wounds, the coppery scent of blood hanging in the air. Scratch and bite marks covered it. His throat half gone from the death blow. A surge of emotions and sensations flooded him. A touch of dizziness hit. His vision blurred. What the fuck? Death had never fazed him. Not once. He enjoyed killing. He always had. What—

Except this was his brother. He'd killed his own brother. The male had been a sick, perverted, twisted, pathetic, disgusting piece of shit... but he'd still been his brother. His anger and darkness, the needs of his black soul, his bloodlust... they'd finally pushed him too far. He hadn't just taken a life—he'd taken the life of his own blood. A hollow ache consumed Hunter, each breath a struggle as the weight of his actions bore down. Waves of rage, bitter and salty, and agony crashed over him. He spat the last of Sam's blood from his mouth as he backed away from the corpse. This life, despite the crime Sam had committed... this life had not been his to take. They should have taken it to the queen. She should have been the one to deal with it, not him. Not to mention what he'd been present for... Conscious or not, plastered or not, he'd been present for it. And he hadn't stopped it. Oh, yeah. He would definitely pay for this. He would pay the ultimate price for all of this.

Hunter didn't spare either Clay or Azazel a single glance as he turned to leave. He disappeared into his camouflage, ignoring Clay as the male hollered after him. He would return to the village and accept his punishment freely. Just not yet. There were only two people alive whom he truly cared about. One was back in the village. The other... if he didn't go see her now, he would never get the chance to again. She was the only one who had ever brought him any peace. He craved peace, a solace he felt he required even more urgently than oxygen itself.

With each step, his wrath and self-loathing swelled, a bitter taste filling his mouth as it consumed him. His eyes turned blacker than they'd ever been. Adrenaline rushed through him. His pulse raced. His chest ached. He had a sour taste in his mouth that had nothing to do with Sam.

Over. Everything was... over.

Because the control he thought he'd finally gotten a handle on... had been nowhere in reach after all.

Fourteen

T hank every god in the fucking universe, he had a session scheduled with Narcissa today, because he needed... *something*. Something he couldn't even put a name to, really. Outside of just knowing he needed to be with her. Narcissa brought him peace in a way nothing and no one had ever even come close to doing before. And with the way he felt right now, that was so much more than just a necessity. Hunter's blood felt as if it were scorching, coursing through his body. The tightness in his chest remained, a constricting pressure that wouldn't ease. Despair clawed at his insides, a relentless storm threatening to tear him apart. He was on the verge of an explosion of epic proportions.

On the way to the brothel, Hunter stopped at a river and hastily washed off. Hardly caring, he knew he'd missed some blood in his fur. He'd gotten most of it. Neither the wounds he bore nor the claw marks across his face seemed to trouble him. None of it mattered. They would either heal... or he'd be dead soon and it wouldn't matter.

Once he reached the establishment, Hunter made his way up to the second-floor reception. He was right on time for his and Narcissa's session—how the fuck had he managed *that* so well? And he had already paid for his sessions, so he did not stop at the desk. However, he'd barely made it to the hallway when Shalla called out to him.

"She's still in a session. It's running a little longer than initially expected, so I need you to wait a bit."

Hunter's eyes darkened, and he ground his jaw together so hard it almost cracked. *Really?* This had to happen *now*? *Today of all fucking days?* It took a lot of willpower not to give a shitty response. He'd never once been rude to Shalla, though; she didn't deserve that. And getting kicked out was *definitely* not his goal. He could wait—provided he didn't think for a *single fucking moment* about *why* he was having to wait.

He only nodded his head in response to the receptionist. Hunter leaned against the empty space, arms crossed, and with a sigh, he was determined not to do anything stupid, forsaking the comfortable chairs along the wall.

Shalla's gaze flicked from Hunter to the guards stationed by the top of the staircase. She reclaimed her seat at the receptionist desk and returned to her normal duties. The minutes continued to tick by as other clients exited rooms and stopped at the desk to schedule, if they desired.

One guard monitored him at all times, which was annoying as fuck. But if they needed the extra assurance that he wouldn't be difficult or flip out or something like that, all power to them. As long as they didn't come at him when he wasn't doing anything to warrant it, they wouldn't have any problems.

Ivory and the male she'd serviced stepped into the hall from one bedroom and made their way to the waiting area. Her eyes immediately settled on Hunter. Not that she approached right away. Instead, she waited until her client was out of sight.

Hunter ground his jaw again, watching the female approach him with the exaggerated sway of her hips that she always used when she saw him. Even though he didn't look directly at her, he could still see her from the corner of his eye. She really shouldn't fucking bother. Maybe it was just the mood he was in, but she seemed desperate as fuck. She could just be trying to grab onto an opportunity to get an extra payment, but he didn't think so.

"Hey, Hunter. You look a little stressed. I'd be happy to offer some relief. I've got time."

Gods, this was the last fucking thing he needed. No, what he *needed* was for whatever fucking *prick* was in Narcissa's room to get the *fuck out* before he stormed down the hall and ripped the fucker's head off and—yeah... that was *so not* going to help any-fucking-thing. With a deep breath meant to calm his nerves, Hunter's gaze, almost black, quickly fell upon Ivory. Both of her eyes were ringed with a faded-green and her nose had obviously been broken recently. Not that he gave a shit where the injuries had come from. Hunter stared forward again. "No. I am not interested."

"I know I must look a mess, but I promise it won't hinder my ability to service you."

Gods, he had to get her the fuck away from him. "Do not beg. It does not suit you." Hunter reluctantly flicked his gaze back to hers, his breath ghosting over her face as he leaned in closer. "It has nothing to do with your face. Look at *mine*. Have you forgotten what happened the last time I looked like this?" And his eyes were blacker than they had been during that session with her. The emotions, like gnarled roots, were planted deep within. The rage coursing through him was so palpable that it felt hot enough to see. Over twenty-five years, and he didn't think Ivory had ever seen him *this* pissed, *this* upset. Athos, a canine guard on duty by the stairs, took one step toward them. It took everything in Hunter not to let loose a snarl. "We are just talking, Athos. Your assistance is not needed," he said, without taking his eyes off of Ivory.

"Whoever pissed in your drinking water this morning—the attitude does not belong here. Get rid of it, or get out."

"As I said. We are *only* talking." Hunter's voice, cold and resolute, left no room for doubt: nothing would ever happen between them.

Athos flicked his gaze to Shalla.

"Ivory," Shalla called out.

"It's all good." Ivory snickered and sauntered off.

Hunter almost smirked when Shalla gestured for Athos to return to his station. *That is right; be a good doggy and do what you are told.* He wasn't in the mood to smirk, though. He wasn't in the mood for anything good. If he possessed an ounce of decency, he would depart immediately, carrying his wrath and unhappiness to torment someone else. Anyone else. But he didn't have any decency. And he wasn't a *good person*. Good people didn't kill their brothers. And Hunter refused to go to his death without seeing her. If he ever fucking got in there, that is. A quick glance at the clock above Shalla's desk told him he'd been waiting exactly forty-seven minutes and fifty-three... fifty-four... fifty-five seconds.

What the actual fuck was taking so long? Hunter rubbed the bridge of his nose, then, with a sigh, settled back against the wall, his tail twitching erratically with the sharp sting of annoyance.

Shalla quickly flicked her gaze down to the appointment book. She got to her feet and crossed over to where Hunter stood. "I have Nina available, if you don't want to keep waiting."

Polite. He could be polite. Shalla deserved nothing less. And he absolutely could not make it appear that what he felt for Narcissa went anywhere beyond sexual satisfaction. "I appreciate that. But Nina has a lot of difficulty handling me on a good day. This is *not* a good day." As if his demeanor and expression weren't a dead giveaway as it was. Had he ever come in here with fresh wounds on him, let alone on his face like this? He couldn't recall, but he didn't think so.

Shalla nodded to him. "Alright. Just thought I'd offer. I'm sure Nia won't be much longer."

"I sure hope not."

Several more minutes ticked by. Hunter flicked his gaze briefly to the clock again. He'd officially been waiting over an hour now. He fought back a growl of frustration, rotated his shoulders, and heard the satisfying crack of his neck. Gods, he was a fucking live-wire right now. He needed to see her, and he needed to be in there *now*. Taking a deep breath, he felt his chest expand, and then slowly released the air, trying to calm his racing heart. If he wasn't careful and lost his cool, all of this waiting would be for nothing because he really would get thrown out on his ass.

Narcissa's familiar and comforting scent wafted over him. Footsteps sounded down the hall. Without moving, Hunter's gaze snapped to the left, immediately falling on Kylen as soon as he rounded the corner from the direction of Narcissa's room. The male strode down the hallway, his collarbone-length white-blonde hair flowing freely, dark purple eyes glinting, and a wide smile upon his face. Stopping in the reception area, he dropped a velvet bag onto the desk. "For my additional time."

"Of course," Shalla said. She tucked the payment in a drawer to the side. "Would you like to tack on an extra hour for your next appointment?"

"Yes, I believe I would." Kylen folded his arms across his chest. "Perhaps you can even move me to the end of the day so I don't keep anyone waiting."

Do not react, Hunter repeated like a fucking mantra in his head.

Though he'd love nothing more right now than to remove that smug grin from the motherfucking prick's face with his claws or teeth. Or both. As pissed as he was right now, Hunter would do just about anything to meet the fucking pussy outside these walls. He'd become adept a long time ago at disposing of bodies undetectably. Those he was paid to eliminate were gone without a trace, their stories ending as they were never seen or heard from again. It was a nice thought. A *really* nice thought. But he was in deep enough shit at the moment.

His black eyes and tense body were already present, which was a fortunate attribute in the situation. Hunter pushed off the wall and strode toward the hallway, the tension still etched on his face. "If she has any other clients scheduled after me, cancel them." He might have put a little too much emphasis on the word clients, his voice rising slightly, though he tried not to.

Shalla leaped from her chair and sprinted around her desk, positioning herself between him and the hallway. "Hunter, wait. She'll need a few minutes or so to clean up."

Did she think someone else's *mess* concerned him? Besides, Narcissa had already had a few minutes, judging by the casual way Fuck Face had strolled down the hall and into the front room. "I have waited long enough."

"Fine." Shalla stepped out of the way.

Kylen waited until Hunter had stalked past him and had just gotten into the hallway before he spoke. "It is such a shame when someone takes something that does not belong to them, is it not?"

Hunter turned around and stared right at the piece of shit. Though his voice remained calm, his expression hadn't changed in the least. "Your life does not belong to me. Perhaps I should take that."

"You could certainly try." Kylen smirked. "Though I do not think you would get very far."

Shalla stepped between the two of them. "Continue, and I will have you both banned." Her attention focused first on Hunter, and then on Kylen. "You've been scheduled. Now, leave."

If he'd been in even a slightly better mood, he might have laughed. Or done the closest thing to it he could do. Fucker didn't know what he was capable of. But that was okay; hardly anyone truly did. The ones who had the *most* knowledge in that regard were dead. Pretty boy could think whatever he wanted. If the two of them ever met outside these walls... well, he would show the pussy *exactly* how far he would get.

Keeping his pitch-black eyes trained on the other male, Hunter nodded to Shalla before continuing down the hallway, walking backward a few steps before turning. Following his prolonged wait, the male's pathetic display of any effort plunged his mood into a deeper darkness. The further he got down the hallway, and the closer to her room, the more everything that didn't center on Narcissa flew straight out of his mind. With everything boiling together into one big pot of shit, he didn't think *dangerous* came close enough right now to describing him.

He stalked down the hallway, took a right, and didn't waste a single moment as he made his way with great purpose. He was the predator, and she was his prey. Narcissa was about to witness the consequences of someone else trying to take his prey. When they shoved in his face that they'd taken what belonged *only* to him. In the vastness of forever, they might have her for a fleeting moment, but he possessed her. Not just her pussy, but her *everything*. He *owned* her. And it was beyond time she admitted that.

Reaching Narcissa's room, he opened the door and shut it firmly behind him. His jaw immediately clenched so hard the pressure was like a vise, and he wouldn't have been surprised if he broke a fang. That male's *fucking scent*. The smell saturated the room, as if the walls, floor, and bed had absorbed it. The fragrance of her soap, still clinging in the air, mixed with the damp smell of steam, drifted from the bathroom. There was a song playing, the sound filling the air. A stripper pole stood near him, in the middle of the room. The bondage horse was out as well, soaked and glistening with fluids. Her bedding was disheveled, with the top blanket crumpled and almost falling off the bed.

As Hunter took every bit in, his mood worsening by the moment, the bathroom door slid open. With a towel around her, still drying her hair, Narcissa moved into the bedroom, and looked up. Her hands stilled, the silence amplifying as her gaze landed on him.

Hunter strode forward, ripped the towel off of her, and threw it to the floor. He gripped her chin and met her gaze with the twin black pits that made up his own. "I dislike being kept waiting," he growled low.

Narcissa bowed her head, dropping the towel in her hand. "I apologize, Sir."

While it was unmistakable that the singing voice was hers, it was only as Hunter stared at her that the words of the song registered in his mind. A vein pulsed in his forehead. Or maybe it had started before he entered, but everything going on in this room just made it that much more pronounced. Not only did she play her singing for that motherfucking prick—and songs like *that*—but she danced for him too, if that stripper pole was anything to go by. Between all of that, plus the bed, the bondage horse, and Kylen's fucking scent every-fucking-where, Hunter just wanted to set the entire fucking room on fire. Not only that, he wanted—no, *needed*—to hurt someone. It was a good thing pain turned both of them on.

"Turn off the music. Get out the cross. And a swing, if you have one." If she didn't, he'd make do. He had no patience to wait for the bondage horse to be cleaned or the bedding to be changed. And he wouldn't stand here and watch while she touched a single drop of cum that didn't belong to either of them. They just wouldn't be using either of those today. Though he'd definitely consider her standing on the floor with her wrists chained to some part of the bed. There was the queening bench to consider, too. Oh, yes. He could definitely make the other equipment work just fine.

"As you wish, Sir." Narcissa crossed the room, her footsteps muffled, and opened a hidden panel on the far wall. With the push of a button, the music abruptly stopped, leaving an echoing silence. Another one, and a fully installed swing set lowered from the ceiling of her bedroom. She shut the panel. The echo of the click disappeared as she went into her closet, emerging with the towering bondage cross.

Hunter watched every single thing she did, not taking his eyes off of her once. No matter how much rage and self-loathing boiled inside him, he couldn't help but stare at her when they were together. It didn't take Narcissa long to set up the cross. Then, mimicking the actions from their sessions, she kneeled and bowed her head into the submissive pose. Hunter strode across the room, his gaze fixed on the wall where the toys, restraints, and other instruments lay, their cold steel glinting. He wouldn't need much to begin with, but he knew he'd be returning to this wall at least a few times throughout this session.

First, he grabbed a simple, black-silk blindfold. Then he removed the flogger from her wall. There wouldn't be any easing into this session. Not with the way he felt today. Hunter approached her, standing behind her, the silence broken only by the soft click of the flogger as he set it on her makeup table. With the blindfold over her eyes, he secured it at the back of her head with a firm knot. "Can you see anything? Nod your head for yes; shake your head for no." Back in their second session, he mentioned that when he felt this way, he only wanted to hear her safe word, if anything at all. Some speaking would be unavoidable, but that was okay. And she had the hand signal she'd shown him, for if she absolutely needed to come and couldn't hold back. He would show her no mercy. And he would push her limits beyond anything he had ever done.

Narcissa shook her head 'no.'

Hunter didn't say a word as his fingers, though not hard enough to block her breath, clamped around her throat and hauled her upright. He turned her to face the cross, its looming shadow falling across her as he positioned her body against the metal. His foot pried her legs apart, moving her feet to the edges, then he turned his attention to her hands. Stretching her arms above her head, he wrapped her fingers around the smooth, metal rings. Hunter buckled the first leather cuff around her left wrist, and then did the same to her right, making sure both were secure and locked.

A soft gasp escaped Narcissa as his claws traced a line down her back and thighs, before he kneeled on the floor behind her. His claws grazed down her left leg until they reached her ankle. While tightening the ankle strap, he bit down on her ass cheek and savored the taste of the blood droplets that emerged. The taste of her skin, and the sound of her moan, caused an immediate hardness in his cock.

Hunter ran his claws down her right leg, reaching all the way to her ankle, before sinking his teeth into her right buttock as he secured the ankle strap. His tongue caressed her skin once more, savoring the taste of her sweetness as his arousal intensified. Hunter stood from the floor and snatched the flogger, the leather cool to the touch, from where he'd left it on her makeup table. He dragged the flogger across her skin, starting at her arm, then moving down her spine and finally over her ass. With no warning, he struck out at first one ass cheek, then the other. The sound of the tails on her backside and the sight of her flushing flesh brought a rush of pleasure to him. Not to mention, the way she moaned again. Hunter wasted no time before striking out across the top of her ass. After that, he sucked on two fingers of his spare hand and ran it between her thighs, caressing her slit twice before retracting his hand. Then, he started all over. With flawless precision, he delivered each blow, his movements controlled as he struck his target exactly where he was aiming. He continued to trace his fingers up and down her slit a few more times before repeating the pattern with the flogger.

Narcissa's moans and groans didn't stop with each strike he landed across her flesh. They only got stronger, louder, sending pulses of electricity through his veins. He had a hunch that would only become more intense the longer they stayed on their current course. The flogger's tail struck her right thigh with a wet thud. Stepping up behind her, Hunter slid two fingers deep inside her. He pumped them in and out of her while his tongue caressed and his fangs scraped up her spine. He withdrew his fingers, and his tongue traced a path up her neck, finally teasing her earlobe. Her arousal filled the air, causing his cock to throb with anticipation, even though they had just started. As a matter of fact, it was time to push things to the next level.

Readjusting his stance a little, Hunter began a figure-eight pattern across her back. A backhand diagonal stroke began, arcing from the top down, with a distinct movement from left to right. Then, with a swift overhand diagonal stroke, it descended from the top, arcing downward from right to left. He repeated it, and then the stinging sensation of his strike spread across her backside and thighs. The many directions he took with the flogger brought a multitude of glorious moans and groans out of her.

Moving in closer, Hunter inserted the flogger handle into her pussy from behind, initiating penetration. Narcissa wasn't soaked, but she was wet enough that it wouldn't be uncomfortable. While doing that, he reached around in front of her and vigorously stimulated her clitoris. After several strokes, he removed it from her sex and resumed his position. Narcissa's fingers curled around the rings her wrists were bound to, *almost* bringing a growl out of him, before he repeated the entire pattern. Each blow intensified as the tails contacted her skin, and the air was filled with the sound of the impact. It wouldn't be long before he drew blood with every stroke.

The flogger moved rhythmically across Narcissa's skin, tracing a pattern between the figure-eight, arms, top of her ass, thighs, calves, and ass. He kept thrusting the flogger handle into her while his fingers pleasured her clit, intensifying the rhythm and strength of his actions as he began anew. He held nothing back as he struck out at her again and again. Near the end of the figure-eight, the first break in the skin, his groin tightened, and he almost came. Fuck yes, *that* was what he wanted. *Needed.*

Narcissa gripped the rings a little tighter and whimpered a moan.

His cock twitched again. Hunter repeated the pattern fully. Across her skin, bloody lines emerged, staining her in multiple spots. After the third repetition of the pattern, Hunter couldn't help but taste the blood on her arms and the top of her back as he pleasured her with the flogger handle and stimulated her clit. The sweet taste exploded on his tongue, invigorating his taste buds as he savored every sweet drop of crimson. He wasn't ready to move on just yet.

Another whimper left her mouth, but Narcissa didn't speak. Such a good girl.

Hunter repeated the pattern, creating the illusion of many thin crimson rivers cascading down her body. Fucking beautiful. The flogger set aside; he stood behind her, and in one fluid motion, he embraced her, his touch light as his hand came to rest on her belly. He cupped her breast, feeling the soft warmth beneath his fingers. After giving her nipple a firm pinch, he slid his hand up, wrapping his fingers around her throat. He slid his other hand between her thighs, burying three fingers deep inside her. With each deliberate motion, he skillfully targeted her G-spot, intensifying her pleasure as he explored her depths.

Her vaginal walls throbbed with a force that mimicked the relentless rhythm of a second heartbeat. His cock pounded harder, aching for release. But he wasn't ready just yet. When he came, his cock would be buried deep inside of her. In a moment, he might need to move her queening bench here. If he unlocked her ankle restraints, she could stand on it and he could leave her wrists bound. It would leave her at the perfect height for him to fuck her up against the cross. Not something he'd ever done before, but it sounded fun. Hunter's hold on her throat tightened as he intensified the rhythm of his fingers inside her.

Her neck arched back ever so slightly as her moans became huskier. The scent of Narcissa's arousal intensified. Her pussy was so fucking hot and wet, his dick was begging to be put to use. The pounding in her vaginal walls intensified further with each beat.

Hunter's erection became increasingly rigid, and the sensation was almost unbearable. More pulsating throbs traveled up and down his length. He knew she was teetering on the edge, about to lose control of her body. He didn't need words to know that; he could read the subtle nuances of her body. As soon as she flashed that hand signal, she'd get exactly what she needed. Increasing his pace and the force of his movements, Hunter delved his fingers inside her, repeatedly stimulating her G-spot with a curling motion. His thumb skillfully caressed her clit, syncing with the motion of his fingers inside her. He squeezed, and his grip on her throat tightened, just a little more.

Narcissa brought her forefinger and thumb together, creating a circle with her left hand. She bit her bottom lip and whimpered.

A shudder shot down his spine. Hunter removed his grip from her throat and his fingers from her pussy. He didn't have any desire to wait any longer, and her need had reached its peak. He sucked his fingers clean, then strode over to the foot of her bed, where the velvet of her queening bench gleamed. Picking it up and moving it over to where the cross stood was an easy feat. He unbuckled both ankle straps; the sound echoed in the silent room, and then stood. Hunter gripped her hips and lifted her, giving her just enough height to push the queening bench forward, so it touched the cross. After she firmly planted her feet on the bench, he dug his claws into her hips and penetrated her deeply. "Come," he growled.

A cry of pure ecstasy escaped Narcissa, and her body responded without a moment's pause. A release of cosmic proportions exploded out of her. His orgasm erupted, a powerful wave that stole his breath as it washed over him. As his head fell back, Hunter closed his eyes, feeling his fangs elongate. Wave after wave of cum gushed out of both of them. His dick, both of their thighs, and the bench got soaked. His claws remained buried deep in her hips, his grip unyielding as they moved toward their mutual release. Then he fucked her. And he didn't ease into this, either. Her wrists were bound to the cross, and his grip on her hips restricted her movement, making it impossible for her to do anything as he thrust forcefully and rapidly inside her.

Narcissa gripped the rungs tighter. The sounds of her moans and groans reverberated, amplifying through the enclosed area. Maybe he wasn't making much noise, but she naturally made enough for the both of them.

His claws dug further into her hips, causing blood to trickle down her thighs, while he thrust his cock with increased intensity and speed. Keeping her body motionless only heightened the intensity of his cock thrusting into her core, the walls of her pussy pressing against his shaft with every movement. He needed more. More of her blood. More of her taste. As he kept thrusting, Hunter closed his mouth over her shoulder, the sharp bite of his fangs breaking the skin. Narcissa cried out in pure bliss as his mouth filled with the warm, rich taste of her blood. His taste buds ignited with each bite, as if a sudden jolt of electricity had passed through them. If his eyes hadn't already been pitch black, they would have shifted to that now. Though he had a feeling they weren't *just* black pits of despair any longer. The overwhelming lust he always felt for her would be shining through now, too. Despite the lingering negativity he felt when he entered her room, Narcissa had a way of healing him that was like no other. She had a way of bringing peace to his soul, his mind, and his body.

Releasing her shoulder, Hunter licked across her skin, swallowing every drop of crimson he could. The metallic tang of her blood was like a potent drug, one he craved with every fiber of his being. His thrusts never faltered as he traced the line of her neck with his tongue, nipping gently at her ear before moving to her shoulder. He needed so much more. Her shoulder wasn't where he really wanted to bite her, but it would have to do. He bit into her right shoulder as he withdrew from her pussy and thrust his cock deep into her ass. She was so much tighter back here. He sucked on her shoulder, savoring the taste of fresh blood on his tongue, while thrusting into her again and again.

The sounds Narcissa made heightened even more. With each thrust, her cheeks squeezed tightly around his cock. Hunter didn't have any desire to stop, and they weren't anywhere near done. Even though he planned to move them soon, he wouldn't do so until she had brought him to another powerful orgasm. With each moment, his arousal spiked higher and higher. It wouldn't be long before he'd need to come again. Hunter yanked his claws from her hips. One hand gripped her throat as the other delved deep between her thighs, inserting three fingers. His thrusts into her ass continued relentlessly as his fingers simultaneously pleasured her pussy without missing a beat.

His fangs left her shoulder, and blood dripped from his chin as his grip on her throat grew tighter. With each thrust of his cock into her ass, his fingers delved deeper into her pussy. His fangs elongated as a hiss threatened, though it didn't quite make an appearance. Just as she'd done before, Narcissa flashed the hand signal, telling him she needed to come.

There it was. *Fuck yes.* Hunter buried his fingers in her pussy, repeatedly stroking her G-spot, as his cock continued to pound into her ass. His grip on her throat remained tight, and the kiss he gave her neck was stained with blood, as he hadn't wiped his mouth or chin, but he didn't think she'd mind. Oh, gods, he wanted to bite her here... at her throat. Where her pulse thrummed beneath his lips. The urge was almost too overwhelming to ignore. He wouldn't give in, but *gods did he want to.* "Come," Hunter growled, his voice thick with desire just before a massive orgasm erupted from him, flowing out of her and coating their skin.

Narcissa's release came in a series of powerful waves, each one more intense than the last, causing her to scream in ecstasy. Her cum saturated his fingers and flowed down to mix with his own. During their release, Hunter continued to penetrate her relentlessly and kept stimulating her G-spot without pause. Hades, that scream echoed in the still air... He buried his face in her neck, inhaling her sweet scent, unsure how he kept from sinking his fangs in again, as deeply as possible. Once the last drop of cum had been expelled, Hunter withdrew and tasted it from his fingers, emitting a soft groan. To him, the flavor of her climax was like a delightful burst of sweetness on his tongue.

He left her restrained to the cross, standing on the queening bench, as he returned to the wall with toys and restraints. They would definitely utilize the swing, but not just yet. He picked up the restricting neck to wrist restraint, then the buzzing dildo that strapped to the thighs. Returning to her side, he carefully set the items down, then held her close with an arm while his other hand untied her wrists from the cross. After helping her down from the queening bench, he guided her to kneel on the floor before him. First, he got the collar buckled around her neck. It was tight, but not enough to cut off her air supply. He buckled her right wrist, then her left. Hunter tightened the strap so her hands were about midway up her back, then he teased her lips with a soft stroke of his tongue, tasting her sweetness. Narcissa gently nipped his tongue.

He reached for the vibrating dildo, teasing her with gentle nips on her bottom lip as he guided it between her thighs and into her. His tongue dove into her mouth, cutting off her moan as their tongues intertwined.

Simultaneously, Hunter got the straps buckled around her thighs and turned the vibrator on as high as it would go. A groan escaped Narcissa's mouth as his lips left hers. Hunter abruptly rose to his feet and, with no warning, he grasped a handful of her hair and pushed his cock into her mouth, going all the way until the tip touched the back of her throat. From his tall vantage point, he could easily spot her hand signal, a silent plea for her to come. Without easing into this, either, Hunter fucked her mouth.

A purr rumbled deep in Narcissa's chest. *Holy fucking shit*, the intense vibrations traveling up his shaft instantly reignited his arousal, making him as hard as a rock once more. Hunter tightened his grip on her hair, but kept a steady rhythm with his hard thrusts. He didn't want another orgasm to come too quickly. He wanted her to find at least one release before he came all down her throat. Then, they'd be putting that swing to good use. In several ways.

Narcissa folded her tongue around the underbelly of his cock. Soft groans escaped him as it moved up and down his shaft with every thrust. It was the first time since he'd come in here that he'd made more than just a slight noise, or no noise at all. His eyes rolled back in his head and he had to force them not to stay like that. He wouldn't be able to see if she flashed the hand signal. He quickened his thrusts into her mouth, his grip on her hair tightening slightly.

She held her tongue, encircling his cock. He nearly hissed as her teeth grazed the base of his shaft, a sudden, sharp intake of breath revealing the new level of pressure. *Holy fuck*, that felt good. On the next thrust, she extended her tongue and wrapped it around his balls, giving them a squeeze before retracting it. Just that simple motion brought him to the edge of a moan, but it didn't quite make it out of his mouth. With a firmer hold on her hair, Hunter intensified his pace, thrusting more forcefully into her mouth. A husky moan left Narcissa's mouth, jerking his arousal even higher. He needed so much more. He desired to listen to her moans and cries of pleasure as she reached climax once more. Then he needed to flood her mouth with his cum.

Hunter exhaled sharply as her teeth grazed against his shaft, creating an even more intense feeling. He was already so close to another orgasm, the pleasure building to a fever pitch, ready to erupt. He could hold it back, feeling the pressure building, until they came at the same time again. His grip on her hair became tighter as he drove his cock into her mouth with increased vigor. *Holy fucking shit*, she felt so good...

Narcissa let out a purred moan, which jerked his orgasm right to the edge. Then she extended her tongue, wrapped it around his balls, and squeezed them tighter than she had before. Electric pulses surged through him as his cock throbbed in her mouth. As she retracted her tongue, Narcissa stroked it along his pulsing shaft. His eyes rolled back into his head again. It took him a moment to straighten his gaze, to the point he wasn't actually sure how long she'd been using the hand signal before he saw it. Hunter couldn't hold his orgasm back a moment longer either.

"Fuck... come." He barely said the words before his body was wracked with an orgasm, accompanied by a deep, guttural moan. With a tight grip on her hair, he ensured her head stayed still as she continued to suck his cock, swallowing his cum as it flowed down her throat. Her moans echoed around him as an intense orgasm overtook her, causing her body to tremble with ecstasy. Her cum soaked the dildo, running down her thighs and covering the floor. He didn't take his eyes off of her once throughout the entirety of their mutual release. The fresh scent of her climax had his fangs elongating further.

As their orgasms subsided, Hunter withdrew his cock and used his other hand to feel the taut belt against her skin. He steadied her on her feet, then scooped her up in his arms. As he lifted Narcissa and took her to the swing, her groans persisted from the vibrating dildo inside her. Setting her on her feet, Hunter unbuckled the restraint and set it aside. He quickly arranged her on the swing, exactly where he envisioned her. The first strap circled her back, and the second wrapped around her thighs. Her legs went in the bottom loops, and her wrists in the top ones. He tightened the loops around her wrists, limiting her movement a little further, before kneeling down on the floor in front of her. While the dildo continued to vibrate vigorously inside her, he lifted her legs onto his shoulders, clutched her ass with his claws, and sucked on her clit.

Hunter stroked his tongue over her nub, nipped it with his fang, then sucked on it hard. He repeated the pattern, the rhythm of his actions echoing through the air, never pausing for a single moment. His claws loosened their grip on her ass, running roughly over both cheeks before clenching again. *Holy fucking shit*, she tasted so good. The lingering flavors of their passions rekindled his senses, igniting his taste. All he could think about was that he needed so much more of her. Capturing her clit in his mouth again, Hunter let out a growl against it. He watched her face as her back arched, his gaze fixed on her as she strained against the leather straps. Gods, she was fucking gorgeous. Strung up like this, completely at his mercy, covered in her blood and their cum. Hunter dug his claws deeper into her ass, making more blood trickle down his fingers, while he repeatedly flicked the tip of his tongue against her clitoris.

A deep, guttural moan left her mouth. Narcissa's hand signal appeared once more. Hunter wasn't about to let anymore of her cum go to waste. While keeping his tongue on her clit, he efficiently removed the dildo straps from around her thighs, switched off the vibrator, and smoothly removed it from her pussy before placing it next to them. Cum from her previous orgasm dripped to the floor. A low growl vibrated up his chest as he licked slowly up her slit. "Come," he practically snarled. As his tongue delved into her pussy, exploring her intimately, his hands tightly gripped her thighs, his claws drawing blood that flowed down her skin.

In the throes of pleasure, Narcissa moaned in ecstasy as a powerful climax surged through her, spilling into his mouth. Without ceasing his growling, he devoured her with his tongue, relishing every single drop of her essence. It seemed to take forever to end. Not that he cared in the least. When the last wave had flowed down his throat, Hunter pulled his tongue from her pussy and bit her clit. "Again," he growled, the sound echoing in the closed space as he drove his tongue back inside her sex.

Her body tightened as she released, the sensation bursting forth and filling his mouth. Even as his erection pulsed, he knew he wasn't prepared for the release. Though he would be at that point soon enough. He remained fully engaged in pleasuring her, eagerly consuming every bit of her arousal. After her release was over, Hunter eagerly lapped at her core and sucked firmly on her sensitive bud. Still, he needed more.

Narcissa tugged at the restraints on her wrists, her toes curling inward and her legs straining against his shoulders. Continuous noises left her mouth. One claw plunged into her thigh, causing blood to flow, staining her leg and dripping onto the floor. He slid two fingers deep inside her while his tongue moved rapidly, pleasuring her intensely. *Holy fucking shit,* she was absolute perfection. He would never get enough of any part of her. He needed more of her taste in his mouth now. The intensity of his fingers in her ass increased along with the speed of his tongue plunging deeper into her pussy. Hunter raked his claws down the length of her leg. It didn't split her open, but more trails of blood ran down, the metallic smell permeating the air.

Narcissa arched her back as a purred moan left her mouth. He didn't relent in any sense of the word as his lips and tongue begged her body for yet another release. Not that it would be her last one. They were far from finished. Hunter gazed up the length of her body and felt the heat of her flushed skin and basked in her expression of pure ecstasy. As she squeezed her legs tighter, he saw her flash him the signal again. Hunter continued the steady rhythm of his fingers as he briefly withdrew his tongue from her sex to nip at her clit. "Come." He shoved his tongue back inside her and let loose a deafening growl.

Her ecstatic cry reverberated through the room as her intense orgasm surged into his mouth. As her back arched, Narcissa tugged at the restraints, her ass cheeks clenched around his fingers, and her grip on his shoulders became even tighter. Hunter's growl didn't cease for a moment. Nor did he stop fucking her ass or her pussy. His eyes didn't once leave her face. Not a single drop of her orgasm went anywhere but down his throat. After devouring the last morsel, he stood and settled himself between her thighs, his erection nudging the opening of her. His claws dug into her thighs as he thrust his cock deep inside her. They both let out a deep moan as he penetrated her vigorously, with no restraint, his cock thrusting into her repeatedly.

Gods, she felt so fucking incredible. Each thrust into her sent an exquisite sensation throughout his entire body. The metallic scent and the sticky warmth of her blood on his fingers ignited his mind. He'd done everything he could today to memorize everything about her. The noises she made. Her face, scent, and taste, both of her blood and her cum. The exact color of her skin, the silky cinnamon-brown strands of her hair, the scar on her waist, and the other newer one on her thigh. The roses tattooed on her right arm and the ornate design of woven vines on her left leg. There was only one part of her left he had yet to drink in during this session. He hadn't taken her blindfold off yet. Because as soon as he did, as soon as he stared into her eyes, Hunter had a feeling he was going to break. The rage, agony, and self-loathing that had fueled his need for a session like *this*... bit by bit, just touching her, hearing her, smelling her, tasting her...

Narcissa was washing it all away. Seeing her eyes would snap his control into a million pieces and scatter them to the wind.

His chest burned with a furious heat, a caged beast clawing to escape its confines. Once this session was through, once he walked out that door... that was it. He wouldn't ever be able to come back. He would die for killing Sam. It had been an unsanctioned kill. Something that wasn't allowed under their new leader. They couldn't kill without cause; they were supposed to bring stuff like that to the queen. But he'd been too eager to spill blood with his own fangs and claws once he knew what had been done. He knew he'd forfeited his life. He knew that after this he would never see Narcissa again.

Hunter let out a groan as he felt her muscles tightening around his cock, enhancing the pleasure of every thrust. Her back arched as she tugged on the straps, and the feel of her legs pressing against his hips intensified his desire to be closer to her than before. One hand covered her breast. The other pushed her blindfold up, allowing her eyes to meet the light, before sliding his hand to the nape of her neck. It was the only place he looked. Right into that beautiful jade-green-and-gold gaze. The blindfold could have fallen to the floor, for all he knew. Hunter didn't care. He couldn't look away. He needed to memorize the intricate details of her eyes, from their shade to the way they sparkled.

Wetness, warm and salty, dripped from his eyes. Hunter didn't stop fucking her, nor did he try to figure out what it was. Probably sweat. He'd been going hard at her for he didn't know how long. His vision blurred, and he blinked hard, trying to clear the haze. Gods, what the fuck was wrong with him?

Though the rhythmic sounds from Narcissa ceased, the rest of her body still reacted to his touch. At least, part of it. Her vaginal muscles tightened and relaxed around his cock as her legs clung more firmly to his hips. Almost as if she feared letting him go. Hunter's grip on the nape tightened, and his fingers massaged and kneaded her breast. He teased her nipple, then lathered her other breast with the same attention. His cock never stopped drilling into her core, nor did his eyes stray away from hers. He didn't just need to re-memorize everything about her—he needed to drown in her. Keep every single part of her with him when he left this room and went home to his death.

Without a second thought, Hunter reached for her wrists, his fingers fumbling as he loosened the confining straps. He gently pulled her hands through the loops, and their warmth soon rested on his shoulders. As the hand at the nape slid up to tangle in her hair, he reached down and gripped her ass, his fingers digging into her flesh. Hunter tugged her closer, then he licked over her bottom lip before slipping his tongue into her mouth to dance with hers. A half-strangled moan left him as her taste exploded on his tongue all over again.

Narcissa nipped his tongue, then swept hers across the back of his fangs. He couldn't stop another strangled moan. His body jolted as a bolt of lightning surged through him, electrifying his senses and heightening his arousal. Her hands slid to the back of his shoulders, clinging to him tightly, her fingers digging in. As she increased the contractions of her vaginal muscles, her deep moan mingled with the kiss.

Between everything she was doing, he was on the verge of another orgasm. And it was going to be more powerful than any other he'd had today. As the kiss deepened, Hunter's thrusts quickened, mirroring the growing passion. He didn't focus on anything but her. Nothing else mattered, or even existed, but the two of them. And this last bit of time they had left together.

Narcissa hooked her legs under his ass, utilizing the swing for added momentum to move her hips against him, skillfully riding him as he thrust into her. As her vaginal contractions intensified, the intervals between them shortened. A deep growl rumbled in his chest, shaking him, and it only became louder as she dug her nails into his shoulder blades and whimpered. It all felt so incredible. She felt so incredible. He was barely holding his orgasm back at this point.

They broke the kiss, their eyes meeting, and he held her gaze for what felt like a full minute. From their initial meeting, their connection blossomed, growing more profound in that singular, shared moment. "Come with me, Narcissa. Come with me now."

Her nails, now digging in, brought his climax within reach. As her release erupted, drenching everything with its essence, his own exploded, setting his soul ablaze. As Narcissa screamed out his name, Hunter let out a roar that echoed through the air. They both flew apart, waves of pleasure exploding out of them simultaneously. It saturated her sex, her thighs, her ass cheeks, and the swing until they were all dripping wet. Hunter didn't think he'd ever had an orgasm of this magnitude. It truly seemed to have no end.

Trembles swept through his body in waves. His arms squeezed her, a desperate plea, their bodies molding together as if they might disappear into each other, a last stand against the inevitable. As if, were they to let go, their very souls would shatter. Before their orgasms concluded, Hunter pressed his forehead against hers, feeling the warmth of her skin, squeezed his eyes shut tight, and just held her. He sent up silent prayers to the gods, begging them to spare him the pain of letting her go, leaving the room, and going home to die.

Gods, he did not want to say goodbye. His eyes stung when he realized he had no choice but to proceed. Something wet dripped out of his eyes. His skin prickled with the chilling certainty of impending doom. He didn't have to say goodbye just yet. He could take his time cleaning her up, stalling for as long as he could. His punishment could wait long enough for that.

He didn't know how long they stayed like that, with his forehead pressed against hers, and her fingers running up and down the back of his neck. He didn't have any desire to move. But they couldn't stay like this forever. A slight groan left him as he pulled his cock from her pussy and kneeled down before her. There was absolutely no fucking way they were using the bed. But he wasn't willing to wash away the remnants of their lovemaking. Not when this was the last opportunity he would have to taste her. His tongue moved slowly across her belly, pelvis, sex, and thighs, cleaning every drop. He remained on his knees and moved around behind her; the silence amplified his movements.

Hunter stood up from the floor after he'd finished licking her clean, and he moved to stand in front of her. With extreme care, he freed her legs from the swing's restraints, and then helped her to her feet, steadying her. Without a word, he gently lifted her, enjoying the feel of her in his arms, and crossed the floor toward the bathroom. Narcissa slid the door open when they reached it, and he carried her inside and into the shower. He kept one arm around her as he adjusted the shower's temperature, feeling for the perfect balance between warm and cool. He kissed her forehead, then the cold air hit him as he stepped from the shower to fill the tub.

Narcissa's eyes remained on him as she stood beneath the spray. The water sluiced down her body, washing away the remnants of their time together, and the puncture wounds healed, leaving her skin smooth. With the bath prepared, Hunter stepped back into the shower, the last drops of water still clinging to his skin, as he gathered Narcissa into his arms. He carried her to the tub slowly, the weight of her in his arms, understanding this was his last chance to hold her close. He eased her into the water, and the sound of the water lapping against the side of the tub filled the air as he kneeled on the floor behind her. Without a word, he massaged her shoulders and her neck.

As she looked back at him, she placed her hand on his to quiet them. "Why don't you get in the tub with me?"

Hunter paused, captivated by her radiant gaze before he spoke. "I plan on it." His voice cracked, a tiny, lost sound that echoed the hollowness within him. As much as he'd been trying to hold his emotions back, he didn't think he was doing such a great job any longer. "I just wanted to take care of you first."

"Alright. Will you then talk to me and explain what's going on? And what happened to you?"

"Yes. I will tell you what happened and answer your questions. I just need to take care of you first." In the only way that he could. This would be the last moment he would experience this. "Is that okay?" Hunter had never spoken to her like this before. He could see the fear in her eyes, that she knew something was wrong, and it troubled her. If only he knew how to take that feeling away, he would do so instantly. But telling her the truth of what was going to happen was only going to make it worse. That couldn't be helped. He couldn't run from his punishment, and he would never lie to her.

Narcissa lifted his hand, then gently pressed a kiss to his palm. "Yes," she replied as she faced forward.

"Thank you," he whispered. After he placed a soft kiss on the side of her neck, right over her pulse point—a place that he would never get to mark—he returned to massaging her. And he took his time. His hands and fingers moved gently, yet with determined precision, across her skin. It was the longest he'd ever spent on a massage. Not just for her, but for anyone. Once he was finished, Hunter carefully climbed into the steaming tub behind her. He drew her onto his lap, his embrace warm and secure as her back met his chest. "I did something really stupid," he whispered.

Covering his hands with her own, Narcissa intertwined their fingers together. "I take it that it has something to do with the claw marks across your face?"

"Yes." Hunter rested his cheek against the top of her head. "I got into a fight with my oldest brother, Sam. I baited him until I pissed him off so he would fight me."

"Was there a reason you baited him?"

"Yes, he, um..." Gods, how was he going to put all of this into words that made sense, when some of it didn't even make sense to him? Start from the beginning, maybe. At least, as much as he could remember. "Last night, I went to talk to Hayden's female. I needed to apologize to her. When Hayden introduced us over a *penumbra* ago, I was a real dick. So, I went to apologize. I ended up getting really... really drunk."

"So, you got wasted while talking to her, or started drinking while apologizing and then continued drinking afterward?"

"I... do not really remember... much of anything from last night. But I do not think I was drinking before I went to see her at her club. I think I started drinking... after we started talking... maybe. I think I got wasted while I was talking to her. But I might still have been drinking when I left... or drank more after I left. Fuck, I do not know." He sighed. "After I left her club... I must have been heading home. That is the only thing that makes sense. But I remember running into Sam... and my father. I do not remember where, just that I ran into them."

Narcissa's thumb moved rhythmically against his skin. "Logically, if you ran into them after you left the club, then it would either have been in the marketplace or the surrounding forest. Do you remember anything regarding the sounds you heard? Were there a lot of people talking or shopping? Or scents from other nearby stores? Or was it quieter, more woodsy?"

Hunter closed his eyes and thought back to the night before. He couldn't remember how long he'd been walking, the silence broken only by his own footsteps, before his father had stepped out of... somewhere. All he remembered about that was a shadow. "Quieter. I could still hear stuff... from the marketplace, I think, but it was more distant. And it was dark. No lights or stars or moon, so I must have been in the forest already. I remember only my father first. I do not remember hearing him... but I smelled him before I saw him. He said...” What had he said? Helping... Something about... “I think he said he needed my help with something.”

“Did he say what he needed your help with, or did he keep the request general?”

Hunter squeezed his eyes shut, trying to remember what happened, but it was just a blurry mess. “I do not remember, but I know I followed him ... to the left, I think. Not that I know why. I do not know how he convinced me, either. When we got to Sam, they had...” His head lowered, almost without him willing it, and he buried his face in the softness of her neck. “They had three females with them. I did not even track what they looked like. Just that two of them were passed out. They said... no, it was my father, he said...” Fuck, what was it? The words were just a garbled mess in his head. Hunter barely registered a flash of something from Sam. The male snickered the whole time. *“He is so fucking plastered, he does not even know where he is.”* “... home. I think... something to do with home.”

“Maybe they were taking them home? Or that there was a problem with their home? Or that they were far from home and required escorts?”

He recalled his father’s words—“help” and “home”—echoing in his mind. Maybe... “I think... I think it was something about helping them home. Sam... he put one female in my arms. One who had passed out. Told me to carry her. Then we started walking. They said more stuff, but I do not remember any of it.” He recalled something wet against his mouth—and it hadn’t been water. *“Are you getting thirsty? Here.”* Then, someone held a jar to his mouth. Whatever had been in it, he’d gulped it down. “One of them gave me more spirits on the way there.”

“Where is ‘there’? Do you remember anything about the smell? If it changed from a woodsy scent? Or anything about the trek?”

“No. Not much at all about the walk there. Except...”

“She wants you, you know. This one.” Sam nodded down at the female in his arms, the only one currently awake. “Look at how she is looking at you.”

The female Azazel had was draped over his shoulder, his hand gripping her ass. “Just think how much fun she is going to be when we get back to her place.”

There was more to it than that. Some back and forth. Despite his best efforts, Hunter couldn’t make any sense of it in his own mind. “They started talking to me... about how one female wanted to have sex with me.

I know I did not, though. I was not with anyone last night. It does not matter how drunk I get, I would never rape someone."

"I know you wouldn't," Narcissa said.

"I remember little more from last night. But this morning, when I woke up, we were in a cave. The wall held all three females in chains. And Sam... he was on top of one of them."

"What happened next? Did you yank him off, or was this where you started goading him to get him off?"

"I did not get the chance. Clay had shown up. Or tracked us. I am not sure if he came on his own or if he was sent to look for us as a job. But he pulled Sam off of the female and threw him across the room. Well, cave. The noise did a good job of getting me more coherent. It woke Azazel up, too. I did a visual check, and that was when I realized exactly how dire the situation was." Hunter took a moment to compose himself, breathing deeply, and then resumed speaking. "The females were Seelie. It was pretty obvious their families are either very well off, or they are nobles. Sam and Azazel thought the entire thing was hilarious, especially how pissed me and Clay were. I got up off the floor and went straight for Azazel. For as long as I can remember, he has had this key hanging around his neck. I always wondered what it went to. Found out this morning. I do not know how many times he has done that before—kidnapped females and held them there. I yanked that chain straight off his neck. Azazel got all pissed off, but Clay slammed him up against the wall and held him there. Sam tried to grab hold of me, but I punched him in the mouth. Knocked one of his fangs out. Then I went to unchain the females."

Narcissa was quiet for a long moment. As if churning things over in her mind. "They were dead, weren't they?" she asked finally.

"One of them was, yeah. And she only had Sam's scent all over her. So, I knew he was the one who killed her. All three of them were... mutilated. Head to toe, bruises, claw marks, bites... and they had all been marked." Hunter bit his tongue, the sharp pain and metallic taste flooding his senses. Even someone like him would never do something so repulsive. They would all lose their lives for that alone. It wouldn't matter that he hadn't actually harmed any of the females. He'd been present for every moment. Too drunk to do anything. "As soon as I realized the one female was dead, and who had killed her... I snapped. I went back and grabbed Sam by the throat. Dragged him outside. Azazel tried to get in the way, but I threatened him, too. Goaded Sam until he fought me. I won. And I killed him. So, on top of what happened to those females... I also killed my brother. It was not self-defense. I pushed him into fighting me, with full intention of killing him. I broke my queen's most sacred law. And there is only one punishment for that." Hunter didn't think he had to say it. Speaking the one word out loud wasn't necessary for Narcissa to know that his punishment would be death.

"Would his punishment have been the same?"

"Yes. But punishments are to be dealt out by the queen. She made it a point when she made that law to state as such. If she abided vigilante justice, people would drop like flies around there for past transgressions. I should have taken it to her, not taken care of it myself. It was not my place to do that. Not only that, but I am not stupid enough to think the families of the females will not demand retribution for what was done. While I was fighting Sam, Clay held Azazel back and made sure the other two females could get away. Their families will know what was done. I stole their retribution for the death of their female. I was there... through all of it. Too drunk to even know what was happening. I could have stopped it. Instead, I carried a passed-out female to a cave... where they chained her up and raped her all night long."

"Except this isn't a past transgression. This just happened. Yes, the nobility will want retribution, but that doesn't mean..." Narcissa pulled her knees to her chest, the silence amplifying the weight of her unfinished sentence. "They kept feeding you alcohol. You said that. They didn't want you to know what was happening."

"I was already drunk, Narcissa. So drunk, I could not even see straight. That is on me. They took advantage of my inebriated state, but I have no one but myself to blame for getting that way." As he wrapped his arms tighter around her, Hunter nuzzled deeper into her neck, breathing in her sweet scent. "Yes. It means that. You are right. This is not a past transgression. It just happened. *After* she made her law—and made the consequences fully known to all. She has only been the leader of my village for a month. This is the first time something like *this*... will have to be dealt with. She is young, and she is female. There are still some in the village who supported Markham. Those who are just waiting for her to fuck up, look weak. Something she cannot afford to do. She is going to have to make an example of me. Azazel will get the same punishment. Clay... he should be okay. He arrived there only this morning. He was not part of it. Except not intervening when I killed Sam. And he ensured the other two could make their escape." Hunter's lips gently brushed her neck, then lingered, savoring the moment. "I should have gone straight home. I just could not..." His throat tightened, and it took him a moment to swallow before he could continue. "But I had to come see you... one last time."

The surrounding air was thick with the bitter scent of tears. Moments later, he could feel them dripping onto his cheek, soaking into his fur. Narcissa's breath hitched, like a sudden, sharp intake of cold.

Yeah... he knew exactly how she felt.

"I am so sorry," Hunter whispered against her. "Sorry I came to you like I did. Sorry, I screwed up. It was not supposed to be... like this, and I screwed everything up." He gently turned her around, his strong arms holding her close as he cupped her face. Looking into Narcissa's eyes, he futilely wiped the tears from her cheeks. Part of him had always known what reflected out of those jade-green orbs, but he couldn't openly admit it to himself. The feeling that had brewed inside him, between them. The one that nothing and no one could diminish in the least. Hunter finally knew what it was. He loved her. Oh, gods, he loved her... A cold, hollow void opened in his chest as the reality of his feelings and their situation became a suffocating weight. "I am so sorry, Narcissa," he whispered. Hunter's lips lingered on hers and her forehead before he pulled her in close, his arms wrapping tightly around her.

Narcissa sobbed, her body wracked with emotion as she curled into his chest. Her pain was so tangible. All he could do was continue to hold her. Hunter buried his face in her hair and stroked the back of her head and her spine, feeling the wetness of her tears soak into his fur as her agony poured out. He'd never been a comforting person. But pulling away from her right now wasn't something he could even think about doing. He needed her as close as possible to him, for as long as possible. There wasn't anything he could say that could make any of this better. And if he could have spared her from any of it at all, he would have done so in a heartbeat. Taken every drop of her pain and added it to his own.

But things just didn't work that way.

There would come a time when he couldn't stay here any longer. Where he would have to get up out of this tub, dry off, cross the room... and leave her for the last time. He wasn't ever going to be ready for that.

Hunter didn't know how long they stayed like that. Or how long it took for her tears to ebb. Except the water at some point had cooled, so she placed her hands in and heated it up.

"I killed my father," Narcissa murmured into the silence.

Her words should have shocked him. Except they didn't. She'd told him her father was dead. And told him some things that made him glad the male was no longer breathing. Narcissa would have had a good reason for what she'd done. Likely the male was abusing her again, or worse... Or harming her mother or brother. Something that led to her having no other choice. "What happened?"

"Deacan had left with my mother and brother. I was supposed to finish packing some things for us and then leave right after them. But my father... he returned sooner than I expected. And he wasn't alone."

Hunter's jaw clenched, his teeth grinding together, but he forced himself to remain calm. Whatever had happened, she was still alive, but her father was gone. "He had sold you to someone." He didn't need to phrase that as a question. Based on their past conversations, the direction her words were going seemed rather obvious.

"He still had the payment in his hand." Narcissa brushed away the last of her tears, her fingertips still damp. "My father dragged me out to meet him. I knew nothing about the male, but I got a bad feeling about him. When he tried to inspect me, I fought back. The more he tried, the harder I fought. He got upset, snatched his payment from my father, and stormed out. My father backhanded me, knocking me to the floor."

The expression in Narcissa's eyes shifted. As if she disappeared into the past, at least somewhat. As much as he wanted—needed—to know, he also wanted to allow her to tell him in her own time. But as the seconds ticked by, Hunter fought the urge to blurt something out. If Narcissa hadn't continued, he would have.

"Until that moment," she said, her words almost coming out as whispers, "I never considered how quickly one's life could change in a matter of minutes."

Gods, the only reason he could want the male alive would be to experience the pleasure of killing him. Hunter caressed her cheek with the back of his hand. His thumb quickly caught the tear, just as it was about to fall from the corner of her eye. He remembered that lesson being taught often in Métamorphe, the place where he grew up. Nothing was ever certain. And things could change in the blink of an eye. "I take it things got pretty brutal rather quickly."

"He grabbed me by the throat and slammed me against the wall." She paused for a moment. "He said, 'No male wants a female who can't fully submit. I shall simply ensure your virtue remains intact. Then, when I find your mother, *she* will pay for your failure.' At that moment, I knew... I only had one choice."

Part of that statement she'd told him a few weeks back. But not all of it. Hunter's eyes turned pitch black, the veins in his forehead pulsing with rage. What that piece of filth had done to her, said to her... Somehow, he held his growl back. "You had to kill him." Hunter stroked her cheek again. His fingers danced across her lower back and the curve of her ass. "You did what you had to do to save yourself. Your mother and brother, too. There is nothing wrong with that. He deserved everything that he got. Your ability to survive what he put you through just shows how strong you are. Everything you endured at his hands only shows how very weak he was."

Narcissa slowly sat up, her eyes locked onto his. "You had to kill Sam. Please, just... listen. I know what law you said your queen made very clear when she took over. I don't expect you'll go unpunished, but I have to believe it won't be—" She swallowed. "Yes, you were drunk. Yes, your body was physically present. The thing is... Sam and Azazel had already kidnapped those females, which means they would have brutalized them whether or not you were there. And yes, you said Clay yanked Sam off of one of them, which made you coherent, but you don't know what brought him there. What if he'd shown up, and you weren't there? With the actions both you and Clay took, two of those females escaped. Do you think Sam and Azazel would've allowed that to happen if Clay had shown up by himself? Would he have been able to fight them both? Even if you hadn't goaded Sam, with you and Clay trying to set the two females who survived free, a fight between the four of you... it would've been inevitable. Yes, I had to kill my father—to protect my family. But I didn't have to hide his death. That's what I did. It took me a little while, but I got his body out of Jade Gardens and I buried it. To my knowledge, my queen never found out. That's neither here nor there, I just..." Her words trailed off for a moment. "I understand, and I don't blame you. No matter what happens when you face your queen... I don't blame you."

Narcissa truly hadn't had a choice. She had been in a 'life or death' situation, and she'd chosen to live. And he couldn't say a single thing about how she'd hidden the male's death. How many times had he done that over the years? And he'd had no stake in those deaths other than that they would fill his pockets. With what he'd done this morning... he'd had several choices. And he'd chosen the worst one. He could have incapacitated Sam instead of fighting him, gone straight back to the village and spoken with Devin after freeing the females, or never have gotten drunk last night—at least, not as drunk as he'd gotten. So many things he could have done differently. But Hunter didn't want to argue about any of that. Hashing out the situation wasn't how he wanted to spend the rest of his time with her today.

That she didn't blame him... that, no matter what occurred when he went home, she wouldn't blame him if he truly never could return... it eased him in a way he couldn't explain. "Thank you," Hunter whispered. He took her face in his hands, then his lips met hers with a soft kiss before he looked into her eyes again. "I need you to promise me something. Can you do that, Narcissa?"

"I can promise to try."

He swallowed the hard lump, desperately trying to keep the tears from welling up and spilling over. "Promise me that after today... you will not let that light in your eyes go out. You will not let your heart go dark or your soul die. I do not want you to forget me. I want you to remember the things that I know I made you feel. The things that you made me feel. I want you to remember that they are possible. And I never want you to forget... that you are so much more than *this*." Not that he had ever looked down on her, not once, for her occupation. But Narcissa deserved so much more than four walls and a string of clients who didn't truly care about her. Who didn't love her the way he did.

Tears welled in the corners of her eyes. Propping up on her knees in his lap, Narcissa stroked her fingers along the nape of his neck and pressed her forehead to his. "I promise." More tears trickled down her cheeks.

A gentle purr came from him. Narcissa was the only one who had ever made that sound, along with so many others, come out of him. "Thank you. I just... I need to know... that you will be okay. That you will make sure... that you will be okay. You are strong. You are *so strong*." Hunter wrapped one arm tightly around her, his fingers gently caressing the nape of her neck. His eyes stayed right on hers. He never wanted to look away from them. Ever. "A few times, when I could not sleep... because my heart and soul were telling me how badly I missed you, even though my mind would not always listen... I went to this set of caves in the boundaries of the shape shifter territory. There is this one particular cove there where the color of the rocks makes the water look almost exactly the same color as your eyes. I would sit there and... just stare into it. Thinking about you while trying not to think about you." A soft, partially strangled chuckle came out of him. Hunter didn't even know why he'd said those words just then. His goal wasn't to make her feel worse about any of this. He just hadn't bothered to hold back.

"For me," Narcissa said, "it started as a random thought on the days we weren't together. Those thoughts became more frequent... until I began dreaming about you. I tried not to, but that only strengthened them. Sometimes, I'd even go to sleep with the necklace you gave me... just so I could encourage them."

That shouldn't have made him smile. But regardless, Hunter couldn't stop the smallest lift to the corners of his lips, however bittersweet it was. "I know this is not fair. None of this is fair. And I am so sorry. I wish more than anything that I could just pick you up and carry you out of here right now. That neither of us would ever have to look back. But I know that is not possible. I guess... I just want you to know that I wish it was."

Narcissa brushed a soft kiss across his lips. "So do I."

"I tried to avoid things, too, that would make me think of you, but it never worked. Things still reminded me of you, and I thought about you more. When I did dream, it was about you, too." Even after their last session, while memories had surfaced about other things, they'd been rather short recollections, cut off by happy moments with her. Even though it left him feeling a bit disoriented each time he woke, he'd loved every moment of seeing her beautiful face in his sleep. He didn't want to dwell any longer on the uncertainties or the dreams they held. The number of his desires was so vast that he could spend hours cataloging them without exhausting the list. "I am not leaving just yet. We still have this... this time together. It is not nearly as much as I would like to have with you... but I am so glad that we have it."

Narcissa cupped his jaw and stroked his cheek with her thumb as she gazed into his eyes. "From the moment you walked into my room, we've had each other. Nothing will ever change that. What we feel, what we've woken up in one another—no one can ever take that from us."

Hunter leaned in close, enjoying the warmth that radiated from her touch. No one had ever touched him this way before. Even the females who had touched him before, none had left a mark as profound as this. No one had ever made him feel like Narcissa did when they touched. He had never wanted that. It was more than that, though. In that moment, the feel of his skin against her palm held the promise of something deeper. He felt her touch upon his very soul, a familiar comfort he had known countless times before. "No, they cannot." Hunter caressed her cheek, his touch tender. "And you will always have me. Even if... it is only in spirit... know that I will *always* be with you."

Narcissa said nothing at first. Just continued to meet his stare with that mesmerizing gaze of hers. When she opened her mouth again, it wasn't to speak. Instead, a song poured from her lips. He had to fight to keep his eyes from drifting shut. The sound of her voice, like a sweet melody, was the most intoxicating thing he'd ever heard. From the first time he'd heard it, it had stirred something within him that nothing else ever had. But he didn't want to take his eyes off of her for even a single moment. Narcissa was too beautiful, and he had so little time left to drink her in. As she sang, his eyes stung with falling tears, but he remained motionless, lost in her melody.

From the moment he had stepped into her room, just under a month ago, something had changed in him. Something he hadn't even realized was happening. A switch had flipped inside him. Narcissa had awakened his emotions. His ability to feel things other than hatred, self-loathing, rage. She had offered him things he'd never received from anyone before—never allowed himself to receive before—and had expected nothing in return. Helped him realize he could love. Shared pieces of herself with him that she'd shared with no one else. And he had done the same.

They'd fallen apart in one another's arms, then put each other back together again with a tender, loving touch. Something he hadn't even known he had the capability for. But with her, he did. Before meeting Narcissa, Hunter had never realized what a broken mess he was. Exactly what the decades of abuse had done to him. When he walked through her door, she mended the cracks and holes within him, like a gentle hand soothing a wounded soul. In her, he had found a soul that matched his own. His perfect soulmate, handpicked by the gods. No matter what happened going forward, nothing and no one could ever take that away from them.

Narcissa's voice rose with the chorus, her repeated words echoing through the space. With each lyric she sang, her voice swelled, until the meaning behind every word was etched in her eyes and echoed strongly in her aria. Tears streamed down her face, but her voice soared above them, singing with all her might. Moving into the chorus again and laying it all out, she gave it everything she had.

Growing up, music had never been a part of his life. It hadn't been allowed. Even when he'd gotten older and been around it outside of the village, he'd never paid it much attention. But he listened to every word that flowed so beautifully out of her. Every single one she sang to him. Narcissa had chosen the perfect song for them. Those words captured the essence of their journey together, despite its brevity. Through the highs and lows they had experienced with each other. Their need of one another had become an obsession. Narcissa had been the first person he'd ever wanted—*needed*—to share pieces of himself with. And she had been the first person he'd craved pieces from in return. But it had gone beyond even that. He'd wanted to own and possess every single bit of her. And he had wanted to give every part of himself to her as well. He'd wanted to bare himself completely to her, and have her do the same. Completely open to each other. No walls between them. None of the lies they told to the rest of the world.

And so, they had.

Hunter's gaze didn't leave hers once, the emotion swelling more and more in both of their eyes, as she belted out the love song to him. He'd wanted nothing from anyone. Least of all love, affection, or comfort. Nothing. He'd never wanted to get close to anyone. Never wanted a mate. Wanting no one he could ruin or destroy like he'd always hoped he wasn't doing to his twin. But Narcissa had embraced even the deepest, darkest parts of him; every single demon that was hidden inside his soul. Her only response had been, *I will burn with you.*

He didn't want things to end. Not like this. He wanted so much more out of life. So much more of a life... with her. Something Hunter never would have thought he'd want with anyone. To spend every day by her side. Wake up with her in the morning and go to sleep with her at night.

To talk with her. Learn more about her. Know her thoughts, her hopes and dreams. To protect her always. To love her.

More tears fell from his eyes, but Hunter didn't wipe those away any more than she wiped away her own. He just held her, one arm around her, the other hand against her cheek. And he listened to her sing to him. Something he could do forever and never tire of.

As Narcissa continued, the words she belted out didn't just apply to her. They applied to him, too. There wasn't anything they wouldn't do for one another. Sacrifice for one another. No chance they wouldn't take to spend their lives together. They would do whatever it took to protect each other. They would risk their lives for one another. Die for one another. Whatever risks they had to take, they would be worth it. Even if they only got one more moment together, it would all be worth it.

If he truly had to die today, Hunter wished he was dying for her. Not for something so stupid as no impulse control. For killing his brother. So idiotic. He didn't know how much time they would have had left together, and he'd cut it so short. Even though the pain of their situation ached in his chest, he wouldn't trade a second of the time they had shared. Not one memory, one look, one taste, one touch. The only thing he would change right now... was for them to have more time.

Just as she'd done twice already, Narcissa transitioned into the chorus one last time. Telling him just how much she had him. Every word she sang, which echoed in the chambers of his heart, filled his entire being. Her voice reached his very soul. As her song faded, Hunter's forehead met hers once more, their gazes locked. "I have got you, too," he whispered. "Every single bit of that... it is all true for me, too. There is nothing I would not do for you."

Narcissa stroked the back of his neck, renewing the purr that vibrated out of him. "I love you," she whispered.

As the three words left her mouth, his chest seized, the ache blooming like a dark flower, as did a radiant glow emanating from within, a euphoric sensation he couldn't describe. He thought he'd felt peace before in her presence. But it was nothing like this. The words were so very dangerous, but like her, Hunter couldn't allow them to part ways without saying out loud what they both knew in their hearts and in their souls. "I love you, too," he whispered. He brushed his lips across hers, then lingered, his gaze locked on the jade-green pools that held flecks of gold. "Be with me... one last time, before I go."

Narcissa responded with just one word—"Yes." As she caressed his cheek, she met his lips with hers, putting all the love she had into the kiss.

Hunter did the same. Not just the pain and heartache he was feeling, but the love and adoration he had for her, too. Narcissa lowered her body a little, but not too much. Just as she was in no hurry, neither was he. Or even in a rush to truly begin. This would be the last time—their very last time—and they both wanted to savor every single moment. The kiss, though slow, was a whirlwind of intense feelings that left them breathless. Her body flushed as his warm hand against her cheek drifted to softly intertwine in her hair. Hunter wrapped his arm tighter around her, and they both groaned, their bodies reacting to the friction. The wide range of emotions flowing through them both was enough to make him dizzy. But he wouldn't change a single moment of this, either. Except that it had to end at all.

The pressure of her pussy against his cock made it stand at full attention. A groan escaped them as his throbbing erection filled her completely. Fuck, the feel of her was nearly enough to make him come right then. But he wouldn't. Not yet. Deepening the kiss, Hunter slid his arm from around her. Tracing a path down her back, his fingers finally landed on her rear. Gripping one cheek tightly, he rocked her back and forth against his shaft. A sound, both a throaty moan and a growl, rumbled from him as she swept her tongue along the back of his fangs, then the base, and their tongues met once more.

Narcissa wrapped her arms around his back and gently sifted her fingers through his wet fur. His purr was so loud now, it practically echoed around the room. She curled her toes against his firm thighs, tucking her feet beneath him so there was absolutely no space between them. With his grip on her ass, Hunter kept each thrust slow, but as deep as possible. His cock pressed hard into her core with each pass. Holy fucking shit, she felt incredible.

As many times as they'd been together over the past few weeks, there was something about this time that differed from all the others. Something raw, intense, and more passionate than their intertwined breaths had ever conveyed. Maybe because nothing compared to how they were at that moment. With no walls between them whatsoever, completely aware of everything they felt for one another. But it was even more. It was like they were making love for the very first time.

Hunter tightened his grip, but kept his pace. He bent his knees and secured his feet on the bottom of the tub to gain better leverage for reaching further inside her. Holy fuck, he was already close to coming. But he was going to hold out for as long as possible.

With each stroke, the intensity magnified. Her core blazed even hotter around his cock. Another deep, throaty moan left him as she swept her tongue along the back of his fangs. Narcissa broke the kiss and rested her forehead against his as she continued to meet each of his slow thrusts, her hips swaying. "Mark me," she whispered.

His fangs lengthened, the sensation like a thousand tiny needles pricking at his gums. His eyes darkened, though they didn't go fully black. Hunter didn't make a move to follow through, though. Not just yet. True, he knew his fate was sealed, and the weight of their last goodbye hung heavy in the air. She had already marked him once. So, he couldn't see any reason to hold back what he'd been fighting against. Even so, he needed to be absolutely certain before taking any action. He continued thrusting, and she kept moving her hips against his, the rhythm never breaking. Hunter brushed a soft kiss over her lips, his fingers tracing the curve of her cheek. "If you are sure..." he whispered. He brushed his tongue over her lower lip, and then he kissed her again, gently. "... tilt your head for me."

Narcissa swept her hair back, revealing the curve of her neck, and tilted her head, offering herself to him. A low growl emanated from his chest, rumbling through the air. A throbbing pulsed in his fangs, and the darkness swirling in his eyes grew with it. The slow movements were constant; their hips never stopped their dance. After a final gentle kiss, Hunter trailed his lips and tongue, tasting her skin as he descended her jaw and throat, stopping where he felt her pulse racing. His grip on her hair tightened a little as he tilted her head more. While he'd made no decision to utter the words, that didn't stop them from leaving his mouth. And he would never take them back.

"Every time you think of me... know that you will always be loved. And you will *always* be mine." Hunter sank his fangs into her neck, and with a wet sound, sucked hard. The taste exploded on his tongue, a burst of flavor that was more potent than anything he'd ever experienced. Every synapse in his being lit up as if an explosion had gone off inside him. He couldn't say how hard he bit her, but he could taste the metallic tang of her blood as it flooded his mouth and spilled down his throat. He couldn't contain the primal roar, a sound that was more aggressive and urgent than any he'd ever produced, just as he couldn't stop the explosive climax that surged through both of them, mingling with the warm water around them.

In that moment, his body expressed both the depths of his love and the sharp sting of their shared pain. That *this* first... would also be a last. It wasn't just him marking her as his; it was also marking their end. The last time he would hold her, make love, and share a bath, he would be in that room, together for hours within those familiar walls. That he would look into her eyes. They would exchange words and touches. Despite his desire to stop, fresh tears still streamed down his face.

A couple of minutes after the last of their orgasms subsided, he pulled his fangs from her neck, the coppery scent of blood still fresh. Hunter nuzzled the mark he'd given her, stroked his tongue over it, and captured a trickle of blood that had slid down. There weren't words to express what it meant to him that she had allowed him this in their last few minutes together. It would be the only time he could do so. She wouldn't be able to keep the mark past the moment he left this room, but she had allowed him to claim her as his. "My Narcissa," he purred against her. She would always be his. No matter what the future brought for both of them, Narcissa would *always* be his.

She stroked the back of his neck, coaxing out another purr as his muscles relaxed under her touch. "Always," she whispered.

Hunter wrapped his arms tighter around her and held her as close as possible. He kissed the spot on her neck and inhaled, enjoying the subtle perfume of her skin. He wanted to drown in her. Not just her scent, but her taste and the feel of her as well. As much as he wished he never had to leave, that wasn't their reality. And while he could run from his punishment, go into hiding, and never face what was waiting for him, that just wasn't him. Hunter had never been one to shy away from repercussions. No matter how horrible, how depraved, how unwarranted they were. It was his burden to bear, and bear it he would. At the very least, Clay deserved that much. He wasn't a bad male. He deserved to have someone vouch that he hadn't been a part of anything that had happened to the females, except for ensuring they could get free. And while he didn't feel like killing Sam was the wrong thing to do, their laws stated otherwise. He'd made a choice a month ago to remain in the village after Markham's death. He'd broken Devin's cardinal rule. Facing the consequences head-on, unflinchingly, was just the right thing to do.

Pulling back to meet her gaze, Hunter wiped away the tears that fell, his thumb brushing against her soft cheek. In her eyes, he saw the reflection of the male he never knew he could become. She had allowed him to have a brief glimpse of the male he could have been... without the way he'd grown up. Without the abuse. She had allowed him to find the male within himself. As much as his heart was breaking in that moment, a genuine smile spread across his face. Something he'd given no one before. Just her. Only her. But he didn't want his anguished-filled and sorrowful expression to be the last thing she saw on him. "You have made me very happy, Narcissa. So very happy. Something no one else has ever done before. For as long as the rest of my life lasts... I will spend every moment thinking of you, and how truly wonderful you are."

Leaning into his touch, Narcissa continued to run her fingers up and down the back of his neck. "You've made me happy, too, Hunter. Happier than I ever thought I deserved. I will never forget you. You'll always be in my mind, my heart, and my soul."

"You deserve everything." Hunter brushed a light kiss over her lips, his fingers tracing the curve of her cheek. "I want you to do something else for me. I want you to keep trying to get free. If you are successful, whether you are let go or you escape, take your family and go to my queen. Regardless of my crimes... as my mate, she would keep the three of you safe."

Narcissa stared at him. Thoughts swirled behind her eyes, but she didn't vocalize any of them. Slowly, she nodded. That nod was a promise, a commitment to try, and though freedom seemed out of reach, it gave him a glimmer of hope. "Thank you." Hunter pressed a soft kiss against her lips, lingering for a moment, before resting his forehead against hers again.

Everyone had their own path in life. Their fate. Their destiny. His world was filled with the bitter taste of pain, the crushing weight of heartache, the stench of degradation, and the terrifying screams of nightmares. The hint of a promise of hope for things that would only ever end up getting ripped away from him in the end. It was part of why he'd lived his life the way he had. Been the person he'd been. Narcissa had softened his heart and cleansed his soul. While it would probably be better for him to go back to the person he'd been before he met her—just in order to get through what he was facing, what *they* were facing—he didn't know if he could be that person any longer. Nor did he think he wanted to.

Thinking back to that recent session, where they had switched roles, where everything about him had been shattered... As horrible and excruciating as it had been, Hunter was glad they'd gone through with it. It had taught him so much about the female in his arms that he loved with all his heart. He'd learned how she could ground him. Bring him back from any nightmare that had taken root in his mind. She could grab hold of them with a tight grip and jerk them away. Gather up the darkness within him and cleanse it completely. She could use her touch to heal his scars—not the ones on the outside, embedded in his skin, but the ones on the inside, on his mind and heart and soul. This female in his arms had healed him. The only person in his life who had ever truly made him feel like there wasn't a single thing wrong with him and who he was.

And it had taught him so much about himself. That he could put himself in another's hands. Capable of trusting another. Of allowing someone else to care for him. And it didn't make him any less of a person for allowing her to do that for him.

"You do, too, Hunter. Regardless of what you think, you deserve so much more than you've been given."

"Maybe in a different universe. But not in this one. There is very little I have ever done in this life that could be considered good. Even protecting my brother... the things that I did... they were not the acts of a good person." And that didn't account for the things that had been done to him. That he'd accepted and allowed to be done to him. The things he'd been paid to do. He'd felt that he had good reasons for all of it, and had enjoyed much of it—maybe even most of it. But that didn't mean anyone could excuse them. "I think I have just been a stain on this world for a very long time. But that you see me differently means more to me than I can say."

"You have never been a stain to me, Hunter. You never could."

"That just shows how good of a person you are, that you can see me that way." Hunter's lips met hers in a soft, fleeting kiss. "You know, when I first started realizing that I was getting close to you—before that, actually, the first day we met—I told myself that if we had not met in this place, and things were not the way they were... that if we were in an actual relationship together, I would have destroyed you. Because that is just the type of person

I am. The more time we spent together, the more the selfish part of me did not care. And the other part of me... knew that you would not care. That even if we both destroyed each other, we would happily go down in flames." His face softened, and a small smile bloomed. "I do not know if that is a good thing or a bad thing. But what I know is that I am so grateful to have found it. Even if it was just for a short time. And I would not change a single moment of the time we have spent together. Even knowing that it is ending. If I could do one thing over, it would be what happened this morning. But only so that we would not have to say goodbye right now."

"That first day... I told myself that you would become my favorite client, but that I could remain professional. As I realized it was so much more than I could've ever anticipated, and that became less and less of a possibility, I considered a few times what it might've been like if we'd met under different circumstances. You're right. We would've destroyed each other, and I wouldn't have cared. But I think that's why we met this way... when we did. I'm extremely thankful for it. In a way, I don't know that I could fully describe." A tiny smile graced Narcissa's face as she gave a nod. "If there was something I could change, I'd go back a little further... so we wouldn't ever have to say goodbye."

He knew exactly what she meant. She would've made it so they could've left together the moment they realized their feelings for one another. "I told myself that you were going to be my favorite, too. The best submissive I have ever had. That you were perfect. Exactly what I needed." He paused for a moment. "I thought I could remain professional, too. We see how well that went." A soft chuckle left him. Sobering a little, he let out a deep sigh. "I wish we never had to say goodbye, either, Narcissa." He wished for many things. Things he felt like she was wishing for too. When they realized they had felt anything for one another, they could have left together then. Or that he could lift her from the water, her skin slick, and carry her out the door into the unknown. That he didn't have to return home and face what was waiting for him. That they had so much more time together. So many things. "Even though a lot of things are ending... at least we both know that the way we feel about one another will never change. We are always going to have that. We are always going to have the *lacunas* we have spent in this room. The words we have spoken to one another. All the firsts we gave to one another. The touches, the scents, the tastes." Hunter gently tilted her head, his tongue tracing the shape of the mark on her neck. "And this. This mark, and the one you gave me. Just because it is... our end... does not mean everything is ending."

Narcissa said nothing in return. She just ran her fingers up and down the back of his neck. Gods, his heart was about to shatter into tiny, infinitesimal pieces. A bitter taste of loss coated his tongue, and knots twisted his insides, making him want to disappear. Through everything he'd endured, nothing had ever felt like this. Knowing she was feeling it, too, just made the sensation that much worse. He needed to be strong for her, mirroring the quiet fortitude she possessed. That was how they'd been from the start—instinctually being what the other needed, no matter what that meant. As much as Hunter felt the urge to tell her again how sorry he was, he refrained. No words could truly express the magnitude of that, and she already knew. Talking about it anymore wouldn't change it or make it better. Hunter pulled her closer, his arms wrapping around her as he softly kissed her head, then her neck. For as long as they had, before he had no other choice but to go... he just wanted to hold her.

Hunter didn't know how much time had passed. Long enough that the water had cooled, Narcissa had warmed it, and it had gone cold once more. Hunter reluctantly pulled back, just enough to meet her gaze, his thumb gently caressing her cheek after placing one last kiss over the mark upon her neck. "As much as neither of us wants to... I think I should probably go." A brand-new pang of agony struck his chest, yet he fought to maintain a neutral expression, concealing his pain.

"I know," she whispered.

As he wrapped his arm around her, Hunter caressed her cheek and tenderly kissed her lips. His tongue danced with hers as he deepened the kiss. A low groan left him. It took every ounce of his being to resist taking things further. As much as he wanted to, that wouldn't be the best thing right now. He pressed his lips softly to each corner of her eyes, a tender kiss over her heart, and then rested his forehead against hers. Hunter slowly stood up in the tub, taking her with him, the water still clinging to their skin after several lingering moments. The air was chilly as it rushed in around them, but it was so much more than just that they were soaking wet. This meant they were that much closer to his leaving the room and never seeing one another again. He knew if he didn't force himself out of the tub, he'd never get out. That was exactly what he did. He kissed her again before stepping out of the water, the scent of the bath and their bodies still lingering as he grabbed towels. Passing one to her, he dried himself off.

Narcissa clutched the clean towel to her breasts. At first, she did nothing but stand there and watch him. He didn't take his eyes off her for a moment as he dried off his fur. He couldn't fathom missing a single moment of their last time together. It would just be one more beautiful view to take with him when he left this room.

After a few moments, she stepped out of the tub and drained the water. However, instead of drying off, she simply wrapped the towel around her body and stared. Their gazes remained on one another until he'd dried off his fur as much as he could. Closing the short distance between them, Hunter tilted her head back a little so their gazes could more easily meet. Then, he used his towel to dry her hair off. Once he was finished, he tossed the towel into the hamper and drew her against him again.

All he wanted to do was pull the towel away from her body, pick her up, and fuck her up against the wall. But there just wasn't time. He'd already been here too long. It would just never be enough between them. Never enough touches, kisses, tastes, times their bodies came together in an explosion of ecstasy. Never enough. His soft kiss lingered on her lips, and he pressed his forehead to hers one last time, with a deep sigh. As much as he knew this was goodbye, Hunter just couldn't seem to bring himself to say the word. Not yet. Not just yet. "I love you, Narcissa."

Her fingers, lightly tracing the curve of his muscles, curled around his biceps as she clung to him. "I love you, too, Hunter. So much more than I thought possible."

He stroked the mark he'd left, sliding his fingers up her back and feeling the warmth of her skin. As his eyes remained locked on hers, he gently pressed his lips against hers. "Mine. Always. No matter what."

And now came the point where he *really* had to be strong. Being strong meant doing things you couldn't fathom, but knew you had no choice but to do. The things that no one else could do. The things that were painful and ripped your heart out. That you were terrified of doing, but you did them anyway. After one last kiss, Hunter let go, the lingering scent of her skin filling the air as he stepped away.

His heart hammered as he took each step toward the bathroom door, then toward the door to her room, as if his ankles were being held down by some substantial weight. Walking away from the woman he loved required a greater effort than he had ever known, each step a struggle. The female he knew without a single doubt he would never see again. A hollow ache consumed him, mirroring the desolate emptiness that stretched endlessly before him.

Narcissa trailed him, her footsteps echoing softly as he got halfway to the door. The scent of fresh tears tinged the air. "Always mine, Narcissa. Do not forget that." Gods, how was he actually going to leave?

"Never." That one word emerged in a croaked whisper.

The tone of her voice shattered his heart even more than it already was. Hunter turned, and with a gentle hand, brushed the tears that were now making wet streaks down her face. He didn't allow himself to linger any longer than that, though. As heartbroken and terrified as he was to walk out that door, he knew it had to be done. They didn't have any other choice but to part ways. He couldn't make this any worse for her than he could already tell it was. With one last fleeting kiss, Hunter retreated to the door. With his hand on the knob, he faltered once more. His gaze met hers, but this time, he couldn't force a smile onto his face. He just stared at her with longing as all their dreams of what they'd wanted for their future drifted further away.

"In case I truly do not get to return, Narcissa... thank you for everything you have done for me. Even if I can never explain all of it to you, even if you never fully understand... just know that I am grateful." It was the last thing he said before he forced himself to leave. Without giving her a chance to answer him, Hunter used every ounce of strength he had to open the door, step out into the hall, and then close the door behind him.

It was a good thing he was a natural at hiding what was behind the mask he wore on his face. Each step was a labored breath, the weight of his despair nearly dragging him to his knees. It had nothing to do with what he was facing, and everything to do with what he was walking away from. Leaving Narcissa behind was leaving a huge part of himself behind, too.

Gods, please... please... let something save us both...

Fifteen

The door hadn't even shut all the way before Narcissa stepped forward. Clutching the towel tightly, she sprinted across her bedroom to the door. Her hand hovered over the doorknob, and the tears rolling down her cheeks punctuated the silent sobs that shook her body. As much as she wanted to chase after Hunter and drag him back to her room, she had to let him go. This was the hardest thing she'd ever had to do. Narcissa pressed her head against the door, her fingers tracing the wood as the hot tears streamed down her face.

Her body racked with sobs, each breath a fresh wave of agony. Oh, gods. That very well could've been the last time they ever saw one another. Why didn't she fight more? Why didn't she try harder to get him to stay? They could've figured something out. Without a second thought, she ripped the towel from her body, flung it to the floor, and reached for her silk bathrobe. Her hand reached for the cold doorknob once more.

No matter what she told herself, she knew Hunter would never run. To beg and plead with him would have been a waste of breath, making him feel guilty. That was the last thing she ever wanted to do to him. With a sharp intake of breath, Narcissa rubbed her chest before abruptly throwing open the door. Running after him would be bad on so many levels. But she couldn't just stand there. The longer she continued, the more she felt her chest tighten, making it difficult to take a breath. Narcissa darted across the hall and practically pounded on Grace's door.

The door flung open. Grace's eyes widened. "Oh, gods, get in here. What has happened? What is wrong?" The female wrapped an arm around her, ushered her inside, and the click of the lock sealed them in. With a gentle hand, her friend led her over to the bed and sat her down on the end, the soft mattress yielding under her. Grace gripped both of Narcissa's hands. "Talk to me."

"I can't breathe." The words were lost in the torrent of her tears, and she cried even harder. How could she just let him walk out? Just let him leave? Her breath hitched with a sob as the hollowness in her chest echoed the emptiness that surrounded her. All hope of even trying to piece them back together walked out of her room, and she did nothing to stop him. Nothing to hold on to him tighter.

"Come here," Grace said. The female gently pulled her close and slowly rubbed her back. "One breath at a time. I am right here. I am not going anywhere."

Although she understood the words, they seemed foreign to her at the same time. Nothing about this situation made any sense. Even though she wanted to believe Hunter would return and wouldn't forfeit his life because of a piece-of-shit like Sam, it became harder and harder for her to accept this. Her breath hitched as a chilling realization dawned, and her body seized with silent, shuddering sobs. Narcissa leaned against Grace, curling up to the female because she didn't know what else to do. She'd never felt this helpless before.

Grace continued rubbing her back slowly. "Just let it all out. Everything is going to be okay."

Gods, she wanted to believe that so badly. That it would be okay. That the punishment Hunter expected wouldn't come to pass. While she couldn't stop the sobbing, somehow, she got words out. "I don't know that it is. Hunter killed Sam."

Shock flooded her friend's face as she recoiled, her eyes wide. *"What?!* What happened? Tell me. Tell me everything, please."

Although her tears didn't cease, they eased enough that she could find her voice, and it got a little easier to breathe. Narcissa recounted what Hunter had told her, or at least what was relevant. Even as she retold the story to Grace, it made no sense how Hunter saw his reaction as anything other than right. That dead female Seelie deserved justice, and he delivered it. Just as the other two did. Narcissa wiped her eyes, but the tears still streamed down her face. Gods, he just couldn't be blamed for this. No matter what the law indicated. "I tried to argue that Sam's death sounded justified, but Hunter just kept telling me the same thing—the circumstances wouldn't matter. He'd broken his queen's most sacred law, and it only had one punishment."

Grace's hand flew up, fingers splayed as if to contain a gasp. "No... No, no, no... *No.* He cannot... That *cannot* be... He *cannot*... die, not for *them*." Her friend pushed off the bed, the creaking of the springs echoing, and dashed to the door. The moment her hand wrapped around the knob, she paused, her breath catching in her throat. The female squeezed the doorknob hard as tears filled her eyes. "Is he gone?" she choked out. "Did he already leave?"

Clarification wasn't necessary. She knew exactly what Grace meant by her question. As their emotions intensified over the last few sessions, she'd never focused on how she could feel Hunter's presence, even after he departed. Would she feel it when he was killed? With a sob, Narcissa nodded, her voice lost in her own despair. It was all she could do. Hunter had already left the building and started his way down the mountainside. There were so many things she could've done, but he would never go into hiding. And if she'd told him about Elisa, more problems would've resulted. "I'm sorry. Gods, I'm so sorry."

"No... No, no, no..." Grace slid down the door and all but crumpled to the floor. Her tears overflowed and poured free. "I have to see him... I have to see him," she sobbed. "I have to tell him I am sorry... how sorry I am."

Nothing could lessen the sting of the guilt that consumed her at that moment. For not breaking her promise and telling Hunter about Elisa. Narcissa pushed herself off the bed, walked over to Grace, and sat beside her. Without delay, she wrapped her arms around the female, holding her close. "I'm so sorry." She'd been selfish in keeping that information to herself. Whenever she even thought about saying anything, all she could think about was the number of issues that could arise. Both short-term and long-term. If Hunter got through the current situation, telling him would've ensured his death.

"I am sorry, too. I am so sorry." The two of them embraced one another, holding the other close. "He cannot die. He just cannot," her friend choked out. "What has he told you about his queen? Maybe he will not... Maybe she will understand."

Some of the information she had about Devin had come from Hunter. Some of it from Fallon. But she didn't know if it was enough to determine what the queen would and wouldn't do. Though she was in the same boat as Grace—Hunter couldn't die. "Devin... she's supposed to be like the queen of the nymphs, someone who just wants the best for her people. I know a lot has changed in Métamorphe. It wouldn't be the place you remembered. The Informant position is gone, forced matings were abolished, slates on prior crimes were..." Her words trailed off as something Hunter told her in their last session replayed in her mind. Fuck, what had he said exactly? Narcissa closed her eyes and took a deep breath, attempting to calm her racing heart. The booming thunder clawed at her, and icy dread coiled in her stomach, making every word a monumental task. "He said, 'If they harm another without cause, they will pay the ultimate price.'"

Grace nodded gently, attempting to wipe away the tears that streamed down her face. "But it was not without cause... right? Sam... he killed that female. Would that not be seen as cause? And Sam doing that... he would have died anyway, yes?"

"I said the same thing, but he didn't seem to think that would make a difference. Because he'd goaded Sam into fighting... that he should've gone to the queen with what happened instead." It hadn't been all she pointed out. She'd mentioned several possibilities as Clay had been there. The tears kept coming, even as Narcissa frantically brushed at her reddened face. "It's going to depend on what the Seelie demand... and what Devin will give them. Seelie nobility don't forgive easily, and always want more than most would deem acceptable." The new queen would be in a difficult position. Not only would she have her subordinates looking at her, but the Seelie as well. All would have to be satisfied. And the Seelie nobility had their own set of rules and expectations. "I have a friend who used to be among the nobility before his family disowned him because they discovered his proclivities, which didn't live up to their standards."

"I do not know the new queen. I have heard she is canine and quite young. Not someone who was even born when I lived there. But... if she kills him just for that, then she is no true queen. Just like Markham was no true king. It does not sound like Hunter did anything wrong. All he did was kill a murderer and a rapist. I may not know much about Hunter, but I know in my heart he is good. A *good* male. Those two... Azazel and Sam—they are demons of the worst kind. All they ever did was abuse people. Anyone they could get their hands on."

"He is a wonderful male, a great male. I know he doesn't believe it, but it doesn't change the facts." Narcissa shook her head. It would take her a lifetime to convince him of that. If he ever believed her. A faint smile played at the corners of her mouth. "I know little about Devin, just what others have told me. I know she's young, but from what I heard she went through for the village..." Her words trailed off again. As she and Grace talked, her fear of Hunter dying steadily diminished. Still, confirmation would be necessary. "Do you think I would feel it?"

"I do not know. I know very little about that kind of thing. Mates, love, anything like that. I know some basic stuff I overheard while I still lived in the village, but I had no examples." Grace's breath caught as she glanced up at him, freezing in place. The female's eyes widened, fixed on Narcissa's throat, where the glint of Hunter's mark was visible. "Um... do you feel him yet? Or him, you? And have, um... have his eyes glowed?"

Narcissa's fingers traced the still-tender puncture wounds on her neck. "I can sense his presence, but that's about it. At least, I think. I mean... I've never really had to question emotions with him. His eyes haven't glowed; that's kind of been our point of no return." She knew what would happen then. With the back of her hand, she cleaned up her face a bit more. It had gotten slightly easier as they spoke, like Hunter wouldn't lose his life. Even easier to believe it. "We don't exactly have soulmates in my species. As far as I know, anyway."

Grace gave a barely perceptible nod as she once more wiped at her damp face. "From what I have heard, everyone has a soulmate. Not that I have any wish to find mine, nor do I think I ever will. I do not think it has anything to do with what species you are." She wrapped her arms around her knees. "Okay. Um... maybe not, then. If you just feel his presence and his eyes have not glowed. I would think you would not feel it if... *that* happened. Though, as you felt his presence... maybe you would instinctively know... but you would not feel the pain. Does that make sense?"

Everyone has a soulmate. Narcissa repeated the words in her mind. If that was the case, then why hadn't she ever heard of them in her species? Most of the nymphs here were younger than her, except maybe Shalla. But she wasn't certain the female would speak to her. At least, not regarding this. "Yeah. That makes sense." But it wouldn't be enough. "His schedule brings him back in four days." And he probably wouldn't have confirmed, though he had paid through the end of the month. "Clay is still seeing Jezzy. If Hunter doesn't keep his appointment, I'll talk to Jezzy and borrow a few minutes of her next appointment with Clay. That's the only way we'll know for sure."

"Okay. Hopefully, he will say. And be truthful about it." Grace wrapped her arms tightly around her knees. "You cannot keep that," she whispered, nodding to the mark on her neck.

The next few days would be hell. Narcissa ran her fingers across the mark. She definitely couldn't keep it. Though she was somewhat surprised, it hadn't triggered the magic. Not knowing how to claim him as her species did might have been for the best. "I know." Though it pained her to think about healing the puncture wounds, she knew it was a must. With immense effort, she called on water and guided it over the mark on her neck, where it stitched the puncture wounds closed. "We'll have to keep each other in check until we know."

Grace squeezed her hand. "Yes, we will. It will be difficult, but I know we can do it." Pulling her hand back, she wrapped her arm around her knees again. A soft smile spread across her lips. "So... Hayden has a female, too?"

Gods, she was grateful to Grace. Though they still addressed one another, even alone, by the names they'd used for years at the den, it was nice to talk so freely with the female. Her gaze remained on the floor. No matter how hard she tried to forget, she couldn't stop the thoughts from racing through her mind. It was as if she wiped Hunter away as she removed his mark. "I guess so. He's never mentioned it before now."

"It is so strange to think of either of them being old enough to have a mate. They were just so young the last time I saw them. And when they were born... they were so tiny, we did not even know if they would make it. Me and the shaman. Our mother died before she got Hayden out."

"Yeah. Hunter told me they were four when you were supposedly killed." Among other things, the two of them had spoken about that before. "It's hard to imagine him as tiny. Probably as difficult as it is to imagine either of them grown up with mates." Narcissa pulled her knees up, and laid her head on them, the soft fabric of her robe brushing her cheek. "Though I can understand how you feel. I have a younger brother, too."

"It is wonderful and heartbreaking all at the same time, all things considered." Leaning against the door, she shifted her weight and stared off into nothingness. "Hunter started taking care of Hayden the moment they were born. I never told them this, but even as infants, Hunter would refuse food until Hayden had eaten. He would get this look in his eyes..." she laughed softly. "There was no arguing with him, even then. I have seen nothing like it in my life, especially there in the village. For those who had to live as orphans especially, if one did not eat as soon as food was produced, they usually missed out."

That definitely had to make her special. She argued with him rather easily. Sometimes without regard. It was part of what brought them closer to one another. He enjoyed it when she pushed back. Narcissa offered the female a smile, barely there, like a whisper. "That's one thing he told me that has changed in the village. Though he still eats the same thing he always has, the queen ensures everyone has enough to eat."

"That makes me really happy. I worry about them... so much."

Right then, she did, too. She worried that if something happened to Hunter, it would shatter Hayden's world. Gods, she prayed for everything to turn out alright. That Hunter would survive this and maybe, one day, things would change for both of them.

Grace cleared her throat a little. "What is your brother like?

"Um, Dion is child-like. He has mental issues, so he doesn't really see or understand things the way we do."

Her friend slowly nodded. "I am sure that can be both a curse and a blessing some days, depending."

"Yes, it could be. I haven't seen him or my mother in thirty *solaris*, so while I hope things have gotten better, I don't really know." That was with great purpose. The workers in the den were supposed to be the only family they had. As far as anyone knew, that was the truth.

"I hope that they have." Grace gave her hand a brief squeeze, a gesture of reassurance. "That is why I asked Ivory about Hunter so often. It was not much at all—and most of what she said were things I would have rather not heard—but it was something, at least. It has been so long since I have seen either of them. Were it not for the blood bond, I wonder if I would even recognize them."

Oh yeah, she could imagine some of what Ivory had told the female. She had gone to Ivory herself when she first looked into taking Hunter as a client. "Blood bond?" Two words, and they seemed rather self-explanatory, but that didn't mean her assumption was accurate. If it meant what she believed, then only one explanation remained.

"Mmhm. Shape shifters can sense their blood. The closer the link, the more intense the sensation. I would feel Hunter's presence stronger than I would Clay's, because Clay and I are half-siblings, not full, like Hunter and I are. Whatever magic protects this place seems to prevent it from working here, though."

"How did you find out Hunter was coming here?"

"People talk." Grace shrugged lightly. "At first, I thought nothing of it when I heard a new shape shifter had come here who wanted to learn about the BDSM lifestyle. And that he was a natural. That is nowhere near my preference, so it was of no concern to me. I think he saw a few in those first few *solaris*, but I cannot really remember. I never paid much attention. They did not flaunt their sessions with him or his name, and the only schedule I looked at was my own. A couple of *solaris* later, or however long it was, when he started seeing Ivory... Well. Not that I think I need to elaborate, but she talked often, loudly, and frankly about her new client. When I had time to talk to her privately, I asked her a few clarifying questions about his looks just to be sure."

"Nope, not necessary at all. In fact, the less I have to think about how she speaks about him, the better." Otherwise, she might want to strangle the female again. Even just the last couple of days had driven her crazy. While she didn't know who set Cheshire on Ivory, it had been entertaining. "Sounds like how I found out about Clay. I just asked Hunter if all of you looked more like your mother than your father."

"That would definitely be an easy way to figure it out. I do not know what his mother looked like, but he had to have taken after her." Grace shifted a bit, wrapping her arms tighter around her knees as she spoke.

"His eyes kind of make him stand out from any other shifter that's come through here." It was exactly how she identified Clay. At that moment, it was a good thing. Gave her someone to go to with this impending punishment. Narcissa peered at Grace. "You still have some sweets lying around?"

"Always. A couple of my clients keep me pretty stocked."

"Normally, mine do, too, but I kind of ate it all." Her stress levels had been at an ultimate high over the last week.

Grace pushed herself off the floor, a small smile playing on her lips, and walked toward her closet. "What are you in the mood for?"

"Chocolate or some mango candies, if you have those."

"I have strawberry; no mango. I have chocolate, though." Opening her closet door, Grace stepped inside and got into her dresser. She didn't use the piece of furniture for clothing, as she didn't need any. Instead, it was stocked with a variety of fascinating objects. Collecting a few bags of candy, she left her closet and carried them over to the bed. "It is clean," she said as she sat down on top of the bedding.

Gods, she still had to do that, didn't she? Which would include completely wiping away Hunter's scent from her bedroom, too. Fuck, she hated this. Narcissa got to her feet and joined Grace on the bed. Crossing her legs, she sat and munched on the chocolate, its rich aroma filling the air as she stared across the room. "I thought about telling him you were here. Then I thought about the repercussions and that it would mean breaking my promise to you."

Grace's gaze dropped to the bedspread, and she absentmindedly reached into a bag, the rustling of the wrapper the only sound. "As much as I might wish for him to know I am here... to see him again... both of them... I know that would just create problems."

Yes, it would. Likely for both of them. Not that she knew what problems would arise from what had occurred earlier with him. But she'd opted to take the risk. It was that one promise, that one request... She didn't know if she could fulfill it. "He asked me to keep trying to..." Her words trailed off, but no doubt Grace understood what she didn't say.

"Does he honestly think that is possible? Or was it just wishful thinking? Trying to keep the hope alive, or something like that?"

"I think he wanted to believe it was possible. I didn't have the heart to tell him it wasn't, so I promised to do what I could. But the look on his face..." Narcissa put a piece of chocolate in her mouth. Yeah, he'd understood what she couldn't put into words. There was no way out. At least, not the way Hunter would want for her. "He doesn't want me to shut down. He wants me to live the life he says I deserve."

Her friend clasped her hand. "Well... at least I can help make sure you do not shut down."

Returning the squeeze, Narcissa offered what she supposed might pass for a smile. She didn't trust people easily. After the betrayals she'd faced in her life, it only made sense to limit the knowledge given to others. While Grace and Silva had become her friends, and Silva a great shopping partner, none of them ever got personal. Even Fallon didn't know all that much about her. Hunter had been the first person she ever talked to about her past. And now Grace. "Thank you. For being here. I don't imagine any of this has been easy, but I'm glad I have you to talk to about all of this."

"Of course. And thank you, too, for telling me all that you have. I am glad I have you to talk to about him as well. Well, them, I should say. To know that Hayden is okay... it eases me in ways I do not have words for."

"I understand. Hope only goes so far." It was still all she had regarding her brother and mother. Hunter had offered, and she'd been afraid of what would happen. Now, she was scared, but in a whole other way. *Gods, please, please, keep Hunter safe.* She honestly didn't know how she'd survive without seeing him again.

"It does. Some days, I wonder how it has sustained me all this time."

Taking another piece of chocolate, she stared at it for a minute. "You do your damnedest not to think about them. Fill your time so much that you don't have a second to steal for yourself. Otherwise, it leads to an opportunity to think about them... and wonder what they're doing right at that moment." As the candy dissolved on her tongue, she thought first of Hunter, then Dion, and finally, her mother. She didn't know how close Métamorphe was to the den. Or how long it would take Hunter to get back to his village. What would happen once he got there? That just made her think about his words and her family. It had been over thirty years since she'd seen or spoken to her mother and brother. Had there been any changes to her brother's routine? Had her mother ever fallen in love and taken another husband?

"I cannot tell you how many times I have done that very thing over the *solaris*." Grace got up off the bed and went to her closet. With a stretch, she cleared a few books and gathered a small stack of five journals. Leaving her closet again, she went back to the bed and settled onto it. "I have never done a very good job of not thinking about them. Wondering about them." Setting all but one journal down, she flipped through it until she landed on a page about halfway through. "I wrote about them both over the *solaris*. Tracked their birthdays and wrote them a message on that day.

Wrote about what they might be like, what things they might enjoy doing. Stuff like that. Of course, it took a couple of *solaris* before I could start doing that. I did not know how to read or write when I came here."

Narcissa watched as Grace stared down at the page and traced a finger over the words on a page of one journal.

'You two are seven today. Over two solaris since I have seen you. I wonder what you look like now, and how much you have changed. What kinds of things you like. If by some miracle you two are happy.'

It was strange to see their similarities and differences in a situation that shared commonalities. Grace had four years with her brothers, and once the female had learned to read and write, began writing them letters. Although she arrived with that knowledge, at no point had she ever done that for her brother. Instead, she focused on earning as much as possible so his care could continue without issue. "How did you even end up here?"

Grace closed the journal slowly, the leather cover making a soft thump as it landed with the others. She pulled a piece of chocolate from her pouch, and the rich smell of cocoa filled the air as she put it in her mouth. It wasn't until she'd swallowed that she answered. "Azazel sold me when I was nineteen. I was nearing the point where I would no longer be valuable to him there in the village. Those who grew up like I did... their lives did not last very long. Especially with how limited our medical care was. Supplies were just too scarce. No one really wanted to mate me. Partly because they could tell my submissiveness was largely just an act, and partly because I cannot get pregnant. They could not further their line. So... he sold me often to other Informants there, as much as he could. But one slip from one male..." Grace shrugged. "He just wanted to get as much money out of me as he could before an *accident* occurred and his coin flow came to an abrupt stop."

For a split second, she almost questioned how Averine could've gone along with that. Then she recalled her own initiation into the den. Right. Their so-called mother-figure... She cared as long as the workers made her money and followed the rules. Though it made her pray Azazel met a horrible end. The male deserved nothing less. "I'm so sorry, Elisa." It was strange saying Grace's true name after all these years that they'd been friends, yet it felt right.

A tiny smile played across Grace's lips. "I am sorry, too, Narcissa."

"I imagine this place was a bit of an adjustment from what you were accustomed to in your village."

"You could definitely say that." She fished out another piece of chocolate. "I think my head spun for a good solid three *cycles*, at least." Grace chuckled softly. "Maybe more. But... honestly, I did not even mind it, really. Generally, I screwed fewer males in a day than I had in Métamorphe. I got to explore what I liked and did not like, and had some measure of control over what I did. It turned out that I enjoy it when two females have sex. I had regular meals and an actual bed to sleep in." Popping the piece of chocolate into her mouth, she chewed slowly. "I did not have to fear that every day would be my last day. That was... really nice, too. And I think took the longest to get used to. The only regret I have ever had... was having no choice but to leave them behind in that place."

Gods, that sounded awful. Despite what Hunter had said about Deacan, things could've been far worse for her... and for her family. "Those who have people on the outside... there's no choice but to cut off all contact, even if you come here voluntarily." Narcissa shook her head. "Don't regret that you had no choice. Maybe... it was just a way for the three of you to come back together one day." If the gods had a heart, that's how things would work out.

"Maybe. I hope so. I regret that because... I cannot imagine what they have gone through all these *solaris*. Azazel did not claim them, but that does not mean he did not abuse them. His nature is wholeheartedly abusive. There are some days I want to curse the gods for ripping us apart. On other days, I honestly believe I would have been dead by now had I remained there. So, in a way... he did me a favor by selling me here. I just wish they had not believed I was dead all this time. That it had been possible to have at least some form of contact with them. I know that would never have been possible, though. Not with me here."

Well, she was right about that. They couldn't have had a relationship with her here. It was the same with her family. She couldn't contact them in any way whatsoever. And she was right about Azazel. He had abused them... more Hunter so he could protect Hayden from it as much as possible. But she wouldn't confirm Grace's suspicions. "Maybe just take comfort in the knowledge of the good things happening for Hayden as we hope for Hunter."

"Yes. You are right. It is wonderful to know that things are at least going well for him. And I will send up extra prayers to the gods for Hunter, that all of this turns out okay, and he does not..." Grace sighed and leaned against the wooden bedpost. "I begged him to let me take care of them. When they were born and our mother died. He would not let me, though."

Gods, listening to the way Grace talked about things, she wanted to get them both out of here. But if Hunter... Fuck, she couldn't think like that. Narcissa dragged a hand down her face. "Azazel hasn't changed at all over the *solaris*. From everything I've heard, he's only gotten worse." She still had cleaning to do. Talking to Grace about everything made her feel better, though. More hopeful for Hunter.

"Oh, gods." Grace shook her head. "I do not see how that could be possible. For him to be *worse.*"

"I won't go into everything, just that I believe he's worse. I mean, look at what happened in just the last twenty-four *lacunas*. He and Sam raped and desecrated three Seelie females without regard." Not to mention the way they tortured Hunter as he grew up, but she wouldn't share that information with Grace. Hunter had told her those things in confidence, and it was something she planned to take to her grave.

"That is not unusual, though. At least, not from what I remember. They used to brag about their... exploits rather frequently."

"Seems like the world would be a little better without both of them." It would certainly be better for Hunter and Hayden. The gods and goddesses would rid the world of all people like that if they cared at all.

"I wholeheartedly agree." With a satisfying clink, Grace took another piece of hard candy out of the pouch and put it in her mouth. "It really makes me wonder why anyone, let alone a leader who is supposed to be good, would allow them to keep on living. After all they have done..." She shook her head. "Some people are not capable of change."

"Hunter questioned that, too. I believe he thought maybe she was trying to give them a chance to atone for their past indiscretions." With a shrug, Narcissa reached for a piece of chocolate, her fingers brushing against the smooth wrapper. "A bunch of them left. You know... some of our new bodyguards." She rolled her eyes.

"I recognize a few of them. Not that I knew them well, I just knew all the Informants when I lived there. Felines and canines did not really mix unless they were on the job." She shrugged a little. "I steer clear of them as much as I can, and they pretend not to see me if we cross paths. Probably because two of my brothers come here, and I am sure they have contracts of their own. Things to prevent them from causing trouble. I overheard a couple of them talking once, though, out in the courtyard, just after they started working here. It was the middle of the night, and they were smoking something. I did not linger, but I heard them say something about how they never would have bowed down to a, insert some unsavory language here, female."

"I can't say that surprises me." Not in the least. "Hunter made me promise not to be anywhere around them. Even told me which ones were the worst." She'd also inquired about special abilities, but if they both avoided the entire group, that seemed best. Plus, it was what she promised Hunter she would do.

"That is good. He would know better than I. It has been quite some time since I have been around them, before they began working here. But I can hazard a guess as to why they would not wish to stay in the village under her rule. Outside of just being unwilling to bow down to a female."

Yes, Hunter made that pretty clear to her as well. Narcissa glanced toward the door. Really, she should get going. She didn't know how long she'd been in here, but she still needed to clean her room. All the equipment and toys that they had used. Her fingers traced the back of her neck, then drifted over the spot where the mark had been, now smooth and unmarked. Talking to Grace had made her feel better. It had also allowed her to grasp onto the hope that this wasn't the end for Hunter.

They couldn't change what had happened. As for what still had yet to pass... all they could do was pray. No matter how long she stalled, it wouldn't affect any of that. Uncrossing her legs, Narcissa got to her feet. "I'm going to go back to my room. It's still a bit of a mess."

"Alright. I am free the rest of the day, in case you need to come talk some more. Otherwise... I will see you at dinner?"

Normal. She had to act normal, which would include her attending dinner with Grace and Silva, like they did every night. "Right. We need to eat even if we don't have an appetite." She started toward the door, her footsteps echoing, and paused halfway there. "I knew he was going to be with Ivory. Well, someone anyway. I didn't expect it would be Ivory. Or that I would run into them."

Grace retrieved another piece of chocolate from the bag and chewed it, the sound echoing softly. "Why *was* he with Ivory, anyway? Regardless of the rules of this place, if you two truly care about each other so much, why did he do it?"

"Last-ditch effort." Three words, and they didn't seem to explain much. Though Grace might understand, Narcissa opted to clarify. "A few sessions ago, we realized the direction things were heading. So, we tried to find ways to make things professional between us again." Now that she thought about it some more, all of their attempts had likely been in vain. Nothing had ever truly been professional with them. Not even in their first session together. It may have seemed like it, but it was the furthest from the truth. "He hated every second he was with her. Told me all he'd been able to think about was me. That he couldn't do it again." What happened as a result didn't need to be mentioned. Grace had smelled him all over her. "When he comes back..." Yes, she had said 'when,' because she refused to believe he wouldn't be back. "I don't know how long we'll have until... Once that happens, he won't be able to return."

"I am so sorry, Nia. I know those words come across pretty empty, but I truly am." Grace rose from the bed and, grasping the bags of candy and the books, carried them back to her closet. "Would it not be better... for him not to come back at all? Stop returning before... that happens? I know little about mates, but I know it is supposed to be a once in a lifetime thing. And that to live without your mate once you have found them... Like I said before, I had no examples, but... it is supposed to be excruciating." Grace put the candy away, and then after pausing, she carefully put the books back on the shelf. "It has to be hard enough now. But after that bond is completely formed..." She let her words hang. Finishing the sentence wasn't really necessary.

Hunter had told her several things regarding his eyes glowing. Exactly what it meant. How difficult things would be for him. That it could be painful if he closed her off. He would have to do that, wouldn't he? Except they didn't know when. Just soon. That had been before all the events of the past day had happened. Still, Grace had a point. "You're right. That would be best."

The female leaned against the doorjamb of her closet. "You know you can talk to me whenever you need to, right?"

"Thank you. I appreciate it. More than I can truly say." Not once since they'd become friends had they ever spoken the way they had in the last few days. There had been a reason behind it. One that Grace understood. Today, of all days, it had been needed. Narcissa nodded to her friend before the click of the door signaled her exit.

Hunter's mood didn't change as he traveled back to Métamorphe. He felt utterly ruined. Likely looked that way, too. Not once throughout this trek had he even tried to put the mask back on his face. The one he always wore to hide his emotions. It was no longer something he cared about.

When he reached the boundary line and slowed to a stop, two guards emerged from the forestry, their movements a rustling of leaves as they shifted into their humanoid forms. One lifted a bag from their back and pulled out two sets of shackles. A cold, clammy hand squeezed his chest, stealing his breath. It was all Hunter could do to keep from backing away. Not that he allowed himself to. Through the rigidity that had overtaken his body, he shifted to his humanoid form and forced himself not to protest as the guard approached with the shackles. When they stood in front of him, he had to push harder to hold out his arms, the metal of the shackles feeling heavy as they were placed around his wrists. Then again, as a second set was placed around his ankles. He'd only seen them once, when the prison was being built, but he knew exactly what they were. They prevented shifting or any other magical ability from being used.

With both sets in place, the guards took up position on either side of him and led him through the boundaries. Hunter didn't say a word, and neither did they. What was the point? There was only one person he was here to speak to, and even that wouldn't make a difference. He knew exactly what was waiting for him.

His mouth remained closed as they reached the village and they led him to Devin's home. Up the short staircase he went, and then through the door, down the echoing hallway. The guards brought him to the meeting room at the hall's end, then departed, the door clicking shut behind them.

Hunter stood at the end of the table and clasped his hands behind him. His gaze flicked from Milla to Cynric, then ended on Devin before he bowed his head. "Your Majesty."

"Hello, Hunter. I have heard testimony from a few. I have also spoken to the females' families. Official interrogations will be tomorrow morning. Azazel and Clay are both already in the prison, which is where you will spend the night as well. However, before I have you taken out there, would you like to tell me where you have been? And why it took so long for you to return?"

Hunter lifted his head and met her gaze. It was a moment before he spoke. She'd heard testimony from a few. She knew what had happened. Likely exactly who had done what. He had nothing to hide. And he wouldn't shy away from what he'd done. "I was not running, Your Majesty, nor did I ever intend to. I knew the possibilities, the likely consequences of killing Sam. The consequences if I was implicated in what was done to the females. That I was present... throughout the whole thing. I may have been inebriated, and then passed out, but I was present. I freely accept any punishment that is coming to me. Whatever that may be." He paused for a long moment. "There was someone I had to see one last time... while I still could. Someone I had to say goodbye to. I meant no offense by my delay."

Devin remained silent for what felt like an eternity, though only a minute or two had passed. "I appreciate the explanation. As I have told both of your brothers and your father, I will not give out any punishments until I am absolutely certain I have gotten the whole truth. I have brought in an impartial third party that is going to assist with that."

Hunter's despondent expression didn't change, but neither did his resolve. He gave a slight dip of his chin in acknowledgement. "Yes, Your Majesty."

More silence passed, then seemingly out of nowhere, Milla said, "That won't be necessary. Just give me a moment."

Had she and Devin been having a private conversation? Must have been. Hunter didn't know if the queen had possessed that ability before taking the position, but she certainly had it now. And used it more often than some around here appreciated. It didn't really bother him, though. His mind was closed airtight, always, except for that sliver that allowed telepathy to be used. His thoughts were always safe from others.

Milla clapped her hands together, the sound echoing, and slowly drew them apart. A pocket of air grew between her palms as she did this, a subtle pressure. A faint silver line on the outer edge barely made it noticeable. When she had it big enough, she threw her hands wide, and the pocket she'd created expanded to surround the four of them. The shimmer was much easier to see now, not just to their sides and above them, but even beneath their feet. "That should do."

Hunter's eyes widened, but his face was an emotionless mask. That was a nifty ability. One that, for sure, came in handy.

"I am going to save most of my questions for tomorrow." Devin spoke to Milla, then nodded toward Hunter. "Go right ahead."

"My questions are focused on a single portion of the testimony I received from one victim. According to her recollection, you looked at one female and said, 'You are not Nia.' Is she the one you had to see? At the brothel?"

Hunter frowned, the lines on his forehead deepening. Not that he was unwilling to answer; he was just confused. The brothel hadn't been mentioned until right now. At least, not out loud. People knew he went there, but he had told no one where he was going. He hadn't even mentioned it to Clay before taking off this morning. And he couldn't, for the life of him, remember saying *that* line. That wasn't surprising. While he'd remembered a good chunk of things while relaxing in the tub with Narcissa after their session, most of any kind of dialogue was still lost on him. He'd remembered a couple of things said, but that was it. Why did Milla want to know? He wouldn't lie. He'd never been a liar, and he wouldn't start now. "Yes. That is who I went to see."

"How were you first introduced to the brothel? Is it something you heard people talking about and found on your own, or did someone who already went there have to be with you?"

"I had heard a few males here in the village talking about it. One of them was my older brother, Clay. I was nineteen when I stole money from my father and tagged along with Clay one night when I knew he was going. We got there, and he introduced me to the receptionist. I have been going ever since. From what I have always understood, it is invitation only. Someone else who is already a client must vouch for newcomers."

"From there, you just told the receptionist what you wanted or preferred, and they recommended someone? Or did you have to meet with the owner first?"

"I have never met the owner. But the rest is accurate. Before I could meet with any of the workers, though, I had to pay, and then I had to read the posted rules and state that I agreed to them."

Milla opened her mouth as if to speak, then snapped it shut. "That's all I have." The *for now* went unsaid.

"Okay." Inhaling and exhaling a deep breath, Devin focused on Hunter. "I am going to have you taken to the prison now, alright?"

Discomfort plagued Hunter's features, something that hadn't shown on his face before, but he couldn't seem to hold back now. It was a hazard of his upbringing—it was excruciating being in restraints or in a cage. Something Narcissa had learned plainly during their switched session. Finally, he nodded. "Okay. How... how long did you say I will be there again?" *How long... until my death.*

"For now, just until morning. Interrogations will be held, and we will go from there."

Hunter dipped his chin once more. "Am I allowed to see Hayden?"

"Yes, visitors will be minimal, though. Outside of guards, I am only allowing whoever brings evening meal out, and family, which is just Hayden. I told him that Rainbow could accompany him. Once you are taken out there, I will let him know."

"Okay. Thank you, Your Majesty."

"Of course." Devin called the guards back in, and they led him out.

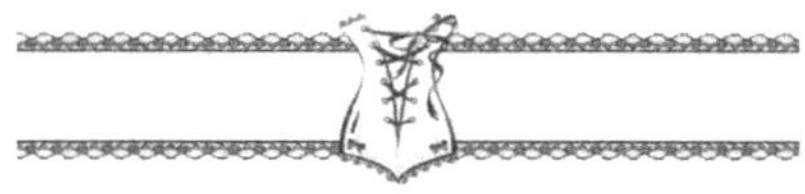

Hunter paced back and forth within his single prison cell. As much as he could without touching the bars, that is. Devin had requested iridium bars when the prison was built. Turned out, the metal was like poison to their species. If it touched them, they would burn, and their natural healing ability wouldn't be able to do anything for it. He turned before he hit the bars and paced in the other direction. Over and over. He couldn't seem to help himself. Between the shackles on his wrists and ankles and the bars surrounding him on all sides, it went so far beyond irritation. Hunter felt as though he could tear himself apart, his skin prickling with agitation.

The door of the prison opened. He'd been expecting Hayden and Rainbow, but that didn't mean he was ready for his twin to see him in this kind of emotional state.

"Well, well, well," Azazel said from across the room in his own single cell. "Look who decided to grace us with their presence. And with your female in tow, whom you have so rudely failed to introduce to me thus far. I suppose after the trial tomorrow there will be plenty of time for us to get to know one another."

"Fucking delusional prick," Clay grumbled under his breath. In his cell, he lay on his back, arms folded beneath his head, legs bent, and his feet firmly planted. His eyes were closed, but he obviously wasn't sleeping.

Hunter didn't respond to Azazel's comment. If the fucker wanted to believe he'd be alive after tomorrow afternoon at the latest, all power to him. The male—not that he could really be called that—was the only one who believed he wouldn't lose his life.

Hayden kept his arm around Rainbow as they walked up to Hunter's cell. "Hey."

"Hey," he responded, not stopping his pacing.

Rainbow smirked over at Azael. "I don't associate with psychopaths or liars." Her eyes locked onto him, and she cocked her head, her expression questioning. "Hi, Hunter."

"If you do not associate with psychopaths, why ever are you speaking to my son?"

Stopping his pacing for only a moment, Hunter glared across the room at Azazel. "Do not fucking call me that, you sick bastard," he growled. "Raping a female you bought and paid for does not make you a father." He resumed his pacing, and with a frustrated sigh, ran his hands roughly over the top of his head. "Neither does any of the other shit you did."

"I made you strong."

"Oh, is *that* what you were doing? Well, if that is the case, I would have been just fine being weak."

"Weak males died here, and quickly. Well..." Azazel smirked as his gaze settled on Hayden's back. "... most of them. If you had not spent so much time playing bodyguard..."

The tension in Hunter was so thick you could cut it with a knife, and his twin mirrored his worry with a frown. He could tell that Hayden was doing his best to ignore every word that came out of Azazel's mouth. He and Rainbow hadn't come here to see their sperm donor.

"Just ignore him, Hunter," Hayden said.

"So, does it count as breaking a promise if it's done to save a life?" Rainbow asked.

"Huh?" Hunter turned around, the sound of his footsteps echoing as he paused in his pacing. He flicked his gaze to the female. She'd said something. "You said hi. Sorry. Hi. And... what? What promise?"

"Dude, you have *got* to chill." Though Clay's eyes were closed, he could track everyone's movements with an uncanny sense. He was a natural-born tracker. "You are either going to make the guards dizzy, or annoy the fuck out of everyone here, or both."

Rainbow maintained her composure. "You came to my club last night, Hunter. We talked for almost a *lacuna*. I promised to keep our conversation to myself. I have uttered nothing regarding the details, just told Devin and Hayden that it occurred."

"Oh... right. I remember the club. And talking to you. Just not... most of the dialogue. Most of it did not come back to me." But if he'd asked Rainbow to keep the conversation to herself... fuck, he could only imagine what had come out of his mouth. "Thank you, though."

Hayden frowned. He glanced briefly over his shoulder at Azazel, decided against saying anything to the male, and faced forward once more. Between wondering if memory loss was always a thing with him when he drank too much, and thinking about how this would be the last chance for him to have a real conversation with their father, Hunter knew his twin wasn't having an easy time with any of this. At least Hayden knew that trying with Azazel, even now, wouldn't change anything. And from what he was getting from his twin, Hayden was actually okay with that. About fucking time.

"If you have something to say, Hayden," Azazel sneered, "spit it out."

"I have nothing to say to you," Hayden said, without looking over at him. "Hunter, Devin said she is going to send out some food later."

"I am not hungry," Hunter replied.

"You need to eat."

"I know. I do not think I can stomach anything right now."

"I know what I could use right now, and it is not food," Azazel said.

"Not a single fucking person asked you, nor cares, what you want or need." Clay's eyes remained closed, but he was, apparently, staying fully in-tune with the conversation.

Rainbow squeezed Hayden's hand and faced Azazel. A grin spread slowly across her face as she studied him. "Yeah, you might as well forget that idea for your last meal because you *definitely* won't get that. In my culture, we try to honor those whose lives are ending with an extravagant meal, but considering you lied about what happened, I don't see that happening. I'm curious. Are you *so* afraid of death that you'd lay the blame on your progeny? Please don't tell me you don't fear death. I can see it in your aura. About as clearly as I can see your lifeline."

She held up a finger. "That's not the only thing I see. I know you saw me the first day I came. Now, granted, I didn't get as good a look at your aura as I do now, but there were a few things I quickly identified. One, you're a liar. Two, the only person you've ever cared about is yourself. Probably explains why you couldn't get a female who will voluntarily sleep with you. Three, the number of lives you've taken. I thought there would only be one more, at least given what I know of what occurred. Surprise, surprise, I'm studying your aura here, and it appears you've taken more. At least two. Now, you're probably asking yourself how I could know this because you don't quite understand what it means to read an aura. I'd explain, but why bother?" Rainbow clasped her hands at the small of her back. "You won't live long enough to take the time to grasp the concept."

Even though he was still furious, Hunter couldn't help but admire Rainbow's strength. He'd seen no female stand up to Azazel and speak to him in that manner; it was no less than the *male* deserved.

Clay chuckled. And he didn't even try to hide it. With his arms resting on his knees, he sat up, surveying the room slowly. First, he looked at Azazel, who had a smirk across his face; then at Hayden, whose fists were clenched; and finally, at himself.

"Keep thinking that. My life is not over yet," Azazel retorted. "That was a *fascinating* assessment. But your sight must be flawed. I am afraid of nothing. And I have taken *a lot* more lives than just two. But..." He smirked. "... that was in the past."

Hunter had to make a conscious decision not to roll his eyes. "No one fucking believes that, or anything else that comes out of your mouth, so why keep spouting bullshit?"

"Maybe it makes me feel good." Azazel chuckled low. "It has been quite some time since I have taken a life. But I will say this—I enjoyed it. Every single time." He fixed his gaze on Hayden, his smirk growing. "I enjoyed it when I took *hers*."

Though Hayden's body tensed and his breath hitched, he didn't break his gaze. It was obvious whom Azazel was speaking about—their sister's death. That Azazel would bring it up again just showed exactly what kind of person the male was.

Hunter fixed his gaze on his twin. "Do not listen to him, Hayden. Words will not save him, and he can no longer hurt anyone physically, so he is going to cause pain with words. That is what cowards do."

"I know," Hayden said quietly.

Ignoring everyone else, Azazel kept his eyes on Hayden. "I know you want to know what happened to her, Hayden. Why she was there one day, gone the next. Why she never returned home."

"I know she is dead. She is at peace, and I have made my peace with that. I do not need to know anything else."

"Oh? Did you know she begged for her life to end? After I watched over a dozen males have their way with her, she begged for it all to just be over... and I ensured she got exactly what she wanted. Then I walked away with more coin than I would have earned here in this village in a *solaris*."

"Shut up!" Hunter snarled. His claws dug deep into his palms, and the coppery scent of blood filled the air as it dripped to the floor. A glistening sheen of tears covered Hayden's eyes, and that only fueled his anger.

"Hunter, do not touch the bars," one guard said firmly. "Azazel, that is more than enough. Keep it up, and I will call the queen down here."

He must have gotten too close without realizing it. Hunter took a step back from the bars before resuming his earlier pacing, the dim light making his shadow dance along the floor.

Rainbow tapped her chin. "Here's the thing about auras. No matter how much you lie, they don't. You can't alter its truth to fit your perception. Let me give you an example. I said you'd taken two lives. I didn't say, *period*. In fact, if you actually paid attention to my words, I inferred you had taken *at least* two lives since the first day I saw you. See, there are these little black dots that exist in your aura. A new one populates for every life you take. If that doesn't convince you that what I'm saying is true, how about this? With your lies, the colors in your aura fluctuate. I can tell you that *part* of what you stated regarding their sister is a lie. What's even better is that, since I was watching your aura while you flapped your mouth, I can even tell you which part. Now, I know the queen brought in a neutral party to sort this mess out tomorrow. I'm wondering... if we asked her, do you think she'd question you about what you did with Elisa? Because you didn't kill her." She stared at Azazel, her gaze intense, daring him to say otherwise. "I'd stake my life on that."

A slow smirk spread across Azazel's face. "I did not say *I killed* her. I said she begged for it all to be over, and I ensured that happened. Her life *ended* that day. Whether or not I killed her, whether or not she is still alive, that hardly matters. With what she endured the last time I laid eyes on her... you should pray that she truly is dead, Hayden. She would certainly be better off that way."

Hayden turned around slowly, his eyes fixed on the male. His attempt to stay composed was failing miserably. "What did you do with her?" he asked, his voice cracking.

Azazel gave a low chuckle. "Perhaps you should also pray to the gods that I do not lose my life tomorrow. Because if I do... you will *never* know."

Hunter stood there, unable to get words to pass through his mouth for a moment. He hadn't been close to Elisa, but her death—disappearance—had gutted Hayden. It had torn him apart for a *long* time. With a furtive glance, he took in Clay. If he'd known... No. Seeing the look on Clay's face, it was easy to see he didn't know what was happening.

"I'm sure there are ways to find her, as well as the truth of what you did with her." Rainbow turned back to Hayden and took his hand in hers. "Hayden, listen to me. This pile of sea sludge can hold his tongue all he wants, but that doesn't mean she'll never be found or questions will remain unanswered. I have the power of the sea at my fingertips. I promise we'll figure it out."

Hayden squeezed Rainbow's hand, but his gaze remained on Azazel. A single tear traced a path down his cheek, and his body trembled. "Why?" he choked out. "Just tell me why. Please."

Azazel didn't say another word. Just sat there with that fucking smirk. Hunter would have happily used his claws to swipe it off his face, but the cold, hard bars were an unyielding obstacle. "Leave it be, Hayden. Rainbow is right; we will figure it out. I promise you." Provided he didn't lose his life as well tomorrow...

Slowly, Hayden turned around, squeezing Rainbow's hand tighter. He hastily wiped away a tear before it could trace a path down his cheek. He opened his mouth, then closed it again.

"Get that look off your face," Hunter said. "Rainbow would not lie to you, and I never have, either. We will figure it out. Let us just get me off death row first, okay?"

"There is only one person in this room headed toward death, Hunter, and it is not you," Clay said

"If you say so."

"I'm inclined to agree with Clay on this one. I spoke to Devin. Maybe I don't know everything that happened, but you have an alibi for the females." Rainbow wiggled her fingers. "I also told her you had had *a lot* to drink. Though I didn't mention that it was my best stuff. Still, everything I told her... it just seemed to emphasize what I believe she suspected."

Gods, he wished he could fucking remember more. Bits and pieces had come back to him, especially after he'd been in the tub with Narcissa after their session this morning, but not everything had returned. He didn't know Rainbow well, but he knew she wasn't a liar; if she said she could alibi him for the females, that meant it was true. Hunter nodded his head in gratitude. "Did I at least pay you?"

"Do not forget that you killed Sam," Azazel called from his cell. "You will have to pay for that."

"Gods, do you *ever* shut the fuck up?" Clay snapped. "Good riddance. He was not worth the air he breathed, and neither are you."

"You are one to talk, Clayton."

"See, right there is just one of the many differences between me and you—I have never claimed to be worth anything. You made sure I felt like that, same as you did all your kids."

"And yet, Sam is the only one who ever measured up."

"If you mean measuring up to *your* standards, I think we are all okay with that."

Rainbow shook her head, then shifted her gaze back to him. "Yes, Hunter. You actually paid rather well, regardless of the fact that I told you it wasn't necessary. Made my barkeep's night. I told her to keep it all."

Well, good. At least he'd done that right.

Rainbow tilted her head. "Do you think the guards would interfere if I muzzled him?" She asked, hooking a thumb over her shoulder.

Neither of the guards said anything, but one of them allowed an amused expression to take over their face.

"Who knows," Hunter replied. "But I would pay you even more to see that."

"I second that," Clay said.

"Fuck both of you," Azazel snapped. A slow smirk crossed his face. "Oh, wait... I already have. It has just been a very long time."

Hunter couldn't quite decipher the look that appeared on his twin's face—something like shock, disgust, sorrow, and something else all rolled into one. Though he put in little effort to figure it out. He just crossed his arms over his chest, feeling the sharp sting of his claws digging into his palms, and paced restlessly. Right now, he was a mess, every aching muscle and joint betraying the tension he felt. All he wanted to do right now was rip Azazel's throat out.

Clay let out a deep growl. "*Enough*, Azazel. I am fucking warning you."

"What are you going to do, Clayton? You are stuck inside these bars the same as me. Forgive me if I cannot help but... reminisce about the good old times." He chuckled low.

"That you enjoyed that shit, and you want to spend your last night alive bragging about it, just says even more about you than it says about either of us."

Before Hunter could answer, the sound of Rainbow's jaw grinding filled the air as she rotated her wrist. Water gathered around Azazel's mouth, forming a constricting, watery muzzle. The male's eyes were black with rage. Rainbow peered over her shoulder at Azazel. "Much better." She turned her attention back to him. "Payment not required."

Despite the darkness within, Hunter found a moment of levity watching Azazel's ridiculous efforts to scrub away the gag. The muzzle apparently didn't keep him from breathing as he didn't look in distress. Just pissed. Too bad.

Clay started chuckling again.

Both guards took a minute to laugh openly—so loudly that the door opened and the two guards right outside peeked in to see what was going on. The two of them enjoyed the view themselves for a moment before resuming their posts.

"That is fuckin' hilarious," one guard inside said. "What is the matter? Havin' a little trouble speakin' there, Azzy?"

"Much appreciated," Hunter said, nodding to Rainbow.

Hayden looked over his shoulder and just stared at Azazel for a minute. Although it didn't amuse him, he didn't seem inclined to have it taken away. With his arm wrapped around Rainbow, her slight form nestled against him, he turned to face their father. "I do not know what happened to you to make you into the person you are, or if that is just the way you were born... but I feel sorry for you. And I still love you. I know you do not love me, and I know you do not see me as your son, but that is okay. I do not need your love, and I do not need to be called your son. Not anymore. I am sorry you are the way you are, and that you have so much hatred inside yourself. And I am sorry you are going to die tomorrow. May the gods have mercy on your soul, Azazel." After he said those few words, he pivoted, his gaze snapping back to Hunter. His hand reached up and wiped away the fresh tears that streamed down his face.

"Stop wasting tears on him, Hayden. He is just not worth it. He never was." Hunter had always understood his twin's need for that connection—not that it was a need he'd ever had himself—but that had never stopped him from discouraging Hayden from trying to get close to Azazel in any regard. It would only ever have resulted in his twin getting hurt. Or worse.

Rainbow squeezed Hayden's hand. "The people who love you are here for you. Focus on them."

Hayden squeezed her hand back, a silent understanding passing between them. Then he glanced at Hunter, the question in his eyes one he couldn't utter out loud.

Hunter shifted his gaze away from his twin's before speaking to him through their mindlink. *I do not want to talk about it. Ever. So, do not bring up what he said. Understood?*

Hayden's first instinct was to protest, but thank the gods he resisted that urge. *Of course, Hunter. But I am here if that ever changes.*

I know you are. And thanks.

You are welcome.

Hayden looked over at Clay. He stood there in silence for a moment before speaking. "I make good food. If you would ever like to... come over and hang out, I could cook."

Clay's entire face scrunched up in an expression loaded with confusion. "You are... inviting *me*... to dinner?"

"Yeah. If you would like to... just know you are welcome anytime. But it is just an offer. Do not feel like you have to take me up on it. I just thought—"

"Sure, kid. Sounds... nice, actually." Clay flicked his gaze to the wall, where it held. "I remember what your mom was like. Maybe I could... tell you about her sometime."

Hayden blinked quickly as a fresh wave of tears welled up and spilled over. Squeezing Rainbow's hand again, he swallowed hard and still had to clear his throat before he could speak. "I would like that. A lot. Thank you, Clay."

Rainbow practically beamed from ear to ear. It was sickening, in all honesty. "He really is an excellent chef," she said.

"Yeah? I kinda figured. Hard to miss the smells when he is cooking." Clay paused for a moment. "I am good at catching food. So... maybe I bring it, you cook it, Hayden? But... you know, only if Hunter comes, too."

Like, *that* wouldn't be the most awkward dinner in existence. But with the hopeful expression that had appeared on Hayden's face, Hunter couldn't bring himself to decline. "Sure. We could probably... figure something out. Depending on how tomorrow goes."

A genuine smile appeared on his twin's face. "That sounds great. Really, really great."

Hunter didn't have to be looking at Azazel to know that steam practically came out of his ears. *Oh, the horror,* that three of his sons would actually attempt to hang out doing something that wouldn't require bloodshed. No one else in the room cared, though; let the male be angry.

"Have faith, Hunter," Rainbow said. "I'm certain you still have many days ahead of you."

"That makes one of us."

"Two of us." Hayden glanced at Clay. "Make that three."

"Yeah, if you say so." Hunter flicked his gaze to Rainbow. "You have a lot of warm, fuzzy thoughts for someone who acted like a complete asshole the first time we met."

"Oh, I won't argue that your first impression was awful. However, someone who's a self-proclaimed jerkface wouldn't have apologized. And you did."

"Well, I could not have Hayden upset at me forever. Where would the fun in that be?"

"Do you even know how to have fun?" Clay teased.

"As a matter of fact, I do. But explaining *how* I like to have fun would be disrespectful in front of a lady, and would make Hayden uncomfortable."

Regardless of the slight discomfort that hit his twin, a small smile appeared on Hayden's face. He looked over at Hunter. "I need to apologize to you for something."

Hunter raised an eyebrow. "To *me*? What the fuck for?"

"For taking you for granted." He held up a hand before Hunter could interrupt him. "I got... comfortable... with you protecting me all these *solaris*. I know I can take care of myself, but I think a part of me just relied on your protection too much. No matter what was going on, if I was going to get hurt, or worse, you always did the best you could to make sure that did not happen. You are covered in scars, and not just on the outside, because you were taking the hits for me. You should have let me take some for you. I want you to know... you do not have to protect me anymore. You have been sacrificing yourself for me throughout our entire lives. You can rest now. Know that, no matter what, I am going to be okay. And another thing... you really deserve everything you have always made sure I knew I deserve. And more. I really hope that one day you allow yourself to believe that."

Though Clay still stared at the wall, it wasn't difficult to hear every word he spoke. "Everything you did for Hayden... I should have been doing for the two of you. And when the gods call me home one day, I will have to atone for all of my selfishness. None of us are perfect, but you are a good male, Hunter."

Hunter didn't bother to open his mouth because he thought nothing would come out. But yeah, they could fucking stop now. Those weren't words he was accustomed to hearing aimed at him. Honestly, they made him uncomfortable.

Rainbow flicked her gaze to Clay. "You know, Clay, it's never too late to change." She looked over at Hunter. "The three of you have an opportunity. One that many don't get. Not just to change the course your lives have taken, but to be something to one another that circumstances haven't previously allowed."

"That is all I want," Hayden said. "For us to be, well, a family. That is all I have ever wanted. I know, with the way things were before, that was not possible, but that is not the case any longer. You are my brothers. I love you both."

Hunter shook his head. "I am no one that anyone should concern themselves with."

"And nothing you ever say or do could ever convince me that is true." A slight smile lifted one corner of Hayden's lips. "Get over it."

No, no matter how much Hunter might want to believe his brother's words, he just couldn't. After everything he'd been put through over the course of his life, everything he'd seen. All the things that he'd done. Finally, finding someone who was his perfect other half, who loved and accepted him despite all of his scars and his wrongdoings... but to be stuck knowing that she would never be free of her prison and he had a good possibility of losing his life tomorrow. Mere hours ago, they'd said goodbye to one another for what was probably the very last time. The gods didn't care about him. Neither should anyone else. Hunter knew without a doubt that he was toxic. A destructive presence. And no matter how much he might wish that Hayden would see that, he knew his twin never would. He would just have to keep praying that it didn't destroy Hayden. His brother, more than anyone else, deserved true happiness.

"Hey, Hayden. Just because I do not know what is going to happen tomorrow... I want you to know." Hunter paused for a long moment. "I love you, too." His eyes met his twin's, and he saw a stunned expression, with tears welling up in his eyes.

"I have, uh... never heard you say that before," Hayden whispered.

"I know, and I am sorry. Look..." Hunter sighed and ran a hand roughly over the top of his head. "This shit is not easy for me, okay? And I am never gonna be great at it, or probably even good at it. But... I am gonna try." For as long as he had. "You deserve that." And after tomorrow, no matter what happened to him and Clay, the last person he'd spent his life protecting Hayden from could never hurt him again.

The heavy door of the prison groaned open, and two males entered. Garrett, a tiger feline, and Castor, a lynx feline. Garrett had two plates of food in hand, and Castor had one. "Shift change, gentlemen," Castor said as he slid the one plate through a slot in the bottom of Azazel's cage. His gaze flicked from Azazel's mouth—he was trying to speak, but wasn't getting anywhere with the water-made contraption around his mouth—then around the room. "First off, *that* is hilarious, and I want to know who did that. Second off, can he eat like that?"

Garrett didn't say a word as he slid a plate of food into Clay's cage, then Hunter's.

Rainbow grinned and wiggled her fingers. "Guilty as charged, and no, he won't. I'll remove it once we're on our way out."

"Fine by me. The less I hear his mouth, the better. By what I hear, he thinks everyone is as stupid as he is."

Clay let out a quiet chuckle. "That is an accurate assessment.," he mumbled under his breath as he picked up his plate of food and dug in.

Hayden looked at him. He hadn't made a single move to pick up his own plate. "Promise me you will eat."

"How about... I promise to give it my best shot."

"Is that the best I am going to get out of you?"

"Pretty much." Hunter paused for a moment. "Or... I could do you one better. I promise to eat if you promise to get some sleep tonight."

"I think I can handle that."

"If nothing else, I know Rainbow will make you. Or, you know, wear you out enough you just pass right the fuck out." He almost laughed when he sensed the embarrassment from Hayden.

Rainbow's cheeks flushed. "You know, for five seconds, I felt bad that you'd have to deal with his mouth after we leave. I don't feel so bad anymore."

"Me, neither," Hayden mumbled, studiously ignoring that Clay was snickering again.

Hunter, with his innocent face, picked up his plate and sat on his cot, the metal cold under him. "I said nothing untrue." He shot her a look full of nothing but respect. "Take care of him, okay? He needs you." *More than he ever needed me.* If he *was* sentenced to death tomorrow, at least he could die knowing, without a doubt, that someone was always going to be there to take care of and protect Hayden, no matter what. It was the best he could hope for at this point.

"I'll always take care of him, but that doesn't mean he won't ever need you." Rainbow tilted her head. "Can you do something for me, Hunter? I know it's outside of what you're accustomed to, but should tomorrow go how I believe it will for you, if you *ever* need help with anything, please ask. We'll do whatever we can for you."

"Absolutely," Hayden said, tightening his hold on her.

Hunter's hand stopped with a bite halfway to his mouth. He flicked his gaze back and forth between them, settling finally on Rainbow. "How about... I make no promises... except to think about giving it a shot?"

"Alright, but know that whatever the *issue* is, there are people who can help."

Hunter stared at her for a moment, then shifted his gaze away and shoved a bite of food in his mouth. He wasn't sure how true that was, but it also wasn't something he could think about right now, either. Narcissa was all he'd thought about since he'd left her this morning. Her, and the huge possibility that he'd never lay eyes on her again. Once he'd hit the boundaries and been presented with these fucking shackles, he'd also been thinking about the huge possibility that his twin might have to say goodbye to him for good, too. His chest hadn't stopped aching for hours now. A cold, paralyzing grip squeezed his chest, a chilling presence that haunted his every breath. A feeling he couldn't seem to shake. "Thanks, Rainbow. I will keep that in mind."

Rainbow nodded, then lifted her gaze to Hayden. "Are you ready to go?"

It took Hayden a moment to shift his eyes from Hunter to Rainbow. "Yeah, I am ready to go." He gave her a light squeeze and glanced back at Hunter. "We will see you in the morning."

Hunter nodded. "Night, you two."

A small smile appeared on Hayden's face. That wasn't something his twin was used to hearing from him, either.

"Good night." Hayden looked over at Clay. "Good night to you too."

Clay said nothing, just nodded.

Hayden tightened his hold on Rainbow, and with one last glance at Hunter, he guided her toward the door.

"Good night, guys." As they exited, Rainbow flicked her wrist over her shoulder and released Azazel's watery gag.

The male's growling yell immediately echoed through the cold, stone prison room. Hayden's voice popped up in his head.

If it gets to be too much, just let me know. We can get Devin involved.

I will be fine, Hunter thought back. *Not the first time I have had to listen to his mouth. He will either wear himself out or Castor will knock him out.*

Something that didn't end up being necessary. After Azazel spouted shit for a few minutes, he dug into his food. He didn't get but a few bites in before he keeled over in his cell. Not dead, just passed out in a deep sleep. Bless whoever had prepared that plate.

Sixteen

"Do you have any last words before I make my ruling?" the shape shifter queen asked.

"I have told you nothing but the truth, Your Majesty," Hunter replied. "There is nothing more to add."

"Nothing more?" Narcissa questioned. How could that be possible? "That can't be true! You should have plenty more." Despite what little she could see, even from how close to everyone she stood, she saw enough. The number of shape shifters gathered for the trial, along with a small group of Seelie. Though that didn't surprise her, given what had occurred. What bothered her, aside from Hunter's refusal to defend his actions, was the sneer across the face of the male standing next to Hunter. While there weren't more than a few feet between them, it almost appeared as if this was going exactly how he wanted.

"Are you sure?" the female questioned, emphasizing the last word. "Once I make my ruling, no further testimony will be allowed."

"I am certain, Your Majesty. I have nothing else to say."

"Yes, you do!" Narcissa shouted. "Don't you dare take this lying down, Hunter!" He couldn't do this to her. Something had to be done, but what could she do if he wouldn't fight? She hadn't seen what had happened. And she had no way of discovering the truth. Fuck. There had to be something they hadn't seen. Some way around this.

"Then I have made my decision. For the charge of murder, I find you guilty and sentence you to death."

"No!" Narcissa screamed. Though it didn't seem as if anyone heard her. This couldn't be happening. The queen couldn't find him guilty. "He did nothing wrong!" Narcissa stretched out her hand, expecting to feel the familiar thrum of earth magic, but the silence was deafening. "Shit," she muttered. Why couldn't she summon it? Something stilted it, not that she knew what. Nor did she have time to figure it out. She charged through the noisy crowd, the sounds of their protests fading as she shoved people to get to Hunter. Their time together couldn't end like this.

Instead of getting closer to him, she only seemed to wind up further away. Despite her best efforts, an unseen force drew her back with an irresistible pull. Stopping in her tracks, she glanced over her shoulder and surveyed her surroundings. Nothing looked familiar. Not that she could identify a single detail. Every tree and bush, a swirl of green and brown, blurred into an indistinguishable mass.

What the fuck was happening? As she focused back on Hunter, her breath grew ragged, then a deafening crack split the sky as a bolt of lightning struck him down. "NO!" Narcissa screamed. She rushed toward him, but a powerful grip seized her arms, preventing her from moving. "Let me go! Let me go!"

The crowd parted, and she saw Hunter's lifeless body sprawled out on the ground, just a few feet away. "Don't leave me, please! Please! Please!" The world dissolved into a blurry haze as she sank, her body wracked with silent sobs.

Narcissa bolted upright with a gasp. A hollow ache resonated in her chest, mirroring the rhythmic beat of a silent drum. Fuck. Where was she? A silken thread brushed her palm, and she looked around, taking in her surroundings. Her bed. These were her sheets, she felt. Her gaze fell upon the candlelight, its warm glow emanating from her bedroom door. Oh, gods. Not again. With her knees pulled up, she ran her hands across her head and grasped a handful of her hair, its weight suddenly noticeable. "What the fuck?" she mumbled. Was her hair wet? That wasn't possible. Her species didn't sweat. Unless... shit. Had she summoned her water magic in her sleep?

Tossing the covers aside, she climbed out of her bed and headed to her bathroom. She slid the door open, strolled inside, and stopped in front of the sink. Narcissa turned on the water, the spray cool against her palms as she splashed it on her face and through her hair. This couldn't keep happening. It was only getting worse. But what could she do? Not sleep? That wouldn't be good for anyone. Turning off the water, she reached for a fluffy towel on the rack and patted her face and hair dry.

Obviously, she had to get sleep, but how? She'd tried the herbs earlier and they had helped little with the nightmare. Maybe something stronger? It probably wouldn't be any better. Finding out what happened to Hunter would help, but it could be days before she got any news. After wiping the water from her face and hair, she tossed the damp towel toward the laundry basket. Until she could get answers, she had only one other option. She couldn't sleep alone. Maybe not even in her bed.

Narcissa left the bathroom, gently closed the door, and reached for her silky, dark-blue bathrobe, feeling its soft fabric. It wasn't the one she normally went for except at night. As she slipped it on, she twisted the bathroom lantern's dial, then walked across the room to dim the lantern by the front door. After opening her bedroom door, she glanced up and down the hallway, and then quietly walked to Grace's room. At least she didn't have to worry about the door being locked. Though she hoped Gracie didn't mind her barging in while the female slept.

Gently turning the doorknob, Narcissa slipped inside the female's bedroom. "Grace," she whispered. "Gracie." She shut the door behind her, trying to muffle the sound as much as she could.

Rustling from Grace's bed indicated she'd bolted upright. The leaves and curtain surrounding her bed shifted, then the female looked down over the edge, her body taut with tension. "Nia? What is it? Is everything alright?"

"Nightmare. I can't sleep." Though it seemed maybe her friend had one as well. They couldn't exactly share any of this with Silva. They truly had only each other to lean on until they had answers. "Think I could, uh... sleep in here with you?"

"Yes, of course. Come on up."

With a slight dip of her chin, Narcissa's footsteps echoed as she made her way across the room to the ladder. She climbed up and slid into the bed next to the female. "Thank you."

"Of course. You know I am always here if you need me." Grace scooted over, the blanket rustling slightly as she made room, and offered her a portion of its warmth. "It was a bad one, I take it?"

Accepting the blanket, Narcissa got as comfortable as she could. "The worst." That didn't even begin to describe how bad the nightmare was. Every single night for the last three nights. With only one minor difference.

Tucking her legs and using an arm as a pillow, Grace settled in as comfortably as she could. "Do you want to talk about it?"

Narcissa peered over at her for only a moment. She couldn't talk about it while looking at Grace. This was Grace's brother. But this wasn't something she could discuss with just anyone. "I watch him die. Not that he even tries to fight. So, I try for him... but I can't do anything. No matter how fast I run... how much magic I summon... I've never felt that helpless."

"At least it was only a dream. An awful one, but just a dream. If I know anything about Hunter, it is that he is a fighter. Even if he does not fight for himself."

She felt the comfort of the female's hand on her shoulder. "You didn't hear him talk about what he'd done, though. I'm not sure he even had any hope that the queen wouldn't punish him for what happened with Sam." Tears pricked the corners of her eyes. Fuck. She couldn't cry over this. Not when she didn't even know what had happened. "I know it's a dream. That's what I tell myself afterward. He's fought these *solaris* for Hayden, so this won't be any different. But it doesn't stop the feeling."

"I know what you mean. I hold the same fears within myself. We just have to hope that the new queen will be merciful." Though Grace used the right words, there wasn't much conviction in them.

Her ability to hope ran thin these days. In a lot of ways. Even if Hunter survived, how much longer would they have together? Gods, she couldn't think about that. With a trembling hand, Narcissa wiped the tears that silently tracked down her cheeks. "I'm going to talk to Jezzy tomorrow and see when Clay's next appointment is. Might get some information from him. Or Fallon, if I see him sooner."

"If they can tell you anything... please let me know?" Grace shifted her hand to Narcissa's back and rubbed slowly.

"Of course." It would be better if she could get Clay to talk to her. "We should try to get some sleep." They both had long days tomorrow.

"Good idea. I hope it will be easier for you now."

"You, too." Though if she closed her eyes, would she still see one of the different ways she'd already witnessed Hunter die? Maybe. Yes, they both needed sleep, but she couldn't quite make the attempt. Not yet. "Have you dreamed about them? All these *solaris* that you've been separated."

It took Grace a minute to respond to the question. "Yes. Many times."

"Do you ever dream about being reunited one day?" They couldn't control their dreams. She usually forgot her dreams, but she distinctly remembered a few dreams over the years that featured her brother and mother. They'd become more common since Hunter's sessions began. Something she did her best to hide.

"I have. Though I do not know if they appear accurately in my dreams or not."

Yeah, that made sense. All this time away from her brother and mother, she supposed things could be different. The shamans could've found a better way to treat Dion. Maybe he lived a normal life. Which could mean her mother might've gotten the chance at love. The same applied to Grace and her brothers. "I guess it's hard to discern how they might've grown up. Or changed." While the female had asked her questions about Hunter, they had to be mindful of their conversations. Who knew what the walls could hear?

"Yes. They were so young when I last saw them. They are grown males now. I am sure... they are nothing like I remember them."

That was likely true. With all she'd learned about Hunter, she couldn't quite imagine what he was like at such a young age. "What was he like back then?" Really, she probably shouldn't ask, but she couldn't help it. There were so many things they just couldn't talk about. But this... they could. Their little secret.

"Very serious, even then. They had to fend for themselves unless someone snuck them food. Which, there were a couple of males that did, but they could only do it so often. Hunter would never eat even a single bite until Hayden insisted he was full. He rarely slept because he felt the need to always watch over Hayden. He even began training on his own at three. Not so that he could prove himself, like would be the case with most males there, but so that he could do all he could to protect his twin." A tiny smile played across her lips. "I would sneak in when I could to tell them bedtime stories. Hunter would sit by the door and keep watch. He would pretend not to listen, but... I like to think that he did."

She didn't have the heart to tell Grace any differently. At least, from what Hunter told her, he stood guard to protect Hayden. He always had.

"The first time he mentioned Hayden to me, he described him as the only good person in the family." Something Hunter had always wanted for the male.

Her forehead creased slightly. "Hunter does not think he is a good person?"

"No, he's always believed he's full of darkness." She didn't even think he felt he deserved her love. "He apologized to me so many times for screwing up. Not that I faulted him for hurting Sam, especially with all he told me."

"Sam deserved everything he got. If there is any darkness inside of Hunter, it is because of him and Azazel."

"I tried to tell him that, but he just pointed out that it wasn't his place to deal out Sam's punishment." She prayed someone killed Azazel. That male deserved nothing less.

"In my opinion, it was his place or Hayden's above anyone else's. Just knowing what kind of male Sam was, I can only imagine what they endured at his hands. I only hope Azazel receives the same, and as brutally as possible."

"The Seelie family that lost a child may not see it that way." Especially if they were nobility. That could be what caused her nightmares. Her experience with the Seelie showed her how unkind they could be. They'd seek revenge for what happened. But would they find Hunter at fault, even if he had done nothing? That was the part that worried her.

"I only have experience with a few Seelie nobles, but they were all pleasant enough except for one." Grace paused for a moment. "But Azazel was involved, too, right? Could they not get retribution through him? Sam may be dead already, but Azazel is not. He is just as much at fault."

"That's true. They certainly could." But what if he had spun some tale while Hunter had spent time with her here? There were so many variables she couldn't account for without more information. Gods, she hated this. Being able to find out what happened couldn't get here fast enough.

"But you do not believe that they will. At least, not totally." Grace gave her arm a gentle squeeze, her fingers lingering briefly. "We just have to have faith... and pray. That is all we can do right now."

"I'll try." She'd promised Hunter that she'd keep her spirits up. If nothing else, she had to stick to that as best she could. Narcissa glanced over her shoulder. "Thank you, Grace. I don't know if I could get through this alone."

"You will never have to, Nia. I will always be here. Promise." Wrapping her hand around hers, Grace gave it a squeeze as well. "I am always here to talk, too."

"I'm grateful for that." It certainly made things easier, having the female to talk to regarding Hunter. Even though they had to be careful about what they said. That didn't matter. As long as she had Grace, she could handle that.

"I am grateful for you as well. More than I can say." Grace squeezed her hand once more, then curled up more beneath the blanket. "We should try to get some sleep."

"Alright." They definitely should. Maybe now, with her mind truly settled, she could pass out. Narcissa burrowed further under the covers, and as she did, she found her mind replaying the intimate whispers she'd exchanged with Hunter.

"Good night."

"G'night," Narcissa mumbled. Warmth spread through her chest as she closed her eyes, replaying their joyful adventures with a gentle sigh. Though it took longer than she would've liked, a peaceful slumber finally came, claiming her.

Narcissa's bathroom surrounded him. Hunter held her close in the warm water of the tub. She ran her fingers up and down the back of his neck. His face was nestled against her throat, his lips against the mark he'd given her. Narcissa's intoxicating scent was all he could smell; it overrode everything else, completely taking over his senses. There was water dripping nearby. However, the tub's faucet was off, as was the sink, both silent. The shower wasn't turned on, and no water came from the nozzle. Strange...

Outside of the constant drip, drip, drip *of the water, all Hunter could hear was the steady beat of Narcissa's heart. Despite the nagging feeling that danger lurked, he remained calm. Hunter couldn't bring himself to focus on anything else but her, though. The warmth of her skin against him. Her slender form in his arms. Her cinnamon-brown hair draped across his shoulder, back, and chest.*

Without warning, the room was plunged into darkness; the shadow swallowing every detail. Even with his exceptional vision, Hunter could no longer see anything but the two of them and the tub they were nestled in. His voice sounded around them, as if it were someone else speaking. It almost sounded as if it was even echoing around the room.

"Even though a lot of things are ending... at least we both know that the way we feel about one another will never change. We are always going to have that. We are always going to have the lacunas we have spent in this room. The words we have spoken to one another. All the firsts we gave to one another. The touches, the scents, the tastes." His body moved as if by instinct, or as if controlled by another, as he gently tilted her head to the side. His tongue traced over the shape of the mark on her neck. "And this. This mark, and the one you gave me. Just because it is... our end... does not mean everything is ending."

Hunter brushed a tender kiss across her lips. He pulled his hands from the water, took her face in his hands, and met her gaze once more. His voice echoed in the small space, sounding distant and unfamiliar, as if it was coming from someone else in the encroaching darkness. "I need you to promise me something. Can you do that, Narcissa?"

"I can promise to try."

"Promise me that after today... you will not let that light in your eyes go out. You will not let your heart go dark or your soul die. I do not want you to forget me. I want you to remember the things that I know I made you feel. The things that you made me feel. I want you to remember that they are possible. And I never want you to forget... that you are so much more than this.*"*

The salty scent of her tears, welling in her eyes, almost choked him. Propping up on her knees in his lap, Narcissa stroked her fingers along the nape of his neck and pressed her forehead to his. "I promise." More tears trickled down her cheeks.

A deeper crack appeared in his heart.

"Always mine, Narcissa. Do not forget that."

Absolute silence descended, broken only by the faintest breeze. Hunter could no longer hear the frantic thump of her heart against her ribs. The dripping sound from its source had stopped, and there was a heavy quiet.

But it didn't last long. Powerful booms resounded off the invisible walls, as if someone—or more than one person—sought to break down the door. Hunter tried to pull Narcissa close, but his legs felt like lead. A monstrous crash sounded, followed by the sound of splintering wood. Thundering footsteps came closer and closer. But he couldn't move. And he couldn't see who was coming for them. Or for her.

"Always mine, Narcissa. Do not forget that."

Figures emerged from the shadows with obscured faces, their forms connected by hands and bodies. They grabbed at her, wrapping their fingers around her flesh in a grip so tight she immediately bruised. Narcissa's scream was cut short as she was ripped from his arms and dragged from the tub. As hard as Hunter jerked and fought against his invisible bindings, he couldn't break them. "Narcissa! No!"

"Hunter! Hunter! I'm sorry! I'm so sorry! I love you!"

"Narcissa!" he roared.

He felt trapped as the walls of Narcissa's bathroom closed in on him. From somewhere in the shadows, he could hear her furniture and equipment turning to dust with a soft, persistent hiss. She was pulled farther and farther away from him until he could no longer see her. But he could still hear her screams.

Then, lights out.

When things became clear again, the bathroom was long gone. Now, he was back in the prison. How had he gotten here? Where was Narcissa? He couldn't see anything but shadows instead of other people. Shadows and the bars that he couldn't touch surrounded him. From within the darkness, Azazel's voice resonated. That wasn't right. That shouldn't be right. Azazel was dead.

"Did you know she begged for her life to end? After I watched over a dozen males have their way with her, she begged for it all to just be over. And I ensured she got exactly what she wanted. Then I walked away with more coin than I would have earned here in this village in a solaris."

"Where is she?!" Hayden screamed. "Where is Elisa?! What did you do with her?!"

Azazel's chuckle boomed around him. "Perhaps you should also pray to the gods that I do not lose my life. Because if I do... you will never know.*"*

But he'd already lost his life. Azazel was dead. Hunter had watched him die, then watched his body burn into ash. He was dead... DEAD. Azazel couldn't hurt them anymore...

His father's paw appeared from the darkness, claws fully extended. They swiped through the air, followed by Hayden's agonized yell. Blood splattered across the floor, the metallic scent filling the air.

Azazel laughed again, but the screams of a female soon overrode that noise. It was Elisa. Had to be. Not that he could remember her voice, but instinct was telling him he was right. As the coins jingled, some of them skittered across the wooden floor. With a sickening crunch, the sound of flesh being torn apart filled the air as Elisa's screams escalated into raw agony. He launched himself at the bars of his cage, the sound of metal against metal filling the air as he disregarded the immediate, excruciating pain. His fur disintegrated first, followed by blisters that covered the flesh of his hands. Before his very eyes, his hands melted. Every bit of skin, muscle, and sinew dripped off of him, until there was nothing but bone left. His ferocious roar echoed through the mostly empty space.

Through the pain that clouded his vision, and all other senses, Azazel's voice echoed again. "Fuck both of you. Oh, wait... I already have."

Drowning in darkness again, a sharp, searing pain seized him. Hunter felt it over every inch of his body, inside and out, as if a physical presence. Though he could see nothing, the scents and noises around him changed. Sweat. Blood. Semen. Claws sank deep into his hips; the crunch of bone was a sickening sound. His body was invaded again and again. Grunts and growls from Azazel. Snickers and lewd comments from Sam and others who surrounded them.

"I already have."

Out in the woods.

"I already have."

Down by the river.

"I already have."

In Azazel's hut. His head tilted back, and he felt the sting of the spirits as they were poured over his face.

His agony persisted, and his sight remained obscured, while the piercing screams of Narcissa and Elisa echoed around him. As Elisa's voice faded into a choked gurgle of blood, all he could hear was Narcissa's frantic screams for help. His Narcissa. Screaming for him.

Her screams didn't stop. Ripped away from his attackers, he was thrown into the middle of Métamorphe's clearing, the ground hard beneath him. Shackles appeared on his wrists and ankles. Spotlit by the sun's rays, Narcissa stood before him, a radiant figure just a step out of reach. She was shackled, too, but each arm was held in a tight grip. Devin appeared, though her eyes were red. As red as Markham's would get sometimes when he used his abilities.

"Hunter. For your crimes, I sentence you—"

As the queen's voice trailed off, jaws closed around Narcissa's throat. Hunter's scream filled the air, twisting his voice to a strained, hoarse sound. Fangs bit down on Narcissa's throat and—

Hunter shot up in bed, and the sudden movement made him fall off, landing on the floor with a thud. Sweat stung his eyes as he pushed himself up, his hands and knees trembling. His eyes darted around, taking in every detail before they finally rested on the window. Blinking rapidly, he focused on the sun, its orange light just beginning to bleed over the horizon. Once he could fully take that in, he allowed his gaze to scan the room. He focused on the wood that made up the walls. A rock kept the bedroom door open, so he wouldn't feel the suffocating weight of being closed in. Through the door, he could see the dining room, sunlight spilling across the polished table. The wall displayed drawings Hayden had commissioned. The only one Hunter wanted to see wasn't there. And it never would be.

Two weeks. It was just two weeks of house arrest. He could do this.

No, the fuck he couldn't.

He forced himself to his feet and stumbled toward the kitchen, the urgent knocking on the front door finally penetrating his daze. The nudges in his brain. Hayden tried to break into his head. No way he hadn't felt everything.

Dream. It was just a dream. Just a dream. Narcissa was alive. *Alive!* And Azazel was *dead*.

Making it into the kitchen, Hunter gazed upon the spotless countertops. He threw open the fridge. Completely empty. Every single cabinet. Nothing. Not a fucking thing. Not accurate on any front, but there was just nothing he wanted. *The* thing he wanted. Not a drop of fucking spirits in this house.

Because he was banned from them. For a fucking year. On the queen's orders. Another part of his punishment.

With a resounding slam of the cabinet door, Hunter pivoted and marched into the dining room. With a shove, the chair went over, clattering against the floorboards. His claws dug in, gripping his head with a force that was impossible to break. He paced through the dining room, his footsteps echoing, then across the front room, and back again. All the while, ignoring Hayden's nudges and knocks on the door.

As much as it shattered him, he forced his mind to bring up what Narcissa had looked like right before he'd left her room. Just as heartbroken and terrified as he was. But alive. She was *alive*. This separation was only temporary. Two weeks—nearly one-and-a-half now—and he could return. Wrap his arms around her. Bury his face in her neck and inhale her scent. And show her with his body just how much he loved her.

For as long as they had left.

Hunter's footsteps echoed as he paced the front room, the floorboards groaning under his restless feet. Caged. As big as his house was, all he felt was fucking caged. The pounding on the door got louder, more insistent. As did the nudges in his head. As much as he didn't want to, he let Hayden in. Not that he allowed him to speak first.

I am fine. Just leave me alone. Please.

Fine. *Right*. Probably the first actual lie he had ever told his twin.

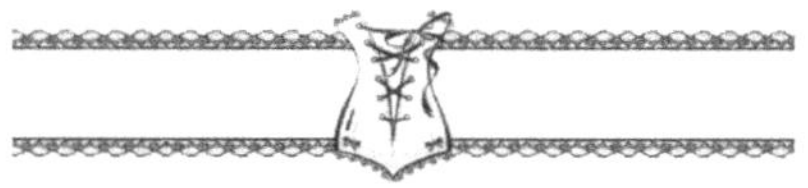

Narcissa crossed one ankle over the other before reversing the position. No matter how she repositioned her body in the chair, she couldn't get comfortable. The book shut with a soft thud as she arched her neck, leaned back, and closed her eyes to the silence. The warmth of the sun on her face couldn't lift her spirits, sadly. Nothing she did helped.

Four days had passed since the last time she'd seen Hunter. He'd never missed a session prior to today. That didn't bother her. It was the lack of knowledge regarding his well-being. Was he alive? What happened when he returned to his village? As she'd told Grace, she'd spoken to Jezzy the day before. Although the female agreed to give her a few minutes alone with Clay, he didn't come back until the next day.

The waiting was killing her.

Maybe if she got away from the bench and attempted reconnecting with the earth, it would help. All she could do was try. She had to get out of her own head. The proprietress couldn't discover the attachment she'd developed for Hunter. With a surge of energy, Narcissa rose to her feet and strode toward a nearby tree. The distinct click of her high heels resonated with each step she took. She stopped outside the grassy area, the soft grass beckoning her, then slipped off her heels, picked them up, and took a step forward.

She felt the coarse blades of grass press against the soles of her feet. A soft smile settled across her face. It reminded her of the last time she'd seen her mother and younger brother.

The wind rustled as the sun-dappled leaves crunched beneath their feet. Narcissa halted in her steps and pointed to a small group of tall trees. "That looks like a pleasant spot. We should sit there." She'd intended today's adventure as a picnic and introduction. A friend of hers agreed to take care of her family in her absence. Hopefully, everything went well.

"We can eat now, Cissa?" her brother asked.

"Yes, we can, Dion. Let me just clear the leaves. Okay?" She gave Dion a moment. It always took a second for him to comprehend what she meant. With anyone, really. His mind worked differently from everyone else. Not that she nor her mother loved him any less for it. After confirming his understanding, Narcissa called upon her earth magic, sending the vibrant leaves swirling and conjuring fresh grass around the tree's roots.

Dion's hands came together with a resounding slap after he let out a hearty, booming chuckle. "Again, Cissa! Again!" he cheerfully pled.

Seeing the way his green eyes sparkled, she couldn't deny his request. Especially as she had to leave her family soon. Who knew when she'd ever get to see them? Or if she'd see them one day after this at all. "Alright, but just once." Using her magic, she reversed the process, and then made the leaves disappear, and regrew the grass.

Dion leaped, reaching for the falling foliage as it swirled gently downward. He chased after the leaves, but didn't run off too far. Monitoring her brother, Narcissa watched out of her periphery as the leaves drifted off into the sky. They danced along as if they had no cares in the world. The life that wouldn't exist for her. That didn't mean she couldn't give that to her family.

Her mother hooked her hand around Narcissa's arm. "This was a wonderful idea, my dear. You did not have to do this for us."

"Yes, I did, Mama." Although they hadn't discussed it, her mother knew she planned to leave. Someone had to provide financially for all the care Dion required. That responsibility had fallen to her since they'd parted ways with her father over a hundred years ago. It was the only way both her mother and brother remained safe. No one could know they had survived. Not even their queen.

"Come along, dear." Her mother patted her hand, lifted her dress, and started toward the tree. "We did not spend all morning on the bread to let it go to waste," her mother called over her shoulder.

Narcissa wiggled her toes against the cool, tickling blades of grass. Although the sun's rays shone through the glass roof above, dew didn't get into the building. Not even in the cooler month of Autumnus. They were only at the beginning. Things would change a bit as they entered wintertime, but that was still a few months away. Gods, that meant she hadn't seen her family in over thirty years. They'd enjoyed that picnic at the end of summer.

She sighed, the sound echoing softly as she sank onto the ground beside the tree. A leaf fell, landing in her hair. She plucked it free and twisted the stem with her fingers. She couldn't decide which was worse: Hunter, a constant thought, or her mother and brother, whose memories flickered in her mind. Both could get her into a lot of trouble.

Not that she could control either.

Dion paused in the chase he'd given a drake. His body tensed as he gazed at the darker part of the forest over his shoulder. "Heavy footsteps. Seventy-five paces away. Seventy-four, seventy-three... Cissa?"

Jumping to her feet, Narcissa rushed over to her brother's side as he continued counting down the distance between them and the newcomer. She gently rested a hand on her brother's shoulder, her fingers brushing against the fabric of his shirt. "Hey. It's okay. That's just the friend I told you about." It was imperative that she calm him before Tiza's arrival. Otherwise, everything would blow up in her face before it even got started. None of them could afford that happening.

"Your friend?" Her brother tilted his head. "Which one?"

"The one with the pretty hair. Do you remember?" Months had gone by since she'd introduced them. Not that back then she imagined Deacan would

leave them nothing upon his death. At least she'd found somewhere for her family to go. Even if it meant they had to live without her.

Her brother's jade-green eyes brightened. "Yes!" he proclaimed loudly. "I touched his pretty hair."

"That's right." While she hadn't gotten the chance to warn Tiza ahead of time, the male had taken her brother's reaction to his hair like a champ. If it had bothered him, Tiza hadn't uttered a word about it. Instead, the male had simply smiled warmly at her brother. She'd met no one so kind before. Although Deacan had taken care of her family for a hundred years, it hadn't come without a cost.

"I like him," her brother replied. "Fifty paces."

The four of them had gone off to Tiza's home after spending some time together. She'd stayed for three days, helping her family get settled. Once it appeared they would get along just fine, she'd left and found her way here. Narcissa pressed the back of her head against the rough bark of the tree trunk. Gods, she had to stop thinking about this. If only she hadn't developed feelings for Hunter, none of this would've come up.

Gods, tomorrow couldn't come soon enough. Then maybe she could shove every ounce of love she felt for him into the recesses of her mind. Along with the things she recalled about her family. Then she could let go of the last promise she'd sort of made to him.

"You deserve everything." Hunter brushed a kiss across her lips, his fingers tracing the curve of her cheek. "I want you to do something else for me. I want you to keep trying to get free. If you are successful, whether you are let go or you escape, take your family and go to my queen. Regardless of my crimes... as my mate, she would keep the three of you safe."

Narcissa stared at him. Her thoughts briefly returned to the conversation she had with Shalla. 'You need to get that out of your head. Don't ask, don't even think about it,' the female had said to her. She couldn't bring herself to break his heart by telling him they were trapped, but she could promise to try. Even if it was one promise she wasn't sure she could keep. Slowly, she nodded. "You do, too. Regardless of what you think, you deserve so much more than you've been given."

She even left out the part about his sister. The one he believed dead, but who was very much alive. Narcissa dragged a hand through her hair, feeling the strands slip through her fingers as she drew her knees to her chest and pressed her face against them. What the fuck could she do?

All these promises. The one to Grace, another to Hunter, and the most important one she'd ever made—to herself and Tiza.

"Are you positive you want to do this?" Tiza asked, the scent of his floral cologne filling the air as he swept his teal hair over his shoulder.

"No, but I have to do something. Dion requires a lot of attention. That doesn't include the cost of his regular shaman visits." His temper could get out of control if they didn't keep him medicated and on a strict daily schedule. One that he followed like clockwork. "My money is almost gone. Work in the marketplace... it just won't cut it."

Tiza took her hands within his own. "That doesn't mean we can't figure it out. We'd find a way, Narcissa."

"As much as I appreciate your support, this is the way." She'd promised herself a long time ago that her family would want for nothing as long as she lived. The gods had seen fit to give her a long and strong life. She just had to keep up her end of the deal. "I'll have most of my earnings routed to you. Whatever you need to cover Dion's expenses." Narcissa produced a deep-blue velvet pouch and held it out to him, the fabric soft. "This should take care of the next cycle. It'll give me time to get set up."

He let out a heavy sigh and accepted the bag. "I don't like this, Narcissa, but I see I can't change your mind." Tiza enveloped her in a tight, warm hug. "Be safe, my friend."

"I will," she whispered as she returned his embrace. "Take care of my family." After stepping out of his arms, Narcissa gave a curt nod before disappearing into the deep, quiet forest.

The promise she'd made to herself. That's what she had to focus on. Lifting her head, she brushed her hair back, inhaled the earthy scent, then exhaled slowly. Narcissa collected the book she'd brought along, her high heels, and stood. Remembering what mattered the most, and why she'd come to the den in the first place, would carry her through. Hopefully tomorrow, Clay had some good news to share. If not, well, she'd think about the people who depended on her. It was all she had.

Narcissa strode to the footpath, slipped on her shoes, and started toward the door. Before going to her bedroom, she took one last look at the courtyard, the scent of flowers filling her nose. Hunter was a dream. A good one, but still a dream. That was what she had to think about. Nothing more.

Hunter's head hung over the toilet as he vomited up the nearly nonexistent contents of his stomach. Again. It had been like this periodically since he'd been forced to quit drinking a few days ago. Getting better, though, a bit more every day. Seemed to be the only thing that was. It would probably help if he could put adequate amounts of food into his stomach, but that wasn't happening. He just had no appetite for food. What he wanted—needed—was inaccessible to him.

Nine days, seven hours, and thirty-seven minutes until his house arrest would end and he could go see Narcissa again. She was what he needed above all else. The only thing that could calm him. Ease his constant pain. Make him feel... normal. Like he wasn't some fucked-up piece of swine for all the shit he'd done, and that had been done to him. Narcissa was the only one who had ever made him feel like he was worthy of being loved. And that he could truly love someone else in return.

Nine days, seven hours, and thirty-five minutes. Thirty-four, thirty-three. It would be his mantra until he finally stepped outside the walls of his home again.

And four-hundred-eighty days, seven hours, and thirty-one minutes until he could legally drink spirits again.

He sure as fuck wouldn't survive for the rest of his life with no way to shut the demons away. Time was running out for him and Narcissa, and that time had been cruelly shortened. Once they were separated, his only solace from the impending agony would be the numbing taste of alcohol.

Gods, if it weren't for Hayden, he might seriously consider ripping his throat out as soon as his soul fully betrayed him. Because a male without their mate was no male at all. They were nothing. He'd seen it before. Bardin's death was the most recent example.

His body shook as he pushed himself up off the floor. Took him three tries, but he managed finally. After flushing the toilet, he stepped into the shower. Hunter only turned the cold nozzle on, and then he leaned against the shower wall, feeling the icy water cascade over him. The chill in the air failed to register, yet it was the only remedy for the uncomfortable, feverish sweats. Another byproduct of alcohol withdrawal. He didn't have anyone else to blame for this. He'd done this to himself, self-medicating with alcohol for decades just to quiet the thoughts in his head. The voices. The memories. He was going to have to learn to live without the vice for now. Or deal with more prison time on top of it. It was only temporary, though. Long-term temporary, but temporary.

As the water continued to completely soak Hunter's fur, a knock on the door came simultaneously with a nudge in his head. Reluctantly, he opened up just enough to receive the words.

Hunter... I am here to get things ready for dinner, Hayden thought to him through their mindlink.

Fuck. Right. That fucking dinner he was supposed to sit through with his twin and Clay. Couldn't they just pretend he was there? Not like he would bring anything to the table conversation-wise. And the steak was probably going to go to waste again because he wouldn't be able to do anything but nibble at it. Then it would sit in the icebox again until it dried out and tasted like shit.

Hunter...? Is it... alright if I come in?

No, it wasn't okay. He didn't want to fucking do this. Hunter dug his claws in, savoring the coppery tang of his blood as he gripped the back of his neck. Most definitely not the blood he wanted to smell. Fuck. No. He couldn't disappoint Hayden like this. His twin had been through enough in the past few days. His incarceration and trial. Sam and Azazel's death and ceremony. The truth about Elisa, such as it was, only brought more unanswered questions and doubt. As much as Hunter might despise even the idea of this... Hayden needed this.

Yeah, sure, Hunter finally answered back. *Come on in. I am in the shower.*

Thank you. The front door swung inward, then clicked shut with a muffled sound. *A shower is good.*

Right. Not like he was actually washing up or anything. Though he really probably should. *Yeah.*

Clay should be here soon. He said he is bringing steak and fish. I just have a few other things I wanted to get set up. Take your time, though, okay?

Yeah. Thanks. Momentarily closing down to his twin, Hunter forced himself to pick up the bar of soap. This wasn't the scent he wanted. He wanted *hers. Her* scent coating him. Not this... whatever the fuck this was. Some kind of woodsy scent he couldn't put his finger on in his current state of mind. Whatever. It would get him clean. But as he grabbed his sponge and loaded it up with suds, all he could think about was Narcissa. When they had sat together in her tub, she had loaded up a sponge and gently washed him.

Gods... that session was one he could never forget. Even long after he truly and completely healed from everything it had brought up from the deepest recesses of his mind. But those memories weren't what he thought of. As Hunter set down the bar of soap, the water cascading over his skin, and ran the sponge over his body, he fixated on the memory of Narcissa, when she had done this to him. It might have been the only thing that allowed him to keep his hand moving. One step at a time. Cleaning off his body for the first time since this fucking house arrest had started. Though he vaguely registered Hayden doing the same. Or at least sponging him down during the first or second day when his withdrawal had been the worst. He'd thrown up more at that point. In between babbling about shit, not that he could say what. And it hadn't come up between him and his twin.

Cedar with a hint of jasmine. That's what he needed his soap to smell like. Something to remember the next time he could travel to the marketplace. Hunter's hand stilled with the sponge at his shoulder. He'd stroked her cheek and traced patterns on her hip. Their gazes had remained connected. Jade green with flecks of yellow. He inhaled and exhaled a deep breath. In the same order as Narcissa had done, he washed his body.

First, his right shoulder. She had straddled him before washing his left. Then his neck, chest, ribs. Stomach, left arm, and right. Left side and hip, then the same on his right. His armpits and pelvic region followed. Left leg. It had tickled when she ran the sponge over the bottom of his foot. He'd told her he wasn't sure he liked it.

"No? Is it too close to smiling?"

Hunter washed down the front of his right leg, then worked on his thighs. She'd slid her hand under his leg, and he'd bent his knees. The look on her face had revealed her complete terror at Hayden's culinary creations. After Hunter finished the underside of his legs, he turned his attention to the tight muscles in the back of his shoulders. Narcissa had sat behind him by now. Once she was done with the back of his shoulders, she'd taken the sponge lower. And she'd told him he was nothing like his father.

"I think you simply did what you had to do to survive. Not just for you, but for Hayden. Because, surely, he wouldn't have made it without you. Not with what you've told me about him. You made the sacrifice so Hayden didn't have to. Azazel would never have done that. You're the one who took what he did and used it as fuel. It didn't tear you down. You used it to strengthen yourself, better than anything Azazel could ever hope to be. That's the simple truth."

If only that were really true. Hunter washed his dick and ass before rinsing off the sponge. One thing he'd learned through his time with Narcissa and over this incarceration was that, in reality, deep down, he wasn't strong at all. Strong physically—absolutely. Strong emotionally—never. Why else would he have had to self-medicate all these years? Why else would he be completely unable to deal with his inner demons, even still? If he couldn't bury the memories, pretend none of it had ever happened, he couldn't function at all. And how utterly *weak* that was.

In that room, just the two of them, Narcissa had set his demons free and didn't just heal the wounds they'd inflicted. She'd healed his soul. So, why did he still feel so broken?

"For the record, I don't think there's anything wrong with you."

"You are in the minority then, if you believe that."

"I can accept that."

Hunter finally set the sponge back on the shelf. He cupped his hands and filled them with cool water, then splashed it on his face, the invigorating wetness scrubbing his palms up and down. After repeating the action multiple times, he shut off the water and groped for a towel.

"About fucking time!" Clay hollered from the kitchen. "Get your ass out here; we are starving!"

Do not listen to him, Hunter. We are fine, Hayden thought to him.

Fuck. *Fuck.* At some point, he'd inadvertently opened his mind back up. At least to some small degree. Enough that his twin could get words through to him. How the fuck had that happened? And how much had Hayden gotten from him? However much his twin didn't let on. And Hunter didn't answer. After drying off his fur as best he could, he hung his towel on a hook next to the shower, the metal cool beneath his touch. He pressed his palm to the icy wall, pinched the bridge of his nose, and took deep, shuddering breaths as the familiar wave of nausea threatened to wash over him. Nope. He would not get sick again. He'd just have to take it easy at dinner. Nothing new.

With one more deep breath, Hunter opened the bathroom door and stepped out into the hall. He didn't rush as he made his way into the kitchen.

By the table stood Clay, pitcher in hand, his nose scrunched up as though he smelled something unpleasant. "You blow chunks again?"

Hunter nodded once. "That you still smell that is uncanny."

"Curse my amazing nose right now." Clay set the pitcher down on the table. It had a reddish-pink tint. Hayden was always making flavored water of some kind or another. This one smelled like a combination of raspberries and strawberries.

A couple of baskets of rolls, a large bowl of salad, two platters of sushi rolls, some soup that Hayden had been working on for a week, and a second pitcher of purple water were spread across the table. The scents coming from the kitchen indicated there was fish just about finished cooking, along with a steak. His stomach grumbled and rolled, alerting him to his hunger while simultaneously warning him that any food consumed would not remain. Great. This was going to be just *so much fucking fun*. He felt utterly awful, his body aching and his mind clouded, wanting only to be near the one person he had zero access to right now, and avoiding conversation.

Oh, yeah. This little experiment, or whatever the fuck it was supposed to be, was going to turn out just *fucking fantastic*. Hunter reached up, pinched the bridge of his nose again, and rubbed his tired eyes. All he could do was be as polite as possible while he tried to get through this.

Hayden stopped in the doorway between the dining room and kitchen. Worry furrowed his brow, creating a deep crease on his forehead. "Would you like me to mix up those herbs for you?"

"No, thank you. I am through the worst of it now." Hopefully.

His twin opened his mouth, likely to make an attempt at protesting his decision, but Clay beat him to the punch.

"Do not be a pussy. Take the fucking herbs. Because the last thing I want you doing is getting sick when I am trying to eat my dinner."

Hunter raised an eyebrow. "Weak stomach?"

"Hardly. But wasting food—and good food, by the smell of it—should be criminal."

True, especially with how they'd grown up. It didn't matter that things had changed around here; sustenance was still a thing of value and always would be. "Will you shut the fuck up about it if I take the damn herbs?"

"Possibly. But you are going to take them either way, because you need to eat."

"He is right, Hunter. You have barely eaten in *umbras*."

Clay hooked a thumb over his shoulder at Hayden. "What he said. That, and you have never been one to worry Hayden on purpose. Not that I know of."

Resisting the urge to roll his eyes, Hunter grumbled under his breath as he headed into the kitchen.

"Whatever you need, Hunter, I can get it," Hayden said, half-following behind him.

"Please do not coddle me. I feel like shit; I am not dying." Even though it felt like it. He pulled a cup out of the cabinet, the wood cool beneath his fingers, and filled it with water from the tap, the rushing sound filling the kitchen. As he slowly sipped the drink, the taste of the drink made him wince, and he regretted snapping at his twin. None of this was Hayden's fault. And his twin had gone to a lot of trouble to put this meal together. He really needed to at least *try* not to be an asshole. "Everything smells great. Do not be surprised if I eat little, though."

A slow smile spread across Hayden's face. That possibly could have been the first time he truly complimented Hayden on his cooking. "Thank you. I can, um... I can always put whatever is left in the icebox, so you can eat it later."

"Yeah. Sure. That would be great."

"Can we eat already?" Clay called out.

"No one is stopping you," Hunter said, taking another sip of water.

"Well, Hayden wants us to eat *together*, so get your ass over to the table, please." Clay smirked, then headed into the kitchen. He grabbed a towel, then, with a grunt, opened the oven and removed the steaming fish. After setting the tray aside and turning off the stove, he started arranging the food, including the steaks, onto the plates Hayden had laid out. He flicked his gaze over to Hunter, then made a *shooing* motion with his hand. "Go. We have got this."

And if that sight wasn't the weirdest fucking thing he'd ever seen in his life. Both Hayden and Clay were in the kitchen, getting a meal ready together. Hunter shrugged, refilled his cup, then headed back into the dining room. Whatever. If they wanted to carry the last of the plates in, they could have at it. He sat at the head of the table, the familiar wood cool beneath his hands as he took a sip of water, before leaning forward. His gaze passed over the spread of food again, settling on the salad. Not something he could ever remember eating before, simply because it hadn't ever interested him. He'd tried a couple of different vegetables over the years, but none of them had appealed. Staring at the leafy green things in the bowl, his curiosity piqued. Hunter reached out and snagged one, bringing it to his mouth. And... yeah. That was nasty. He chewed and swallowed, though his face betrayed none of the internal struggle. Hayden and Clay were reentering the dining room. Grimacing at something Hayden had put together for their meal—or, gods forbid, spitting it out—would definitely hurt his twin's feelings. He just wouldn't put any on his plate. Not that he'd been planning to, anyway.

His plate of steak appeared in his vision. Hayden's hand had placed it in front of him, along with a second cup that held the herbal mixture. Hunter gave a slight nod of thanks, but didn't dig in yet like he normally would have. The damn steak was so fucking huge, it nearly overtook the plate. There was no way he was going to eat even half of that right now. But he choked down at least half of the herbal mixture. That was some kind of progress, at least.

Hunter half-zoned out while Hayden and Clay took their seats with their plates of meat. Hayden just had fish, while Clay had fish... stacked on top of a steak.

"You really can use another plate if you want to, Clay," Hayden said, as he filled a couple of cups with flavored water. "I do not mind taking care of the dishes."

"That is good, because I have never done them before." Clay chuckled, and the sound echoed slightly as he picked up his knife and fork. "Nah, this is good."

Hayden's eyebrows raised slightly. "You are going to eat them... together?"

"Sure. Who knows, they might taste good together." He smirked. "Only one way to find out."

Hayden watched as Clay cut a bit of both, raised his fork to his mouth, and popped the whole mouthful in. He chewed slowly, then swallowed. "I think I am going to go with... interesting. Not sure the flavors are supposed to mix, but they are not bad."

Hunter extended a claw and cut a small piece off the edge of his steak. He had silverware, of course, but using his claw was such a habit. Picking up the piece, he pulled it into his mouth and chewed slower than he'd ever chewed on a piece of food before. Already, he could tell it wouldn't sit well on his stomach, but he had to try to at least get something in. As he went to cut off a second piece, Clay reached over and picked up his knife, setting it on the edge of his plate.

"So, what are all those again?" Clay asked Hayden, as if he had done nothing. He nodded at the platters of sushi rolls.

"That is called sushi. Rainbow taught me how to make it. We have made several kinds together, but I just made a couple, in case either of you wanted to try them."

"Rainbow. That is your... mate, right?"

Hayden practically beamed. "Yes, that is her name."

A slight look of discomfort passed over Clay's face. Like Hunter, he wasn't used to being around people who could easily get so cheery. "So, what *exactly* is in them? The sushi?"

Hayden pointed to one platter. "That one is the Lunar Roll. It has seaweed, rice, crab, avocado, and cucumber in it. But I made some without the seaweed, too, just in case. I think it is an acquired taste. And that one has seaweed, rice, shrimp, and salmon inside, with tuna, salmon, and yellowtail on top of it. Similar to the first one, just with more layers, and I made some without the seaweed, too. It is called the Rainbow Roll."

Clay raised an eyebrow. "Rainbow, huh?"

"Relax," Hunter said as he raised a third small bite of his steak up to his mouth. Completely ignoring his knife. Maybe another day, he'd get *adventurous* enough to use one to slice up his dinner. "It is not like you are eating his mate. They just have the same name." Immediately, he flicked his gaze to Hayden. "Sorry. If that offended or anything." His gaze dropped back to his plate.

Hayden briefly gripped the back of his neck. "Um... it is okay. Thank you for apologizing." His eyes darted from Hunter to the sushi, then to Clay, back to the sushi, and finally landed on the shadowy liquid between them. "Oh. That is eel sauce. To dip the sushi rolls in. It has a sweet and salty taste."

Clay nodded slowly. "Right. Hmm. I will give them both a try. Once I get some room on my plate."

Without even realizing he was doing it, Hunter checked out of the conversation then. His finger traced through the juice from his steak. Gross, maybe. But he half didn't notice, half didn't care. He wasn't sure how long he sat like that before Clay kicked him under the table.

"Eat."

Hunter briefly looked up at him. "I did."

"Three bites."

"You are counting how much I eat now?"

"When you are starving yourself with or without meaning to, yeah."

"That is not what I am doing. Just feel sick. Eating makes it worse." Hunter glanced over at Hayden. "I am trying, though. Promise. And it is good."

"I know you are, Hunter. And thank you." Hayden paused for a minute. "We can... talk about stuff. If you want. Anything you want."

"That is not something I am up for." He'd rather endure the excruciating pain of breaking all his fingers and toes than utter a single thought. "But appreciate the offer."

"Of course. Anytime."

Hunter cleaned off his finger, then forced himself to slice another piece off of the steak. He barely looked up when Hayden placed the warm rolls next to his plate. Pieces of his brothers' periodical conversation reached him, but Hunter barely paid attention to any of that, either. The sooner this was over, the sooner he could just go back to bed. It was that or pacing. And he was too tired to pace.

In between talking about some kind of poultry meal he'd put together, Hayden reached over and broke the rolls up into pieces. Hunter, his interest piqued, idly watched him without a word. Once his twin had finished, Hunter took a roll and dunked it into the rich juices from his steak. Better than sticking his finger back in it. He chewed slowly, swallowed, then picked up another. It settled just a little easier on his stomach. Maybe this was the answer. There were pieces of potato and other vegetables, by the looks of it, in the soup, but maybe he could handle the broth. It would put something else in his stomach, anyway.

Hunter finished the first roll, and part of the second before he stopped. After taking a slow sip of water, he stared at the enormous slab of meat, still untouched on his plate. Normally, the thing would have been long gone by now.

"That... was fucking fantastic," Clay said as he set his utensils down on his plate. "Even those sushi things were not half bad."

Hayden's face brightened, as if a lamp had been switched on. "Thank you, Clay. We can do this anytime you want. Or... you know, I can just... cook for you, if you would prefer that."

"Nah, I think I can handle a few dinners. Maybe..." He shrugged. "... maybe you can even teach me a thing or two. I am not very good at cooking for myself. I get by, but it is nothing like this."

If it was possible, Hayden's smile got even wider. "Yeah, absolutely. I would be happy to."

Clay gestured down at his plate. "That steak reminded me of how your mom made them."

Hayden's eyes immediately went misty, and he blinked a few times. "Re... really?" he asked quietly.

"Uh... yeah. Really. The way she could prepare venison had it practically melting in your mouth. Yours was not exactly the same, but pretty damn close."

"Yeah?"

"Mmhm. Giselle—your mom—she loved to cook. Never having said so out loud, I could just tell."

"How?"

"She always seemed more at peace after being in the kitchen. I guess I cannot really say if it was the cooking itself, or just being around all those other females, but I think it was the former."

That had been a nice thing for Clay to tell him. Though Hunter could do without the tears about to pour out of Hayden's eyes. He didn't need to feel that depth of emotion from his twin. Especially not when he was trying to bury so much of it within himself.

"What else... can you tell me about her?" Hayden asked.

Without waiting for their brother to answer, Hunter pushed his chair back with a loud screech and stood up. He picked up his plate and both of his cups. Mid-sentence, Clay's gaze flicked over to him, watching as he made his way slowly into the kitchen. Not that Hunter acknowledged the look both he and Hayden gave him. He placed his plates on the counter, then wrapped up the remaining steak, before putting it in the cold icebox. Hunter rinsed out his dishes, left them in the sink, and dried off his hands. Then he left the kitchen and headed down the hallway to his bedroom.

A chair scraped slightly, then stopped.

"Let him go," he heard Clay mutter.

Though he didn't want to be bothered, Hunter left his bedroom door propped open. He crossed the room, crawled into bed, and curled up on top of the bedding. The light of the moon reflected off the wall. Was Narcissa staring at the moon right now? Did she miss him? Was she having trouble sleeping? Did she think his life had ended? Gods, if he could only tell her the truth. That his punishment wasn't as dire as all that. Soon... Soon, he could go back there and show her that he was still alive. That they still had time to figure things out. To be together... somehow. They still had time...

Seventeen

Narcissa stepped out of the courtyard, walking by the back rooms as she headed for Jezzy's room. It had been six days. Six long-ass days since the last time she'd seen Hunter. After a night of nightmares, she sought refuge in Grace's room. As Hunter had missed his appointment, and she couldn't tell if he was alive or dead, this was her only option. If only Clay's appointment hadn't coincided with Kylen's. Not that she gave a shit. So what if it meant she'd snuck out of her own bedroom and left him waiting.

This was too important.

She didn't have time to remove her black suede knee-high stiletto boots, so she walked as quietly as possible down the hallway, the heels clicking softly against the floor. Narcissa gently tapped on Jezzy's door, then pushed it open, not bothering to wait for a response.

"You couldn't have given me two seconds?" Jezzy faintly snapped as Narcissa slipped into her bedroom.

"Not exactly. I'm on a bit of a time crunch." Which didn't matter, because Clay wasn't in here yet. Damn it.

With a roll of her eyes, the female secured her bathrobe and folded her arms across her chest. "You just need a few minutes, right?"

"Yes, that's all I need." Unless Clay questioned what she wanted to know for any reason. A possibility she hadn't entirely considered, but the risk would be worth it.

"Alright. He should be here shortly." Jezzy crossed the room with a determined stride and paused at her bedroom door. "I'll be back in about five minutes. That should give you plenty of time."

"Thanks, Jezzy. I owe you one."

The female waved it off and left the bedroom.

Thirty seconds passed before Narcissa paced the length of Jezzy's room. The rug, a plush oasis in the room, muffled the sharp click of her stilettos on the hard wooden floor. Fuck, she needed Clay to get here sooner rather than later. Not because she left Kylen waiting in her bedroom. The dread of not knowing Hunter's fate twisted her stomach, and she couldn't find a moment's peace. No matter how much she tried to maintain control, each day it got a little harder. She didn't know how much longer she would last without knowing.

As the door swung open, Clay entered the room. His footsteps almost immediately froze. With his eyes narrowed, he pushed the door closed with a slow creak. "What the fuck are *you* doing in here?"

Stopping mid-pace, Narcissa let out a sigh of relief. Thank fuck, Clay finally showed up. She was getting really fucking antsy here. "I just need to talk to you. Five minutes tops, and then you can have your session with Jezzy." For whatever they did. Call her selfish, but at that moment, she didn't really give a fuck.

Clay leaned back against the door, the wood groaning slightly under his weight, and crossed his arms over his chest. "Talk to me about what?"

Well, wasn't this going to be fun? Had he always been an ass? Granted, she *did* kind of just take over his session. Not that it mattered, because he had information she needed. "Hunter." Gods, it was the first time she'd said his name outside of Grace's room or hers. Narcissa paused for a second, but nothing happened. Small favors.

His eyebrows shot up. "You know, I was asked about you a few days ago. Six, to be exact. If I knew you, or knew if you were associated with him. Not that I had an answer to that." With a shove, Clay crossed to the bed and settled onto the queening bench sitting against it. Leaning over slightly, he rested his forearms on his knees, and clasped his hands together. His eyes scrutinized her for a moment. "You look like you are about to get *really* mean if I do not answer your questions. And no one working here would come after a client to ask questions about another client, related or not, unless there was something more than a worker-client relationship going on. So... I am going to take a guess and say... you two are into something you should not be?"

Who the fuck had asked questions about her? Not important. Narcissa folded her arms across her chest, the leather of her stiletto creaking as she contemplated how much to reveal. As much as it pained her, she needed him. "Something to that effect." Although she could've said more, she opted not to. Yes, knowledge of Hunter's well-being was a must, but that didn't make her heartless or a bitch regarding Clay. While she had no clue how much progress Jezzy had made with him, she also didn't want to stifle any the female might have made.

"Okay. What do you need to know?"

Good, he asked nothing more, since she couldn't really say a lot. At least, she shouldn't. Nor should she be in here, but it had become too much for both her and Grace. Okay. Her question needed to be simple, but straightforward. "What punishment did he receive?" Narcissa steeled herself for his reply, her knuckles turning white as she balled her hands into fists against her frame.

"Well, he thought he was going to die right until sentencing was actually given. I think he almost passed out when the queen gave him his. He just got house arrest for two *penumbras*, though. Yes, he broke the law, but the circumstances being what they were..." Clay shrugged. "Oh, and he is banned from drinking alcohol for a *solaris*."

House arrest. Two weeks. "Oh, thank gods." Her shoulders dropped, and her muscles relaxed as a sense of relief coursed through her. With her hands now resting on her hips, Narcissa stared at the floor, fighting back the tears that threatened to fall. She could cry later when it was just her and Grace. It provided scant relief, so she crouched down, and clasped the back of her head as she buried it between her knees. *Holy fuck, he's alive.*

A few tears pricked the corners of her eyes and rolled down her cheeks. He was alive. No drinking—yeah, she was fully on board with that plan. Two weeks. She'd see him in another eight days. With a deep inhale and exhale, she let out a gentle, airy laugh. Finally getting a hold of herself, she rose to her feet and strode across Jezzy's room, into the female's bathroom. Throughout her... episode, for lack of a better term, Clay had done nothing but sit there, frozen. "I'm sorry," Narcissa called out. With a couple of tissues, she dabbed her face, feeling the soft fibers against her skin, and then headed back into the bedroom. "The last six *umbras* have just... I'd rather walk through Hades's realm than deal with that again."

"It is all good. You, uh... you really care about him, huh?"

Yeah, he could say that. Not that *care* was a strong enough word in this case. Far from it. As if her small breakdown hadn't been enough of an answer. Still, Narcissa nodded. "Something to that effect."

"Well, I would not say he is doing all that great, but he is alive. So, there is that. Hayden—his twin, in case you do not know—makes sure he eats. Though it has been rough going a time or two, from what I understand. I thought it was just because of the alcohol withdrawal, but now I am thinking it is probably more than that." He re-situated, then Clay leaned back against the bed frame. "What else did you need to know?"

Shit. That wasn't good. Not that she could say things had been much different for her. If it hadn't been for Grace and Silva, she probably wouldn't have eaten anything over the last six days. Was there a way she could use Clay to get word back to Hunter? No, Hunter had described Clay to her, but he hadn't mentioned that Clay actually went to the brothel. And he sure as fuck didn't need to know how she and Clay knew one another. Eight days. Hayden was making sure Hunter ate. At least there was that. She'd just make sure he had the best 'welcome back' that she could think of. A smile spread across her face, bright as the morning sun. "Um, nothing. That's all I needed. No, wait." There was one more thing. Something she could find out for Grace. "What about Azazel?"

A slow expression, almost a grin, spread over his face, and the tips of his fangs showed. "Dead. Totally willing to give you the details on that, too."

Not really necessary. Nor did she have the time to get them. "Good. I hope it was slow and painful." At least he could give her that much.

"Very. And humiliating for him. In my opinion."

"Probably not as much as he deserved." Even without details, she could say that. And it would be the best news she could deliver to Grace. "Thank you." He'd given her all she asked for and more. And she had a client to get back to. Whoops. "Obviously, this goes without saying, but we never had this conversation." Narcissa started for the door and paused. She glanced back at Clay. "I'd say that Hunter's the exception to that, but it's probably best he doesn't know how we know each other."

"What conversation?" He rested his arms on the armrests of the bench. "Are you sure you do not want me to say anything to him? I will never say a word to him about... *that,* but I am sure I could come up with something."

Hmm, how could she pass up an opportunity to get a message to Hunter on the outside? Clay could be discreet. If nothing else, they at least agreed on one thing. With what had popped into her head earlier, she had just the thing to pass along. "Actually, I have a message for him." Something needed to accompany her words, though. Oh! She knew exactly what to do. Keeping her back to Clay, Narcissa slipped her hands under her dress and wiggled out of the thong she'd worn for a good hour. Kylen didn't really need to tear them off. "Tell him, 'Build your energy now. When you return, I'm giving you the bad-girl treatment.'" It might sound dirty and confusing to Clay, but to Hunter... well, he'd get the picture.

"The... Okay... I do not think I want to know what that means... but, you got it."

"For the record, he described you to me. Might help you come up with something to tell him."

"Yeah, that will help. I will take care of it."

Narcissa set the tiny piece of fabric on a nearby table by the door.

"Your panties? Seriously?"

Facing him, Narcissa gestured to the little black dress, the fabric clinging to her as it zipped up the back, and the sleek knee-high boots. "Do you see anything else on my person I could give him?" A smirk stretched across her face as she folded her arms across her chest. "Besides, he'll like it."

"Point taken. On both fronts."

Yeah, definitely not something else they needed to discuss. Her eyes gleamed, and a gentle purr echoed in her chest as she walked toward the door. She paused with her hand on the doorknob, the polished metal cool against her skin, and looked back at him. "Thank you, Clay. For everything. It means more than you can imagine." Knowing that Hunter was alive didn't just alleviate all she'd felt for days, but it would help Grace, too. The sister none of them knew was alive. That gave her one additional pause, something she could ask on Grace's behalf. "Hayden's female... is she a good person? Someone who makes him happy?"

"Well, Hunter just told you everything, huh?" he teased. "Yeah, I think so. I mean, I do not know her well or anything, but I have always been observant. It seems like she has been good for him. And from what I have seen, she makes him happy. She might actually be the *only* thing making him happy right now. He is still a bit of a mess over everything that happened, but getting better. Rainbow is keeping him pretty grounded. Outside of what Hunter is going through, I think he is still dealing with Sam and Azazel's deaths. Hayden might have been the only person who actually gave a shit about either of them. Not because he liked them, just because that is the type of person he is. He is going to be fine, though, and we are all better off."

Yeah, Hunter had told her a lot. More than she'd ever reveal. Except for Hayden's female's name. What kind of name was *Rainbow*? Her eyebrows furrowed a bit. Was the female happy-go-lucky or something? "I'm glad to hear Azazel's dead. He deserved it." For a multitude of reasons. It was good to know Hayden would be alright, though. "I'll leave you to your appointment now."

"Thanks. Take care of yourself, Nia."

"You, too, Clay." With a dip of her chin, she stepped out of the room, pulling the door shut behind her just as Satin and Jezzy strode her way. Well, that was good to know. Narcissa acknowledged the two of them. "Mind if I ask, what number?"

Jezzy raised an eyebrow. At no point over the last couple of decades had Narcissa ever questioned her about a client, even one she passed onto her.

"Two," Satin responded.

Hmm, only two. Just the beginning. They probably had a way to go before Clay fully transitioned. Although... Narcissa stepped up to Satin, stood on her tip-toes a little, and whispered in his ear. While Jezzy had been working with the guy for a bit, there were things she knew about him that others didn't. If Satin stepped up his game and used it, he might give Clay a bit of an extra push.

Satin's eyes widened ever so slightly, and he nodded at her words. "Oh, I can *definitely* do that."

Settling back on her stilettos, Narcissa grinned. Clay would appreciate her suggestion. "Have fun." She wiggled her fingers and made her way back down the hall.

"Sure," Jezzy replied.

Maybe she'd check with them later and see how it all went. At least the news he'd shared gave her some comfort. She might even sleep in her own bed tonight. With a subtle nod to the guard, she pushed through the heavy oak door and continued into the courtyard. Before she climbed back through her bathroom window to her patiently waiting client, she needed to update Grace. Narcissa walked through the door on the other side of the courtyard, her footsteps echoing softly, passed Silva's room, and stopped in front of Grace's. She rapped on the door with her knuckles. Seemed the best way to keep her client from discovering her location.

The door opened about a minute later. Grace opened the door wider and ushered her in. After closing the door, she opened her mouth as if to speak, but then she shut it once more. "Is everything all right?"

"I don't have a lot of time, so I'll get straight to it." How long had she kept Kylen waiting? Probably longer than she should have. "Hunter is fine. He's under house arrest for a couple of *penumbras* and banned from alcohol for a *solaris*. Oh, and Azazel is dead."

Grace's hand shot out, her palm pressing against the wall. Tears welled in the corners of her eyes. "Thank you... very much for telling me."

"You're welcome. I figured you'd want to know sooner rather than later. Alright, I'll see you in a few *lacunas*. Need to get to my client." Before backing away, Narcissa gave Grace's hand a reassuring squeeze, a silent promise. "He's fine, and we only have a little over a *penumbra* before he's off house arrest." No way would Hunter miss a session after that.

"Let me know how he is... after you see him. Thank you again. I will see you later."

"I will." Quietly, Narcissa slipped out of her friend's room and made her way back to the courtyard. Her bathroom window faced it, so she could climb in through there.

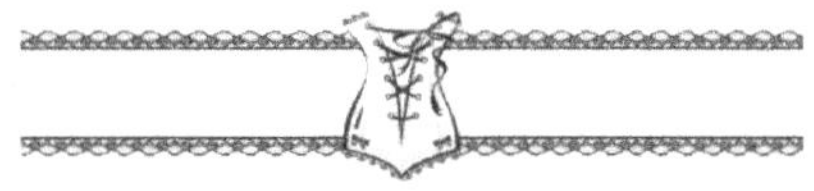

Leaning back against the pillows, Narcissa flipped the page, the scent of old paper filling the air. After what happened in their last session and the one he'd missed, she didn't know if Fallon would show up for today's or not.

All of her professionalism the last time they were together had gone out the window. She'd broken one of her own rules. All because of Hunter. She wouldn't change her history with Hunter, but she'd change the painful events that unfolded between her and Fallon. It was why she'd done the unthinkable and had Fallon reassigned. Given how long she and the male had been together, Shalla allowed her to handle the change however she saw fit.

The words in front of her competed for her attention with the delicate strap of her peep-toe high-heeled sandal. Narcissa smoothed it out and then, with a sigh, returned her attention to the book. In case Fallon showed up, she'd dressed for their session. Today she'd selected an outfit he'd purchased for her. A tan, elegant, spaghetti-strapped lace romper. It perfectly accentuated her breasts. So as not to make it too easy, she'd pulled on a pair of tan shorts. Those, combined with the tan and floral decor of her heels, complemented the outfit well.

After some time, the door opened and closed, though Fallon didn't appear. Which meant he'd come in camouflaged again. Narcissa waited patiently, keeping her eyes half on the page of her book.

Fallon cleared his throat quietly before removing his camouflage. His gaze was aimed at the floor. "I... I do not think I can... do this. My apologies. I should just..." He turned toward the door, abandoning his words, and placed the satchel of fragrant herbs onto a shelf with a gentle thud.

"Fallon, wait." Narcissa tossed the book in her hands aside and climbed off the bed. Fallon's shoulders tensed. "Can we talk? Please?" They'd spent nearly thirty years together. She'd known him long enough to know how much he blamed himself for what had happened. It didn't matter if the fault lay with her. Though, from the brief glimpse she'd gotten, this was so much worse than she expected.

Without turning around, Fallon nodded. "Okay."

"I know you blame yourself, even though it's not your fault. What happened... it's all on me. I took advantage of you and pushed every button I knew you had to get what I wanted. While I don't think I can apologize enough, I hope that, one day, you'll forgive me." Narcissa paused, lingering near the bed as she wrung out her hands. "Obviously, this changes our relationship in ways I don't know if we'll ever get back. Although I hope that's not the case. You're one of the few friends I have."

A few minutes passed before Fallon spoke. When he did, his words came out quiet. "I can never place the blame anywhere but on myself. It does not matter what the cause was, or what buttons were pushed. I nearly killed you... and there is nothing that can change that. No amount of guilt, regret, or anything else felt by either of us... will ever take back what I did to you." Fallon inhaled deeply, then exhaled with a visible tremor. "You are... the only friend that I have. I wish I knew how to... fix things between us."

The two of them were essentially the same, molded from the same material. No matter what the other said, they would always take the blame upon themselves. Something that would probably never change. She didn't deserve his kindness right now. "I know we've been together a long time, but... maybe it's time for someone else to meet your needs. Please don't think this is a reflection of you. I just think... you deserve better."

"Of... of course," he whispered. "Um..." As he reached up to wipe his face, he tried to be discreet, attempting to hide his emotions. "You are the only one who has ever... willingly given me what I need. But... of course. I understand. Will I still be able to... see you again after this?"

Oh, gods. She'd told him too soon. Damn it. She just kept messing things up. Narcissa took a couple of steps forward. "Of course. I'm always here for you, Fallon. I'm not blaming myself, so you don't, or assigning you to someone else to punish you. That is the furthest thing from the truth. I wasn't even close to death. That's not why I used my safe word. I could've healed myself with ease. Fallon, I..." Her words trailed off. Had she even explained any of this better? Or simply made things worse? Narcissa dropped a hand to her hip and let out a heavy sigh, the sound echoing softly in the quiet room. "I've always thought that one day I could make things better for you. That I could help you, I don't know... find yourself, maybe." Was that the right way to describe it? She knew how much he hated the type of sex he had to have. Very few females in the den liked the idea of rape fantasies. While it wasn't among her favorites, she enjoyed the pain, which did wonders with it.

"You say you were not close to death... so you must not have realized how close my claws came to your spine."

No, she hadn't realized that. Not even once all the pain had truly registered during their last session.

Fallon held his neck as his head gradually dipped downward. "I know you have always wanted to help me, Nia, but... I do not think there could ever be any real help for me. I know what I am. What I am always going to be."

It was pointless to argue with him regarding blame. Something she'd learned a long time ago. "I'll never believe you're beyond help, Fallon. I'm just not the right person to get you there." Something she should've seen much sooner. In that sense, she had truly failed him. Not that he'd accept that, either. So, she didn't say it.

Fallon finally turned around, the tension visible as he crossed his arms over his chest. "Did you... have someone in mind already? Is there even anyone else here that would be... willing?"

"I do, and I've already talked to her about it. She joined the den a few *solaris* back, and she's looking forward to taking you on as a client. We set time aside for you today in case you wanted to meet her."

"How much..." His words trailed off as he worked his jaw a moment. "How much did you tell her?"

"I told her everything I thought she needed to know. Different scenarios you and I have played out over the *solaris*. Things you like, things you don't. Your triggers. I answered questions she had, too." Stuff that any well-trained worker needed to know before they took on a new client. While there were some similarities between her and Nina, there were *a lot* of differences between them.

"And she is... *looking forward* to... having *me* as a client? What if I..." Fallon paused. "What if I hurt her... like I hurt you?"

"You won't. I promise." Narcissa couldn't explain it, but something about the woman made her think Nina would be a perfect match for Fallon. "She has more experience with your particular fantasies. And enjoys them."

Fallon rubbed a hand over the top of his head. "I will trust you on that. I..." His eyebrows pinched together. "I guess I could... meet her. Though I still want to see you. If I can. Even if I have to pay for it. That is... if you would still want to. I do not have anyone else to talk to about, well, anything."

"I still want to see you, too, Fallon. We're friends. That won't ever change. At least, I hope it doesn't." They had a connection that she'd always need. He was someone she'd leaned on throughout the years. Narcissa slipped her hands into the pockets of her shorts. "If you don't like Nina, then we'll figure something else out. Okay?"

"Okay," he whispered. Fallon flicked his gaze up to hers for a moment. "You are far too kind to me, Nia. You do not have to say it, either; I know we will never agree on that."

"No, we won't." At least they could agree on that. With a slight nod, Narcissa gestured to the door. "Are you ready to meet Nina? Or did you want to hang out here a little longer?"

"I can go meet her now. I guess that would be... okay."

"Okay." Narcissa started for the door. "And just so you know, we don't have to hang out in here when we spend time together. We could always meet in the courtyard and bask in the sun a little."

"That would actually be really nice. At least... well, at least for now."

"Then we can do that." Whatever he wanted. She owed him that much. More actually, but he'd never accept it from her. Just like he'd denied her help with the damage she'd caused him. "I'll show you how to get there before we go to Nina's." They could even walk that way.

With a subtle nod, Fallon trailed behind her, carefully closing the door with a soft click. "I did not even know there was a courtyard here."

"I think only those who utilize it know about its existence." She led him to the left, her footsteps echoing in the hallway, until she reached the door and pushed it open. It surprised her that he hadn't noticed it out the window in her bathroom. He'd used it several times over the years.

"And we can take books and things out there?"

"Absolutely." Narcissa strolled forward, leading him into the courtyard. With a dip of her chin, she gestured toward the vibrant collection of trees, flowers, and the gentle burbling fountain. Despite the scattered benches and inviting spots to relax, she'd never spent much time here. Maybe once or twice a week. At least, since their time in the marketplace had become a bit more restricted. She had to get sun and fresh air somehow, and this worked as a little oasis for the workers.

Fallon's gaze swept over the courtyard's features before a subtle smile played on his lips. Not that it lingered. "It is nice out here."

"Yeah. There's a pleasant spot in the corner there." Narcissa pointed it out. "Makes it easier to deal with all the light that filters in from above." Something she couldn't really handle a lot of, though she could in small doses.

Fallon flicked his gaze over to where she indicated, but didn't comment on it. Halfway across the courtyard, his fingers brushed against her shoulder. "Nia..." His voice trailed off, and it took him a minute to continue. "I do not think I will ever be able to apologize enough, either. And while I know you feel as though my apologies are unnecessary... I hope, one day, you will forgive me, too."

Narcissa paused in her steps. She lifted her gaze to him. It hadn't occurred to her until that moment that, with neither of them blaming the other, how could they ever truly forgive one another? Could they both be looking at this the wrong way? She tilted her head. "Maybe we need to try forgiving ourselves. I know that probably sounds strange, but it makes sense. I don't think it's your fault, and you don't think it's mine. As far as I'm concerned, there's nothing to forgive, Fallon. I don't believe you did anything more than what I wanted you to do." She'd simply let it go too far.

"I do not feel as though you have anything to apologize for, either. I am not very good at forgiving myself. For anything. It is part of the reason I left Métamorphe. That and... fear of the possibilities if I stayed."

"I'm not very good at it, either. Maybe it's something we can work on together." Although she couldn't say it, she believed, in some part, it was why she had come to the den. While her family needed her financially, they lived a much better life without her physically around. This was a place where emotions didn't exist. And she liked that, because she didn't deserve them.

"I would like that."

"Alright then." Narcissa started forward, and Fallon followed her. What more could she say? She didn't even know how they'd forgive themselves. It wouldn't be easy. That much she could admit, at least to herself.

"So... you really think she will be a good fit for me?"

Not a question he needed to ask. She wouldn't have set this up if she didn't think so. Conversation had a way of quieting his mind somewhat, though. "Yes, there's just something about her and how she carries herself. My gut tells me that the two of you will fit well together." Narcissa glanced at him, her eyes flitting back and forth as they walked along the path. "I'm never wrong about these things." It had happened in the past. Usually with one-offs that she'd taken on, but this was different.

A small smile touched his lips. "Somehow, that does not surprise me." Fallon briefly shifted his gaze toward her. "Change is just a weird concept for me, I guess. Not something I am used to. Everything was the same throughout my entire life. Now it seems as if everything wants to change all at once."

"I get that. But sometimes it's inevitable. We move through different stages of our lives. With that comes change." Even the things happening around the den seemed out of place in one way or another. Not that she could explain any of it. Most days, she just kept her distance and watched. It was better that way.

"I have never really felt like I went through different life stages. Not until recently, anyway. In some ways, I feel like my life moved from one kind of monotony to another. Though I get to do more things now. So, I guess that is good."

"I'm not sure if we ever truly recognize them. At least, not until some kind of change happens. Then, it's easy to take notice. You get used to stuff being one way or another, then something throws it all off kilter. Maybe even alters your path." Hopefully, for the good, but she didn't say that. It could be hard to feel like things were good under certain circumstances. "Maybe you're still in a fairly young life stage. There's nothing that says they have to last for any particular amount of time, or that they have to occur at any particular age." Narcissa opened the heavy door that they'd been walking toward, the wood groaning in protest. She dipped her chin to the guard on the other side and gestured for Fallon to go first.

Taking her cue, he passed through the doorway before her. Though he glanced at the guard, his gaze didn't linger. The shape shifter said nothing nor acknowledged Fallon. He waited for Narcissa, and the echoing sounds of their footsteps filled the hallway as they walked together. "I guess so. I kind of feel as though I should not still be trying to get my bearings. Like, enough time should have passed by now that…" His words trailed off and he shrugged. "I guess I feel like I should be used to all the changes by now."

"Really? It's been what—a *cycle*? Is that really long enough to get used to drastic changes? I mean, we're not talking about small things that you can just brush off to the wayside. These were life-altering." The new guards here proved it. And the change he was about to go through wasn't small, either. She'd had him as a client for thirty years. That wasn't a short period.

Fallon shrugged again. "I was raised to adapt to anything and every-thing without hesitation. My life depended on it. This is just the first time I ever remember feeling… kind of like I am in the middle of a colossal body of water and I do not know how to swim. If that makes sense."

"It does. The question is, how long do you tread water before you attempt to swim? Our base instincts are all about survival. For the first time, the opportunities presented to you go beyond that." Her pace slowed as they approached Nina's room.

"And there is where I find myself completely lost." Fallon slowed his pace beside her, his gaze darting nervously toward the door nearest them. He paused, staring before finally turning back to her. "I am sure I will find my way at some point. I just have to... look for the path for the first time in my life."

"I have faith in you." Narcissa stopped in front of Nina's door. It was completely unlike hers. Dark green with curlicue floral lines along the border. She rapped on the door with her knuckles. A moment later, it swung open.

A female with light-brown hair, partially pulled back from her pointed ears, and emerald-green eyes gazed back at them from the other side. A short, blue dress with a floral pattern adorned her, its vibrant colors contrasting the slight green tinge of her skin tone. The dress had triangular slits along each side, and a halter that tied around her neck. Her feet were clad in a pair of matching heels, ready to take her anywhere. "Hi," Nina said.

"Hello." Narcissa flicked her gaze to Fallon. "Fallon, this is Nina. Nina, Fallon."

"It's good to meet you." With a bright smile, Nina held her hand out to him.

Fallon blinked a few times. Then a few more. His mouth opened and closed in a silent, fishlike gesture, then opened again. He appeared to be stunned into a momentary, breathless silence. At last, he stretched his hand out, and their hands clasped with a gentle pressure as he accepted hers. "It is a pleasure to meet you."

Nina swept her tongue across her bottom lip. "Please come in." Releasing his hand, she stepped aside, and the scent of old wood filled the air as she opened the door wider.

Narcissa couldn't help but grin. The nuances in both of their reactions hadn't gone unnoticed. Yep. These two would be a good match. "Of course." She shifted her attention to Fallon. "Though, I believe I'm leaving you in very capable hands. So, I could just take my leave... unless you really want me here."

Fallon's eyes shifted rapidly, from her to Nina and back, before landing squarely on her, as if making a hard decision. "Oh, um... it is up to you. But I think we..." His focus shifted once more to Nina. "... we will be okay?"

"Oh, absolutely, Nia." Nina grinned.

"Alright. Have fun, you two." Narcissa clasped her hands behind her and strolled down the hall, her footsteps echoing softly. What would she do with the time she now had available? Hmm... maybe she could go down to the rehearsal room.

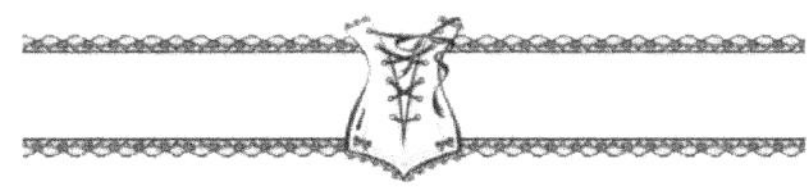

Hunter lay in bed, half-zoned out, as he listened to Hayden move around the front room. Though he'd eaten a bit more today, his energy continued to be depleted. As if something sucked it out of him, and he couldn't get it back. The vomiting and sweating had finally ceased, though. Gods willing.

A slightly muted buzz tickled his veins before a knock came at the door, but Hunter didn't move. Hayden could get it, or Clay—the only one outside of his twin that could cause him to feel such a thing—could go away. While his curiosity was slightly piqued at what the male was doing here, he was in no mood to talk to anyone. As usual, especially lately. His ears perked up at the sound of the faraway voices. A minute or two passed, and then the sound of footsteps echoed down the hall. Hunter's nose twitched.

Clay paused in the doorway, a frustrated shake of his head accompanying his grimace. "Is this all you plan on doing all day, every day? Shitty way to spend your house arrest, if you ask me."

Hunter slowly struggled to sit, the weight of his body pressing against the mattress as his legs went over the side of the bed. "When you get put on house arrest, you can make suggestions."

"Nah. I do not plan on getting into that situation, thank you very much."

He pressed his palms into the bedding and locked his elbows, the muscles in his arms straining to prevent his body from collapsing back onto the mattress. His eyes gravitated naturally to Clay's bag. For some fucking reason. "What do you want?"

"So nice and polite to your guest," Clay said sarcastically. Crossing the room, he leaned his hip against the footboard of the bed, the wood groaning softly under his weight. "Just brought you something, that is all."

Hunter raised an eyebrow. "*You* brought *me* something?"

"Did I stutter?" Clay put his hand on his bag. "Did you know I still go to the den?"

His gaze flicked up to Clay's face, then back to the bag, his eyes narrowed. "Never paid much attention, to be honest."

"Well... I do. I was there today, and your *friend* asked me to pass along a message to you. Along with a little gift to go with it."

His fr—Hunter's eyes flared briefly, then immediately darkened. For the first time since all of this had begun, hope and warmth flared within him. Narcissa. Narcissa had sent him a message... and a gift. "And this came together how?"

"You described me to her, I guess?" Clay shrugged. "They must all have a good idea of who each other's clients are, or know how to get the info, because she hijacked the beginning of my session today to ask about you. Wanted to know if you were okay." He smirked. "How sweet is that?"

Hunter almost told him to shut the fuck up, but he wanted—no, *needed*—to know what the message was. And the gift. "Well?"

Clay opened his bag—finally. Narcissa's scent automatically hit Hunter full-force, giving him an immediate erection. A growl almost escaped him, but he clenched his jaw to prevent the sound from echoing and possibly breaking his window. *Oh, Hades,* **yes.** Bless all the gods, she had sent something with her scent *all over* it.

His brother reached into the bag and produced a piece of small, black, lacy fabric, the delicate pattern catching the light. He tossed it to Hunter, who snatched it right out of the air. A pair of her panties. Fucking *perfect*. Resisting the urge to bring them to his nose and sniff the fuck out of her scent—for now; that was something he could do once Clay had left the room, among other things—Hunter felt a slight smirk appear on his face as he flicked his gaze back to the male. "And the message?"

A somewhat uncomfortable expression crossed his face. "She... well, she said..." Clay chuckled a bit. "This is word-for-word, mind you. 'Build your energy now. When you return, I am giving you the bad-girl treatment.' Do not worry, I did not ask what the fuck that is."

His smirk widened. The bad-girl treatment, huh? *So* many things came to mind at that. And every single one of them put such a beautiful image into his head. "I can tell you, if you want," Hunter said, only half-teasing.

"Nope, I am good. I do not need to know anything about your sexual proclivities." Clay closed his bag with a snap and pushed off the footboard, the wood creaking softly. "On that note, I am going to leave you with... that, and... see you later."

"Best idea you have probably had all day." As Clay made his way back toward the hallway, Hunter leaned back, the bed's springs groaning softly. "Close the door, please. I am about to need some *serious* privacy."

The look that appeared on Clay's face nearly made him laugh out loud. But he had *much* more pressing matters to attend to. Like the thick erection that was getting harder and harder between his thighs. As soon as his bedroom door was closed, Hunter buried his face in Narcissa's panties and inhaled deeply. Lava coursed through his veins, ignited by the intoxicating scent of her. Licking his palm until it was coated with his saliva, Hunter reached down and wrapped his fingers around the base of his rigid cock. His growl transformed into a low moan as he adjusted his hold along his shaft, pressing his thumb at the tip of his dick before gliding his hand back down.

With a grunt, he planted his foot on the bed and pushed up his hips with the next stroke. And the next. And the next. Stroke after stroke along his cock, each one harder and faster than the last. At no point did he stop inhaling the scent of Narcissa's panties. Nor did he stop envisioning her in his mind. The way she looked splayed out on the bed for him. Bound to the bondage horse. Locked onto the cross. Each time she moaned. Begged. Screamed when she came. The way it looked when she cried out his name.

Holy shit, he was already about to come. Fucking pathetic, but he didn't care. Not now. On the next stroke, Hunter squeezed the tip of his dick. That one little motion was all it took. He didn't let out a roar, but his growl rattled the window panes as his orgasm burst out of him. His release coated his pelvis, his hips, and even parts of his stomach. Hunter didn't stop pumping up and down his length until the very last drop emptied out of him. Then he just lay there, catching his breath. It would be a minute or two before he was ready to get up and clean himself off.

When he slid out of bed, the first thing Hunter did was hang Narcissa's panties off the corner of his headboard. Something he would easily see every time he entered his room. Have easy access to every night before he laid down to sleep—because who fucking cared if it was her panties? They were still coated with her scent and would, hopefully, help him sleep easier. Wouldn't that be nice?

Smirking, he glanced at the fabric once more before leaving his room and heading down to the bathroom. He would have to treat that strip of fabric with care. Because the next pair of her panties he got a hold of would most certainly not fare very well.

Gods, two weeks had been way too fucking long. Fourteen days—three missed sessions—of feeling like he'd been burning alive in Hades's domain. Being without Narcissa had become a perpetual agony he didn't know what to do with. Had it not been for Hayden damn near forcing him to eat, Hunter couldn't say if he would have even bothered making the effort. Likely not.

The words Clay—of all fucking people—had passed along to him had periodically played over and over in his head; though he heard them in Narcissa's voice, not his brother's. 'Build your energy now. When you return, I am giving you the bad-girl treatment.' What could she have planned for him today? Once again, all manner of things entered his mind. The outfits she'd so-far worn—and he'd ripped off of her. The equipment and toys they'd used. Even the different positions he'd devoured and fucked her in.

Hades, he had to get ahold of himself or he'd have a raging erection before he even stepped foot outside his home. It was already nearly impossible not to bolt out the door and sprint to the den, as it was.

After making sure he had everything with him, Hunter readied himself to leave and opened the door. Not that he exited just yet. His head tilted just slightly to the side. Marcell was headed this way. The male hadn't ever come to pay him a visit. Made him wonder what warranted this one. Intrigued, he stepped onto his porch, the wood cool beneath his feet, closed the door, and waited.

It took Marcell *way* too long to make his way up here. And even longer to open his mouth and *speak*.

After a couple of minutes of silence, Hunter couldn't help but break it. Either that or he broke the male's face. Because he needed to leave and get to the den. *Now*. "Did you need something, Marcell?"

The male gripped the back of his neck. "Yes, I do." His voice came out quietly and dripped with nervousness.

Hades save this male right now, because his patience was waning. Quickly. "*And*? What do you need?"

"Um... Actually, I... I was wondering if..." Marcell's voice trailed off.

"Not to be a complete and total dick right now, but there is somewhere I need to be. Right this very moment. So, if you cannot get on with it, or walk and talk, this is going to have to wait until another time."

"The den," Marcell blurted out. His voice dropped, becoming a hushed murmur. "The brothel. I heard that you... visit the establishment... frequently. Is that correct?"

And... his interest was certainly piqued even more now. "Yes, that is correct." Hunter paused for a moment. "Are you saying you want to go to the brothel, Marcell?"

The male's face flushed crimson, like a ripe summer tomato. "Yes, um... I mean... well..." He inhaled and exhaled a deep breath. Then another one. "Yes... I would like to go... there."

"I see." He waited for Marcell to speak again, but the male said nothing. "I am assuming you know the rule of 'by invitation only,' then."

Marcell nodded slowly. His gaze lowered. "I lost my... my mate... a very long time ago. I am not one for... well, casual sex, but... I just... I suppose I am just... quite lonely lately, and—"

"You do not need to explain anything to me." In fact, that was far truer than he would say out loud. Regardless that it had happened before his time, Hunter knew every detail. When one loses their mate in such a brutal manner, it was hardly a secret that was kept. More often than not, it was a story used as a warning to other females in the village. At least, that was how it had been in the past, before Devin had become queen. "I am going there now. If you have time, tag along. Even if you do not go through with a session today, at least I will be able to vouch for you so you can return at your leisure. After today, I will not return for four days."

Marcell nodded slowly again. "I have time now."

Hunter gave a nod in return. "Good. Then let us go. I have a session myself that I am *quite* anxious to get to."

Eighteen

Fourteen days had been far too long without seeing Hunter. Despite what Grace had previously suggested, Narcissa fully intended to have her time with him today. At the end of their session, she'd mention the idea of seeing each other less. Until then, she completely lived up to the message Clay should have delivered to Hunter.

Narcissa surveyed her room, making sure the arrangement of objects was exactly as she liked. She'd pulled out all the stops—every piece of equipment they'd ever used, along with every toy they'd ever utilized, was out. It had taken some effort to leave the working space, but she'd managed it. The cross stood close to her closet, its presence a stark contrast to the colorful clothes within, while the bondage horse sat near her make-up table, and the swing creaked softly from the ceiling. The queening bench sat against the dresser closest to the door. There had even been a few restraints added to her bed.

As for her, well, she completed the 'bad-girl treatment.' For today's session, she'd selected a piece of sheer crimson lingerie. Thin straps crossed her shoulders before attaching to a wide band that was secured at the back with a bow. The floral pattern took nothing away from the lacy material. It only seemed to emphasize the string bikini thong she had on underneath. To bring it all together, she added the necklace he'd given her after their first session, a matching belly-button ring, and a pair of strappy, crimson stilettos that zipped in the back. Her makeup was the final touch. She'd painted her eyes and lips crimson, too.

Sensing Hunter's approach, Narcissa took her place and kneeled on the floor in a submission pose.

The door opened. Hunter stepped inside, shut it behind him, and froze. Narcissa felt his gaze on her, though she couldn't see what held his attention, following the angle of his stare. Nothing but her. Like a delicious hum across her skin. It took every ounce of willpower to keep her eyes from meeting his. Especially as his breathing quickened and his heart raced. Then a low growl started deep in his chest, rising higher and higher in volume until it echoed around the room. Fuck, she had missed that sound.

With a swift movement, Hunter closed the space between them, his grip firm as he drew her to her feet. With how dark his eyes were, it didn't surprise her in the least when he led her to the bed, turned her around, and ripped her thong off. He didn't waste any time from there. He intertwined their fingers as he thrust deep inside her, their hands tightly clasped together.

"Oh, fuck!" he cried out.

"Fuck!" Narcissa cried out simultaneously as he fucked her hard and fast. Gods, yes. She needed him in a way she hadn't ever needed him before. They'd been apart for far too long. She clenched his hand as she matched his powerful thrusts with her own rhythmic movements. Her vaginal walls pulsed around him, and a loud moan escaped her as she arched her neck. "Gods, I missed you."

His cock repeatedly thrust into her core with force. Hunter's grip tightened, and each thrust grew more intense, kindling a deep, internal blaze within her. "Fuck... I missed you, too. Turn your head."

She did so immediately. As their lips met, the taste of his tongue sent a spark of electricity through her. Fuck, she'd missed him. Not just how incredible he felt, but his taste, too. She'd nearly forgotten how extraordinary everything with him felt. A sense of euphoria bloomed in her chest, sparked by his presence. As the kiss grew more intense, Narcissa moved against him with increasing urgency. At the rate they were going, it wouldn't take long before a massive orgasm detonated inside of her body.

Hunter moaned into the kiss. Releasing his hold on one of her hands, he reached down and gripped behind one knee, moving it up onto the bed. *Holy fucking shit.* The modification permitted him to advance further, drilling into her with even greater force. But, fuck, she needed more. It seemed like he did, too. With their lips still fused together and their tongues entangled, she did the only thing that came to mind, giving him exactly what their bodies required. Narcissa pushed her foot off the floor and, with a grunt, lifted her other knee to the soft mattress. Arching her back, she raised her ass a bit, and with a groan, rocked her hips back with greater force. Her vaginal muscles clenched and relaxed repeatedly, amplifying every movement of his cock. A deep, husky moan poured into the kiss at the sensations flooding her nerve-endings. Her orgasm was already right there on the edge, but she wasn't quite ready to let it go. Not that she could hold out much longer, either.

Hunter met her moan with one of his own, just as full of hunger and passion. His hand slid around in front of her, finding her clit and rubbing it vigorously. Breaking the kiss, he nipped at her bottom lip. "Gods, you feel so fucking good," he growled out.

"Fuck... so do you." Narcissa couldn't hold her orgasm back any longer. Not that she didn't try. But it hadn't just been her heart that had missed him. Her body had as well. She knew exactly what to say to make him cave and join her. "May I please come, Sir?" Narcissa purred.

He practically snarled. Hunter hoisted himself onto the bed, first with one knee, then the other, inching Narcissa forward. As he shifted, she hooked her legs over his. He then increased the pressure on her hand and intensified the stimulation of her clitoris. Hunter stroked his tongue up her throat as he ground his cock into her core. "Come all over my dick, Narcissa," he whispered in her ear. He bit down on her shoulder as a colossal orgasm exploded from him, accompanied by a deafening roar.

As Narcissa cried out his name, her release flooded out, soaking his dick, their thighs, and the bedding below. Her entire body shook from the power behind the orgasm, and it was just the first for both of them. They had two weeks to make up for. And she fully intended for them to do just that.

He moaned as he removed his fangs from her skin, licked his lips, and stroked his tongue over the puncture wounds he'd left. With his fingers still caressing her clit, he groaned as he withdrew his cock. Hunter bit through first one strap, then the other, of her lingerie. He took the ribbon in his teeth and, with a gentle tug, separated the two halves, unveiling her upper body. He quickened the pace and intensity of his fingers on her clit while also using his teeth to tear apart the remaining lower half. A low growl left him as he bit down on one ass cheek, then the other. Then he sucked and licked, his fangs grazing along, all the way up her spine until he reached the nape of her neck.

Fuck, everything he did had her gearing up for another orgasm. Hunter took the back of the necklace between his fangs and pulled on it; not enough to cut off her air supply, but enough that it bit just slightly into her skin. It brought a moan from her mouth.

He released the chain and nipped at her ear. "Where do you want me to tie you up while I devour this pussy?"

That was a good question. She'd gotten out so many wonderful pieces of equipment. The swing was a good option, and he could use the queening bench to sit. But it had been quite some time since they had used the bondage horse. And if they went back there, they could start a nice brief tour of the equipment, toys, and memories all at the same time. Narcissa purred again, her voice a soft rumble as she gazed over her shoulder, and he responded with a low growl of approval. "The bondage horse, Sir, seems like an *excellent* idea to me."

Hunter's tongue traced the curve of her throat. "Mmm. That seems like an *excellent* idea to me as well." Wrapping his arms around her, he picked her up, the soft fabric of the sheets brushing his legs as he backed up off the bed. As Narcissa encircled his waist, her body molding to his, his hands found her ass, and their gazes met, a silent conversation passing between them. Hunter carried her to the bondage horse, and as he nuzzled his fangs along her skin, she shuddered, her body arching into his. Narcissa groaned. Fuck, she missed this with him. As he set her down, he gently tugged at her belly button ring before reaching her pelvis, inner thighs, and ultimately, her pussy where he teasingly nipped her clit.

"Get in position, Narcissa," he growled out.

The most beautiful words she'd heard in what felt like forever. Oh, she'd get in position, all right. As she kept her eyes on him, Narcissa slowly lowered her back onto the bondage horse, feeling the cold leather against her skin as she stretched her arms and tucked her legs, placing her body on display.

Hunter licked his lips, then put the restraints on her. Each touch as he belted the straps pulled a moan out of her. He began by gently sucking each breast, then tightened the strap over her ribs. The cold metal of the belly button ring felt like ice as he gently tugged it before he belted the strap across her hips. As his fangs grazed her inner thighs, she could feel his warm breath, and then he belted the straps across her thighs and ankles. With her legs spread wide apart, Hunter nipped at her nub before moving around to her head. He growled, his voice a low rumble as his lips crashed against hers, his tongue delving deep while her wrists were secured by the soft-leather cuffs.

Fuck, lightning jolted across every nerve-ending in her body. Narcissa nipped at his tongue, savoring the moment before sweeping her tongue along the back of his fangs, which caused him to moan. Holy fuck, she'd nearly forgotten how much she enjoyed doing that.

Hunter broke the kiss, gently sucking on her lower lip, and then trailed his lips back down her body, creating a slow path until he reached her inner thighs. After getting back on his feet, Hunter backed away, only to grab the queening bench and set it up at the end of the bondage horse. As he sat down, his claws slowly traced the length of her body, coming to a stop at her inner thighs.

The sensations caused her to arch her back, straining against the cold-leather restraints. Fuck, it felt like it had been forever since his claws had touched any part of her body.

"I missed you," he growled. "Very much." His tongue stroked slowly up her slit.

Oh yes, she knew just how much he missed her. Well, at least that he *had* missed her a lot. That he fucked her seconds after he entered her room confirmed the truth of his proclamation. Still, it wasn't quite enough. "I believe you should show me just how much you missed me... Sir," Narcissa said, punctuating the last word. Something she rather enjoyed doing. Eventually, it would become his name, but not yet.

"Oh, I definitely plan on it, sweetheart."

Holy fuck, she loved hearing that word come out of his mouth. Almost as much as she loved when he uttered 'yes, ma'am.' Before she heard him say them, she never knew words like 'sweetheart' or 'ma'am' could be so fucking sexy. Hunter's claws gently traced back up her inner thighs while he licked her slit once more. A deep rumble vibrated from him. With no warning, he shoved his tongue deep into her pussy and fucked her with it.

As a husky moan left her mouth, Narcissa's back arched, her fingers curling against the rough feel of the cuffs around her wrists. The thing about the bondage horse—it restricted her movements, which meant she couldn't quite ride his tongue. Not that she didn't try.

His claws traced a line up her inner thighs, leaving a trail of fire in their wake, before returning to her hips. With a playful tug at the belly button ring, he moved closer, his hands now cupping her breasts. As he drove his tongue deeper into her pussy, the sounds he made grew louder.

Holy fucking shit. She didn't know what drove her crazier or what she missed more. Jolts of lightning speared her core, pulling an orgasm closer to the edge. Gods, he felt incredible. She just couldn't get enough. With each tug at her restraints, Narcissa pushed her breasts more firmly against the palms of his hands.

A rumble of satisfaction left him. Licking up her slit, Hunter nipped at her nub and sucked on it hard. Then he took it between his teeth, the tip of his tongue flicking against it relentlessly. His claws traced slow circles around her nipples. Her orgasm had already been riding the edge. But that certainly yanked it forward. Narcissa clenched her thighs and vaginal walls so tightly, she thought she might burst. She knew how much Hunter hated to waste cum. Between the continuous vibrations against her clit and the look on his face, he wanted her orgasm right then. "May I please come, Sir?"

Letting go of her clitoris, Hunter sensually licked up her slit once more, maintaining intense eye contact with her. "Yes, Narcissa. You may come." Then he thrust his tongue into her wetness and released a primal growl.

His noises had always done something to her body. That hadn't changed one bit. Releasing the tension in her muscles, Narcissa moaned his name as a powerful orgasm swept over her and spilled onto his tongue. One intense wave after another cascaded into his waiting mouth. Her restraints bit blissfully into her flesh, and she writhed against them, arching her back and rocking her hips. Hunter grasped her breasts without letting a single drop spill from her pussy.

Even when her orgasm ended, she didn't stop rocking her hips as much as possible, nor did Hunter stop fucking her with his tongue. One time wouldn't be enough… for either of them. It had never been. But this time they had a lot to make up for. And she fully believed they'd get it.

The sting from the restraints that held her down was absolutely magnificent. Between the way he kept at her with his tongue and his hold on her breasts, another orgasm wasn't far off. But she needed more. She had been deprived of him for far too long. "Harder," Narcissa purred. A sound that she knew drove him wild. His growl deepened. Driving at her harder, Hunter's claws pricked her skin while his grip on her breasts became tighter.

"Oh, gods!" Her orgasm yanked itself out of her so fast, she didn't have time to acknowledge it. Punching out of her body and erupting into his mouth, coating his tongue like lava. It wasn't as powerful as the last two, but it still had some force to it.

Hunter let out a growling moan, the sound echoing in the stillness as he devoured every single drop. His tongue danced along her slit as he grinned, a glint of mischief in his eyes. Licking his lips, Hunter's fangs grazed her inner thigh, then her pelvis, stomach, ribcage, until they reached her breasts. "Mmm... you did not ask permission to come that time." Delicately, he savored one breast, swirling his tongue around her nipple before releasing it from his mouth. "Should I punish you... or should I let this one slide because you taste *so fucking good*?" His mouth closed around her other breast, giving it the same gentle suckling as before.

A soft moan left her mouth. No, she hadn't. And it had been totally worth it. As for letting it slide, where would the fun be in that? In fact, she was fairly certain that, before this session was over, she'd absolutely do it again. It had been quite some time since she'd disobeyed him... since he'd punished her. It definitely wouldn't be the *bad-girl treatment* without a punishment. "Oh, I believe I should be punished, Sir." To emphasize her point, she purred, purposely drawing attention to her crimson-painted lips.

His gaze flicked immediately to her mouth. Hunter took her lower lip between his fangs, then his tongue swept across hers, and he released her lip. "Mmm. I believe that can be arranged." Standing tall, he moved toward the wall, his eyes scanning all of her toys. Hunter selected the first nipple clamps they'd used, then the vibrating dildo that strapped to her thighs, and finally, the vibrating butt plug. He also grabbed the finger vibrator they'd used during their fifth session before making his way back to the bondage horse. "I think leaving you restrained right here will work nicely. What do you think?" he asked as he set the vibrators down and got the nipple clamps in place.

Narcissa groaned. It wasn't her answer, but she had little time to reply to him. Given everything he grabbed, her current position would work fine for at least two of the toys. Well, three, unless he intended to use them together. "Mmm, I think that depends on what order you plan to use them." The butt plug wouldn't work at all with her ass against the bondage horse. Even if her legs weren't tucked back the way they were, it wouldn't quite work. He'd have to flip her over, which would kind of defeat the purpose of the nipple clamps. And the finger vibrator would work great with the butt plug, but not so great with the vibrator.

"I was thinking these"—Hunter tugged first one, then the other nipple clamp—"and this"—he picked up the vibrator and trailed it from between her breasts, to between her thighs, and stroked it up and down her slit—"for your punishment. Then I thought we could switch things up a little before we move on to something else—another piece of equipment." Setting the vibrator down, he picked up the butt plug and the finger vibrator. "Before we move on, I plan to turn you over and fuck this sweet pussy of yours with the plug in your ass, and this right here—" He briefly activated the finger vibrator against her clit before switching it off.

Holy fucking shit. The images alone that popped into her head turned her on even more than she already was. *Especially* when he mentioned fucking her with the butt plug in her ass. That made her purr. Too bad she hadn't thought to put the Ben Wa balls in before all of this started. They would've enjoyed those fuckers, just like they had in their fifth session together. "I completely agree, *Sir*. This will work nicely."

Hunter's hand trailed up her body and settled at the base of her head. He clenched a fistful of her hair, yanking her head up, just enough to meet his gaze. Leaning over, he put their faces just an inch apart. "You purr like that just to drive me completely fucking insane."

Yes, yes, she did. Well, sometimes. Other times, it just happened all on its own. Hunter nipped at her bottom lip. She couldn't help but purr as he kissed, licked, and sucked his way down her body. His growl vibrated against her flesh. He paused at her breasts, giving a sharp tug to both nipple clamps with his fangs before moving further down.

"You fucking love it." And he knew it just as much as she did. Oh, and yes, she purposely left off the word 'sir' in that little commentary. There were several things Narcissa did that drove him insane, and they both enjoyed every single last one of them. If they could spend the next couple hundred years doing them, well, wouldn't that be a dream come true? Even then, it still might not be enough.

Hunter's eyes darkened. Without a word, he nipped at her nub, then stood up fully. As he slid the vibrator deep inside her, his gaze remained locked on hers the entire time while securing the straps snugly around her thighs. Then, as he stood above her head, he raked his claws back up her body, the metal of the nipple clamps scraping against her skin again. He took his cock in hand and gently brushed her lips with the tip before moving his hips back. "You are going to suck my cock, Narcissa, until I come down your throat. You may not come until then."

Oh, fuck, yes! And she was going to enjoy every second of torturing the both of them. Hunter scraped his claws a bit more forcefully down her body, and dug them in deeper across her inner thighs. A deep growl rumbled from him as a few drops of blood bloomed on her skin. Gods, she loved that. With a loud moan, their gazes locked on one another, and she licked her lips. As one hand teased her, the other hand reached for the vibrator, switching it on to the initial, soft setting. Only the first setting, huh? They were both going to enjoy this punishment as he drew it out as long as possible.

Leaning over a little, Hunter pressed his cock against her lips. One hand went to grip the end of the bondage horse, while the other stayed at her pussy. "You should be doing something else with that tongue, sweetheart."

"Only my tongue?" Narcissa licked the tip of his cock, pulling a growl out of him. She'd done the same thing the last time she painted her lips crimson. Of course, that had been to torture him, and this... well, not to torture him, but to tease a little.

"You know better than that." As Hunter kept his pace nice and slow, he turned the vibrator up to the second setting, and he rubbed her clit harder.

Narcissa groaned. That she did, but she enjoyed tantalizing him. Now, she wasn't quite ready to do *exactly* what he desired, but a sneak peek wouldn't hurt. Her mouth enveloped his cock as she used her tongue to caress the underside of his shaft.

Hunter moaned deeply, his breath hitching, as he turned the vibrator up another notch to the halfway setting. While his cock rested at her mouth, he delicately traced his claws along her inner thighs and teased her nub with his tongue.

Fuck. They were equally playing dirty, and she loved it. Given the restriction of her movements, the difference in their height worked well for this. Hunter could practically straddle the bondage horse, even with her strapped to it. The way he leaned over a little more, he was damn near close. Her hips lifted ever so slightly, pressing against the straps as she wrapped her mouth a little further up the length of his cock before sucking back down. He growled as she stroked the underside of his shaft with the tip of her tongue. Extending it a bit more, Narcissa flicked the tip of her tongue against the skin behind his balls, which had his growl deepening.

Once more, Hunter traced his claws along her inner thighs, teasing her with his tongue on her clit, playfully biting it with his fangs, and finally pulling it into his mouth with a strong suction.

Holy fucking shit. That drove her insane. Jolts of pleasurable pain shot straight to her core. Just as she knew what would push him to the edge, he knew what would push her there, too. Lifting her head as much as possible, Narcissa wrapped her mouth a little closer to the base of his shaft and purred, sending vibrations all along the length of his shaft. He snarled, the noise shifting into a moan as she grazed her teeth down the length of his cock, dragging the tip of her tongue along the underbelly at the same time.

Hunter dug his claws into her inner thighs, teasing her clit with quick nips before devouring it eagerly. With no warning, he bypassed the next setting on the vibrator and turned it all the way up.

If she didn't know better, she'd say he struggled a little. Otherwise, he wouldn't have skipped a setting like that. Two could play that game. She hadn't yet pulled out all the stops. That could be fixed. With a deep-throated hum, Narcissa expertly ran her tongue along the underside of his cock in a continuous motion.

A deep, growling-moan erupted against her pussy, a vibrator all on its own. Hunter had yet to thrust his length into her mouth, as often occurred with the blowjobs she gave him. But he wouldn't be able to resist much longer. No more than she would. Though she held her orgasm back, everything he did pushed her closer to the edge. At the mere thought, Hunter's hips surged forward, plunging his cock into her mouth with force, hitting the back of her throat over and over. He straightened up a little, and his claws left a burning trail across her. After giving the nipple clamps several tugs in quick succession, he removed them from her nipples and set them aside with a metallic clang. His fur grazed her breasts as he leaned over, settling into place. As he growled, he simultaneously dragged his claws along both inner thighs while sucking on her clit.

Holy fuck. The combination of everything—she needed him to come right then. Narcissa didn't let up as she licked up and down the underside of his cock. Instead, she went at him full force by adding in an alternation between humming and purring. It wouldn't take long now.

A strangled growl left him. While continuing to pleasure her clit, Hunter silenced the vibrator, released the straps, and removed the toy from her pussy. "Fuck... Narcissa... come for me." He had barely closed his mouth over her sex before his orgasm erupted from him like a geyser. His body shook against hers as wave after wave jetted out of him, pulling a moan out of him unlike any he'd ever uttered before.

Simultaneously, her own orgasm erupted out of her body, surging out of her as if a dam had ruptured. As wave after wave left her body, every nerve in her body was alight with a sensation like fireworks. Narcissa worked him through his release, swallowing as much of it as possible, doing everything that could be done not to let a single drop go anywhere but down her throat. The noise that came out of her in the process wasn't anything she could describe. Not any more than the sound she heard from him. A glorious noise that vibrated through her entire body and lit up every synapse in a way she'd never felt before.

After they both fully consumed each other's pleasure, he sensually licked up her inner thighs and withdrew his cock from her mouth. With a slight adjustment, he leaned in, his breath warm against her skin, and gently bit her lower lip. "I need to be inside you right fucking now." His tongue darted inside her mouth, and their tongues met as he blindly removed her restraints.

Oh, gods, yes. Narcissa moaned deeply during the kiss. Tasting herself just moments after she had his taste down her throat, holy fuck did it turn her on. One of many, many things she enjoyed with him. It only heightened her desire. She didn't just need his cock buried inside her pussy; she needed to wrap her legs around his waist and ride him hard.

Once the last restraint was off of her, Hunter shifted the position of her legs and sat her upright on the bondage horse. With the kiss deepening, his hands tangled in her hair, feeling the strands slip through his fingers. A low rumble escaped him as he gently nipped her tongue before pulling away from the kiss. "Turn that beautiful ass of yours around. Once we are done here, I want to move on to something else."

Oh, that much was a given. She hadn't pulled out every single toy and piece of equipment they'd ever used without the intention of their taking a tour. Gazing at him through hooded eyes, Narcissa arched her back and dragged her leg across his hip toward her body, sliding her stiletto through his fur. His fangs extended, and a predatory gleam sparked in his eyes. "You say the sweetest things," Narcissa purred.

"Mmm, only to you, sweetheart."

His eyes didn't leave her once as she swung her leg over the bondage horse and slowly laid down against it. Getting into position put her ass on full display. Hunter leaned over and bit her left ass cheek, leaving a stinging mark, then did the same to her right. A slight gasp left her mouth. Afterward, he positioned the butt plug precisely at the entrance to her rear end.

"I could devour you every second for the rest of my life and still be starving." His tongue moved leisurely up her spine before his fangs lightly grazed her shoulder while inserting the plug inside her and activating it.

Narcissa peered over her shoulder at him. "The sweetest things," she repeated. She absolutely understood and claimed that sentiment. No amount of time with him would ever be enough. She would always want more. The vibrations from the butt plug began igniting her synapses. "Fuck, Hunter," she moaned. "I need you inside me."

A low growl escaped Hunter's throat before he nipped her shoulder, and then he tenderly lapped up the fresh, metallic scent of her blood. A smirk spread over his face. Hunter put the finger vibrator on and held it against her clit. "Only if you moan my name again." Then he turned it on, too.

It had been the first time since he had walked through her bedroom door that she'd uttered his name. And, fuck, it felt damn good. She could moan it again if he wanted. Because no matter how she said it, all she planned to use for the rest of the session was his name. "Hunter," she said in a husky voice. Their gazes locked, and she arched her back, her skin flushed against his. "Hunter," she moaned. "Hunter," she purred. "Fuck me like you missed me."

A rumbling purr of satisfaction vibrated out of him. His erection, thick and hard, prodded against her, arousing her from behind. Hunter gently took her lip, his fangs grazing the skin as he sucked on it slowly, and then let her go. "Yes, Ma'am," he purred.

Holy fucking shit. Those two words drove her wild with need for him. More than the vibrations from the butt plug or the finger vibrator ever could.

He didn't put any of the restraints back on her. With the finger vibrator still in place, Hunter wrapped his other arm around her waist and let out a moan as he penetrated deep inside her. With deliberate slowness, he withdrew his hips and entered her until she enveloped him entirely. Then he repeated the motion. "*Fuck,*" he growled out, "you feel so fucking good, sweetheart."

Fuck, the images that ran through her mind. If he thought she felt good now, he had felt nothing yet. Narcissa moved her hips against his, matching the rhythm of his slow thrusts. She hooked her feet onto his thighs, a grip that let him sink into her. With each penetration, she contracted and released her vaginal muscles around his cock. "Fuck, Hunter... you feel amazing."

With each of his thrusts, a low growling moan escaped him, growing louder with each one. "I fucking love how you say my name." Hunter pressed the vibrator harder against her clit. He seized her wrist, his touch sending a shiver through her, and guided her hand to his neck. "Dig your nails in, Narcissa," he growled in her ear. "I want to bleed for you." Taking hold of her breast, he pushed deeper inside her, moving at a deliberately slow speed.

Oh, she could absolutely do that. Doing just as he desired, Narcissa got a good hold of him. She nipped his lower lip, pulling a growl out of him. But it wasn't enough. She needed more of him. *All* of him. With a gasp, Narcissa squeezed him, her nails finding purchase on his neck. Rocking her hips back further, she felt Hunter intensify the power of his thrusts, driving his cock deep inside her. Narcissa swept her tongue across his lower lip and purred. A deep moan escaped him before she met his lips, their tongues tangling in a heated embrace.

His grip on her breast tightened. As he deepened the kiss, Hunter used the finger vibrator on her clit, grinding his pelvis against her ass with each connection of their bodies. Gods, the way he felt had her body on fire. Coupled with the vibrations from the toys, her synapses lit up like the night sky. Narcissa covered his hand on her breast, their fingers intertwined, and she gave a gentle squeeze to his hand and her breast. She dug her nails in until a warm, wet sensation blossomed beneath her fingers. Fuck, she could feel an orgasm pushing against the edge. But it could be held back a little longer. With a moan, she kissed him more deeply and increased the rhythm of her hips. Even then, his pace remained agonizingly slow.

Hunter's teeth playfully grazed her tongue as he leaned back from their kiss. With their lips still touching, a silent intimacy hung in the air, leaving hardly any space between them. "Does it feel like I missed you enough yet, sweetheart? Or do I need to fuck you harder?" With a deep growl, he withdrew his hips and thrust his cock harder into her.

As if that wasn't an answer to his own question. Narcissa groaned against his lips. "Oh, baby, I'm *definitely* feeling like you missed me." Not that proof had really been required. It was there from the second he entered her room—in every sound, every touch, every look. Completely stealing her breath away.

His eyes darkened. "Good. Because I really... *really* fucking did."

Narcissa thrust her tongue back into his mouth, a sudden, wet invasion. Her nails dug into his neck, and she drove her hips backward with more force. As she rocked against him, her vaginal muscles clenched, heightening the sensation of his thrusts. Their deep, unending kiss devoured his moans and groans. Amidst it all, Hunter turned off the finger vibrator and set it aside.

Although he'd spoken the words, they hadn't been necessary. Or everything he meant behind them. All the things they couldn't utter verbally, they said with their bodies in the way they connected repeatedly. It was also in his touch. How his hand slid up her stomach, continued to her sternum, and further until he reached her throat. It was in the way he deepened the kiss more, practically devouring her until everything around them disappeared. At that moment, all that existed between them were their emotions—completely raw and all-consuming.

Fuck, she couldn't hold her orgasm back any longer. A deep moan escaped her as she kissed him, and a tremendous wave of pleasure rippled through her, engulfing his cock. Hunter's grip on her breast and throat was like a vise, tightening with each breath. A ferocious snarl left him as his orgasm followed right behind hers. He continued to thrust his hips, his shaft pounding into her relentlessly as a steady stream flowed from him, filling her completely. His release was so copious that it overflowed from her, mingling with her own as their thighs became soaked.

When their mutual orgasms finally found their end, their bodies trembled against one another. *Holy fucking shit.* That had been more tremendous than anything she could've imagined.

Hunter's deep rumble echoed around them as he broke the kiss and nipped at her lower lip. "Mmm. Do you enjoy being naughty for me, Narcissa?" As his fangs met her neck, a shiver coursed through his entire being. "So... so very naughty for me."

Tingles traversed her spine. As much as either of them might desire that, she couldn't allow him to mark her again. They were already biding their time, enjoying every second they had with one another, which also meant they had to be careful of their actions. That didn't mean she couldn't long for it, though. A slow grin spread across her face. "I promised the bad-girl treatment to you, Hunter."

"That. You. Did." He slowly slid his hand down her body, his fingers grazing her skin until he found her clit, and rubbed it in a slow, deliberate rhythm. "So... how should I punish you this time? Hmm... Decisions, decisions." Slowly, he smirked. "What about... a spanking... with a bit of a twist?"

Hmm, if the look on his face was anything to go by, they'd both enjoy it. Possibly even something that hadn't quite been done before. Narcissa snaked her tongue out across her lower lip. "You have me quite intrigued."

"I *love* intriguing you, sweetheart." Hunter turned off the vibrating butt plug and removed it from her ass, a small sound escaping her as she felt the change. He turned her around, helped her from the bondage horse, and gave her ass a squeeze. "Go over to the cross and face it. I want you spread-eagle, with your arms above your head, holding onto the rings."

Oh, she *really* liked where this was going. A few interesting ideas about the direction he intended to take things flashed through her mind. Narcissa didn't utter a word. His eyes stayed glued to her ass as she strode over to the cross. Placing her hands on the rings in the middle of it, she spread her legs wide. Hunter groaned as she arched her back, which caused her ass to stick out. She looked over her shoulder and stared at him. "Like this? Or should I move closer to it?"

His eyes met hers, and the corners of his mouth turned upward into a smirk. "Oh, no. You stay right there. That is *exactly* how I want you, baby girl."

Oh, she really enjoyed being called that, even more than she liked 'sweetheart.' She'd have to remember to tell him at the end of their session. From now on, if he wasn't using her name or calling her ma'am, he should *definitely* use 'baby girl.'

Hunter took his time crossing the floor, keeping his gaze right on hers every step of the way. Once he got there, he stood behind her and placed his hands on her hips. Starting from her neck, his lips, tongue, and fangs grazed a slow trail down her flesh. She moaned as he bit down on both of her ass cheeks. Fuck, she loved when he did that.

Hunter moved around to sit on the floor in front of her. He leaned back against the cross as he met her gaze again. "Here is how we are going to do this. I will not restrain you. You are going to have to hold your position the entire time. I am going to devour your pussy while you count out every spanking I give you. But I will not put any limits on it. I am going to spank you until you beg me to let you come."

A slow smile spread across her face. "Mmm, we could be here for a while, baby," she teased.

His eyes darkened further. "Oh, I plan on it. But before we begin..." He closed the space between their faces, gripped her neck, then bit her lip before thrusting his tongue into her mouth with a guttural growl.

Fuck, she loved kissing him, the feel of his tongue entangled with her own, and the taste of his mouth. One of the many things she'd never get enough of with him. Especially those fucking growls of his that sent tingles down her spine. Moaning, she nipped his tongue and swept hers across the back of his fangs. Maybe he couldn't mark her again, but he sure as fuck could bite her again.

As the kiss continued, Hunter grazed his claws down the full length of her back and over her ass. With a hard smack, he contacted her ass cheek, the sting a familiar sensation. *Oh, gods, yes.* With a groan, she uttered, "One." Then, she entwined their tongues again, the taste of him familiar on her lips, and pressed her ass a little more into his warm hand. The electrical currents that went through her body had her longing for more. Hmm, she might have moved a bit. Whoops. He might have to add to her punishment. Or come up with another one after this.

As he pulled back from the kiss, Hunter's growl vibrated against her lips, and he gave her a knowing smirk. "Do not forget, you have to stay still."

She didn't need a reminder. Disobeying him was much more enjoyable than standing still. Though she could tantalize him in other ways. He made it so, so easy, too. He pressed a kiss on her jaw, his tongue tracing a path down her neck, his fangs barely brushing against her collarbone. Teasing her nipple with his tongue and teeth, he grasped one of her ass cheeks. Then he pulled his hand back quickly, and the sound of the smack echoed in the room.

"Two," she purred without moving.

As he moved to her other breast, he answered her purr with a growl and gave it the same attention as the first. Hunter bit down on her nipple as he scraped his claws across her ass, then continued down her stomach, pausing at her belly button ring. With his eyes locked on hers, he gently tugged the jewelry with his fangs as he smacked her ass once more.

Fuck, that lit her synapses up. "Three," she moaned out. Hmm, would it cause a stronger sensation if the belly button ring was longer? Something to think about at a later time.

Hunter nipped at her pelvic region, then each of her hips. He let out a low growl while running his claws across her buttocks, teasing her clit with his tongue, and delivering another firm smack to her rear. A shudder went through him.

She loved the slight tease. How many was this? Not enough yet, that was for sure. "Four," Narcissa groaned. Although she hadn't moved again, it wouldn't last forever.

Slowly, he teased his tongue into her pussy. A deep groan left him. As his claws pierced her ass, blood flowed down her cheeks, while his tongue meticulously explored every crevice inside her. Hunter pulled his tongue from her and licked up her slit. With a bit more force, he struck her ass again as he bit down on her clit simultaneously.

Oh, gods. Narcissa didn't know what got to her more. "Five."

Hunter growled against her clit as he nipped at her nub again. "Your ass is going to be *very* red before we are through."

Before she could respond, Hunter switched hands and drove his tongue back into her sex as his palm connected with her other ass cheek.

Holy fucking shit. Somehow, not that Narcissa knew how, she held her position when all she wanted was to ride his tongue. "Six," she moaned out.

He emitted a low growl as he delved into her pussy once more, slipping a finger into her rear and moving it in a slow, rhythmic motion, before running his tongue along her slit.

Holy fuck. She wouldn't last much longer without having to ride his tongue.

His eyes smoldered as he looked up and met her gaze. "Say my name, Narcissa," he growled out as he spanked her again.

Oh, that could *absolutely* be done. The intensity in Hunter's eyes told her that he needed her to challenge him. His gaze flicked to her mouth as she snaked her tongue out across her top lip. "Seven," she purred. "Hunter."

He growled as he added another finger into her ass, ramping up their pace and vigor. It pulled her orgasm a little closer to the edge. Though she wasn't at the point of begging yet.

"*Fuck,* I love that. Again. Say my name again, Narcissa." This time, when his hand connected with her ass cheek, his claws dug in, drawing more blood.

Narcissa moaned deeply. He'd have to work harder to make her beg. Something he had done before. Maybe he needed a reminder. Narcissa licked her lips. "Eight," she said with a purr, intentionally leaving his name off this time.

A deep rumble vibrated from him. "Eight, *what*, Narcissa?" Hunter took her clit between his fangs and let loose a growl. She barely kept from crying out his name. His claws dug deeper into her ass cheek as he fucked her harder with his fingers. As he slid his tongue deep inside her, his low growl resonated through her core as he started penetrating her in that manner as well.

Narcissa lost all control and cried out his name. He withdrew his claws from her ass, then intensified his next strike on her rear while pushing her closer against his mouth. The sound of his palm connecting with her skin echoed around the room, ripping a half-growl, half-snarl out of him.

Holy fuck, it made her want to ride his tongue more. "Nine, Hunter," Narcissa moaned.

"Mmm, good girl." With another growl, he slid his tongue back inside her, edging her closer to another orgasm. He slid his fingers from her ass, his hand gripping her thigh as he brought her leg over his shoulder. Though he held her, Narcissa drove her stiletto into his back just before his hand fell, its force echoing the earlier impact on her.

Holy fucking shit, that practically yanked her to the point of begging. Not just yet, but they weren't far off. "Ten, Hunter."

His moans filled the room as he explored every part of her with his tongue. Hunter's claws dug into her thigh, their sharp tips teasing her skin as he intensified his movements with his tongue. He licked her slit, teasing her clit with the tip of his tongue, before diving back in.

Narcissa dug her stiletto into his back harder. She could have told him 'harder,' except they'd done this dance before and she rather enjoyed it. Even though his tongue continued to move leisurely, each thrust into her pussy remained intense. It didn't even impact his growls or the hard swats to her ass. "Eleven," she groaned out. "May I please come, Hunter?" Something she knew he would deny. The need for a release was there, just not quite to the point he wanted.

Hunter dragged his tongue from her pussy. He licked up her slit and nipped at her clit. As Hunter met her gaze, he dug his claws deeper into her thigh, sending thin streaks of blood sliding down her skin while he sucked hard on her nub. "Hmm... not yet, baby girl. I told you I am going to spank you until you *beg* me to let you come. That did not sound like begging to me." His tongue delved back into her pussy as his palm contacted her ass once more, with even more force than the previous time.

Oh, it definitely hadn't been begging. Though that nearly had her there. Just a little more. "Twelve," she moaned. The sharp point of her stiletto dug into his back, and she shivered as his growl reverberated against her. "May I please, please come, Hunter?" Narcissa curled her fingers around the ring she held onto. Still, he wouldn't let her just yet. She wasn't quite where he wanted her to be. To be fair, it wasn't quite where she wanted, either. But, almost.

Hunter tightened his grip on her thigh, digging his claws in deeper as he withdrew his tongue. He leaned in close, and with a low growl, he tugged on her necklace with his fangs. He bit down on one of her breasts, and she moaned as he brushed his tongue over her nipple, and then licked down her chest and stomach. Gently tugging on her belly button ring, his fangs moved sensually along her skin, grazing down toward her lower region. "Not yet." As he landed another hard blow to her ass, he drove his tongue back inside her and dug his claws into her cheek.

Her stiletto dug in until blood beaded beneath her shoe. Hunter cried out against her. Holy fucking shit, he'd certainly taken her there. They'd been able to read each other's bodies since the beginning. And he'd handled hers beautifully. "Oh, gods," she cried out. If he hadn't been holding her thigh so tight, her hips would've likely moved all on their own. "Thirteen. Please, please, baby, please let me come."

Ever so slowly, Hunter's tongue traced up her slit, then teasingly nibbled on her nub. "Mmm, is that what you need, baby girl? Do you need to *come*?" His claws sank harder into her thigh and ass as he flicked his tongue repeatedly against her clit, sending electrifying sensations straight to her core.

Oh, he was playing dirty. No doubt he could sense the need in her as much as she sensed it in him. Pressing her calf tighter against his shoulder, the heel of her shoe bore into his back more. Her eyes met his, and she purred, "Yes, I do, baby."

Hunter's fangs elongated a little, and he let out a snarl. "Then come for me, Narcissa." He tightened his grip further and emitted a deep growl while thrusting his tongue back into her sex to pleasure her.

As a massive orgasm pulsed through her body, Narcissa cried out his name, feeling it explode all over his tongue. Fuck. It was so powerful and intense; it felt like a volcano had erupted inside of her as wave after wave gushed into his mouth. Her grip tightened, and the cold, metallic ring dug sharply into her skin. Even her leg clenched harder against his shoulder.

His relentless growl filled the room as his tongue eagerly lapped up every drop of her release, ensuring nothing went to waste. Once he'd taken every drop, he stroked his tongue up her slit and licked his lips. "Mmm. Nothing could ever come close to tasting as sweet as you." Hunter kissed each of her inner thighs before starting a trail back up her body. "Where do you want me to fuck you, Narcissa? Right here, or in the swing?"

With her eyes on his, she carefully weighed the options he presented. While she certainly enjoyed the swing, she also enjoyed riding him, too. And he was right there, ready and waiting. All she'd have to do is lower her body. But they couldn't leave the swing out of the tour. "Mmm, I have a better proposition. I fuck you here and you fuck me there."

With eyes as dark as night, a low growl rumbled in his chest. Hunter licked his lips as he slowly lowered her leg from his shoulder. Giving her hips a gentle squeeze, he leaned backward until his back met the cross. "I love the way you think."

She didn't waste time on words. Instead, Narcissa placed her hands on his shoulders, fused their lips together, and slowly lowered her body. Their tongues intertwined as she enveloped his cock with ease, thanks to his reclined position and her intense arousal. Together, they groaned. Holy fuck, he always felt amazing. Hunter tightened his grip and lifted his hips.

With her legs wide, she hooked her feet beneath his thighs; the muscles flexing beneath her touch. Slowly, Narcissa rocked her hips, riding up and down his length. Not once did the kiss break. She deepened the kiss with a sweep of her tongue, relishing the feel of his fangs as his growl intensified. Holy fuck, even as close as they were, it didn't seem close enough. Narcissa pressed closer to him as she continued to ride his cock.

Hunter planted his feet flat on the floor, changing their angle slightly. *Oh, fuck.* The change was only minor, but that was all it took. His hips rose, setting a slow rhythm, which let her spread her thighs wider. As his claws traced a path down her body, she sifted her fingers through his fur, clinging to the nape of his neck.

Not once had Narcissa ever imagined she'd have something like this—an equal exchange between both sides of her desires. Where control shifted between the two of them, unless he needed to be in full control—something she could absolutely relinquish. Either way, it never diminished how perfect it all was with him.

His claws traced paths up and down her skin as his other hand kept moving. With his free hand, he threaded his fingers into her hair as the kiss became more intense and he moved more forcefully against her. Narcissa moaned as he shifted sideways suddenly and laid back on the floor. Fuck, yes. It opened everything up so much more. She clasped the back of his thighs tighter, widening her legs to intensify the rhythm of her hips. To enhance the intensity even more, she squeezed and then released her vaginal muscles in sync with his thrusts. Tightening her hold on the nape of his neck, Narcissa dug her fingernails into his flesh. Jolts of lightning fired across every synapse, lighting up every nerve ending inside of her and setting her body on fire.

Hunter dragged his claws down her back, then clasped her ass, sinking his claws in until the coppery scent of blood filled the air. As his hips crashed into hers, he nipped at her tongue, then her lower lip. "Holy fuck. Harder. Dig your nails in harder."

'Holy fuck' was right. She could absolutely comply with that. Her nails sank into his skin, and soon blood pooled beneath her fingertips. The pleasurable pain, coupled with the renewed scent of his blood, had him snarling. Her hips swayed with increased fervor and determination. "Oh, fuck, Hunter, don't stop. Please don't stop!"

Not that she believed he would. His claws dug further into her ass cheeks as he thrust his cock more forcefully into her. "Fuck! Harder, Narcissa. Fuck me harder, baby girl." After biting down on her lower lip, Hunter reconnected their tongues in a fervent kiss.

Oh, gods, yes! Deepening the kiss, Narcissa tightened her hold on the back of his neck and adjusted the positioning of her feet. Her stilettos dug in, and the world seemed to narrow as she rocked against him, faster, with a driving, hungry rhythm. Not once did she let up on clenching her walls around his cock. *Holy fuck!* The sensation of each stroke of his shaft had her synapses lighting up at both ends. An orgasm sat ready and waiting on the edge.

Hunter jerked his head back right as his fangs punched even further out of his mouth, and he hissed.

Holy shit. Every time his fangs lengthened, it took everything in her not to ask him to bite her. They had risked so much already, but there was no way they could go without seeing one another. Instead, they made the most of the time they had together.

He grabbed her hair and yanked it, his fingers tightly gripping her as he kept one hand on her. "Come for me, Narcissa. Come all over my dick." At the same moment, his release erupted, mirroring the wave exploding out of her. Hunter didn't take his eyes away from hers once as his roar echoed around the room and she screamed his name at the top of her lungs. Their releases were so massive that both of their thighs and the floor beneath them became saturated.

When both of their releases had ended, Hunter pulled her off of his dick and brought her overtop of his face. He gripped her knees tightly, spreading her thighs apart, and delved deep inside her with a guttural growl. His tongue devoured her, his fangs grazing along her outer lips.

Licking up her slit, he nipped at her nub and growled as he met her gaze, their juices coating his lips. "Swing. Now."

Staring into his eyes, Narcissa placed one hand on either side of his head and lifted her knees from the floor. Bent at the waist, she brushed a kiss across his lips and grinned wide. "Yes, Sir."

While she hadn't expected him to bring her overtop his face like that, it had worked out rather well. As much as she enjoyed his taste alone, theirs together was so much better. Before straightening her body, Narcissa gave him one more soft kiss. Once she stood up straight, she did exactly as he demanded and strode over to the swing.

Getting up from the floor, Hunter followed. He made quick work of getting her in the swing, so he could do just as she suggested and fuck her hard. He turned her around so her back was to him and placed her hands in the stirrups. A strap circled her chest, above her breasts, with another wrapping around her waist. Even if she lost her grip on the stirrups, she wouldn't fall.

His claws grazed her ass cheeks, then moved to her stomach, finally resting on her inner thighs as he cupped them. He lifted her feet off the floor, his grip tightening as he wrapped her legs around his thighs. Not that he immediately buried his erection in her pussy. He enticed her with the sensation of his cock gliding along her opening, caressing her clit, and teasingly penetrating her multiple times. They were both very good at tantalizing one another. Not that it ever lasted for too long.

Without warning, Hunter slammed his cock deep inside her. In the throes of passion, Narcissa's cries of pleasure filled the room as he thrust vigorously and rapidly into her. Her heels dug into his cheeks as she curled her feet against his ass.

"Fuck," he growled out. "Harder, Narcissa. I need to bleed for you." His fingers tightened around her inner thighs, digging his claws in deep enough to draw blood. The speed and force of his thrusts intensified.

There had been a difference in his word choice. The word *need* had more power behind it than *want*. If one *needed* something, they simply couldn't survive without it. As long as she could, she would ensure he never went without what he needed. Narcissa's knuckles turned white as she clutched the straps. She felt the material digging into her palms as she pressed her stilettos harder into his ass cheeks, and the smell of his blood overwhelmed her senses. As he thrust, a prolonged, guttural moan escaped him, intensifying with each clench of her vaginal muscles and her rocking motion against him using her hold on his backside.

"Fuck yes. Gods, you feel so fucking good." He dragged his claws from her inner thighs down to her knees.

The sting pulled a deep groan out of her. Hunter spread her legs wider, not that it impacted the hold she had on his ass. In fact, it allowed her to dig in more, especially as he drilled his cock into her pussy with greater speed and ferocity. "Oh, fuck... don't stop."

"Never. Fuck... Holy fuck..." Hunter's claws sent blood dripping to the floor. "Harder... I need... dig your heels in harder."

His request had barely left his mouth when her body automatically complied. Narcissa dug her stilettos in so hard, blood trickled down his ass cheeks and onto her legs. He gave an even louder, more strangled moan. Between the way he pounded into her and the continuous bite of his claws, her body had quickly been driven toward another orgasm. "Oh, fuck... oh, gods... I'm gonna come, Hunter."

"Fuck... me, too. Come for me, baby girl, come all over me. Fucking drown my cock in your cum."

Narcissa screamed his name as an orgasm of colossal proportions erupted around his cock. His fangs elongated even longer than before, and Hunter let out a feral hiss as his orgasm exploded out of him the same moment hers did. Both were so massive, they were like a volcanic eruption and a broken dam all in one.

Hunter pulled his cock from her sex, lowered her legs from around him, removed her from the swing, and picked her up in his arms. He fused their lips together with a deep growl as he carried her over to the bed. He laid her back on the edge, his lips and tongue tracing a path down her throat and collarbone. A hand caught the back of her necklace, drawing it taut and pressing the cool metal against her skin. A moan escaped Narcissa's lips as she arched her neck. The sounds she made for him had always been the most natural in the world. This time was no different.

Hunter gave a deep rumble and took her breast in his mouth. His teeth gently nipped at her nipple while his tongue swirled around it. Fuck those noises that came out of him. Narcissa had heard nothing more exquisite.

"I am not finished with you yet," he growled as he moved to her other breast, giving it the same attention.

It should be impossible to need someone so much. No matter how much of one another they had, their desire for more simply didn't have an end. They had both just had extremely explosive orgasms—something no one else had ever given her—and yet it wasn't enough for either of them.

Their tour definitely wasn't over yet.

She raked her nails up his arms as he growled; the sound echoed in the close space. Then, her legs slid along the warmth of his thighs, finally hooking onto his hips. Her stilettos sank into his ass cheeks, eliciting a low, animalistic growl from him. Not once did her eyes stray from him as he continued his trail down her body, going exactly where she expected. Though, she didn't anticipate the stop at her belly button ring, which he tugged, before moving on to grip her ankles and spread her legs wide.

Hunter pressed her stilettos hard into his shoulders. As their gazes met, he licked his lips and gently cupped her breasts with his hands. She arched her back as his claws dug in and he drove his tongue deep inside her pussy. *Holy fucking shit.* No matter how many times he went down on her, it always felt like the first time. And this time, she was in a perfect position to ride his tongue. Narcissa shifted her weight, feeling the muscles bunch beneath her, and she drove her heels into his shoulder blades. She held him tightly, arched her back, and moved rhythmically against his tongue.

Gauging how slowly he drove his tongue in and out of her pussy, he planned to take his time. And she was perfectly all right with that. They didn't need to rush through anything. Narcissa matched the rhythm of her hips to the pace of his tongue. As his claws dug harder into her breasts, she raked her nails up and down his arms, drawing blood. To ensure nothing got left out, she dug her stilettos in more as well.

"Oh, gods," Narcissa moaned.

He skillfully traced his tongue along her folds, finding her most sensitive spot, and sucked on it intensely. He briefly consumed her before repeating the process. Continuing his assault, his claws scraped from her breasts, up to her shoulders, down her sides, and then up once more.

Her back arched with each path he took. She tightened her grip on his shoulders and pressed down firmly with her stilettos as he resumed pleasuring her with his tongue, causing her to increase the intensity and speed of her movements. "Fuck, Hunter... don't stop... I'm gonna come!" Not that they'd be anywhere near finished with this part once they got through this release. Oh, no, far from it. In fact, she had an idea he was certain to enjoy.

This time, his claws dug deeper, and the scent of her blood filled the air as it seeped down her skin and soaked into his fur. He let out a continuous growl as he drove at her even harder. Words of approval didn't need to leave his mouth. His approval came in his body's response. His name escaped her lips in a loud cry as she experienced a powerful orgasm that pulsed through her body and spilled into his mouth, trickling down his throat. Like many others this time around, this orgasm didn't seem to have an end. Once he'd swallowed the last wave, Hunter pulled his tongue from her sex. As he removed his claws from her breasts, he licked his blood-stained lips. His tongue traced a path up her stomach and over her breasts, meticulously removing every trace of blood, as he stood up.

He gripped a handful of her hair, pulling her up as he pressed their lips together in a deep kiss, letting her taste their shared essence, before rising to his full height. With a firmer grip on her hair, he positioned the base of his shaft and teased the tip against her lips. "I need your mouth around my cock until you swallow every drop of my cum, as I just swallowed every drop of yours."

Oh, he was going to get that, but not just yet. As Narcissa stroked the tip with her tongue, his cock twitched, and he let out a growl before she licked her lips. "I have a better idea. You lay down on the bed, and while I wrap my mouth around your *cock*—" she punctuated one word before she continued on, "—I'll ride your face." Along with a few other things, but those were the primary objectives.

His face slowly spread into a smirk, and his eyes gleamed with a mischievous glint. With a tighter grip on his shaft, Hunter moaned softly while gliding his hand up and down his length at a leisurely pace. "Do you need my tongue back in your *pussy*—" he paused after punctuating that one word, "—that badly already, Narcissa?"

Gods, she fucking loved it when he teased her like that. Especially when he emphasized the word 'pussy.' Biting her bottom lip, she had an answer. One that couldn't be more perfect if she tried. As she stared at him through hooded eyes, Narcissa stuck her middle finger in her mouth, grazed her teeth to the knuckle, and sucked the rest of the way to the tip. His eyes followed her hand as she trailed it down her throat, traced a circle around her nipple, and continued down the valley between her breasts. By the time she reached her pussy, his lips had parted, and he was damn near panting. As she slipped her finger inside her pussy, his fangs sank into his lower lip. "I wasn't ready for your tongue to leave yet," she purred.

Hunter gripped the top of the bedframe. He found her eyes and increased the pace of his strokes. "Perhaps, if you beg me for my *tongue...* or my *cock...* or *both...* you will get exactly what you want."

The look on his face said it *all*. Narcissa lifted her stilettos onto the bed, spread her thighs wide, leaned back on her hands, and lifted her ass, pushing herself further into the soft mattress. Her hand stayed pressed into the bed as she bent her knees and spread her thighs wider, exposing herself completely. "I'm done begging for the day."

A low growl came from him.

As much as she enjoyed watching him stroke his cock, she could see exactly how much he was panting for her already. And she wasn't about to go easy on him. His gaze followed her the entire time as she slipped two fingers, this time, into her mouth and sucked on both of them. Once more, she traced the trail down her neck, circled her nipple with her fingers, followed the valley between her breasts, and gradually moved downward until she reached her core. His fangs dug harder into his lower lip. "You'll give me what I want. Until you do, you have to stay right where you are... and *watch*." This time, Narcissa pushed both fingers deep inside herself and let out a moan.

His growl became deeper, more carnal. Hunter maintained his slow pace as he stroked his cock, his gaze fixed on her pussy. "Maybe I want to watch. Maybe I want to watch you make yourself come... before I fuck your mouth and have you ride my face."

Narcissa watched his face, even as the movements of his cock became more intense. Yes, she imagined he *wanted* to watch. Thrusting her fingers in and out of her pussy, she matched the rhythm of his strokes with a groan. "But can you keep from touching me while I touch myself?"

He licked his lips hungrily. "I do not know. I can certainly try, though." His grip on the iron frame of the bed tightened.

Narcissa drove home her point, lowering her back to the mattress as she moved her hips against each thrust of her fingers. With a free hand, she encircled her nipple and then gently squeezed it between her fingers.

Hunter groaned as he kept his strokes in rhythm with the thrusts of her fingers. "Do not stop, Narcissa."

Definitely not stopping this. Not by the look on his face. Even if his hand had stilled on his cock, the rapt attention he gave her would've been enough to encourage her to continue. Giving her nipple a quick pinch, she squeezed and massaged her breast. But it wasn't enough. Not any more than her two fingers felt like enough.

Hunter let out a deep growl as she inserted a third finger into her wetness. On every lift of her hips, Narcissa quickened the pace of her thrusts. Each time, he did the same with the strokes to his cock. He held onto the bed frame, his eyes following the movement of her tongue as it traced the curve of her breast, and then flicked across her nipple. "Fuck," he growled. "Fuck, yes. Make yourself come, baby girl. I want to taste every drop while you take every inch of my cock."

Retracting her tongue, she let out a husky moan. "Oh, gods." Her orgasm sat so close to the edge. One more push, and she wouldn't be able to hold it back. Narcissa intensified her movements, rocking her hips and thrusting her fingers harder, while twisting her nipple and digging her nails into her breast. "Fuck! I'm gonna come, Hunter!"

With a snarl, Hunter let go of the bar, the metal frame clanging as he fell to his knees on the bed. She somehow held her orgasm back just long enough for him to adjust his position. The way she'd positioned herself made his height ideal. It allowed him to crawl up on the bed, place his knees on either side of her feet and put his hand beside hers, all while continuing to stroke his cock. Meeting her gaze, he increased the speed of his strokes and moaned. "Fuck yes, baby girl. Fucking come for me."

Narcissa called out his name as she pitched over the cliff, her release completely coating her fingers and the mattress beneath them. Simultaneously, his shot up the length of his cock and exploded out of him. Hunter released a powerful roar that reverberated throughout the room as his climax covered her breasts, stomach, hand, and even her intimate areas and thighs. Marking her without *marking* her. He barely reached the end of their pleasure before seizing a handful of her hair, tilting her head back, and trailing his tongue up her throat. His teeth grazed her lower lip before his tongue dove in, a frenzied dance with hers.

Holy fucking shit, he didn't waste any time. Not that she blamed him. Teasing one another like that only heightened her desire to have his cock in her mouth. If that urge hadn't burned so deep, she would've certainly done something with his cum on her body. But he'd gone in for the kiss first.

With a lingering taste on her tongue as Hunter broke the kiss, he flipped them over; her straddling his mouth; her face inches from his cock. He gripped her thighs tightly, digging his claws in, and pressed his mouth against her. With a fierce growl, he plunged his tongue deep inside. Her hands found his ass, squeezing tightly, and she took his cock into her mouth. He cried out against her pussy as she deep-throated, taking him all the way to the back of her throat. His taste remained prominent, but their combined tastes lingered beneath that from when he fucked her on the swing. Fuck, it lit up every nerve-ending in her body.

With a forceful thrust of his hips, he pressed his claws deeper into her thighs, as if desperate for one last taste of her essence to sustain him. Oh, gods. His touch, accompanied by the lingering taste on her lips, ignited a burning desire within her. Every lick of his tongue had her core burning hotter and hotter. Gently grazing her teeth along his shaft, Narcissa let out a groan before starting anew by sliding her tongue along the underbelly of his cock.

His claws raked down her thighs, a burning sensation traveling to her knees. With a tight grip, Hunter positioned her legs wider over his face. He licked her moist folds, teasing her sensitive spots with his fangs, before delving his tongue back into her warmth. *Holy fuck*. Already, she was gearing up for yet another release. As she moaned around his cock, Narcissa dug her nails into one of his ass cheeks and dragged them up the back of his right thigh.

Their primal, guttural noises grew louder as they consumed one another, driving at each other with unrelenting passion. A symphony of sensations entangled them, and they endlessly pursued the ultimate pleasure, culminating in a shared, exquisite climax. As they simultaneously flew over the edge, her juices gushed into his waiting mouth, and a continuous stream jetted out of him, flowing down her throat. Neither of them stopped until they'd swallowed every drop offered.

, Hunter moved her to the side of the bed, the cold metal of the cross a stark contrast to the warmth of the sheets. With no hesitation, he loosened the chain and fastened the restraints around her wrists, leaving her arms suspended.

Which didn't surprise her. She sensed a deep need within him. Unlike anything she'd ever felt before. A moan escaped her mouth as his arm encircled her belly and his fingers tightened around her throat. He sank his teeth into her shoulder before thrusting deeply inside her. *Holy fucking shit.* If his prior actions up to that point hadn't been enough to confirm what she sensed from him, then his hard thrusts certainly would have done the job. Narcissa rocked her hips back against him, her wrists straining against the cuffs.

It didn't take long for his continuous growl to fill the room. With a barely perceptible squeeze around her neck, he raked his claws into her flesh as he thrust into her. Hunter slid his fangs from her shoulder, the coppery scent of blood hanging in the air, and then grazed them up to her neck. He placed a kiss on her throat, and his cock slammed home. Each breath against her neck came out in a hard pant.

A shudder shot down her spine. She nearly tilted her head, but no. He couldn't mark her again. Regardless that the desire to have him do just that lingered heavily between them. Narcissa jerked her restraints. As she lifted her heels and drove them into the back of his thighs, his growl became a low, guttural rumble. Every nerve in her body was ablaze with the fierceness of his thrusts. With a husky moan, Narcissa rocked her hips back to match his speed. At that moment, a feeling of wholeness washed over her, like shards of glass reforming into a beautiful mosaic. Warmth spread through her, each piece clicking into place, a symphony of renewal and hope.

Hunter buried his face in her neck, his fingers loosening their hold as he angled her hips and braced himself against the cross. His movements intensified as he forcefully drove his shaft into her center repeatedly. "Oh, fuck... Narcissa..."

Gods, he always felt amazing, but there was just something about this time that seemed different. More spectacular than normal. With their bodies so much closer together, it allowed his cock to reach so much deeper. A groan escaped Narcissa's lips as her head fell back against his chest. She increased the rhythm of her hips, keeping pace with his thrusts. "Fuck... Hunter... don't stop."

His grip on the cross and her midsection became tighter, a silent promise hanging in the air. Each time she sheathed his cock completely, he ground into her core. His body shook against hers. The scraping of his claws against the metal, as well as her hip, echoed as he tightened his hold.

"Oh, fuck, I need you. Narcissa... Mine," he growled. His mouth closed over the side of her neck; her pulse thrummed against his lips.

Such simple words, but he didn't have to explain the deeper meaning behind them. Because she was his and he was hers. She needed him the same way he needed her. Not that the words found their way to her mouth. They never could. Settling for just these few scant hours every few days would never be enough. Not when she wanted to lie in his arms at night, spend actual time with him, have him any time they desired... things Narcissa never thought she would ever long for. Things they couldn't ever truly have, regardless of what they felt for one another.

Maybe she could show him with her body what she couldn't vocalize. She arched her back and, with a subtle groan, Narcissa dug the heels of her stilettos deeper into his thighs, pulling harder on the restraints. He groaned against her throat. His hand slid from her side to cover one of her breasts as he dug his claws in all over again. The subtle change gave her the freedom to deepen the sway of her hips while pressing herself closer to his arm. Fuck, if that didn't make her core burn hotter, even more so as her vaginal muscles gripped his cock like a vise with every thrust.

As he sucked harder on her throat, a fang barely pierced her skin, which drew a moan from him. Hunter leaned his upper body toward the cross, causing her hips to tilt back slightly and enabling him to thrust even deeper inside her. Holy fuck. It yanked her orgasm right up against the edge. But it was far too soon. She didn't want their time to end. Not yet. Ever. Though, with how their bodies responded to one another, she'd only be able to hold it back for so long. Pushing her breast more into his palm, Narcissa tilted her head, giving him more access to her neck.

With no warning, his fangs plunged in deep. Hunter roared against her as her sweet, heady blood filled his mouth, coated his tongue, and flowed down his throat. As he sucked her throat, bruising her skin, he clutched the cross and held her tighter. Marked her for the second time. His hips didn't stop once as he rammed his cock into her core again and again.

Some kind of strangled, moaned purr left her mouth. The intense peace, along with the fierce sexual bliss pouring through her body, was enough for her to fly. Clamping her vaginal muscles tight around his cock, Narcissa barely held her orgasm back. It teetered so damn close to the edge that when she finally let go, it would be more massive than anything she'd ever experienced. Regardless, her hips didn't stop meeting each of his thrusts, no matter how hard he pounded into her.

His fangs slid from her neck with a groan. Then his tongue trailed along her neck, over his mark, as he swallowed what blood had spilled. Hunter nuzzled against the puncture wounds and purred, "Mine," against her throat. Releasing her breast, he cupped her cheek and turned her head so their gazes met. Hunter pressed his forehead to hers. "Come for me," he whispered. "My Narcissa... come for me."

Silence hung heavy in the air as their mutual releases erupted with a powerful burst. Her vaginal muscles clamped tight onto his cock as their juices gushed out, cascading down their thighs, spilling onto the bed beneath them. She couldn't stop it. She couldn't stop any of this. All she could do was gaze into the bright-blue glow emanating from his eyes. Hunter's mouth hung open, his cock jerking repeatedly, his body shaking against hers, as their orgasm continued, once again, seemingly with no end.

There had been no turning back the moment the words came out of his mouth. It didn't matter that both her heart and soul shattered into a million pieces. While she mentally and emotionally understood what that glow from his eyes meant, all she physically felt was him. Staring at him through ragged breaths, her world dissolved into a blur of tears as an echo of silence enveloped her fractured existence. Narcissa didn't immediately realize her feet had lowered from the back of his thighs to the mattress. His eyes weren't supposed to be like that—not yet. No! They were supposed to have more time before it happened. It shouldn't be this soon. Not when she had just gotten him back. Not when the magic in her contract hadn't yet been triggered.

Because *this*... it wouldn't matter that it occurred in the privacy of her bedroom.

Averine would know.

And consequently separate them.

After a shaky breath, Hunter exhaled, the sound barely audible in the quiet space as he lowered his head. He squeezed his eyes shut tightly. Lifting his head, he looked at her with a tender gaze, gently wiping away a tear and then kissing away the other. He opened his mouth, then snapped it shut again. After a moment, his lips met hers, a soft touch that lingered as he reached up and unbuckled the restraints from around her wrists. Then he pressed his forehead to hers one last time, slid his cock from her sex, and moved off of the bed. All he took was one step, though. His fingers curled around one bar of the cross so hard he'd likely have indents in his palms.

No words. She didn't have any words. Nothing could make any of this better. It didn't seem he had any, either. But she couldn't let him leave without saying something... anything. Especially with the issues that could arise because of it. When they had spoken of this as a possibility before, he'd told her it meant he wouldn't be able to come back. For his own safety—and for hers—she needed him to stick to that.

A hollow ache consumed her, the world fading into a blurry watercolor of gray. Oh, gods. She'd never known this kind of pain before...

No, that wasn't true. The last time they'd been together. When he believed he would lose his life.

But this wasn't the same thing.

Yes, they wouldn't ever be able to see one another again. But at least she'd know he was alive. It would have to be enough. Would it be?

Sitting back on her heels, Narcissa glanced over at him and climbed off the bed. What could she say to make this better? She stared at his back, watching the rise and fall as he stood there. Still, with no words coming to her, there was only one thing she could do. She wrapped her arms around him from behind.

Hunter placed his free hand over both of hers and gently squeezed. "I will always love you, Narcissa. Always. It does not matter who... walks through that door. You... you will always be mine." He gave her hands another squeeze. "Keep those promises you made to me last we saw one another. You will not let the light in your eyes go out. You will not let your heart go dark or your soul die. You will remember everything we made one another feel. The warmth and healing we brought to one another's hearts and souls. You will never forget your worth. And you will never stop trying to get free. Promise me again. Please."

Her breath hitched, and the world seemed to shrink as the agony clawed at her insides. Resting her head against his back, she wanted nothing more than to promise him she would keep trying to get free. That she wouldn't resign herself to the decisions she'd made thirty years ago. Or that she wouldn't have to shut down just to get through days that had become a chore she no longer wished to do. A life that she'd give anything to change.

Just so they could be together. Narcissa did the only thing she could to protect him. No matter how much pain it caused her.

"I'm so sorry, Hunter," she whispered. With one more hard squeeze, she unwound her arms from his waist. Her throat ached, and she retreated from him, each step echoing the sorrow in her heart. "You need to go."

His entire body went rigid. She hated what she'd done, but she knew what was coming. Without a word, Hunter released his hold on the bed. He didn't look back at her. Or say a single word. He just crossed the room, opened the door, and left for the last time.

As much as Narcissa wanted to chase after him, to say more than what she had, she didn't. She didn't tell him how much she loved him. That nothing could ever make her forget him. Or that she wished she could promise him what he wanted, or explain why she couldn't.

Without saying a word, Narcissa let him walk out of her bedroom. It pained her to no end not to say what she'd really wanted to tell him, but it was safest for both of them. A red haze clouded her vision, and she welcomed the searing agony as a weapon.

Taking a slow breath, she shut every emotion down. Her love, her pain, her desire... none of it could make an appearance. Not only that, but she had to quiet all the things she didn't say in her head.

Focusing her senses, her gaze flicked to the ceiling. There wasn't much time. Emotionally and mentally shut down, she called water over her body, feeling it wash away the session's lingering passion as she moved to her closet. Taking a shower was out of the question. Nor would there be time to clean up the mess in her room. There would just be enough time to get dressed and wipe the makeup from her face.

Usually, she took her time selecting an outfit to wear, but she didn't have that kind of time. Instead, as quickly as possible, Narcissa slipped off the crimson high heels she had on and grabbed a pair of dark blue jeans, a peach low-cut halter, and a pair of dark denim high heels. She'd barely finished getting dressed before there was a knock on her door.

"Just a second," she called out before giving herself the once-over. No visible puncture wounds, a clean face, and no emotion showing in her jade-green eyes. Set to go, Narcissa ensured she closed up her closet and strode across the floor to her bedroom door.

Her conversations with Averine since she started with the den had been minimal. While she had her suspicions about how this one might go, she didn't know for sure what exact actions would be taken.

Just that, however it went... she would never see Hunter again.

Nineteen

Narcissa—Nia—allowed her hands to hang loose and held her head high as the guards escorted her to the third floor. Her high heels echoed with a sharp click as she walked beside them. Ascending the staircase gave her the additional time needed to fully prepare herself for what lay before her. She shut off every emotion that attempted to linger inside her heart. None of that mattered at the moment—only her livelihood. She'd do whatever it took to reassure Averine of her commitment to the den.

One guard opened the door at the top of the staircase while the other remained behind her. Narcissa strode forward toward Averine's office. The door was already open. Not that it surprised her. Given what happened, of course, Averine awaited her. Aside from their initial contact, she hadn't met with the woman more than a handful of times. It coincided only ever with updates to her contract. Trouble rarely found her. At least, not outside that one time she almost died. Not that she could be faulted for that.

This... well, prior actions couldn't be changed. She could control only what happened going forward.

Nia took the last few steps into Averine's office. The guards remained on the other side and closed the door behind her. "You wished to see me."

Averine lifted her gaze from the register on her desk. She returned the quill pen to its holder and steepled her fingers together. "Yes. Sit."

The female's reaction didn't surprise her. Nor did the demand. Although she could claim that she and Hunter had done everything possible to prevent this, thinking over the last couple of months, they hadn't done the one thing that would've ensured his eyes never glowed. They'd refused to separate. Not that she'd verbally acknowledge any of that. Instead, she offered Averine nothing more than an appropriate response: "Yes, ma'am." Nia strode forward, sat in the chair, draped one leg over the other, and clasped her hands in her lap.

"I suspect you are aware of why I summoned you here. Correct?" The woman pushed the chair back, the scraping sound echoing as she stood up. She strode around the desk without taking her dark-brown eyes off of Nia.

Obviously, the glow of Hunter's eyes had triggered the magic in this place. While she could feign stupidity, it likely wouldn't accomplish much. Nor could she risk losing this job. Or something worse happening because of a lie. "Hunter," Nia stated. "Not that his reaction was in my control."

"You must think me a fool." Averine stopped in front of her large oak desk, the scent of the wood filling the air, and leaned back against the edge. "Or do you simply believe I'm unaware of your prior transgression with him?"

Clenching her fingers tightly together, she tensed. Shit. Did the woman know about all of them? No, Averine hadn't used the plural term. Okay. *Everything is okay,* Narcissa told herself. She could respond, admitting nothing. It was better if she didn't. Then, through their conversation, she could determine how much Averine actually knew. Multiple transgressions existed. They'd slept together after that one session he'd had with Ivory. It took every ounce of effort to keep the disgust off her face. That didn't include their previous session together, where things had become far more personal than they ever had before. And he'd marked her twice. "Of course not," Nia replied.

"Then it stands to reason you encouraged him." A faint smirk played on the female's face. "*That* is in your control." Averine gripped the edge of her desk and crossed one ankle over the other. "So, what do we do about it? One transgression, Nia, I might forgive, but a second... something that should've never occurred. That... well, it seems best we find a way to *correct* that behavior. Unless... you no longer feel up to your work." The female tilted her head. "Which I imagine would disappoint many of your clients."

It was her fault. She'd gotten close to Hunter. Grown to care about and love him. Something that should never have happened. When the possibility of leaving him arose, she held on, her grip tightening around him. The consequences of her actions were now abundantly clear. Hunter would also face his own consequences—if he ever returned.

Desperate, Narcissa swallowed, her throat scratchy, each movement a struggle against the impending doom. Of all her clients, she cared about only one other. Though Fallon would get along fine without her, it didn't mean the same for her family. They depended on her income too much. She had no other choice. "I'll do whatever you wish to prove myself, Mistress. I'm committed to the den. To the work. To you."

"That's good to hear, Nia." Averine pushed off her desk. "First, Hunter will be reassigned to Nina. Pass along any information you see fit. Second, you'll work the night shift in the club downstairs—without pay—for the next week, along with maintaining your regular schedule. That should cover the financial loss of the free session he received from you."

As far as punishment went, she could handle all of that. While she cared little about the temporary demotion, it was better than the alternative. Workers had disappeared for having made some of the same transgressions. "Yes, ma'am."

"Oh, and if Hunter argues or refuses these changes, he will be banned. For life. And you will be sent elsewhere. Understood?"

"Yes, ma'am." What else could she say? She couldn't question what would happen to her. Nor could she express that Hunter wouldn't like any of this. It didn't matter whether it was true. Gods, she prayed he didn't return. If she had to numb herself out just to go forward, so be it. Because if Hunter came back... it would break her. It might break them both. And neither of them would ever recover.

"Good. Now, go pass this along to Shalla. I'll know if you don't." Averine returned to her seat at the oak desk and let her eyes trace the lines of the book laid out across it.

"Yes, ma'am."

Two of her favorite words. And she'd never despised them more.

Nia rose to her feet and headed for the door. With each click of her six-inch heels on the hardwood floor, her heart sank like a nail being hammered in. The door opened before she even reached for the doorknob.

"Nia? One last thing."

From the doorway, she glanced back at the woman, her gaze lingering for a moment. Whatever Averine planned to tack on couldn't be good.

"If you miss one night at the club or break another rule, I know a few guards who'd eagerly handle your punishment. Understood?"

One of the many things that occurred in the background that no one talked about. Not just because they couldn't, but because some of them simply didn't know. It was one thing to fake a rape fantasy. A whole other thing to experience it.

"Yes, ma'am," Nia muttered.

Without another word, she exited Averine's office, turned to the right, and headed for the front staircase. It was best if she got these changes with Shalla over with now. Then she could return to her room, sink into her bed, and inhale the familiar scents of her and Hunter that remained. At least, until she had to clean everything up. After that, she would lock the memories away. It was the only way she could handle the agony of losing him.

That's what happened. Their time together had officially gotten cut off. As if it had never existed.

Halfway down, she paused, her fingers tracing the worn grooves of the banister. Her entire body stilled. A cold vise squeezed her chest, and a whimper escaped her lips as darkness threatened to consume her. Her grip on the handrail tightened until her knuckles turned white.

Gods, that was exactly what had to happen. She had to forget their time together. Shut down completely. Otherwise, she'd never get through another day. She'd never imagined this when she joined the den three decades back. Shaking the shock off, Nia continued her descent.

As she hit the last step, a prickling sensation ran up her spine, raising the hairs on her neck. Nia glanced around the room. Shalla remained ever so alert at her desk. Two guards were on duty—one posted at the bottom of the staircase and the other posted by the second-floor door. It opened, and in walked Hanita. Not a client she expected to see soon.

But a welcome distraction.

Nia crossed over to the receptionist's desk. She had to take care of business first. Then, she'd divert her attention away from the pain burrowing in her heart.

Because freedom was just a myth. Now, survival was all she had left.

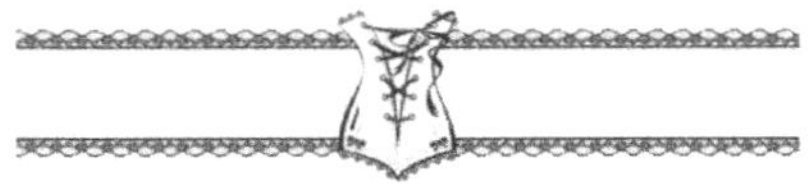

Putting one foot in front of the other, Hunter began the long walk to the village. With every step he took, he allowed his mind to relive every one of his last moments in Narcissa's room. Every ounce of pain he had felt. The things that had led to his decision—the only one he could make. To shut not only *her* out, but to shut everything out.

Each moment was a reminder that this was the way things had to be going forward.

There was no going back.

He felt every moment vividly, as if he were back in that room. One arm was wrapped around her, clutching her breast, while the other hand gripped the rough cross of the bed. Felt his fangs sink into her throat. Tasted her blood coating his tongue, her flesh as he suckled at the mark he created. Heard her strangled moan purr as if it resonated in the surrounding air. The vice-like grip of her pussy around his cock. Both of them holding their orgasms back to ensure they were more explosive than ever before. The soft *slick* of his fangs easing from her throat. He had savored the metallic taste as he licked his lips, then carefully stroked his tongue over his mark, swallowing every drop of blood, before softly nuzzling the puncture wounds. *Mine,* he'd purred. He had cupped her cheek, turned her head, met that glorious gaze of Narcissa's and pressed his forehead against hers. *Come for me,* he'd whispered. *My Narcissa... come for me.*

Had that been the moment? That declaration? Had it opened the floodgates? Snapped the last remaining sliver of control?

They'd come together, and just as he'd predicted, it had been beyond euphoric. Utterly divine. As if the two of them had been lifted out of this plane and placed in a realm only accessible to them. So different from the rest of the world not existing. As if in that moment between them, the gods themselves had blessed them.

It had been unlike anything either of them had ever experienced. Remarkably so. The releases he had found with her had been indescribable. But it had been something different altogether. And he knew she had experienced nothing like it before, either. Because in that moment their powerful orgasms erupted out of them, his eyes had glowed. Brilliant blue, not subtle, reflecting off the walls and the bedding beneath them. Like the ocean had turned into a fiery blaze and surrounded them.

His heart had stopped as he realized he could feel her. *All of her.* The anguish and heartbreak that had consumed her, the way their souls had linked and completely intertwined, the blood that rushed through her veins. Each beat of her heart. Every breath she took as if it were his own.

Intent on keeping his even pace, Hunter embraced the memory of every sensation. The constriction of his lungs, stabs to his chest, the perception that his heart had been carved right out of him, and the knowledge that it was *over*. His relationship with Narcissa that never should have been. It had never been allowed. Never *would be* allowed. He had broken all of his rules, *and hers.* Broken the rules of the one sanctuary he'd had for three decades.

Everything he had been fighting against—shattered in an instant. One moment of lost self-control—something he had always prided himself on.

One idiotic moment to bring it all crashing down on both of them.

His life had ended.

And there was nothing he could do about it.

His entire being had shattered.

And there would never be a way to put the pieces back together again.

Not anymore.

One foot in front of the other. One foot... in front of the other.

Crack.

Hunter didn't feel the pain in his chest as the memories continued. A scene playing out in his head. Reliving every moment.

His thumb gently brushed the tears from one of her eyes while his lips kissed them away from the other.

He had said nothing. Because there had been nothing to say. No apology to be made. No words that would suffice. Nothing to make the situation better. No way to reverse what had been done. The betrayal of his body and his soul.

Before he had met Narcissa, he had never wanted a mate. Never wished to belong to anyone. To have his soul forever tied to another's. It should have been such a joyous moment. But he had cursed the gods for their cruelty. To bring him to the one person who had been perfectly made just for him. The one person who knew him like no other. Who embraced his demons, his insecurities, his vulnerabilities. Who stitched together every internal wound and made him whole, in a way he never had been. Only to rip them completely away from one another. Freeze them in an impossible position with no way out. No path to reconciliation. No way around the stone wall that separated them from freedom and a future together. The realization that they would live, yet be separated eternally, that their souls were connected but their paths diverged, inflicted a deep, unprecedented pain. Not even when he thought he would lose his life had the pain been so tremendous.

He'd brushed his lips across hers, lingering for a moment. Released her from her restraints. Pressed his forehead against hers one last time. Slid his cock out of her sex. Moved off the bed. Taken just one step. His fingers had curled around one bar of the cross, confined to that spot as he'd contemplated how the fuck he was supposed to cross the room. How the fuck was he supposed to walk out the door. How the fuck was he supposed to *accept this*.

Pain that wasn't his own had lanced through him before Narcissa had wrapped her arms around him from behind. He'd squeezed his eyes shut. Recalled everything he'd told her nearly three weeks prior about what his eyes glowing would mean. He would feel every bit of her pain. Her emotions. Her *arousal*. Unless he closed off to her completely. It was something that would only bring him further pain. A male without his mate... forcibly separated... never to be near her again. It wasn't sustainable for life. Eventually, his soul would wither, and his heart would give out on him. Hopefully, keeping himself closed off from her would prevent her from feeling any of it. She didn't deserve that pain, or the knowledge of his death, when it came.

Hunter reiterated his thoughts from that moment. There would be no way he could *ever* come anywhere near this place again. Given the chance, he would kill anyone who dared to touch Narcissa without a second thought. Do everything within his limited power to steal her away. His actions, allowed to run unchecked, would bring about both of their deaths. There was nothing he could do that would get them anywhere except into a fiery grave.

I will always love you, Narcissa. Always. It does not matter who walks through that door. You... you will always be mine. Keep the promises you made to me last we saw one another. You will not let the light in your eyes go out. You will not let your heart go dark or your soul die. You will remember everything we made one another feel. The warmth and healing we brought to one another's hearts and souls. You will never forget your worth. And you will never stop trying to get free. Promise me again. Please.

But Narcissa hadn't promised him. Not like she had the first time, as he'd held her in the bathtub.

I'm so sorry, Hunter. You need to go.

You need to go. Four simple words, when they weren't strung together in a sentence like that. No promises. No verbal return of her love. He knew Narcissa loved him. But those weren't words he could ever hear from her again. No. All he had gotten from her, the last words he would ever hear her speak—*I'm so sorry, Hunter. You need to go.* The words had utterly destroyed the last vestiges of his composure. He understood why she'd only said what she did. But it hadn't stopped the overwhelming agony inside him from rising higher. From threatening to stop his heart and bleed him dry. He'd been wrong earlier. Nothing had ever hurt more than *that.*

And that was the moment he had done the only thing he could do. Not only to protect her, but to protect himself. No matter how much more pain it caused him. Hunter had shut her out. Slammed a door on the connection that had been forged between the two of them.

But it hadn't been enough. It wouldn't be enough not to feel her. He'd had to ensure he felt *nothing.* Otherwise, he never would have been able to force himself to leave.

So, he had shut *everything* down. Shoved every single emotion into an iron room and placed an impenetrable lock upon the door. It was a lock he couldn't even think about undoing until, at the very least, he was far away from that place. Far enough away... and all alone. But if he was intelligent... it was a lock he would never open ever again.

Hunter slowed and stopped, his eyes fixed on the open space ahead, the silence broken only by the chirping of unseen birds. The den was no longer visible. He'd ensured he wouldn't be able to feel Narcissa any longer, and that she wouldn't be able to feel him. He'd left her room without another word. Ignored the door that opened across the hall, as well as the person who stood in the doorway. Kept an even pace, with a blank expression. Nothing had shown because there was no longer anything there, not on the surface or beneath it. He'd reached the end of the hall, taken a right to get to the hallway that would lead him to the waiting room, and passed the personnel staircase on his right just as it opened and guards exited. But he didn't break his stride as they moved past him and headed down the hallway behind him. He'd just kept right on moving. Exited into the waiting room. He didn't speak a word to Shalla as he crossed the floor and headed to the exit. The words died in his throat; he no longer had a reason to speak to the female. He had no further appointments to confirm. Not anymore. A few more paces and he had left that place for the last time.

Even behind the walls of the iron prison he'd locked every emotion into, Hunter recognized the torment raging inside. The urgency. The instinct. Even with every ounce of self-control and discipline firmly in place, he nearly headed back the way he'd come. But he stopped himself in time. It would be futile.

Every moment he relived in his head was a reminder that this was how things had to be. There was no other way. He had *no choice* but to go home and never return to that place again. There were no options to free her from her confinement. There were no options that ended in their having a life together. Narcissa had made that abundantly clear. More than once.

"You make me forget... everything. All the darkness... the bad stuff... the evil in me. When I am with you... it is like it does not exist. And when you touch me... you make me forget what covers me. It has never been like that with anyone else."

"For the first time in my life, I feel like I can see myself. Like I'm not broken or damaged. When I'm with you, it's like we're the only two in existence. You touch me... I feel like I'm more than just a warm body. I've never had that before."

"You are more than that to me, Narcissa. So much more. I have never wanted to be with anyone. Not that way. Not for more than sex. I am too damaged, broken, scarred, both inside and out. I have never been with a female who could see past that. But you do. What I have grown to feel for you, there is nothing I would not do to keep these feelings from going away. I would break every rule, take any consequence to be with you."

Narcissa laid her head against his chest. "I don't want what I feel for you to go away, either. We can have that..." She opened her mouth and snapped it shut. Hunter felt the separation before she even moved, his cock sliding free from her. As she sat on the bed and pulled her knees up against her, he felt a chilling wave of dread wash over him. She didn't have to say the words for him to know he'd been right. He definitely did not want to hear the answer to the unspoken question.

"You mean a lot to me, Hunter. The things I feel for you… I didn't think any of it was possible. But this is the only place we can have that. None of it can show out there."

Hunter's gut twisted, a surge of fiery acid burning its way up his throat. His chest constricted, as if a vise was squeezing the air from his lungs. That icy dread grew, and it felt as though he had been plunged into the biting cold of an icy river. This pain… this… rejection… no, this was definitely not a pain that was enjoyable.

"I see," he muttered. He sat up slowly on the bed, his fingers gently touching the puncture wounds she'd left at his pulse point. She'd fucking marked him. Even without that, a fragile hope flickered within him for things he'd never imagined he was worthy of. Gods, he'd been so fucking stupid. Really fucking stupid. Of course, this thing between them wouldn't go beyond this room. How could it? He was who he was, and she was who she was. Apparently, not even something as extraordinary as what they'd just shared could change that. But the fucking mark… How fucking selfish of her had that been? "So… you get to claim me, but I do not get to claim you. You marked me—which I can only assume you have knowledge of what that means for my species—but I do not get to do the same. Despite what the both of us freely admit we feel for one another, what we have brought out of one another, the parts of ourselves we have given to one another… I have to continue to share you with…" A grimace, tight and angry, twisted his mouth. "How many clients do you have?"

Her jaw clenched. His eyes tracked her as she got off the bed, crossed to the closet, removed her heels and put them away, then covered herself with a black robe. Ah. So, that was how it was going to be. Not that he could really blame her. The tone of their conversation had shifted in the blink of an eye. Unable to sit on the bed any longer, Hunter stood up off of it and leaned against the nearest post, his arms crossed as she turned to face him.

"You think this is easy for me? You think I don't want to just run off with you? It's not that simple. You come in, pick who you plan to screw, pay, fuck, and leave. That's the extent of your involvement. Little different for those of us who are here. You can't even imagine what it's like. They even get a hint that we feel anything for each other, they'll put as much separation between us as possible. That doesn't even consider why I'm even here. Why I have spent the last thirty solaris of my life letting a string of endless people use my body."

"I never once said this was easy for you. Or that you did not want to leave with me. But you obviously will not, so that is a moot point. Whatever consequences or punishments would rain down on you because of this"—he gestured back and forth between them—*"obviously overshadows anything you might feel. If they have that strong a hold on you, control you that much, to the point you will not even attempt to fight for something you so clearly want as much as I do—which is a phenomenon all on its own, by the way, that I would even want this for a single moment—then fine. It is what it is. But do not act like I do not understand. Whatever reason you came here and stayed... I am sure it was a good one, whatever it is. I started coming here for a multitude of reasons, just one of which for what this place can offer that I could get nowhere else. Because that is all I deserve, Nia, a quick fuck that I have to pay for. I am no good to a female for anything else."*

And she proved that a bit more right now. Her job was more important and more necessary to keep, the punishments and consequences too much to bear, to fight for what they obviously had. Even after all their declarations. Even after what she'd done. That she wouldn't leave with him, that she'd stay and continue to work here, insist that they could only ever have a relationship in secret while she continued to screw however many others... that wasn't even what he was the most pissed off about right now.

"Even knowing all of that, knowing how this was going to end up, how this was going to have to be... you still did this." Hunter tapped the side of his throat harshly. *"You still claimed me as yours. There are some in my species who take marking lightly, but not me. Not in this spot. When I am with a female, I am exclusive with them by choice, but this... You obviously have no idea what this meant to me. You did this knowing I would never get the same exclusivity from you. There was no chance of it ever happening. That was cruel, Nia. It was cruel, and it was selfish."*

No, what was *cruel* was what the gods had done to them. Any action on his part to change things would culminate in one or both of their deaths. *Nothing* was worth her death. At least this way... she would survive.

Was this what it felt like to have claws split your heart in two?

Hunter turned away and continued his trek. His conscious mind barely registered the passing scenery, but his subconscious soaked in every detail of the journey.

When he reached the village, he had already decided. There was no freeing Narcissa from her prison. There was no future for them. She had told him to go. He had to respect her decision. Even if it killed him. If she had wanted him to free her... she would have asked. But there were things at stake that he didn't understand. Because she wouldn't—or couldn't—tell him.

Hunter paid no attention to anyone or anything as he made his way home. He opened his front door, stepped inside, closed the door, and bolted it. He went straight to the fireplace, the scent of ash filling his nostrils, and kneeled on the cold floor. Made quick work of starting a fire. Stood to his feet and went to his bedroom. The small, black, lacy thong Narcissa had sent to him still hung on the corner of his headboard. Every night before sleeping, he would take them off, but they always went back to the same place.

He stood in his bedroom doorway for the longest time, just staring at them. If he was truly going to commit to a future he had no choice but to accept... he couldn't have anything around that would remind him of *her*. Crossing the room, he scooped the panties off the headboard and returned to the front room. Without hesitation, he tossed the fabric into the flames. Then he turned around and returned to his bedroom. Underneath a corner floorboard, he found what he was looking for. Countless bags of gems and coins lay buried deep beneath the wood, unseen and shielded from prying eyes. He collected a bag of gems, checked the contents, and then switched it with another. Having found what he was searching for, Hunter closed up the floor and returned to the fireplace.

First, he opened the black velvet bag, bent over, and emptied the contents onto the floor in front of the grate. Dozens of tiny diamonds spilled across the wooden boards. The image embodied the tears he could no longer release. Tossing the bag aside, Hunter unsheathed his claws and dragged them diagonally over his heart in two directions, creating an 'X'. He did the same to both sides of his throat, and over both of his inner thighs. Over every mating mark point. Symbolic. For the loss of his mate. She wasn't dead, but she was lost to him forever. It might as well have been the same thing.

With blood dripping from the open wounds, he kneeled on the floor, legs spread to ensure the blood from his thighs had plenty of room to coat the diamonds. The gemstones dug into his knees, but he welcomed the pain. He leaned in, the rough stones scratching his knuckles as he pressed them into the shimmering diamond pile. Lowered his head. The steady *drip-drip-drip* and the crackle of the flames were the only noises in the room.

It was hours later, long after the fire had burned down to ashes, that Hunter moved again.

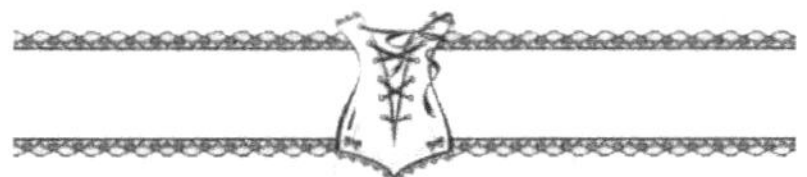

Nia set a delay on the music player in her room. She had everything set for Kylen's arrival. His preference for things hadn't changed in years. They always started with her performing for him on the stripper pole, followed by a lap dance, which eventually led them to the bed. Occasionally, he changed things up, but that only applied to the toys he liked to use. Right now, it all worked for her.

Routine kept her focused and her mind clear. Most of the time. Over the last couple of weeks, Hunter had made his way into her thoughts once or twice. That she handled easily. She shoved him deep into the recesses of her mind, locking him away with a finality that echoed in the silence. If only it was that easy when he haunted her dreams. Nia swallowed, the dryness still present in her throat, and glanced at the time she'd chosen.

One minute.

Perfect. With each step she took, her heels tapped against the dark floor as she strolled across the room to the stripper pole. She slowly eased her body onto the ground, feeling the rough texture of the cold wood beneath her. Yes, one minute was perfect. It gave enough time for the cold to seep into her bones and focus her thoughts. Of all her clients, Kylen would notice if something appeared off. She couldn't allow that. She had a job to do. One that served her well.

This wasn't the time to miss Hunter. Not the things he'd done to her body or how they spoke to one another without judgment. It didn't matter how perfect they were for each other. Something she had to keep reminding herself of nearly every day. It's why she'd chosen this song. A piece she'd recorded a few days earlier. No, the song didn't belong to her, nor the words. Just the voice. And the emotion.

It served as a reminder. One she desperately needed to hear. Because she had to remember—a relationship with Hunter was toxic. His presence was a venomous threat to her livelihood and family. She'd needed to part ways with him. It didn't matter how much she loved him. That kind of emotion was for the weak. And she wasn't weak. She was a strong professional.

The music started, rebounding softly off the walls. Her voice echoed, and as she lifted her upper body, the cool metal of the stripper pole greeted her touch. Nia swept her hands down her hair, face, and neck. Reaching behind her, she unhooked the back. For this evening's show, she'd selected a black velvet dress with long, lace sleeves. It hooked around the nape of the neck and accentuated every curve of hers. That didn't even include the lingerie she'd chosen to wear underneath. A lace leopard print with a multitude of black strings wrapped around her abdomen and hips. The G-string panties connected to a pair of black, thigh-high stockings. Something she believed Hunter—shit, no. This was for Kylen. Kylen. She had to remember that.

The door opened just as she arched her neck and unzipped the back of the dress. From the corner of her eye, Nia saw Kylen walk into her room and approach the queening bench she had set up in front of her. With her back arched against the cold, metal pole, she rose to her knees, delicately pulling one sleeve down her arm, and then the other. Her gaze fell upon Kylen as he sat on the queening bench and brushed his white hair away from his shoulders. As she continued her show, she felt his dark-purple eyes boring into her.

Dropping to all fours, she crawled around the pole until she faced it. Nia gripped it with both hands, the texture a familiar sensation, and with one hand higher than the other, she swung into a standing position. She ran a hand up the length of her leg as she straightened her body. Hooking her thumbs into each side of the dress, which currently sat bunched around her hips, she inched it down her body. Once it hit the floor, she took only one high-heeled foot out and hooked her leg around the pole. She executed a slow spin, which flung the dress across the room. Briefly noting where it landed, Nia switched legs mid-spin and extended the other for a moment, and then brought them both together.

She swung around the pole until her tribal-print platform heels hit the floor. Coming into a standing position, Nia tightened her hands on the pole. She swiveled to the left, her back pressing against the warm metal, as she brought one knee to the ground and bent the other. Then she spun in the opposite direction. She kicked her right leg out, brought it over the left, and released the hold she had on the bottom part of the pole as she straightened her body.

Kylen was the only client she had that she performed for like this. It simply wasn't something any of her other clients requested. Though she imagined Hunter would've—Fuck! No! This wasn't happening. Focusing on the sound of the music, Narcissa tuned into the words coming from the speakers: "Do you feel me now?"

Monotony.

That was what had become of Hunter's existence for the past thirteen days.

Wake up. Bathe. Eat. Work around the village or for the queen. Eat. Sleep.

Wash, rinse, repeat.

An endless cycle of nothingness that allowed him to function. Because the alternative was chaos and savagery.

He hadn't even bothered to cook the slab of meat in front of him. Right now, the temperature of his meal was the least of his concerns. His belly would get full, and that was the essential point.

Hunter's claw sliced into the raw meat with ease. He rolled his shoulders, feeling the sudden tension that had settled in his muscles. Not just in his back, but in his thighs and wrists as well. Not the first time something similar had occurred. But he otherwise ignored the sensation, just as he had every other time. Hunter brought his claw to his mouth, licked off the blood, then rubbed his wrists one after the other. He stabbed the piece of meat he'd cut from the slab and brought it to his mouth. Chewed slowly and swallowed. Licked the blood from his lips.

Wash, rinse, repeat.

Bite after bite entered his mouth and traveled tastelessly to his stomach. Periodically, he rolled his shoulders and rubbed his wrists again. Nothing out of the ordinary. He felt nothing, not the racing thoughts, the loud thumping of his heart, nor any warmth in his veins. His claw sliced through the meat, the only sound in the room, then scraped against the plate. No soothing, feminine voice. And touch. No scent of cedar with a hint of jasmine. No jade green or gold.

Just those occasional twinges that were nothing... but could be everything. Not that he allowed those thoughts to enter his mind. Or *any* thoughts to enter his mind.

Nothing... Nothing that would remind him of the one he'd left behind. The one he'd walked away from, forever. The life he'd turned his back on, as if it meant naught. Nothing that reminded him of what he'd stopped fighting for.

Because what he had left behind meant more *alive* than *tortured and dead*.

Hunter brought another bite to his mouth. He chewed slowly, not tasting a single drop of the blood that filled his mouth and coated his fangs. He swallowed—and nearly choked as a jolt of intense pleasure coursed through his belly and between his thighs.

That was *definitely* out of the ordinary.

Forcing the bite down, Hunter sat there immobile for several moments. Just waiting.

A fluke. It had to be. Because he had shut down. Both to his emotions, and to *her*. There was *no way* he should have felt a *single fucking thing*.

Could it be from Hayden? Had he somehow opened up to his twin and was getting residual sensations from him?

No, not only had he never done that before, but while his twin was in the village, Rainbow was not. So, it couldn't be—another jolt, more intense than the last, speared through him. A groan escaped Hunter as he balled his hand and slammed it down, the wood vibrating beneath his fist. No, *no*. He strained to keep out the intrusive sensations that were desperately trying to break through. His fist slammed down on the table again, and the plate jumped as it clattered against the rough wood. Blood splattered across the back of his hand, warm and sticky from his steak. For a moment, the fierce pleasure that had welled up, settled. Nothing left but a dull hum in his veins. He had an erection now, but that could be handled—a burst of pleasurable pain cracked across the middle of his back. Hunter's back arched as a twin burst of pain tingled across his ass. His ears twitched as, for a moment, he could have *sworn* he heard Narcissa moan. But that was *impossible.* She was not here. Nowhere near this village. She was back *there,* locked up in that *place.* Métamorphe was not a place that she would ever get to see.

Without realizing it, he'd gripped so tightly to the edge of the table, the wood bit into his palms. Hunter's breaths were ragged as they left his mouth. Using his feet, he shoved his chair back and stood to his feet—nails bit into one of his ass cheeks as, simultaneously, teeth buried themselves in his other.

Hunter's body didn't register the shift before he was crashing to the floor. He landed hard; the impact reverberating through the wood, his chair toppling over with a loud clatter.

His fingers tightened around the corner rings as he steeled himself, before the leather crop cracked against his ass, the sound echoing in the silent room. The sting was more intense than before, bringing a more pronounced moan out of him this time.

"Oh, yes, Hunter. I enjoy hearing those sounds come from you." Narcissa struck each ass cheek twice with the crop, and then across one of his thighs. She kept the same power behind it as she had with the previous crack.

Hunter couldn't hold back the hiss. The delicious sting seemed to travel through the full length of his cock. But then she bit one of his ass cheeks and moaned. His hands clenched so tightly around the rings that his knuckles cracked. His eyes flipped black—though not in a good way—and he let out a snarl. He fucking loved being bitten, especially when she did it. But not there.

Wind whistled through the cracks in the walls of the meager hut. Hunter stared down at the half-rotten wooden slats. Already, his elongated claws had left deep gouges in the wooden floor. No matter what was said—or done—there was no fucking way he was looking up from this floor. No fucking way he was going to make a single sound. He wouldn't give any of them the fucking satisfaction. Not Clay, who sat in his room, not participating while he pretended everyone else wasn't there. Or Sam, who stood in the corner of the front room, arms crossed, laughing and goading the others along. Not the two Informants Azazel had brought in to "watch the show." And definitely not Azazel himself.

Hunter's body jerked with each powerful thrust the male made into his not-quite-transitioned body. It took every ounce of strength he had to remain on his hands and knees while he was fucked from behind. The smell of spirits and blood and cum damn near choked him. He focused on the metallic taste of his own blood, which had pooled in his mouth.

One of the other Informants tossed an empty spirit jar into the doorway of the bedroom. "Watch what he does when you do this."

After a moment of shuffling, fangs sank deep into Hunter's ass cheek. He yelped loudly and instinctively jerked away. Azazel buried his claws deeper into his shoulder, jerking his ass back against his pelvis and sending bloody streams down his collarbone.

The laughter that filled the room became all he could hear.

"Ten coins says he cries soon."

"What qualifies as 'soon?'"

"The next... eh, let us say, five minutes."

"I will take that bet."

The male bit into his ass again and—

"Fuck. More, sir."

Hunter's eyes popped wide open. As impossible as it was, he jerked his head this way and that. Looking everywhere. Searching for what—who—could absolutely not be here.

He could still feel the excruciating pain of the fangs in his ass. Even reached behind him and searched for blood. Nothing. There was no blood there. No one had bitten him. He wasn't back *there*. He was *here*. A full-grown male. Azazel was dead. Fucking dead. He had watched the motherfucker burn into ash.

Narcissa wasn't here, either. A sharp pain pierced his chest, as though his heart had been stabbed.

What the fuck was wrong with him? Was he losing his fucking mind? He'd expected it at some point, but like *this*?

Hunter dug the heels of his hands into his eye sockets. *No, no, no, no, no. No more. No more memories. No more... Hades, please...*

Something tickled his shoulder. Removing his hands, he glanced down. There were puncture wounds on his shoulder. Blood had trickled down over his collarbone and dripped a little to the floor. Had he done that to himself?

Suddenly, all he could feel was an overwhelming *need*. A need... that wasn't his own. Hunter's back bowed against the floor as a fiery sensation coursed through his veins. He let out a moan and hastily covered his erection with one hand, clutching it firmly.

"More, please, Sir," Narcissa pled.

Hunter pressed his hand against his eyes again. "You are not here. You are not here. I am alone." With a groan, he stroked his cock, unable to resist the urge. Whatever would take this burn, this demand, from his body.

It didn't seem to matter. Inexplicably, waves of pleasure mingled with pain surged through his lower back and ass, intensifying the rising orgasm. Sensual agony sent another surge of heat across his body, driving him higher and higher. His body moved on its own, flipping him onto his side. As the pain cracked across his ass and his back, Hunter let out a moan. But then it felt like his ass was bitten again, this time, harder than before, and—

"Barely past your growth spurt, and this is already your favorite toy. Maybe I should take it away. No, I think not. I like what it does to you when I do this.*" The strokes of his cock got harder and faster.*

Hunter whimpered, then bit down on his tongue so hard he could taste the metallic tang of blood filling his mouth.

Azazel laughed. "Yes. That is what I like. Everything you are feeling right now—that disgust, that self-loathing, that fear—I can smell it. And it smells so good."

"NO! NO! NO!" Hunter lashed out, no idea what his blows found purchase with. He felt the sting of fingernails foreign to him, piercing his palms. Panting, he bore down mentally and did everything in his power to push the warring sensations from his brain. The horror at what Azazel had done to him, coupled with the pleasure that coursed through his mate.

"No," he moaned. "No, no... no..."

He panted as the invisible blows connected with his back, bruising his flesh. "Fuck... fuck..."

"Please, may I come, Sir?"

"You are not here! You are not here! Leave me alone!"

But those last words held no weight. Because he wanted her here. Wanted to be with her. Wanted to be the one making her feel the things she was feeling right now. The one that was quickly pushing her to the point of no return—Hunter's lips parted as his pants became more audible. He jerked in and out of the fetal position, his head connecting with one of the table legs, then the floor. Maybe. He couldn't be sure. Gods, he could *feel* her riding his tongue... her glorious pussy pressed against his lips... And he could *taste her...* His moan echoed around the room. Now, he could actually hear the cracks as something smacked his ass. Hard. His grip on his cock tightened, but in his mind, it wasn't his hand gripping and pumping against his cock. It was Narcissa. And he was pounding into her, ready to come and fill her ass with his seed. Jolts of lightning lit up his synapses, setting a blaze off in his body.

This time, he barely stopped the growl that threatened to escape as she purred again. Fuck... He firmly pushed the vibrator deeper into her core with his heel, simultaneously increasing the speed and intensity of rubbing her clit as he struck her back with the whip. His hand lingered on her sex as he continued to strike her back with the whip. Red mark after red mark appeared. He wanted nothing more than to fuck the shit out of her right now. Use his cock to take possession of her in every way, shape, and form. But he wouldn't break first. Not this time.

Each crack of the whip against her skin intensified with every strike. As soon as the first streak of crimson blood appeared, trickling along her skin, something snapped within him. A massive snarl and a loud moan reverberated around the room, the sounds bouncing from wall to wall. The two together sounded utterly divine. Drawing blood had always turned him on. He'd never given a thought to why. But this... drawing blood this way... it did things to him that using his claws to draw blood didn't do. Not that he could explain that, either. His hand lingered at her core as he leaned over her, tracing his tongue up the expanse of her back, his fangs skimming her skin as he consumed the blood he had drawn.

Narcissa arched her back, the chains rattling a little more. She let out another groan. "Will you fuck me, please, Sir?"

Holy shit, he wanted to fuck her. He absolutely wanted to fuck her. This was the first time she had ever pleaded with him for that, her voice laced with desperation. She'd begged him for a lot of things, but that was the first time she had used those particular words. And he absolutely loved it. He needed to be inside her just as much as she needed the same thing, though he wasn't quite ready to give in just yet. Not that it would likely take more than another moment or two before he wouldn't be able to wait any longer.

The whip cracked across her back, and as the blow landed harder than the last, his control frayed, a snarl escaping him as a fresh line of crimson bloomed. He allowed it to trickle down to her waist, right above the belt, before he swept his tongue across it, capturing every drop. Licking up her neck, he bit down on her earlobe. "How badly do you need me to fuck you, Nia?"

She purred. "Intensely, Sir," *Narcissa replied, with a pleading tone to her voice.*

Holy fuck, what those two sounds did to him. As his other hand tugged at the nipple clamps, he stroked her clit, feeling the heat of her body. "Have you learned your lesson today?"

"Yes, sir."

Another blow to his ass, harder than before.

"Fuck... may I come, please, Sir?"

Hunter salivated as her juices coated his tongue. Holy fucking shit. *Fuck yes, baby girl, you can fucking come.* His body twisted as he felt the searing pain of nails piercing his thighs. A deafening cry reverberated throughout the room as an intense orgasm washed over him, covering both him and the floor. But it was like he could taste a wave of Narcissa's cum filling his mouth. He swallowed greedily, his mouth and tongue searching for what wasn't really there.

With an endless stream of moans, Narcissa did as requested. With a minor shift of her legs, she secured the hook and then jammed her heels into his backside with maximum force. The aroma of his blood filled the air. Not only that, but her heels digging in so hard also lifted her hips closer to his. Another purred moan slipped from between her lips.

Hunter's growl was a low, guttural sound as he snapped a hand to her throat. He squeezed, not enough to cut off her airway, but enough to send her heart rate skyrocketing. His claws dug deeper into her buttocks, crimson droplets seeping between his fingers, while the intensity of his thrusts grew. "Look at me." *Where had those words come from? His mouth. They'd left his mouth... and he couldn't take them back.*

Narcissa immediately complied. The arch of her neck lowered until their eyes met.

It didn't matter that his eyes were shut. Those jade-green irises with flecks of gold were all he could see. Something scraped against wood. Hunter's body connected with something hard. But he didn't stop pumping his fist up and down his length. As if he had no control over the motion. His hips thrust repeatedly into his grip, as if her pussy or her ass were a warm embrace around his cock. And he needed *more*. So much *more*.

"Fuck," Narcissa purred.

"Oh, fuck... Fuck yes," he moaned.

A deep, guttural growl rumbled from his chest. He liked what she'd said to him, not to mention the way she'd said it. A lot. Not that he was going to admit that out loud. Hunter spun, fangs displayed, and secured her wrists with one hand, while his other hand forced her chin up. His cock was still fully erect. "You like saying things like that to me, Nia?"

Her heated gaze met his. "Among other things. Would you like an example?" Her tongue snaked out across her lips. "If you're a really good boy, I'll give you a reward."

As he pushed her back onto the bed, a growl emanated from him, vibrating the very air around them. Raising her arms, he held her wrists, the pressure a stark contrast to the soft mattress beneath them, as he straddled her, his knees a vise. "And what kind of reward would you give me for being a really good boy?"

"Given how much you like having your mouth on my pussy, an hour before your next session, I'll insert vaginal beads and even have a couple of clit vibrators out for your use." She tilted her head. "I'll even let you pick them out before you leave today. How does that sound as a reward?"

Oh, she knew exactly how much he enjoyed having his mouth on her pussy. With a growl, Hunter seized a handful of her hair, pulling her head back sharply. As he used his knees to spread her, he lightly teased her slit with the head of his cock. Fuck, she was wet. "And how am I supposed to earn this reward?" He leaned in, tilting her head back to give his tongue access to the sensitive skin of her neck. "I am not very good at being a good boy. I am much better at being bad." He bit her earlobe, then licked her neck again.

A loud moan left her mouth. Nia's legs found purchase on his thighs as she wrapped them around his hips. "I want you to fuck me hard while I dig my heels into your ass. So, it isn't too easy. While I may have multiple orgasms, you cannot have more than two to fully please me." The same tilt to one side of her mouth reappeared with a glint in her eyes. "I suggest you make them count," she purred.

The pleasure coursing through his body mounted to impossible heights. Between the torrent of emotions he felt from Narcissa and the phantom blows that struck his own body, he was quickly losing his grip. His thighs and his ass hummed with the repeated stings.

The rough bark of the tree had scraped his palms raw. But Hunter didn't move as much as was possible. The whip sliced into his back again. The muscles in his shoulders rippled with the blow.

"Stop. Again."

Another blow. Rivers of blood trickled down his spine.

"To be able to endure pain without flinching is a gift from the gods. If you can master this, then nothing will ever be able to take you down. Again."

Oh, gods. He was going to come again. *NO.* The memories lingered, bitter and acrid. Not *good.* He didn't want to think about those things. He didn't want to think about anything but—

A shudder went straight down his spine. Fuck, that purr of hers. He kept the head of his cock from doing more than a delicate dance against her opening. Hunter's tongue traced a path along her neck as his grip on her wrists grew firmer. "No one... has ever told me how many times I can come. What makes you think you get to tell me that?"

With a groan of anticipation, Nia leaned in, her breath tickling his ear. "Because..." she purred. "I know how badly you want that reward. Only good boys get rewards." She nipped his ear.

A powerful shiver ran down his spine, all the way to his groin, causing his cock to give a small twitch. Hunter sucked in a breath. Holy fuck, that felt good. He growled against her neck as he brushed his erection a little harder against her pussy. "You are not playing fair."

She ever-so-slightly increased the pressure of her hold on his hips. "I never said I would." Nia's tongue darted out, briefly touching the sensitive skin of his ear. "Now, are you going to be a good boy?"

Oh, she definitely wasn't playing fair. He pinned her wrists to the mattress on either side of her head, trapping her. Staring down at her, he licked his lips. He really enjoyed holding her down like this. Restraints without restraints. "I do not know, Nia. Perhaps we should find out." Without uttering a single word, he forcefully penetrated her, releasing a guttural moan as he entered her deeply. "Fuck..." he growled out. He started doing exactly what she wanted.

Nia groaned loudly. Gods... Fuck yes, that was exactly what he wanted to hear. She tightened her grip on him, digging her heels in, and moans and groans echoed in the air. His fangs extended at the way she arched her back, bringing her breasts nearer. Fuck, he wanted to bite them. Difficult at this angle, though. He widened his thighs and pressed her wrists down, escalating the intensity and rhythm of his thrusts. "Come for me."

As she dug her stilettos further into his ass, Nia's cry echoed through the room as a powerful orgasm surged through her, covering his cock with her release. "Fuck!"

"Fuck yes, just like that, Nia," he groaned. "Fucking come all over me." With growing intensity, his thrusts became even more forceful. Her body jerked each time he rammed his cock into her core. Oh, he was going to pull as many fucking orgasms out of her as he could before he finished. The session may not have started off great, but it would certainly end that way.

With her wrists pinned down, he couldn't hoist her up, no matter how hard he tried. But she took care of that. With a firmer grip, Nia pressed her stilettos into his backside and subtly shifted her hips, increasing the depth of his penetration. "Holy fucking shit. Fuck, don't stop!"

"Ahhhhh! NO, fuck!" Hunter twisted in on himself, his movements jerky as he unwittingly buried his claws into his skull. "Make it stop... Make it stop! Hades... please..." He jerked, flopped, and kicked, his limbs flailing wildly, knocking over everything in his path. But it didn't stop the sensation of his ass being filled and vibrations shooting through him. "Fuck... fuck... *please...*"

"Hold him down! Fucking hold him down! I warned you, you fucking bastard. I warned you what would happen if you interfered again."

Splinters sliced into Hunter's cheek as his face was pressed into the wooden floor. He snarled and roared, fought with everything in him, but—just like always—he lost the fight. His wrists and ankles were held down so tightly that blood puddled around them from the depth of the claws in his flesh.

"One of these fucking days, you are going to get—"

Azazel slammed into him, and the impact stole his breath, nearly forcing a scream. His body wasn't made for an invasion like this. Not yet, anyway. He was only twelve. He couldn't take this. He couldn't take this...

"—it through your fucking head. What I say is the fucking law. Twin or no fucking twin. Learn to obey me, or I will take his life before your eyes, and make you watch."

"Turn that beautiful ass of yours around. Once we are done here, I want to move on to something else."

Gazing at him through hooded eyes, Narcissa arched her back and dragged her leg across his hip toward her body, sliding her stiletto through his fur. His fangs extended, and a predatory gleam sparked in his eyes. "You say the sweetest things," Narcissa purred.

"Mmm, only to you, sweetheart."

His eyes didn't leave her once as she swung her leg over the bondage horse and slowly laid down against it. Getting into position put her ass on full display. Hunter leaned over and bit her left ass cheek, leaving a stinging mark, then did the same to her right. A slight gasp left her mouth. Afterward, he positioned the butt plug precisely at the entrance to her rear end.

"I could devour you every second for the rest of my life and still be starving." His tongue moved leisurely up her spine before his fangs lightly grazed her shoulder while inserting the plug inside her and activating it.

Narcissa peered over her shoulder at him. "The sweetest things," she repeated. "Fuck, Hunter," she moaned. "I need you inside me."

A low growl escaped Hunter's throat before he nipped her shoulder, and then he tenderly lapped up the fresh, metallic scent of her blood. A smirk spread over his face. Hunter put the finger vibrator on and held it against her clit. "Only if you moan my name again." Then he turned it on, too.

It had been the first time since he had walked through her bedroom door that she'd uttered his name. And, fuck, it felt damn good.

"Hunter," she said in a husky voice. Their gazes locked, and she arched her back, her skin flushed against his. "Hunter," she moaned. "Hunter," she purred. "Fuck me like you missed me."

Hunter cried out loudly. Tears he couldn't feel streamed down his face. His mind was fracturing. Between the agony and the pleasure. Between what the memories made him feel and what his mate was feeling. What was real? Was any of it real? Or had he just completely lost it finally, and this was the result?

Another orgasm slicked his thighs, pelvis, and the floor surrounding him. His foot squeaked against the wood as he tried to get away from... something. All of it. Everything. He needed *reality.* More than air in his lungs or food in his belly. More than any of his other senses. He needed something *real.* Something tangible. Something—

"There are times I will need to be in control—fully in control—and I will need you to embrace that." With his tongue, he followed a path up her stomach and along her ribcage, before moving on to suck on her breasts and tease her nipples. "But I recognize the dominant in you as well. And you know how much I enjoy that part of you too." Hunter licked her collarbone, then

her neck, and finally, gave a tiny, playful bite to her ear. "Even though it is… extremely difficult for me to relinquish any control whatsoever. But I thought that today, we could do a bit of both."

Minus the noises that came out of her mouth as he'd trailed his tongue up her body, Nia didn't utter a word. Reaching over to the bedside table, he grabbed the extenders. After releasing her cuffs from the chains, he attached the extenders, then attached those to the chains at the top of her bed. Hunter lowered her to her knees, the clang of the chains echoing in the silent room as he checked the restraints. She could move as much as she needed to, but her arms would remain above her head. No touching. That was important for this session. He absolutely craved it, but that had become part of the problem. "Your arms will remain restrained above your head. But today, you are going to be a bit more in control than I have ever allowed before."

Hunter lay down on the bed, his muscles tensing as he allowed himself a moment of hesitation before pulling her close. He had never been in this position before. Not once. Never. His cock was angled upwards, firmly pressed against his stomach as he moved her pussy along the length of his pulsating erection. He couldn't stop the groan that escaped him. Holy fuck, she felt good. Even like this, it felt … fuck; it felt good to have her on top of him.

"Today, Nia… I want you to fuck me. And you had better make it good."

"I'm going to fuck you so good, you won't want it any other way," Nia said, following it up with a purr.

Those words, not to mention that fucking mouthwatering purr that followed, just about did him in.

With a slight stretch, she adjusted her legs and hips, positioning her feet under his backside. "Sir," she punctuated as she swayed back, his cock head brushing against the entrance to her pussy. One thrust would bury him deep inside her.

Hunter let out a deep groan. Holy fucking shit, he couldn't wait. He'd never wanted this from anyone. But right now, it was all he wanted from her. Definitely not how this plan was supposed to go.

But there was no turning back now.

"I am going to come as soon as I get inside you." Grabbing onto her hips, Hunter buried his cock deep inside her. As promised, a massive orgasm erupted from him, shaking his entire body. "Oh, fuck!" he cried out in unison with her. He let out the loudest moan yet, his head immediately pressing back into the bed, and his body arching with the strain. With each jerk of his cock,

his claws dug further into her flesh. Holy fuck, holy fuck, holy fucking shit! Before it had even ended, he thrust his hips up into hers as hard as he could. "Fuck me, Nia."

She hooked her shoes tighter, her stilettos digging into his thighs, and moved her hips. A long, drawn-out growl rolled out of him. Oh ... fuck. Her movements were completely unhurried as she rolled her hips against his. Holy shit, he went so much deeper inside her. It took another minute before his climax concluded. As it did, he tightened his hold on her hips and met her thrusts, keeping his pace just as slow as hers.

Fuck. Fuck. Fuck. He should hate this. Not being fully in control. Having a female on top of him. Being in a vulnerable position like this. He should absolutely hate all of this. But that was far from the truth. Nope. Not even close. Not even a little. It couldn't possibly be just because he enjoyed the position. Nope. He wasn't stupid enough to believe that. It was because she was on top of him. Nia rocked her hips against his, rode him, fucked him.

Bad... this was bad... This was so bad. But... oh fuck, it was so good.

There was a pounding on the door. He barely acknowledged the disturbance, but somehow, he registered Hayden's voice in his head. Not that he understood a fucking word his twin was saying to him.

Get the fuck away, Hayden, now! You step one foot through that fucking door and I will do to you what I did to Sam.

Hunter didn't mean to say the words. Didn't mean them at all. And he would apologize to Hayden later. At that moment, he felt like he was losing control, a state he'd never reveal to his twin. It was bad enough that Hayden had felt it from him. Or had he simply heard the noises? His yells and the crashes?

"Things are going to be so different from now on. Going forward, you're mine. All mine."

No. No, no, no... He knew that voice. Hunter knew that voice.

His shoulder slammed into the wall. When had he stood to his feet? He gripped the sides of his head, and the blood trickled down his face, warm and sticky. It dripped to the floor, but Hunter didn't see it. Didn't smell it. His chest met the wall forcefully as he felt Narcissa's arousal building up inside him and finally erupting. He moaned and growled and panted as his release coated the floor at his feet. It covered him now. Covered in his own cum and sweat. And blood. Why was he bleeding? What had he done to harm himself?

The restraints around her, once tight, had been loosened. He could no longer feel the pressure around his midsection or wrists. Around *her* midsection or wrists. Hunter blinked fiercely, but it didn't clear his vision any. He could feel her falling... falling... landing on something soft. Constriction on his—*her*—wrists. A heavy weight on top of her. Broad shoulders. Knees spread her thighs wide. Pressure on her mouth—

"NO!" he roared. His fist crashed through the wall, splintering the wood. Wood cracked with a loud bang, and splinters rained down around him like tiny daggers. He grabbed the nearest object and hurled it with all his might. A mighty crash shook the room. Whatever room he was in now. Hunter, without a care in the world, struck out angrily at everything within his grasp.

"Oh... *fuck!*" The largest burst yet of arousal took him to his knees and sent spots dancing across his altered vision.

His grip on the cross and her midsection became tighter, a silent promise hanging in the air. Each time she sheathed his cock completely, he ground into her core. His body shook against hers. The scraping of his claws against the metal, as well as her hip, echoed as he tightened his hold. "Oh, fuck, I need you."

In that moment, it completely escaped his attention that his words weren't just regarding her body; he needed every single part of her. Mind, body, and soul. Needed to own and possess her. But he needed the same from her. He needed her to possess and own every single part of him. Not just during the few hours they spent together in this room, but forever. Every moment for the rest of their lives. He needed her. More than air, food, or water. More than anything.

"Narcissa..." Holy fucking shit, he didn't know what demand was rising within him. That wasn't true; part of him knew. But that part was in the back of his mind, a place he couldn't reach right now. All he knew was that he needed to answer the call. That he might go insane if he denied the instinct that threatened to take complete control. "Mine," he growled out. Gods, he was fucking panting; the throbbing in his fangs was even more intense now. His mouth closed over the side of her neck; her pulse thrummed against his lips. He wasn't sure how he kept his fangs from sinking in, fighting the urge to taste the warm flesh. A whimper escaped as he barely withheld yet again.

She arched her back and, with a subtle groan, Narcissa dug the heels of her stilettos deeper into his thighs, pulling harder on the restraints. He groaned against her throat. His hand slid from her side to cover one of her breasts as he dug his claws in all over again. The subtle change gave her the freedom to deepen the sway of her hips while pressing herself closer to his arm. Holy fuck. Regardless that his orgasm sat right at the surface, he wasn't ready to come just yet. He needed to draw this out for as long as possible.

As he sucked harder on her throat, a fang barely pierced her skin, which drew a moan from him. Hunter leaned his upper body toward the cross, causing her hips to tilt back slightly and enabling him to thrust even deeper inside her.

Pushing her breast more into his palm, Narcissa tilted her head, giving him more access to her neck.

With no warning, his fangs plunged in deep. Hunter roared against her as her sweet, heady blood filled his mouth, coated his tongue, and flowed down his throat. As he sucked her throat, bruising her skin, he clutched the cross and held her tighter. Marked her for the second time. His hips didn't stop once as he rammed his cock into her core again and again.

Some kind of strangled, moaned purr left her mouth. Narcissa clamped her vaginal muscles tight around his cock. Her hips didn't stop meeting each of his thrusts, no matter how hard he pounded into her.

His fangs slid from her neck with a groan. Then his tongue trailed along her neck, over his mark, as he swallowed what blood had spilled. Hunter nuzzled against the puncture wounds and purred, "Mine," against her throat. He couldn't hold back his orgasm any longer. And he could sense it was the same for her. Both of them teetered on the very edge. Once they fell over together, it would be more magnificent than anything they had yet experienced, or even shared. Releasing her breast, he cupped her cheek and turned her head so their gazes met. Hunter pressed his forehead to hers. "Come for me," he whispered. "My Narcissa... come for me."

Silence hung heavy in the air as their mutual releases erupted with a powerful burst. Her vaginal muscles clamped tight onto his cock as their juices gushed out, cascading down their thighs, spilling onto the bed beneath them. Hunter's mouth hung open, his cock jerking repeatedly, his body shaking against hers, as their orgasm continued, once again, seemingly with no end.

The release felt utterly... divine. As if the two of them had been lifted out of this plane and placed in a realm only accessible to them. So different from the rest of the world not existing... it was like this moment between them, the gods themselves had blessed them.

And then he realized. His mind took in the bright-blue glow reflected in her eyes. And his heart stopped.

For a blissful moment, the bright-blue glow surrounded Hunter, and he felt the comforting sensation of Narcissa in his embrace. It took a few minutes before he understood what he was hearing. Water?

He blinked rapidly, but it didn't help. His vision took its fucking time coming back to him. When it finally did, he looked around, but everything was blurred. That didn't mean he couldn't see, though. His mouth dropped. Heavy breaths left him. At some point, he had ended up in the bathroom. Everything in here had been destroyed. Toilet, sink, shower, which was where the water was coming from—the broken faucets... Flooding the room and... yep... it had spread down the hallway. Hunter's eyes widened as he followed the path, taking in the scenery. Large holes marred the hall, a testament to destruction, scattered in the walls and floor. Through the doorway, the living room was a disaster with holes riddled everywhere. Shattered furniture. Ripped parchment of what used to be photographs that Hayden had insisted on putting up. A chunk of the kitchen table. A shattered plate with blood on it from remnants of his dinner... that had settled by the front door... that was nearly cracked in two.

He looked down at himself. At the ejaculate that covered his lap and parts of his chest. His bloody thighs and hips. His head throbbed. Blood was dripping from his forehead, splattering on the floor with a soft thud. There were splinters embedded in his hands. His knuckles were bloody and likely broken.

It was like his brain took a minute to catch up with everything he was seeing. And everything he was still feeling. Hunter's breath caught as a fresh wave of tears started of their own accord and poured down his cheeks. *Agony.* Pulsating, all-consuming *agony.* Outside of the overwhelming arousal he hadn't been able to get rid of—arousal that had not been his own, but he had felt the full effects of—it was the most wretched thing Hunter had ever felt in his life. More painful than the whippings and the beatings. Even more painful than the rapes. More painful than the memories he tried to keep locked up tightly and buried deeper than Hades's domain.

Hunter wrapped his arms around himself and dug his claws into his shoulders, all the way to the bone. His tears fell like a torrential downpour, each drop a painful reminder of the emptiness that consumed him.

He forced it all out on a roar that shook the very foundations, splintering the walls and shattering the tile flooring.

His mate... his Narcissa... had been with someone else. His mate had been with another male. Had been with... *him.*

And Hunter had felt it *all.*

Twenty

As they exited Meraki, Narcissa added two more bags to the heavy load of three already digging into her arm. She enjoyed the slight burn of its weight. Though it was far from the most she'd ever carried around before. Right now, she needed to feel every lick of pain possible. It was the only thing that could silence the endless thrumming in her mind. A soothing balm to her racing thoughts.

"Do you want to talk about it?" Silva posed.

Yes and no, but they were far too exposed for her to address anything properly. The only people she might consider opening up to about her inner turmoil would be Silva or Grace. Narcissa did not want to bring it up when they were back at the den, stifling as always, leaving her with few options. "Let's head toward the bazaar."

A chill—unexpected and unsettling—shot down her spine. Something was off. Rounding the corner, she glanced back to see nothing beyond the guards accompanying them, their footsteps echoing.

"You're deflecting." Silva gave her a pointed look as they got closer to the nearby stall displaying a vibrant collection of seashells.

"No, I'm not." To drive her point home, Narcissa shifted the sunglasses from atop her cinnamon-brown hair, their dark lenses reflecting the world around her. Except she was, and he knew it. They'd spent far too much time with one another over the years for them to truly hold secrets. Mostly. There were things he'd never know—Hunter, and her family. She'd do whatever it took to protect those thoughts from ever being discovered. Not that Silva and Grace were unaware of what transpired a few weeks back. Come to think of it, two weeks to the day had gone by since the last time she'd seen Hunter. As the passage of time truly struck her, the crisp click of her heels turned into soft taps as her pace slowed. *Fuck, I can't think about that.* She shook her head and smoothed a hand down the sleek, tight skirt of her form-fitting dress, the fabric rustling softly.

"If you don't talk to me, Nia, I'll get Gracie involved when we return."

Her brows snapped together, a deep crease forming between them, her jaw clenched tight. This was the problem with people who knew you well; they also knew which buttons to push. "Fine. My last client yesterday—he had a meeting with Mistress afterward."

"You don't think—"

"Yes," Narcissa replied before he could even conclude his statement. Not that it was remotely necessary. "Except, Mistress has mentioned nothing since it occurred." That gnawed at her, a prickly unease far sharper than any vow she'd made to the den. At least this way, if Hunter ever returned, she stood a chance of glimpsing him. The back of her neck prickled with a sudden, inexplicable awareness. Narcissa halted, browsing the assortment of curiosities at the stall. It wasn't so much that anything caught her attention, but more so that she could discreetly scan the bustling bazaar, its vibrant atmosphere teeming with merchants and travelers. Someone was watching them. Another guard? That made little sense. The tips of her ears twitched. It couldn't be...

"Then you're worrying for nothing. If he'd succeeded, then Mother wouldn't have waited." Silva cracked a grin. "Besides, we both know you enjoy variety too much for that to happen," her friend teased.

"Right," she muttered. Even if it was no longer true. She *had* enjoyed variety. All that changed with Hunter. Not that she dared mention or give that too much thought. Sex with anyone outside of him lacked, well, everything—connection, control, and genuine pleasure. After her time with Hunter, the session with any client felt like a desperate attempt to reclaim her lost sense of control. Gods, she shouldn't be thinking like this. As a distraction from the indistinguishable faces in the crowd, Narcissa picked up a trinket, her fingers tracing the smooth curves of the ceramic. No matter which direction she searched, she didn't see him. There was no way he was here. She'd just imagined sensing him. A cruel illusion that tricked her into believing the impossible.

"Why doesn't it seem as though you believe that?"

"What?" Shit. What had Silva prattled on about? Narcissa blinked, her eyes narrowing, her brow furrowing in confusion. After he confirmed she had worried about Kylen for naught, she barely registered his words.

A soft *whoosh* reached her ears. Tucker's gaze snapped to the left a mere moment before Narcissa turned to see a short, stumpy male with their head cocked, as if looking at something invisible. Without moving from his position, Tucker panned his gaze to the right, and narrowed his eyes.

Narcissa's jade-green eyes grew wide, reflecting the shock on her face. Hunter was here. He was just camouflaged. Why hadn't she thought about that? How many times over the years had Fallon used that ability when he'd come into her room? She should've figured it out sooner. Her heart hammered against her ribs. Despite not being able to see him, the feeling of his closeness was tormenting. She despised everything about their position; the choice she had to make between him and her family.

"Nia," Silva's voice had grown closer. "What has you so distracted? Is it—"

Pivoting toward her friend, she pressed a finger to his lips, cutting off his question. There was no need for him to pose it. Narcissa stared daggers at Silva, attempting to communicate her desire for him to be quiet through her harsh expression. Of the four guards with them, Tucker likely knew Hunter was present. The male would've caught his scent already, even if he hadn't uttered a word. Unlike their physical prowess, trolls didn't possess an acute sense of smell.

Silva's glare was a sharp blade of disapproval, highlighting his displeasure with the situation she'd created. Even if he understood it. She'd shared that she had to drop Hunter as a client with both him and Grace. While she hadn't disclosed the reason, she supposed they'd figured it out themselves. For the past few weeks, the two of them had observed her, just as a parent would a baby, as she drifted, numb, unaware of the growing anguish within her heart.

Until yesterday. Kylen's antics had changed all that.

She couldn't allow this precious, transient moment to slip through her fingers.

Was he under the impression that his disapproval meant anything to her? Narcissa removed her finger from his lips and then poked Silva in the chest. "After everything we've been through over the *solaris*, you're going to do nothing. Agreed?"

Silva scoffed, the sound sharp and bitter as his eyes narrowed. "I don't like this." Her friend scrubbed a hand across his face.

"When have we ever been in a suitable position?" His time at the brothel extended well beyond hers. It wasn't as if things had improved. He knew that more than anyone. Yes, they had privilege, but it still only went so far. If Silva expected her to push through, he had to give her this. Gripped by the renewed agony, Narcissa knew she couldn't go on any further. Not without breaking a few rules.

"Five minutes, Nia."

"Ten," she retorted.

The male cursed under his breath. "Fine," he snapped. "But be quick about it."

Beaming brightly, she released the figurine in her hand and pressed a kiss to his cheek. Her high heel made a sharp sound as she turned, eyed Tzane and Tucker, and then purposefully strode over to them. "The two of you, come with me."

Tucker turned his narrowed gaze to hers. "Are you *sure* that is a good idea?"

No, it was a horrible idea, but she couldn't stop herself. Narcissa, with a questioning look, tilted her head at Tucker and raised an eyebrow. Did she dare admit how bad this was? It could land her, even Hunter, in a heap of trouble. Bring more to their stoop than they were already facing. With a subtle exhale, she released a soft breath. She bypassed his question and worked with the choices they had. "That isn't the real question. It's whether you'll stand down and let me do it. Your primary charge is ensuring I return in one piece. That will happen. Do not doubt that." Narcissa glanced from him to Tzane and back again. "So, for once, do what's right. I know Jade has been trying to drill that into you." Her gaze softened. "We all hear rumors." Nothing was truly private in the den.

Tucker ground his jaw and lowered his tone to a near-whisper. "If you even *think* about trying anything stupid... you know that we will have no choice but to stop you. *And him.* Please do not make us do that."

"I just need to see him." Even though it was foolish, it was the reality she lived. Narcissa prayed that, for once, the gods would heed her desperate pleas. If only for a few minutes. That was all she needed—a few minutes to see him and talk to him. Though her fingers itched to trace the lines of Hunter's face, she would restrain herself. "Now, I'm going to walk in his direction and you're going to keep your distance."

Tucker's brow furrowed more. "So long as you remember that your life is not the only one on the line, Nia. And some rules have too great of consequences to break." With that, he returned to his full height and gestured ahead of them.

He didn't have to tell her everything that she had put at risk. It included things he knew nothing about, nor did he need to know. They'd agreed on how to move forward. Narcissa faced the direction she'd seen the stumpy dwarf, focusing her senses to locate one person in the lively crowd. Hunter's deep voice carried on the wind, reaching her ears above the noisy chatter of the bazaar.

Sunlight danced in her eyes, mirroring the joy that bubbled within her. Dear gods, she'd heard nothing so exquisite. Narcissa marched forward without hesitation, Tucker and Tzane keeping a semi-distance away from her. Each step carried her closer to the person who soothed her aching heart.

"Hunter?" Narcissa muttered. She could feel his presence—a faint thrum against her skin, a sensation that told her he was close, though his distance was unknown. Shit. In the bustling bazaar, there were countless nooks where he could be concealing himself—a nearby alleyway, the jamb of a storefront, or even amongst the many ongoing conversations between merchants and customers. To the right, there was a fruit stand, its ripe fruits glistening, then a table displaying colorful fabrics and scarves, and behind it, a cart of flowers. Each establishment bustled with the presence of its loyal clientele. Her heart raced faster with each frantic attempt to find him. "Please..." she begged. "I just..." Her words trailed off. Was this selfish of her? Yes. He had left a few weeks back, but it wasn't as if she could fight for him. Not in the way they both desired.

"Five silver coins," a male voice spoke.

A jingle of coins preceded Hunter's voice. "You can keep the change if you can do me a favor."

Tucker took a few steps forward and discreetly nudged her to the right. Toward the flower vendor. Narcissa merely dipped her chin, silently thanking Tucker. As her gaze fell on the older dwarf, she noticed he was holding out a single blue rose, its petals still glistening. She caught the sweet sound of Hunter's voice.

"Could you give her the rose? Please? She is headed this way. Not quite five-and-a-half feet tall, thin, cinnamon-brown hair, jade-green eyes with gold flecks, and flanked by a troll and a canine. Please. I would appreciate it."

With a careful swallow, Narcissa tried to moisten her parched throat. She clutched the bags draped over her arm, a silent effort to control her swirling emotions. Fighting with all her might, she strove to maintain composure. "Hunter... I know you're here." Even whispered, she knew he heard her.

The vendor tilted his head toward her. "Are you certain you do not wish to give it to her yourself?"

It took several moments. For several *long* moments, while Narcissa held her breath... and prayed.

Then Hunter's camouflage fell, and he turned around. His hands gripped tightly on his upper arms, as though he had to hold himself together lest he fall apart. "Nia," he whispered.

It wasn't her name, but Hunter wouldn't use that among mixed company. Not that it mattered. The sight of him almost made her buckle, her legs weak beneath her. A cacophony of emotions swirled deep inside her. Joy and pain clawed at her, each vying for control and threatening to consume her. Leaving only a few feet, Narcissa closed most of the distance, her heart pounding in her chest. It took great effort not to wrap her arms around him, to hold him close. She feared that if she did, she might never let go. This had to be enough.

"Hi," she choked out. A single word—and it didn't seem like enough. As her heart broke for what they couldn't have, she blinked back tears that threatened to spill over.

"Hi." Hunter's fingers twitched. He gripped tighter on his upper arms. "I miss you," he said, his voice gravelly, breaking.

They stood close, but inescapable mountains formed a divide. What she wouldn't give to climb the fuckers, especially as the three most beautiful words she'd heard in a while left his mouth. Narcissa didn't dare get closer. As it stood, this was a risk. One she had to take. "I miss you, too," she whispered, her voice cracking ever so slightly. "I..." What else could she say? That she loved him. No, it would only make things worse. The worst part was knowing how each other felt, even though they couldn't change their circumstances. She clutched the bags in her arms tighter, struggling against the hopelessness of their situation. Gods, what was wrong with her? Coming over here and talking to him felt like an incredibly selfish act. "I'm sorry." Narcissa brushed away the tear that traced a cold path down her cheek, her eyes falling to the ground.

"I know. I am sorry, too."

Her eyes snapped to his brilliant-blue gaze. What could he have to apologize for? Coming into the marketplace? It wasn't as if they could've known the other would be here. Not anymore than they could've known what would happen when they'd first come together. They didn't do either of those things purely for personal reasons. Fuck. If they wanted to be truly selfish, they'd do everything they wanted in that moment.

Hunter glanced back at the rose still held in the vendor's hand. "Please..."

"Yes, of course, sir." The dwarf's gaze locked on her as he offered her the blue rose. "For you, ma'am."

Narcissa blinked, the sting of unshed tears making her vision blurry. For her? Hunter had picked it out for her? It was the same color as his eyes. She glanced from the older male to Hunter, and as she did, she swept her fingers across her cheeks, wiping away the tears she wouldn't shed. It wouldn't hurt to take the flower. They brought stuff back all the time from the marketplace. Except eventually it would die. The delicate petals would fall off. She didn't think she could bear to watch that.

"I can encase it if you would like," the male suggested.

"You could do that?" Narcissa asked without diverting her attention from Hunter. This moment between them had to last what felt like a lifetime. The moment would soon pass, and Silva would arrive, having allowed her the ten minutes she asked for.

Hunter shifted his gaze to hers again. "Do it, please. I will pay whatever it costs."

"No," Narcissa stated firmly, her hand rising as she cut off Hunter's offer, and she stepped forward without hesitation. "I'll cover the cost." Then, no one could ever take it from her grasp. Her gaze flicked briefly to the merchant. "Please encase it."

"As you wish." The male dipped his chin to the two of them and went to work.

Hunter stepped forward as well until there were only inches between them. His claws unsheathed and pierced his biceps. Blood trickled through his fur. "I needed you to have something. So, you would know..." Hunter's words trailed off.

It wouldn't take much effort at all to reach out and touch him. Fighting the urge, Narcissa pushed the sunglasses up from her face and into her long hair. It wasn't necessary for Hunter to finish his statement. She knew exactly what he meant. The feeling was mutual. He possessed her heart and soul, the very essence of her being. "I wish things were different." In a multitude of ways. If she could, she'd draw up against him, press a kiss to his lips, and never look back. None of that was remotely possible.

"So do I." Hunter's eyes misted over. But the threatening tears didn't fall. "At least we had... everything that we did."

"That we did." Her mouth tilted up at one corner, almost imperceptibly. As much as she wished she could smile for him, she couldn't muster one. The agony of being so near, yet unable to reach out and touch him, was almost unbearable. Recalling all the time they had together was almost as agonizing. Not that she wanted to forget a second of it.

How much time did they have left? Could she stretch this out a little longer? Over her shoulder, Narcissa glimpsed Silva, who strolled toward them, winding through the bustling crowd. With a soft exhale, she shifted her attention back to Hunter. She didn't want to ruin this, but she had to be certain he knew what would happen going forward. Narcissa swallowed hard, trying to moisten her dry throat before she spoke. "You know... Did they..." Fuck. How the hell could she even ask? By sheer strength, because it was far too important that they were safe. "If you come back," she choked out.

"You know I cannot—" Hunter's words cut off, and he swallowed hard. "Not... now. Not after..."

Narcissa gave a slight, hardly noticeable nod. Gods, the thought of him with someone else killed her. Training Nina for his return had nearly driven her to the brink of madness. It was the only time anything ever broke through the numbness. Her jaw clenched as she chewed on the inside of her cheek, her eyes briefly falling to the dusty ground. Her gaze shot back to him. "Then I'm glad I at least got this."

"I am glad I got to give it to you. And that I got to see you..." Hunter's breathing picked up slightly. His gaze flicked briefly to Silva and the other two guards that accompanied them. He met her gaze again. "Please... take care of yourself. And do not forget your promise to me."

Right. Her promise. The one she'd given him when they both believed he might die. She couldn't bring herself to speak the words and tell him that leaving wasn't an option. Even more so, since she'd recommitted to the den. The request went well beyond that, yet she knew she'd likely break this promise. A familiar hollowness echoed in her chest, each breath a painful reminder of the emptiness awaiting her back at the den. Narcissa clasped her hands together, gripping her purse tightly. Not that it did much to ground her. No matter how much she wanted to give him the answer he craved, she couldn't bring herself to say it. "I'll survive. I'm good at that."

"I know you will. But you deserve so much more than that."

There was a time in her life when she firmly believed that. Now, it was all about her family and what they needed from her. "I've never put myself first. It's not a luxury I have." If she could, she would. Not that he didn't know why things couldn't work. Hunter was the only one she'd told about her brother and mother. If she entertained the thought for a second, she'd suggest he buy out her contract, and together, they could chase their dreams. Even if she could share that information, Mistress wouldn't allow it to happen. Not with what had transpired between them. "You understand that better than anyone. Your brothers need you."

"I do. I understand," he said, his voice low. "I will just have to... find a way..." His eyes filled with tears again. More tears that Hunter wouldn't shed. "... to accept it," he finished.

They were both doing their best to come to terms with the reality of their situation. What other choice did they have? Narcissa turned to see Silva, and with a look, silently begged for a brief extension. His wordless huff was enough of a response, but he held up two fingers, indicating a couple more minutes. Refocusing on Hunter, she took off her sunglasses, the movement a quiet distraction for her hands. Narcissa's breath hitched as she blinked, holding tears back as her lungs constricted, her every muscle screaming with agony. It felt like she couldn't breathe. Fuck. "I wish we could have another *one last*," she whispered. Her hand instinctively went out to touch him, but she swiftly withdrew it. Despite her best efforts to remain silent, the words spilled out. "I'm sorry, Hunter. I would—" Narcissa cut herself off. Tears trickled down her cheeks. He had to know she'd fight for them if she could. Not that she uttered the words. She'd already said enough.

Hunter, after pulling his claws from his arms, wiped his bloody hands on his thighs before enveloping her in a powerful hug.

"Hunter," Tucker's voice held warning.

He flicked his gaze to the male. "I will not fuss when she has to go. Just give us this. Two minutes. *Please.*" Hunter leaned down and buried his face in her hair, inhaling deeply, drawing in her scent. "Do not be sorry," he whispered. "Never be sorry for doing what you have to do. I know. I know everything you cannot say. Everything inside your heart. Your soul. I know *you.* And even though… we cannot be together…" Wetness dripped onto her head. "… you will *always* be mine. And I will *always* be yours. I love you. I know it makes this harder, and I should not say it, but I love you."

Despite her bags, purse, and sunglasses, Narcissa's arms instinctively wrapped around him. A choked sob escaped as she clung to Hunter, her knuckles white, as if trying to keep the world from shattering. Even as she heard Silva mumbling under his breath, she didn't step out of Hunter's hold. "I love you, too," she uttered. Yes, Mistress would punish her for this, and she'd happily accept it. This was the goodbye they should have had. A last farewell etched in their memories. Instead of her rushing him out of her room, sparing him from what came once he left.

Hunter's tears fell harder. He clung harder to her as she clutched at him, her fingers digging into his back. He lowered his voice. Not that it would stop at least Tucker from hearing, but this was the best they could get. This was the best they would ever get. "If there is *ever* a way… you know how to reach me. I would take care of you. I would take care of *them,* too. None of you would ever want for anything."

Yes, she knew how to reach him. Narcissa loved him even more for it, but the rift in her heart only widened further. Every fiber of her being ached at the loss, even as she desperately clung to the fragments of her soul. Despite her attempts to stop them, the tears streamed down her face, hot and relentless. Narcissa prayed he understood that if there ever was a way, she'd take it without question. Not that she could verbalize it. Thinking it was bad enough.

"I will never forget you. You are my life."

"You'll always be in my heart. I'll cherish every memory we've shared." It wouldn't convey her complete message, but it would do.

"As will I," he choked out. Without taking his arms from around her, Hunter kneeled down in front of her and slid one hand to her cheek. "You will *always* have me. No matter *whatever happens.* No one will ever own me like you do." Then he kissed her. Soft, no tongue, but it conveyed all the emotions they couldn't say out loud. It spoke volumes about a longing that time and circumstance had stolen from them.

Though Narcissa longed to savor him further, they had already pushed their limits. The situation would become significantly more difficult if the guards had to intervene, making it crucial to prevent the situation from escalating. Narcissa paused, the kiss continuing, hoping he understood her feelings, extending the pleasantness before separating. She gently pressed her forehead against his, a moment of quiet closeness. There was so much more she wished she could say. But inevitably she had to let go. "Goodbye, Hunter."

Tears streamed down his face, but he didn't make a move to stop them or wipe them away. "Goodbye." Hunter lowered his hand from her cheek and stood. His arms wrapped around himself again as he took a couple of forced steps backward, his breath catching in his throat. Then he drew on his camouflage, hiding himself from view.

Only then did her gaze leave him. Tears silently streamed down her face, each drop a painful echo of that final blow. This was the most excruciating pain she had ever felt. Nothing had ever caused her so much emotional distress. Not even leaving her family behind. Every breath felt labored, the future a suffocating void where hope had withered and died.

With a quiet and gentle tone, the merchant asked, "Ma'am?"

"Nia?" Silva's elbow nudged her, jarring her from her gaze at the space Hunter had occupied.

"What?" Her voice was a shaky whisper, cracking with the sheer force of her emotions.

"Your trinket. Pay for it, and then we'll head to lunch, where you can clean yourself up, make yourself look presentable."

Right. Presentable. Because they were a walking advertisement for the den. An everlasting image of sensual allure. With a sniffle, Narcissa swiped at her wet cheeks, though the tears persisted, and she searched her purse for money.

Lost in a sea of overwhelming emotions, Narcissa was numb and barely registered what was happening. She collected the encased blue rose and added the bag to the collection that weighed down her arm.

"Let us keep it moving," Tucker said.

Silva escorted her toward a restaurant while the guards returned to their positions. He rambled on about something. Her shoulders slumped, each word echoing into a vast emptiness within her, making the world fade away. She'd left Hunter back there with her heart and soul. It was an effort to keep moving, each step a battle against the impulse to run back and embrace him. They arrived at a restaurant, its chatter and clatter a familiar symphony, though she couldn't name it.

Silva, with two guards following her, lightly guided her into the bathroom, which was at the rear of the building. "Go on, love. Beautify yourself. We'll sit for food and wine afterward."

Narcissa watched the door click shut behind her friend, a chill running down her spine. Although they'd left her to manage on her own, they were all huddled together on the other side of the door, within earshot. There was no escape from the suffocating silence. Her jade-green gaze found the mirror, the glass reflecting her tear-stained features in a blurry, fleeting moment. With a surge of fury, she imagined throwing something at the glass and destroying it, even though it wasn't hers to break.

Each breath felt like a lead weight in her chest, the silence amplifying the mournful echo of her decision. The task at hand wouldn't get any easier, no matter how long she lingered in the silence.

Narcissa, against her better judgment, let the bags fall onto the cold, hard floor. All of them except for one. She kept the small container holding the blue rose close by. Hunter's last gift would remain with her. She leaned against the cool, marble counter, closed her eyes, and took several deep, steadying breaths, organizing her thoughts and planning her next move. After what felt like an eternity, she turned on the icy water and used it to wash away the tears before fixing her smeared makeup. Though it wouldn't mend her broken heart, it would conceal the unspoken pain. That would have to do. For now.

Narcissa's focus repeatedly slipped away from their surroundings during the shopping trip and the long walk back to the den. That three-story house with all of its rooms, bustling and loud, had never truly been home. Even with the presence of the people she cared about, she doubted their love would be enough to keep her from falling apart. It didn't mean she wouldn't try. For those who depended on her, she had to find the strength to push through.

The moment they entered the den, Narcissa blew out a heavy breath, her shoulders slumping slightly. Her eyes immediately landed on Averine, standing in the stairwell. With Diablo and Colt standing on either side of her, and Sollix behind her. All three of them with their arms crossed over their chests and self-satisfied smirks on their faces. The scent of old wood wafted from the passage to the upper floors and the female's office. Averine's eyes narrowed as she glared, confirming her awareness.

"The five of you, in my office. Now," Mistress snapped, pointing a finger at Narcissa and the four guards who'd accompanied her.

"Mother—" Silva started, but the female quickly cut him off.

"Don't even try. Go to your room. I'll deal with you later."

"Yes, Mother." Silva squeezed Narcissa's hand and offered her a supportive glance. With a determined stride, he headed toward the long hall, the hum of the club fading as he bypassed it for the employee entrance to the upper levels.

"Of course, Mistress," Narcissa replied. What other choice did she have? At the female's summons, they responded, their movements swift and purposeful. Narcissa followed Tucker and Tzane, the rhythmic click of her heels on the wooden floor a counterpoint to the quiet footsteps of Malak and Yavo. Whatever punishment came their way, she owed them an apology. They'd taken a risk standing around doing nothing on her behalf, just so she could have a proper goodbye.

Once they reached Averine's office, Tucker didn't wait for anyone else before going in. He stepped over to the right of the door, giving the others plenty of room to follow him, and clasped his hands together behind his back.

Diablo was the last one in Averine's office. He shut the door behind him and then took a spot next to her desk. Re-crossing his arms over his chest, he settled his gaze on Narcissa, mirroring the pose as Colt beside him, and as Sollix on the opposite side of the desk.

The males' stance made Narcissa worry about the potential punishment. Those three were not exactly ones for polite exchanges. This was definitely going to get bad.

Narcissa had never felt so isolated, even with the four guards flanking her, two on each side. She shifted the bags, feeling the rough canvas against her skin as she curled her fingers tightly around them. With her head held high, she could feel the tension in her shoulders as she steeled herself. All she could do was accept whatever came her way.

Averine leaned against the edge of her desk and crossed one ankle over the other, a wrinkle appearing on her forehead. "What part of *stay away from Hunter* did I not make myself clear about? Did you think it was a suggestion?"

"No, Mistress. It wasn't intentional." At least, that much was true. Not that she planned to admit the rest of it. Despite sensing his presence, she could have easily avoided him. But she chose to find him instead.

"I'm sorry, did you trip and fall on him?" Averine snapped. "I don't give a fuck if he was there. You were ordered to stay away." Her dark gaze, sharp and assessing, flickered over the four males. "Where the fuck were the four of you? Are you incapable of doing your job? Protecting the ones I send you with?"

Tzane, Malak, and Yavo kept their mouths tightly shut. It was Tucker who spoke. "No, ma'am. We remained with both of our charges the entire time. Our primary objective is to ensure they return home safe and unharmed. We did that."

"Oh, so you saw her with Hunter?" With a shove, Averine moved away from the desk, advancing with a determined stride, the sharp clicks of her heels growing louder. "Do you think I'm ignorant? Or perhaps I'm unaware of what it means when a shifter's eyes glow?"

Narcissa sensed the look of shock across Tzane, Malak, and Yavo's faces without having to see it. She realized the truth from the way Mistress's eyes moved quickly, locking onto each male. This was her mess. It was her responsibility to clean it up. "No one thinks that, Mistress," Narcissa stated.

"Then they must be ignorant. Or they deliberately allowed you to disobey an order. When you recommitted, Nia, you made it clear you understood I forbade you from being around Hunter." Averine clasped her hands together, her expression hardening with a wave of displeasure. "Which is it?"

"I did not realize that was an order that had been made, ma'am," Tucker responded. "He has not been banned from the establishment. It is not my place or my privilege to know which clients are and may not be with which employees, unless that is specifically told to us, or we are told to drag someone out the door. If there was any indication that a fuss or a fight would be made, we would have done what needed to be done to ensure that didn't happen... and dealt with him accordingly. That, however, was not the case. They had a moment, said their goodbyes, and went their separate ways."

"Oh, I see," Averine retorted, her voice a venomous whisper. "What you're saying is I have an incompetent staff, that Shalla failed to inform you that I had reassigned Hunter to Nina, and that I forbade him from having contact with Nia. His last chance to prove he can keep his paws where they belong. Not that he has returned since this occurred."

Shit. The matter was rapidly becoming more and more entangled. She had brought enough people into her convoluted mess. Maybe she couldn't prevent the guards from getting in trouble, but she could protect Shalla. "No, Mistress. The failure was on my part," Narcissa admitted. "I simply thought bidding him goodbye was appropriate."

"Of course," the female muttered as she got in Narcissa's face. "Because he's more than a client who paid to fuck you, right?" Gripping Narcissa's jaw hard, Averine leaned in so close their breaths mingled. "When are you going to get it through your skull? *I own you.*" With a slight jerk, the female released Narcissa's chin.

Her jaw clenched, but she held her tongue, forcing down the words that almost escaped. Arguing against the claim would only make matters worse. The day she signed that accursed contract was the day her life was no longer hers.

"Obviously, some clarifications are required," Averine said as she reclaimed her spot against her desk. "Should Hunter return, he may see Nina. If he has any contact with Nia, I will ban him, and I will punish any who allows it to happen. If I allow Nia any future trips to the marketplace, she is to have *no* contact with him whatsoever. Is that understood?"

"Yes, Mistress," echoed from each male, one behind the other.

"Excellent. Now that all parties understand the rules and consequences, let's ensure the lesson sticks." A subtle smirk played on the female's lips. "You'll spend the next eight nights working in the club, Nia. Every coin or gem you receive will go to the barkeep for the den's use. I expect you to play nice. You need to meet a quota of at least ten per night. After, of course, you return to your room and scrub the stench of that shifter off your skin." She spoke, her voice steady as her gaze fixed intently on each guard. "And as the four of you are so keen on watching her ass, you'll each take four shifts for half the pay, ensuring she does her fucking job. Every other night. Tucker and Tzane, you'll join her tonight. Understood?"

"Yes, Mistress," Tzane said. The other two—Malak and Yavo—echoed the same words right behind him.

It took Tucker a minute to respond. "Yes, ma'am," he said finally.

"Good. I'm glad we understand one another. Now, the four of you are dismissed." Averine plastered a wide, almost manic, grin on her face. "Not you, Nia. I'm not finished with you."

"Yes, Mistress." Of course, the female wasn't. She knew with absolute certainty that whatever the woman said next would be about the three males' hungry gazes on her. From the moment she entered the office, their eyes fixed on her. Nothing good would come from arguing, though. She already had one punishment under her belt; another meant little in the long run. Unless it involved those three.

Tzane, Malak, and Yavo moved immediately to the door. Tucker hesitated. But only briefly, before following the other three.

Averine waited until Tucker had closed the door behind him before she spoke again. "I'm hesitant to believe you comprehend the seriousness of this situation." Pushing off her desk again, the female closed the distance, the clicking of her stilettos growing louder with each step. "That you think I'm unaware of *all* that has transpired between you and Hunter. When I know it all. I know you marked him and that you allowed him to mark you." As she spoke, the female moved in a slow circle around Narcissa, her eyes never leaving her. Her last word faded into the air, and she stood still, positioned directly behind Narcissa. Averine clenched a fistful of Narcissa's thick hair, giving it a hard tug that brought a gasp from Narcissa's mouth. "Given all of that, I'm inclined to let these three tear you apart." As if offering Narcissa a chance to reflect, the female paused, creating a brief silence. "Consider yourself lucky that you're valuable to me right now, and that I don't want that pretty face shredded," Averine continued. "*Don't* misunderstand—this is your *last* warning. Go near Hunter, break *any* of my rules, and these three males, well... they'd love to have at you. Valuable or not, I'll let them bring you to the brink before you can be healed. Understood?"

Except for the short, startled gasp, Narcissa remained completely silent. Though slight, the sting from Averine's grip on her hair was still present. She embraced the pain, her senses heightened by its raw intensity. It offered a brief respite, allowing her to experience something other than the emptiness in her chest. "Yes, Mistress," Narcissa replied.

"I don't believe you." Averine yanked Narcissa's head back, her grip tightening with a cruel swiftness. "Now, try it again, but properly."

The female wanted one word from her. In the thirty years she'd spent in the den, she'd never once uttered it. Unlike Silva, Narcissa had *never* called Averine *mother*. She had a mother—one who birthed and loved her. Averine didn't fit that fucking bill and never would. What would happen if she refused to use it? That was simple. Her jade-green gaze moved from one male to the next, lingering on their faces as they hovered around the desk, their hungry stares making her uncomfortable. The female would follow through on the threat. "Yes, Mother," Narcissa gritted out.

"Excuse me? I didn't quite get that."

"Yes, Mother," Narcissa repeated with perfect clarity.

Diablo's eyes darkened, and he licked his lips. "Can we have permission to give her... just a little taste, Mistress? I would not touch her *face.*"

"Tempting. A tempting offer, indeed," Averine declared. "Given the way you heal, I could let them have at you. Provided they left you close enough to water."

The female paused, as if she were letting the gravity of her words sink in. Narcissa wouldn't beg, no matter what. If that was Averine's expectation, the woman would continue to wait even after Narcissa's passing. She refused to give this bitch any satisfaction. She simply said nothing.

Averine's fingers twisted in Narcissa's hair, yanking it hard. "You're lucky I need you in one piece for the two clients attempting to outbid one another for you," Averine continued. "But I'll tell you what, boys. She's got to meet a quota of ten clients a night at the club—female or male, it doesn't matter to me. Watch her. If she cannot make that even one night, then you're free to have at her for an hour. Just make sure she's left close to water."

As he cracked his knuckles, a wide, maniacal grin bloomed on Sollix's face, a flash of teeth in the dim light. "I'll keep an eye out. I look forward to you missing it."

"So do I," Diablo agreed.

A lewd smirk stretched over Colt's face. "We can just fuck her *in* the water. Then there is no need to stop so she can heal her fragile bones."

Diablo strode slowly over to Narcissa and stroked her cheek with a claw. He hooked it beneath her chin and forced her to look up at him. "I hope Hunter *comes* back. And I hope he goes straight to you. I would love to punish you *both*."

Ignoring their words and Diablo's actions, Narcissa's face remained an emotionless mask. She didn't utter a sound, nor did she react in any manner. She fought the urge to clutch her shopping bags and purse, using every bit of self-control she possessed. It was the only way she got out of this unscathed.

"And we all know he's going to come back," Averine commented.

No, he won't, Narcissa thought to herself. Even as Averine released her hair, she kept her mouth shut, her silence echoing in the room. The males—and Averine—would only get off if she reacted.

The female strode around Narcissa, her shadow falling over her until she stood, face to face, directly in front of her. "Go clean yourself up. You've got work tonight. I expect you on the floor right after dinner."

"Yes, Mother." Narcissa dipped her chin, then took a step back and pivoted on her heel, the click of her shoes echoing as she departed Averine's office.

Tucker turned around when the door opened. His presence momentarily caught her off guard. It meant he'd overheard everything that went down in there. Something she would've preferred hadn't occurred. Why the fuck had he lingered? He didn't owe her anything. They weren't even friends. Yes, she had contact with Jade, but why would that matter? The reason mattered little. Not that Tucker said anything to her as she exited and headed down the hall. Sollix, then Colt, then Diablo left behind her.

"What the fuck are you still doing here?" Diablo asked, his voice low with a hint of amusement. "Vying for the position of her next *savior*?" He chuckled low.

At the end of the hallway, Narcissa paused, Diablo's utterances echoing around her. She peered over her shoulder at Tucker. If he was smart, he'd avoid responding to Diablo and let it go.

Not that the male did so. He smirked. "Even as dumb as you are, you should know better than that."

Diablo shoved him up against the wall, keeping his hand on his shoulder. "You *sure* about that? Why else would you be hanging around out here in the hall, waiting for her to leave?"

Tucker's hand snapped up, his claws burying into the back of Diablo's hand. "Take your fucking hand off me. Now. Before I take your hand off you." He glanced behind the male and laughed. "What is the matter, Colt? Jealous?"

Colt snorted. "What the fuck would I have to be jealous of *your* ass over?"

"That his hand is on me and not you. I know you like it better when he has his whole fist up your ass, but—" He didn't get any further before Diablo punched him so hard, his nose broke and blood gushed down his face.

Seriously? Fuck, no. If this progressed any further, she'd have Jade on her ass. That was the last thing she wanted.

As Narcissa took a step, Averine materialized in the doorjamb, her wrist moving with a swift flick to separate the moronic Diablo and Tucker. With a violent whoosh of air, they were flung away from each other, slamming into the wall. "I don't recall giving either of you permission to spill blood on my floors." Her eyes narrowed and locked onto Diablo. "I've granted you a slew of perks. If you wish to keep them, I recommend getting where you fucking need to be." Her dark gaze swung toward Tucker. "You've caused enough trouble. Are you gearing toward more?"

Diablo's black eyes lightened slightly. "Yes, Mistress." He pushed off of Tucker and headed down the hall without another word, Colt right behind him.

Tucker snapped his nose back into place, then wiped the blood off with the back of his hand. "Nope, not at all, ma'am." He glanced downward, then back up at Averine. "It does not look like any got on the floor." Tucker hooked a thumb over his shoulder. "I am gonna get out of your hair. I should clean up before my shift." He turned to head down the hall. "Have a pleasant night."

"You have somewhere to be as well, Nia. Do you not?" Averine snapped, the sound of her impatience cutting through the tense atmosphere.

"Yes, Mother."

At least, that was over. For now.

Narcissa spun around, her stilettos clicking on the polished floor, and then headed toward the back staircase. This was a nightmare of the worst kind. One that stretched on endlessly, with no escape. If only she knew what to do with it.

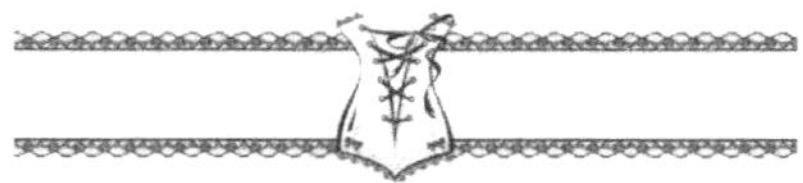

Parting ways with her eighth encounter of the night, Nia let the plastered smile fall from her face. The bass vibrated the floor, a subtle thrum that she barely noticed. Nothing much caught her attention. Not even those gathered at various tables across the club, sipping their drinks. Some chattered loudly, their voices lost in the cacophony, while others, with hungry eyes, watched the scantily-clad workers.

Nia walked up to the far side of the bar. The scent of stale ale hung thick in the air. She paused, then tossed a velvet bag of coins onto the gleaming wood. It landed with a clunk. Her dull gaze settled on the barkeep. "Can I get a shot of nectar?" It was the only thing getting her through this punishment. The end was near.

"Sure thing, sweetheart." Tarron grabbed the heavy bag of coins and locked it away before reaching for a shot glass. "Want to make it a double this time?" His pointed ears twitched, and he scanned the room with a swift flick of his eyes. Tarron filled the shot with nectar and set it in front of her. "You've got to stop getting in trouble like this. You're too good for the likes of us down here."

Most of the staff at the club treated her well. Yeah, this was her second time since Hunter had left that she'd ended up covering this shithole. Not that it was an awful place. The clientele could be more than handsy. They could be incredibly foul, with a stench that made you gag. That didn't even include the transactions that happened in secret.

Nia knocked the shot back, setting the small glass down with a slight scoff. "We're all too good to be down here." Her eyes zeroed in on the two shitheads who kept sabotaging her work, all because they wanted her. The memory of that part of the conversation resurfaced, sharp and stinging. With a tired sigh, Nia shook it off, scrubbed at her face and then pressed her palms onto the counter, feeling the rough edge bite into her skin. "Yeah, Tarron. Give me a double shot this time."

"A double, it is," the Seelie said, adding more nectar to the glass and patting her hand. "How much longer you got now?"

"Two more for tonight. Just another three nights after that." It couldn't end soon enough. It wasn't as if she hadn't known why Averine had sent her down here. The female had one singular reason: it would strip her of her worth, bringing her to the brink of breaking down over and over. The double shot burned as it went down, and Nia pressed the heel of her palm against her neck, working out the tension.

"Make it fast," he muttered under his breath. "And *don't* get picky. Tweedle-Dumb and Tweedle-Dipshit have been trying to sabotage you since night one."

"They get a perk if I don't meet my quota," Nia mumbled.

Two males had eyed her since before she'd taken the last one to the back rooms—a dwarf and a Seelie. With no time to assess the differences between them, aside from the obvious, she pushed off the bar, and started toward the dwarf. He was the closest.

Diablo pushed off the wall away from Sollix and made quick work of crossing the room. He made it to the couch the dwarf sat in before Nia had made it halfway over. "Just a suggestion, mate, but... I would look elsewhere," he mumbled. "If you value not having a disease attacking your dick."

A smile played on her lips as she barely stifled her laughter at Diablo's remarks. Wow. Talk about ignorance.

The dwarf's features twisted in disbelief, suggesting that he didn't believe Diablo. If Nia had had any liquid in her mouth, she would've spit it out given what followed.

The dwarf tilted his head, his gaze shifting from Nia's approaching form back to Diablo. "Inta she a nymph?"

"Pure-bred," Nia purred, her voice smooth like silk, as she came upon them. "Don't mind him, honey. He's just going through something."

She winced, her expression mirroring the ailment he had described. Her jade-green gaze swung briefly in Diablo's direction as she caressed her fingers along the dwarf's jaw. "I thought Cheshire told you to get that looked at. I know you haven't been with us long, but we've got an excellent medical staff. They'll get that cleared right up for you."

Diablo chuckled low. "Who said I was talking about anything sexual? You think I am that stupid? Everyone knows they do not let anyone work here if they have something that needs to be treated. I am talking about what you *do* to your clients." He flicked his gaze back to the male. "We are supposed to keep our mouths shut here, but I hate to see another guy walk out of here after being with her, with something no herbs or tonics can cure. She already lost most of her regular clients over that shit, which is why she is down here working the night shift in the first place."

Was this seriously the best this shithead had? It explained how he'd failed in his mission to prevent her from meeting her nightly quota. As the dwarf's bushy features displayed confusion, she mirrored his expression by drawing her eyebrows together. "Do ya know what he's referrin'?" he asked.

"I wish I did, baby. I'm just down here helping my fellow workers out. No client of mine has ever left unsatisfied or complained about anything. And most of them have been with me for thirty *solaris*. They're all serviced extremely well, including the one that just walked out." She'd rarely faked any response they ever received from her. It only ever happened with a few until recently. Not that any of them recognized that shit. A grin played across Nia's face as she bent over, drawing the dwarf's eyes to the enticing curve of her breasts. "And you look like the kind of male who likes to play hard. I'm all for that. If you want to, I'll grab us a couple of shots of nectar, and then we can slip into a little nook in the corner." As she stood, she slowly straightened, the cool air raising goosebumps as her nails scraped lightly along her thighs. "Or, if you want to take this... persona non grata male at his word, I'll move to someone else who desires my time. The choice is yours." As Nia turned, she felt the sudden, firm grip of the dwarf's hand on her wrist.

Diablo sucked in a breath through his fangs. "Man, these females really know how to lie through their teeth," he muttered under his breath. He glared at her, his brow furrowed. "Thirty *solaris*? Are you fucking kidding me? You *really* cannot do any better than that?" He scoffed. "Last client she had, a feline shape shifter, has not been back in *penumbras*. And he has been a repeat customer for decades. Shoulda seen the guy when he came back the day after the last time he fucked *her*. He was walking bowlegged after what she did to his dick. Last I heard from his brother—" Diablo locked eyes with her. "—the male is so sick he cannot even get out of bed." Diablo shook his head and stood to his feet. "Whatever. Do not say no one tried to fucking warn you. It is your funeral." He shook his head again. "All over getting your dick wet. Fucking waste."

Even though she remained silent, Nia's jawline tightened with suppressed emotion. For two seconds, that piece of shit almost had her. Except she knew Clay intimately. Not that Diablo would have access to that information. Or that they'd even spoken occasionally. The male wouldn't have a damn thing to do with the likes of Diablo. Just like the females in the den. Nor did she believe Hunter was sick the way the dickwad described. Hayden wouldn't allow that to happen. She kept all of that to herself and instead focused on what she could say.

Nia plastered a smile on her face and then looked at the dwarf. "I'll get us some drinks, baby." Peering across the way at Tarron, she dipped her chin and held up two fingers. The male would understand. She grinned widely before Diablo, defeated, could escape. "For the record, nymphs are immune to those kinds of diseases, but I guess since the females around here won't touch you, it wasn't important for you to know."

Diablo put a hand on the back of the couch as he turned back. "Like I said, I was not talking about a fucking disease you can contract by being fucked. Just what you like to do to your clients. You know, like you did to him. Poor guy. You will not see him again. And you have the audacity to call other people around here *sick fucks*." He focused back on the dwarf. "Look, there are plenty of other females around here, so you would not have to worry about anything. They fuck just as well, if not better, and they are cheaper, too. So, if you fancy any recommendations, just let me know. I was just looking out for my fellow male, but hey—" He shrugged. "—you do you." Diablo started to walk away, then he turned, leaned down, and spoke to Nia in a low voice, his breath tickling her ear. He spoke just loud enough so that only she would hear him. Dwarves didn't have the best hearing. "Just so you know… I am not lying about that. Not everyone in my species knows this, but a bonded male *literally* cannot live without their mate. Their bodies start to shut down. Piece… by piece… by piece.

Until their hearts stop. Seen it a few times in my life. It is fucking brutal to watch. But oh, so fun. Why do you think so many of us close ourselves off? Who the fuck would want someone else to have that kind of fucking power over them?"

Nia's heart seized in her chest, as if time itself had frozen. The silence descended, a suffocating blanket that silenced every noise, every movement, as if the room itself was a predator, swallowing her whole. *No, Diablo is lying. Hunter won't die.* These were just words, an attempt by Diablo to rattle her. But they couldn't penetrate her resolve against this trial if she didn't let them. The male would say anything to succeed. She refused to give him the satisfaction. As if to defy her anger, Nia jutted her chin, her shoulders stiffening. "He's decided what he wants. It's time you walked away, while you still can."

"Come on, lass," the dwarf rumbled. His calloused hand gave Nia's wrist a tug, pulling her down onto the well-worn couch beside him.

Diablo didn't say another word. Just headed back over to his station while his eyes scanned the floor.

Nia was deep in thought and barely registered the waitress's arrival with a tray overflowing with shots. Despite her claim, the weight of Diablo's words lingered in her mind. The ringing in her ears persisted, a maddening echo in the space she shared with the dwarf after Diablo left.

No, he's not right. Yes, she and Hunter had to stay away from one another, but that didn't mean he would die. That wouldn't happen. It couldn't.

Right?

The dwarf's thick voice snapped her from the endless cycle that weighed her heart down. Nia's gaze lifted to the female.

"Apologies for the delay," the female said. Slowly bending over, and showing more than a healthy amount of cleavage, she set three shots down on the table in front of them.

Thank the gods. She'd need that third to get through what came next. "It's all good." Nia plastered a smile on her face, trying to ignore the knot of worry in her stomach. There was work to do.

"Just let me know if you need more." She shot the dwarf a wink before righting herself, then sauntering off to return the tray to the bar, her hips swishing back and forth with each step.

"Aye, lass," the dwarf replied as he lifted two glasses, handing one to Nia.

Thank the gods, Tarron had sent that female over. The waitress provided a pleasant diversion for the dwarf, allowing Nia to focus on silencing the chaos bouncing around her skull. "To an evening full of hard fun," Nia declared as she tilted her head, feeling the cold glass against her lips, and downed the fiery liquid. Without a second thought, she set the empty glass aside with a clink and reached for the next. The fire in her throat was the remedy she needed.

Nia leaned across the dwarf, the soft fabric of her dress brushing his chest. The glasses clinked on the rough wooden table. "Come on, let me show you a place for privacy." Taking his hand in her own, she eased to her feet.

One down, one left to go.

Then, three more fucking nights of this horrific shit. And it was all over. At least she felt nothing. Without Hunter, numbness was all she had. If she had to serve as another warm body, so be it. Though she despised its darkness, she was compelled to endure every moment. She'd do whatever it took to take care of her family.

Twenty-One

After just one bite of the food Hayden had provided, Hunter's stomach churned, and he struggled to keep the contents down. He lurched up, almost head-butting his twin in the face. "Fuck," he muttered.

"Hunter, let me help you," Hayden said, barely concealing his distress.

His twin tried to hook his arm around him, but Hunter weakly pushed at his hand. "Get off me."

"No, you can barely move. If you need to get sick, let me get a wastebasket or help you to the bathroom."

"Do not... want any help," he replied, his voice barely audible.

"I do not care. I will not let you fall on your face or throw up all over yourself. Lie back, please. Let me get you some water."

"Get—" Hunter swallowed back the rise of bile. "—the fuck away from me, Hayden."

Tears filled his twin's eyes. "I am not leaving you. You are my brother. I am going to take care of you, just like you have always taken care of—"

"I said get the fuck aw—" He barely got the words out before his stomach threatened to betray him again with a violent roll. He retched and lurched, but could only get his head over the edge of the bed before the sickness took over. Barely anything came up, because there was barely anything there. So, the dry heaves started pretty quickly. His stomach contracted repeatedly, his mouth filling with so much saliva, he gagged.

Hayden immediately sprang into action. After making sure Hunter wouldn't go to the floor, he rushed out of the room, the wood floors creaking under his weight, then he quickly returned with a glass of cold water and a couple of cool cloths. Hunter was still being attacked by dry heaves.

His brother set the items down on the floor. Ignoring his feeble struggle, Hayden put his arm around him and held him through the worst of it. Then he eased him back against his pillow. "Stop... stop fussing, Hunter. I am going to help you whether or not... whether you like it." He couldn't keep the emotion out of his tone anymore. After wiping up the sickness on the floor with one cloth, Hayden picked the glass of water up. He gently supported Hunter with his arm, and then carefully brought the cup to his lips.

A thin stream of water dribbled down to Hunter's chin. He didn't even try to drink. All of his strength had completely left him.

"C-come on, Hunter. You have to *try*."

What was the fucking point? Hunter knew he was dying. There was no stopping it. Without Narcissa, with no hope of being with her or even seeing her again... his body was shutting down. He could feel it in the sluggish flow of blood in his veins. His heart's slowed-down beat. The constant pounding migraine. A pain throbbed in every bone of his body. The increasing difficulty in stringing thoughts together. The graying that had come over his fur. Without being able to eat, his weight had practically fallen off of his body. What little he had eaten had refused to stay down. Fevers and sweats had plagued him. Had been lying in bed constantly in a near-lifeless state.

Why try? The sooner his body gave up completely... the sooner he would be at peace. Free to wait in the in-between for his mate until she joined him. Then they could go to the afterlife... finally together.

Tears trickled down Hayden's cheeks. "I am going to get Aradia."

"No," he mumbled.

"*Yes*, Hunter." Hayden picked up the second cloth, folded it, and placed it across Hunter's forehead. "You *have* to let her look at you. She can help; she will know what to do, I know it."

"No, Hayden. No..."

"Hunter—"

"I said no!" His words came out with more volume than they had in days. Exhaustion speared through him, weighing him down. Hunter closed his eyes. "No. There is nothing... she can do. No one can help me. Not anymore."

"I do not accept that," Hayden choked out. "I will *never* accept that."

That was just too damn bad. Hunter didn't respond out loud. Because there was nothing more to say. No treatment or medication could heal what had been done to him. Heal the shattered pieces of his heart. The tatters of his soul. The deep, unending hole inside of him. He'd never understood the mate bond. Always thought *true love* was a foolish endeavor that only idiots pursued. Until it had smacked him in the face with the truth. There was no code to be had in the matter. And you couldn't survive without your mate. The separation alone was enough to rip you to shreds. There was no way to fix the sickness. No way to put his body back together again. No way to stop the deterioration. Not without her. Not without Narcissa. And that was simply impossible.

The despair and hopelessness inside of Hayden intensified. Another jolt of fear hit, burrowing deep inside him, taking root. It spread throughout every inch of his body, sending an icy sensation through his blood. But then, stubborn determination fought back with unexpected strength. Not that he should be surprised.

Pushing up off of the bed, Hayden headed out of the bedroom and toward the front door without another word.

Close to the house, Rainbow and Aradia approached. Seemed his brother's mate had beaten him to the punch. Hunter could hear every word spoken between the three. The one thing that hadn't declined was his hearing. Which was a pity. He didn't like the way Hayden's heart and breathing sounded. Too erratic, too strained. But he just didn't have the strength to make things okay for his twin this time.

"I don't know what's wrong with him, Aradia, but Hayden isn't the only one worried about him. So am I."

"Why was this not brought to my attention sooner?"

"He's spent the last week pushing Hayden away. Hunter insisted we do nothing, that we just let him be. We've tried to give him space."

"Well, this is obviously not the time for *space*."

Probably not. But none of their attempts were going to do a damn bit of good.

He should be out there on the porch, helping his twin calm himself down. Not lying in here, half-dead, causing his upset.

"He... he thinks he... is..." Hayden's voice trailed off. His brother finished the sentence mentally that he couldn't bear to say out loud. *He thinks he is dying.*

"No, I suppose not," Rainbow said, obviously responding to the shaman, not his twin. "Aradia's here now. We'll figure it out."

"He is in his bedroom," Hayden started, his voice low. "He, um... he has not really moved... except to throw up. I got him to eat one bite of food, but he just threw it up. Then dry heaved. He..."

"Just take me in to see him. We will sort this out."

The front door closed. Footsteps sounded down the hallway. Hunter didn't look up as the three entered the room. Didn't react to what Rainbow said.

"His fur has lightened," she mumbled, sliding her arm tighter around Hayden's waist.

He didn't acknowledge the inaudible gasp that came from Aradia. Or the shock she tried unsuccessfully to keep off of her face. Nor did he move a single inch as the shaman strode swiftly across the room and set her bag down on the floor. Sitting on the bed, she took Hunter's wrist, feeling the slow, erratic beat of his pulse beneath her fingers. "Hunter. I need to check your vitals and do some tests. Tell me if you can hear me, and if you understand."

Hunter just lay there, staring at the wall. Thinking of Narcissa. Of all their times together.

When they'd first met. With her kneeling on the floor in the submissive pose in nothing but a pair of sheer underwear. How perfectly exquisite he had found her. So ignorant of what Narcissa would become to him.

Two days after that. The time and care he had put into finding *the perfect* piece of jewelry for her. Her favorite color, unbeknownst to him. She'd been wearing all red. The two-piece lingerie set and matching heels. He'd even put a red blindfold on her that day. And he'd punished her when she couldn't stop *purring* during aftercare. Two more hours of absolute bliss.

Three days later. Midnight blue from head to toe. Wearing the necklace he had painstakingly selected for her. For the first time ever, he had yearned to reach the peak of pleasure simultaneously with his partner.

His forehead had touched hers as they came for the first time. The first time, he had been afraid that things might become *personal*. He had first wondered what kissing someone would be like. The all-consuming peace he had found with her. Reveling in it. Afraid of it. Unable to deny it.

Rainbow ran her fingers through her mate's fur, making gentle circles across his back.

"He can hear you," Hayden whispered. "He just…"

Hunter was blocking Hayden from everything; his mind was a fortress of silence. What little strength he had left was being poured into that. Into protecting his most private thoughts. About the only times in his life when he had *truly* felt alive. Where he had lived for *himself*, for the first and only time in his life.

Four days after that. A sexy fucking one-piece lingerie and heels, all white. Both of them had tried so hard to mute things down. Their reactions, their movements. Everything. It hadn't worked. At all. She had sat behind him. *Touched his scars.* And he had *liked* it. He should have known right then how deep things had become. How entrenched he was in everything she was and everything she did for him. Everything she made him feel. They had talked. More than they ever had before. Discovered things about one another. And he had *submitted to her*. Even in just a small way, but he had. How had he not realized then how utterly attached he was?

"He can hear me, but does not wish to respond. Understood," Aradia said as she gently lowered Hunter's wrist and removed several items from her bag.

Hayden slid his arm around his mate and held her closer. "His fur… it did not look like that… just yesterday. I do not know how…" Reaching up, he tried to wipe the tears from his eyes, but it didn't help.

Four days after that. The thong and lace-halter set that left not a damn thing to the imagination, especially with the vee that dipped all the way to her belly button. Royal fucking purple. The black boots with a ladder pattern on the back. Her crimson lips he'd been dying to see wrapped around his cock. He had taken her braid down during their session, eager to feel the softness of her hair against his fingertips. The first time he'd ever put clit jewelry on someone. Their back-and-forth exchange. Both trying to keep the upper hand. Their dominance, a tête-à-tête. Until they both gave in. And allowed themselves to lose it in spectacular fashion. How hard he had fought not to mark her that day. The faintest brush of her lips against his; their first kiss. *"We should pretend this session never happened, Nia."* He'd gotten so drunk that night after going back to the village.

Rainbow snuggled a little more against Hayden as she watched Aradia.

And another four days. Nothing but those silver panties and heels. And the necklace he'd told her to put on. The matching belly button ring. The first time he'd taken what she'd worn between his teeth and tugged. Her cinnamon-brown hair had cascaded down her back. On the bed, blindfolded, with her wrists bound. The first time he had *ever* been beneath a female. It was supposed to bring him out of his comfort zone. Break the spell she had over him. Instead, he hadn't been able to get enough. So much so that he'd unbound her wrists and ripped her blindfold off of her. The first time she had ever said his name. *Purred* it. *Screamed* it. The frenzy it had released inside of him. The kisses they had shared. Devouring one another in every way. The first time she had told him her real name. She had marked him, sending an indescribably mutual chaos, peace, and ecstasy throughout him. Hunter had known then that she was *his*. That she would *always* be his. Despite their conversation as the session had ended.

Aradia jotted Hunter's temperature down on her medical pad. Hunter didn't need to see the number to know that it was far too low. A healthy shape shifter feline was never this cold. Aradia took his wrist in her hand again to track his pulse and his respiration, silently counting the too-few beats and his breaths.

Five days later. Because Nia had had a day off, he'd had to wait an extra day. The black dress with cutouts all the way up the sides. Barely there, black lingerie underneath that he'd untied with his fangs. Tall, black heels with red stilettos. The day he had let each of his vulnerabilities show. Had gone completely and totally out of his comfort zone. The day his demons had free rein on his mind, taking him away to another time and place more than once. But Narcissa had always brought him back to her. He had been completely and totally shattered that day. But Narcissa had picked up every single piece and put him back together. She had held him in the tub, with his face tucked into her throat, and caressed the back of his head and his ears. He had told her every dark, dirty, disgusting secret he had. Her fingers had never ceased in their movements. She'd told him more about her family that day. And he had told her more about his. They had shared a soft, slow, unfrenzied but wildly-passionate kiss. Unlike anything they had ever shared prior. Extraordinary, after how difficult the session had been. She'd washed him slowly, tenderly. Before he had left that day, they had made love.

Without a word, Aradia laid his wrist back on the bed and jotted down more notes. "You said this first began about a *penumbra* ago, correct?" she asked as she picked up a disc to take Hunter's blood pressure.

"Yes," Rainbow replied.

He had seen Narcissa again the very next day. After another failed attempt to halt what had become completely inevitable. She had been in jeans, a pink long-sleeved top, and pink-and-gold heels. They'd snuck into a downstairs performance room, talked, and fucked on the stage in front of the stripper pole.

"This... whatever this is... yes. About a *penumbra* ago," Hayden said, in agreement with his mate. "But it was a few *penumbras* ago, really, that he came home... different."

"Different how?" Aradia placed the disc in the appropriate spot and waited patiently for the numbers to appear.

Three days later... he had killed his brother. And fled to the den to be with the only one who could make him come to terms with what he'd done. With everything he had given up. It had been the hardest and roughest session he and Narcissa had ever had. Restraints. The bondage cross. The swing. A flogger he had used to whip her back to shreds. Even fucked her pussy with the handle. He'd fucked her up against the cross. Repositioned her, put a vibrator in her pussy, and had her suck his cock. Then, he had his way with her on the swing, while spilling her blood with his claws. Every emotion, every reality of their situation, had hit him in a torrential wave. While fucking her, he had re-memorized every single part of her. And he had cried. Cried at losing what little they could have. Cried at losing what they would never have again. He had taken care of her in the tub. And he had confessed to her. Narcissa had sung to him, and he had reveled in her beautiful voice. They had made love slowly in her tub. And she had told him to mark her.

"I do not know where he went, but when he came home, he went immediately into his house. After that, he just seemed... withdrawn. Subdued. Just... not his usual self. I do not know how to explain it any other way. But anytime I asked him what was wrong, he would just say that it was nothing and he was fine. Then, a *penumbra* ago, he…" Hayden's words trailed off.

The day he had utterly destroyed his home, from one end to the next. Except for some inexplicable reason, his bedroom. The day he had threatened Hayden not to come inside his home *or else.* Hunter had let no one inside. Not even the queen.

"Every time you think of me… know that you will always be loved. And you will always be mine."

Then he had done it. And it had been glorious.

"I love you, Narcissa."

"I love you, too, Hunter. So much more than I thought possible."

Then they said their goodbyes.

"In case I truly do not get to return, Narcissa… thank you for everything you have done for me. Even if I can never explain all of it to you, even if you never fully understand… just know that I am grateful."

"He went through changes before all of that. They just…" Rainbow's words trailed off. "Hunter had relaxed a little. Maybe become more comfortable with himself." She bit her bottom lip as her gaze lifted briefly to her mate. "We believe he fell in love with someone, but he's never spoken about it."

Aradia glanced back and forth between the two of them. The disc beeped. Flicking her gaze to the monitor, she jotted those numbers down, too. "I see," she mumbled. Aradia picked up the oxygen monitor and slid it onto the tip of one of his fingers.

Goodbyes that didn't last. Hunter hadn't been killed that day. He had been given an unexpected pardon. And he had come back to Narcissa again.

After the most painful two weeks he had ever experienced in his life. Until now.

As they'd made love on her bed, they'd poured every ounce of love and passion into their touches. Showed one another how much they had missed each other. Every word they'd spoken to one another had said all the things they couldn't say out loud. They had spent hours together that day. Showing one another just how deep their love went. It had been too much. That last sliver of his self-control had snapped. And when he'd marked her, his eyes had glowed. And they had both known it was over.

Hayden opened his mouth, but closed it again. Hunter knew he desperately wanted to ask if Aradia knew yet what might be wrong. But he was afraid he already knew the answer. Hayden tightened his hold on Rainbow.

Aradia jotted his oxygen level down as well. She looked at Hayden and Rainbow, flicking her gaze between them. "So, you do not know for sure if he has a mate bond?"

Rainbow blew out a soft breath, her shoulders sagging slightly. "A couple of *cycles* ago, when I mentioned to Hunter what I'd seen regarding his emotions surrounding a female, he refused to discuss it, but he didn't deny it, either. He *has* fallen in love with someone. We don't know who it is, but I can say without a doubt there's some kind of... complication with whomever he's given his heart to."

Hayden stared down at her in shock. "He... he has?"

Hunter didn't want to think about what had come after that. Not any of it. So, he chose not to. Instead, he remembered Narcissa's face. Her touch, her scent, her voice. How she made him feel. The tender way she cared for him at his most vulnerable. The way she had always, from the very beginning, taken everything he had to give her and begged for more. Because it had never been enough for either of them. Nothing had ever been enough. And it never would be again.

Though Hunter fought against it, the very last time he had seen her filled his mind. The hunch to her shoulders. The light was gone from her eyes. Despair was like a persistent cloud, clinging to her. As she'd left the marketplace, Hunter had gripped the edge of a building, his claws gouging into the brick. It took more self-control than he knew he possessed not to go after her. Watch her walk away from him. Knowing he could never get near her again.

"If that is true..." Aradia sighed heavily. Removing the oxygen monitor from his finger, she picked up a tourniquet. Aradia was quiet as she got it tied around Hunter's upper arm, then prepped a needle and tubing, as well as a few vials for his blood.

A fresh jolt of fear went through Hayden. He flicked his gaze back to the female. "What? If that is true, then what?"

Tucker's last words to him— *"Keep your distance, Hunter. You do not know what the punishment is for workers who break the rules. I cannot tell you what those are, but trust me—if you really love her, you will let her go."*

And so, he had.

Now, he was dying without her. Which was for the best. They were utterly and completely lost to one another. And he simply couldn't go on like this. Not in this reality. He couldn't live with this pain.

Aradia waited until she got the vials filled with blood, stoppered, and put away in her bag. Then, she slowly packed up all of her supplies. Once finished, she patted Hunter's hand and stood to her feet. "Let us go into the other room and talk," she breathed.

Hayden immediately shook his head. Tears filled his eyes and poured down his cheeks. "No. No."

Taking her mate's hand within her own, Rainbow urged him out of the room. "Come on, my love. Let's hear what she has to say."

With a slight nod, Hayden allowed himself to be led from the room.

Even though they were out of his sight, Hunter still heard everything. Curse his fucking hearing. If only that would go as well. There were a few subtle shifts as everyone settled into seats and got comfortable, as much as possible.

"I will not beat around the bush," Aradia said, using the same gentle tone as before. "And while I am still going to run all the tests, I do not believe they are going to be necessary."

"Why would they not be necessary?" Hayden choked out. "What is wrong with him? What can we do?"

"I know we are still working on educating everyone about our history. So, what I have to tell you is going to come across as a shock." Aradia inhaled and exhaled a deep breath. "Hunter is displaying all the signs of a bonded shape shifter who has lost his mate. The time frame is different for everyone, but when this happens... their bodies shut down. It is a slow transition at first, but there comes a turning point when things happen rapidly."

"I do not... understand," Hayden whispered.

"Is there a possibility of it... changing?" Rainbow asked. "If we can find this female and resolve whatever complication has arisen?"

"I have strong suspicions that will not be a possibility," Aradia replied. "If he were just separated from his mate, I do not believe he would decline in such a manner. It is not something I have ever seen before, and I have lived a very long time. Even mates separated due to Markham during his reign did not decline like this unless their mate had passed away. I think Hunter has truly lost her… whoever she is."

"There has to be something we can do, though," Hayden pled. "There has to be some kind of treatment or medicine."

The despair in his twin's voice sank Hunter lower than he already was. Not that he knew how that was possible. Instead of remembering Narcissa the way she'd looked the last time he'd seen her, Hunter brought her up in his mind during their time together. Running through every moment all over again. The way she'd moved. The way she'd touched him. Her voice when she'd sung to him. *"I have got you, too."* The way she had embraced every deepest, darkest part of him. Every single demon inside of his soul. And instead of running, she had always clung tighter. Teaching him that, despite everything in his past, he deserved someone like her. He deserved her love. He deserved happiness. It was the gods that, once again, had laughed in his face for ever harboring such a belief. For ever believing that he deserved more than painful, empty loneliness.

"Hayden. I know you remember when Bardin passed away. Remember what he looked like when he was brought back to the village. Nothing else causes a shape shifter's fur to lighten in such a way, not this quickly. You indicated this was a change that occurred overnight. This… is what our species goes through… when we have nothing left to live for. When the other half of our soul has been taken from us. At our core… once we have found our soul mate, that is what keeps us going. Our bodies depend on that bond remaining intact. Once broken… there is no known treatment that can bring us back to life."

"But you said… the tests… this could be something else…"

"Hayden, I need you to listen to me. I need you to understand what I am saying. Hunter is refusing to let anyone in. Even you. I am sure he has his reasons; everyone in these situations does. But with no information about who his female might be, we have no way of confirming if she still lives, or even how to find her. I do not believe that Hunter is going to live much longer. And I believe the only thing we can do now… is make him as comfortable as possible."

"I do not accept that. *I do not accept that!* There *has* to be something we can do! Anything! I will do anything! Tell me what medicine you need, and I will get it. I do not care what it takes or what it costs. I will not lose him. Do you hear me? *I will not lose him.*"

"*If* we can find out who she is, and she *is* alive, things could turn around?" Rainbow asked.

"That depends," Aradia answered.

"On what?" Hayden choked out.

"If she can get here in time."

"And if she cannot?" Hayden didn't wait for an answer. Because he already knew. Hunter was dying in the next room, and he didn't know what to do to help him. He didn't know where to start. Though he desperately wanted to. Sobs took over and shook Hayden to his core.

As much as Hunter accepted what was happening to him, what he felt from his twin broke his heart anew. There hadn't been a single moment in their lives that Hunter hadn't been there for him. Provided for him. Protected him. They were polar opposites, but they had always been together. From their first breaths, they had never spent a day apart. He didn't want to leave his twin behind. But he just didn't have the strength to stay. What was Hayden going to do without him?

But then he remembered the words his twin had spoken to him. A little over five *penumbras* ago, when he'd been locked in the prison.

"I got... comfortable... with you protecting me all these solaris. *I know I can take care of myself, but I think a part of me just relied on your protection too much. No matter what was going on, if I was going to get hurt, or worse, you always did the best you could to make sure that did not happen. You are covered in scars, and not just on the outside, because you were taking the hits for me. You should have let me take some for you. I want you to know... you do not have to protect me anymore. You have been sacrificing yourself for me throughout our entire lives. You can rest now. And know that, no matter what, I am going to be okay."*

He would be okay. Hayden would be okay... even after he was gone. Hunter could rest now... as he waited for the end.

"What kind of timeframe do we have?" Rainbow asked.

Aradia inhaled a deep breath. "*Umbras. A penumbra*, if we are lucky. But his vitals are not making me very hopeful that we have that long."

"No, no, no, no, no," Hayden sobbed.

"Honey, listen to me," Rainbow said firmly. "We'll figure it out. We can talk to Devin, let Clay know what's happening. We're not alone in this. Neither is Hunter."

Hunter, Hayden thought to him. *Please, please... just talk to me. Please.*

I am sorry, Hayden, he thought back. *I am really... really sorry.*

"He just... told me... he is sorry," Hayden sobbed. "I do not... know how to get through to him."

"Listen to me," Rainbow started. "I get what he's thinking, but that doesn't mean we give up on him. We just may not be the right people to get through to him. We'll do everything in our power to find this female and get to the truth."

"Okay," Hayden whispered, his voice cracking. "I am sorry... I did not mean to... fall apart all over you."

"It's okay, honey. How could this not upset you?" The female paused for a moment. "Aradia, do you think one of your granddaughters could stay here with Hunter, just to monitor him, while we go talk to Devin and Clay?"

"Of course. I will have them bring things over to get an IV set up as well." There were slight noises, indicating that Aradia was readying to leave. "Just because his body is ready to give up, does not mean we have to let him."

"Thank you, Aradia," Hayden said. "We should go. We should talk to Devin first, or divide and conquer. I can go find Clay, or should we talk to them both simultaneously, maybe? That would save time."

"Why don't we start with Clay?" Rainbow responded. "That way, if he knows something, the three of us can go to Devin."

"Thank you again."

"Of course," Aradia spoke. "Go on ahead. My granddaughters and I will handle things here, while you two handle things out there."

Listening to them out in the living area, Hunter closed his eyes. Not that he was going to sleep. Sleep had eluded him for some time. No amount of fluid was going to turn things around for him. Especially with what Aradia had said. Narcissa wasn't dead, but they were separated for the rest of their lives. His body was steadily reflecting his heart and his soul. And his life wouldn't last much longer. Unless an impossible miracle happened. All they had left was their memories. And Narcissa had his last gift to her. Something she would always have to remember him by. It would just have to be enough.

Hayden would be alright. He had his mate.

That mate bond could get you through anything. But it could also irreparably shatter you.

Narcissa stared at the back of Fallon's painting, where she'd hidden the note from Hunter. Her heart was pounding. Sixteen words that she couldn't get out of her head. Not that she hadn't tried. This was supposed to be the end for them. They didn't get the dream. Right? Shalla had convinced her that there was no way out of her contract. It was more than just a piece of paper. The magic in it bound her to this place for the rest of her life. But if he wasn't giving up, how could she? That's what the note meant, didn't it?

The words replayed in her mind: *You were the only one who ever saw the good in me. We are not done.*

A tiny, fleeting smile touched the corner of her mouth. From the beginning, Narcissa had known he was unlike any other. There was something she couldn't quite put her finger on back then. A small, unexplainable feeling flickered like a flame in her gut. It was the same feeling that had flooded her the first day he had entered her room. One that had grown significantly as they'd gotten to know one another. It was something she'd never experienced with another person.

Yes, she'd seen the good in him. And he'd seen it in her.

Was that why this felt too good to be true? Or why she was so captivated by the faded, yellow parchment? While that was something Hunter would say, she'd never seen his handwriting. How did she know the note had even come from him? Narcissa, still reeling from the conversation with Jezzy, thought back on the exchange.

The bedroom door slowly creaked open, the sound reverberating in the quiet. "What part of 'go away' do you not understand?" Narcissa called from her bed, her voice muffled as she burrowed deeper under the covers. She didn't want to talk to anyone. Or for Silva or Grace to drag her out of bed again. What was the point? She did her job, letting clients do what they wanted, bending to their will. Day in and day out. It was all she had left.

"I think you're going to want to see me," Jezzy said, the click of the door echoing as she closed it.

"I doubt that," she muttered. A raw, desperate breath escaped her lips as the darkness threatened to overwhelm her, the fading light of hope struggling against the encroaching shadows. A chilling void opened within her, and a suffocating silence pressed against her chest. Nothing could ease the agony consuming her soul. Except for Hunter, but they couldn't be together.

Jezzy stifled a groan. The wooden floor protested with each step she took, creaking as she approached the bed. "Look, I have gone back and forth over this. I was warned, told to stay out of this, but… this just seems like something you'll want."

Her eyes shifted to the harsh angles of the female's jaw. Her breath hitched as she met Jezzy's unwavering dark-green stare. There was something in it she couldn't decipher. It made about as much sense as Jezzy's words. Narcissa had known the female for years, and she'd seen nothing like this in that gaze before. Her eyes focused on the black, rectangular box her friend clutched. At least, that she recognized.

With a groan, Narcissa sat up, letting the covers fall away to reveal her dirty nightgown. "What are you talking about? And what does any of that have to do with candy?"

"The day your punishment began, word got around about what happened. Not all the details, but we all know that things between you and a client went too far. Anyway, I guess someone told Jade about his relationship with… my client. So, she paid me a visit and told me not to get in the middle of it, especially if any messages came for you." Jezzy's mouth curved up at the corner, a subtle hint of a smirk, as she lifted the box of candy. "But you and I both know I'm not the best at following orders."

Without a second thought, Narcissa threw the covers aside, feeling the soft fabric fall away as she bounded out of the bed. Her heart hammered against her ribs, the frantic rhythm like a drum in her ears. It couldn't be. Had Hunter truly sent her a message? Had he come up with a way for them to get out of this? That wasn't possible. Her eyes darted back and forth between Jezzy and the black box. "I don't understand. Why would you take this risk?"

"Because." The aroma of rich chocolate filled the air as Jezzy removed the box top to reveal six truffles dusted with a white, sugary coating. As she took out a single piece of candy, her gaze locked on Narcissa. A piece of parchment rested there, tucked neatly beneath the truffles. "If you can find a way, then maybe there's hope for the rest of us."

They all signed contracts and non-disclosure agreements, each bound by magic. It hadn't occurred to her that others might want a way out as much as she did. Or that she could provide a path forward. Not that Narcissa had a damn clue how they could escape their restraints. The magic caused agonizing pain, far worse than what she felt when her leather cuffs bit into her flesh.

How could they get around that? She had little in the way of answers. The rest of her conversation with Jezzy echoed in her thoughts.

Narcissa stared at the faded, yellow paper with dark, scribbled lines. It couldn't be. With a gulp, she held back the wave of tears that threatened to escape. "How did you get this?"

"I told you—my client. One we've shared."

Clay had delivered this? Hunter had actually gone to Clay with a request? It wasn't as if they hadn't used him before as a go-between. She'd done it during their two-week separation. What if this wasn't hope? What if it was just another goodbye? Their last goodbye and Hunter was truly dying? Gods, she didn't know what she would do if that was the case. Staying away from Hunter broke her heart in two, but his death—the thought alone—that she couldn't handle. Narcissa's eyes welled up, her hand trembling as she retrieved and unfolded the note, grief washing over her.

A gentle knocking on her bedroom door broke the silence, pulling her back to reality. Blowing out a heavy breath, Narcissa bit back a groan. The last thing she wanted was to deal with Silva or Grace right now. No one else except her clients—until Jezzy—had come to her door over the last few weeks. Although she wasn't consumed by her feelings, she still lacked the strength to tell them anything at this moment. "Go away."

"We need to talk."

What the fuck? Shalla *never* came to her room. The last time they'd even spoken, Narcissa had sought the female out. *Oh, gods.* What if Shalla had an update regarding her contract? No, no, no. It would be a more terrifying prospect than the darkest thoughts currently swirling in her mind.

"I'm coming in, Nia. I hope you're decent." The sound of the doorknob turning resonated.

"Fine," Narcissa muttered. It wasn't as though Shalla had offered her any alternative. *Gods, please don't let her tell me Kylen gained exclusivity.*

Though if that happened, she supposed Averine would announce it herself. Or summon her to the third floor. Neither of which had happened.

With a silent click, the door shut, the subtle sound swallowed by the quiet. Shalla's high heels echoed sharply across the hardwood floor, the sound bouncing off the walls, announcing her every move in the room. "How long do you intend to remain in that bed?"

The answer was simple—until she could decipher a way out for her and Hunter. Not that she imagined Shalla wanted to hear that. Nor did she want those words to get back to Averine somehow. That didn't mean she couldn't stall, giving herself time to come up with a better response. "Why?"

"Because your neighbors have complained about the stench."

Her green gaze focused on the blonde-haired female, the sconces casting a fiery glow on the long locks. What the fuck kind of statement was that? Silva and Grace wouldn't complain. They'd yank her from her slumber and shove her, protesting, into the shower. Which they had already done several times over the past week. Both of them had even washed her hair. Then why would Shalla say that? Narcissa slowly sat up, the cold wood of the headboard against her back. "Bullshit. Why don't you tell me what you really want?"

"You've been in that bed now for, what, nearly twenty-four *lacunas*?" Shalla strolled around the room, her eyes darting from one piece of equipment to another, while her hands remained clasped at the small of her back. "Stewing in an endless sea of juices. The aroma here has shifted. It's grown a bit... grotesque. I'm surprised you can stand it."

Narcissa's gaze followed every step the female took as she traveled between furnishings. Each piece still bore a faint scent of her last client, serving as a reminder of what she had to do to survive, to provide for her family. Memories of Hunter often surfaced, overpowering the dread that made her skin prickle. Lately, it had been happening less, forcing her to wallow in her own squalor. The putrid scent of each piece Shalla touched made Narcissa's flesh crawl as she watched the female move about. The stench in the air grew thicker and more pungent. Dear gods, how could she have allowed this to happen? How could she not have followed her normal cleaning routine? Her body numb, Narcissa clawed her way from the bed, desperate to escape the confines of her misery.

Stopping at the chaise's edge, Shalla pivoted sharply, the fabric of her dress swirling. As the corner of her mouth lifted in a smile, a glint sparkled in her bright-green eyes, accentuating the scar on her right cheek. "Shower first. We can talk while you do that, and then you can address this mess."

"What?" What was the female prattling on about? Why the fuck did it matter which order she handled things? That made little sense. Especially when she'd get dirty again, her clothes stained with even more grime. No, she had to take care of the mess she'd left untouched first. Then she could scrub her skin raw.

"I promise. It'll be worth your while."

Five words—Narcissa fixated on the expression taking shape on Shalla's face. It was somewhere between a silent plea and a twinkle of hope. It changed everything. Whatever had transpired between them before no longer existed. "Fine. I'll get a shower going, but then you talk." Not during or after, but while the water ran, covering their voices, and before she got naked.

With a dip of her chin, Shalla stepped to the side. "That's acceptable."

Good. The female didn't have any other choice. Shalla had invaded her space, not the other way around. Narcissa strode into her bathroom, the open sliding door offering a clear path. She didn't know what required such evasive maneuvering, but the lack of knowledge wouldn't stop her, either. She slid the glass door back and got the shower running in no time. The gentle trickling of water echoed through the room, releasing steam into the air. "Now, talk."

"Remember what I said earlier about accepting your fate?" Shalla began, her heels clicking a staccato rhythm as she approached. "I was wrong."

With a sudden movement, Narcissa turned, her focus immediately on the female, her eyes growing in surprise. "What?" Those words sure as fuck weren't something she expected. The female had been nothing but honest when they first had that conversation. What led Shalla to change her mind?

"My previous failure had set me on a single path, so I never considered another opportunity would present itself. Which led me to dismiss you rather quickly when you last approached me." Shalla lifted a hand, cutting off questions. "I can't disclose the details. All you need to know is that I've got something in the works that will affect us all. I don't have a timeframe, so it'll require patience on your end."

Patience? Right. Not something she was all that great at. With a sigh, Narcissa gripped the back of her neck, trying to massage away the knot of tension. So many questions. None of which she could get answered. Even the rushing water couldn't hide all the other noises. This required a great deal of trust.

Her gaze flicked into her bedroom, past Shalla. From her position, the note was hidden, yet its message was permanently etched in her memory. He'd told her he wouldn't give up. She needed to reply somehow—to let Hunter know she got his message. That she'd do whatever it took for them to be together. Even if it meant waiting. Narcissa bit the inside of her cheek. "Can you get something to him?"

"Yes, but choose your words wisely. It's prudent he doesn't react before we're ready and ruin everything. Understood?"

"Of course." Her reply served one purpose—hope, for both of them.

That was all they needed to get through this.

A little hope.

Beep. Beep. Beep.

The steady noise of Hunter's monitors should have been utterly maddening to him. But, wouldn't you know it, he just didn't have the strength to get annoyed by it. An unknown number of days and nights had passed since Cassandra and Iridessa had returned and gotten him set up with not one, but two IVs. One with fluids, the other with Hunter didn't know what. There were multiple monitors attached to his body: some on his chest for his heart and lungs, one on his forehead for his temperature, others on his biceps, stomach, and head to monitor different functions.

He should have been so uncomfortable. But all he felt was... tired. So tired. And defeated.

Why couldn't his body just get the fuck on with it?

His fingers twitched of their own accord. But Hunter shut the subconscious notion down. He wouldn't do that again. His twin was going to be a father. He couldn't put Hayden through that again. Not after...

"What the—" Hayden strode swiftly across the room and lifted the IV that was no longer attached to Hunter's arm like it should be. His gaze scanned his twin's body, from top to bottom. The male's eyes darkened as he took in the other detached IV, and the monitors that were no longer connected to Hunter's chest or head. "What did you do? Hunter? What did you do?!"

'Please... Leave me alone,' Hunter thought to him. 'Hayden... Just let me... let me go... please.'

"No! NO!" Fire blazed in Hayden's darkened eyes. The only thing that had overridden his twin's anger was the worry. And the fear. The all-consuming fear that the removal of his brother's lifeline had caused things to take another turn for the worst. "I. Refuse. To let you go. It is not your time. It is..." Hayden choked up. "No."

'I... cannot... I cannot fight... anymore.'

"Then I will fight for you," Hayden said firmly. Though his body shook with a nervous tremor, his hands remained steady as he reattached the IVs and monitors. "Until you are strong enough to fight for yourself again. For yourself, and for her."

All Hunter had wanted—still wanted—was to go to sleep and not wake up again until he was on the other side. The only place he would ever see his mate again. How was that too much to ask?

But he couldn't sleep. Couldn't eat. Could barely think—and thinking was all he had left to do. He certainly couldn't move. He had endured the humiliation and disgrace of soiling himself repeatedly, lacking the strength to lift his head, or even his arms, to get out of bed. Unable to speak, he was left with no way to call for assistance, and reaching the bathroom down the hall felt impossible. How many times had Hayden lifted him up so his sheets could be changed? Twice—no, three times. Before they'd put a catheter in so it didn't happen again. They'd wanted to before that. After the second time, Hunter had stopped protesting and just let them do it.

It shouldn't have taken this long. His body should have already fully given up on him. Could all the medicine and fluids really be doing enough to keep him stable? Had to be. It certainly wasn't his body that was refusing to give up. It already had. Piece by piece, he was slipping away. The only thing he had left was his memories, which ran on a repeat in his mind. Mostly about Narcissa and their time together. But he thought about Hayden, too. Growing up, taking care of his twin. He thought about

Elisa a little, too. Not much, because he really didn't have all that many memories of her. But he thought about her a little.

The front door opened, then closed. Hunter could make out soft murmurs down the hall, but he didn't decipher them. His gaze slowly drifted toward the window. Right. It was about that time for his vitals to be checked again. Like it would make a difference? It had been clear that day that Aradia held no hope. She wanted to—desperately. Just as everyone did. Hades, even the queen had been checking on him semi-regularly. But Hunter wasn't naïve. There simply wasn't any hope to be found.

The words Aradia had spoken went through his head. When she'd come back that day with Hayden and Rainbow, after getting his blood test results. She had sat down on the edge of his bed again. *"I have never attempted to reverse a situation like this. Normally, once someone enters this stage, if they have not already, they accept rather quickly that their end is rapidly approaching. That is not the case here."* Her last words came out rather forcefully. *"We are going to do everything that we can to get you out of critical condition. However, I do not know if the situation can ever be fully reversed. In other words, I have no knowledge if any part of your condition is going to end up being permanent. Several of your organs have already shut down. That being said, there are herbal remedies that may help repair the damage. I just cannot say how long you would have to take them. Or if you would ever safely be able to stop taking them. But we have to get you to the point of being able to ingest liquids first. That is our first step. So, I am going to get you set up with some more IV fluids and nutrients, and..."* She'd gone after that. Talked about keeping him stable for the time being. But that the result really depended on him. Whatever will he had to go on. Though Hunter hadn't openly responded to her, he'd heard everything she said. And asked Hayden telepathically to tell her that he understood.

But he hadn't said anything more than that. It hadn't been necessary. Especially not to his twin.

Soft footsteps sounded down the hall. Hunter didn't shift his gaze from the window. They'd left the curtains open for him, and the warm sunlight spilled onto his bed, which they'd moved closer to the window. Thankfully, his bedroom didn't face the village. He didn't want anyone gawking at him.

Hunter's nose twitched at the growing scent, and his brow furrowed lightly. What was he doing here?

"Hello, Hunter. Is it alright if I come in? I have something I need to speak with you about."

His gaze drifted and landed on Marcell, whose form was silhouetted in the entryway. The male stood tall, broad-shouldered, seeming to nearly fill the doorway. And he wasn't even necessarily a large male, by feline standards. Maybe it was just his perception at the moment. Hunter shut his eyes and said nothing. Did nothing.

"I promise... you are going to want to hear what I have to say."

Nope, he seriously doubted it. But the sooner he heard Marcell out, the sooner the male would leave. Opening his eyes again, Hunter's chin dipped the slightest amount. At first, he wasn't sure if the male noticed the tiny movement. Marcell entered the room, the sound of his footsteps echoing, and grabbed a chair to the right of the doorway as he moved toward the bed.

Marcell set the chair down with a soft thump and sat. "I have something for you as well." A strap hung across the male's chest. Pulling it, he shifted the bag onto his lap. "Hades, it pains me to see you like this." Marcell opened the bag with a slight tug. "I have heard of your troubles. I want you to know that... I understand." There was a deeper meaning to those words, but fuck if Hunter knew what it was. "A plan is in motion," the male said, the leather bag's scent filling the air as one of his hands disappeared inside. "Not just for her, but for all of them."

That got his attention. Hunter's muted gaze shifted to the bag as Marcell pulled out... a book? What the fuck?

"I cannot give you any of the details. Nor do I need anything from you but patience." Marcell opened the book, revealing a piece of faded, yellow parchment folded in the middle to conceal its contents. "It is most important that you not return until the proper moment." He held the parchment out to Hunter, but when he didn't move, Marcell unfolded the parchment, the crisp paper rustling in the quiet room, and laid it on the bed, right in front of his face. "Read it. Please."

Still, Hunter didn't move. Return? Return where? He flicked his gaze downward to the parchment. Surely, Marcell didn't mean—

I won't give up if you don't. — N

And right below that flowy letter—a crimson-colored kiss.

Hunter's heart stopped in his chest, skipping a couple of beats. The monitor beeped louder and more swiftly. His trembling hand reached for the parchment, the rough paper crackling as he pulled it from the covers.

I won't give up if you don't.

Tears streamed down his face, the salty drops soaking the pillow beneath him. Not that Hunter did anything to stifle them. He clutched the note tighter, feeling the paper's rough texture against his skin, all the while carefully preventing his tears from staining it. His Narcissa had sent him a message. She had found a way. Hunter pressed his lips to where hers had left that beautiful crimson mark. Narcissa...

Gods, he could almost smell her.

"Hunter? Do you understand what I said to you?"

It took a lot of mental strain to comprehend what the male was saying.

Marcell gripped his forearm tightly. "It is imperative that you not return until the proper moment. Do you understand? It could ruin everything."

Somehow, he forced his gaze from the note and met Marcell's. "I understand," he said, his voice coming out hoarse and soft as a whisper.

The male squeezed his arm again. "So do I. I would be the same... if I lost my lifeline. Now. Patience. Alright?" The grip on his arm tightened further. "And you must promise yourself not to give up." Marcell smiled. "How would it be for everything to fall properly into place, only for us to lose you? Have faith. You will see her again."

"When?" Hunter choked out.

Marcell pulled his hand back to his lap, replaced the book in his bag, and closed it. "I cannot tell you that. Only because I do not know myself. Which is why this will require patience from you. From both of you."

Both of—"You have spoken to her?"

"No. But I am close to someone who has."

Shalla. Had to be. She and Marcell... they were working together. Working to find them all a way out. All of them... including Narcissa.

Hunter had been wrong.

There was hope to be found.

That was all they needed to get through this.

Just a little hope.

Slowly, he nodded.

Weak and fragile, Hunter pushed his arm beneath him, feeling as if his bones might crumble at any moment. He pushed with all his might, aided some by Marcell's steadying hand, and rose up on his elbow. Marcell sprang into action, propping another pillow behind him to help keep him upright.

"Patience," he muttered, his eyes on the note again. Those seven beautiful words from his mate. "I can have patience."

"I am glad to hear that."

Aradia appeared in the doorway. Hunter hadn't even heard her approach. Her eyes widened slightly. Looking Hunter over, from head to foot, a small smile played on her lips. "Now, this is exactly what I have been hoping to see."

Twenty-Two

It had been one month precisely since Hunter had stepped foot inside the walls of the den. His *plan* to keep his emotions buried—the only way for him and Narcissa to survive—had been pulverized just about two weeks afterward. When he had felt—Hunter slammed the door on that memory. Again. It was something he'd had to do more than once.

How many times had he wished he were a stronger male? Strong enough to do what needed to be done? He had never been weak. Never. Not until his entire being had become weak for her. That it didn't disgust him was a true testament of how deeply his feelings for Narcissa went.

As if everything over the past couple of weeks didn't say that plainly enough. Which meant this was the very last place he should be. But he couldn't stay away any longer. Even if this was the very last time he laid eyes on his beloved mate... staying away was killing him. Hades, *this* might kill him, too.

But it was a situation he had no choice but to rectify. One way or another.

They'd reassigned him to Nina, but Hunter had no intention of being with the female. Which, apparently, was not a secret, though he'd uttered not a single word to the effect. Shalla had escorted him to the female's door, but before she departed, she turned and threw him a knowing glance.

"If you find Nina's room is lacking, I'm sure you might find the court-yard a bit more suitable. The door there at the end of the other hall grants you access."

As if he didn't know exactly what that meant.

As he made his way through the den, Hunter ensured that there would be no suspicion if anyone were to lay eyes on him. His pace was slow and even. As he walked to the courtyard, his eyes scanned the intricate carvings of the decor. He'd forced himself to remain there for a few moments before he'd continued on his way. Not that he'd be able to explain how he could exhibit restraint.

Not a single soul laid eyes on him, and he finally reached the all-too-familiar door of his Narcissa's room. His gaze remained fixed on the door, but his heart hammered against his ribs in anticipation of the person on the other side. A dangerous thing in his condition that couldn't be helped. Hunter wrapped his fingers around the doorknob. For the first time since he'd been here last, his body felt a little less cold. Without hesitation, he opened the door and silently entered the room, closing the door just as quietly behind him.

Staring across the room, the sight of Narcissa brought a wave of relief; her presence was a calming balm. It was as if, regardless that he felt her without being able to *see* her, it had been difficult to know for sure if she even still existed. If all of his wonderful memories of their time together, all the horrid agony they had both endured in their separation, hadn't all just been some terrible joke the gods were playing on him.

But, no. There she was, in the flesh. Her cinnamon-brown hair cascaded down her back. She wore a white, off-the-shoulder, lace crop top over a white tank, paired with low-slung, faded jeans with white lace, and white stilettos fastened by a thick ankle buckle.

While Hunter registered, she stood in her closet; he didn't take any of the surroundings in. No, that wasn't true. He saw the rose he'd gifted to her two weeks ago in the marketplace. Perfectly preserved in a glass case on her dresser. Her hand was wrapped tightly around it, making it impossible to overlook. But his eyes didn't drift away from her face once. *Oh, gods...* her beauty took his breath away. As it always had. Even with the sorrowful expression in her eyes, she was an absolute vision. One that invigorated not just his body—that had become quite gaunt with the weight he'd lost and the constant feeling of death—but his soul as well. She was a goddess. His treasure. His baby girl.

Fuck, he shouldn't be here. But he couldn't bear to leave.

Setting the case on her dresser, Narcissa turned toward him. "Hunter?"

His eyes momentarily drifted closed. She'd voiced it as a question. It was difficult to believe, just as he did, that what they were experiencing was real. Hunter, his eyes locked on her, closed the distance, each step echoing in the sudden quiet. Her scent... *oh gods,* her scent. Slowly, Hunter kneeled down in front of her. One hand went to her waist, a tentative touch of his thumb brushing across her soft skin. His fingers brushed her cheek, and then the base of her neck, where he could feel her pulse racing. A shudder swept through him.

Leaning forward slightly, he rested his forehead against her chest, right over her heart. "Narcissa."

As she wrapped her arms around his shoulders, the gentle strokes on the back of his head sent a wave of warmth through him. His heart swelled, the sensation both powerful and unfamiliar. The relief at just having her close to him again. Her caress pulled a quiet purr out of him, his body's natural response to her touch.

"I missed you," she admitted.

"I missed you, too." With a slight tilt of his head, Hunter gently kissed her breast, his lips just above her tank top's edge. For probably the first time, there wasn't a sexual overtone to the gesture. Regardless that his dick was already hard as stone just from being near his mate again. "I know I should not be here." He slowly swept his lips up her collarbone, then nuzzled his face against her neck, feeling the warmth of her skin. Inhaling a deep breath, another shudder swept through him. "Staying away any longer was impossible. I needed to see you. I need... you."

"I need you, too," Narcissa replied, her voice low.

Gods, those words from her... A shudder jolted through his spine. Placing a soft kiss against her throat, Hunter pulled back just enough to meet her eyes. Those words were the opposite of what either of them should have said. Just being here at all was dangerous. Wrong. But if *this,* being with Narcissa, was wrong... how could they ever want to be right? His forehead met hers, and his thumb softly traced the curve of her cheek. While a thousand lines ran through his mind, none of them seemed right for this moment. They should talk though, right? That was important. It wasn't like this could last. If Averine somehow got wind that he was here—and not with Nina as he was supposed to be—what little time they had would become nonexistent. Being caught in this room meant facing expulsion and a permanent banishment from the den. The only time they had was right now.

She had to know how much he needed her. Cared for her. Loved her. But words continued to escape him. Which meant he was going to have to show her.

His lips met hers, a feather-light contact that was almost a phantom sensation. It was so powerful it would have floored him if he weren't already kneeling in front of her. His tongue gently swept across her lower lip before he drew it into his mouth, his fangs delicately grazing her skin. Holy fucking shit, the more he touched her, the more *alive* he became.

But then, he had truly been dying without her.

He stood from the floor, and his arms wrapped around her as he explored the taste between her lips. As Hunter lifted her, her legs came around his waist. He held her close, feeling the gentle pressure of her breasts against him. He had Narcissa pinned against the wall before he could fully process what he was doing. His tongue danced slowly, a gentle exploration against hers at first. Rougher, more demanding, he took possession of her as his hands moved through her hair. His fingers tangled in her cinnamon-brown locks as he deepened the kiss with a carnal growl. Hunter held on to her with everything he had, as if she was the only thing holding him together. The only thing keeping him from falling. From shattering completely.

Because she was.

Their bodies heated against one another, burning hotter than the sun. Hades, it was beautiful.

Hunter moaned into the kiss, his fingers tangling in her hair as she embraced him, digging her heels into his ass. Her nails scraped against his shoulder, and then her fingers danced up the back of his head. The feel of her fingers sifting through his fur was fucking incredible. Oh, gods, he had missed her so fucking much. And there was only one way to show her.

Deepening the kiss even more, one hand left her hair and slid between them. He didn't stop kissing her as he grabbed the top of both her shirts, right at the curve of her breasts, and ripped the fabric away with his claws. He shuddered as her bare breasts were revealed; the sight took his breath away. No bra. There would be time to worship them as they deserved later. Right now, there was so much more to attend to.

His hand wandered down her ribcage, across her stomach, brushed the belly button ring, and finally rested on her jeans. As the kiss continued, he fumbled with the button until it snapped. His claws, sharp and deadly, shredded the fabric with a loud rip as he frantically tried to get at what was underneath. What he desired. Needed. Craved. What the both of them had gone *far* too long without. Her heels could stay on, but nothing else. He needed her to be completely bare of anything but him. A growling moan escaped him, his fingertips grazing the delicate lace of her thong. Holy fuck, it barely covered anything. He could feel hints of her skin through the holes in the fabric. White—it was probably white. Narcissa always matched her clothing and undergarments.

With a groan, Hunter let go of her hair and clutched her bare ass. He intensified his touch, pinpointing her clit through the fabric and applying a firm, slow pressure. Oh, fuck... *fuck...* The fucking fabric needed to go.

A growl, heavy with need and desire, rumbled from him as Narcissa dug her heels deeper into his ass cheeks, the metallic tang of his blood now thick in the air. *Fuck, yes...* Oh, gods, that was exactly what he needed. He tightened his grip, his claws digging deeper into her flesh. Her hips moved faster, grinding against his fingers, and his rubbing quickened to match her pace. It wasn't enough, though. Not nearly enough.

Narcissa's fingers tightened around his shoulder as she ripped the lace material of her thong with her other hand, discarding the shreds onto the floor.

Hunter gripped his shaft, pressing the head of his dick right at her entrance. "I need you. I need *all* of you. Now," he growled. With no other warning, he slammed his cock inside of her as hard as he could. "Oh, fuck! Narcissa!" He thrust vigorously and swiftly in and out of her. The head of his shaft slammed into her core with each forceful push. He tightened his grip on her ass, feeling her blood pulse beneath the fur of his fingers as he grabbed a handful of her hair and forcefully pulled her head back.

"Mine." Hunter nipped at her shoulder. "Mine." He stroked his tongue up her neck. "*Mine,*" he practically snarled in her ear.

"All yours," Narcissa moaned. Her heels pressed firmly against his ass as she moved her hips in sync with his powerful thrusts. As she ran her fingers along his arm, she clenched her nails into his biceps and held on with all her strength.

"That is right, baby girl. You are all mine." And he was absolutely all hers. *Holy fucking shit.* Hunter let out a deep moan. Each time she met one of his thrusts, a massive jolt slammed through his shaft and into his balls. The sensations grew stronger with each squeeze, and despite his desire to delay the moment of their release, he was close to the edge.

"Fuck!" they hollered simultaneously.

As his cock relentlessly penetrated her, Hunter pushed two fingers into her tight rear entrance. Bracing himself against the wall, he widened her thighs with his hips, increasing both his speed and the force of his thrusts. His dark eyes locked with hers as he claimed her mouth, his tongue exploring her depths. Holy Hades, how could it still not be enough?

Narcissa moved her hips with precision, synchronizing with both his thrusts and fingers, purring a soft moan.

Holy shit, that fucking sound... Hunter groaned as he deepened the kiss, his body both taking and giving what they each needed. His cock and fingers moved seamlessly together, with one thrusting in as the other pulled back almost completely, and vice versa. Narcissa met every single thrust. When he could no longer contain himself, he broke the kiss, their lips softly brushing against each other. Their eyes met, and the air crackled with the heat of his desire. "Come with me, Narcissa. Come with me." He uttered those words only before a powerful release shot up his shaft and erupted with a thunderous roar.

As though her body was his to command, she came right along with him, colossal in its magnitude. Their fluids mingled, drenching their bodies and trickling down onto the ground beneath them. Not that either of them ceased the swing of their hips, nor did he stop the penetration of his fingers. Even after this release was done, they were far from finished.

Hades, just to look upon her face again as she came for him. It was an utterly celestial experience. He tightened his grip around her, feeling her soft skin, before pulling her from the wall and turning toward the bed. He paused at the edge, then climbed onto it, before gently laying her down. Still connected, his body enveloped hers as he deepened their kiss, their tongues intertwining in a slow, passionate rhythm.

This was so different from anything he'd ever experienced. Not just with her, but with anyone. Ever. It went beyond the fact that he had bonded completely with her. They'd been together with no walls before, but this... Hunter had no words to describe it. So, he didn't even try, and just reveled in the moment's beauty.

Their movements were slow and gentle, a stark contrast to the urgency that would soon consume them. They needed to release their pain. All of it. Before it could engulf them in the darkness once more. Because no matter what they both wanted, this was temporary. Unless they figured out a miracle. Or whatever plan had been put in place, somehow, magically came through.

Narcissa widened her thighs and wrapped a leg higher around his hip, while Hunter's arm cradled her lower back and the other hand tangled into her hair. Her fingers danced over the taut muscles of his back as she ran them up and down. Her touch on his scars caused a slight, involuntary shudder to ripple through him. The way she touched them wasn't to point them out or bring attention to them. It was a soft, loving touch. His heart swelled, an unfamiliar emotion blooming within him like a vibrant flower.

She arched her back, synchronizing with his movements as he entered her repeatedly. He moaned while kissing her, feeling the tight contractions of her inner walls around his cock. Holy fuck... gods, she felt so good. Even though he didn't go any faster, his thrusts gained a bit more power. His claws scraped just slightly against her scalp. Hunter nipped at her tongue, a low growl rumbling in his chest, and then their tongues met once more. The tip of her tongue swept across one of his fangs, drawing a bit of blood. Hunter sucked on her tongue, the metallic tang of blood filling his mouth as he swallowed greedily. Gods, he'd fucking missed that taste. *All* of her tastes. Her skin, blood, and cum. He needed it *all*.

His growl intensified as she purred into the kiss. Fuck, she knew what that sound did to him. As he tucked his knees in tighter, Hunter increased the force of his movements while deepening the kiss. Even with the pressure from her stiletto on his ass cheek, it didn't elicit the desired response. "Harder," he growled against her lips. "Make me bleed for you, baby girl."

"Yes, Sir," Narcissa said with a soft rumble deep in her chest.

A satisfied purr vibrated from deep within him. Fuck, he loved that. He'd missed that sound so very much, too.

Shifting her other leg higher on his hip, she firmly pressed each stiletto into his ass, utilizing the added leverage to intensify the motion of her hips against his. He hissed as she raked her nails down his back, a sound that echoed through the otherwise silent room, and his head jerked back. "Fuck... fuck, yes," he growled. Hunter tasted the metallic tang of her blood after nipping her lip, and his claws dug into her hip. He dragged his claws, leaving a trail of crimson from her waist to her shoulder. It wasn't enough, though. From either of them. Not only did he need to bleed for her, but he also needed her to bleed for him.

"Gods, yes!" Narcissa bit his bottom lip, pulling at it until a crimson stream flowed, the coppery scent filling the air.

Gods, he fucking loved that.

She gouged her stilettos into his ass, lifted her hips, and held the position. "Fuck," they moaned simultaneously. His dick reached much deeper inside her at this angle.

Each time she tightened her pussy around his shaft, his growls reverberated throughout the room. Fully upright on his knees, he forcefully pulled her hand from her shoulder to her breast, clutching it and digging his claws in, causing her blood to well up and trickle down her skin. His other hand slipped between her thighs, where he located her clit and began rubbing it vigorously. "Holy fuck, you feel so good, sweetheart."

Though his emotions had been 'turned back on,' so to speak, for a couple of weeks now, he hadn't yet opened up to her. It was something he'd longed to do, but had known better than to do, at the same time. But now, he didn't want to hold back. With anything. Hunter tightened his grip on her breast while flicking the nail of his thumb over her nipple repeatedly, escalating the speed and intensity of rubbing her clit. "I love you, Narcissa." Then he opened up fully to her, allowing her to feel every single bit of the love, desire, and need he had for her. Something that would never cease, as long as his heart remained beating.

Hunter knew she couldn't open up to him in the same way. Whatever held her here, if she opened up to him, it could trigger that; a surefire way of Averine knowing exactly what was going on. They were playing with fire as it was. Hopefully, that he'd opened up to her already wouldn't trigger anything. It was too late now, though. And now that he'd done it, he couldn't fathom turning back.

But even though she couldn't, her response was utterly perfect. Narcissa cupped his jaw, and he leaned into her touch, his eyes never leaving hers. "I love you, too, Hunter."

Those four words from her lips brought a genuine smile to his face. One unlike any he'd ever made before. Not that he'd really ever smiled much, but he was practically beaming.

Narcissa fused their lips together and entwined their tongues, her moan commingling with his growl. Gods, she tasted so fucking good. His growl became more erotic as she widened her thighs and pressed her heels firmly into his ass. Even more so as an orgasm exploded out of her pussy. One after another, waves of pleasure flowed out of her, soaking his shaft, their thighs, her buttocks, and the bedding below. He needed to taste it. Needed that sweet, sweet taste in his mouth, drenching his tongue, and flowing down his throat. Holy fuck, he needed it. And he couldn't wait any longer.

With her orgasm concluded, Hunter freed her breast, and then his lips lightly grazed her tongue while he separated her legs from his waist. He lay on his back on the bed, and then with a gentle tug, he brought her down; her legs framing his face. Hunter dug his claws into her hips and ran his tongue along one of her inner thighs, savoring the taste of her essence as he moaned. "Mmm, fuck, I really missed this, sweetheart."

"Fuck. Me, too." Narcissa dragged her nails up his thighs and over his ass, the sound of her nails against his skin mixing with her soft moans as she twirled her tongue around the head of his cock.

His head kicked back on his neck, pressing into the bed. Holy fucking shit... *yes*. Hunter growled as he cleaned her juices from her inner thigh, his tongue tracing the pulse in her femoral artery. Gods, he wanted to fucking bite her. Mark her. Claim her all over again. Without hesitation, he dug his claws further into her hips, thrust his tongue inside her, and released a fierce growl that reverberated through her body. Fuck, yes. *Fuck, yes.* She was perfect. Every inch of her, both inside and out, was pure perfection.

"Fuck!" Narcissa sensually licked up each of his thighs, playfully biting at the pulse point while cleaning up the blend of their essence from his skin.

A jolt of lightning went straight through his cock each time. *Holy fuck.* His grip on her hips tightened further, and a warm, crimson stream flowed down her thighs. With a low, guttural sound, she pleasured him by sucking on his balls and grinding her pussy against his tongue. His moan against her pussy was uncontrollable. His tongue delved deeper and moved with a heightened fervor as he pleasured her. Hunter licked her, teasing her clit before plunging his tongue back inside, repeating the tantalizing cycle. One hand broke free from her hip, arcing back before delivering a stinging slap to her rear.

"Harder," Narcissa demanded.

She wanted harder? Oh, he could *definitely* do harder. Hunter removed his claws from her hip, and then, with a swipe, they tore down her back before embedding in her thigh. He recoiled his other hand and struck her backside again; this time the impact resonated more powerfully. A carnal growl, thick with desire, rumbled from his chest and echoed against her as he devoured her with renewed fervor. His body took control, his feet remaining still on the bed as he forcefully thrust into her mouth. Holy shit, it wouldn't be much longer before he came.

With a firm hold on his ass and her nails digging into his flesh, Narcissa engulfed him in her mouth, deep-throating him.

"Oh, fuck!" Holy fucking shit. He had missed the way her mouth felt around his cock, the pressure of his dick against her throat, and her nails digging into his flesh. Her tongue sensuously explored every inch of his shaft, causing him to involuntarily close his eyes in ecstasy. "Fuck! Do not stop!"

Narcissa tightened her grip on his ass while extending her tongue to encircle his shaft entirely. He snarled against her pussy as she purred. *Holy fuck, yes.* She knew exactly what that fucking did to him. Her thighs parted further as she moaned, rocking her pussy against his eager tongue. Gods, he was so fucking close. Again and again, his palm contacted her ass, his claws sinking in deeper each time, increasing in intensity with every strike. "Fuck, come with me." After biting down on her clit, Hunter increased the pressure on her sex with his mouth and thrust his tongue in deeply once more.

Rocking back against his tongue, a massive orgasm surged through her body and gushed into his mouth. The moment she came, his orgasm burst forth and spurted down her throat. The tight suction of her cheeks around his shaft and her firm grip on his balls heightened the intensity of his release. Hunter continued to eagerly explore her wetness with his tongue, unrelenting as her orgasm seemed to stretch on endlessly. His growl echoed around the room as he held her sex to his mouth, unwilling to let a single drop go anywhere but down his throat. His hips kept moving, thrusting up into her mouth repeatedly as wave after wave of his release poured out. Narcissa kept her mouth wrapped around his cock, swallowing every drop.

Just that one orgasm in his mouth wasn't nearly enough. He needed so much more. But there would be time for that later. Right now, he needed his dick as deep inside her as possible.

Once he'd cleaned off her pussy, Hunter ripped his claws from her ass and lifted her off of him. The motion ripped her nails from his ass as well, drawing more blood, but that was exactly what he wanted. He got her on her hands and knees and got up behind her. With a tight grip on his shaft, he guided it to her anus and entered smoothly in one swift action. "Holy fuck!" Oh gods, she was so fucking tight. Holy Hades, he'd missed this, too. With one hand anchored to the bed, the other hand found its way between her thighs. He firmly and swiftly massaged her clitoris while his erection quickly established a consistent rhythm. Hunter groaned her name as he thrust into her behind and teased her clit with his fingers.

"Fuck," Narcissa groaned. With each of his thrusts, she met him, balling the bedding beneath her hands as she rocked her ass against his cock. With each thrust, she squeezed her ass cheeks around his pulsating shaft. "Gods, don't stop."

That wouldn't be happening. At least, not for a very long while. Hunter grazed his fangs over her shoulder with a deep growl. Fuck, this felt so amazing. "Fuck... Narcissa," he moaned. Extending his hand, he inserted three fingers deep into her pussy, thrusting with them while his cock made forceful, rhythmic movements inside her.

Arching her back, she cupped one of her breasts and rolled her nipple between her fingers. Her hips swayed in time with his thrusts, her body responding to his touch. "Fuck... Hunter."

When his name left her lips, a deep growl resonated in response. "I love when you moan my name, baby girl. Say it again." He intensified his movements, penetrating her with more power and speed, employing both his cock and fingers. His fangs grazed over her shoulder once more, and then slowly traveled up her neck. Fuck, he wanted to bite her... *Needed* to bite her. To see his mark on her again... A shudder swept down his spine.

Narcissa's fingers pressed into the soft flesh of her breast as she clutched the bedding. "Gods yes, Hunter," she grunted as she rocked her hips back, slamming her ass against his cock.

He removed his fingers from her and delivered a firm smack to her pussy. Pulling out of her ass, Hunter thrust his cock deeply into her sex. He didn't take any time to work up to a steady rhythm this time. He relentlessly thrust into her, the rhythm unbroken with barely a pause in between each motion. "I need you to come so hard you fucking drench my cock." He covered her hand with his own, the warmth of her skin against his. As his claws sank into the soft flesh, she continued to knead it with her hand, feeling the slickness of her blood. The scent of her filled his nostrils, and his fangs throbbed with a growing ache. *Holy shit...*

"Hunter!" she cried out in pure ecstasy.

With fangs bared, he hissed, the sound echoing around the room. Before he could think, the instinct came crashing down, a tidal wave of sensation. Not that he could say he would have tried to stop it, given the chance. As her orgasm erupted, Narcissa's head fell back against his shoulder, her breath coming in ragged gasps. Her climax coated his cock, their thighs, and the sheets beneath them in a series of intense waves. And his fangs sank deep into her throat. A predatory and possessive snarl ripped from his throat, the sound bouncing off the walls of the room. Hunter bit down, tasting the metallic tang of blood as it trickled down her throat.

Her orgasm hadn't quite ended yet when her entire body stilled. Even then, it took Hunter a moment to do the same. Not that his fangs immediately retracted from her throat. And then one solitary word came out of her on a whisper.

"Blue."

An enormous pain speared through his chest, forcing Hunter to squeeze his eyes shut. Her safe word... something she had never used with him before. *No... No.* His breath quickened with each rumble, the predatory growl emerging once more, though softer this time. At that moment, he couldn't have said how his mind overrode his instincts. He finally pulled his fangs from her throat, the taste of iron still lingering in the air. He licked his lips, the coppery tang of blood still fresh as he wiped away the remnants. His mouth opened, as if to speak, but he swallowed the words, his eyes fixed on the darkening mark on her skin. "Narcissa... no... please," he whispered. He couldn't walk away from her. Not again. He didn't have that kind of strength.

"Please," she said, her voice strangled.

The scent of her tears, salty and heavy in the air, mixed with the tremor in her voice, broke his heart. But nothing caused him more pain than what she said next.

"Please get off me," Narcissa mumbled.

Those four words played over and over in his head, on an unending loop. Each movement was a heavy burden, Hunter's chest aching as he slowly withdrew, a wave of desolate grief washing over him. "Do not ask me to leave you," he choked out. "Do not. I cannot... I cannot do that. I am not strong enough."

Narcissa climbed off the bed. His eyes followed her as she darted across the room, the click of the bathroom door echoing behind her. She'd run... from him. No, he wasn't supposed to be here. Yes, he'd put them in even more danger by marking her again, but he hadn't been able to hold back. His instincts had completely taken over, taking the choice away from his conscious mind. Hunter stared at the closed door, the silence punctuated only by his own ragged breath. Oh, fuck, this hurt. He slowly got off the bed, each movement creaking against the stillness of the room, and moved toward the bathroom door. "Narcissa."

While he heard a quiet muttering, whatever Narcissa said wasn't directed at him. Hunter pressed his clammy palm and forehead against her bathroom door. He'd never wanted a mate before. Never wanted a relationship of any kind. Relationships were dangerous. They made you *feel* things, which made you vulnerable. They forced you to open up and share parts of yourself that you wanted to hide until they could be destroyed. Without a doubt, he knew he wasn't good for anyone. He was dangerous, too. That he'd come here, to Narcissa's room, proved that more than anything else he'd ever done. More than the people he'd killed; the blood he'd spilled. He'd turned his soul black, and he'd done it willingly. All for Hayden. All so his twin wouldn't have to endure the disgusting, degrading things he had. He'd left all the good with his brother, leaving only evil for himself.

Being with Narcissa was the only thing that had ever made him forget about all of that. The only thing that had ever made him think he might actually have something good inside of him. It had all been an illusion, but Hunter didn't care. He couldn't leave her again. He just couldn't. He *needed* her. More than he'd ever needed anything or anyone before. More than air to breathe, food to eat, water to drink.

Without her, he was nothing. And his soul had been wasting away.

"Narcissa..." His voice cracked. Normally, he would have at least attempted to clear it, but he knew it wouldn't do any good. "I cannot walk away from you. I just cannot. Whatever that means... Walking away from you is resigning myself to the most painful death imaginable. If I cannot have you... I may as well rip my heart out of my chest because it will kill me. It is already killing me. I tried to stay away, I swear I did. I just could not any longer." Tears welled as he pressed his forehead against the door, the wood cool against his skin. "I have not been able to breathe without you. I cannot eat. I cannot sleep. It has taken everything in me not to come back here and rip out the throat of every male who even dares to think about putting their cock where *only* mine belongs. Because you are mine, Narcissa. I do not care about the repercussions. I do not care what it takes. What I have to do. What I have to endure. You are *mine,* and I cannot bear to live one more single day without you."

Hunter heard shattering glass and frantically tried to open the locked door. Of course, it was locked. A coppery scent filled his nostrils; he smelled blood. His knuckles throbbed. Oh, gods, what had she done? "Open the door, Narcissa." She said nothing in response. He pushed the door with a pathetic shove; the wood groaned slightly under the pressure. "Open this door right now, or I am going to leave it in splinters."

The sound of her heels clicking against the floor echoed, like a clock counting down, ticking away at the seconds they had left together. A *click* indicated the door unlocking. It slid open, and there she stood.

The look on her face was enough to make him nearly weep with sorrow. Gods, what were they going to do? Hunter's arm went around her, and without a word, he led her toward the sink. He turned on the water, watching it run red as he gently washed the blood from her knuckles. While he did so, his eyes gravitated to the shower and the tub. They had memories there, too. Glorious memories. But the memories just weren't enough to sustain him any longer.

Turning the water off, he drew her into his arms and tilted her chin up so their eyes met. "Do not ask me to walk away from you," he whispered. "Please, Narcissa. We will figure it out. Somehow. We... we have to."

"What if we can't?"

Hunter reached up and caressed her cheek. "We must believe that we can. Some way, somehow, there has to be a solution. I know the gods can be cruel, but I cannot believe they would have brought us together, and allowed us to open each other's hearts, only to rip us apart in this way. You have made me feel things I never thought I could. Made me believe things about myself I thought could never be possible. I know I have done the same to you. You are my savior, Narcissa. My life. There is no turning back for me. No living without you. It is an impossibility."

Narcissa opened her mouth—a melodic voice went off in her head. One she hadn't heard in decades. Her eyes narrowed as she snapped her mouth shut. What was their queen doing here? The reason didn't matter. The female summoned her, which meant she had to respond. Hunter's brow furrowed as she stepped out of his arms. She reached for her black silk bathrobe, shrugged it over her shoulders, and headed toward her bedroom door.

"What is it?"

Though she tried to answer him, the words just wouldn't come out of her mouth. Narcissa opened the door and exited into the hallway. A few other doors opened, other nymphs stepping into the hall just as she had.

Hunter followed her to the door, and they all made their way to the second-floor waiting area. Those who were nymphs bowed. Males dropped to their knees and bent at the waist, lowering their heads. Females got down on their knees, pressed their asses to their heels, and bowed until their foreheads touched the floor.

At the end of a hallway, Dyeera's gaze scanned over all who had gathered. "Rise, my children."

Narcissa blinked; the bright light momentarily blurred her vision as she stood. Hunter immediately put a protective arm around her. The nymph queen truly stood before them. It wasn't as if anyone else could've summoned them the way the female had. Was this the answer Shalla intended? Their way out? It couldn't be. Could it? How would the queen grant their freedom from the den? She had so many questions, and she couldn't ask a single one.

Averine stood near the nymph queen. And beside her, whispering in her ear, stood a male, canine shape shifter. Someone Narcissa vaguely recognized. He'd been in the queen's employ for quite some time. The bracelet he wore on his wrist denoted as much.

Hunter glanced around at everyone gathered and tightened his hold on Narcissa. She rested her hand atop his, their hands fitting perfectly as she threaded their fingers together, giving them a gentle squeeze.

Dyeera, with a glower on her face, peered over her shoulder at Averine, and returned her attention to the canine. She whispered something back to him. He gave a curt nod before standing to his full height at her side, hands clasped behind him. Steeling herself, Dyeera focused on her people. "I have questions regarding your treatment here that require answers. While *solaris* have passed since I saw many of you, I expect you to respond with complete honesty as long as you're comfortable providing the information."

Was this truly happening? With a slight frown creasing her brow, Narcissa surveyed the faces of those gathered. Though she saw Red and Ivory, the vision was fleeting, like a whisper in the wind, and she didn't pay them any attention. If this was really the moment they awaited, then where was Shalla? This had to be what the female had referenced. It made the most sense. Except the female was nowhere to be seen. Unfortunately, Shalla had shared no part of the plan with her. With good reason. They couldn't have risked the information getting out. It was why she had referenced nothing in the note she'd sent to Hunter last week.

Though it took some maneuvering, due to their height difference, Hunter leaned over and tucked his face into her neck. His lips brushed softly across the mark he'd left on her. A slight shiver shot down her spine. It was a reflex she couldn't control.

"While I have learned some of how Averine has… welcomed you… with auctions and initiations, there is still much I do not know regarding punishments," Dyeera said. "Let us start simple. How many of you have received a punishment?"

Narcissa scanned the crowd, noting the worry etched on their faces, determining how the various individuals answered the queen's question. Almost all of them bore the mark of a penalty they had faced. Some sheepishly raised their hands, their knuckles white, while others averted their eyes. As much as she didn't want Hunter to react, this wasn't something she could hide from him. Or the queen. Her heart hammered against her ribs, a frantic rhythm in her chest. Hunter brushed his thumbs soothingly against the backs of her hands and pressed a loving kiss to her throat. Despite his attention, an icy dread settled in her stomach, and she could only imagine Hunter's reaction to the truth. Narcissa steeled her shoulders, held her head high, and with a deep breath, eased her hand into the air, forcing back the rising emotion.

A low, menacing growl left Hunter as his gaze flicked to Averine. He tightened his hold around Narcissa.

The situation could be worse, but at least Hunter hadn't shot across the room to kill Averine, bypassing the queen. Though if her mate got his hands around that female's neck, Narcissa didn't doubt he'd successfully end her life. As everyone did, she lowered her hand, her fingertips lightly tracing the fur of Hunter's forearm, trying to reassure him.

"Thank you for that information," Dyeera stated. "Would any of you willingly disclose what transpired regarding your punishment?"

Not likely. Everyone had signed NDAs. The enchantment surrounding those things kept them from revealing secrets about the den's business. If they somehow surpassed it, they suffered for it. Would the queen do something even without details? Or would she require some kind of proof? Narcissa took a deep, shuddering breath, then exhaled slowly, the tension easing as she swallowed the saliva that had pooled in her throat. There was only one way to find out. Consequences from the NDA be damned.

"I will," she started. "I had to work in the club downstairs, meeting an additional quota outside my regular clients." A powerful jolt of pain, like a lightning strike, lanced through her head. Her face contorted in a grimace as she dug her nails into Hunter's arm, ignoring the pain that threatened to consume her. "If I failed... if I didn't prove my loyalty to the den, three males had permission to use me as they saw fit." As she finished her testimony, a wave of agony washed over her, like a beast clawing at her brain. Narcissa bit her lip, holding back the scream that threatened to escape, tears welling in her eyes.

Seething, Hunter gently—but swiftly—eased her to the ground, then straightened to his full height of nine-seven. He turned toward Averine, his fangs and claws elongated longer than Narcissa had ever seen them before. "*Release. My. Mate,*" he snarled.

"Mate?!" Ivory exclaimed.

"Whatever fucking hold you have on her," Hunter continued, "*break it. Now*. Or I swear to all the gods, I will rip your head and heart from your body, feast on your remains, and quench my thirst with your blood."

Dyeera spun on Averine with a flash of anger in her eyes, marching toward her as she gestured back to Narcissa. "Is this what you do? Is this how you take care of my people?"

The proprietress unclasped her hands with a slight shrug. "I told you there are consequences for breaking the rules."

Dyeera's green eyes narrowed at Averine as determination hardened her features. "Then, perhaps, it is time I address these pesky contracts and non-disclosures. I won't *allow* them to impede the truth." With a forceful impact, Dyeera drove the end of her staff into the hardwood, causing a magical shockwave to spread throughout the building.

Narcissa's gaze lifted, but everything seemed to ripple before her. The agony eased a bit in her head. Not completely, but that didn't impact the value of her statement. She was prepared to accept any pain that came her way if it would liberate them all. Anything that allowed her and Hunter to live their lives. Narcissa slowly rose to her feet, her eyes fixed on the queen as she approached, the scent of roses lingering in the air with each step the female took.

Dyeera stopped in front of her. The queen's fingertips traced her cheek as a wave of magic washed over her, lessening the pain. "You bear incredible strength. Tell me, what crime did you commit?"

There were many ways to answer that. She'd spent time with Hunter without charging him. They'd seen one another and spoken in the marketplace. Except, everything that happened all stemmed from one truth. "My client and I," she began, "fell in love."

Hunter's fangs and claws shortened significantly. He turned back toward her and took her hand in his own. "Are you alright?"

"Yes." Narcissa's grip on his hand was firm, offering silent reassurance. Her eyes flickered from her mate to Queen Dyeera, her heart pounding. "Thank you, Your Majesty."

"Of course, my child. You should not suffer for something that cannot be helped." Facing the gathered crowd, Dyeera spun around.

The hushed murmurs of the people filled Narcissa's ears as a nearby door opened. She stole a glimpse over her shoulder. Maybe this *was* what Shalla intended after all.

"Would anyone else disclose the punishment they received? Or do any of you know what happens if the crime is more egregious than... love?"

"That is par for the course, Your Majesty," Aniya, another of the nymphs, stated. "At least, regarding the fundamental rules for the workers. As for the more flagrant actions, no one knows. Many are never seen again."

"That isn't entirely accurate," Shalla said, her voice clear as she emerged from the doorway, with a feline at her side. With their hands clasped tightly together, they made their way down the hall.

Reaching the crowd, the male feline bowed his head to Queen Dyeera, holding the motion for several moments. "Good day, Your Majesty." His gaze flicked to Hunter. He gave a nod before slipping his arm around Shalla's waist.

Hunter returned Marcell's nod and put his arm around Narcissa.

Dyeera dipped her chin, acknowledging the male before all her attention turned to the female with him. "Sashallina," the Queen said, her voice echoing slightly as she stopped before them. Dyeera brushed the white-blonde hair away from the female's shoulder. "My beautiful daughter. Just as stunning as ever." The faintest hint of a smile touched the corner of her mouth. "It's wonderful of you to join us."

"My apologies for the delay, Mother," Shalla stated, resting her hand atop the male's grip. "We're here now, and I know the answer to your question."

Narcissa's eyes widened, right along with Hunter's, and snapped in Shalla's direction. *Mother?* Not only had the female *not* disclosed anything regarding the plan, but she hadn't uttered a word regarding that relationship. Narcissa peeked around the corner and noticed the look of pure shock on Averine's face. That was probably why.

The queen leaned in close, her eyes filled with a secret, and lowered her voice conspiratorially. "You were supposed to report your findings to me."

"I know, Mother," Shalla responded. "That's what led to what I faced. I thought I'd found a guard I could trust to send word back to you with what I'd discovered. It turned out I was wrong. Averine had me sent to the poppy fields away from the isle. I'm uncertain of their exact location, but I wasn't the only one she sent. We were the lucky ones. Some didn't get that chance at all. Nor were they ever able to return."

Shit. Narcissa's eyes popped wider. Was that what Averine had meant by sending her away from the den? It explained why Shalla had initially urged her to end things with Hunter.

Dyeera peered over her shoulder at Averine. "I'm aware of the place."

"You sent your birth daughter here to my establishment and have the audacity to question how I run things?" With narrowed eyes, Averine smirked, a dangerous glint in her gaze. "Seems hypocritical."

Dyeera took a final, furtive look at her daughter before heading toward where the proprietress waited, the air thick with tension. "Although Numir vouched for you, I didn't fully trust you. When I decided to test your... tactics, my daughter volunteered. We both want what is best for our people." Dyeera cut Averine off with a dismissive wave of her hand before the female could speak and glanced at the canine at her side. "Tell me, Jaxon, how much truth have we heard from the testimony provided by our people?"

Jaxon slowly took his eyes from Averine and shifted his gaze to Dyeera, lowering his head slightly. "Everything they have spoken is the truth, Your Majesty. Though... *much* has been left out. Not that I would deign to give details without consent."

The Queen took the first step, beginning a slow circle around the proprietress. "And what have you discerned from Averine, the subject of our inquiry?"

"Well, she was not happy to see you, for one. Though I'm sure that went without saying." Jaxon flicked his gaze to Averine. "She is a liar, somewhat outright, somewhat by omission. From the beginning, this is what I've deduced. She provided each of the workers here with a place to sleep. Food to eat. A rehearsal space to practice in. However, that place to sleep was often a shared room with minimal personal space. Only a select few of the sex workers—none of the guards—have been allowed a personal room, and I imagine it had much to do with earning it, and popularity with the clients, more than anything else. The food was nutritious, but rarely were any of the sex workers allowed to eat their fill. They are under strict diet regimens and mandatory weight checks, as well as having restrictions on certain foods. Likely depending on their species, as all species react differently to different nutrients. There are physicians, but they are not here for the care of the employees. They are here for the money and for their own personal reasons. They are contracted, as much as every other employee here. Their job is to ensure that the employees can work safely, and that no diseases are contracted or passed along. Nothing more. That includes pregnancies. I can't put a number on how many were... disposed of. But perhaps Averine can do that for you, Your Majesty."

He paused for a moment, gathering himself. "She did not truly care for our people, nor has this place ever been safe. There were expectations, and threats if they were not met. Examples were made, so that everyone here would understand how serious she was, and that she would allow for no... mistakes. When a newcomer arrived, Averine assigned someone to guide them, but they could not share the initiation details. They knew nothing of what they would endure until they were experiencing it. Averine witnessed at least a few of those... initiations. For those who might have posed real trouble during the ordeal. Things went worse for those who were not virgins prior to their arrival. As such a... *commodity* was not present, there was much less care put into what happened to them. If they survived, good. If not... it was no skin off her back, from what I understand. Illiterate people were not told their contract's true contents. Am I right, Averine? I got it all, correct? Or would you honestly even attempt another lie at this point? Oh, wait. One more thing. Not everyone came here willingly, did they? In fact, there is quite a large number who were brought here *un*willingly, sold to you, and then forced into servitude."

Narcissa squeezed Hunter's hand. None of that could've been easy for him to hear. Even some of it was difficult for her, and she'd lived through a portion of it.

"He's not wrong, Mother," Shalla added. "Not all of them were forced to work here. Some were taken directly to the plantation. That's what we call the poppy fields. She had an arrangement with Aragar. His men have delivered people to her in the past."

Dyeera stopped in her tracks. "When you came to me all those *solaris* ago, requesting the power to help create this establishment, I asked what it meant to you. What you hoped to achieve. You took a breath, carefully choosing your words. Your hesitation told me all I needed to know, but I trusted Numir and knew he wouldn't have vouched for you lightly. Though it wasn't a small ask. As many who came before and after you can attest, there is always a price, and I always collect. Do you recall what you paid for my services? The demand I set before you?" As she began her circular walking pattern again, the queen gestured with her hand, halting Averine mid-sentence. "Your fear of my arrival says you do. As does your preventing my daughter from her reporting..." Dyeera glanced at her daughter. "How long ago was that, Sashallina?"

"Nearly eighty *solaris* have passed since that occurred, Mother." Shalla brushed her fingers along her right cheek, feeling the soft texture of her skin. Her eyebrows dipped low.

"If you had kept to our agreement, then three hundred *solaris* might seem long enough. Instead, you violated it. Given the amount of your transgressions, Averine, shutting down this establishment is the *least* of your costs."

"Your Majesty, if I may," Narcissa said. The queen halted her movement once more. All eyes focused on her. Narcissa squeezed Hunter's hand, a silent promise of strength. Not only for her own resolve, but to fortify his spirit, too. This was doing more than just setting them free, giving them a life together. As much as she yearned for that, this establishment provided for so many others. Like Clay, who was still finding his way. Or Fallon, who feared what he might do if this place didn't exist. "I know this place hasn't lived up to what Averine promised you, but that doesn't mean it can't. Despite her actions, it has offered, not just nymphs, but all the other species across the isle, a haven to explore sexual natures and certain proclivities that most would look down upon. With your permission, I'd like to take over the leadership and turn this into the haven it was meant to be."

Hunter's gaze shifted downward, turning thoughtful. A small smile spread over his face, and pride beamed from his gaze.

"That seems like a sound request," Dyeera replied. "Jaxon. Your thoughts?"

Slowly, Jaxon stepped forward, getting closer to Narcissa, though not too close. His gaze focused on her. "While I'm sure you may not have had time to think much about it... what are your initial thoughts about what you would do with this place, were you given permission to take it over?"

That was a damn good question. While she immediately had a few ideas, Narcissa didn't know what all she would have to address. Or what it would take for them to accept her offer. "The majority came here voluntarily. For those who didn't, I'd begin by checking in with them and seeing if they wanted to continue in their current position. Then I'd address the clientele. Not everyone has a choice in who they see, and that needs to be handled posthaste. As for the club downstairs... I'd change it. Maybe into..." Her words trailed off. With a furrowed brow, Narcissa worriedly chewed on the inside of her cheek. They didn't need another place for sexual desires to be met. What could she put in its place?

"A burlesque," Jade suggested. "You'd also want to address the substance issue." A sly smile played on her lips as she glanced at Averine before lowering her head in a respectful bow to Queen Dyeera. "Averine has used it as a place to sell opiates and hallucinogens derived from the poppy fields for many *solaris.*"

Of course, there was a drug issue. She'd seen the exchanges, but the guards had prevented her from gathering any information. Her mind was elsewhere over the two weeks she'd spent in there, far from anything outside of her punishment, as their constant scheming distracted her. Narcissa dipped her chin, acknowledging the female's statement. "I like that. A burlesque. Thank you, Jade. I'd also address some of our security issues, terminating the positions of guards who don't understand the word 'no.' Beyond that... if my mate agreed, I'd make him head of our security. I'd also convert the rooms on the lower level, change them into a place outsiders could... temporarily use... for those with... unique proclivities, and I'd do away with auctions and initiations."

Shalla smiled, her pride evident on her beaming face. "Nia has the capacity to run this place right. She doesn't just have an eye for detail, but she is excellent at reading the needs of people. Even when they can't see it themselves. And she has the respect of the workers. All things crucial in running a business like this."

Ivory scoffed, her lip curling as she rolled her eyes in annoyance.

Jaxon flicked a brief gaze at the female. He focused back on Narcissa for a couple of minutes in silence.

Hunter spared Ivory nothing more than a passing glance, but said nothing.

"How long have you been employed here?" Jaxon asked. "Nia, was it?"

"Her name is Narcissa," Hunter spoke up suddenly.

Jaxon inclined his head. "My apologies. Narcissa. How long have you been here?"

Hunter's correction of her name and their support brought a smile to her face. Along with a sense of... she couldn't tell for sure. For the first time, she swore she felt emotions that didn't belong to her. Narcissa shook it off. Something to address later. As for Ivory, if the female were smart, she'd keep her mouth shut. The NDA no longer protected the female regarding her financial activities surrounding Hunter. Something Narcissa would share with her mate. He deserved to know how Ivory had used the knowledge she gleaned over the years as his so-called submissive. "Thirty *solaris.* Compared to some, it doesn't seem that long, but during that time, I have moved clients successfully to other workers who were a much better fit. Whether they were someone I'd only seen once, or spent *solaris* with. If I required help, I'd seek recommendations from others, who may have more contact with staff, or have more knowledge surrounding this establishment. I'm not afraid to put in the work. Too many people depend on this place for me to do nothing and allow it to close."

Jaxon raised a brow. His gaze went momentarily back to Ivory before returning to Narcissa. "Thirty *solaris* may not be a long time to some, but it is where I originally come from. And how would you deal with employees who did not take kindly to the new ownership? Or pushed boundaries with the removal of certain... threats?"

Another good question. It required no explanation. The queen sought his advice, and Narcissa expected him to investigate properly before making a formal decision. "If anyone here doesn't wish to serve under new leadership, they're free to leave. I won't hold them here against their will. That's not my style. Same if they push back on another's removal. If one who is being removed pushes back... make no mistake, I can throw them out myself." Among other things, but she didn't say that. Hunter knew what she could do without the constraints on her powers. Just as she knew what he could handle. He'd told her what had happened with his brother, Sam. And she'd told him what she'd done to her father. "I protect what's mine," Narcissa stated, her words sharp and unyielding.

Jaxon smiled. He turned his gaze to Hunter, but only for a minute, before focusing on Queen Dyeera. "I believe she would be an acceptable choice as a new proprietress. Both who have spoken to support her were truthful in their words. I believe that not only will she run this place acceptably, but she will do so with the good of the people in mind. *Not* only for how they can fill her pockets." At that, he shot a glare at Averine before returning his gaze to Dyeera. "She won't care about getting rich from her new position. She'll care that her employees and their clients are cared for and cared for *well*. And that if they ever wish to leave, they can do so. From everything I've gathered, she not only has the respect of the workers, but she knows them well. Their wants, their needs—especially those unique to them. Alongside her mate—who I believe would be an excellent choice as head of security—they will remove all problematic employees, as well as rectify any… misconduct that has been occurring within these walls. Above all else, she will care about them the way you want someone in charge of your people to care. There may well be bumpy roads ahead with the shift in ownership, but I believe the two of them could handle anything that came their way."

Dyeera surveyed those gathered. "You disagree, Volette?"

Thrown off by the question, Ivory's eyes widened. Her shoulders tensed as she tightened her arms across her chest. "Not at all, Your Majesty. Nia would be a fine choice."

Narcissa blinked, a sudden fill of hope and a momentary rush of weakness colliding within her. Both were as foreign as Ivory throwing in her support. It didn't just appear that all workers had gained their freedom, but she and Hunter might actually have a life together. Something she hadn't dared to dream was a possibility. This all still seemed surreal, yet it was actually happening. Hunter tightened his hold around her waist, and she felt the warmth of his touch as she gripped his hand in return.

"I have never been in charge of anything before," Hunter said to Jaxon. "I have no doubt about my capability of doing the job. I simply wonder where your confidence stems from, when we have only ever met the one time."

Jaxon turned toward Hunter, staring at him for a minute without speaking. "Suffice it to say… I see more than most. I may have met you only once before now, but the strength of your bloodline runs through your veins. And I am not talking about your father. Despite what you think, you *have* been in charge of something before. Even if you didn't view it as such. I believe you, as well as Narcissa, would both make excellent choices in the running of this place… as it is made new."

Hunter stared at the male for a couple of moments and then left a nod as his only response.

"Very well," Dyeera said as others joined them, the sound of their footsteps getting closer from the hallway and staircase. Her gaze flicked briefly to the newcomers. "Narcissa, you will take over the den, serving as the new proprietress, and Hunter, you will aid her, serving as the new head of security. As before, my magic, along with that of my daughter, will help you along as you take this journey." The queen turned, and her eyes, like glittering emeralds, locked onto Averine, commanding her attention. "They have presented you with an opportunity. Given your transgressions and the violation of our agreement, two choices sit before you. One, relinquish all rights to this establishment and serve out the remainder of your life, however many *solaris* that is, in my prison. Two, execution here and now before these witnesses."

"Over my dead body will I ever hand my rights over to that cunt. Or anyone else, for that matter. I've dedicated *solaris* to this establishment, doing what was necessary to build it into the empire it has become. I'll die before I relinquish a damn thing." Averine's dark gaze narrowed, her eyes flashing with anger as she glowered at the queen. "You'll have to kill me first."

A menacing snarl ripped its way from Hunter's lips, and his eyes flashed darker than onyx.

Jaxon turned an apathetic gaze on Averine. "I don't think she'll have a problem with that."

Dyeera dipped her chin, a gesture of silent acceptance. "So be it." And she drove the end of her staff into the ground for the second time.

Averine's surprised eyes widened. Green fire swirled, the scent of burning roses filling the air as it enveloped the female. It swiftly turned her body into a pile of ash, silencing her agonizing screams.

Focused intently on what transpired, Narcissa paid little mind to the murmurs of those gathered. She hadn't realized the crowd had grown to include more of the other staff, such as sex workers, cooks, and guards. At least, not until all that remained of Averine was nothing more than cinders. Though she had heard the stories, she hadn't ever witnessed the queen claim a life before. It was over almost as quickly as it had started.

And like her, Hunter had watched it all. As ash replaced what had used to be Averine, Hunter's legs trembled. His gaze gravitated to Queen Dyeera. His knees gave out on him and connected with the floor. Tears pricked at the corners of his eyes. With his arms still around Narcissa, he drew her even closer. "Thank you," he mouthed to Dyeera.

Dyeera dipped her chin at Hunter, acknowledging his words, as she strolled over to where her daughter and the feline male stood.

The soft sound of Narcissa's silk bathrobe swishing accompanied her as she slowly turned around, wrapping her arms around Hunter's neck. *Holy shit.* They were truly free. And taking over. Something to address later. She had a secret to deal with before they could figure out anything else. "We should go back to my room. There's something I need to talk to you about," she whispered to him.

Hunter nodded against her. Reaching up, he dragged a hand down his face. "There is something I should talk to you about, too," he said, his voice low. "Yeah. Let us go back to your room."

Gods, if it had something to do with his current appearance—the weight loss and pallor of his fur—Narcissa didn't know if she could handle it. Except Hunter was here, well and alive. Maybe if she focused on that, then whatever he had to tell her of how bad things had gotten, she could hear it. She might even share what she had endured. It would be wise to tell him. He deserved to know. Before they did any of that, she should figure a few things out.

Narcissa's gaze swept over the crowd as she peered over her shoulder at the gathered faces. They hadn't exactly gone anywhere, just murmured among themselves, awaiting instructions. Okay. She could do this. Squeezing Hunter once more, Narcissa stepped out of his hold and faced the other workers. "Jade, Tamara, cancel any remaining appointments for today. Refund them their money for their appointment today, but schedule a time for them to see the proprietress tomorrow. Say nothing to any clients regarding the change." That would give her time to assess client records and worker files. "Zunabar, take Yavo and Druid with you to clear the clubs out downstairs." She watched as the five she'd called out acknowledged her orders and then turned to the others. "As for the rest of you, return to your rooms and get cleaned up. We've got a lot to address."

Smiling, Hunter put his hands to the floor and pushed himself to his feet.

Thankfully, they all dispersed without issue. And there weren't any clients in the waiting room. Even better. Except for Hunter and Marcell, no one outside of the staff witnessed what transpired. Well, and those the queen brought along. It made things much easier. "Razi, Kelraz, start going room to room and clearing out clients. I don't care if it's interrupting time." Narcissa turned toward Hunter, then paused, her gaze drifting away in a moment of afterthought. "Except for Grace's. I'll handle that one personally."

Hunter held his hand out to Narcissa, waiting patiently until she returned to his side. "Is there anything else you need to do right this moment?"

"No." At least, not that she could think of. They'd have to address everyone together, but they could do that later. When she wasn't in a bathrobe. And after they'd talked. Narcissa placed her hand in Hunter's, lacing their fingers together as she peered over at Shalla. They should speak as well, but she didn't want to interrupt the... reunion.

Hunter glanced briefly over as well. He tightened his grip a bit on Narcissa's hand as he led her down the hall. Not that he spoke until they were well away from those gathered. Hunter sighed. "I have been sick. Which I know is quite obvious from my appearance." He paused for a moment. "The shaman in my village does not know... how much I will get better."

Gods, those males were right. Narcissa refused to think much about that now. Hunter was alive and by her side. "We can always talk with other healers. Do whatever it takes to ensure you fully regain your strength." Blowing out a deep breath, she squeezed his hand. "I didn't fare all that well without you around. My friends... Shalla... they helped, but that note you sent... it meant more than all of their efforts."

Hunter's brow furrowed. "Being away from you after my eyes glowed... with no hope, then, of ever seeing you again... my body reacted as if... you had died. It started after we last saw one another. Then, a little over a *penumbra* ago... the decline got very rapid. By the time the shaman was informed and she made a house call... a few of my organs were no longer working properly. And still are not. My kidneys, liver, and heart. But I have been receiving treatment, and Aradia has plans for further care. I will be okay. But we can talk to whomever you think we should. I have been stubborn enough about my health in the past. Something I know I need to change. Your note helped me get through. Marcell told me to exhibit patience. Thank the gods, things went the way they did today, because my patience just ran out, I guess." Hunter gazed down at her as they continued toward her room. "I had no strength... to think about doing anything. Not even to... send a message to you. As much guilt and shame as that brings me. Though, I think my brothers and sister-in-law played their hand in that. Normally, it would anger me for others to speak for me, but I am glad they did."

Her steps slowed as she lifted her gaze to Hunter. How could she not have realized how close she had come to losing him completely? Even though the males had tried to dissuade her, she hadn't believed Hunter would quit, even when she had. Narcissa blinked, a sob catching in her throat as tears traced paths down her cheeks. Dear gods, things could've been so much worse. It still seemed surreal that they were even walking down this hallway, side by side, together. As she wiped the wetness from her face, a small smile played at the corner of her mouth. "I guess they know you well. It seemed like something you would say. Then Shalla came to me... told me she had something in the works. That I needed to exercise some patience. I spent a lot of time in bed after the last time we crossed paths. Showering, cleaning... none of it mattered. The note and Shalla's words... gave me the courage to hope." She rubbed at the ache in her chest, which seemed out of place. They were together now, with a bright future ahead of them. "I'm glad they all intervened. I don't know if we'd be here if they hadn't."

Hunter stopped completely, then halted her steps as well and turned her to face him. "I am glad, too. And I am glad that my brother stopped listening to me. I told him I did not want intervention at all. That I did not want the shaman to look at me. I just..." Hunter sighed. "... My only desire was to hurry and die. I never thought I would see you again in this life. I wanted to hurry along to the next... because I knew I would see you there at some point. It seemed easier, less painful... to just let go." He kneeled down before her, putting them closer to eye level. "I never used to apologize, ever. Take responsibility for things I had done wrong. But I believe that is something I need to change, too. I hope you can forgive me... for losing hope. And for giving up. Not just on myself, but... on us. On our future. I am sorry, Narcissa."

"I'm sorry, too, Hunter." Narcissa brushed the back of her knuckles across his cheek. "I think my time here made me complacent. It just wasn't something I realized until you came into my life. Then, suddenly, I truly had something to fight for, but I'd forgotten how." Fighting for them was far more than she'd ever had to do to protect her family. "There's a lot we still have to figure out, but I have faith we will." She cracked a smile. "We're too stubborn to do otherwise."

Hunter leaned into her touch. "Damn right, we are." He kissed her palm. "I have done nothing *but* fight for my entire life. It was what drove me for so long. Then, when I finally had something worth fighting for... I will not say I forgot how. But... I do not think I knew how to fight how I needed to. I did not need a physical fight, but a mental one. And that is not something I ever learned how to do. For as long as I can remember, I shut my emotions away because it was too dangerous to deal with them. I locked them away because I could not bear to feel... anything but hatred. Until I met you, and you made me realize what I was missing out on. How much allowing love inside does not weaken you, but strengthens you. And you made me realize just how much I need it in my life. How much I need *you*." Hunter cupped her jaw. "I have changed so much since I met you. Despite how difficult it has all been, I know I would not change any of it."

"Neither would I." Goddess, he was right about all of that. Love strengthened them. It allowed them to get here. It had all truly happened. They had gotten their way out. Narcissa's hand gently covered his, and then she brushed her thumb through his soft fur. A lot had changed in a short period. They still had much to get through, but first, she had to do something she'd wanted to do for weeks now. "Will you go back to my room and wait for me there? I need to take care of something, but then I'll join you."

"Of course." Before he stood back up, Hunter drew her mouth to his and pressed their lips together. A deep, lingering kiss without tongue. Which was good; they didn't need to get hot-and-heavy in the middle of the hallway. There was a lot to get done, and besides, they didn't have any restraints out here. Breaking the kiss, Hunter stood to his feet. "At some point this evening, as much as I hate even the thought of a minute away from you right now, I am going to have to return to my village briefly. My twin is about to have an aneurysm out of worry. And the shaman, not to mention my queen, are probably going to be ready to kick my ass the moment they see me. I sort of... ripped a few IVs and monitors off before leaving to come here... telling no one that I was leaving, or where I was going."

Narcissa practically gawked at him. He'd mentioned he'd gotten *really* sick. What the fuck had she thought he would've done when he'd grown impatient? Besides, with what she had to share with him... he'd have another reason to return to Métamorphe, even if it was only briefly. "I don't like the idea, either, but I don't want them worrying over you, or unexpectedly making their way here. There is plenty to keep me busy here. Now, go on to my room. I'll be there shortly."

Hunter glanced down and cracked a small smile. "Did I not mention that my patience ran out?" He leaned down and kissed her, then pressed his forehead to hers for a moment. "Do what you need to do, sweetheart. I do not mind waiting."

Curling her fingers around the nape of his neck, Narcissa brushed one more kiss across Hunter's lips. A low rumble left him. It still seemed strange that she could do something so intimate at will. "Twice now." A wide grin spread across her face. They were stalling, but it didn't seem either of them could help it. One of them had to make the first move. Forcing herself to step back, Narcissa created distance between them after releasing her hold. They were near Grace's room, but some magic must have still lingered. Otherwise... well, this would happen much differently. "I won't take long."

"I know. I will be okay. I will be in your room waiting." Hunter forced his feet further away from her. They weren't far from her room. A sudden twinge went through him. Furrowing his brow, he glanced around. Huh. That was strange. But maybe Clay was here somewhere. Outside of him and Marcell, it had only been employees in the lobby. Glancing back at Narcissa, he smiled. "I will see you soon." He reluctantly turned around and headed to her room, the silence of the corridor amplifying his footsteps. When he got there and shut the door behind him, sitting wasn't an option. So, he paced a little instead. Something he wasn't prone to doing, but he couldn't seem to help himself.

It seemed hours later that the door opened. He turned to face it and smiled as Narcissa stepped into view. A frown almost immediately covered his face. The sensation that speared through him... It couldn't be Hayden; his twin would never come to a place like this. Then who...? No... There was no way... It couldn't be... Hunter opened his mouth then snapped it shut as he flipped his gaze to his mate.

"I have something to tell you," Narcissa said, the click of the door echoing in the quiet room. "And I think you may want to sit down for it."

His pulse quickened. Words became completely impossible. Hunter offered a subtle nod before retreating to the queening bench at the foot of her bed, where he sank down slowly. He didn't need Narcissa to say it. He already knew. The words that fucking prick had said to Hayden in the prison came back to him, no matter how hard he tried to shut them out.

"I know you want to know what happened to her, Hayden. Why she was there one day, gone the next. Why she never returned home."

"I know she is dead," Hayden said. "She is at peace, and I have made peace with that. I do not need to know anything else."

"Oh? Did you know she begged for her life to end? After I watched over a dozen males have their way with her, she begged for it all to just be over... and I ensured she got exactly what she wanted. Then I walked away with more coin than I would have earned here in this village in a solaris."

It had saddened him, too. But Hayden... it had utterly shattered his twin.

Hunter looked up and met his mate's gaze. "Tell me."

"Sam lied to you. Elisa is alive," Narcissa stated. "She's here."

His body completely froze. It was one thing to know the truth, but to hear it spoken by someone you trusted, their scent familiar, was a different story altogether. It seemed to take forever before he could move again. He exhaled a harsh breath, and Hunter, overcome with emotion, leaned over, hiding his face in his hands. She was here. Elisa was *here*.

"Where is Ellie?" Hayden asked Sam as their brother walked right past them. Hayden had been searching all over the village, but she was nowhere in sight. Which meant something was wrong. Ellie could never leave the village.

"She is dead, you little fucktwit."

Hayden stilled, as if he'd been turned to stone. "What...?" His voice came out so soft and feeble.

"I said she is dead. Fucking pity, too. She was a hot piece of ass."

Tears flooded Hayden's eyes. "No... no... that is not true. She is not... No, she is not dead."

"Yeah, you fucking pussy, she is. And it was bloody, and really fucking painful for her, too, just so you know."

"You are a dick," Hunter growled out.

"What did you say to me?"

"I said. You. Are. A. Dick."

Sam got right up in his face. His breath was rank, like he'd spent the whole day drinking and eating raw meat and not bothered to clean his teeth. "Keep that shit up, and I will ensure you go the same way as your precious Ellie."

Hunter looked back at Narcissa. "She has been here... the *entire time*? He sold her *here*?" For all the years he'd been coming here, he'd never known. How could he not have known?

"Yes, I'm sure you have a lot of questions. Some I'll be able to answer. Others, not so much. She's right outside, waiting to see you, if you're ready."

Fuck... How was he going to tell Hayden this? After that conversation in the prison, they'd known that Azazel had sold her to someone or some place. But he never could have imagined... It actually made the most sense, though. Azazel had raged about being banned from the brothel not long after Elisa had disappeared. Not that he knew exactly why, but he could guess. Hunter nodded a little. "Yes. Yes, I am ready."

Narcissa cupped his jaw and brushed her thumb across his cheek. With her touch, a sense of calm washed over him, slowing his erratic heartbeat and quieting his breath. Hunter kissed her palm, a soft, lingering touch, before she pulled away and headed for her bedroom door. As she opened the door, he stood up, and rubbed his hands on his thighs.

And there she stood. Looking no different from how he remembered her from the last time they'd seen one another.

Elisa's eyes filled with tears. "Hunter..." she whispered.

"Gods, it is really you..." For a moment, he was thrown back to over forty years ago, to the last time he'd laid eyes on her. Elisa had snuck into the orphan's hut really late at night. He hadn't been able to sleep, which was nothing new. So, he'd just been sitting there watching Hayden sleep. Elisa had made him promise to always look out for Hayden, no matter what, to the best of his ability. He'd done his damndest never to break that promise.

As Elisa entered the room, Narcissa shut her bedroom door with a soft click. With each slow step, Elisa crossed the room until she stood in front of him. "I cannot believe this is really happening," she whispered. "That you are here... and I get to see you again." Elisa brushed the wetness from her face. "I never thought that I would lay my eyes on you again. And Hayden... I have missed you both so much."

Hunter lifted his hand, then let it fall. Even with her right in front of him, this didn't seem real. "We were told that you had died. Until recently, we believed no differently."

"Until recently?"

"Yes." He flicked his gaze to Narcissa. Surely, she'd told Elisa at least some of what had happened. If not, he could explain more later. He looked back at... his sister. Gods... "When I was in prison with Azazel and Clay, Azazel let slip that you had not died. That he had sold you somewhere. He did not say where, though. He insisted that the only way he would reveal where you were is if he did not lose his life. That did not happen, though, and he was executed the next day."

"I am glad of it. Neither he nor Sam deserved to breathe."

All Hunter could do was nod. This was beyond surreal.

Elisa's voice came out whispered, strained, as if she was trying to hold back more tears. "May I hug you?"

Before Hunter even knew what he was doing, he nodded again. Then, her arms, trembling slightly, held him tight. And, surprisingly, his arms followed suit. He laid his cheek on the top of her head. Listened to her heartbeat. Proof of life. That this wasn't some sick joke the gods were playing on him.

"I missed you," she muttered against his chest. "I missed you so much."

"I missed you, too, Ellie." As his sister's tears soaked into his fur, Hunter looked up and found his mate's eyes. Those beautiful jade-green eyes. *Thank you,* he mouthed to her.

You're welcome, Narcissa mouthed back. "We'll figure things out over the coming days for the rest of this reunion."

Hunter nodded. "Good. That would be good. I am going to have to tell Hayden, though. I do not think this is one of those things I could keep from him." He didn't want to, either. His twin had made peace with Elisa's disappearance a long time ago. Azazel's bullshit had reopened all of those old wounds. The sooner he did what was necessary to close them up again, the better.

"No, definitely not," Narcissa replied.

"I cannot wait to see him. And meet his mate."

"She is a good female," Hunter said. "Definitely exactly who he needs in his life."

"I am overjoyed to hear it." Elisa blinked, pulling back slightly as she rubbed her eyes. "I still feel as though I am dreaming."

"I know the feeling." Hunter looked over to Narcissa. There was so much to figure out now. Would Elisa... would she want to stay here? Continue working here? Did she want a home outside of this place? Would she even feel comfortable leaving right away? Likely not. With the circumstances what they'd been under Markham's rule, and that no one from the village had laid eyes on Elisa since her disappearance, he couldn't imagine she'd been allowed to leave in any capacity.

Narcissa joined them, stopping next to Hunter. "Not to add to that feeling, but I should tell you something. Hunter and I... we're taking the den over."

Elisa's eyes widened, and she blinked a few times. "You two are..." Her words trailed off. "So, Averine... she is gone?"

Hunter smirked. "Oh, yeah. She will definitely not be a problem any longer." If only he could witness repeatedly what Queen Dyeera had done to the bitch. Wouldn't that be entertaining? Part of the multitude of things they had to figure out—near the top of the list, he intended to vet every single guard and client. A tedious process, though he expected there would be plenty of amusement in that, too.

A slow smile spread across Elisa's face. "So, you two would be... my bosses?"

"If you decide to continue working here, yes," Hunter said.

"I have ideas on how we can change things around here," Narcissa stated. "If you still want to continue working here, it doesn't have to be in the same capacity. I've seen you dance." She winked. "Like I said. You missed a whole lot of something."

"I, uh... yeah, apparently." Elisa chuckled. "I will have to think about it. I have been doing..." She avoided Hunter's eyes. "... *that* for my entire life."

Her *entire life.* Hunter bit back a growl. He clenched his jaw, pinched the bridge of his nose, and then forced himself to settle quickly. What he wouldn't give to bring that fucker back to life and kill him a dozen times over or more. Inhaling and exhaling a deep breath, he focused back on his mate. Oh yeah, a perfectly easy way to remain calm. Just looking at her washed every ounce of darkness away. Gods, he couldn't believe that all the stress and worry and fear was over for them now. *Over.* "First things first," Hunter declared. "Hayden will not want to wait to see her. And he is going to want Rainbow with him."

Elisa's eyebrows raised. "*Rainbow*?"

"Yes, she is merfolk." Hunter left off that she was royalty; that wasn't really his business to tell. "How should we handle that?" He wasn't privy to what the personnel areas here held, or if there were any places they could set up a private dinner scenario, so Hayden and Rainbow could come here. Elisa's room would contain a bed and the "tools of her trade," so to speak, which could bring up uncomfortable conversation, considering this was their older sister. Unless Elisa was comfortable leaving right now, their options were pretty limited.

Narcissa looked thoughtful. "Um, well, we could start with seeing what we have to work with on the third floor. It belonged entirely to Averine. We might be able to host a private dinner or something there."

"Alright. That would work. I am only going home to talk to Hayden—" And, likely, get yelled at by him, the shaman, and the queen. "—and then I will be back. Unless you want to come with me, but that would be entirely up to you." Either way, he wouldn't be away from her tonight. They'd been apart far too much. Now that they no longer had to be, he had no desire to spend tonight anywhere but with her in his arms.

"As much as I'd love to, I need to go through the contracts that Averine negotiated. Figure out what's what. After I take a shower and get dressed."

A slow smirk spread across Hunter's face. "You know... I need a shower, too, and conservation of water is *very* important, baby girl."

"Oh, dear gods, please keep comments like that to yourself," Elisa begged.

"What?"

"You are my brother. That is the *last* thing I want to hear from you."

"I do not think I have a filter, sis." Wow, it felt weird to say that. *Sis.* "Probably just something you will have to get used to or ignore." He chuckled and peered at Narcissa. "When I get back, would you like some help with that?"

"It would definitely go faster," Narcissa replied. "You know, I think the first one I'm going to go through is Ivory's."

"I think that is an excellent idea. And if I might make a suggestion... I think she needs a demotion. Perhaps she can work in the kitchen. Or clean the toilets."

Elisa snickered. "If you two make her clean the toilets, can we make her a special badge or vest she has to wear that indicates she cleans up shit for a living?"

"And I thought what I orchestrated was bad." A barely audible snicker escaped Narcissa.

Hunter raised his eyebrows at her. "I have to ask... what exactly did you orchestrate?"

"Oh, I might have used a rumor to get Cheshire to attack Ivory and give her a couple of black eyes."

"This did not occur around the time I killed Sam, did it?"

"Maybe," she said, stretching out the word.

Hunter smirked. "She tried to get me to have a session with her that day. Even without the two black eyes and broken nose, I would not have been interested. And I likely would have traumatized her for life."

"That would've been interesting." A smirk played on Narcissa's lips as she turned her gaze to Elisa. "We should tell him, shouldn't we?"

His sister barely held back a laugh. "Oh, yes. We should *definitely* tell him."

Hunter looked back and forth between them. "Tell me what?"

"You've become a bit of a punchline with Ivory," Narcissa said. "Anytime you left her for another worker, she'd take bets on how long before you returned to her. The day after, when she believed you'd left me... yeah... A couple of black eyes and a broken nose was the least she deserved."

"Ah. I see." Though nothing showed on his face, inside he was seething. *No one* turned him into a joke. He focused on Narcissa. "I have a couple of ideas on how to... rectify that situation. It should prove rather entertaining, too."

"I feel as though I should be frightened, but I'm definitely intrigued," Elisa interjected.

"Good," Narcissa stated. "Because you don't know how hard it was not to slap that smug look off her face and not tell her what happened *after* you left her room." Her gaze flicked toward her open closet.

Elisa's eyes widened. "*Oh...* the day that... right."

Hunter chuckled a bit. "*Please* feel free to tell her. In front of everyone, preferably. I intend to handle the issue as publicly as possible." A public humiliation was exactly what Ivory deserved. Reaching out, he caressed Narcissa's hip. This felt completely unreal. Every dream they'd had since he first walked through her door was going to come true now.

"Happily." Narcissa glanced at Elisa. "Yeah, *that* day."

"What day would that be?"

"The day Narcissa figured out my true identity," Elisa answered. "And yet another day that we, as well as a friend of ours, wanted to stab Ivory in the throat. Unfortunately, we are not allowed weapons within these walls, and my natural weapons were taken from me after I was brought here." Elisa looked down at her hands, a faint look of longing appearing on her face.

"Your..." Hunter's eyes flared as his gaze dropped to her hands, then carefully took them in his own. "Your claws... were *removed*?" he growled through gritted fangs. She had to be fucking joking. How could someone do something so fucking cruel? To a feline, it could easily cause infection; too many removed at one time could actually cause death. What the fuck had that bitch been thinking? When Elisa nodded, the darkness in his eyes intensified, and he emitted a low, guttural growl.

Narcissa placed a hand on Hunter's arm. Immediately, he calmed. Which was strange, but probably a wonderful thing. She squeezed Elisa's hand. "We'll see what we can do to rectify it. I don't know how Queen Dyeera altered the magic, aside from breaking everyone's contracts, but we'll figure it out."

Hunter leaned down and kissed his mate. "Thank you."

"Yes, thank you," Elisa added. "It would be nice to have them back again." She smiled softly, then focused on Narcissa. "What happened to her? To Averine?"

"Based on what we saw, I'm going with burned beyond a crisp," Narcissa answered. "The queen of the nymphs showed up to collect payment from Averine. Apparently, for the den. Queen Dyeera gave her a choice and, in the end, the female chose death."

Elisa nodded a little. "Good. Do not get me wrong; I have had a much better life here than I ever would have had in the village. But that does not make Averine's actions right, or any less cruel."

"No, there's so much to change around here," Narcissa said. "I'm just glad Shalla agreed to stick around. Having her and Jade's insight will be helpful."

"I agree." Not that he really knew Jade, but he would always trust his female's judgement. And he was familiar with Shalla. It hadn't taken long for Hunter to get a bead on that female. Not to mention, she would have Marcell by her side. They weren't friends—not that he had any of those—but the male was intelligent, and a good person to have in your corner.

"We have a lot to get done, so we should get started." Narcissa peered at Elisa. "I know you haven't been out since you got here, so maybe for now, stay close by. I don't want you to get overwhelmed or anything. Though when you're up for it, I believe a shopping trip is in order. Because I will need a new wardrobe."

"That sounds... truly wonderful."

"The shopping trip will be on me," Hunter stated firmly. "For the both of you."

"Oh no," Elisa retorted, "that is unnecessary, Hunter. I can pay for whatever I wish to purchase."

"And yet, I insist."

His sister smiled a little. "I will not win this argument, will I?"

"Absolutely not."

"Then it would seem I have no choice but to concede." She smiled over at Narcissa. "Staying close for now is probably a good idea, too. Is there anything I can help you with while Hunter is gone?"

"Help me go through contracts and non-disclosures. Figure out how to make this transition as smooth as possible for the workers and the clients."

"I can definitely do that. Whatever you need."

"I am going to stay just a few more minutes, then I will head out. I will be back, though, as soon as I can."

Narcissa's gaze flicked briefly to Hunter. "Grace's room... I mean, Elisa..." Narcissa shot Elisa an apologetic look. "Her room is right across the hall. I guess we can stay in my room until we get things situated upstairs."

"I do not know if I will ever get used to being called Elisa again. I have been Grace for twice as long."

Hunter reached out and gave his sister's shoulder a squeeze. "You can go by whatever name makes you most comfortable." Holy fuck, right across the hall... She'd been so close... Hunter shook the thought away. "Sleeping quarters are the least of my worries. Things will get figured out when they get figured out. You want to continue living here, then? Or would that just be temporary?"

"Here, at least for now," Narcissa replied. "While we transition. Then... I'd like to see my family. The rest we can figure out afterward."

"Of course." He leaned down and kissed her. "And I am perfectly okay with that." It didn't matter where they ended up, as long as they were together. Something he never imagined he would want, before meeting Narcissa. "I actually have an idea I would like to talk to you about when we are in private."

While they spoke, Elisa tried to be discreet as she looked him over. Not that he couldn't see her out of his peripheral vision, let alone feel her staring at him. She was looking at all his scars. Likely wondering how he'd gotten all of them. And she looked at his brand, too. Though he didn't sense any judgement from her. Her staring didn't bother him, either. Not that he could explain that.

"I welcome ideas," Narcissa said.

"Good. I look forward to sharing them."

Twenty-Three

In the den, Narcissa's fingers danced over Hunter's soft ears and the top of his head, which rested in her lap. While he wasn't saying anything just now, she could tell what was on his mind. The day had been long, and the night had been longer. His weakened and sickened body was exhausted. But despite all of that, he felt good for the first time in his life.

After returning from Métamorphe with a book containing his family's tree, he had stayed up late talking to Grace, and they had gone through it together. They had excluded Sam and Azazel from it. He had passed it on to Grace, insisting that he could have another one made. The image of their mother had brought his sister to tears.

Once in Narcissa's bedroom for the night, they had worked their way through every inch—literally. Which hadn't helped with Hunter's fatigue, but they hadn't been able to help themselves.

Hunter purred quietly as his finger slowly traced the vines of the tattoo on her left leg. "Where did you get your tattoos done?"

"I have an old friend who did them. Another nymph I know." Someone she'd met some time ago. The female used to just do work for other nymphs. Recently, she'd discovered her friend had expanded. "She opened a shop in the marketplace not too long ago. Why do you ask?"

"Just curious. Sort of." Hunter tilted his head back and looked up at her. "Do you think she would consider doing a brand?"

"A brand?" Narcissa raised an eyebrow. "I guess. As long as the person was willing. She'd never mark anyone who didn't want it." Not that she expected that's why he'd asked. They wouldn't force anyone into anything.

Hunter's lips spread into a slow smirk. "Oh, I never ask for anything I am not willing to receive, baby girl. I was thinking of getting... a particular brand. On my neck. Right... here." He brushed his thumb over his throat, across one spot she'd bitten him earlier. A shudder passed through him, and his eyes flashed brightly. "A tattoo would not really work with my fur."

As a slow grin stretched across her face, she purred softly, a sound that was met with his exquisite, rumbling growl. Fuck, he knew what that did to her. It almost made her want him again. Except she could have him anytime she wanted. Something she didn't think she'd ever get accustomed to. And they still had a lot of work to do. Plus, his brother and his brother's mate—pregnant mate, at that—were coming tomorrow. "Oh, I'm sure *that* could easily be arranged. And don't worry. My friend knows how to make it permanent. Fur or not."

"Good." Hunter reached up and stroked her cheek. "I want your mark on me permanently. We should try to find time to go tomorrow."

She ran her fingers over the mark on his throat. Just like the first time, it had happened all on its own. "I think we can do that."

Hunter turned his head and kissed her palm, then looked back up at her. "I was going to tell you about my idea. About the living arrangements. We just got sidetracked for a while." One corner of his lips upturned a bit.

That. They. Had. Narcissa tilted her head. Right. He'd said so after being reintroduced to Grace earlier. They'd just been rather busy since. He seemed to be full of ideas. Not that she would ever complain. It was nice that she didn't have to think about some things. "Oh?"

"Mmhm. And before you object, I can absolutely afford it. What do you think about... a four-story house? One floor for your mother, your brother, and Elisa, each with their own living quarters; one floor for Hayden, Rainbow, and their young; one floor for you and me; and the bottom floor for communal spaces and the kitchen area, things like that. And, yes, I am well aware we would have to talk to all of them first, to see if that would be acceptable, but it would keep all of us near those we do not want to be far away from, but also give each family unit their own space."

Narcissa blinked. Wow. She didn't quite know how to respond to that. It wasn't as if she hadn't lived with her brother and mother before.

Or kept them from discovering her lifestyle choices. But to do that with his family and to have children around their home, too... That wasn't something she expected. None of that included the first part of his statement. *I can absolutely afford it.* While things were different with Hunter than anyone she'd ever been with, Narcissa needed more information before she could agree to something like this. "How can you afford it?"

"Because I have not just been an Informant. For over two decades, I have had another job in secret. It has... mushroomed my finances." He rolled onto his back and pulled her on top of him, and she could feel the heat radiating from his chest as her breasts pressed against it. His fingers traced a slow path up and down her spine, sending shivers down her back. "I would ensure that the walls were soundproof, ensuring plenty of privacy for everyone." He smirked a bit. "I am sure that our particular proclivities are not something you want your family to experience, and that is not something I think my brother could handle hearing. We could have a lift installed as well, for easier access to the upper levels."

The more he spoke, the more money she could see herself spending. Though he still had yet to explain *how* he'd pay for all of this. Or anything about this *secret job.* Narcissa ran her fingers in a slow circle across his chest. He knew the worst thing she'd ever done in her life. And he hadn't judged her for it. Why couldn't he share this with her? Did he think she might look at him differently? "Hunter... you know you can tell me anything, right?"

"I know I can." He brushed a soft kiss over her lips. "But if I tell you this, it cannot leave this room. It is imperative that you tell no one what I do, because it is illegal... across the entire isle, I am sure."

Illegal? That made her sit up just a touch. Some things she could handle, but not everything. There were even some lines she refused to cross. Gods, she hoped whatever he did wasn't one of them. "No matter what you tell me, I'd tell no one things about you." That was true even when Grace asked her about him.

"I know." Hunter inhaled and exhaled a deep breath. "I am a professional contract killer. And one of the very best. Which means I do not come cheap. But unlike others, I will not take a client without valid grounds. And I also tend to be the last resort."

Well, that certainly wasn't what she expected. And it came as a bit of a relief. Narcissa rested her chin on her hand and ran her fingers across his chest in a circular motion. His purr rose just slightly in volume. "Okay."

Hunter raised an eyebrow. "You seem perfectly okay with that. That is not the reaction I was expecting."

"Am I supposed to be against it?" Her eyebrow arched in response. "You said 'without valid grounds.' I presume that means your target has done something that justifies or warrants their death."

"Yes. Always. That is a stipulation I never deviate from. I did just tell you I get paid to kill people. *Okay* is not the response one would get after saying that." His fingers traced a slow path down her spine, then grazed her ass before making their way back up. "I was hoping you would not be against it, though, in all honesty. I enjoy my work. Hayden has never known what I do, as he would definitely object. And while Markham would not have given a single shit, I am technically breaking Devin's law in doing so. But mostly with those who commission me, there is no one else who can help them."

Narcissa stifled a snicker. Perhaps there were several other responses, but it seemed the most appropriate. "Hunter, do you remember the day I told you I killed my father? You reacted as if you understood. Beyond what you experienced with your father and half-brothers. You didn't bat an eye, but looked as if you wished he was alive so you could kill him again... it revealed so much. It was the first time I really felt that I'd made the right call." Not even Deacan had made her feel that way. And he was the only person who knew it happened, aside from Hunter. "I've been in the position where no one believed me. My father was a well-respected member of the community. The type of male who loved his family. Not someone who would hurt them. Men like him... people like him... they don't deserve to live. They have no soul. No heart. As far as I'm concerned, if that's the type you go after, then you're a fucking hero."

"No one has ever called me a hero before."

"That's what you'll always be to me." Narcissa leaned in and gently brushed her lips against his. "You saved me in ways I don't think you even realize. That's before I even knew what you did. Now that I know, it just makes everything that much clearer. You help people who cannot help themselves." So what if he got paid for it? In a way, that had been her job, too. She just helped people differently. And while she would no longer be so directly involved, she could still help people.

"That is because I remember what it was like... to be helpless," he whispered. "Those things... those memories... they may hide in a small, locked cage in my mind, but they will never go away. I was once exactly like the people I take money from. And I sometimes wonder, if someone had saved me... if I would have turned out differently. If I would not have ended up... needing the things that I do. But now I know." Hunter cupped her jaw. His thumb stroked her cheek as he stared into her eyes. "If I had not needed this place, we may never have found one another. Something I will forever be grateful for. You saved me, too, Narcissa. In ways that no one else ever could have."

She hadn't thought about it like that. The decisions each of them made led them here. To this moment. To each other. Narcissa leaned into his touch. "I think if everyone agrees, then all of us living together is a good idea. Maybe we can find a place not too far from here to build." But far enough away that they could separate their work and home life.

"I think that sounds like a wonderful idea. We can talk to Elisa, and Hayden and Rainbow about it tomorrow. After we go to see your mother and brother, we can find the right time to talk to them about it as well. If everyone agrees, we have about... four *cycles*, I believe, to get everything figured out and handled. That is when my brother's semen demons are supposed to be arriving."

'Semen demons.' Not a term she'd heard before. She kind of liked it. "So then, under four *cycles*, actually. They'd need time to get a nursery situated before its arrival."

"That is true. They will want to get that ready. You know, we should probably actually look somewhere triangular between here, Métamorphe, and the marketplace. Clay still lives in the shape shifter village. Not that I ever really expect to be close to him myself, but I know he and Hayden are trying. And Rainbow has a club in the marketplace."

"And definitely someplace where the territory is unclaimed." That way, they wouldn't need permission from anyone to build. Or indebted to someone because they got it.

"Right, definitely. We can set aside some time to go scouting." Hunter stared thoughtfully into her eyes for a minute. "We should probably get some sleep, sweetheart."

"I still feel like I'm dreaming." She pushed up onto her hands and knees, swung one leg over, and straddled him. "Maybe before we fall asleep, we should prove it's not surreal."

Hunter's eyes flashed as a low growl rumbled out of him. "I love when we are on the same page." Sliding his hands to her hips, he gave them a squeeze. "I still feel like I am dreaming, too. I think you should prove to me that I am wide awake."

Without a moment of hesitation, Narcissa fused their lips together, swept her tongue across his fangs, and moaned. He shuddered, a deep growl escaping his throat. She'd never get enough of tasting every part of him. He gripped her ass harder and deepened the kiss as she dragged her nails down his chest and pelvis. Narcissa reached between them as he lifted his hips with a guttural moan, one that only got louder as she gripped his cock and stroked it.

Not stopping with the hand job, Narcissa removed one of his hands from her hips and moved it to the bar at the head of the bed. His fingers immediately wrapped around it. She eased out of the kiss. "Move the other one." It had been quite some time since she'd truly taken him.

A slow smirk spread across his face as his hips lifted again. "Yes, Ma'am," he purred, then followed her instructions and moved his other hand to the bar.

Fuck, she loved that sound. "Good boy," she replied in a husky voice. "Now, keep them there until I say otherwise." Narcissa licked his lips.

He leaned just slightly forward to capture her lips in a kiss, but she was already sitting up. While keeping his gaze fixed on her, he let out a low growl as she quickened her movements and ran her nails forcefully down his chest. His eyes darkened as she slipped two fingers inside her pussy. Hunter's fangs elongated and dug into his lower lip as he watched her fingers go to work.

Thrusting her fingers a few more times in perfect sync with her strokes of his cock, she revved them both up a bit more. Narcissa pulled her fingers from her pussy. He leaned forward slightly, watching as she brought her fingers to her mouth, and then licked them, readying herself to take him.

"I need you," Hunter growled. "Get my dick inside you."

Even before he spoke, she understood what he wanted—a phenomenon that was still strange, but it didn't stop her. With her thighs spread wider, Narcissa skillfully guided him deep inside her with a single fluid motion.

His hands tightened around the bar, and he growled. "Fuck..."

"You forgot to say please," she purred as she ran her hand down her body, inching closer and closer toward her sex.

His eyes darkened further as they followed along. "Please," he purred out. "Please, fuck me."

"Much better," she moaned. Pressing her feet against his ass, Narcissa slid her finger over her clit and rocked her pussy back against his cock. She established a consistent pace, aligning the intensity of her riding with the stimulation of her clit. As she massaged her breast, she rolled her nipple gently between her thumb and forefinger.

Hunter flicked his gaze to her chest. A slight snarl escaped him as his fangs grew longer. He licked his lips as their eyes locked. "May I fuck you, too... Ma'am?"

Fuck. That one word sent shivers down her spine. That didn't even include how sexy as fuck her mate was with each little thing he did. And the control he demonstrated. "Yes, you may." Narcissa extended her tongue, gently brushing it against her other nipple.

"Fuck," he hissed out. Hunter maintained eye contact as he raised his hips and thrust vigorously into her, emitting a moan.

Narcissa groaned deeply. Extending her thighs apart, she pushed her feet against his ass, increasing the intensity of her movements while keeping pace with her finger strokes on her clit. With a moan, her tongue swept across her nipple, the sensation electric. Fuck, if she kept this up, it wouldn't take long for her to come.

His grip tightened even more around the bar until it was almost cutting into his hands. His neck and arms bulged, muscles straining with the effort to maintain his position. Hunter thrust his hips up harder, moving in time with her frantic, urgent rhythm. "Oh, fuck... Narcissa..." he growled. The brilliant blue of his eyes shone, turning their room into a bright, illuminating space. "Fuck... please, do not stop."

"Not stopping." Especially with how gorgeous his eyes looked right then. Something that no longer had to be hidden. Something they didn't have to run from anymore. They could freely love one another without fear of the repercussions. As she pinched her other nipple and fondled her breast, her skin sparkled in the light. With his eyes glowing brighter, he picked up the pace of his thrusts, syncing with her as she heightened the motion of her hips and the caress of her clit. "Fuck," Narcissa groaned.

Her orgasm sat right on the edge. She knew exactly what would push it over—for both of them.

Narcissa, with Hunter's eyes glued to her movements, ran a hand up her shoulder, pushed her hair away, and exposed her throat, tilting her head. "Let go."

Just two words, but they flipped a switch inside of him. Hunter did exactly as he was told—he let go.

He let go of the bar, seized her, and with a swift motion, flipped them, ending with him positioned above her. His hips thrust uncontrollably, driving his cock deep inside her with intense speed and force. One hand clamped down on her wrists, pinning them above her head. He seized her hair in his fist and roughly forced her head to the side. He struck, his elongated fangs piercing her flesh, sinking in deep, as an unearthly roar escaped him, and she responded with a cry of ecstasy. As they plunged off the cliff, a wave of pure euphoria surged through them, eclipsing all else but their connection.

As strange as it was to sense that he wasn't finished, and the desires he still had, Narcissa rather liked it, too. They had made quite a mess. One she'd happily allow him to clean off her body.

Hunter eased his fangs from her throat, not bothering to lick the blood from her skin or his chin. Narcissa's mouth made a soft purring sound before their lips fused together for a deep kiss. Hunter adjusted his position by tucking his knees beneath him and spreading them slightly, widening her thighs as he released her wrists and moved that hand up into her hair.

With her legs locked around his hips, Narcissa used her feet to grip his ass as she leaned back. She maintained her pace, lifting her hips and meeting his every movement with her own.

As his pace slowed, so did the tempo of her hips. They did not lessen the force with which their pelvises collided. Hunter made the kiss languid until it became purely passionate. Each time her back arched, pushing her breasts against his chest, he released a low groan into their kiss. He broke the kiss only to snarl, "Nails." Then his tongue returned, a forceful dance with hers.

She knew exactly what he wanted. Narcissa gripped his shoulders tightly, her nails scraping against his skin until blood bloomed beneath her fingertips. His growls and moans consumed her. Fuck, he felt incredible.

He deepened the kiss as he pulled her closer, his fingers tangled in her hair. As she moved back and forth, her pussy pressed against his cock firmly, squeezing him with each movement. Jolts of lightning shot straight to her core. Their bodies connected in a way that was familiar, yet new. It completely shattered the idea that this could be a dream. This was a fantasy that had come true. Something they'd both craved from one another. Gods, she loved him. More than she had imagined possible. Her skin's brightness illuminated the wall, the light like a soft, pale shimmer.

Hunter pulled back just slightly and met her gaze. His eyes emitted a blue glow, and her skin shimmered, painting the walls with an ethereal aurora. But his eyes were locked on her face. "I love you, Narcissa."

"I love you, too, Hunter." This male had awakened every part of her. The parts she'd kept hidden for her own safety. Even the parts she hadn't known existed. For the first time in her life, she truly felt whole. It was because of him. This definitely wasn't a dream. This was everything she'd never known she needed, and more.

"Gods, do I love you. So very much." Hunter's lips met hers once more, then he gently explored her mouth with his tongue until she welcomed him. The kiss's passion knew no bounds. His thrusts increased in speed. As their bodies crashed, his growl swelled, a low, guttural sound that echoed with each impact. Fuck, she could sense it. They were both going to come.

Narcissa cried out his name as she threw her head back against the pillow. Her body was wracked with a massive orgasm, and his followed in its wake. Pleasure washed over their bodies, flowing between them, down their thighs, and across her ass, dampening the linens beneath. Their noises continued, a chorus that created the most beautiful melody. Their unique love song.

As their bodies stilled, and the echoes of their orgasms faded, he held her close, forehead to forehead, as they gasped for air. His sweat-soaked body trembled slightly. Her nails were still buried in his shoulders, his hands still tangled in her hair. His heart beat perfectly in sync with hers. No words could describe everything Narcissa felt in that moment. It was the most beautiful thing she'd ever experienced. Gods, she'd never get enough of feeling him like this. They truly belonged to one another.

Nothing could ever take that away.

No words were spoken as their bodies cooled down. Hunter pulled away and sat up, drawing her with him as the possibility of motion arose. He climbed out of bed, scooped her up, and carried her into the bathroom. After placing her in the shower, he started the water before filling the tub. After they'd rinsed off the last traces of their exertions, Hunter helped her into the tub, the warm water already smelling of the soap as he slid in close behind. He held her close, a tender embrace and placed a soft kiss just below her ear. "I will help you change the bedding when we get out of here. I just figured one last soak in the tub would be nice before we go to sleep."

"This is nice." Though she didn't think he should help with the bedding. She liked things a certain way. Gods, the cleaning that a four-story house required. She'd handled the mansion well that she'd lived in before the den. "When we present your idea to our respective families, I only have one requirement. I handle the hiring of all staff. At least, regarding the household. Security measures I'll leave in your hands."

"I can deal with that. Although I have one requirement myself in that regard. They all must be discreet. No gossiping, even amongst themselves. Anyone who works for us will be paid extremely well and treated even better. That warrants decorum and professionalism, even when they are not beneath our roof."

They were always on the same page. "Agreed." Narcissa entwined their fingers together. Discretion was a necessity with their sexual desires. Not to mention that they were now in charge of the den. No one needed to know any of that.

Hunter smiled against her. "Good. I know several people I can hire to guard the place, especially when I am not home. They are very skilled; no one will be able to tell they are there, so they will not disrupt daily life."

"That's good. The less my brother sees in that regard, the better." She didn't even know how he'd react to children in the household. It would be interesting, to say the least.

Hunter nipped her throat, then laid his head on top of hers as his fingers stroked her thigh. "What kinds of things will need to be included as we build to accommodate him?"

"A separate playroom, music room, and a quiet room. Loud noises bother him. Clocks will need to be everywhere. He always has to know the time." She didn't expect either of them to have changed. Her brother required constant supervision and a strict schedule. It helped him keep control of his anger, something that one thing out of place could easily trigger. "We'll have to set something up for him outside, too."

He nuzzled into her hair and inhaled deeply. "What kind of something?"

"A greenhouse is what we had before. He enjoys seeing all the flowers and watering them." He purred as Narcissa nuzzled against him a bit more.

"That is simple enough. What about hiring a caretaker or two? I am not sure if that is something he has ever had before, but your mother deserves to have time to herself as well, without worrying about his routine and all of his needs."

"We have to see how he'll interact with a caretaker. As much as I'm sure my mother would appreciate it, Dion handles each newcomer differently. I've tried in the past, but it's never really worked out." None of them could handle his rough patches. The longest one had ever lasted was six months. After that, she stopped trying.

"Because of how he can lose his temper, or for another reason?"

"His temper mostly. Because he's basically a child in a grown male's body, he doesn't recognize his own strength. He's unintentionally harmed caretakers before. Sometimes it was because they angered him, and other times it was because he tried to hurt himself and they didn't know how to stop him appropriately."

"Has he done better with a female or male caretaker? Or has he ever even experienced a male caretaker before?"

"Deacan was particular about the males he allowed in the house. So, we only ever attempted female caretakers." She'd had a guy lined up once, but Deacan had refused to even entertain the thought. "However, the person he and my mother stayed with all these years is a male friend of mine. That may give us some insight if anything has changed at all."

"Good. If that has changed toward the positive, I know one male we could try out. Other than that, I know of a few females who would be well suited as well." Hunter placed a kiss on one mark he'd made on her neck. "None that I have slept with, though, I promise. But I would like to talk to your mother about it, when we all get settled, if that would be okay with you. A new caretaker is not something we should probably try right away. Everyone needs time to adjust to all the changes before we add another new dynamic."

"That certainly makes sense. And I'm glad." Narcissa grinned. "I'm not afraid to put a female in her place... if necessary."

Hunter chuckled against her. "Mmm, I think I would rather enjoy watching that. Sounds really fucking sexy."

"Does this mean we should have a room upstairs just in case?" For the times when they couldn't contain themselves. Especially if they witnessed something that the other did that was a complete turn-on.

"Oh, there will be no 'just in case.' We are *absolutely* going to need a room upstairs."

Narcissa purred. "I love when we're on the same page."

He growled and nipped at her throat again. "So do I, baby girl. So do I. Should we get out and try to get some sleep?"

"I think we should. We've got a lot of work tomorrow. And it's too important to do tired." Though she could think of other things they could do instead, what they did here mattered to many people. She refused to mess that up.

"That it is." Hunter turned her head slightly and pressed a kiss to her lips, the taste of it lingering for a moment.

A warm, tingling sensation spread through her, a feeling of deep-seated contentment. Tonight, and forever, the sleep they would get would be the most restful and comforting of their lives.

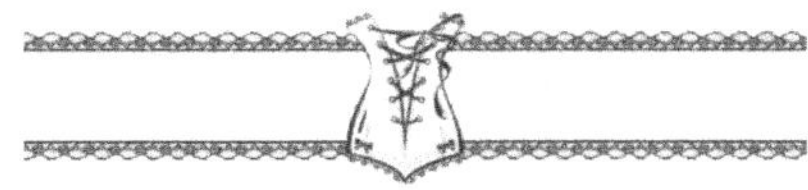

Hunter's eyes snapped open. Even in the low light of the lantern, it took him a moment to adjust to the wakefulness. He blinked rapidly, trying to clear his vision of the lingering, hazy images. They proved more difficult to deter recently. Spirits had always kept them at bay. But he couldn't drink any longer. *For now.* The only thing that made them leave was his Narcissa.

Sleep seemed to make it difficult regardless, though. Lately, sleep had become a fleeting visitor, rarely gracing him with its presence. Especially before today. And deep-rooted habits were difficult to break.

Though with his illness, that was harder to contend with. When he'd returned to the village, and proven to Aradia that he could keep down liquids—finally—she'd provided him with an armful of herbal remedies to take. Several times a day. One of which included a sleep aid that he'd tried, and failed, to refuse.

Hunter carefully set Narcissa aside and quietly got out of the bed. She was sleeping, and a sense of tranquility filled the room, so at least one of them should have an uninterrupted rest. He splashed water on his face in the bathroom, dried it, then set off for a short walk. Normally, this would be the time he'd check on Hayden. But that was only something he could do mentally at present. That was precisely what he did as he crossed the room and exited.

Just across the hall. All this time with Narcissa. All the years at the den. His sister had been so close, and he hadn't known it. Hunter fought the wave of failure that threatened to drown him. There was no way he could have known. Contingencies had been put into place to ensure that no shape shifter even knew Elisa still lived.

Hayden was doing just fine. Sleeping soundly. Fully content. His emotions settled from the news Hunter had brought to him earlier in the evening, as well as what he'd put his twin through.

As silently as possible, he cracked the door to Elisa's—to *Grace's* room. Just a crack, though. He did nothing more than listen. The only sound in the room was the quiet hush of someone's breath, a gentle rhythm in the stillness. Good. She was sleeping, too. And well, by the sound of it. He eased the door shut, listening for the soft click that signaled it was closed.

Not that he could seem to make himself go back to bed just yet. He was restless. A semi-short walk appeared to be the only thing that did the trick.

About half an hour later, Hunter returned to Narcissa's room. He reentered the room, shutting the door softly, and his gaze immediately went to the bed. Narcissa was awake now. Not sitting up, but propped up a bit on the pillows. Her comforting embrace beckoned him to her, her open arms ready to offer solace.

Calling him home.

It would never matter what walls surrounded him. The only place he had ever felt at home was in her arms.

Hunter strode across the cold floor, the sound of his footsteps echoing, and then he crawled back into bed to snuggle close to her. "Everything is okay. Go back to sleep."

He did exactly that—the feel of her skin against his as he pulled her closer, burying his face in her throat. As her calming fragrance embraced him, the gentle rhythm of her heart lulled him back to sleep.

Epilogue

H unter's eyes remained on his mate as she retrieved a file from the drawer of a wooden cabinet on the other side of the office. It had only been two days since they'd taken over the den, and already, they'd made several changes. Beginning with several of the staff members. They had happily demoted Ivory to a janitor position, something his mate, sister, and their friend had, apparently, once joked about. And that had been *after* he'd dealt out the planned public humiliation in the dining hall, in front of at least seventy-five percent of the workers here.

Hunter strode through the door with Narcissa on his arm, his eyes scanning the hall until he found Ivory, seated with her sister, as well as a few others. Perfect. He leaned down to kiss his mate before he removed his arm and crossed the room. Stopping behind Ivory, he waited a beat—and for everyone else's eyes to raise up to meet his—before speaking. "Ivory. Get up."

The female practically fell out of her chair. She almost jumped up and spun around, her eyes wide. "What can I do for you?" Ivory asked tentatively.

Even after she stood before him, and had spoken, Hunter waited another moment more.

"I know you kept the necklace. Bring it to me." Ivory's mouth fell open, but Hunter didn't give her a chance to speak. "I am sure you made enough coin from all the times you held betting pools about me, you can easily buy yourself a new one." He almost left it at that, but then changed his mind. The horrified expression on the female's face was too amusing. As if his mate wouldn't have told him about that? "Better yet... I think I would prefer you

to produce every coin you have earned from turning me into your personal joke. If you do not possess the amount, it will come out of your wages until it is paid in full." Which would likely take quite some time, with the female's recent demotion. Hunter turned away from Ivory, then spun on his heel to face her again. *"Oh, and do not forget, you owe two thousand to... my sister, if I am not mistaken. I will expect that to be paid before anything else."*

Cue the even more shocked look on Ivory's face. While some had already discovered the relationship between him and Eli—between him and Grace, *it wasn't yet common knowledge that they were siblings.*

They were still dealing with some of the staff, but today wasn't about them. Today was all about clients. And getting rid of the ones that did nothing for their new business model.

Narcissa strode over to the desk where he sat and reclaimed her seat in his lap. "We may have to shut a few things down for a couple of *penumbras* to really get everything rearranged the way we'd like. Though I'd prefer if we could avoid that."

"I would as well." Hunter's fingertips danced along her thigh, barely grazing the silky crimson material of her jumpsuit. "I think we could if we just take everything one step at a time. If we figure out exactly everything that we want to change, then we can figure out what accommodations we will need to make so we do not have to shut down for any period. I could probably even get us some temporary help." Coin talked, and loudly at that. And this was important, so it wouldn't be something he would skimp on the payment for.

"That might be useful." Narcissa set the file on the desk. "Do you think we'll have to move any of the workers into the cavern rooms?"

"That might be a good idea. The quicker we can get everything done, and up and running how we want it to, the better." He laid his head on her shoulder and inhaled deeply, the scent of her nearly making him growl low in his chest. "Whose file is that?"

"Kylen's. He should arrive shortly. I thought it might be helpful for our meeting with him."

"Oh?" Hunter drew the file toward them and flipped it open. He'd gone through most of them—both worker and client—but this was one he'd yet to look at. Mostly because even thinking of the spineless male made him murderous. Which was a wonderful emotion for him to have, considering the male's imminent arrival. Narcissa had purposely had the guards escort every client to their office before whatever session they had scheduled. Especially for those whose relationships they had to terminate. As they were about to do with Kylen. She and Grace had addressed the files a couple of days ago while he'd gone off to share the good news with his twin. "It is not very professional of me to be looking forward to his visit, is it?"

"You mean because you get to rub in his face how you got the girl in the end?" Narcissa turned to the notes, the pages rustling with the motion. "He tried to buy out my contract while you were gone."

Hunter's fangs clenched hard together. Not that any other expression showed on his face. "Really now." He scanned the notes on the page. That Kylen had ever thought he had a chance—not just to be Narcissa's only client, but to truly be with her as well—just showed how delusional the prick was. Not that the notes alluded to the latter fact. But it didn't take a genius to figure it out. He doubted Kylen had legitimate feelings for her. The male was just greedy, jealous, and possessive over someone he had no claim to. "Not just that. I simply have an... ultimatum to offer him. Something I have been ruthlessly anticipating."

"Just remember, you can't kill him."

Right. They *did not have the right to do that*. Unless, of course, Kylen provoked things. His mate didn't anticipate that happening, but Hunter couldn't help but hold out some hope. It would be fun ripping the fucker apart, piece by piece. Messy, though. It would take some time to clean up. Maybe he could fuck Narcissa on top of the bastard's remains.

"In fact, if you're a good boy in how you handle things, we've got a *lacuna* or two before anyone comes in after him." Narcissa brushed a soft kiss across his lips.

"Mmm, is that right?" Hunter let out a low growl against her throat. He drifted his hand from her stomach to cover her breast, feeling the soft curves. "I think we can find *plenty* of ways to occupy that time." He grazed his fangs along her neck, and the taste of her skin made his mouth water before he gently bit down over her pulse point. "As for *him*... whether or not he survives this encounter will be entirely up to him. I give you my word."

"Good," Narcissa moaned. "Just don't tear any of my clothes. You'll have to actually take all of them off."

Fuck those sounds of hers. As he moved his tongue along her throat, Hunter increased the pressure of his massage on her breast. "Damn. I do not know whether I have had enough practice for that. Or if I have enough restraint. Are you sure I should be trusted with it? Perhaps..." He bit her throat again, the pressure increasing just a little. "... you should just undress for me."

"A stripper pole. We should definitely have one of those in our bedroom," Narcissa purred as she ran her fingers up and down the back of his head. "But I can make do with what we have in here and give you a little show."

That was an interesting idea. A stripper pole wasn't something he'd ever considered before. But just thinking about it... Oh, yes. He was right there with her. They *definitely* should have one of those. Hunter growled against her. "I cannot wait to see what you have in store for me, baby girl."

The tips of her ears flicked. "Sounds like we have company."

Hunter lifted his head, his gaze locked on hers as he turned her chin, forcing them to meet. "He can wait just a moment." He gripped her chin, their lips meeting in a passionate kiss. Not that he planned to go beyond this. But there was no harm in getting them both a bit more aroused for when they had some private time together.

Narcissa groaned into the kiss. Hades, he never wanted her to stop making noises for him. Never again. Hunter ended the kiss with a low growl, his eyes darkening as she brushed her tongue across his bottom lip. Or maybe it was the way her scent intensified, a wave of heat blasting out from between her thighs. Fuck, all he wanted to do was lay her out on his desk and have his way with her. Repeatedly. His eyes lit up, the soft-blue glow reflecting off the walls.

"It's definitely fun to make him wait."

"Mmm, we can make him wait longer if you would like," he replied, not teasing in the least. Fucker could wait all damn day and it wouldn't faze him a bit.

"As fun as it would be, it wouldn't be professional."

Hunter grumbled under his breath, though it wasn't very heartfelt. "I am quickly going to have to get used to being *professional*. I do not know if I like it," he joked.

Letting out a small chuckle, Narcissa gave him one more quick kiss. "I'm sure you'll learn to survive."

"With you by my side, of course I will." He kissed her neck. "I may not like it, but I do not have to like something in order to do it. I will get used to it."

"Yes, you will."

"I have quite a lot of things to get used to." So many things had changed. And there were more changes to come, too. Not just the new business venture, but his mate. Being able to be with her every day and night. No longer hiding their relationship. Having his sister back. Actually getting to know his brother. Brothers. Learning what the fuck it meant to be an uncle. "I am actually looking forward to all of it."

"That's good." Narcissa adjusted her seat on his lap as the footsteps approached closer. Then came a knock, likely from one guard.

Hunter slid his hands comfortably onto her thighs. Moving no other part of his body, he called out, "Enter."

One bodyguard opened the door, stepping aside to let the visitor into the office. Kylen strode past the male. "By your invitation, proprietress, I take it..." His words trailed off as his gaze settled on Narcissa. "You. What are you doing here?"

"We've taken over," she responded. "For someone who notices so many details, I'm a tad surprised you overlooked the changes already made." She leaned back against Hunter, purposely draping an arm across his shoulders. "I believe the two of you know one another."

"We have met." Hunter slowly stroked his fingers up and down her thigh, though his eyes remained on the male. He flicked his gaze only briefly to the guard, giving him a slight nod to indicate that he could depart, then focused back on Kylen. The guard left without a word, closing the door behind him. "I—or, I should say, we—have an ultimatum for you."

"An ultimatum?" Kylen repeated, shock denoted in his tone. He rubbed his thumb across his brow and flicked his gaze back to Narcissa. "I don't quite understand how this is possible or what *he's* doing in here. I need an explanation. Now."

"Watch your tone," Narcissa stated firmly. "It's recommended that you treat me with the respect I deserve. I'm the new proprietress. And he's here for many reasons. He's my mate and my head of security. You'll show him the *same* respect you show me. Understood?"

Arousal blazed briefly in the male's eyes, and his scent flared. While Hunter held back the threatening growl, he wasn't able to keep his eyes from flipping to pitch black.

Kylen narrowed his eyes. "*You're* the new proprietress?"

"Yes," she answered simply.

"It suits you, Nia. Rather well." Kylen clasped his hands behind his back and strolled around the office. "And he's *your* mate?"

He was wasting time. Hunter was tiring of it rather quickly. Just as he could sense Narcissa was.

"Right again. Though I highly doubt all of this needs repeating. So, shall we move forward with the ultimatum we have for you?"

"Very well." Kylen waved them on. "What is it you wish to discuss?"

It had taken a lot of effort on his part to keep his composure throughout all of that. And only partially because of the air of superiority the male maintained. "Suffice it to say, you will no longer be welcome here. Now, since you have paid for several sessions in advance, you have two options. You can be refunded, leave gracefully and without fuss, and never even think about coming near my mate, our employees, or this establishment *ever* again. Or, if you decide that is not a satisfactory route for you to take and decide that you would rather make a fuss... you can leave flat broke, followed by finding out *exactly* how far I would get with taking your life." Hunter couldn't help the smirk that appeared, at the reference to what Kylen had said to him when they'd spoken.

"No longer welcome?" Kylen retorted. "That seems a bit outrageous. I'd happily switch to another worker. There is sure to be someone in this establishment who would suffice." He shifted his gaze from Hunter to Narcissa. "That seems only fair."

They'd already discussed this at great length. Narcissa tilted her head as if she were pondering his suggestion. A broad smile crossed her face just before she uttered the word, "No."

"Come on, Nia. With all the *solaris* I've been a well-paying client of yours, surely, we could work something out."

"Is there any part of this you're not understanding?"

"Several things. How could you so easily dismiss me? How could you choose him over me, especially after all the time we've had together? What *exactly* does he have that I don't?"

Hunter raised an eyebrow. How nauseatingly passionate he'd gotten with that last statement of his.

"Do you *really* want me to answer that?" Narcissa asked. "Before you respond and embarrass yourself further, there are a few things you should consider. You're no longer a client of mine, so I don't have to convince you that you're a god, kowtow to your every desire, or worry about pleasing you. Now, he was fair in his offers and, like me, he doesn't care for someone wasting his time. With that said, you have thirty seconds to decide, and I suggest you choose your next words wisely before I have you thrown out on your ass."

"I was thinking fifteen," Hunter interjected. His smirk widened a bit. "To answer you, Kylen, at least partially... just one of the *many* differences between you and me..." He paused for a beat longer than necessary. "... she never had to fake it with me. Now, time is ticking away. And Narcissa is absolutely correct in that I do not care for anyone wasting my time. Or my mate's. Choose. Now. But you should probably keep in mind... I was never *just* an Informant. If you want to know what I am talking about, I would be glad to show you. But I would not recommend it."

Kylen narrowed his eyes at the two of them and clenched his jaw. "Keep the money, Nia. Consider it a bonus. I'm certain you'll need every gem. If this is how you plan to treat long-time clients, this place will go under sooner rather than later." He spun on the back of his heel, strode for the door, and attempted to open it, except it wouldn't budge.

"I don't recall either of us giving you permission to leave," Narcissa spoke. "Though if you *ask* nicely, then I might grant your wish."

"In all honesty, I am leaning closer and closer to not allowing that to happen," Hunter added. "The more you inch across that line between keeping your cool and making a fuss." His eyes flashed inky black again. "Something I will *never* tolerate is someone insulting my mate." Though he didn't growl full-on, there was definitely an undertone in his words.

"And I will not apologize, nor will I grovel. Though if you continue to keep me prisoner, then I'll happily share this heinous experience with every Seelie I know and ensure none ever return to your establishment again."

"Feel free." Narcissa waited to see if he'd relent in any manner. As she did, she rubbed her ass a bit against Hunter's cock.

Fuck, she was turned on. And her attention was quickly causing his erection to lengthen and thicken beneath her. "Oh, you are being treated much better than I would treat a prisoner." Neither of them had even tortured him. They were far from taking that route. Unless he kept this up. Hunter let out a low growl against his mate's throat as he slid a hand between her thighs.

Narcissa spread her thighs a little wider as she rubbed her ass harder against his shaft. "You can keep tugging on that door, but it won't open... yet."

"Let me leave," Kylen said through clenched teeth. "Please."

"Now, was that so hard? Let this be a lesson you always take with you." Narcissa grinned wide as she flicked her wrist. "Now, get out of our office. I'm about to fuck my mate all over this place."

Hunter didn't even try to hold the growl back this time. Yes, the fuck she was. "Do not forget what I said, Kylen," he said against her throat. "If you ever come back here, or come anywhere near my mate, our families, or our employees, you are going to find out exactly why fucking with me is the very last thing you would *ever* want to do. Do not let the door hit you in the ass on your way out." He smirked. "Unless, of course, you enjoy that kind of thing." Something that honestly wouldn't surprise him.

Without uttering another word, Kylen left and slammed the door shut on his way out.

"I think that went over rather well," Narcissa smirked. She flicked her wrist to lock the door, stood, and straddled him. "Much better."

Hunter slid his hands to her ass and growled as he gripped tight, Kylen quickly receding from his mind. They wouldn't have to deal with him ever again. "It could have been so much more enjoyable for us, though. He is lucky you were here." And now he had even more to focus on besides her ass. Hunter leaned in, and with a playful nip at her earlobe, his lips soon left a trail of soft kisses down her throat. "So... what *many ways* did you have planned to fuck me *all over* our office?"

"Mmm." Narcissa wrapped her arms around him and tilted her head back. "I thought we'd start with your desk, then mine, and end with that ugly-ass chaise by the fireplace."

They hadn't changed any of the furniture yet, but they would get it handled. He couldn't wait. The other half of this floor needed a complete redo as well. But they would truly make it theirs soon enough.

"I think that sounds like an *excellent* plan, baby girl." Hunter grazed his fangs up her neck, feeling the warmth of her skin, then back down before pressing his fangs into her throat, right over her pulse point. Not enough to draw blood or even leave indents, but enough that she would feel a slight sting. "Does that mean I can rip the chaise to shreds while I fuck you on it? Since it is so ugly and all?"

"That sounds like the perfect way to destroy it. Maybe we should start there first." She nipped at his ear, sending a jolt down his spine. "The question is, if you want to rip my clothes from my body... are you willing to get me another suit?"

Hunter growled as he bit down slightly harder on her throat. "If that means I get to rip your clothes off, I would go clear across the isle for a change of clothes for you." Thankfully, he wouldn't have to go that far.

"Absolutely," Narcissa purred and rubbed her crotch against his cock.

Some mixture of a growl and groan left him. His claws began at her lower back, crawling up her body, and then pausing on the fabric covering her. He needed it gone, and he needed it gone *now*. Clenching the lace, Hunter yanked, the delicate fabric tearing with a sharp sound as it freed her breasts. *Fuck, yes.* His palm enveloped one, while his mouth covered the other. With a gentle bite, he repeatedly flicked his tongue against her nipple.

"Oh, gods!"

Narcissa's actions fueled his growl, making it more intense as she pressed against his erection and clawed at his shoulders, drawing blood. Her arousal heightened right along with his own. *Holy fuck*, he needed to be inside her. And he could feel that their desires, as always, were the same.

Without taking his mouth from her breast, Hunter picked her up and sat her on the desk—right on top of the file. Not that he gave a shit. He would happily make her come all over it. The file deserved no less. Hunter wasted no time, the fabric of the jumpsuit giving way with a tearing sound as he ripped it apart. Then he pulled the pieces off of her legs, dropping them to the floor, before bending her knees and placing her heels against the top of his desk. "Mmm, *much* better," he growled out as he trailed kisses up her inner thigh.

Narcissa dug her heels into his desk as she gripped the edge of it and arched her back. "Fuck yes."

At about mid-thigh, he switched to his fangs, grazing them the rest of the length of her leg. His arms embraced her thighs firmly, maintaining the spread of her legs for him, as he licked all the way up her slit. From his chest, a deep growl resonated. Gods, she'd always tasted so fucking fantastic. Hunter tightened his grip on her legs as he teased her slit and her nub.

"Oh, gods," Narcissa groaned. "Harder."

Hunter let out a low groan as she moved her hips, pressing her wet center against his eager mouth. "Mmm, how much harder, baby girl?" He gently slid his tongue between the outer lips of her sex, teasing the entrance with just the tip.

"A lot," she moaned.

His gaze flicked up to hers and darkened significantly at what he sensed from her. *A lot* harder, huh? He could certainly do that. Hunter tightened his grip around her thighs and extended his claws, which he then sunk into her flesh, as she desired. With a deep snarl, he shoved his tongue into her pussy, as far as it would go.

"Gods, yes," Narcissa cried out. With her heels against the desk, she arched her hips, grinding against his tongue. She tightened her grip on the desk's edge, the wood groaning slightly under the pressure. "Fuck."

He craved only to increase the vigor and pace of his tongue's ministrations. Which was exactly what he did. His claws tore deeper, sending tiny rivulets of blood staining her legs. The scent of her arousal and blood mingling was intoxicating, almost divine.

Her back arched, thrusting her chest forward. The moment she screamed, he felt the intense burst of sensation and the hot, flavorful release on his tongue. With a carnal growl, he devoured her release, making sure not a single drop escaped his grasp. After the last shudder, Hunter lifted her from the desk and carried her to the chaise. Normally, he would have continued until she came all over his tongue again, but he needed to be inside her too badly. And besides, they were far from done.

He positioned Narcissa on her knees, the soft fabric of the chaise cushioning her chest, and then he closed his hand around her throat. Getting behind her, Hunter gave her no warning before he slammed his dick deep inside her. An intense orgasm erupted from him, flooding her with ecstasy and drenching her inner thighs. Fuck, he hadn't realized he was that close.

"Fuck, yes." Narcissa hooked her feet behind his knees and rocked her pussy against his cock.

A guttural growl left him. *Holy fuck*, she always felt so fantastic. As he pulled his hips back, Hunter tightened his hold around her throat and drove forcefully inside her. The rhythmic pounding nearly overturned the chaise as his thrusts intensified. His other hand went to her hip, claws digging so deep the coppery smell of blood filled the air.

"Harder," Narcissa demanded. Not that it stopped her from rocking her pussy back against his cock, meeting each of his thrusts. As she tightened her hold, the wood on the chaise cracked and splintered.

If she wanted harder, he would give her harder. With a violent rip of his claws from her hip, Hunter seized her wrists and pinned her arms against the chaise's back. As he leaned closer to her, he felt her warmth as her breasts met the hard back of the furniture. Not that his thrusts stopped, though they slowed down momentarily. "Be a good girl and *stay*." He raked his claws down her sides, a streak of crimson staining her flesh. Hunter's teeth lightly grazed her ear while his claws sank into her hips. Angling her ass back further, he kept his grip tight as he worked back up to a hard, swift rhythm. Hunter could feel her arousal rising higher and higher. The inner walls of her pussy clenched tight, increasing the friction of each thrust.

"Oh, gods, yes!" she cried out.

A new growl vibrated out of him, this one more intense than the one before. Once more, Hunter tore his claws from her hips and seized her breast, causing fresh wounds to appear on her flesh. He increased the intensity and speed of his thrusts while simultaneously stimulating her clit with his finger.

"Fuck," she moaned.

"Fuck, yes," he growled. "Give me those moans, baby girl." As he raked his claws down her side, Hunter pinched her clit. He buried them in her inner thigh and leaned harder into her, feeling the heat rise as he changed the angle of his thrust. "Holy fuck, I love your pussy." Hunter bared his fangs and snarled as he grazed his teeth along her neck. "Come for me, Narcissa." He hissed, the sound echoing in the confined space, and then struck at her throat.

Holy Hades, the taste of her blood on his tongue jerked an orgasm right to the surface. As she reached her peak, Narcissa screamed his name, her muscles contracting around him. That was all it took to shove him the last fraction of the way off the cliff he'd momentarily teetered on. With a surge, her release burst forth, and she clutched the chaise's top, straining against the wood.

Hunter bit down harder, the warm, thick blood gushing into his mouth as he savored the taste. Her release covered his shaft entirely as his poured into her pussy, soaking their thighs and the cushion of the chaise beneath them. He let out a loud roar while maintaining a rapid and forceful pace as he moved in and out of her. As their orgasms faded, he withdrew his fangs, gently lifted her, and settled onto the chaise. He flipped her over onto him, spreading her thighs wide above his face, gripping a handful of her hair, and pushing his cock into her mouth while simultaneously pressing his mouth to her pussy. As he drove his tongue deep inside her, he landed a brutal smack on her ass cheek.

Immediately, Narcissa purred around his shaft, bringing a guttural moan out of him. Either that, or it was the way their combined tastes exploded on his tastebuds. She was absolutely mouthwatering all on her own, but there was something about their tastes *together* that was even better. Likely both; especially with the head of his cock all the way to the back of her throat.

As she squeezed his ass tightly, Hunter growled in pleasure while she rocked against his tongue. *Fuck, yes.* That's what he needed. The sweetest part of her fucking his mouth. Her groan reverberated down his shaft as he gripped her hair tighter and pressed his claws into her ass cheek, increasing the speed and intensity of his tongue movements. She ran her tongue along his shaft, gripping his ass and trailing her nails up his thighs. Blood welled beneath her fingers.

Hunter's head jerked back, his fangs elongating on a hiss. "Fuck... Suck my cock, baby girl."

With his mouth back at her pussy, she rocked back against his tongue, causing his claws to tear at her ass cheeks a bit. As he struck out at her inner thigh, he slid his thumb into her asshole and penetrated her pussy with three fingers. His snarl echoed through the room as his fangs pierced her skin, while his fingers worked her G-spot vigorously. Holy fucking Hades, she tasted so good. And her ass was so tight, her pussy blazing hot and soaking wet.

Narcissa groaned around his shaft. The heat burning in her core intensified, but he knew she wasn't ready to come. Not yet. Though her orgasm came closer to the edge, she wouldn't give in to it too soon. Hunter used his fingers and thumb to pleasure her in both openings at once, while his fangs extended deeper into her thigh. He sucked vigorously on her flesh while thrusting forcefully into her mouth. His deep groan filled the room as she gripped his balls in one hand and traced her nails from the back of his thigh to his ass with the other. Her tongue encircled his shaft, gliding along its full extent as the head of his cock kept brushing against the back of her throat. Hades, her mouth was fucking perfection.

With a swift motion, Hunter dragged his claws along her ass and down her leg, then administered a sharp smack on her backside before embedding his claws into her flesh again. As Narcissa purred around his cock, the vibrations traveled down his shaft while she delicately licked the underside of his dick.

His fangs released her thigh with another hiss. *Holy fuck*, that felt incredible. Hunter paused, eyes tracing the angry purple bloom on her inner thigh, noting the tiny, red rivulets of blood. He leisurely ran his tongue over the bite marks while withdrawing his thumb from her rear, substituting it with the fingers previously immersed in her pussy. They were coated with their cum and slid in easily.

Thrusting in and out, he covered the outer lips of her sex with his mouth, feeling her tighten her grip on his balls in a non-painful way. *Holy fuck.* Hunter delicately nibbled at her sensitive flesh before his tongue traced up the middle. A deep rumble vibrated from him. Hades, he needed so much more. Letting go of his balls, Narcissa scraped her nails from his inner thigh to his ass cheek. *Fuck*, holy shit, that jerked his orgasm closer to the edge. But it was the way she extended her tongue, stroking the tip down the underside of his cock before wrapping it around his balls that shot his arousal through the roof, and nearly sent him flying over the cliff. Hades, he would never get enough of that.

Hunter maintained a firm grip with his claws buried in her ass cheek while pressing his mouth more firmly against her pussy. He let out a series of moans, alternating with growls, as he pushed his cock into her mouth over and over. He delved his tongue into her core, plunging it in and out with thorough exploration, ensuring no part went untouched. As her hips moved against his mouth, the scent of her fueled his intensity. Fuck, he was about to come. Right along with her. Then he would have her ride his dick until they both came again. Before bending her over that desk of hers and fucking her perfect ass.

With a swift motion, Hunter ran his claws over her ass cheek and thigh, then delivered a loud smack to her backside. Recoiling her tongue, Narcissa removed it from his balls and closed her mouth fully around his shaft. As her teeth grazed his length, she purred, and he felt a shiver of pleasure course through him.

Hunter didn't know how he had held his orgasm back then, but somehow, he had. For a moment, anyway. With her thighs spreading further apart, she pushed harder against his tongue, prompting him to thrust his hips more forcefully. Her orgasm erupted all over his tongue at the same time as his burst out of him, like a fucking geyser had gone off. Hunter pulled his fingers out of her with force, gripping her buttocks firmly as he consumed every bit of his mate's essence, determined not to waste a single drop. As if her nectar were the only substance that could quench his raging thirst.

Just as he devoured her, she consumed him. She didn't let a single bead of his release trickle down his shaft. Swallowing the last bit, Narcissa stroked the tip of her tongue up the length of his cock and popped it out of her mouth. "Yum."

A low rumble left his mouth. Hunter slipped his tongue from her pussy and licked up her slit. "Fucking delicious." He gave her ass a hard squeeze and then eased up some on his hold. "Turn around and ride my dick. I want to watch you fuck me."

Setting her feet on the ground, she swung a leg over and stood. His back arched a bit on a growl as she raked her nails down his chest.

She took a few steps back. "Only watch?" A slow grin crossed her face as her eyes hooded. "Because we both know you're not very good at lying still."

His mouth formed a smirk. Fuck, he loved that look in her eyes. "You know better than that, baby girl. I just figured I would give you a chance to have your way with me... before I bend you over your desk and fuck that perfect ass of yours." Practically salivating at the thought, his tongue snaked over his lower lip.

"What if I want more than just *one* before you fuck my ass?"

His eyes darkened as she purred. Hunter didn't move as he watched her take a few more steps back, then stop at the end of the chaise. Although it was ugly as sin, it was wide enough that she could crawl her way up his body. His tail, which hung off the side of the chaise, flicked swiftly back and forth as she placed her knees on either side of his legs, then bent down close so her nipples just barely brushed across his fur. "You are my Narcissa." The smirk grew as he reached back and his claws tore into the chaise's arm. "You can have whatever the fuck you want."

"Damn right I'm yours. Just like every *single* part of you is *mine*," Narcissa purred.

"Always," he growled low. Though the words could be spoken freely now, they had always belonged to one another. Body, heart, and soul. As it would always be, the feeling would last until their last days. He never pictured himself in such a situation. And he would never try to deny ever again. She was his. And he was hers.

Despite the impossible, his eyes grew even darker as she crawled up his body, her breasts lightly grazing his thighs, shaft, and abs as she went. Hunter dug his claws deeper into the chaise. His body tensed and grew hard as her pussy brushed against his skin. Fuck, he needed to be inside her. "You are perfection," he growled as she straddled him.

"Mmm, so are you."

As she ran her hands up his chest, sifting her fingers through his fur, a low purr rumbled from within him. His hips rose, pushing his erection more firmly against her as she moved against him. Fuck, he loved when she teased him before taking advantage of him. Hunter responded with a combination of growls and hisses as she licked one of his nipples, lightly bit it, and then dragged her nails along his sides. He tore the fabric of the chaise as he dug his claws deeper, while she pushed her sex against his cock and dug her stilettos into his ass cheek.

"I do not know how much longer I can keep my hands here... *Ma'am*." Hunter purred out the last word. "So, you had better get my dick inside your sweet pussy *soon*. Before I do it for you."

"So impatient."

How could he *not* be impatient when she was teasing him like that? He groaned as her tongue played with his other nipple. Not that he had much of a chance to say anything else. Not with the way she angled his cock at her entrance, and slammed her pussy back onto it with a moan. "Fuck!" they both hollered. Hunter raked his claws up the arm of the chaise, ripping it even more, and thrust his hips up hard, driving his cock into her core.

Dragging her nails down his chest, she got a tight grip on his pecs as she sat up straighter. His eyes rolled back into his head. Well, then. That was new. Then again, he'd never been grabbed that way before. But, *fuck*, it felt fantastic. Especially with the way it altered the angle, allowing his dick to penetrate her even deeper. His head fell back with a ferocious growl, and she groaned, digging her stilettos deeper into his flesh. As she rode him vigorously, her pussy pressed against his cock with each movement. But it wasn't enough. "More," he practically snarled out. "Ride me harder."

Narcissa's bottom lip was caught between her teeth as she stared at him, her eyes shadowed. Even with his head pressed back into the cushion, it didn't prevent him from watching her. From seeing every fucking movement that she made. *Fuck,* that expression in her eyes. It would do him in every single time. "Yes, Sir," she purred.

His eyes darkened, then lit up bright blue, like the sun reflected off the ocean at dawn. Two words he'd heard a million times, but they meant so much more coming from her than they ever had before. From her. At this moment. With their lives as they were now.

She slammed her pussy back against his cock over and over, riding him like he was a fucking wild animal that only she could tame. His growls got louder and more savage each time the head of his dick connected with her core. His hips continued to buck up into her, meeting her thrust for thrust. Releasing his grip, he tore into the back and side of the chaise lounge, the sound of his claws echoing as he cried out. "Fuck! Fuck, yes! Make me come for you, Narcissa."

As her nails raked further down his body and dug into his abs, he let out a guttural moan that filled the air. Not to mention the way it altered the angle at which she rode him. Oh, dear gods, he was in fucking paradise. The walls of her pussy contracted, clenching around his shaft and intensifying every single stroke.

"Fuck," Narcissa groaned.

Hunter groaned right along with her, though no words came out of his mouth. He was in complete and utter bliss as she rode him with pure and unadulterated wildness. Gods, he fucking loved her. At that moment, with absolutely nothing between them, nothing lingering over their head, nothing to fight or deal with or handle, every string and condition having disappeared, Hunter freely and willingly gave up his control, relinquishing every bit to her. A sparkle flickered across her skin. His mouth parted, his fangs elongating further than ever before, as he watched her take complete advantage of him. Claim him. Possess him. In every way that she could.

Her tongue swept across his lower lip and brought another moan out of him. His moan shifted into a growl as she spread her thighs wider, dug her heels harder into his ass cheeks and tightened her grip on him. His head lifted slightly to meet hers as she fused their lips together. Not that he closed his eyes right away. Not with how that hypnotizing sheen over her skin brightened. He couldn't keep that up for very long, though. Hunter growled as her tongue swept across his fangs. His claws dug deeper into the lounger, gouging part of the stuffing from it. He'd have let go, except that would have given him the opportunity to really *let go*. And for the first time *ever*, he didn't want to. He *wanted* her to be completely in control right now. To truly take him as she'd never taken him before.

The heat between them crackled, a palpable inferno of desire. Their hips slapped together each time their sexes fully connected. But, fuck, if it still wasn't enough.

Narcissa broke off the kiss as she increased how hard and fast she slammed her pussy against his cock. He didn't need her to speak a single word. Some instinct inside of him knew exactly what she wanted. Needed. What he needed, too. Her mark on him. A loud growl vibrated out of him from deep within. Hunter tilted his head as she trailed kisses along his jawline and throat. And then she bit his neck so hard she drew blood. An earth-shattering roar came out of him, but just like before, a peculiar calm swept through him, emptying every thought from his brain. Except how much he loved her. Through his eyelids, he could register the golden glow of her body brightening. But what shoved him over the edge, other than her teeth buried in his throat, was everything he felt through her as she came. It yanked his orgasm out of him, right along with hers, both of them so much more explosive than any other release they'd ever had together.

Releasing the hold she had on his throat, she stroked her tongue across the puncture marks she'd left and trailed kisses back up his jawline. Hunter moaned. Hades, he didn't know something so simple could feel so good.

"I love you, Hunter."

Narcissa silenced his words with a kiss, her tongue a possessive dance in his mouth. With a growl that rumbled in his chest, he finally let go of the lounger and pulled her closer by her hips. Not that he helped her as she continued rocking against his cock; she certainly didn't need assistance. He moved within her, and she matched his deliberate, unhurried pace. They could take as long as they wanted. Time limits were just one of many things that no longer existed for them. As she deepened the kiss, a low moan escaped both their lips while her nails traced a path from his sides to his back. She pressed her body against his, gripping his shoulders tightly as if never to let go.

Hades, he'd felt nothing like this before. And it was so much more than the physical passion between them. For the first time in his life, he felt utterly and completely... loved. Yes, his siblings loved him, and he assumed his mother had, too. But this was a unique feeling altogether. Not to mention, he freely accepted the love Narcissa had for him. She made him feel as though he actually deserved it. He felt her love in more than just the obvious looks, touches, and actions. It was the little things. The way she openly and freely accepted everything about him. Every single part. Even the very darkest. The little touches and teasing glances when she felt how much he wanted her. The way she woke immediately if a nightmare woke him, not coddling him but ensuring he knew she was there. He knew she would continue this, even though it had only happened twice before. Before Narcissa, a heavy darkness had always shadowed his path. Now, that had all changed.

Hunter grabbed her ass and tangled a hand in her hair, intensifying his thrusts. She rocked her hips back, meeting each of his thrusts. With each thrust, the tightness of her pussy heightened the pleasure pulsating through their bodies. Narcissa swept her tongue across his fangs, purposely nicking her tongue with a deep moan.

His grip on her ass and hair tightened. Hades, he would never get enough of her taste. Hunter growled into the kiss as their bodies moved together as one. In perfect sync, as they'd been from day one. Planting his feet flat on the cushion gave him better leverage to thrust his hips up harder. Shit, at this rate, it wouldn't take either of them long to come again.

Narcissa broke the kiss with a nip of his tongue, followed by a slight change of her position. Hunter groaned as she rode him with a wild rhythm, causing his desire to explode. Their bodies collided repeatedly, and he intensified his grip on her ass. "Fuck..." he growled out. "Do not stop, sweetheart. Ride my fucking dick."

"Not stopping," she groaned.

The sound of his snarl filled the air as she dug her stilettos deeper into his ass cheeks, intensifying the motion of her hips as she rode him with increased ferocity. *Holy fucking shit!* Her gaze zeroed in on the other side of his throat. That was all he needed to see. She'd already marked him once, but he'd take her teeth sinking into his skin as many times as she'd do it. Hunter barely got his head tilted to the side before she struck without warning. Her teeth tore into his flesh, drawing blood once more. Just as the inner walls of her pussy clenched around his dick, he let out a roar loud enough to shake the walls. A massive release exploded out of her, completely coating his cock, at the same moment one detonated out of him. Their fluids mingled, saturating their bodies, the chaise below them, and the surrounding air.

Narcissa didn't stop swinging her hips and slamming her pussy back against his cock until their mutual orgasms had reached their end. She freed her hold on his throat, and as she lapped at the marks, a moan escaped his lips. She dropped her head into the crook of his neck. "Fuck," Narcissa muttered with a heavy breath.

Releasing his hold of her ass and hair, Hunter wrapped his arms around her and nuzzled the top of her head. His chest rose and fell as he held her close, inhaling her sweet fragrance. "Fuck indeed." He chuckled softly. "I love you, Narcissa."

"I love you, too, Hunter." A faint smile crossed her lips. "It's still so strange hearing my name. Not sure I'll ever get used to it."

"I can imagine." His fingers stroked up and down her spine as they lay there together, catching their breath. "I could just call you 'baby girl' all the time. Or '*mine*.'" His fingers slipped lower, grazing her ass before making their way back up. "I like your name, though."

"As much as I like the idea of hearing those regularly, I prefer my name. Just like I prefer saying yours."

"I never thought I would enjoy hearing my name." Hunter tilted her chin up and kissed her. "Until I heard you say it for the first time."

"Guess a lot really has changed for us."

"Yes, it has. All the change... is not affecting me like it normally does, though." Something he certainly attributed to Narcissa.

"That's good." She brushed the back of her knuckles across his cheek. "I guess there really is someone out there for everyone."

"I always thought that was such bullshit, too. For once, I am actually glad to be wrong." Hunter pulled her lower lip between his fangs and sucked on it a little. "Have you caught your breath yet? I still want you bent over that desk."

"Definitely," Narcissa purred.

His eyes darkened more. "Fuck, I love that sound." He nipped at her lower lip as he slid both hands down to her ass and gave it a squeeze. "Get in position... Narcissa."

"Yes, *Sir.*"

A slight growl left him.

Hunter kept his eyes on her as she pushed up onto her knees, groaning a bit when his cock slipped from her pussy. As she walked around the lounger, a smirk played on her lips while her fingers trailed down his leg, and then she strode purposefully to her desk. Hunter turned to the side, his eyes locked on her, never losing sight of her. After she placed her hands on the cold, wooden desk, he finally rose from the chaise and came to stand beside her. He bit into his lower lip, a low growl escaping as he slowly raked his claws up her body. Starting at her ass, over her hips, then up the curve of her spine. His claws raked down her shoulder and the length of her arms. Reaching her wrists, Hunter's grip tightened, and he gently lowered her, her arms now spread, her fingertips grazing the desk's edge. He nipped at her ear and then flicked his tongue against her earlobe. "Grab on."

"Yes, Sir," she moaned. As he instructed, she wrapped her fingers around the edge of the desk and held on tight.

"Good girl," he growled in her ear before standing back up. His fingers traced a path along her body, eventually settling on her waist. Holding her firmly, Hunter guided his erection towards her rear, sliding the tip along the crease. "Tell me what you want, Narcissa."

"For you to fuck my ass until we're both on the verge of another orgasm, and then fuck my pussy until we both explode."

Hunter gripped her waist, his body against hers, and whispered into her ear, "Yes, Ma'am." With no warning, he buried his dick in her ass with a ferocious growl. His shaft went in easily, thanks to the lubrication from their orgasms, but he could still feel how every solid inch of his length expanded her from one end to the other. He nipped at her ear before straightening up and putting a firmer grip on her waist. He held her steady, preventing her stomach from hitting the desk's edge with each forceful thrust, as he quickly intensified the rhythm. Holy *fuck,* she was so tight.

"Fuck, yes," she groaned. Narcissa tightened her grip on the edge of the desk, her fingers digging into the worn surface.

Fuck yes, was right. Holy shit, he'd never tire of how incredible she felt in every way. As he tightened his grip, his claws slightly tore into her flesh. His growls and snarls grew more intense with each slam of his pelvis into her ass. Gods, he felt fucking unhinged. In that moment, the intensity of his desire to possess her, just as she had taken him on the chaise, eclipsed all other thoughts. Releasing one side of her waist, Hunter's palm met her back, pushing her down further, and her breasts met the hard surface of the desk. "Louder," he snarled as he buried his claws back into her flesh. His grip was so tight that blood flowed like a river, staining her hips and thighs. As a louder, deeper growl rumbled from his chest, his thrusts became more forceful and rapid. "Fucking scream for me, sweetheart."

Her fingers dug into the wood as Narcissa gripped the desk tighter. "Harder, Hunter. Harder."

Hunter let out a ferocious growl. Holy fucking Hades, the way his name sounded when she moaned it. As much as he fucking loved her noises, it wasn't quite where he wanted her. They would get there, though. As his thrusts became more intense, his grip on her waist grew even tighter. Each time he drilled his cock into her ass, the desk jerked a little. And this wasn't even as hard as it would get. If the thing broke—fuck it, they were redecorating anyway.

"Fuck, yes," she cried out.

As she clenched her ass cheeks around his shaft, his growl transformed into a moan, heightening the intensity of their shared sensations. Fuck, that felt good. Hunter's claws extended, digging deeper into her flesh, as he released one side of her waist. Grasping the edge of the desk, his claws left marks on the wood as his movements became even more carnal. His hips slapped rapidly against her ass as he pummeled into her, shaking the desk even more.

"Fuck, yes," Narcissa screamed.

Hunter snarled. He watched her, sensing the raw, electric energy that signaled her climax was at hand. It only flared his arousal that much higher. His eyes smoldered as a scorching blaze ignited in his veins. Fuck, he was about to come. Without missing a beat, Hunter smoothly transitioned from her ass to thrust deep into her pussy. "Fuck!" With a savage rake of his claws across her hip and thigh, streaks of blood flowed, and he seized a handful of her hair. Jerking her head to the side, he bared his fangs and hissed, right before he struck. As his fangs sank deep into her throat, Hunter moved in and out of her at a frantic pace. A growl escaped his throat, and as he sucked, her taste ignited every synapse in his brain. His growl shifted to a roar as a tremendous orgasm barreled up the length of his shaft and exploded out of him.

Hunter didn't release his hold on her throat until their mutual release had ended. Their cum had drenched his shaft, their thighs, and the floor beneath them. There was probably some on the desk, too. As their bodies stilled, he slowly withdrew from her, his fangs leaving her throat. With a slow lick to savor his work, Hunter nuzzled the mark, a soft rumble escaping him, and then he turned her, lifting her onto the desk.

Narcissa purred, and a low rumble vibrated out of him in response as their gazes met. Hunter kneeled down before her and spread her thighs. Just because they didn't have sessions any longer, didn't mean he would no longer clean her up afterwards. Something so sweet should never be wasted.

Leaning back a bit, Narcissa reached behind her to open one of the desk drawers. Not that he paid attention to whatever she retrieved. His tongue stroked slowly up her right inner thigh until he'd swallowed every drop of blood and cum that coated her flesh. Then he moved to her left inner thigh, giving it the same attention.

She set a jar of salt on the other side of her leg. "What do you say we make that mark a bit more permanent?"

Without breaking his rhythm, Hunter's eyes darkened as a deeper growl left him. He stroked his tongue slowly up her inner thigh, then her pelvis. "Really? *This* mark?" He nipped at her left inner thigh, then stroked his tongue along the puncture wounds.

"And perhaps this one." Narcissa tilted her head, showing the one he'd made on her throat a little more.

Something halfway between a growl and a purr left him. That she would wish to have his mark permanently on her flesh... And not just one, but two of them... Sitting up more on his knees, Hunter cupped her cheek and pressed a kiss to her lips. "*Yes.* If you truly would like to do that. I would love it."

"That I would." She wrapped her fingers around the jar and held it up. "Care to do the honors?"

"Absolutely." Hunter took the jar from her and opened it. Setting the lid down, he picked up a pinch of salt, feeling the grains against his skin as he smeared it into the mark on her throat. The sensation coaxed another purr from her throat. Keeping his palm there for the moment, he growled, the sound rumbling in his chest, as he claimed her lips in a hard, deep kiss. He broke it off and traced his fangs and the tip of his tongue along her collarbone, over her breasts, and down her stomach. Hunter widened her stance and sucked on her right inner thigh while applying more salt to his branding on her left inner thigh. Her purr changed to a moan, causing him to grip the edge of the desk. Fuck, she was turning him on all over again, especially as both places he'd marked her sealed up and scarred.

Once he was finished, Hunter pulled back slowly and gazed at the marks that would forever be on her skin. His marks. Leaving no doubt in anyone of who she belonged to. It just made him that much more anxious to get the branding done on his throat. He kissed the mark, and then Hunter pressed his forehead to her inner thigh, the skin soft beneath his touch. He repeated the same motion to the mark on her throat. "I love you."

She cupped his cheek, brushing her thumb along his jaw. "I love you, too. Think you're ready to meet my family?"

"I am ready for anything, baby girl. I have you." He kissed her again and nipped at her lower lip. "I cannot say it will surprise me if they dislike me, though."

"I keep thinking the same thing about yours. Except your sister." Narcissa grinned. "Dinner with your family tomorrow night and then a trip to meet mine the next day."

There didn't seem to be a single thing they weren't of the same mind about. Then again, they were truly perfect for one another in every way. "I think this will be the most family interaction I have ever had." He knew Hayden would love her, simply because of how happy Narcissa made him. Though, just being in the den would likely embarrass him. He didn't know Rainbow well enough to say, but even if she didn't like Narcissa, she'd be respectful. He wasn't sure Clay liked anyone really, not that his half-brother's opinion mattered to him, anyway. "I am glad you and my sister get along so well. Though I am still unsure what name she would like to go by. I did not get around to asking her yet."

"When I first realized who she was, I used her real name. Do you know what she said to me? That she hadn't heard it in so long. Maybe we go in between and call her Ellie."

"I like that. Hayden would, too. That is what he used to call her when we were little." It would be a bit of the past and the future mixed in one.

"You should probably get me some clothes."

"Probably." He smirked. "Do I get to pick, or do you have something in mind?"

"Well, you have two options. One, find something that matches my heels, or two, pick out a whole new outfit with matching heels."

"Hmm... well, I love that color, especially on you." Hunter's eyes darkened as he grazed his fingers along the mark on her throat. "I will be back soon."

"I'll be here."

It might have been just three words, but they made him smile. A real, genuine smile. Yes, she would. And so would he. They would never have to worry about being separated ever again. Not by anything. Especially not four walls and rules that couldn't be ignored. Hunter kissed the mark on her neck, lingering in her scent, then rose and walked to the door. "There is a new piece of jewelry for you in my bag, if you would like to wear it." He glanced back at her, a knowing smirk playing on his lips. "Now that personal gifts are no longer out of the question, you can expect a lot more." Without waiting for her response, he abruptly opened the heavy oak door and departed, instructing the guards in a stern voice that no one was to enter until he came back.

It didn't take him long to reach her room, nor to make it to her closet. As soon as he opened the door and got a gander at her clothes collection, though... "What the fuck did I just get myself into?" he mumbled. Holy fuck. How in the gods did someone collect *so many*? And that was nothing compared to her collection of *shoes*. Everything was organized perfectly and precisely. Not only that, they were organized by color. Among other things, by the looks of it. Type. Length. Whether they were lingerie, form-fitting clothing, or casual wear. How high or short the heel was. And then there was her jewelry. Was there anything she *didn't* have in here? He'd never been so glad to have no use for clothing.

Shaking his head, Hunter got to work. He bypassed all the other colors, going straight to the group of red items. Flicking through them, he scanned each item one by one. It took him a couple of minutes to find one that caught his eye. For the occasion, anyway. There were *plenty* of items he'd love to see her in, but not so many he'd want her walking down the hallway in. He chose a red jumpsuit with a zipper that ran over the rear and chest, with a lace-edged triangle cut out in the back. The heels she had were fine, but he went over to the shoes next anyway. There was a pair of stiletto heels that perfectly matched the outfit he'd picked out. They had a strap over the toe and buckled around the ankle. Hunter almost left her closet then, but he couldn't resist giving her lingerie another once-over. There were plenty that matched the outfit he'd picked out for her. One that particularly caught his eye, though, was a thin-strapped see-through lace nighty that would just barely cover her breasts. It would stretch over her hips and had matching garters and panties with it. She could wear the panties now and add the nightie later. Would give him something new to rip off of her.

Hunter glanced over Narcissa's clothing horde once more, shook his head again, and headed back to their office. He nodded to the guards and entered, setting the clothing and heels on her desk chair before embracing her. One hand went over her stomach and the other over her breast. She'd switched out her necklace with the new one—a strand of diamonds with row after row of diamonds hanging from the main strand, surrounding a diamond star. "I knew that would look perfect on you. It will look good with the outfit I picked out for you, too."

"Mmm... yes. It appears you have excellent taste."

"Of course, I have excellent taste. I chose you, did I not?"

"Yes, you did," she purred.

Hades, that fucking purr of hers was going to destroy him.

Her gaze flicked briefly to the fire. Hunter's eyes followed hers. A small smirk appeared on his face as he eyed the flames licking at what remained of Kylen's file. Perfect place for it.

Her gaze landed on the lace panties draped casually across the chair. "Does this mean you want me to wear the rest of this piece of lingerie later?"

"You know me so well." As his fingertips brushed the mark on her inner thigh, he kissed the mark on her throat. "I figured the panties would give me anticipation for what I get to rip off of you later."

"You're right. They will. Alright. I need to get dressed. We have work to do."

"Mmm, yes, we do. And a lot. But I am going to enjoy watching you get dressed before I do anything else." He reluctantly released her, his arms falling away, and settled into his desk chair, which provided an unobstructed view of her as she dressed.

"Really? As I cover everything up?" She strode around her desk to her chair, where he'd laid everything out.

Hunter's eyes didn't leave her once. She had to bend over to take the heels off she had on, then again to slip on the panties. His eyes darkened at the *excellent* view of her ass that he got. "Mmhm."

"Do you know what's interesting about this outfit? It's a bodysuit, which means it can only go on one way." She unbuttoned the back of the top, unzipped the back of the pants, and stepped into them, slowly inching them up her legs.

A low growl came from him. "Mmm, that is interesting." And her ass was going to look *fantastic* in it. Not that it ever didn't. "So that means, when I fuck you in it later before I rip it off of you, I have to start from the top and work my way down? Or just... unzip the back part there? That would work ,too, I think."

"I thought you wanted me to wear the lingerie." She peered over her shoulder at him. "Besides, if you destroy all of my business suits, then you might just have to take me shopping."

"I want you to wear the lingerie. And you will." He smirked. "I can fuck you without destroying your panties, or taking them off. As for your business suits, do you think I would mind taking you shopping?"

"How long did you watch me that day in the marketplace?"

"I am not sure exactly how long. When I first laid eyes on you, there were only three bags between the two of you. I did not stop watching you until you left the marketplace. So, however long that was."

"By that time, I'd collected eight bags. Though I have returned before with sixteen." She grinned as she tugged the pants over her hips and slipped her arms through the openings on each side of the top half of the bodysuit.

"Before seeing your closet, sixteen bags would have shocked me." Hunter chuckled. "I have never come across anything I wanted to buy so much that it would fill that many bags." Or even a fraction of that. He stood and crossed the room. Turning Narcissa around, he slowly zipped up the back over her ass, and then did the button at the top. "As much as I enjoy ripping clothing off of you... I anticipated future shopping trips. So, you do not have to worry about that."

"Good to know. Though I'm more concerned that you don't quite know what you're getting yourself into. Perhaps I can expose you... slowly." A grin spread across her face as she hooded her eyes.

He let out another low growl as he slid his hand down to her breast. Through the fabric, his thumb moved rhythmically across her nipple while his fangs gently brushed from her earlobe to the curve of her throat. "I think I like the sound of that. By the way, as long as it is making you happy, I honestly do not care what I am getting myself into."

"I swear you know just what to say." Narcissa tilted her head a little as she slid her hands up his arms.

A low rumble vibrated out of him as she slid her hands up his arms. "Well..." Hunter leaned down until his face was closer to hers. "... I have always been very good with my mouth and tongue. It is good to know my *skills* extend to my words." He nipped her lower lip and brushed a kiss across her mouth. They'd never get enough of each other. Made him wonder how much work they would actually get done some days.

"I need to get my heels on. We have a schedule to keep, and I'd like the cleaning staff to come in and give the office a thorough scrub down."

"I would *much* prefer giving *you* a scrub down." His smirk widened a bit. "But I can control myself. For now." Hunter released her and leaned back against her desk. He really shouldn't have to say it, but... he just couldn't resist. "Have Ivory be part of the cleaning crew that comes in here. And others that will ensure she does nothing stupid."

"Just lock all the drawers." Narcissa collected the high heels he'd brought in for her. She sat on the desk and slipped on her stilettos, buckling them one at a time.

"The drawers are always locked." As was the office any time they weren't inside it. Trust had to be earned, and it was a difficult thing for anyone to do. Especially in his book.

"They aren't currently. And I have no intention of watching her every move."

"If she fucks up, she knows exactly what the result will be." And it would have nothing to do with working in any field. Red's pleas and promises would only get her sister so far.

Nia got the last strap buckled. "What's on your schedule for the rest of the day?"

"I have a meeting with the guards, as well as a few of the workers. I also plan to spend a little time looking at the blueprints for this place, and I want to speak to the cooks about tomorrow." Hunter held his hand out to her and drew her body against his. "What about you?"

"Jade and I are going over the plans for the burlesque. She has an idea of how to recruit performers. Plus, we need to make a few decisions on how to ensure drugs are completely removed from this place."

They were certainly in agreement there. Drugs would not be allowed. In any capacity. He nodded slowly. "I could bring in someone to assist with that, if need be, but I think we should try to keep it in-house for the time being. Do you have any names of who is using or distributing?"

"No, Jade likely knows them, but that's part of what we have to weed out. Shalla believes the drugs are coming from the fields. I'm leaving it to her and Marcell to handle things on that end."

"That is a good idea. I am sure they will figure things out on that end. If we have to end up searching rooms here, that is what we will do." Looking for drugs wasn't exactly his forte. He could find people with ease, but drugs were a different story. Especially with all the ways there were to conceal them and hide their scent. "I will tolerate a lot of things, but not that."

"We'll interview everyone who worked at the club on the first floor. From what I've learned, that's where it all exchanged hands."

It wasn't much, but at least it was something to go on. "That sounds like a good place to start." Hunter gave her hips a squeeze and pressed a fairly rare gentle kiss to her lips. As he pulled back and gazed into those gorgeous green eyes of hers, it struck him—and not for the first time—just how lucky he was. If his Narcissa hadn't come into his life when she had...

Hayden was mated and happy. Elisa... Ellie... was safe and well, and now living a life she could truly enjoy. In freedom. No one else needed him to protect them and watch over him. Where would he be now if the gods hadn't granted him the gift of love? The gift he had always viewed as a fabrication that had grown from loneliness, stupidity, and hope. Something that didn't truly exist. Something he didn't need, and would never be worthy of, anyway. Thank Hades, he had been wrong. And that his path had shifted away from the one that would end with his body rotting beneath the earth, while his family mourned the curse he had brought to them with his black heart and his destroyed soul. There was so much more to life than the self-hatred he had spent his existence feasting on. And he had found it, everything he never knew he needed, in this beautiful female before him.

"Let us go deal with the unfortunate nature of our duties. The sooner we finish..." Hunter grinned. "... the sooner we can work this room over again."

Narcissa beamed up at him. "I think that sounds like the best fucking idea I've ever heard."

About the Authors

B. Noir is a romance author of the smuttiest kind, delivering anarchy and chaos through one dirty novel after another. Dabbling in the abyss is just a part of everyday life. While she also writes under **Krys Fenner** and **Brigit Rosé**—like the wine, not the flower—debauchery is near to her heart. To learn more, visit her official website: kbfennerrose.com.

Nikki Haras has had a passion for writing since she was a small child. She will use whatever means necessary to get the words down that swirl inside her head, bleeding ink onto the page and breathing life into the characters who demand to tell their stories. When she's not immersing herself in her fantasy worlds, she's a full-time mom of three children and three fur babies, but you can usually always find her with a cup of coffee in one hand and a pen tucked into her messy bun. Always plotting the next amazing scene, fantastic new story, or immersive fantasy world to bring to life. To find out more about Nikki Haras and her upcoming book releases, you can find her on Facebook or visit her official website: https://nikkiharas1988.wixsite.com/mysite

Also by

Prisma Isle Series
by Brigit Rosé & Nikki Haras
Perfectly Reckless
Chaotic Tranquility
Rebel Tides
Prisma Isle Puzzle & Coloring Book

The Atlis Chronicles
by Krys Fenner
Blood Sacrifice
Hunted